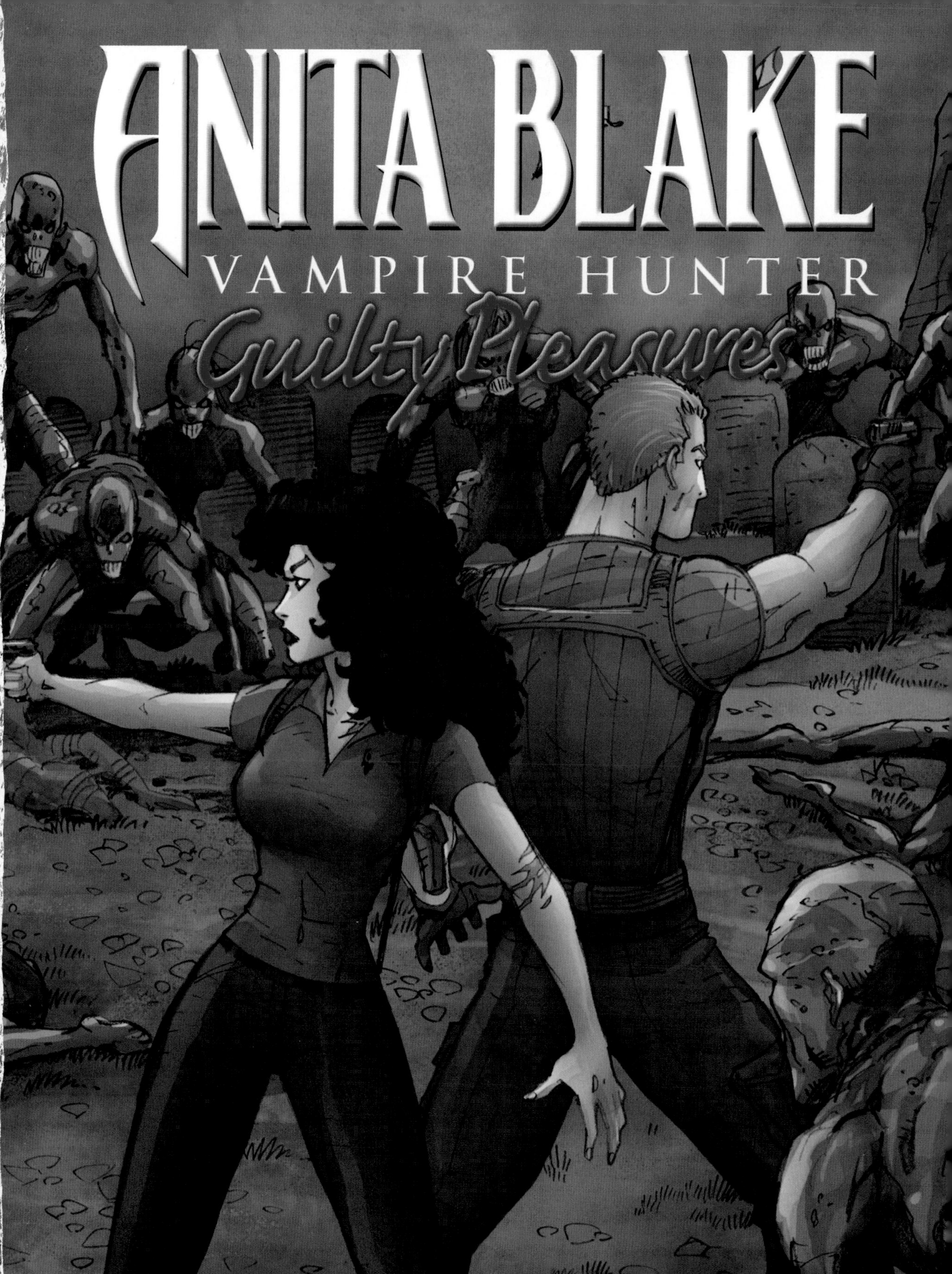

ANITA BLAKE
VAMPIRE HUNTER
Guilty Pleasures

ANITA BLAKE, VAMPIRE HUNTER: GUILTY PLEASURES — THE COMPLETE EDITION. Contains material originally published in magazine form as ANITA BLAKE, VAMPIRE HUNTER: GUILTY PLEASURES #1-12. First printing 2009. ISBN# 978-0-7851-4021-4. Published by MARVEL PUBLISHING, INC., a subsidiary of MARVEL ENTERTAINMENT, INC. OFFICE OF PUBLICATION: 417 5th Avenue, New York, NY 10016. Copyright © 2006, 2007, 2008 and 2009 Laurell K. Hamilton. All rights reserved. $34.99 per copy in the U.S. (GST #R127032852); Canadian Agreement #40668537. Anita Blake: Vampire Hunter and all characters featured in this issue and the distinctive names and likenesses thereof, and all related indicia are trademarks of Laurell K. Hamilton. No similarity between any of the names, characters, persons, and/or institutions in this magazine with those of any living or dead person or institution is intended, and any such similarity which may exist is purely coincidental. **Printed in the U.S.A.** ALAN FINE, EVP - Office Of The Chief Executive Marvel Entertainment, Inc. & CMO Marvel Characters B.V.; DAN BUCKLEY, Chief Executive Officer and Publisher - Print, Animation & Digital Media; JIM SOKOLOWSKI, Chief Operating Officer; DAVID GABRIEL, SVP of Publishing Sales & Circulation; DAVID BOGART, SVP of Business Affairs & Talent Management; MICHAEL PASCIULLO, VP Merchandising & Communications; JIM O'KEEFE, VP of Operations & Logistics; DAN CARR, Executive Director of Publishing Technology; JUSTIN F. GABRIE, Director of Publishing & Editorial Operations; SUSAN CRESPI, Editorial Operations Manager; ALEX MORALES, Publishing Operations Manager; STAN LEE, Chairman Emeritus. For information regarding advertising in Marvel Comics or on Marvel.com, please contact Mitch Dane, Advertising Director, at mdane@marvel.com. For Marvel subscription inquiries, please call 800-217-9158. Manufactured between 8/21/09

ANITA BLAKE
VAMPIRE HUNTER
Guilty Pleasures

WRITER: LAURELL K. HAMILTON
ADAPTATION: STACIE RITCHIE (ISSUES #1-5)
& JESS RUFFNER-BOOTH (ISSUES #6-12)
ARTISTS: BRETT BOOTH (ISSUES #1-7)
& RON LIM (ISSUES #8-12)
COLORISTS: IMAGINARY FRIENDS STUDIO
WITH MATT MOYLAN (ISSUES #1-6) & JUNE CHUNG (ISSUES #7-12)
LETTERERS: BILL TORTOLINI WITH SIMON BOWLAND (ISSUE #5)
COVER ARTISTS: BRETT BOOTH WITH JESS RUFFNER-BOOTH
& IMAGINARY FRIENDS STUDIO AND RON LIM WITH JUNE CHUNG

"VAMPIRE VICTIM"
WRITERS: LAURELL K. HAMILTON & JONATHON GREEN
ARTIST: BRETT BOOTH
COLORISTS: LARRY MOLINAR WITH JESS RUFFNER-BOOTH
LETTERER: BILL TORTOLINI

ASSISTANT EDITOR: JORDAN D. WHITE
EDITORS: MIKE RAICHT, SEAN JORDAN
& MARK PANICCIA

Special Thanks to Melissa McAlister, Ann Tredway, Jonathon Green,
Merrilee Heifetz, Michael Horwitz & Jason and Darla Cook

COLLECTION EDITOR: CORY LEVINE
ASSISTANT EDITORS: ALEX STARBUCK & JOHN DENNING
EDITORS, SPECIAL PROJECTS: JENNIFER GRÜNWALD & MARK D. BEAZLEY
SENIOR EDITOR, SPECIAL PROJECTS: JEFF YOUNGQUIST
SENIOR VICE PRESIDENT OF STRATEGIC DEVELOPMENT: RUWAN JAYATILLEKE
SENIOR VICE PRESIDENT OF SALES: DAVID GABRIEL
BOOK DESIGN: SPRING HOTELING

EDITOR IN CHIEF: JOE QUESADA
PUBLISHER: DAN BUCKLEY

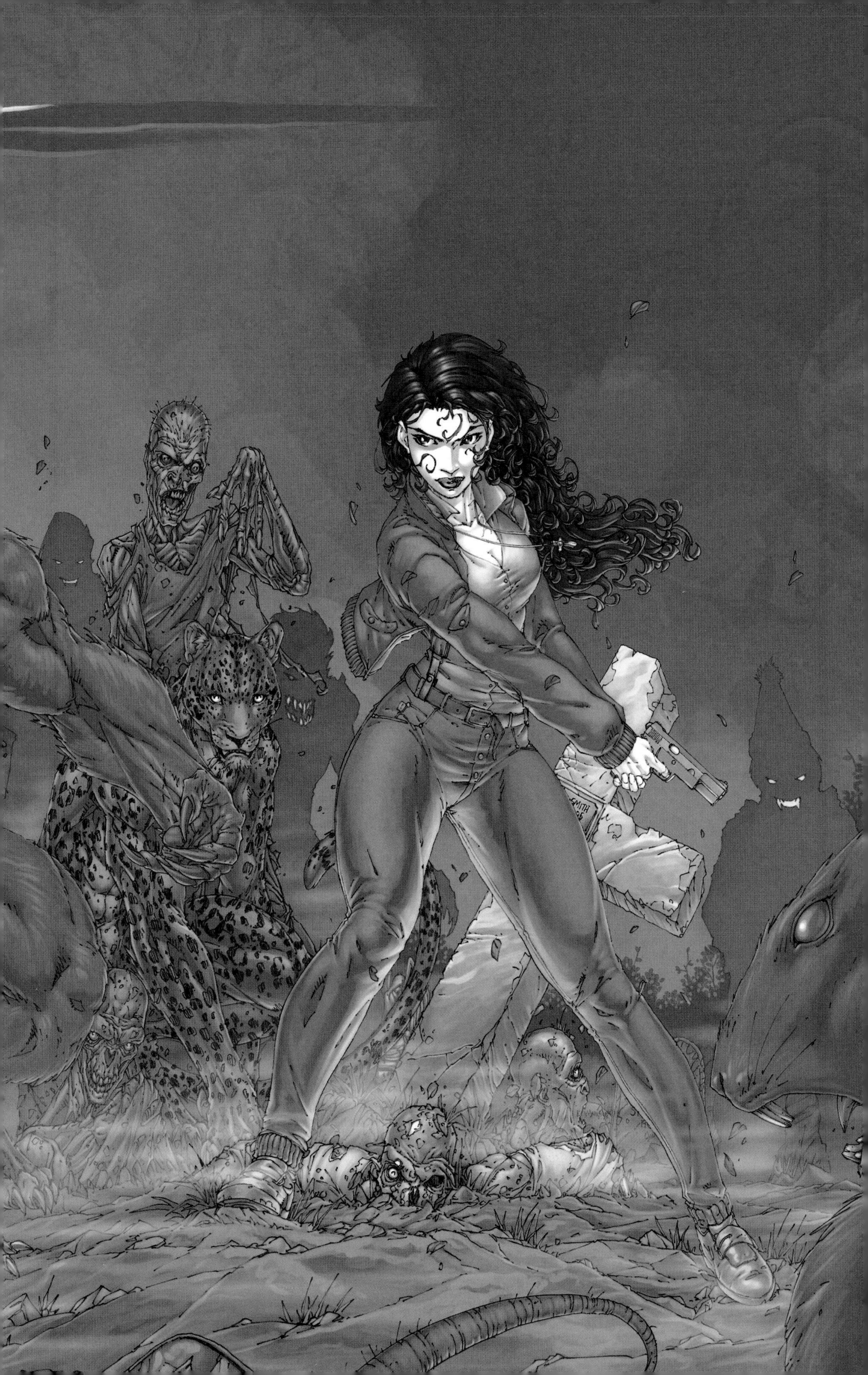

INTRODUCTION

Guilty Pleasures, the novel, began life as a desperate attempt to save my writing career. I had sold one novel, my first, NIGHTSEER, and a handful of short stories, and then suddenly the bottom fell out of the fantasy market. My editor did not want the sequel to NIGHTSEER, or anything else from me. He said that my writing lacked a certain *je ne sais quoi*, which is a quaint little French phrase that as far as I've been able to determine means nothing. No, literally, it meant my writing lacked a certain indefinable something, which being indefinable isn't very helpful for a writer as criticism from her editor. I couldn't seem to sell a short story for love, let alone money. I had my third novel rejected even by my then agent. I honestly wondered if I was going to be a one-hit wonder -- no, not a one hit wonder, that implies a certain level of sales and my first novel barely made a blip on the sales chart. In fact, its lack of sales was one of the reasons my first book editor gave for rejecting my second novel. So, I was worried that I'd be a one book wonder.

In desperation I went into my files of unpublished short stories to see if anything seemed like it might be interesting enough to be made into a novel. I was looking for something that wasn't heroic or high fantasy since no one was buying that. I found this short story, "Those Who Seek Forgiveness," featuring a woman who raised zombies as her job. Her name was Anita Blake, and in this first adventure she was trying to help a bereaved woman deal with her grief by having one last talk with the dead husband. The woman lied about the husband's death and it all went horribly, fatally wrong. I'd gotten a lot of very nice rejection slips on the story. Editors loved it, but didn't quite know what to do with it. The horror magazines thought it had more the feel of science fiction, so I sent it to science fiction magazines that thought it seems more like a fantasy piece, so I tried the fantasy magazines and they thought it was horror, and... Well, you get the idea. Everyone loved it, some editors even suggested other magazines to send it to, but no one wanted to buy it. But it was the most positive feedback I'd gotten on anything in the unsold files, and it was also one of the few stories I had that was set in modern times and wasn't the type of fantasy which no one wanted. So, I sat down to try and make it into a book. To Anita's zombie raising skills I added her being a legal vampire executioner, and the moment I added that she started helping the police and the moment she did that the book began to take form. I always know when I'm on the right track with an idea because it attracts a strong voice for the main character, and I know when I've got the right main character because they will attract a strong supporting cast. It's a little magical, and a lot of brain sweat.

I finally had a book, GUILTY PLEASURES, featuring Anita Blake, vampire hunter. It was the late 1980s. I sent the book to my then agent and she sent it out. The book was rejected over two hundred times. The horror publishers thought it was science fiction. The science fiction publishers thought it was fantasy. The fantasy publishers thought it was maybe a mystery. It was a who/how/what done-it but it was a hard-boiled mystery with horror elements, so the mystery editors thought it was, wait for it, horror, and the ring around the rosy game of rejection started all over again. One mystery editor said, "You can't have a mystery with vampires and zombies in it." One horror editor said, "It's not scary because everybody knows about the vampires. They should be secret." Another well-known mystery editor told me, "A straight mystery with a female detective can't have that much violence in it." A fantasy editor said, "The vampire market is dead and can't bear one more book." (That last is ironic in retrospect with this being one of the hottest publishing trends ever.) I was told again and again that mixed genre does not sell. That my book was mystery, fantasy, horror, and even science fiction and they couldn't market something that mixed that many genres. GUILTY PLEASURES would take over two years and those two hundred plus rejections to finally sell to Penguin/Putnam and it was originally an Ace paperback. The book has now been reissued in hardback, trade paperback, gone through three different covers in America alone, been translated into at least sixteen languages, has sold just under a million copies and was the beginning of a series that would finally land me as the #1 best-selling book in the country, and put me at the #1 slot at the New York Times three times, as of the last book, SKIN TRADE, which is #17 in the Anita Blake series.

I had just finished writing DANSE MACABRE when my agent, Merrilee Heifetz, helped me put together a deal to turn the first three Anita Blake novels into comics/graphic novels. At the time, neither comics based on books OR comics about vampires were selling with much success. And indeed my agent had been trying to sell Anita to a comics company for quite a while before we got this deal…but once they were published, the comics broke records. So once again I had to start the trend and once again I've had the satisfaction of seeing many other authors make the move to comics and graphic novels – in fact, there is now even a New York Times Graphic Novel Bestseller List.

Every frame of art that you see between these two covers went over my desk, and my husband, Jonathon Green's desk. Jonathon was actually instrumental in the comic books because he was a comic geek of long standing and could explain to me how the business worked, and how the art and script worked together. In the early days he had to lay the rough art out with the script beside it and show me how it would all fit together. It was like some huge jigsaw puzzle. Now, I can edit art and script on screen. I can "see" in comic almost as well as I "see" in prose. Jonathon is still better at the visual impact for the comics and I've learned that just because prose and dialogue worked in the novel doesn't mean it works with the comic art. We are blessed with a wonderful adapter Jess Booth, and she is as faithful to the books as she can leaving it to me to add new dialogue or prose as needed. I've found that sometimes you need new words, but I've also found that a good picture is worth more than a thousand words... so much more.

Every piece of art from character design, to roughs, to works in progress (wips), to coloring, to it being brought together with the lettering, to the finished product went through our hands. I touched it, approved it, and worked with the artists, the colorists, the script adapter, everything and everyone. I watched people that I had first imagined two decades earlier come to life in pictures. It was exciting, and God, I wished for the millionth time that I could draw what was in my head. Brett Booth, our original artist, seemed to be able to reach into my head and draw the characters straight out from my imagination. We were sorry to lose Brett to other projects and very happy to be able to keep his wife, Jess on as our script adapter. She also was the colorist on some of the original comic covers, and the combination of Brett's art and her coloring still takes my breath away. Ron Lim came on to finish up GUILTY PLEASURES. Ron is still with us, and is both very talented and very patient as we work on THE LAUGHING CORPSE, the second book as it comes out in comic form and we work towards that graphic novel collection.

Events inspired by the book in your hands:

A brand new Anita Blake adventure, "First Death", a prequel to GUILTY PLEASURES. The new story was co-written with Jonathon. It was fun to have someone else helping with the actual writing. Novels can be such lonely tasks.

Jonathon got his first solo writing credit with "Hollywood Bloodsuckers", a Spider-Woman story.

We went to ComicCon 2007 in San Diego – 250,000 people in one building. Wow. I did a Q&A to a 2000-plus, standing room only crowd with a 30 ft. screen of me, on stage, behind me. So weird. I don't know how actors do it.

I have a deal for a television movie/series on IFC with LionsGate and AfterDark Films.

The 1st hardback collection of GUILTY PLEASURES was the #1 graphic novel in the country the same week as J. Michael Straczynski's THOR was #1 for individual issue. To share a list with the return of the God of Thunder, scripted by the creator of Babylon 5, and also be published by Marvel Comics is pretty awesome.

LAURELL K. HAMILTON
ST. LOUIS, 2009

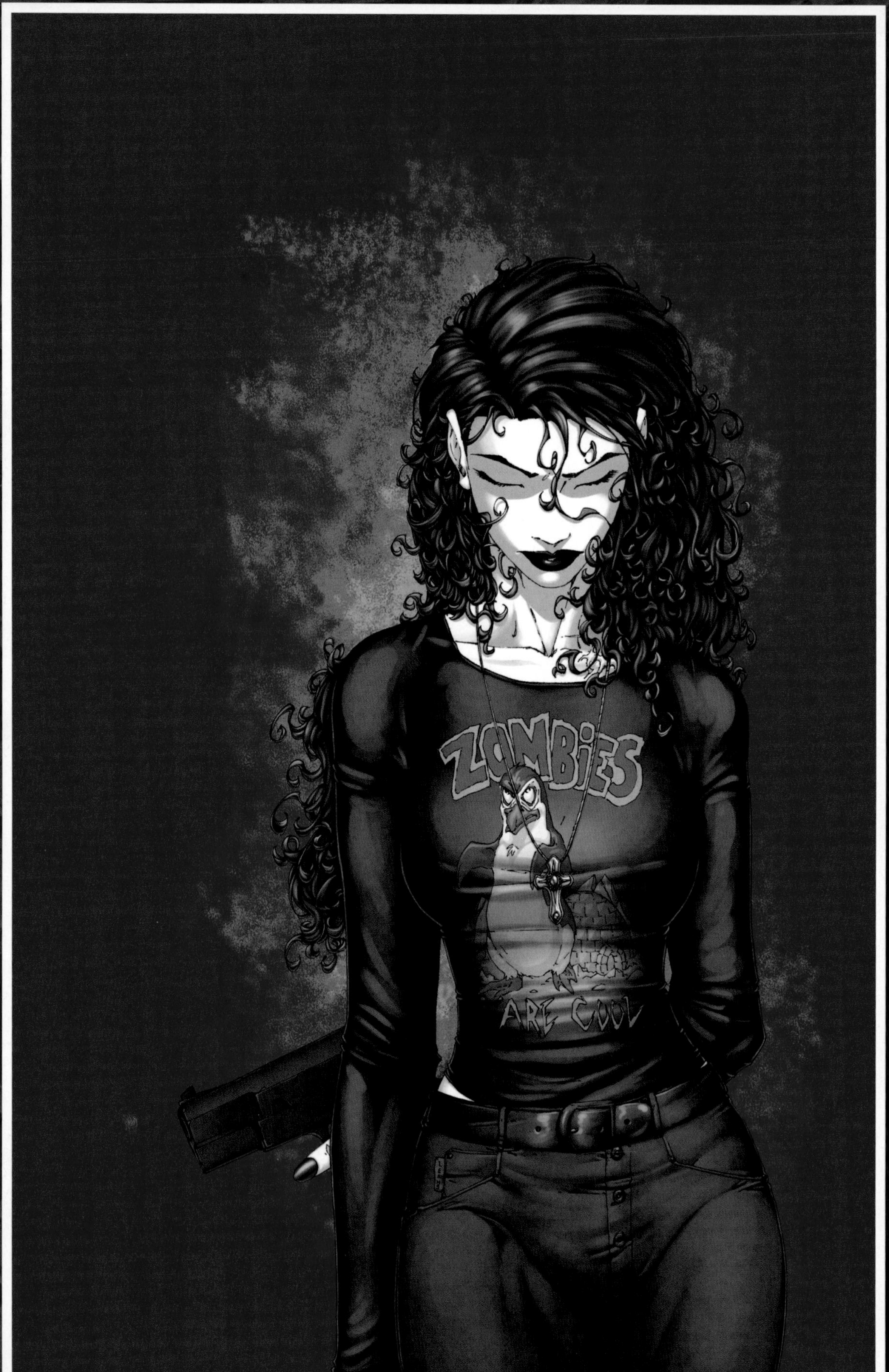
ZOMBIES
ARE COOL

ONE

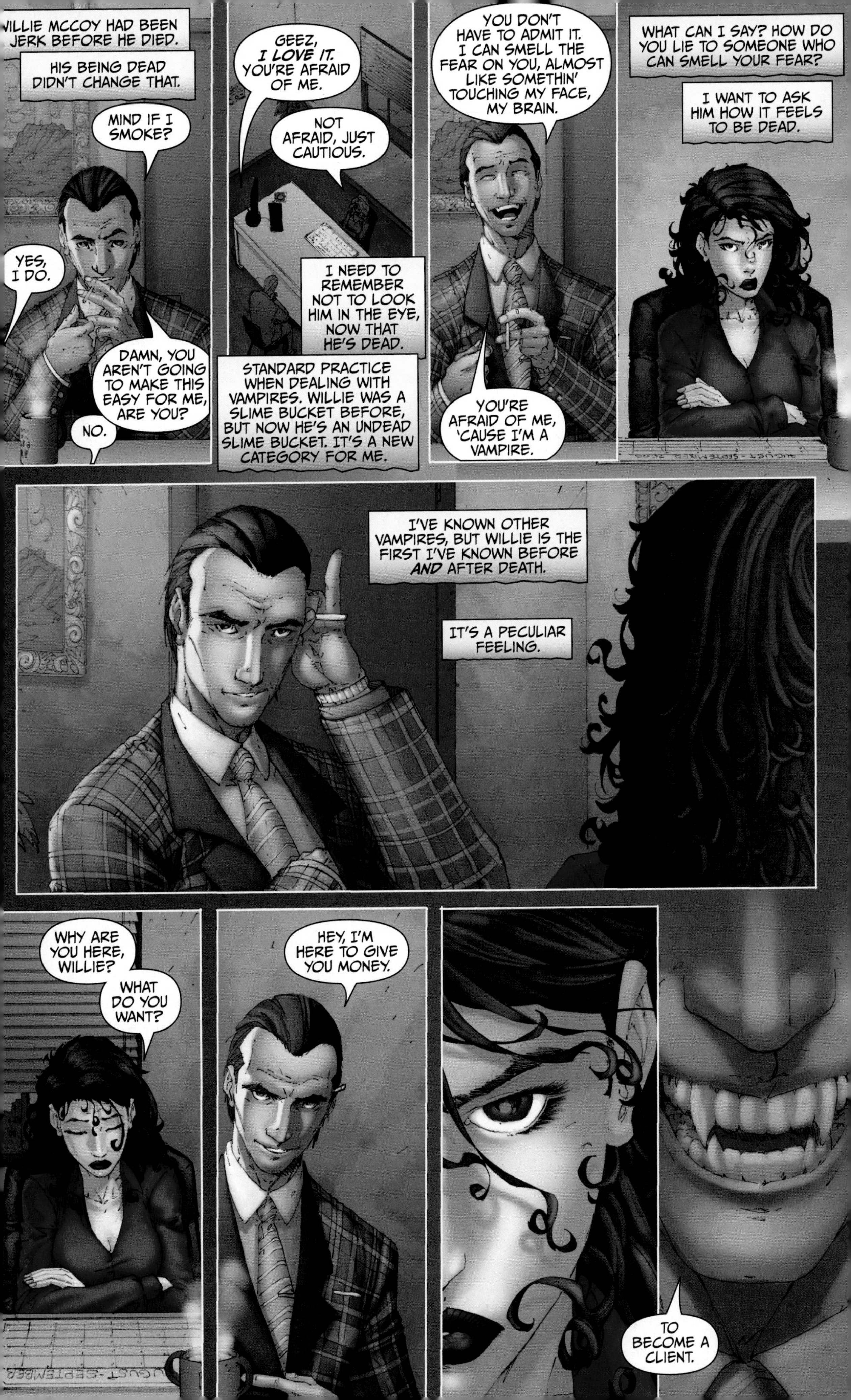

WILLIE MCCOY HAD BEEN A JERK BEFORE HE DIED.
HIS BEING DEAD DIDN'T CHANGE THAT.
MIND IF I SMOKE?
YES, I DO.
DAMN, YOU AREN'T GOING TO MAKE THIS EASY FOR ME, ARE YOU?
NO.
GEEZ, *I LOVE IT.* YOU'RE AFRAID OF ME.
NOT AFRAID, JUST CAUTIOUS.
I NEED TO REMEMBER NOT TO LOOK HIM IN THE EYE, NOW THAT HE'S DEAD.
STANDARD PRACTICE WHEN DEALING WITH VAMPIRES. WILLIE WAS A SLIME BUCKET BEFORE, BUT NOW HE'S AN UNDEAD SLIME BUCKET. IT'S A NEW CATEGORY FOR ME.
YOU DON'T HAVE TO ADMIT IT. I CAN SMELL THE FEAR ON YOU, ALMOST LIKE SOMETHIN' TOUCHING MY FACE, MY BRAIN.
YOU'RE AFRAID OF ME, 'CAUSE I'M A VAMPIRE.
WHAT CAN I SAY? HOW DO YOU LIE TO SOMEONE WHO CAN SMELL YOUR FEAR?
I WANT TO ASK HIM HOW IT FEELS TO BE DEAD.
I'VE KNOWN OTHER VAMPIRES, BUT WILLIE IS THE FIRST I'VE KNOWN BEFORE *AND* AFTER DEATH.
IT'S A PECULIAR FEELING.
WHY ARE YOU HERE, WILLIE?
WHAT DO YOU WANT?
HEY, I'M HERE TO GIVE YOU MONEY.
TO BECOME A CLIENT.

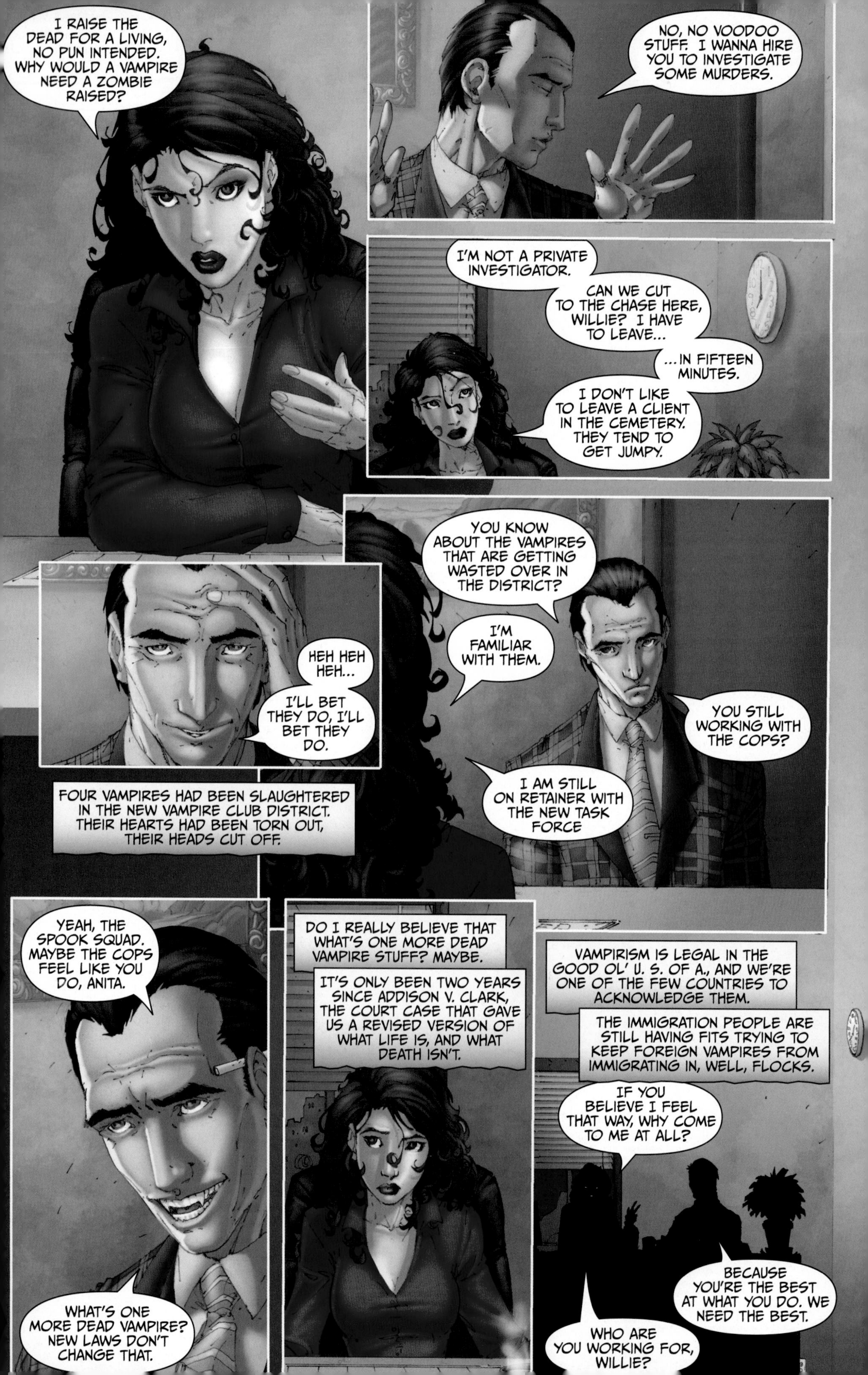
I RAISE THE DEAD FOR A LIVING, NO PUN INTENDED. WHY WOULD A VAMPIRE NEED A ZOMBIE RAISED?
NO, NO VOODOO STUFF. I WANNA HIRE YOU TO INVESTIGATE SOME MURDERS.
I'M NOT A PRIVATE INVESTIGATOR.
CAN WE CUT TO THE CHASE HERE, WILLIE? I HAVE TO LEAVE...
...IN FIFTEEN MINUTES.
I DON'T LIKE TO LEAVE A CLIENT IN THE CEMETERY. THEY TEND TO GET JUMPY.
YOU KNOW ABOUT THE VAMPIRES THAT ARE GETTING WASTED OVER IN THE DISTRICT?
I'M FAMILIAR WITH THEM.
HEH HEH HEH...
I'LL BET THEY DO, I'LL BET THEY DO.
YOU STILL WORKING WITH THE COPS?
I AM STILL ON RETAINER WITH THE NEW TASK FORCE
FOUR VAMPIRES HAD BEEN SLAUGHTERED IN THE NEW VAMPIRE CLUB DISTRICT. THEIR HEARTS HAD BEEN TORN OUT, THEIR HEADS CUT OFF.
YEAH, THE SPOOK SQUAD. MAYBE THE COPS FEEL LIKE YOU DO, ANITA.
WHAT'S ONE MORE DEAD VAMPIRE? NEW LAWS DON'T CHANGE THAT.
DO I REALLY BELIEVE THAT WHAT'S ONE MORE DEAD VAMPIRE STUFF? MAYBE.
IT'S ONLY BEEN TWO YEARS SINCE ADDISON V. CLARK, THE COURT CASE THAT GAVE US A REVISED VERSION OF WHAT LIFE IS, AND WHAT DEATH ISN'T.
VAMPIRISM IS LEGAL IN THE GOOD OL' U. S. OF A., AND WE'RE ONE OF THE FEW COUNTRIES TO ACKNOWLEDGE THEM.
THE IMMIGRATION PEOPLE ARE STILL HAVING FITS TRYING TO KEEP FOREIGN VAMPIRES FROM IMMIGRATING IN, WELL, FLOCKS.
IF YOU BELIEVE I FEEL THAT WAY, WHY COME TO ME AT ALL?
BECAUSE YOU'RE THE BEST AT WHAT YOU DO. WE NEED THE BEST.
WHO ARE YOU WORKING FOR, WILLIE?

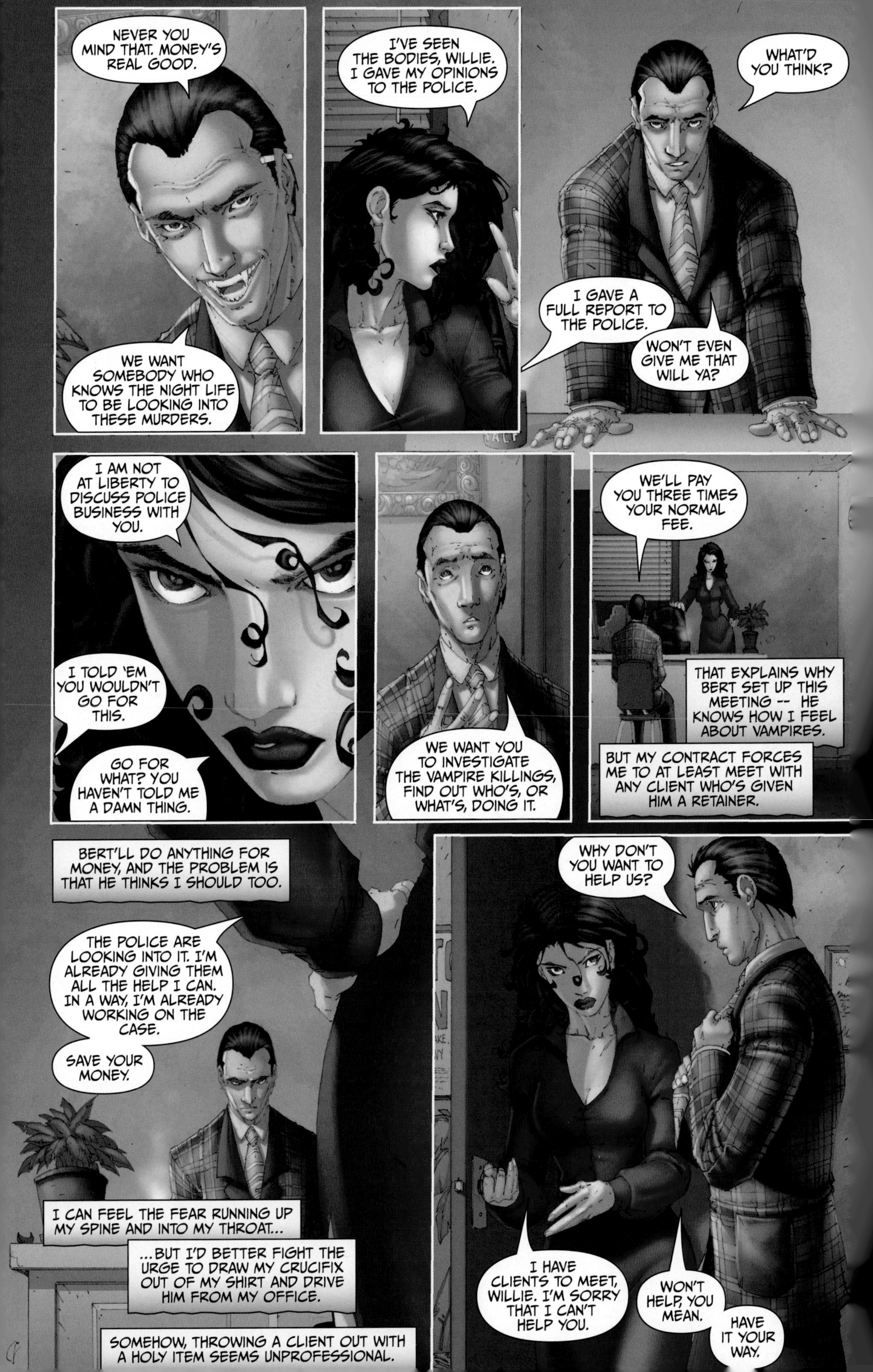

NEVER YOU MIND THAT. MONEY'S REAL GOOD.
WE WANT SOMEBODY WHO KNOWS THE NIGHT LIFE TO BE LOOKING INTO THESE MURDERS.
I'VE SEEN THE BODIES, WILLIE. I GAVE MY OPINIONS TO THE POLICE.
WHAT'D YOU THINK?
I GAVE A FULL REPORT TO THE POLICE.
WON'T EVEN GIVE ME THAT WILL YA?
I AM NOT AT LIBERTY TO DISCUSS POLICE BUSINESS WITH YOU.
I TOLD 'EM YOU WOULDN'T GO FOR THIS.
GO FOR WHAT? YOU HAVEN'T TOLD ME A DAMN THING.
WE WANT YOU TO INVESTIGATE THE VAMPIRE KILLINGS, FIND OUT WHO'S, OR WHAT'S, DOING IT.
WE'LL PAY YOU THREE TIMES YOUR NORMAL FEE.
THAT EXPLAINS WHY BERT SET UP THIS MEETING -- HE KNOWS HOW I FEEL ABOUT VAMPIRES.
BUT MY CONTRACT FORCES ME TO AT LEAST MEET WITH ANY CLIENT WHO'S GIVEN HIM A RETAINER.
BERT'LL DO ANYTHING FOR MONEY, AND THE PROBLEM IS THAT HE THINKS I SHOULD TOO.
THE POLICE ARE LOOKING INTO IT. I'M ALREADY GIVING THEM ALL THE HELP I CAN. IN A WAY, I'M ALREADY WORKING ON THE CASE.
SAVE YOUR MONEY.
I CAN FEEL THE FEAR RUNNING UP MY SPINE AND INTO MY THROAT...
...BUT I'D BETTER FIGHT THE URGE TO DRAW MY CRUCIFIX OUT OF MY SHIRT AND DRIVE HIM FROM MY OFFICE.
SOMEHOW, THROWING A CLIENT OUT WITH A HOLY ITEM SEEMS UNPROFESSIONAL.
WHY DON'T YOU WANT TO HELP US?
I HAVE CLIENTS TO MEET, WILLIE. I'M SORRY THAT I CAN'T HELP YOU.
WON'T HELP, YOU MEAN.
HAVE IT YOUR WAY.

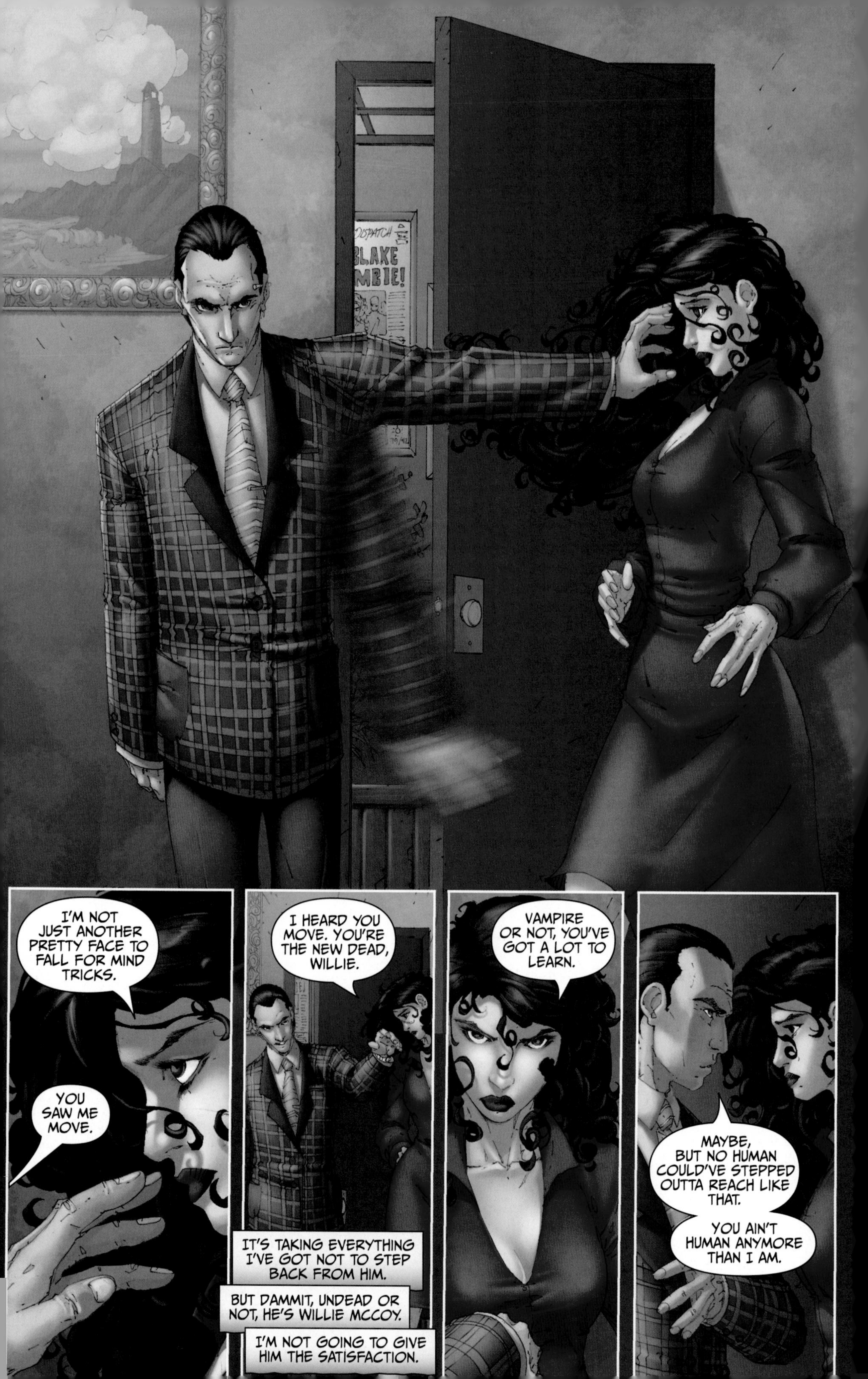
I'M NOT JUST ANOTHER PRETTY FACE TO FALL FOR MIND TRICKS.
YOU SAW ME MOVE.
I HEARD YOU MOVE. YOU'RE THE NEW DEAD, WILLIE.
IT'S TAKING EVERYTHING I'VE GOT NOT TO STEP BACK FROM HIM.
BUT DAMMIT, UNDEAD OR NOT, HE'S WILLIE MCCOY.
I'M NOT GOING TO GIVE HIM THE SATISFACTION.
VAMPIRE OR NOT, YOU'VE GOT A LOT TO LEARN.
MAYBE, BUT NO HUMAN COULD'VE STEPPED OUTTA REACH LIKE THAT.
YOU AIN'T HUMAN ANYMORE THAN I AM.

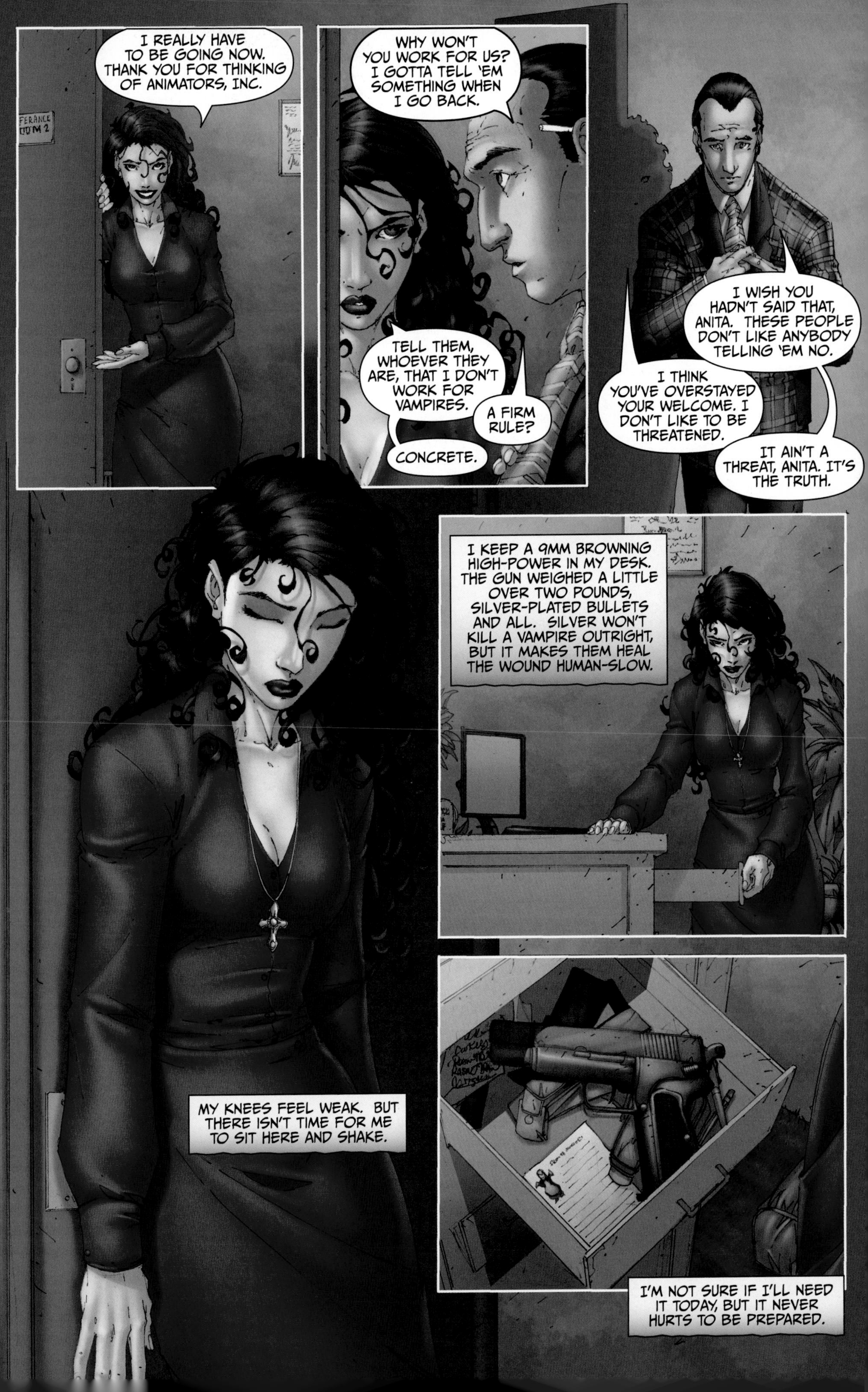

I REALLY HAVE TO BE GOING NOW. THANK YOU FOR THINKING OF ANIMATORS, INC.
WHY WON'T YOU WORK FOR US? I GOTTA TELL 'EM SOMETHING WHEN I GO BACK.
TELL THEM, WHOEVER THEY ARE, THAT I DON'T WORK FOR VAMPIRES.
A FIRM RULE?
CONCRETE.
I WISH YOU HADN'T SAID THAT, ANITA. THESE PEOPLE DON'T LIKE ANYBODY TELLING 'EM NO.
I THINK YOU'VE OVERSTAYED YOUR WELCOME. I DON'T LIKE TO BE THREATENED.
IT AIN'T A THREAT, ANITA. IT'S THE TRUTH.
MY KNEES FEEL WEAK. BUT THERE ISN'T TIME FOR ME TO SIT HERE AND SHAKE.
I KEEP A 9MM BROWNING HIGH-POWER IN MY DESK. THE GUN WEIGHED A LITTLE OVER TWO POUNDS, SILVER-PLATED BULLETS AND ALL. SILVER WON'T KILL A VAMPIRE OUTRIGHT, BUT IT MAKES THEM HEAL THE WOUND HUMAN-SLOW.
I'M NOT SURE IF I'LL NEED IT TODAY, BUT IT NEVER HURTS TO BE PREPARED.

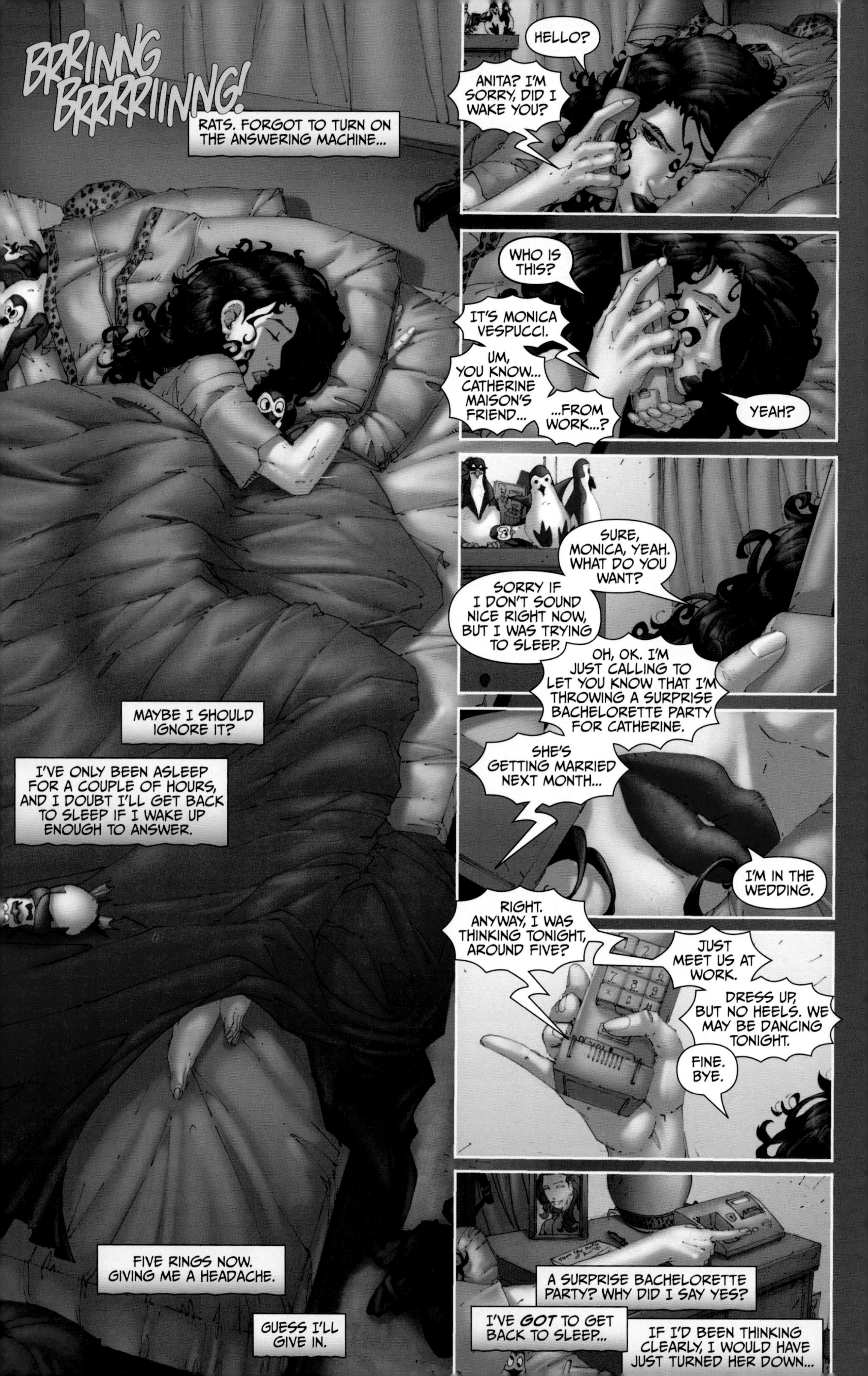
BRRINNG BRRRRIINNG!
RATS. FORGOT TO TURN ON THE ANSWERING MACHINE...
MAYBE I SHOULD IGNORE IT?
I'VE ONLY BEEN ASLEEP FOR A COUPLE OF HOURS, AND I DOUBT I'LL GET BACK TO SLEEP IF I WAKE UP ENOUGH TO ANSWER.
FIVE RINGS NOW. GIVING ME A HEADACHE.
GUESS I'LL GIVE IN.
HELLO?
ANITA? I'M SORRY, DID I WAKE YOU?
WHO IS THIS?
IT'S MONICA VESPUCCI.
UM, YOU KNOW... CATHERINE MAISON'S FRIEND...
...FROM WORK...?
YEAH?
SURE, MONICA, YEAH. WHAT DO YOU WANT?
SORRY IF I DON'T SOUND NICE RIGHT NOW, BUT I WAS TRYING TO SLEEP.
OH, OK. I'M JUST CALLING TO LET YOU KNOW THAT I'M THROWING A SURPRISE BACHELORETTE PARTY FOR CATHERINE.
SHE'S GETTING MARRIED NEXT MONTH...
I'M IN THE WEDDING.
RIGHT. ANYWAY, I WAS THINKING TONIGHT, AROUND FIVE?
JUST MEET US AT WORK.
DRESS UP, BUT NO HEELS. WE MAY BE DANCING TONIGHT.
FINE. BYE.
A SURPRISE BACHELORETTE PARTY? WHY DID I SAY YES?
I'VE GOT TO GET BACK TO SLEEP...
IF I'D BEEN THINKING CLEARLY, I WOULD HAVE JUST TURNED HER DOWN...

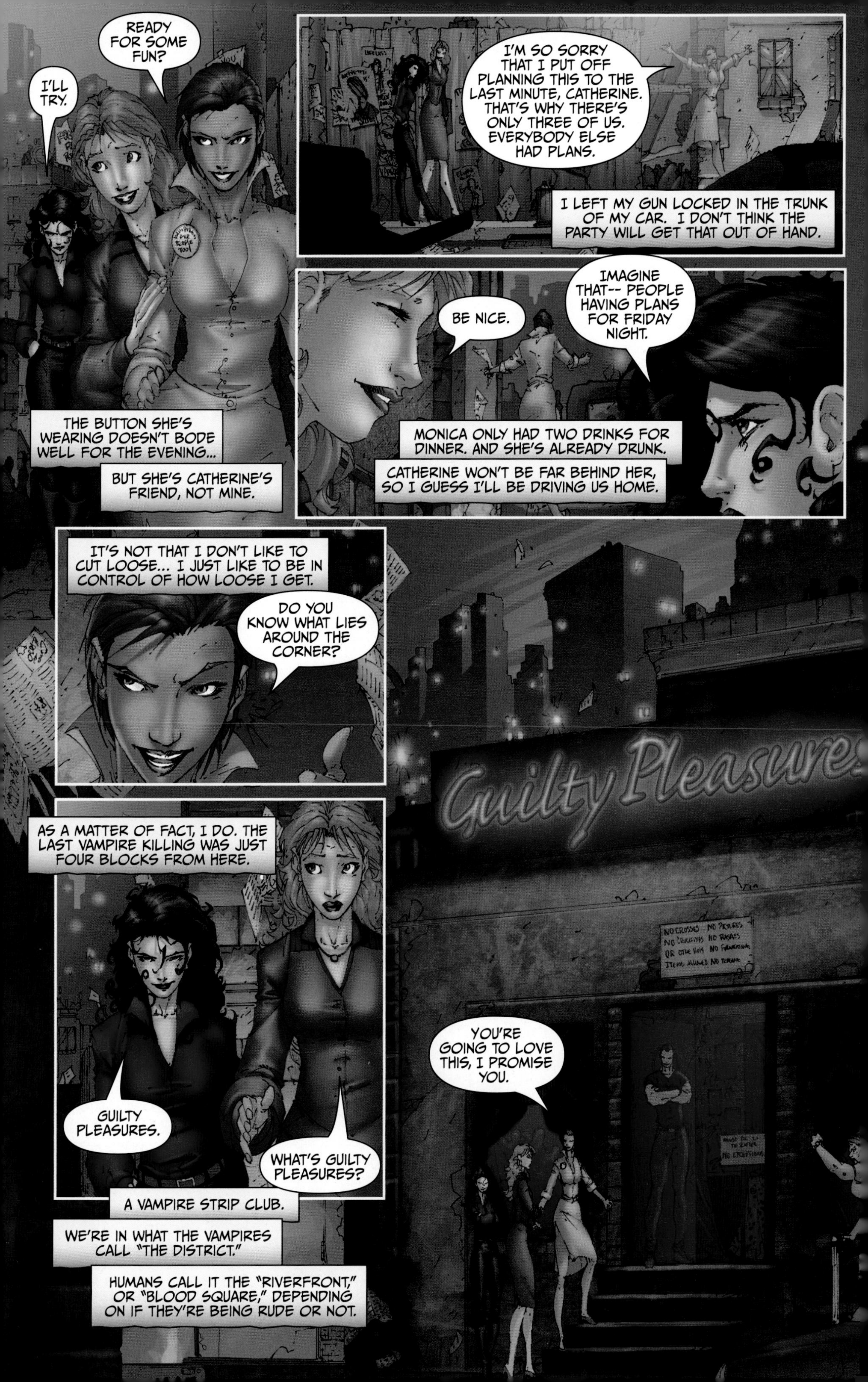
READY FOR SOME FUN?
I'LL TRY.
THE BUTTON SHE'S WEARING DOESN'T BODE WELL FOR THE EVENING...
BUT SHE'S CATHERINE'S FRIEND, NOT MINE.
I'M SO SORRY THAT I PUT OFF PLANNING THIS TO THE LAST MINUTE, CATHERINE. THAT'S WHY THERE'S ONLY THREE OF US. EVERYBODY ELSE HAD PLANS.
I LEFT MY GUN LOCKED IN THE TRUNK OF MY CAR. I DON'T THINK THE PARTY WILL GET THAT OUT OF HAND.
BE NICE.
IMAGINE THAT-- PEOPLE HAVING PLANS FOR FRIDAY NIGHT.
MONICA ONLY HAD TWO DRINKS FOR DINNER. AND SHE'S ALREADY DRUNK.
CATHERINE WON'T BE FAR BEHIND HER, SO I GUESS I'LL BE DRIVING US HOME.
IT'S NOT THAT I DON'T LIKE TO CUT LOOSE... I JUST LIKE TO BE IN CONTROL OF HOW LOOSE I GET.
DO YOU KNOW WHAT LIES AROUND THE CORNER?
AS A MATTER OF FACT, I DO. THE LAST VAMPIRE KILLING WAS JUST FOUR BLOCKS FROM HERE.
GUILTY PLEASURES.
WHAT'S GUILTY PLEASURES?
A VAMPIRE STRIP CLUB.
WE'RE IN WHAT THE VAMPIRES CALL "THE DISTRICT."
HUMANS CALL IT THE "RIVERFRONT," OR "BLOOD SQUARE," DEPENDING ON IF THEY'RE BEING RUDE OR NOT.
Guilty Pleasures
YOU'RE GOING TO LOVE THIS, I PROMISE YOU.

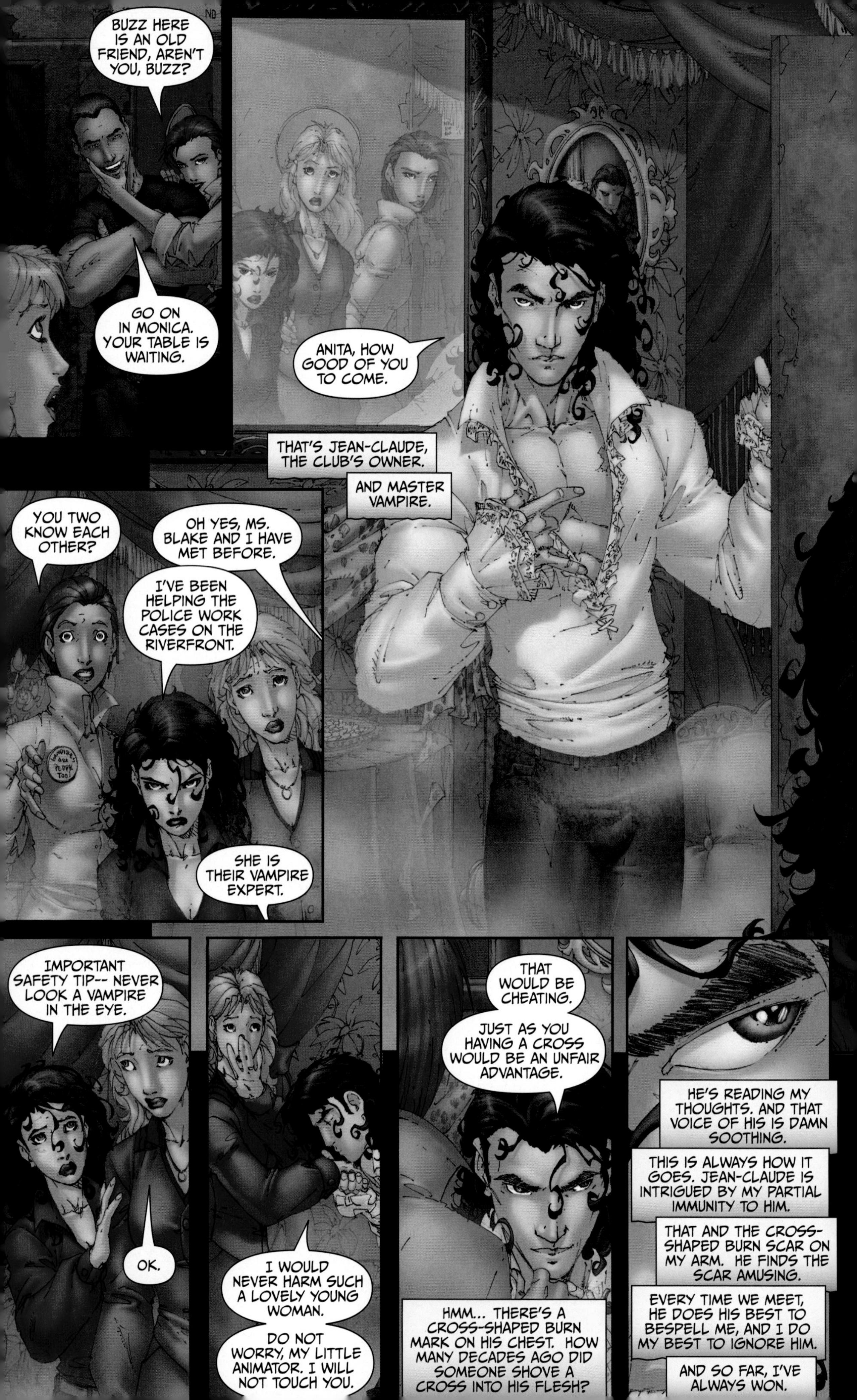
BUZZ HERE IS AN OLD FRIEND, AREN'T YOU, BUZZ?
GO ON IN MONICA. YOUR TABLE IS WAITING.
ANITA, HOW GOOD OF YOU TO COME.
THAT'S JEAN-CLAUDE, THE CLUB'S OWNER.
AND MASTER VAMPIRE.
YOU TWO KNOW EACH OTHER?
OH YES, MS. BLAKE AND I HAVE MET BEFORE.
I'VE BEEN HELPING THE POLICE WORK CASES ON THE RIVERFRONT.
SHE IS THEIR VAMPIRE EXPERT.
IMPORTANT SAFETY TIP-- NEVER LOOK A VAMPIRE IN THE EYE.
OK.
I WOULD NEVER HARM SUCH A LOVELY YOUNG WOMAN.
DO NOT WORRY, MY LITTLE ANIMATOR. I WILL NOT TOUCH YOU.
THAT WOULD BE CHEATING.
JUST AS YOU HAVING A CROSS WOULD BE AN UNFAIR ADVANTAGE.
HMM... THERE'S A CROSS-SHAPED BURN MARK ON HIS CHEST. HOW MANY DECADES AGO DID SOMEONE SHOVE A CROSS INTO HIS FLESH?
HE'S READING MY THOUGHTS. AND THAT VOICE OF HIS IS DAMN SOOTHING.
THIS IS ALWAYS HOW IT GOES. JEAN-CLAUDE IS INTRIGUED BY MY PARTIAL IMMUNITY TO HIM.
THAT AND THE CROSS-SHAPED BURN SCAR ON MY ARM. HE FINDS THE SCAR AMUSING.
EVERY TIME WE MEET, HE DOES HIS BEST TO BESPELL ME, AND I DO MY BEST TO IGNORE HIM.
AND SO FAR, I'VE ALWAYS WON.

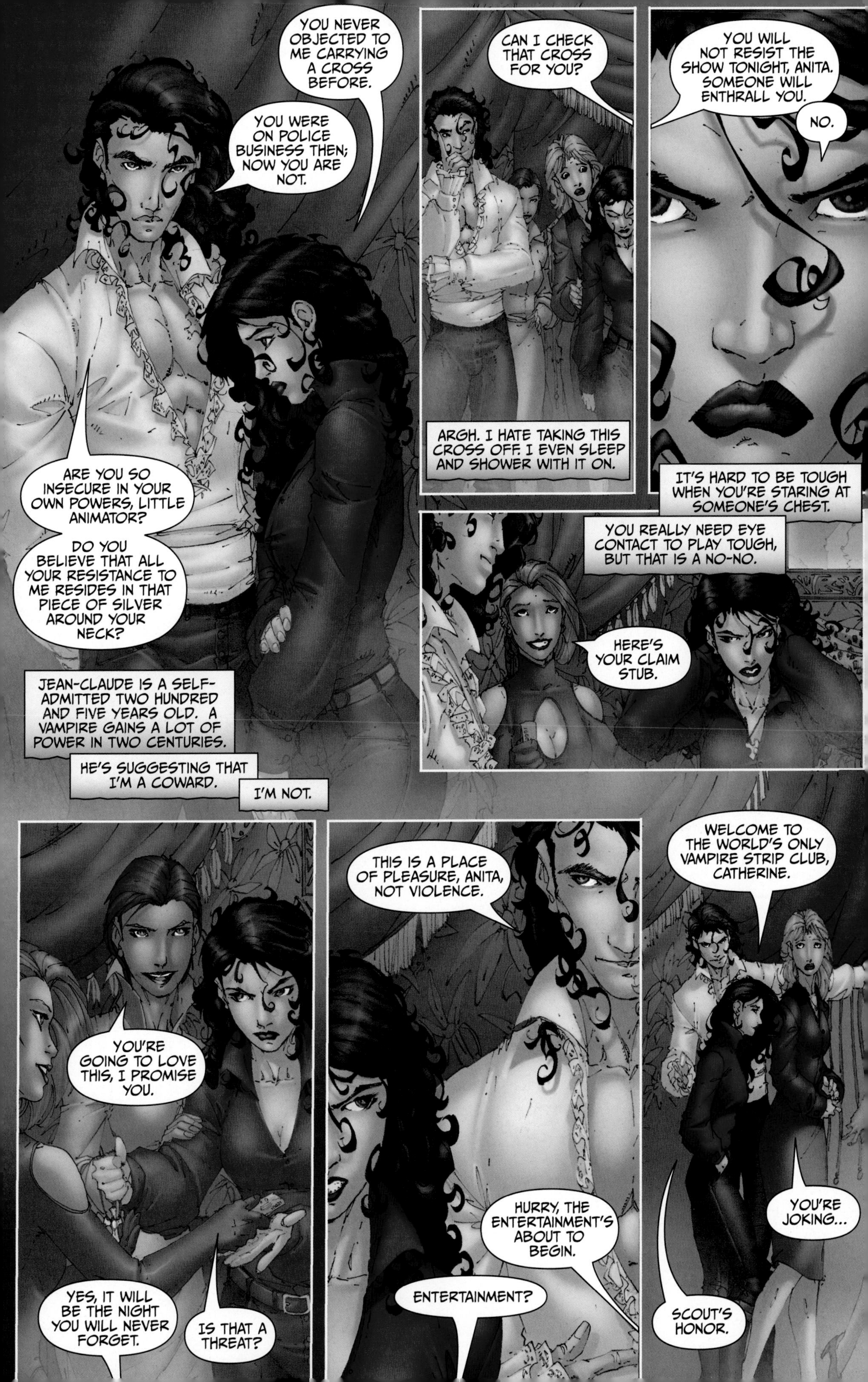
YOU NEVER OBJECTED TO ME CARRYING A CROSS BEFORE.
YOU WERE ON POLICE BUSINESS THEN; NOW YOU ARE NOT.
ARE YOU SO INSECURE IN YOUR OWN POWERS, LITTLE ANIMATOR?
DO YOU BELIEVE THAT ALL YOUR RESISTANCE TO ME RESIDES IN THAT PIECE OF SILVER AROUND YOUR NECK?
JEAN-CLAUDE IS A SELF-ADMITTED TWO HUNDRED AND FIVE YEARS OLD. A VAMPIRE GAINS A LOT OF POWER IN TWO CENTURIES.
HE'S SUGGESTING THAT I'M A COWARD.
I'M NOT.
CAN I CHECK THAT CROSS FOR YOU?
ARGH. I HATE TAKING THIS CROSS OFF. I EVEN SLEEP AND SHOWER WITH IT ON.
YOU WILL NOT RESIST THE SHOW TONIGHT, ANITA. SOMEONE WILL ENTHRALL YOU.
NO.
IT'S HARD TO BE TOUGH WHEN YOU'RE STARING AT SOMEONE'S CHEST.
YOU REALLY NEED EYE CONTACT TO PLAY TOUGH, BUT THAT IS A NO-NO.
HERE'S YOUR CLAIM STUB.
YOU'RE GOING TO LOVE THIS, I PROMISE YOU.
YES, IT WILL BE THE NIGHT YOU WILL NEVER FORGET.
IS THAT A THREAT?
THIS IS A PLACE OF PLEASURE, ANITA, NOT VIOLENCE.
HURRY, THE ENTERTAINMENT'S ABOUT TO BEGIN.
ENTERTAINMENT?
WELCOME TO THE WORLD'S ONLY VAMPIRE STRIP CLUB, CATHERINE.
YOU'RE JOKING...
SCOUT'S HONOR.

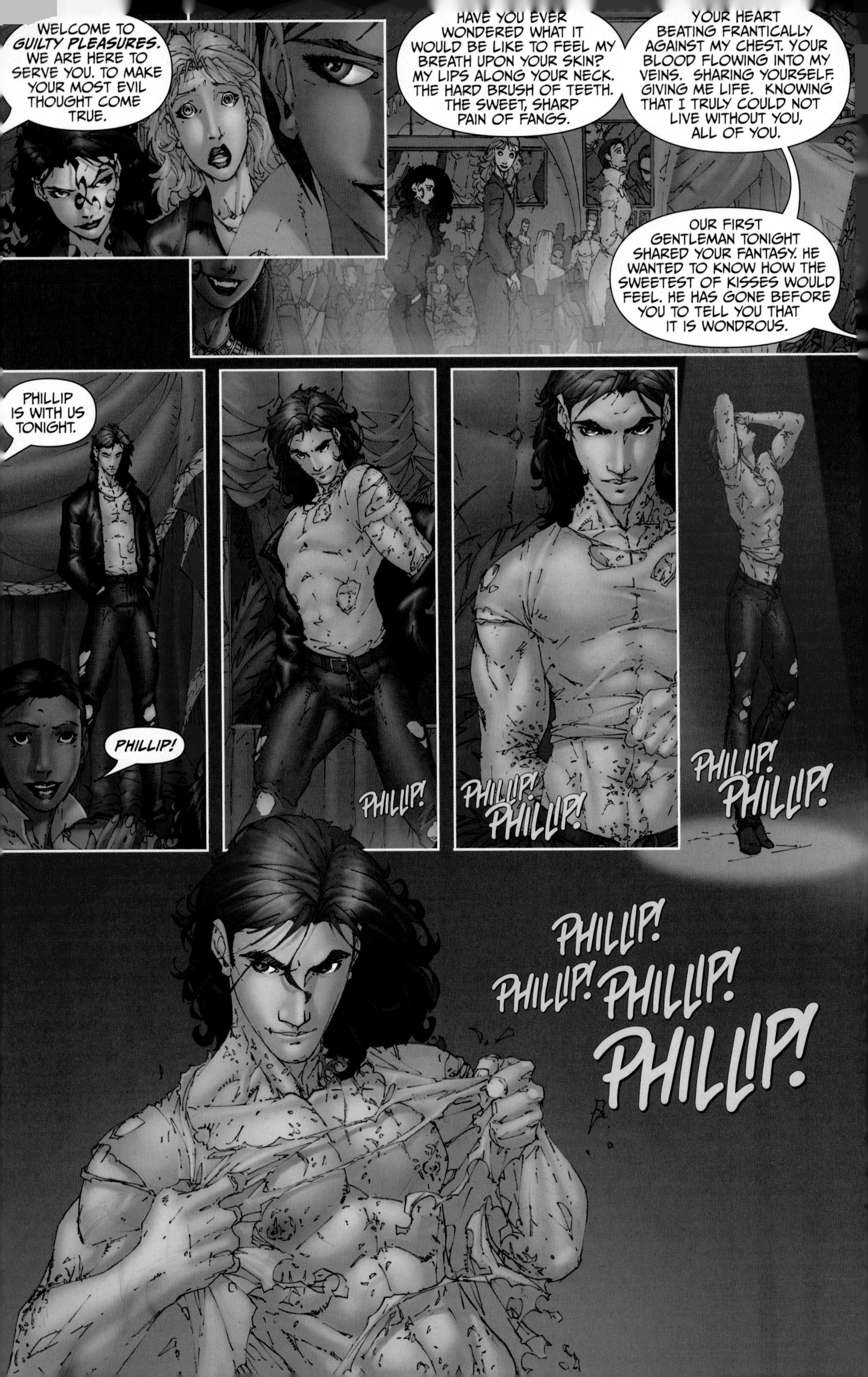
WELCOME TO GUILTY PLEASURES. WE ARE HERE TO SERVE YOU. TO MAKE YOUR MOST EVIL THOUGHT COME TRUE.
HAVE YOU EVER WONDERED WHAT IT WOULD BE LIKE TO FEEL MY BREATH UPON YOUR SKIN? MY LIPS ALONG YOUR NECK. THE HARD BRUSH OF TEETH. THE SWEET, SHARP PAIN OF FANGS.
YOUR HEART BEATING FRANTICALLY AGAINST MY CHEST. YOUR BLOOD FLOWING INTO MY VEINS. SHARING YOURSELF. GIVING ME LIFE. KNOWING THAT I TRULY COULD NOT LIVE WITHOUT YOU, ALL OF YOU.
OUR FIRST GENTLEMAN TONIGHT SHARED YOUR FANTASY. HE WANTED TO KNOW HOW THE SWEETEST OF KISSES WOULD FEEL. HE HAS GONE BEFORE YOU TO TELL YOU THAT IT IS WONDROUS.
PHILLIP IS WITH US TONIGHT.
PHILLIP!
PHILLIP!
PHILLIP! PHILLIP!
PHILLIP! PHILLIP!
PHILLIP!
PHILLIP! PHILLIP!
PHILLIP!

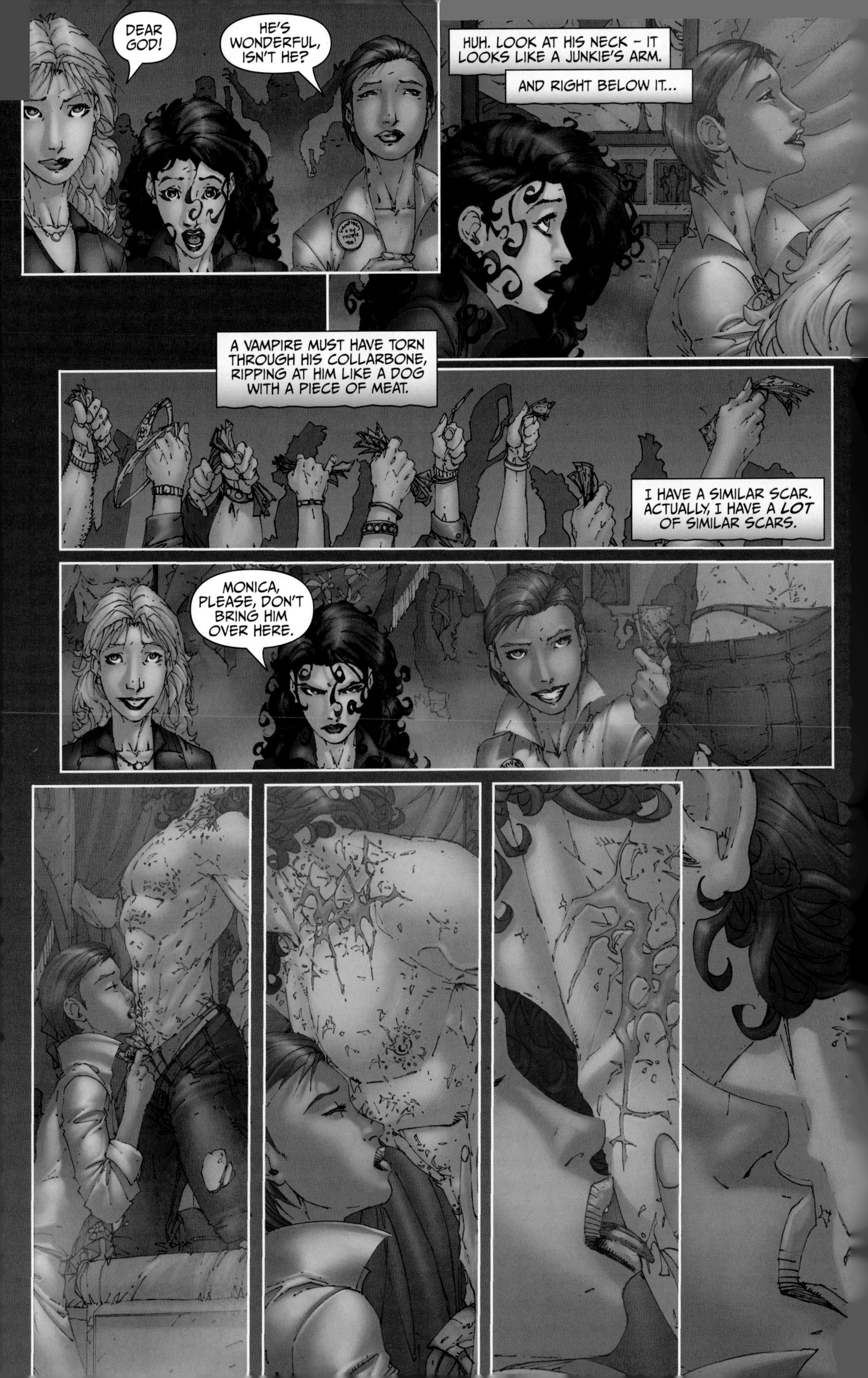
DEAR GOD!
HE'S WONDERFUL, ISN'T HE?
HUH. LOOK AT HIS NECK – IT LOOKS LIKE A JUNKIE'S ARM.
AND RIGHT BELOW IT...
A VAMPIRE MUST HAVE TORN THROUGH HIS COLLARBONE, RIPPING AT HIM LIKE A DOG WITH A PIECE OF MEAT.
I HAVE A SIMILAR SCAR. ACTUALLY, I HAVE A LOT OF SIMILAR SCARS.
MONICA, PLEASE, DON'T BRING HIM OVER HERE.

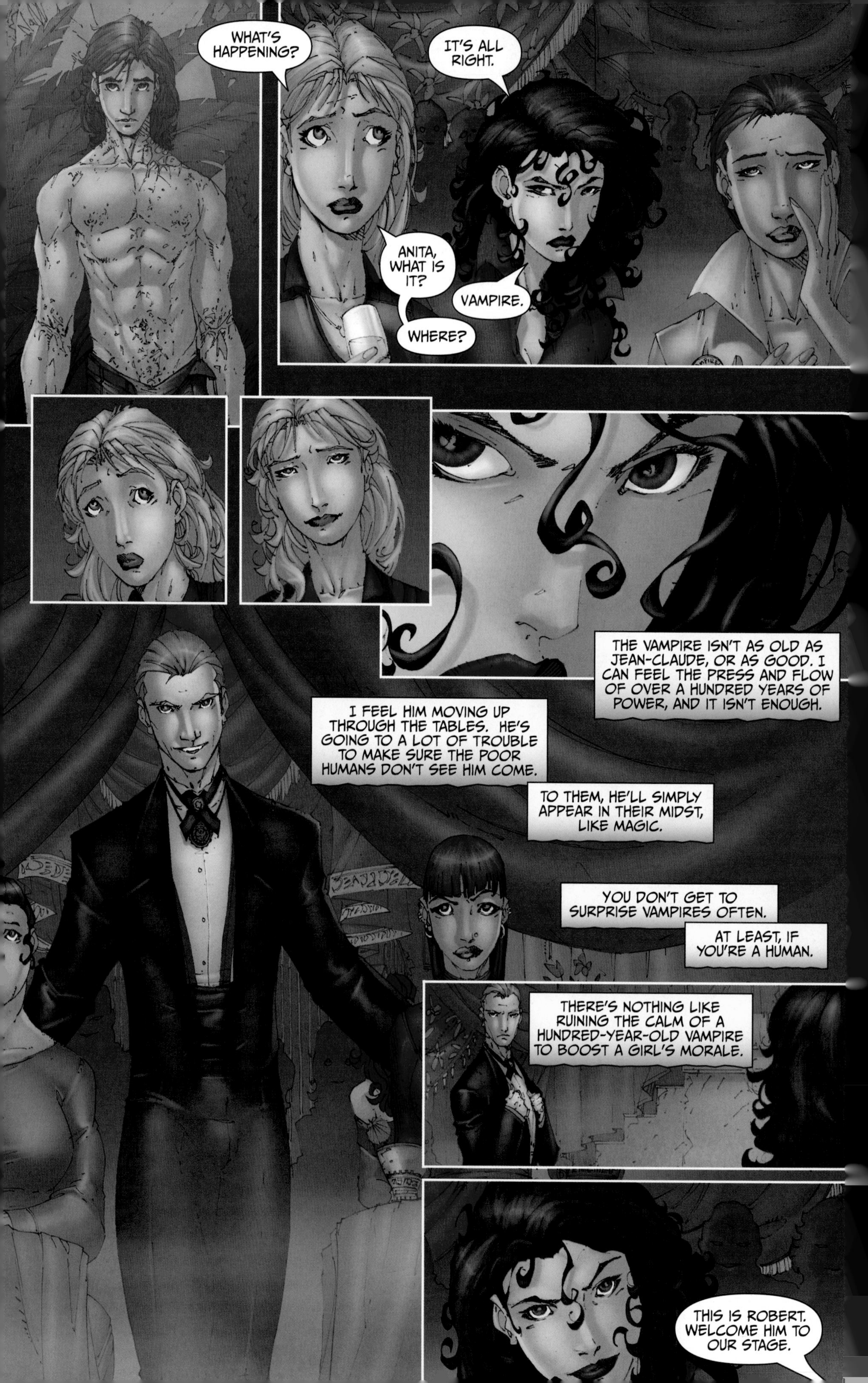
WHAT'S HAPPENING?
IT'S ALL RIGHT.
ANITA, WHAT IS IT?
VAMPIRE.
WHERE?
THE VAMPIRE ISN'T AS OLD AS JEAN-CLAUDE, OR AS GOOD. I CAN FEEL THE PRESS AND FLOW OF OVER A HUNDRED YEARS OF POWER, AND IT ISN'T ENOUGH.
I FEEL HIM MOVING UP THROUGH THE TABLES. HE'S GOING TO A LOT OF TROUBLE TO MAKE SURE THE POOR HUMANS DON'T SEE HIM COME.
TO THEM, HE'LL SIMPLY APPEAR IN THEIR MIDST, LIKE MAGIC.
YOU DON'T GET TO SURPRISE VAMPIRES OFTEN.
AT LEAST, IF YOU'RE A HUMAN.
THERE'S NOTHING LIKE RUINING THE CALM OF A HUNDRED-YEAR-OLD VAMPIRE TO BOOST A GIRL'S MORALE.
THIS IS ROBERT. WELCOME HIM TO OUR STAGE.

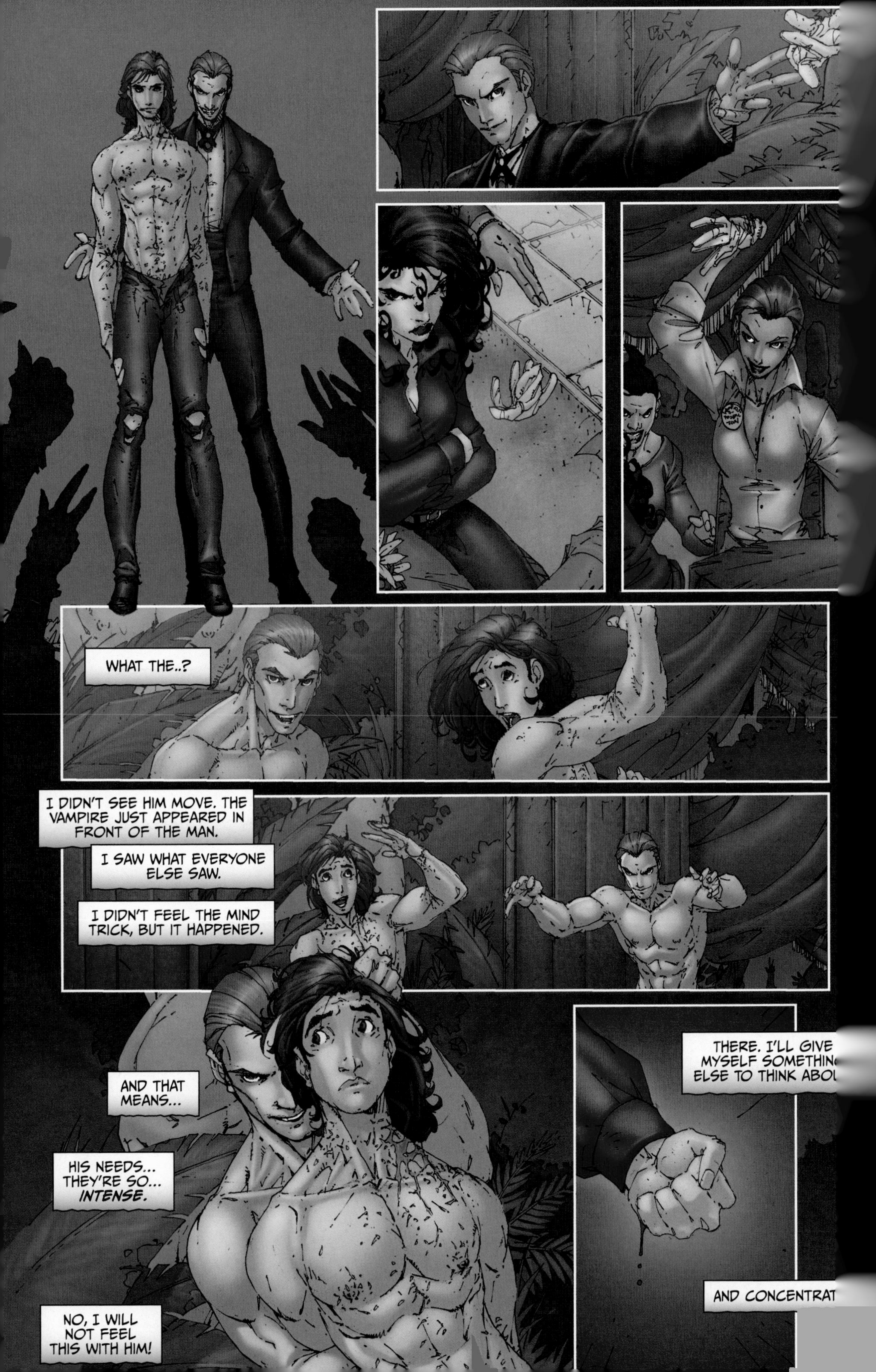
WHAT THE..?
I DIDN'T SEE HIM MOVE. THE VAMPIRE JUST APPEARED IN FRONT OF THE MAN.
I SAW WHAT EVERYONE ELSE SAW.
I DIDN'T FEEL THE MIND TRICK, BUT IT HAPPENED.
AND THAT MEANS...
HIS NEEDS... THEY'RE SO... *INTENSE.*
NO, I WILL NOT FEEL THIS WITH HIM!
THERE. I'LL GIVE MYSELF SOMETHIN ELSE TO THINK ABOU
AND CONCENTRAT

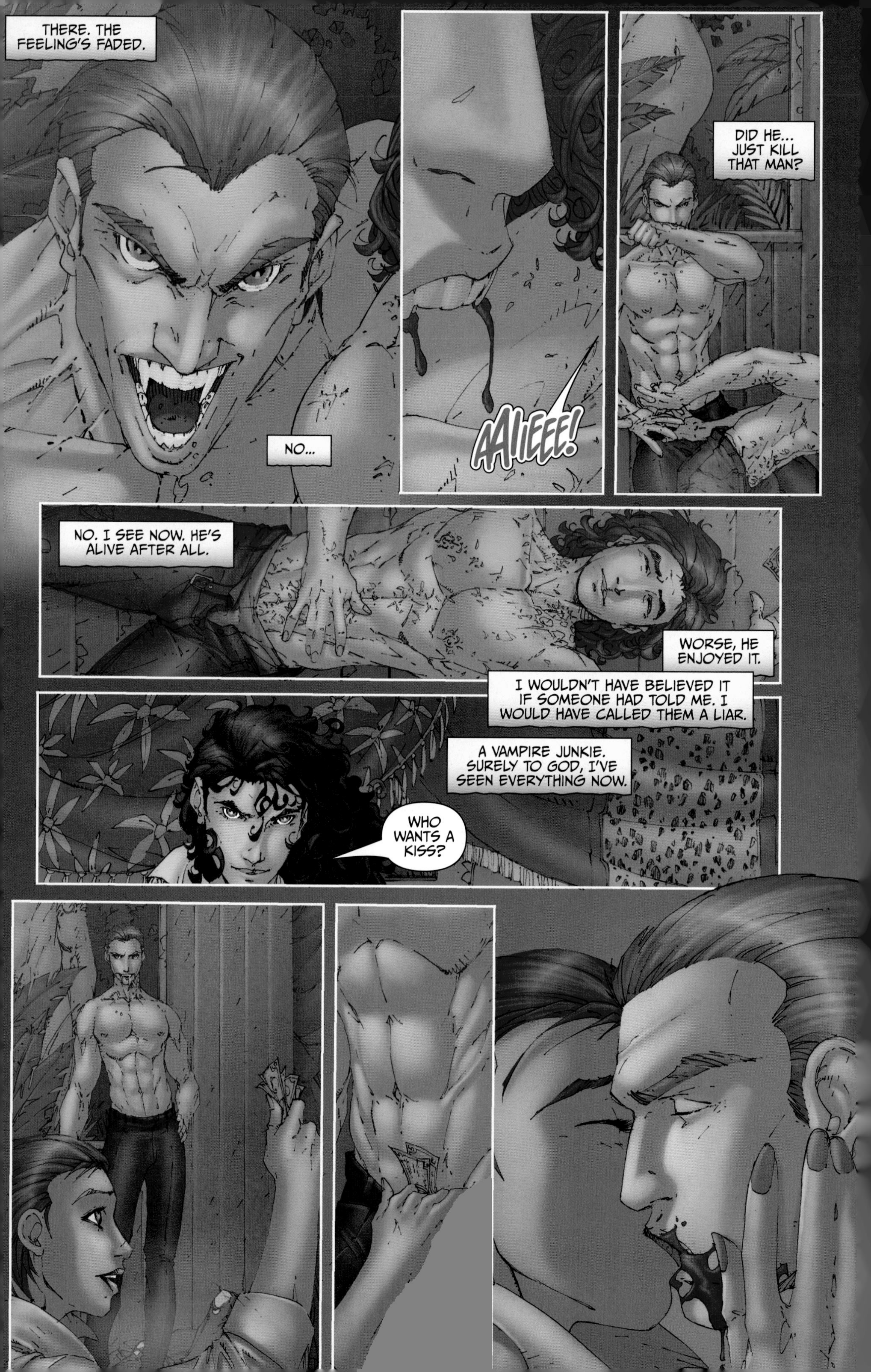
THERE. THE FEELING'S FADED.
NO...
AAIIEEE!
DID HE... JUST KILL THAT MAN?
NO. I SEE NOW. HE'S ALIVE AFTER ALL.
WORSE, HE ENJOYED IT.
I WOULDN'T HAVE BELIEVED IT IF SOMEONE HAD TOLD ME. I WOULD HAVE CALLED THEM A LIAR.
A VAMPIRE JUNKIE. SURELY TO GOD, I'VE SEEN EVERYTHING NOW.
WHO WANTS A KISS?

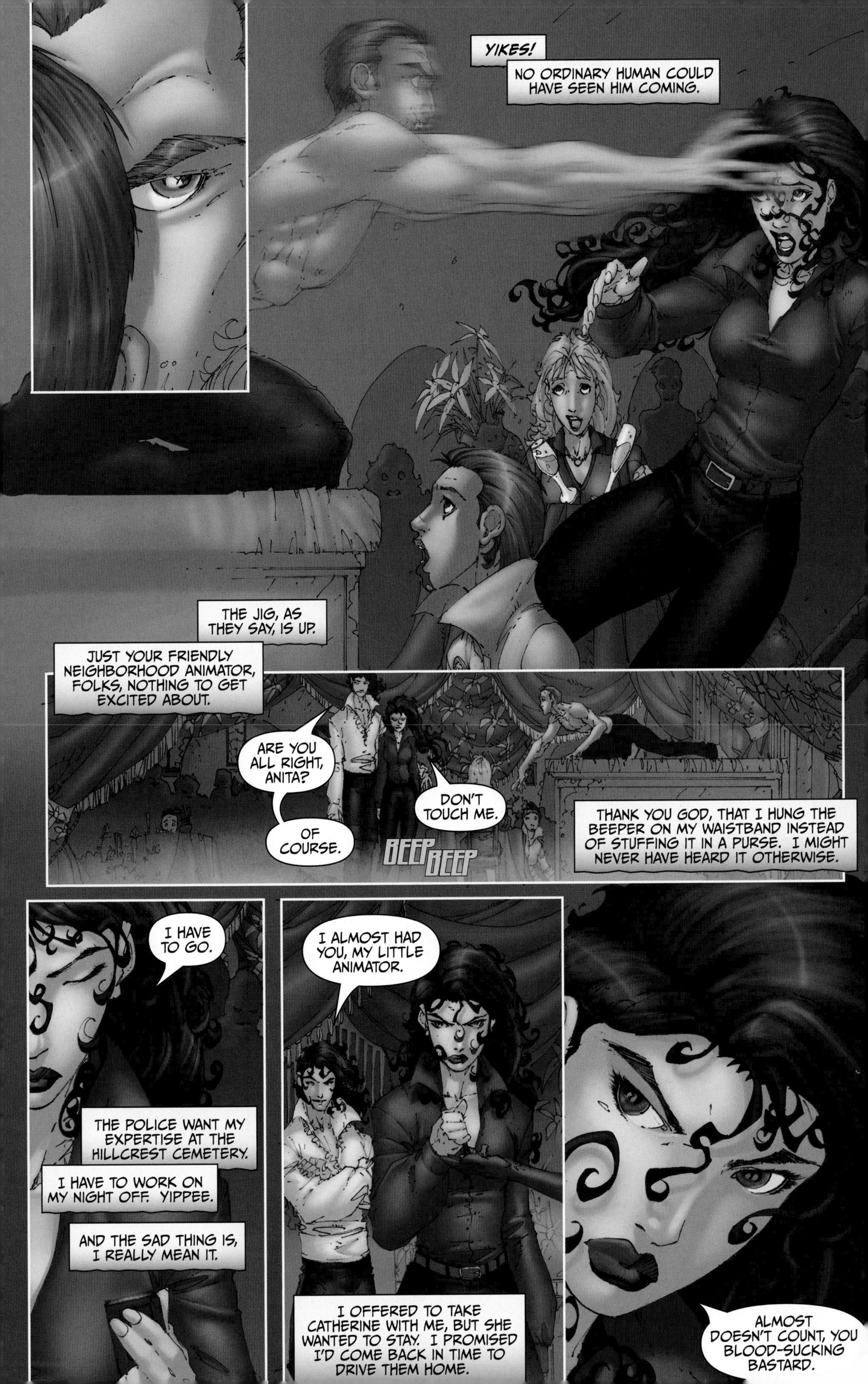
YIKES!
NO ORDINARY HUMAN COULD HAVE SEEN HIM COMING.
THE JIG, AS THEY SAY, IS UP.
JUST YOUR FRIENDLY NEIGHBORHOOD ANIMATOR, FOLKS, NOTHING TO GET EXCITED ABOUT.
ARE YOU ALL RIGHT, ANITA?
OF COURSE.
DON'T TOUCH ME.
BEEP BEEP
THANK YOU GOD, THAT I HUNG THE BEEPER ON MY WAISTBAND INSTEAD OF STUFFING IT IN A PURSE. I MIGHT NEVER HAVE HEARD IT OTHERWISE.
I HAVE TO GO.
THE POLICE WANT MY EXPERTISE AT THE HILLCREST CEMETERY.
I HAVE TO WORK ON MY NIGHT OFF. YIPPEE.
AND THE SAD THING IS, I REALLY MEAN IT.
I ALMOST HAD YOU, MY LITTLE ANIMATOR.
I OFFERED TO TAKE CATHERINE WITH ME, BUT SHE WANTED TO STAY. I PROMISED I'D COME BACK IN TIME TO DRIVE THEM HOME.
ALMOST DOESN'T COUNT, YOU BLOOD-SUCKING BASTARD.

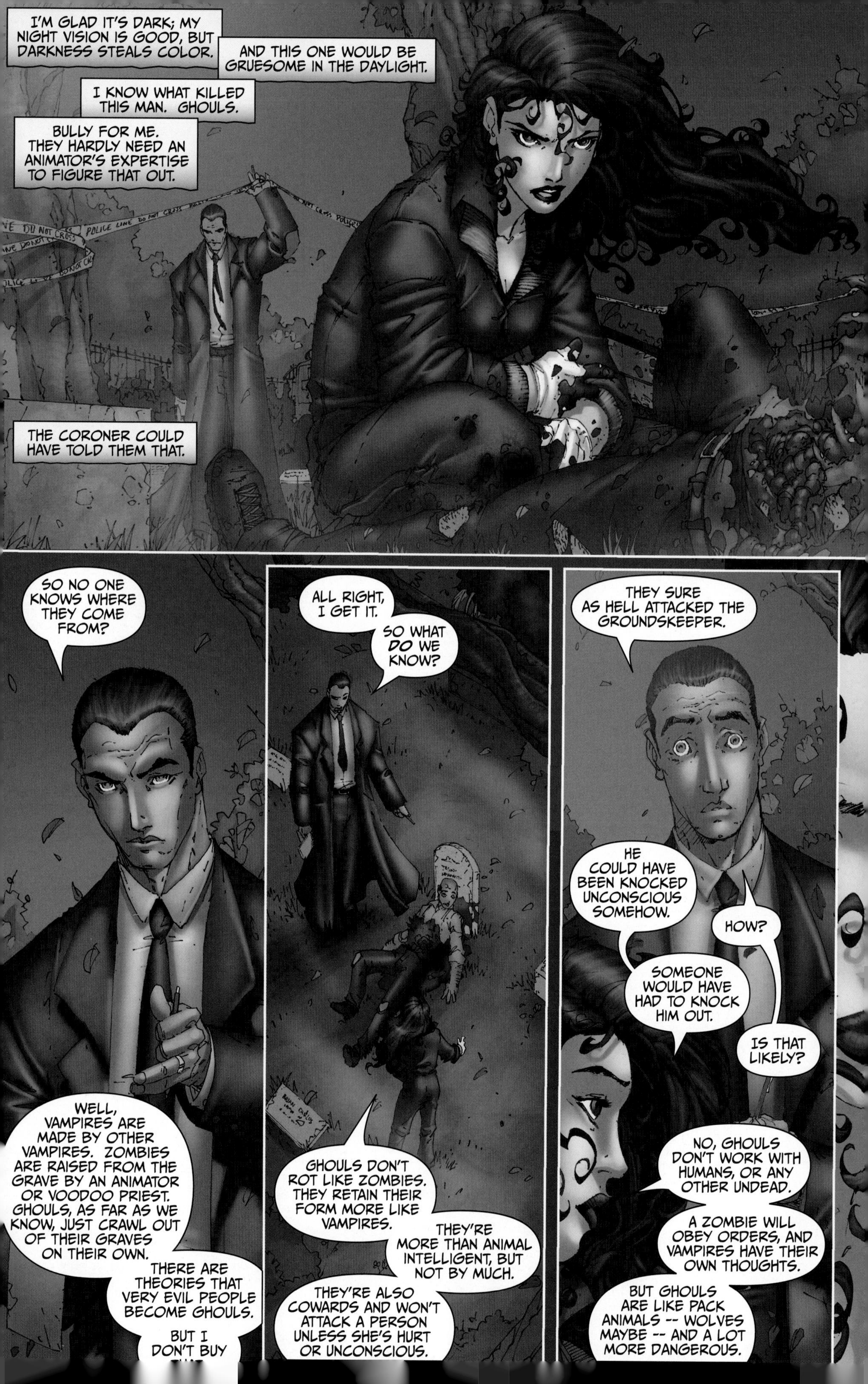
I'M GLAD IT'S DARK; MY NIGHT VISION IS GOOD, BUT DARKNESS STEALS COLOR.
AND THIS ONE WOULD BE GRUESOME IN THE DAYLIGHT.
I KNOW WHAT KILLED THIS MAN. GHOULS.
BULLY FOR ME. THEY HARDLY NEED AN ANIMATOR'S EXPERTISE TO FIGURE THAT OUT.
THE CORONER COULD HAVE TOLD THEM THAT.
SO NO ONE KNOWS WHERE THEY COME FROM?
WELL, VAMPIRES ARE MADE BY OTHER VAMPIRES. ZOMBIES ARE RAISED FROM THE GRAVE BY AN ANIMATOR OR VOODOO PRIEST. GHOULS, AS FAR AS WE KNOW, JUST CRAWL OUT OF THEIR GRAVES ON THEIR OWN.
THERE ARE THEORIES THAT VERY EVIL PEOPLE BECOME GHOULS.
BUT I DON'T BUY
ALL RIGHT, I GET IT.
SO WHAT *DO* WE KNOW?
GHOULS DON'T ROT LIKE ZOMBIES. THEY RETAIN THEIR FORM MORE LIKE VAMPIRES.
THEY'RE MORE THAN ANIMAL INTELLIGENT, BUT NOT BY MUCH.
THEY'RE ALSO COWARDS AND WON'T ATTACK A PERSON UNLESS SHE'S HURT OR UNCONSCIOUS.
THEY SURE AS HELL ATTACKED THE GROUNDSKEEPER.
HE COULD HAVE BEEN KNOCKED UNCONSCIOUS SOMEHOW.
HOW?
SOMEONE WOULD HAVE HAD TO KNOCK HIM OUT.
IS THAT LIKELY?
NO, GHOULS DON'T WORK WITH HUMANS, OR ANY OTHER UNDEAD.
A ZOMBIE WILL OBEY ORDERS, AND VAMPIRES HAVE THEIR OWN THOUGHTS.
BUT GHOULS ARE LIKE PACK ANIMALS -- WOLVES MAYBE -- AND A LOT MORE DANGEROUS.

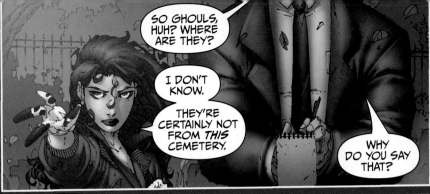

SO GHOULS, HUH? WHERE ARE THEY?

I DON'T KNOW.

THEY'RE CERTAINLY NOT FROM *THIS* CEMETERY.

WHY DO YOU SAY THAT?

THIS CEMETERY IS HOLY GROUND. CEMETERIES THAT HAVE GHOUL INFESTATIONS ARE USUALLY VERY OLD OR HAVE SATANIC OR CERTAIN VOODOO RITES PERFORMED IN THEM.

THE EVIL SORT OF USES UP THE BLESSING, UNTIL THE GROUND BECOMES UNHOLY.

ONCE THAT HAPPENS, GHOULS EITHER MOVE IN OR RISE FROM THE GRAVES. NO ONE'S SURE EXACTLY WHICH.

THEY WOULDN'T BE ABLE TO UNDERSTAND WORKING WITH SOMEONE.

IF YOU'RE NOT A GHOUL, YOU'RE EITHER MEAT OR SOMETHING TO HIDE FROM.

THEN WHAT HAPPENED HERE?

THESE GHOULS TRAVELED QUITE A DISTANCE TO REACH THIS CEMETERY.

THERE ISN'T ANOTHER ONE FOR MILES. GHOULS DON'T TRAVEL LIKE THAT.

SO MAYBE, THEY ATTACKED THE CARETAKER WHEN HE CAME TO SCARE THEM OFF.

THEY SHOULD HAVE RUN FROM HIM; MAYBE THEY DIDN'T.

OKAY, THANKS. SORRY TO INTERRUPT YOUR NIGHT OFF.

THE SECRETARY SAID YOU WERE AT A BACHELORETTE PARTY.

HAVING FUN?

DON'T GIVE ME A HARD TIME, DOLPH.

IF YOU DON'T NEED ME ANYMORE, I'LL BE GETTING BACK.

CALL ME IF YOU THINK OF ANYTHING ELSE.

WILL DO.

YOU BE CAREFUL TONIGHT, ANITA. WOULDN'T WANT YOU GETTING YOURSELF IN TROUBLE PICKING UP ANYONE.

OR ANY*THING*.

YOU HAVE NO IDEA...

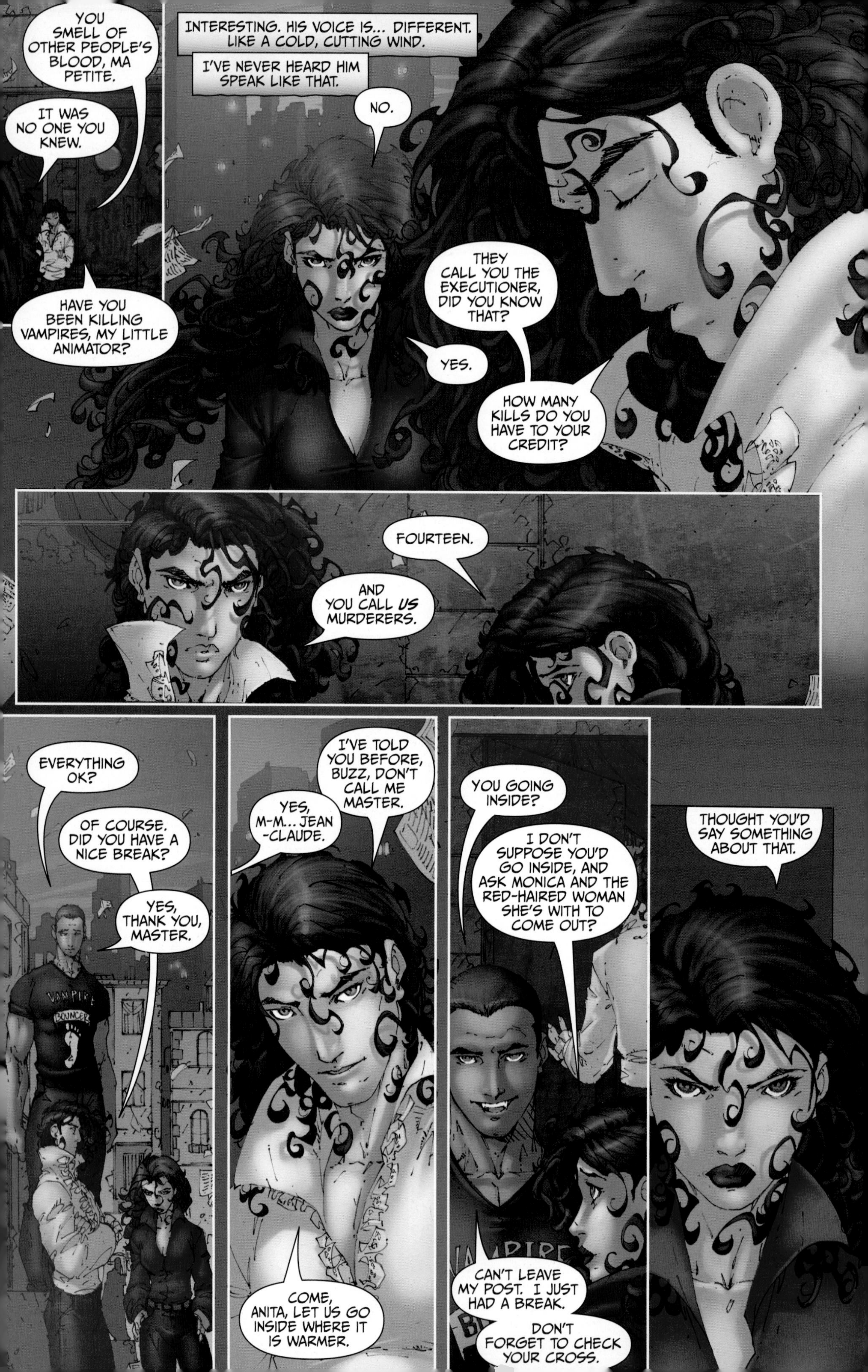
YOU SMELL OF OTHER PEOPLE'S BLOOD, MA PETITE.
IT WAS NO ONE YOU KNEW.
HAVE YOU BEEN KILLING VAMPIRES, MY LITTLE ANIMATOR?
INTERESTING. HIS VOICE IS... DIFFERENT. LIKE A COLD, CUTTING WIND.
I'VE NEVER HEARD HIM SPEAK LIKE THAT.
NO.
THEY CALL YOU THE EXECUTIONER, DID YOU KNOW THAT?
YES.
HOW MANY KILLS DO YOU HAVE TO YOUR CREDIT?
FOURTEEN.
AND YOU CALL US MURDERERS.
EVERYTHING OK?
OF COURSE. DID YOU HAVE A NICE BREAK?
YES, THANK YOU, MASTER.
VAMPIRE BOUNCER
I'VE TOLD YOU BEFORE, BUZZ, DON'T CALL ME MASTER.
YES, M-M... JEAN-CLAUDE.
COME, ANITA, LET US GO INSIDE WHERE IT IS WARMER.
YOU GOING INSIDE?
I DON'T SUPPOSE YOU'D GO INSIDE, AND ASK MONICA AND THE RED-HAIRED WOMAN SHE'S WITH TO COME OUT?
CAN'T LEAVE MY POST. I JUST HAD A BREAK.
DON'T FORGET TO CHECK YOUR CROSS.
THOUGHT YOU'D SAY SOMETHING ABOUT THAT.

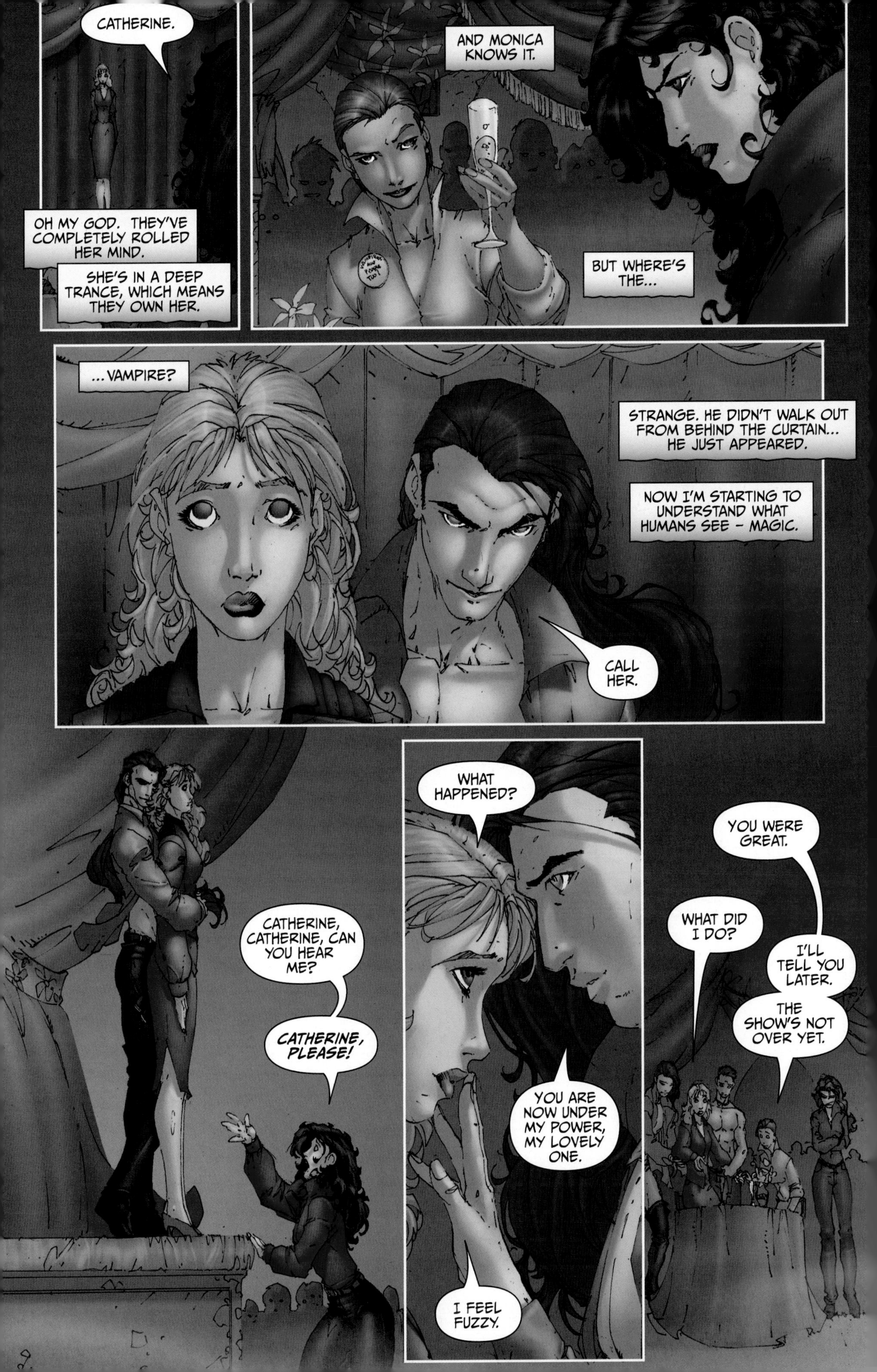
CATHERINE.
OH MY GOD. THEY'VE COMPLETELY ROLLED HER MIND.
SHE'S IN A DEEP TRANCE, WHICH MEANS THEY OWN HER.
AND MONICA KNOWS IT.
BUT WHERE'S THE...
...VAMPIRE?
STRANGE. HE DIDN'T WALK OUT FROM BEHIND THE CURTAIN... HE JUST APPEARED.
NOW I'M STARTING TO UNDERSTAND WHAT HUMANS SEE – MAGIC.
CALL HER.
CATHERINE, CATHERINE, CAN YOU HEAR ME?
CATHERINE, PLEASE!
WHAT HAPPENED?
YOU ARE NOW UNDER MY POWER, MY LOVELY ONE.
I FEEL FUZZY.
YOU WERE GREAT.
WHAT DID I DO?
I'LL TELL YOU LATER.
THE SHOW'S NOT OVER YET.

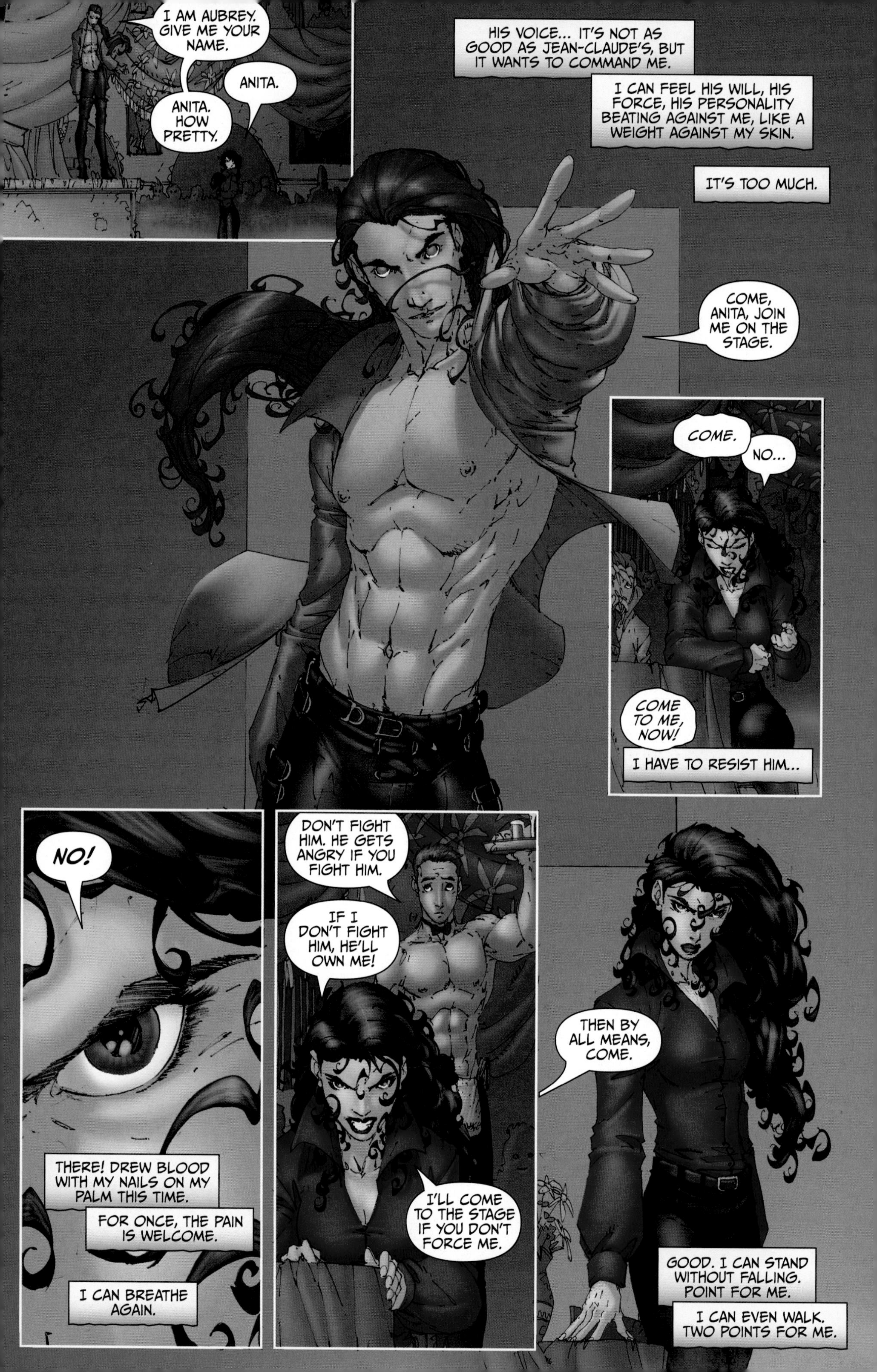
I AM AUBREY. GIVE ME YOUR NAME.
ANITA.
ANITA. HOW PRETTY.
HIS VOICE... IT'S NOT AS GOOD AS JEAN-CLAUDE'S, BUT IT WANTS TO COMMAND ME.
I CAN FEEL HIS WILL, HIS FORCE, HIS PERSONALITY BEATING AGAINST ME, LIKE A WEIGHT AGAINST MY SKIN.
IT'S TOO MUCH.
COME, ANITA, JOIN ME ON THE STAGE.
COME.
NO...
COME TO ME, NOW!
I HAVE TO RESIST HIM...
NO!
THERE! DREW BLOOD WITH MY NAILS ON MY PALM THIS TIME.
FOR ONCE, THE PAIN IS WELCOME.
I CAN BREATHE AGAIN.
DON'T FIGHT HIM. HE GETS ANGRY IF YOU FIGHT HIM.
IF I DON'T FIGHT HIM, HE'LL OWN ME!
I'LL COME TO THE STAGE IF YOU DON'T FORCE ME.
THEN BY ALL MEANS, COME.
GOOD. I CAN STAND WITHOUT FALLING. POINT FOR ME.
I CAN EVEN WALK. TWO POINTS FOR ME.

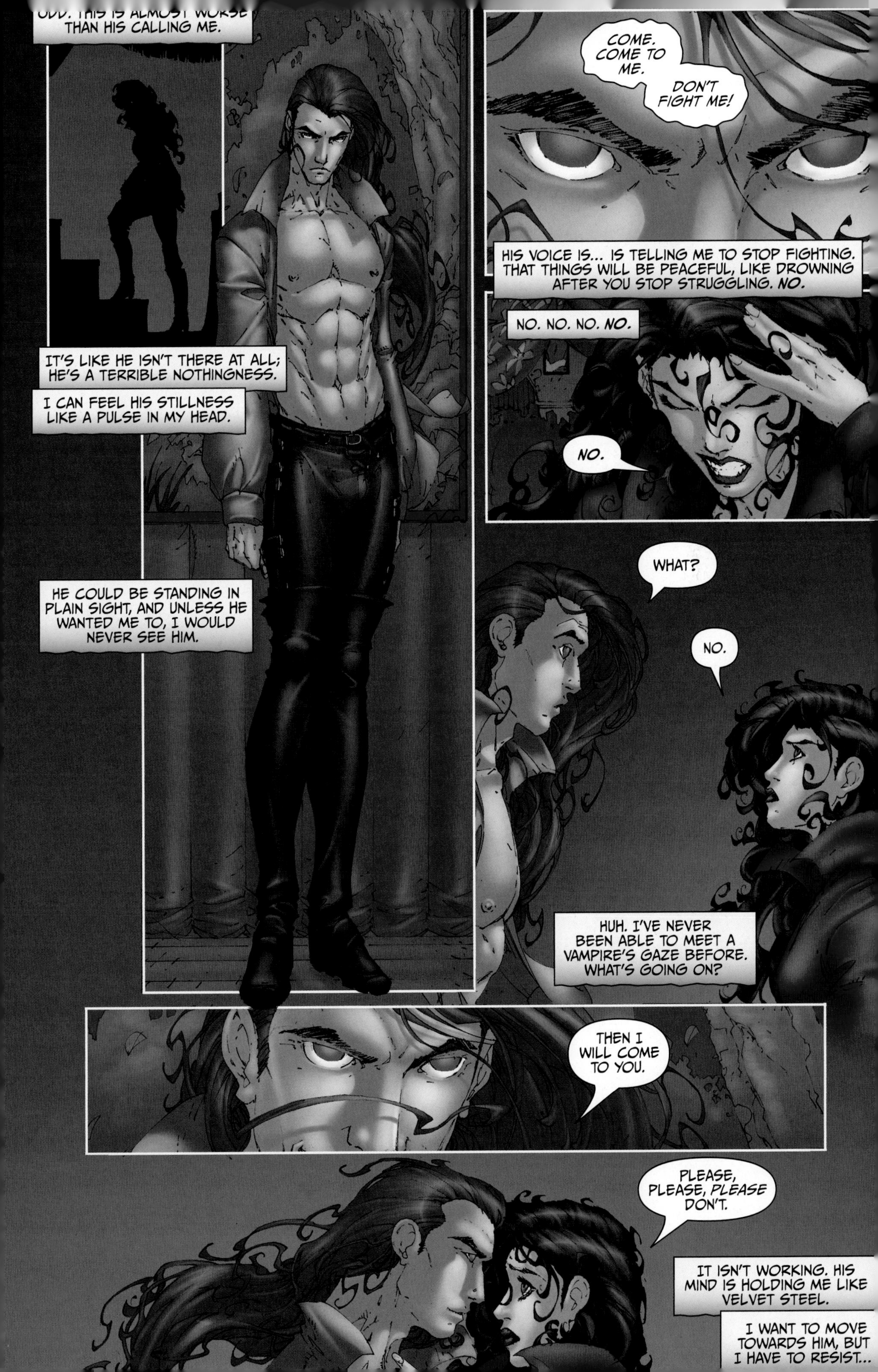
ODD. THIS IS ALMOST WORSE THAN HIS CALLING ME.
IT'S LIKE HE ISN'T THERE AT ALL; HE'S A TERRIBLE NOTHINGNESS.
I CAN FEEL HIS STILLNESS LIKE A PULSE IN MY HEAD.
HE COULD BE STANDING IN PLAIN SIGHT, AND UNLESS HE WANTED ME TO, I WOULD NEVER SEE HIM.
COME. COME TO ME.
DON'T FIGHT ME!
HIS VOICE IS... IS TELLING ME TO STOP FIGHTING. THAT THINGS WILL BE PEACEFUL, LIKE DROWNING AFTER YOU STOP STRUGGLING. NO.
NO. NO. NO. NO.
NO.
WHAT?
NO.
HUH. I'VE NEVER BEEN ABLE TO MEET A VAMPIRE'S GAZE BEFORE. WHAT'S GOING ON?
THEN I WILL COME TO YOU.
PLEASE, PLEASE, PLEASE DON'T.
IT ISN'T WORKING. HIS MIND IS HOLDING ME LIKE VELVET STEEL.
I WANT TO MOVE TOWARDS HIM, BUT I HAVE TO RESIST...

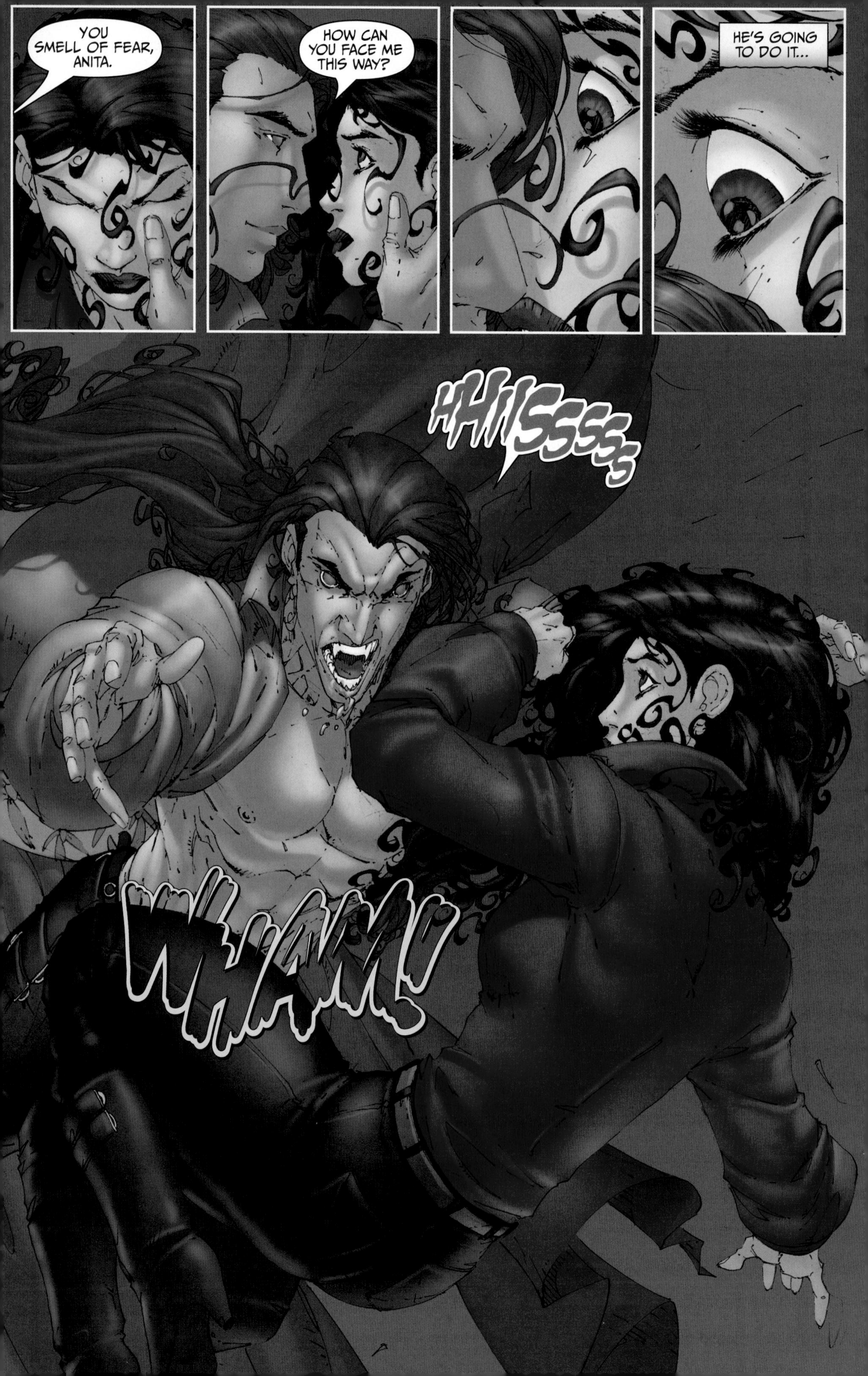
YOU SMELL OF FEAR, ANITA.
HOW CAN YOU FACE ME THIS WAY?
HE'S GOING TO DO IT...
HHISSSSS
WHAM!

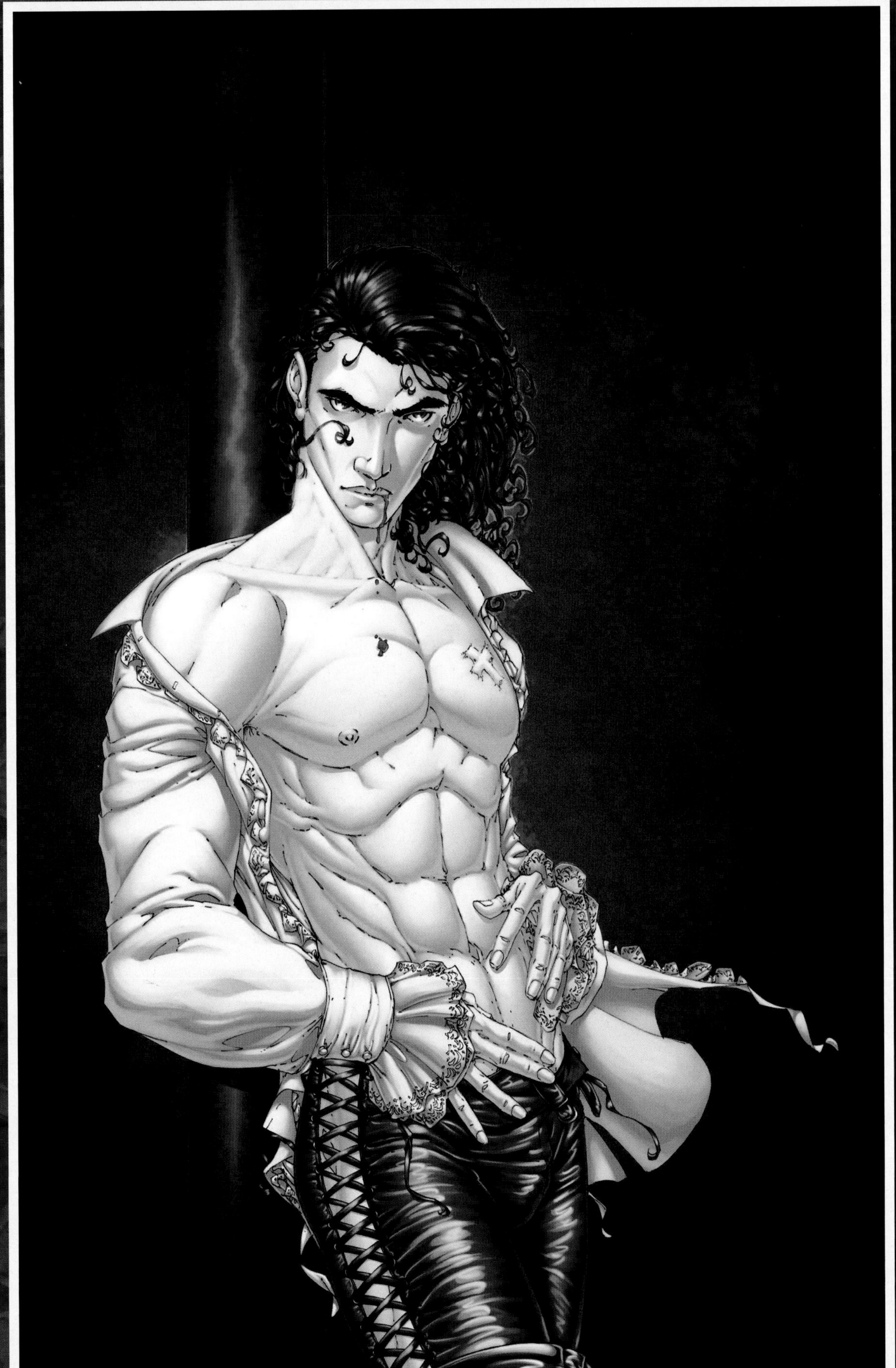

TWO

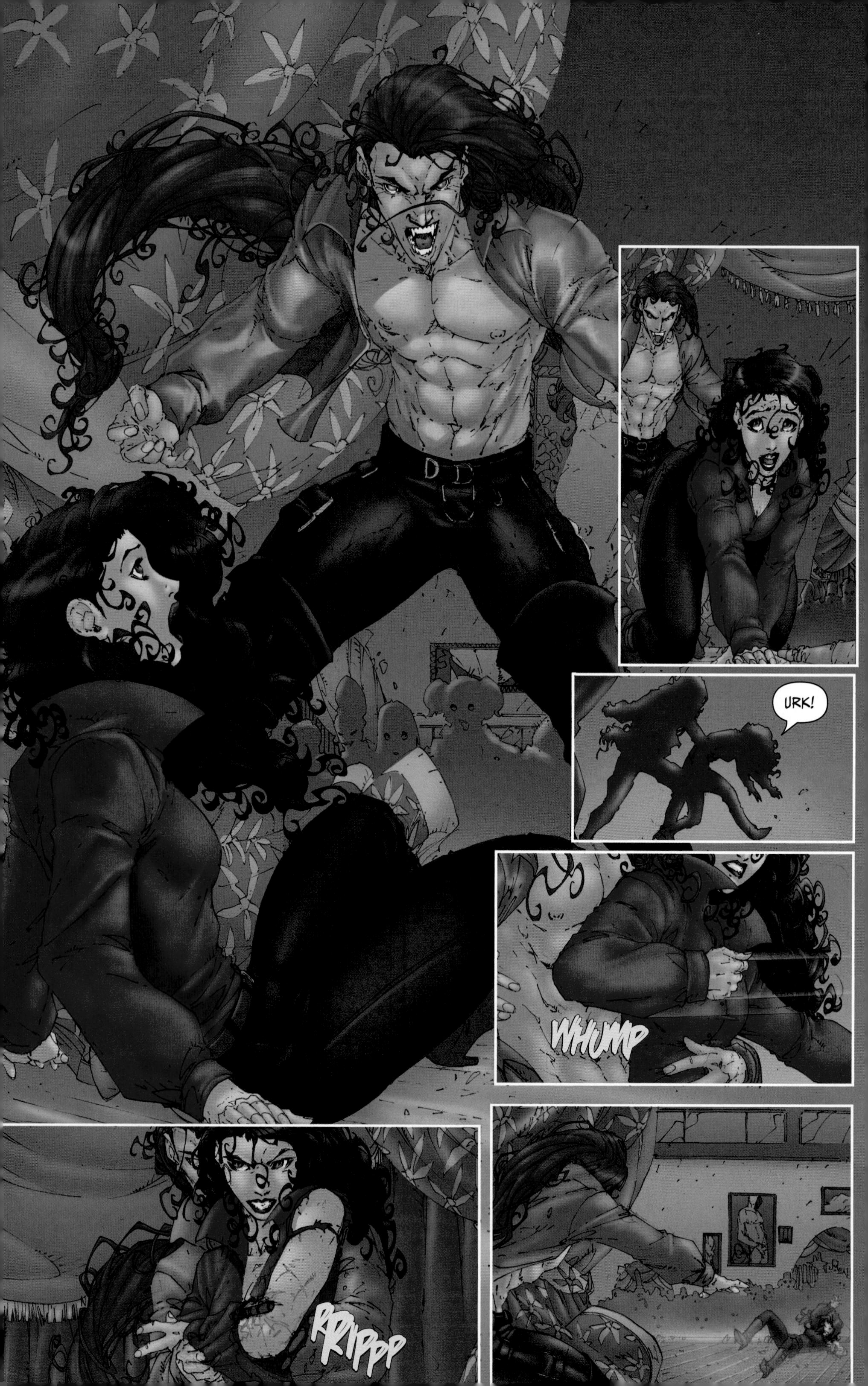
URK!
WHUMP
RRIPPP

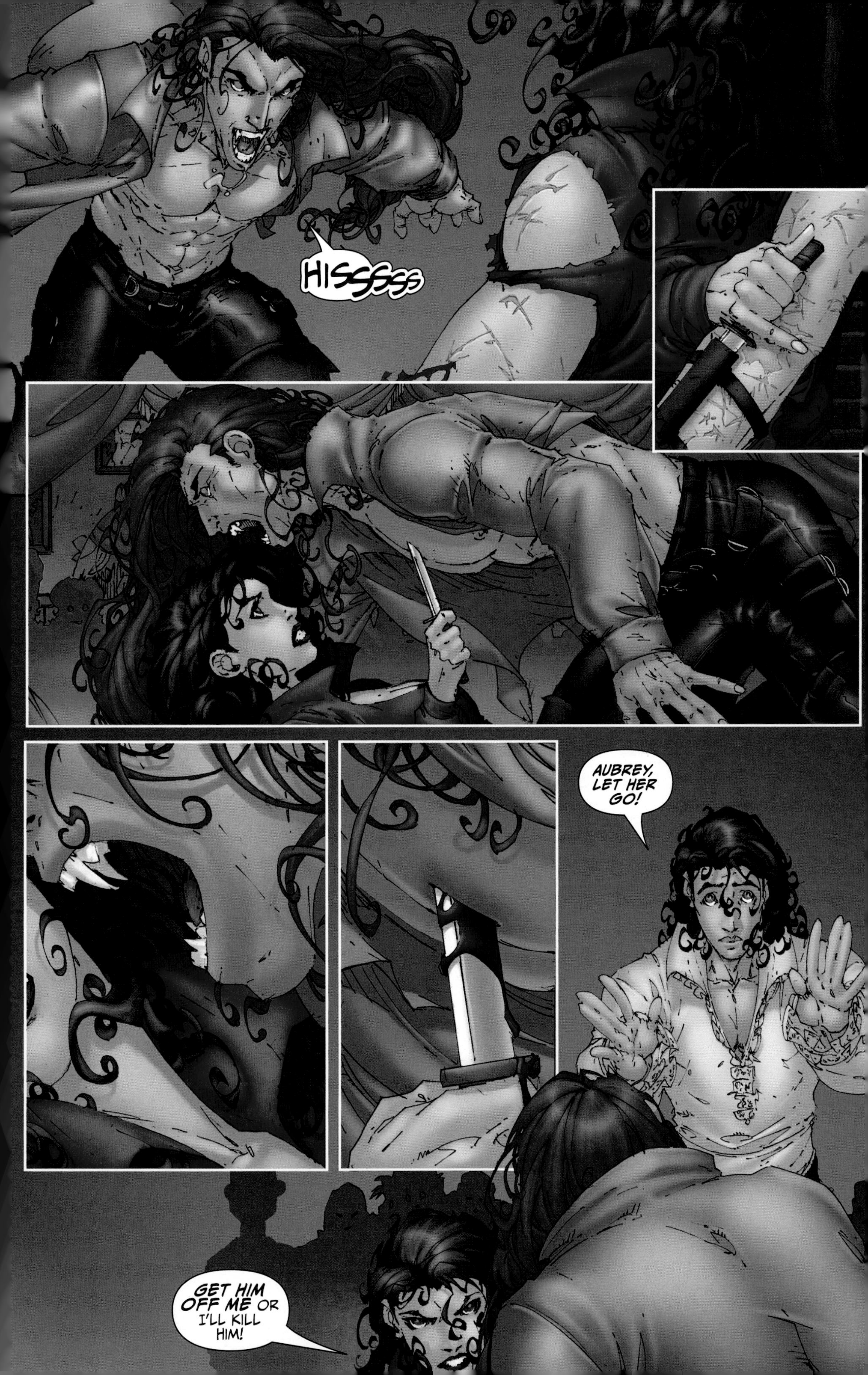
HISSSSSS
AUBREY, LET HER GO!
GET HIM OFF ME OR I'LL KILL HIM!

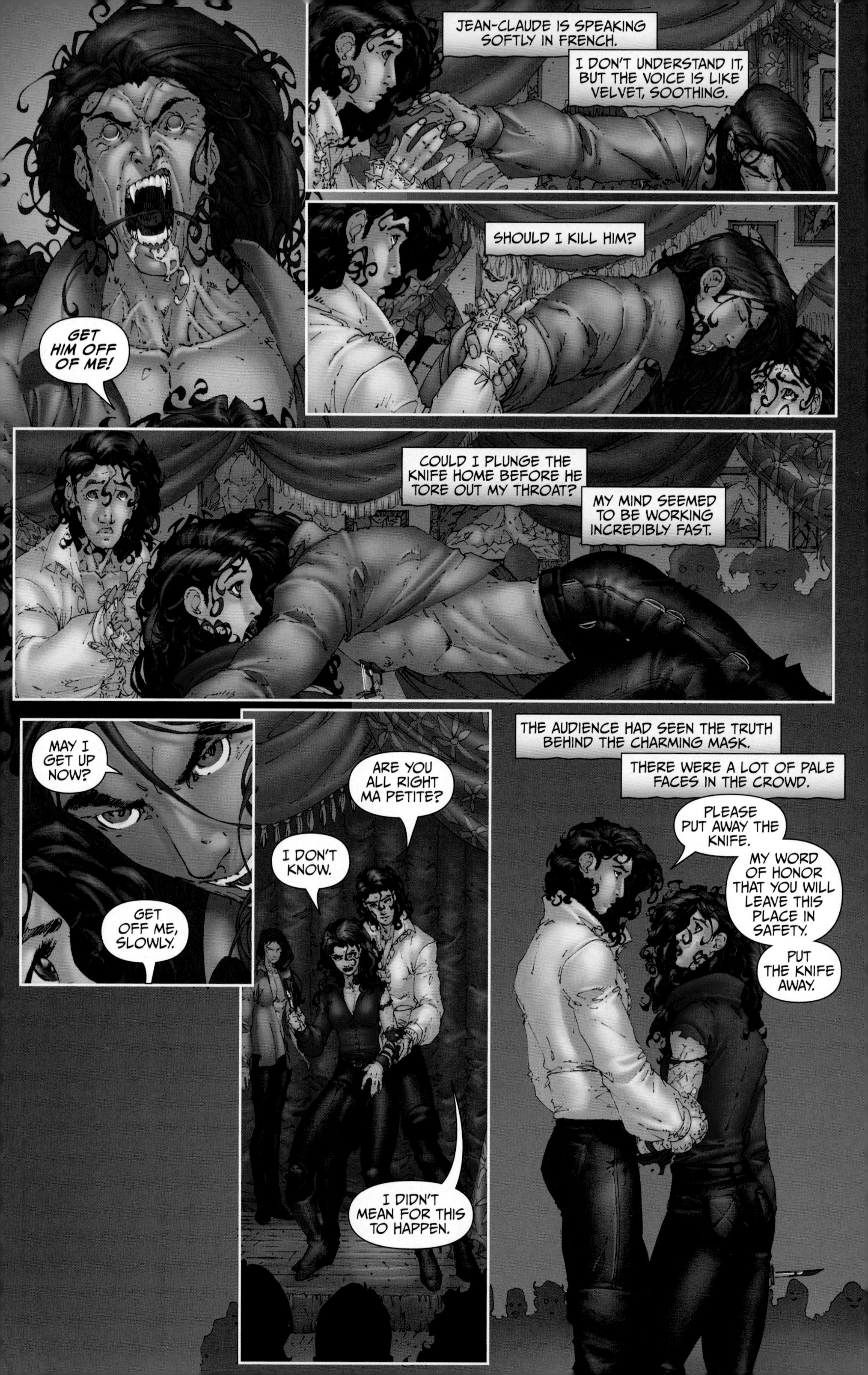
GET HIM OFF OF ME!
JEAN-CLAUDE IS SPEAKING SOFTLY IN FRENCH.
I DON'T UNDERSTAND IT, BUT THE VOICE IS LIKE VELVET, SOOTHING.
SHOULD I KILL HIM?
COULD I PLUNGE THE KNIFE HOME BEFORE HE TORE OUT MY THROAT?
MY MIND SEEMED TO BE WORKING INCREDIBLY FAST.
MAY I GET UP NOW?
GET OFF ME, SLOWLY.
ARE YOU ALL RIGHT MA PETITE?
I DON'T KNOW.
I DIDN'T MEAN FOR THIS TO HAPPEN.
THE AUDIENCE HAD SEEN THE TRUTH BEHIND THE CHARMING MASK.
THERE WERE A LOT OF PALE FACES IN THE CROWD.
PLEASE PUT AWAY THE KNIFE.
MY WORD OF HONOR THAT YOU WILL LEAVE THIS PLACE IN SAFETY.
PUT THE KNIFE AWAY.

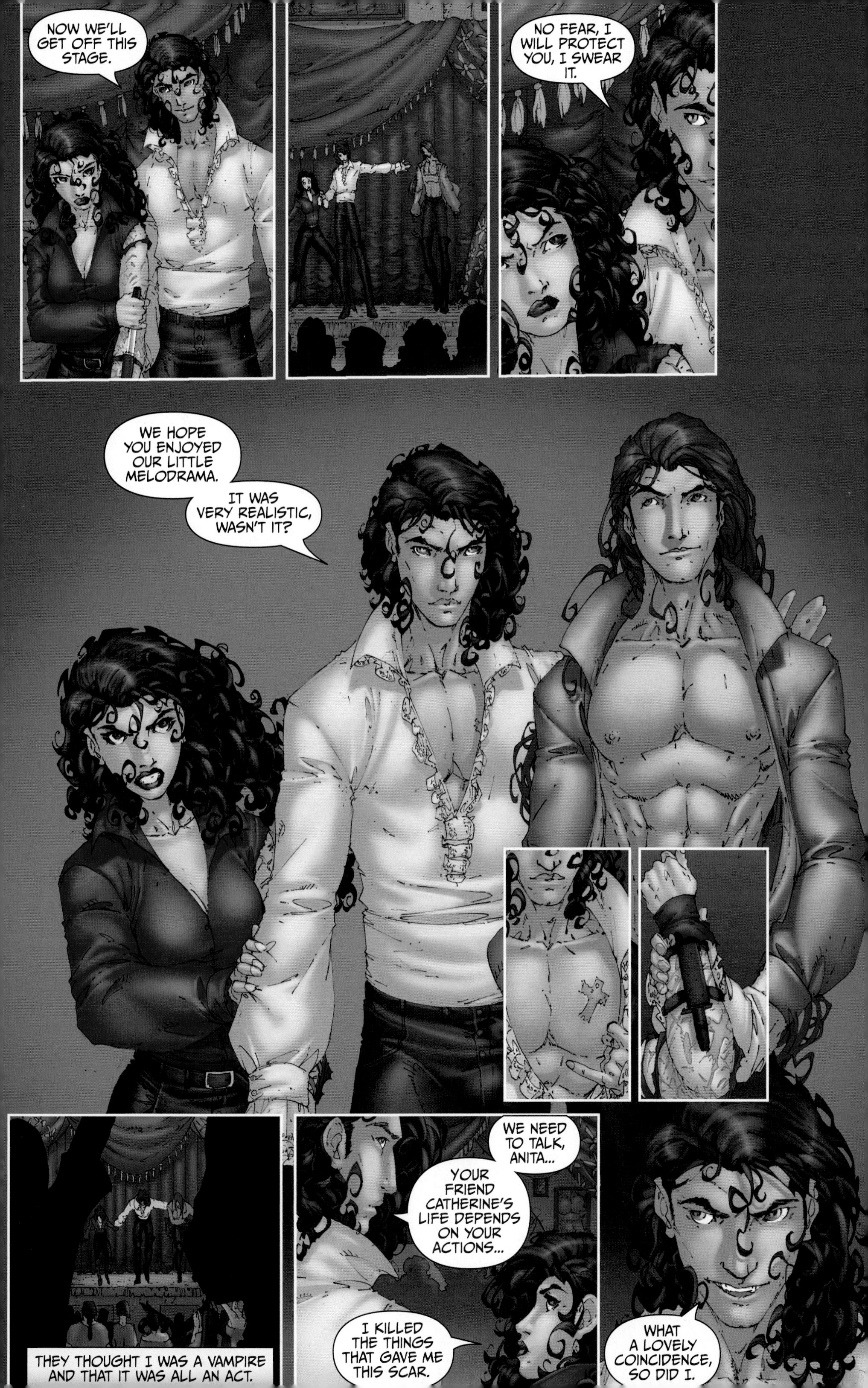
NOW WE'LL GET OFF THIS STAGE.
NO FEAR, I WILL PROTECT YOU, I SWEAR IT.
WE HOPE YOU ENJOYED OUR LITTLE MELODRAMA.
IT WAS VERY REALISTIC, WASN'T IT?
THEY THOUGHT I WAS A VAMPIRE AND THAT IT WAS ALL AN ACT.
WE NEED TO TALK, ANITA...
YOUR FRIEND CATHERINE'S LIFE DEPENDS ON YOUR ACTIONS...
I KILLED THE THINGS THAT GAVE ME THIS SCAR.
WHAT A LOVELY COINCIDENCE, SO DID I.

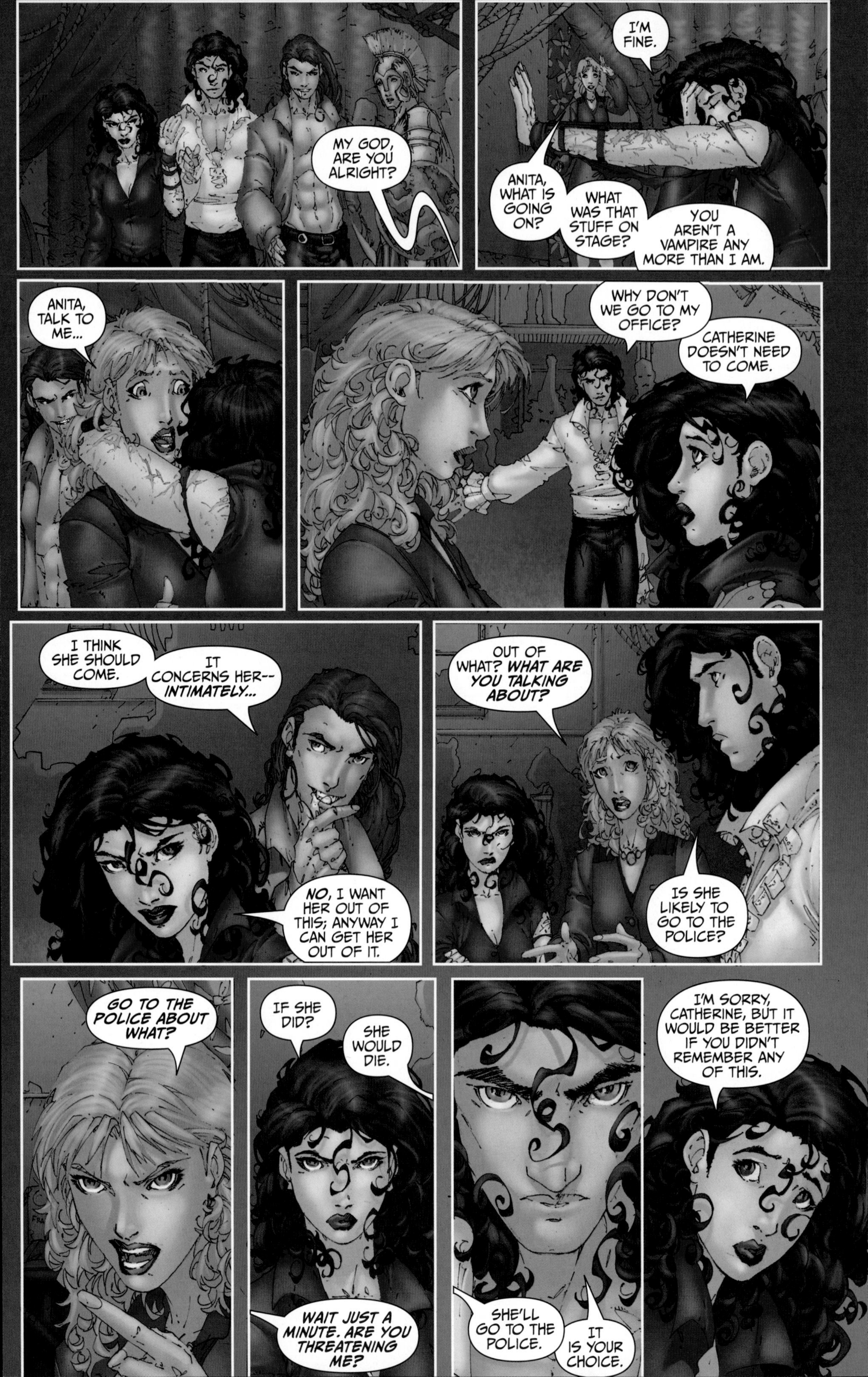
MY GOD, ARE YOU ALRIGHT?
I'M FINE.
ANITA, WHAT IS GOING ON?
WHAT WAS THAT STUFF ON STAGE?
YOU AREN'T A VAMPIRE ANY MORE THAN I AM.
ANITA, TALK TO ME...
WHY DON'T WE GO TO MY OFFICE?
CATHERINE DOESN'T NEED TO COME.
I THINK SHE SHOULD COME.
IT CONCERNS HER-- INTIMATELY...
NO, I WANT HER OUT OF THIS; ANYWAY I CAN GET HER OUT OF IT.
OUT OF WHAT? WHAT ARE YOU TALKING ABOUT?
IS SHE LIKELY TO GO TO THE POLICE?
GO TO THE POLICE ABOUT WHAT?
IF SHE DID?
SHE WOULD DIE.
WAIT JUST A MINUTE. ARE YOU THREATENING ME?
SHE'LL GO TO THE POLICE.
IT IS YOUR CHOICE.
I'M SORRY, CATHERINE, BUT IT WOULD BE BETTER IF YOU DIDN'T REMEMBER ANY OF THIS.

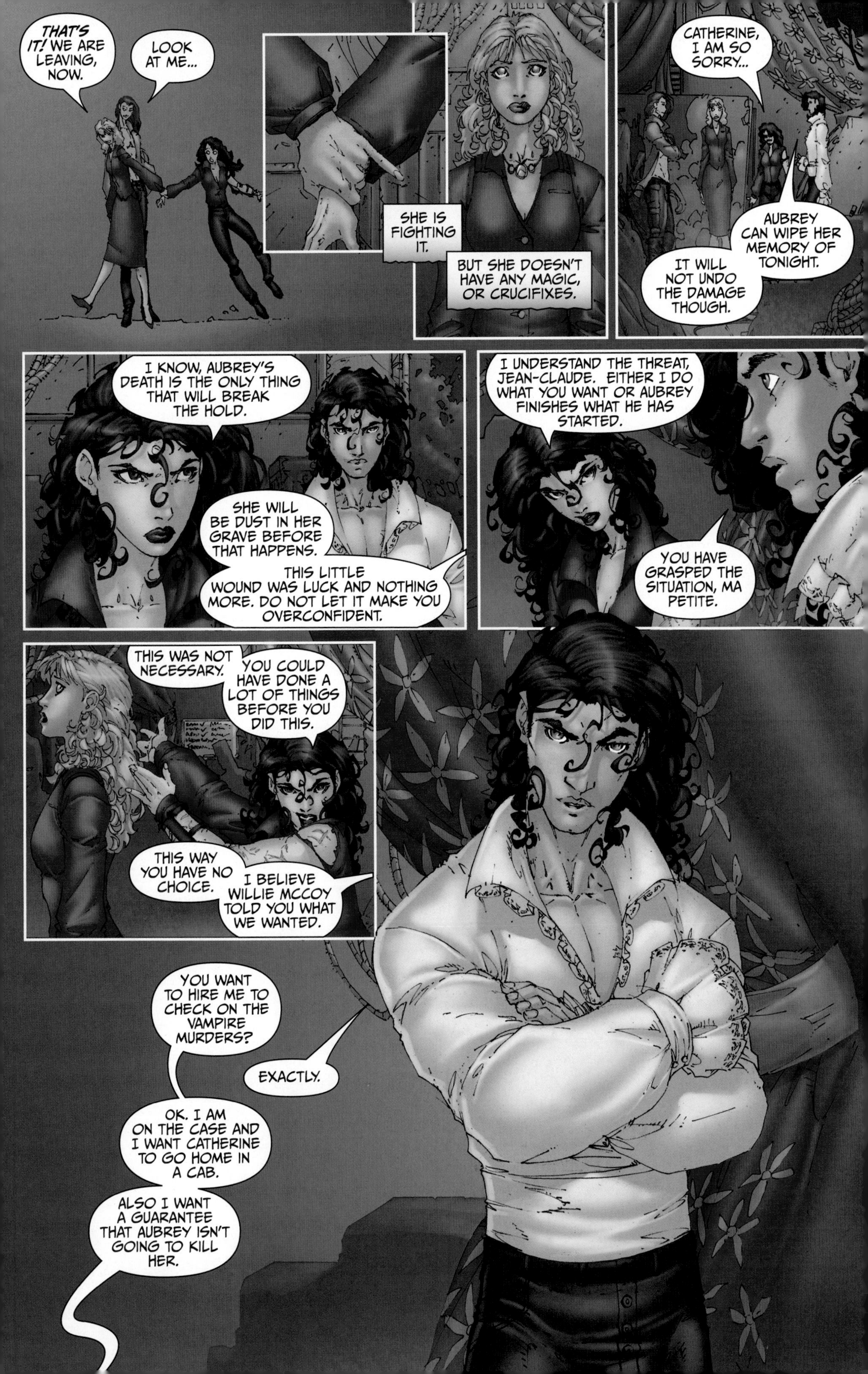
THAT'S IT! WE ARE LEAVING, NOW.
LOOK AT ME...
SHE IS FIGHTING IT.
BUT SHE DOESN'T HAVE ANY MAGIC, OR CRUCIFIXES.
CATHERINE, I AM SO SORRY...
AUBREY CAN WIPE HER MEMORY OF TONIGHT.
IT WILL NOT UNDO THE DAMAGE THOUGH.
I KNOW, AUBREY'S DEATH IS THE ONLY THING THAT WILL BREAK THE HOLD.
SHE WILL BE DUST IN HER GRAVE BEFORE THAT HAPPENS.
THIS LITTLE WOUND WAS LUCK AND NOTHING MORE. DO NOT LET IT MAKE YOU OVERCONFIDENT.
I UNDERSTAND THE THREAT, JEAN-CLAUDE. EITHER I DO WHAT YOU WANT OR AUBREY FINISHES WHAT HE HAS STARTED.
YOU HAVE GRASPED THE SITUATION, MA PETITE.
THIS WAS NOT NECESSARY.
YOU COULD HAVE DONE A LOT OF THINGS BEFORE YOU DID THIS.
THIS WAY YOU HAVE NO CHOICE.
I BELIEVE WILLIE MCCOY TOLD YOU WHAT WE WANTED.
YOU WANT TO HIRE ME TO CHECK ON THE VAMPIRE MURDERS?
EXACTLY.
OK. I AM ON THE CASE AND I WANT CATHERINE TO GO HOME IN A CAB.
ALSO I WANT A GUARANTEE THAT AUBREY ISN'T GOING TO KILL HER.

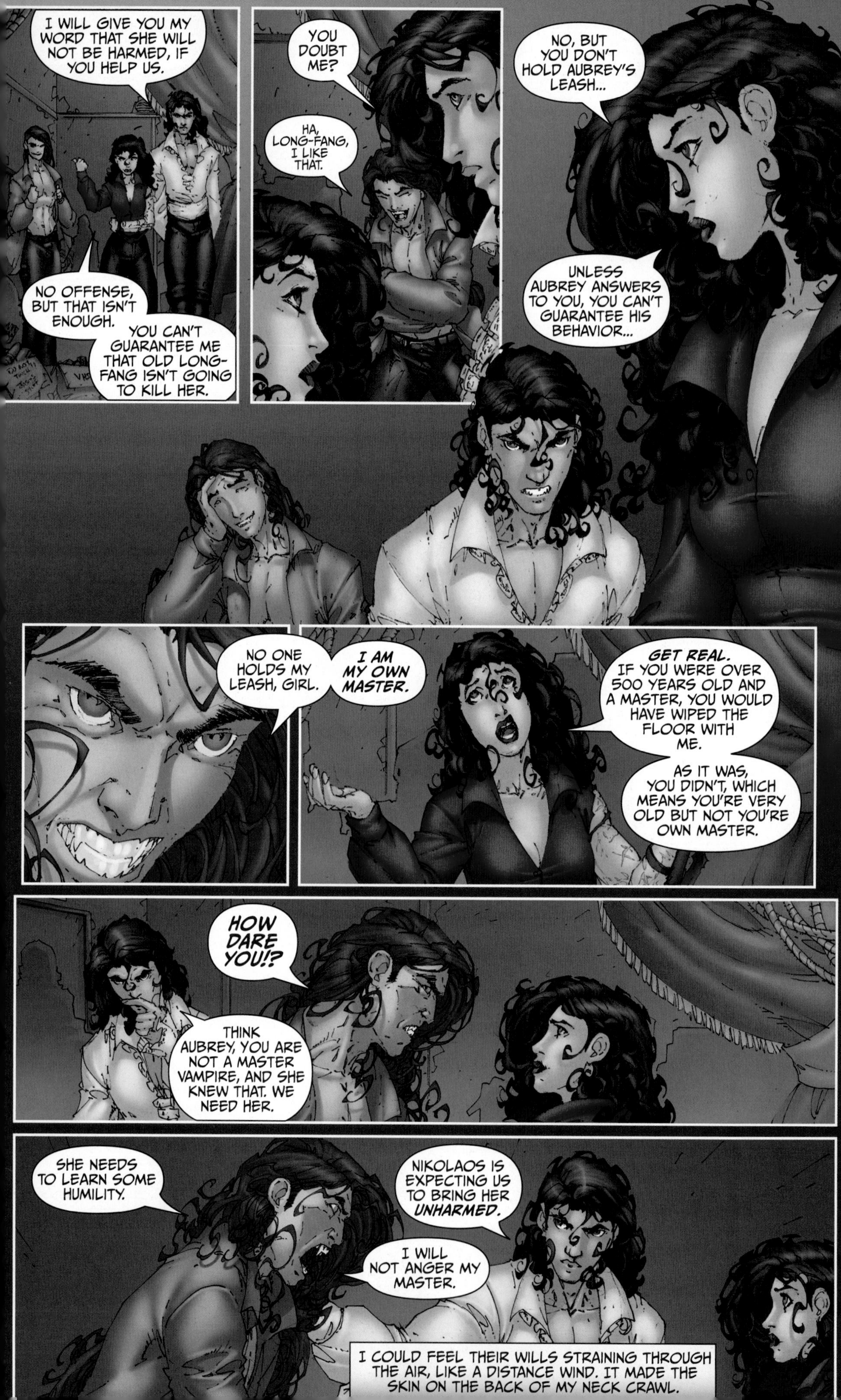
I WILL GIVE YOU MY WORD THAT SHE WILL NOT BE HARMED, IF YOU HELP US.
NO OFFENSE, BUT THAT ISN'T ENOUGH.
YOU CAN'T GUARANTEE ME THAT OLD LONG-FANG ISN'T GOING TO KILL HER.
YOU DOUBT ME?
HA, LONG-FANG, I LIKE THAT.
NO, BUT YOU DON'T HOLD AUBREY'S LEASH...
UNLESS AUBREY ANSWERS TO YOU, YOU CAN'T GUARANTEE HIS BEHAVIOR...
NO ONE HOLDS MY LEASH, GIRL.
I AM MY OWN MASTER.
GET REAL. IF YOU WERE OVER 500 YEARS OLD AND A MASTER, YOU WOULD HAVE WIPED THE FLOOR WITH ME.
AS IT WAS, YOU DIDN'T, WHICH MEANS YOU'RE VERY OLD BUT NOT YOU'RE OWN MASTER.
HOW DARE YOU!?
THINK AUBREY, YOU ARE NOT A MASTER VAMPIRE, AND SHE KNEW THAT. WE NEED HER.
SHE NEEDS TO LEARN SOME HUMILITY.
NIKOLAOS IS EXPECTING US TO BRING HER UNHARMED.
I WILL NOT ANGER MY MASTER.
I COULD FEEL THEIR WILLS STRAINING THROUGH THE AIR, LIKE A DISTANCE WIND. IT MADE THE SKIN ON THE BACK OF MY NECK CRAWL.

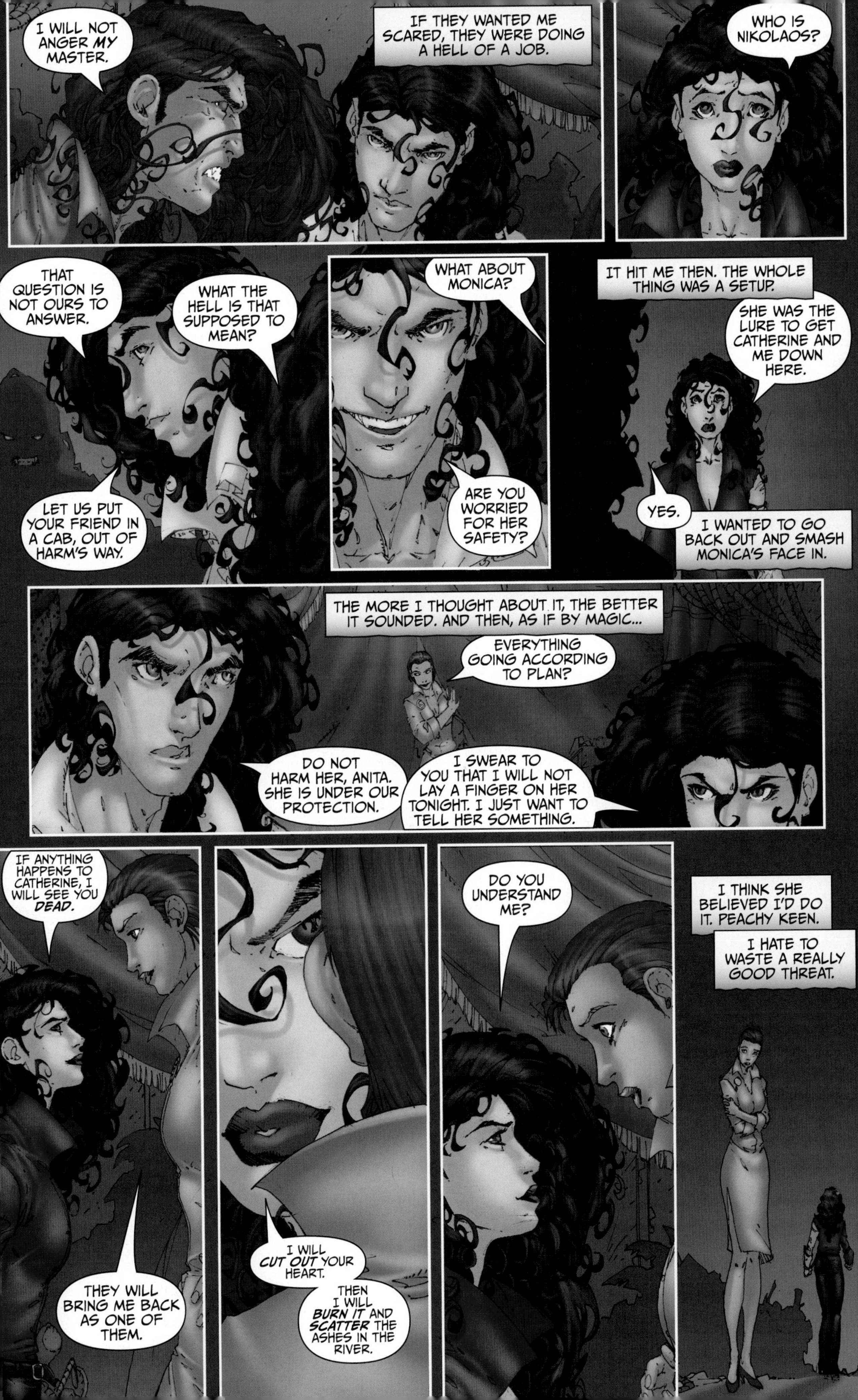
I WILL NOT ANGER MY MASTER.
IF THEY WANTED ME SCARED, THEY WERE DOING A HELL OF A JOB.
WHO IS NIKOLAOS?
THAT QUESTION IS NOT OURS TO ANSWER.
WHAT THE HELL IS THAT SUPPOSED TO MEAN?
LET US PUT YOUR FRIEND IN A CAB, OUT OF HARM'S WAY.
WHAT ABOUT MONICA?
ARE YOU WORRIED FOR HER SAFETY?
IT HIT ME THEN. THE WHOLE THING WAS A SETUP.
SHE WAS THE LURE TO GET CATHERINE AND ME DOWN HERE.
YES.
I WANTED TO GO BACK OUT AND SMASH MONICA'S FACE IN.
THE MORE I THOUGHT ABOUT IT, THE BETTER IT SOUNDED. AND THEN, AS IF BY MAGIC...
EVERYTHING GOING ACCORDING TO PLAN?
DO NOT HARM HER, ANITA. SHE IS UNDER OUR PROTECTION.
I SWEAR TO YOU THAT I WILL NOT LAY A FINGER ON HER TONIGHT. I JUST WANT TO TELL HER SOMETHING.
IF ANYTHING HAPPENS TO CATHERINE, I WILL SEE YOU DEAD.
THEY WILL BRING ME BACK AS ONE OF THEM.
I WILL CUT OUT YOUR HEART.
THEN I WILL BURN IT AND SCATTER THE ASHES IN THE RIVER.
DO YOU UNDERSTAND ME?
I THINK SHE BELIEVED I'D DO IT. PEACHY KEEN.
I HATE TO WASTE A REALLY GOOD THREAT.

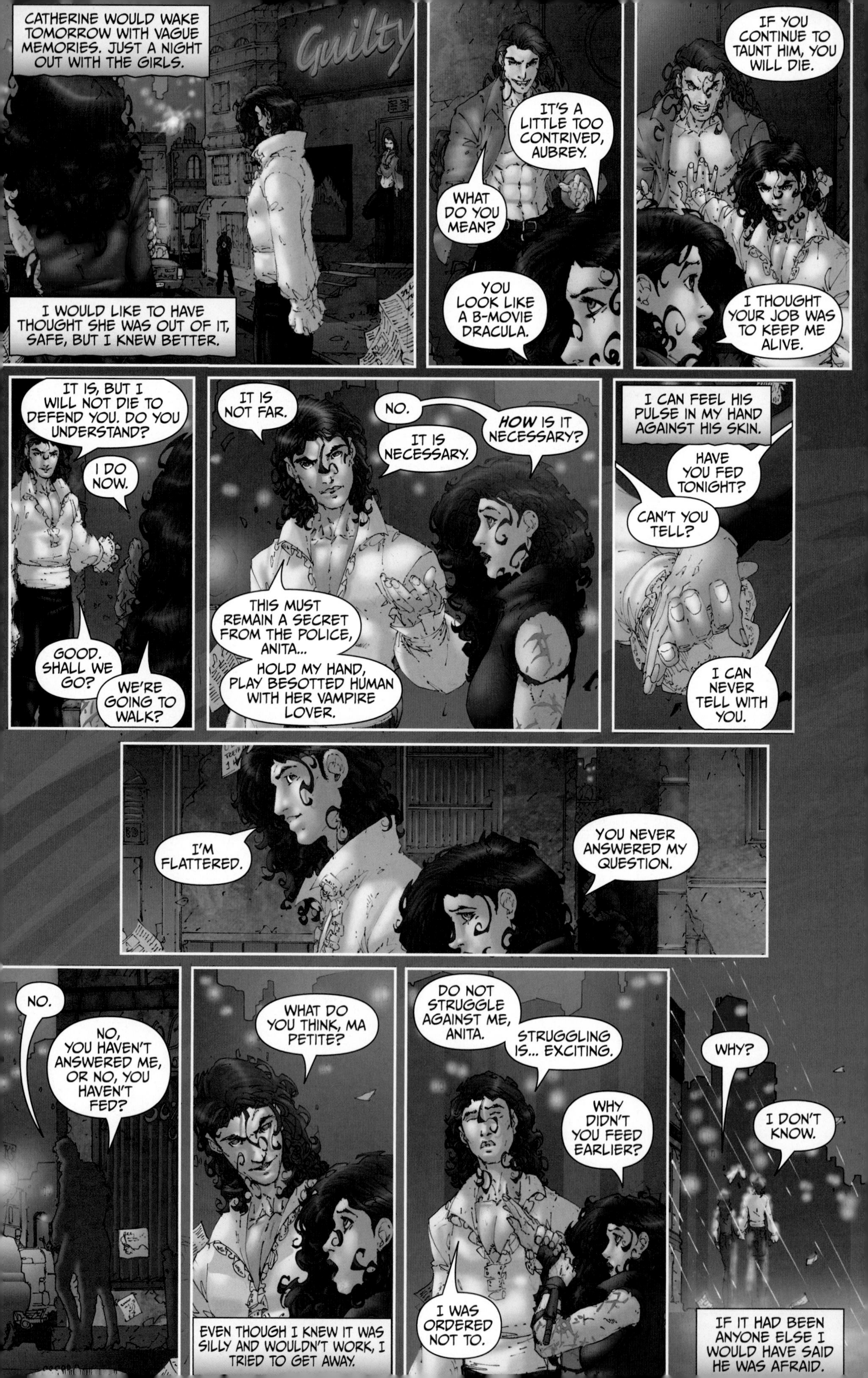
CATHERINE WOULD WAKE TOMORROW WITH VAGUE MEMORIES. JUST A NIGHT OUT WITH THE GIRLS.
Guilty
I WOULD LIKE TO HAVE THOUGHT SHE WAS OUT OF IT, SAFE, BUT I KNEW BETTER.
IT'S A LITTLE TOO CONTRIVED, AUBREY.
WHAT DO YOU MEAN?
YOU LOOK LIKE A B-MOVIE DRACULA.
IF YOU CONTINUE TO TAUNT HIM, YOU WILL DIE.
I THOUGHT YOUR JOB WAS TO KEEP ME ALIVE.
IT IS, BUT I WILL NOT DIE TO DEFEND YOU. DO YOU UNDERSTAND?
I DO NOW.
GOOD. SHALL WE GO?
WE'RE GOING TO WALK?
IT IS NOT FAR.
NO.
IT IS NECESSARY.
HOW IS IT NECESSARY?
THIS MUST REMAIN A SECRET FROM THE POLICE, ANITA...
HOLD MY HAND, PLAY BESOTTED HUMAN WITH HER VAMPIRE LOVER.
I CAN FEEL HIS PULSE IN MY HAND AGAINST HIS SKIN.
HAVE YOU FED TONIGHT?
CAN'T YOU TELL?
I CAN NEVER TELL WITH YOU.
I'M FLATTERED.
YOU NEVER ANSWERED MY QUESTION.
NO.
NO, YOU HAVEN'T ANSWERED ME, OR NO, YOU HAVEN'T FED?
WHAT DO YOU THINK, MA PETITE?
EVEN THOUGH I KNEW IT WAS SILLY AND WOULDN'T WORK, I TRIED TO GET AWAY.
DO NOT STRUGGLE AGAINST ME, ANITA.
STRUGGLING IS... EXCITING.
WHY DIDN'T YOU FEED EARLIER?
I WAS ORDERED NOT TO.
WHY?
I DON'T KNOW.
IF IT HAD BEEN ANYONE ELSE I WOULD HAVE SAID HE WAS AFRAID.

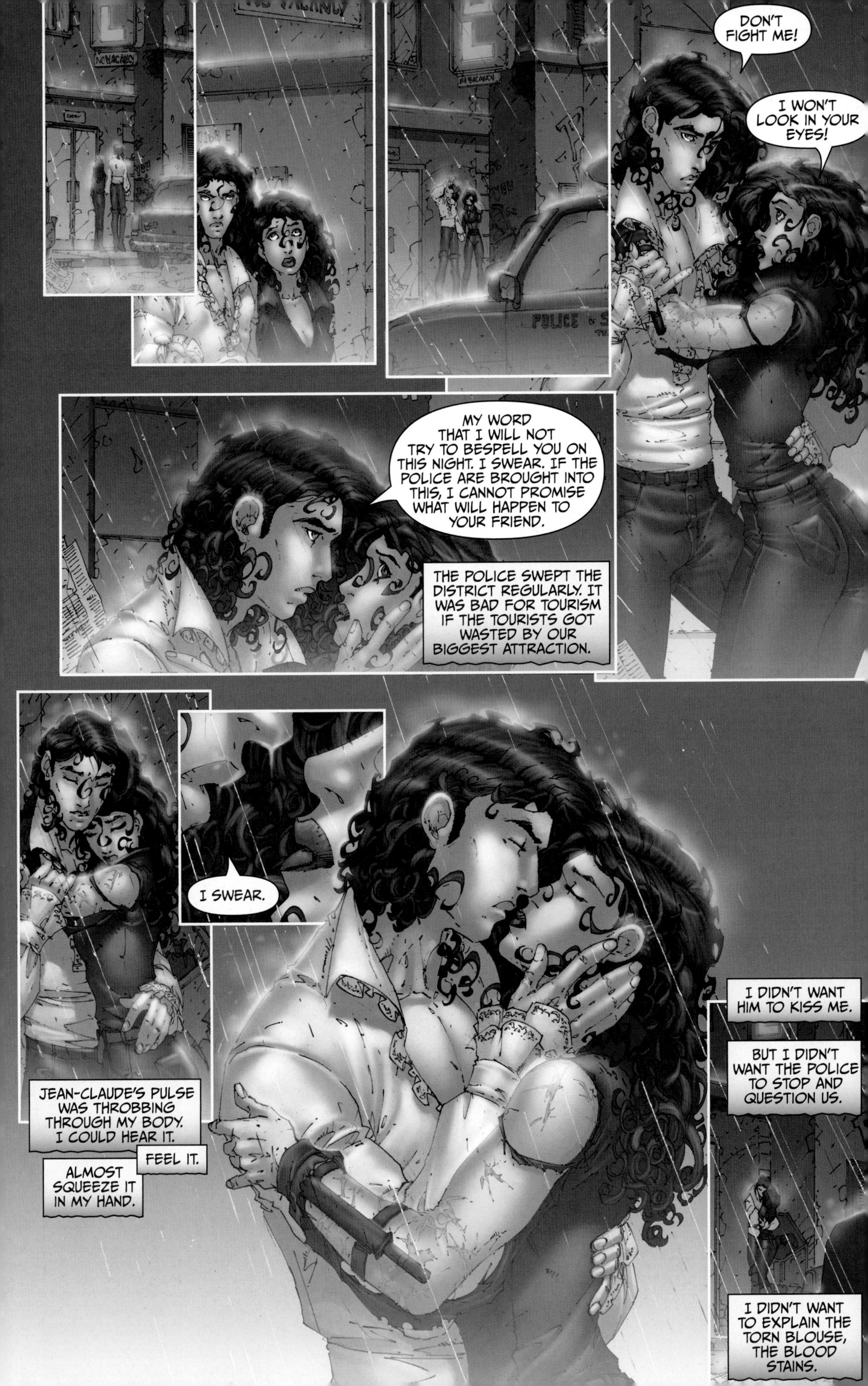
DON'T FIGHT ME!
I WON'T LOOK IN YOUR EYES!
MY WORD THAT I WILL NOT TRY TO BESPELL YOU ON THIS NIGHT. I SWEAR. IF THE POLICE ARE BROUGHT INTO THIS, I CANNOT PROMISE WHAT WILL HAPPEN TO YOUR FRIEND.
THE POLICE SWEPT THE DISTRICT REGULARLY. IT WAS BAD FOR TOURISM IF THE TOURISTS GOT WASTED BY OUR BIGGEST ATTRACTION.
I SWEAR.
JEAN-CLAUDE'S PULSE WAS THROBBING THROUGH MY BODY. I COULD HEAR IT.
FEEL IT.
ALMOST SQUEEZE IT IN MY HAND.
I DIDN'T WANT HIM TO KISS ME.
BUT I DIDN'T WANT THE POLICE TO STOP AND QUESTION US.
I DIDN'T WANT TO EXPLAIN THE TORN BLOUSE, THE BLOOD STAINS.

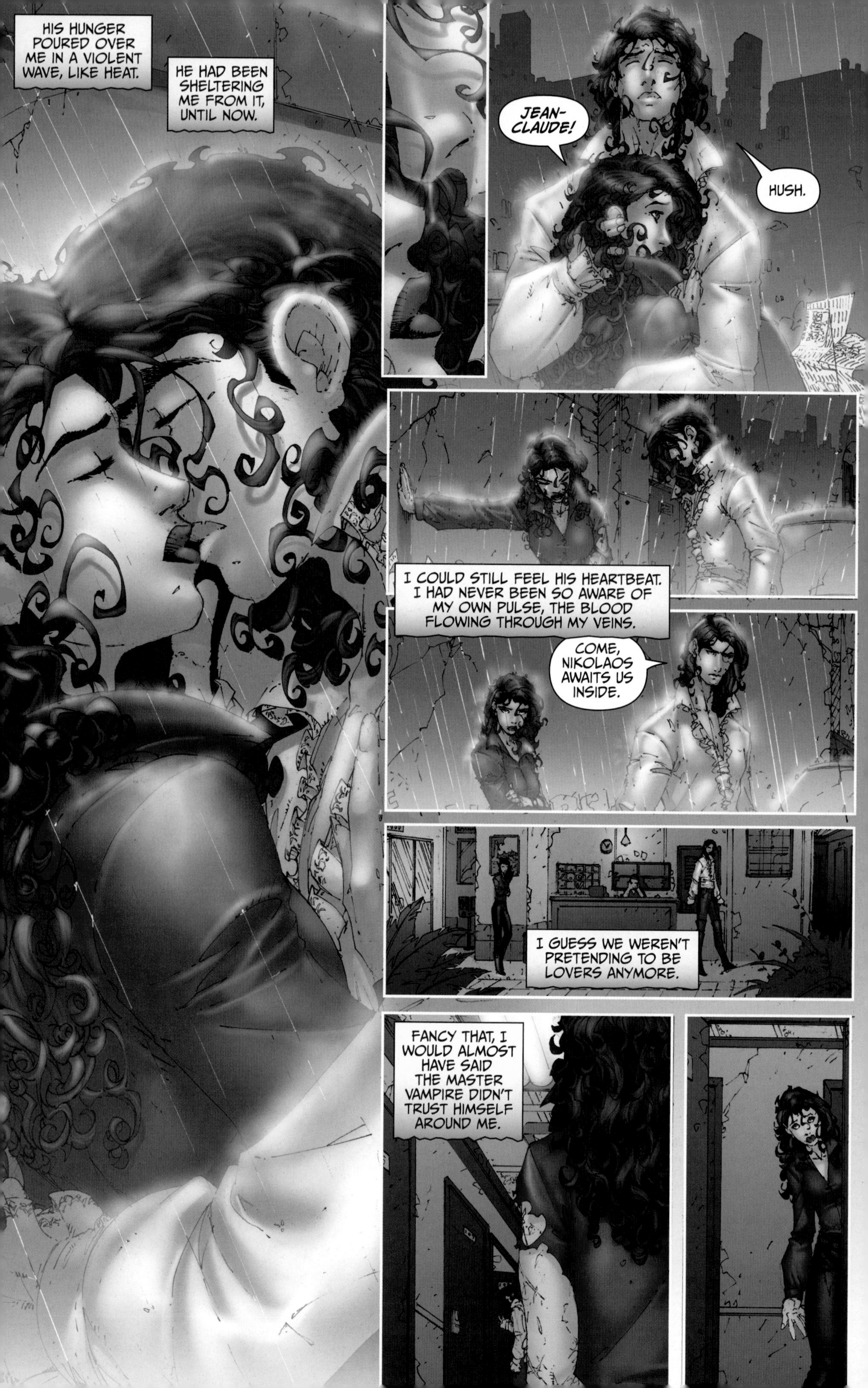
HIS HUNGER POURED OVER ME IN A VIOLENT WAVE, LIKE HEAT.
HE HAD BEEN SHELTERING ME FROM IT, UNTIL NOW.
JEAN-CLAUDE!
HUSH.
I COULD STILL FEEL HIS HEARTBEAT. I HAD NEVER BEEN SO AWARE OF MY OWN PULSE, THE BLOOD FLOWING THROUGH MY VEINS.
COME, NIKOLAOS AWAITS US INSIDE.
I GUESS WE WEREN'T PRETENDING TO BE LOVERS ANYMORE.
FANCY THAT, I WOULD ALMOST HAVE SAID THE MASTER VAMPIRE DIDN'T TRUST HIMSELF AROUND ME.

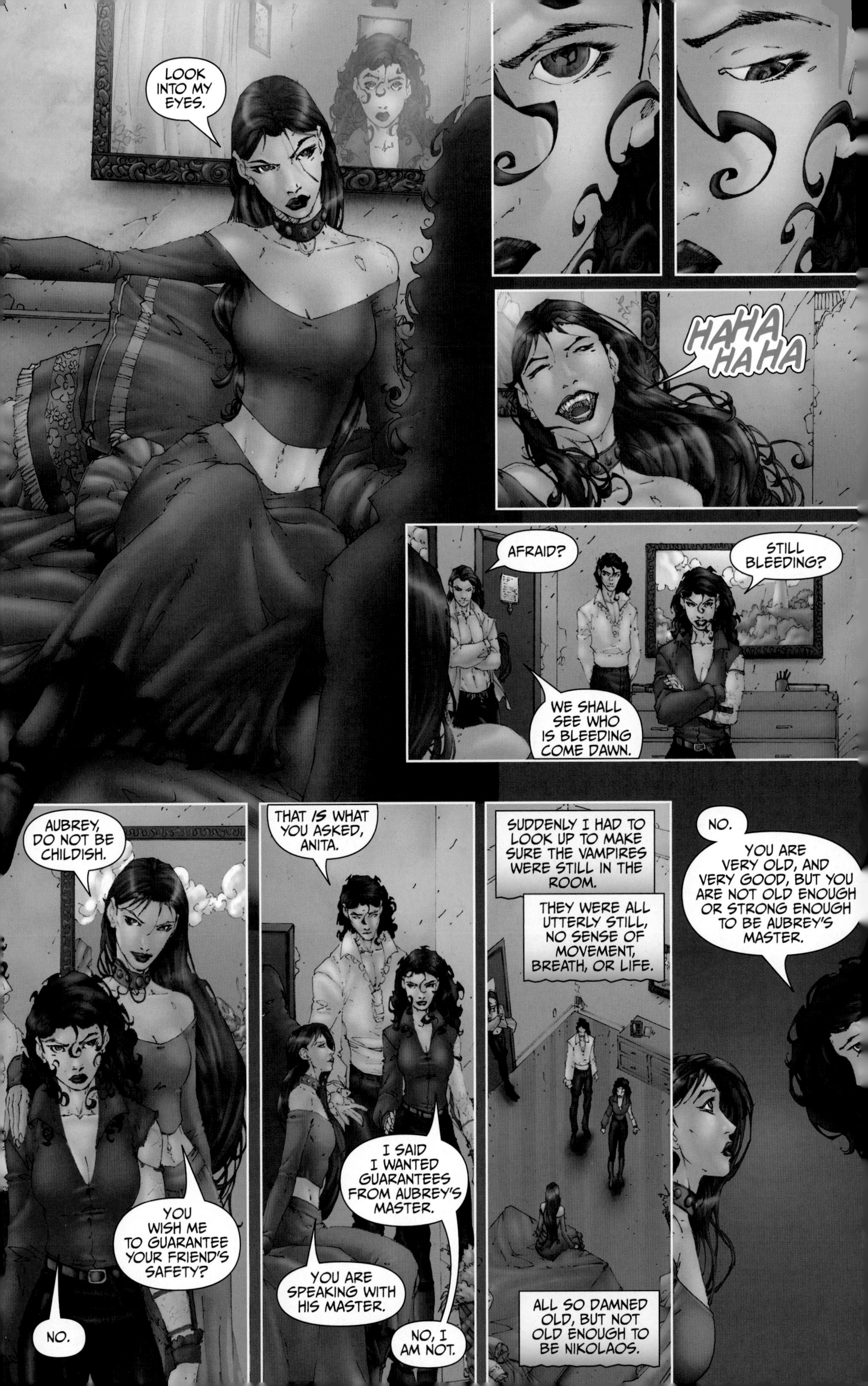
LOOK INTO MY EYES.
HAHA HAHA
AFRAID?
STILL BLEEDING?
WE SHALL SEE WHO IS BLEEDING COME DAWN.
AUBREY, DO NOT BE CHILDISH.
YOU WISH ME TO GUARANTEE YOUR FRIEND'S SAFETY?
NO.
THAT IS WHAT YOU ASKED, ANITA.
I SAID I WANTED GUARANTEES FROM AUBREY'S MASTER.
YOU ARE SPEAKING WITH HIS MASTER.
NO, I AM NOT.
SUDDENLY I HAD TO LOOK UP TO MAKE SURE THE VAMPIRES WERE STILL IN THE ROOM.
THEY WERE ALL UTTERLY STILL, NO SENSE OF MOVEMENT, BREATH, OR LIFE.
ALL SO DAMNED OLD, BUT NOT OLD ENOUGH TO BE NIKOLAOS.
NO.
YOU ARE VERY OLD, AND VERY GOOD, BUT YOU ARE NOT OLD ENOUGH OR STRONG ENOUGH TO BE AUBREY'S MASTER.

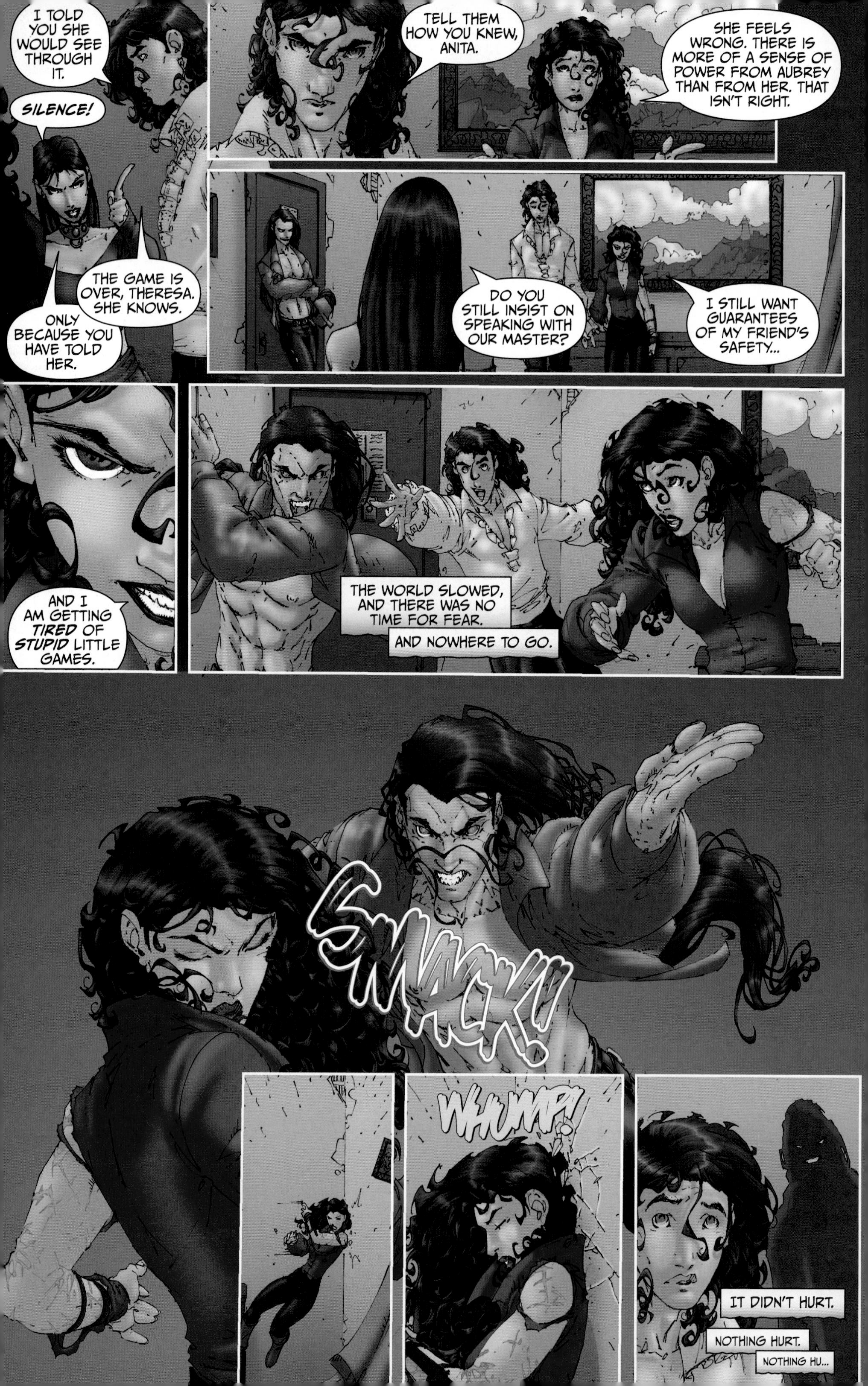
I TOLD YOU SHE WOULD SEE THROUGH IT.
SILENCE!
THE GAME IS OVER, THERESA. SHE KNOWS.
ONLY BECAUSE YOU HAVE TOLD HER.
TELL THEM HOW YOU KNEW, ANITA.
SHE FEELS WRONG. THERE IS MORE OF A SENSE OF POWER FROM AUBREY THAN FROM HER. THAT ISN'T RIGHT.
DO YOU STILL INSIST ON SPEAKING WITH OUR MASTER?
I STILL WANT GUARANTEES OF MY FRIEND'S SAFETY...
AND I AM GETTING TIRED OF STUPID LITTLE GAMES.
THE WORLD SLOWED, AND THERE WAS NO TIME FOR FEAR.
AND NOWHERE TO GO.
SMACK!
WHUMP!
IT DIDN'T HURT.
NOTHING HURT.
NOTHING HU...

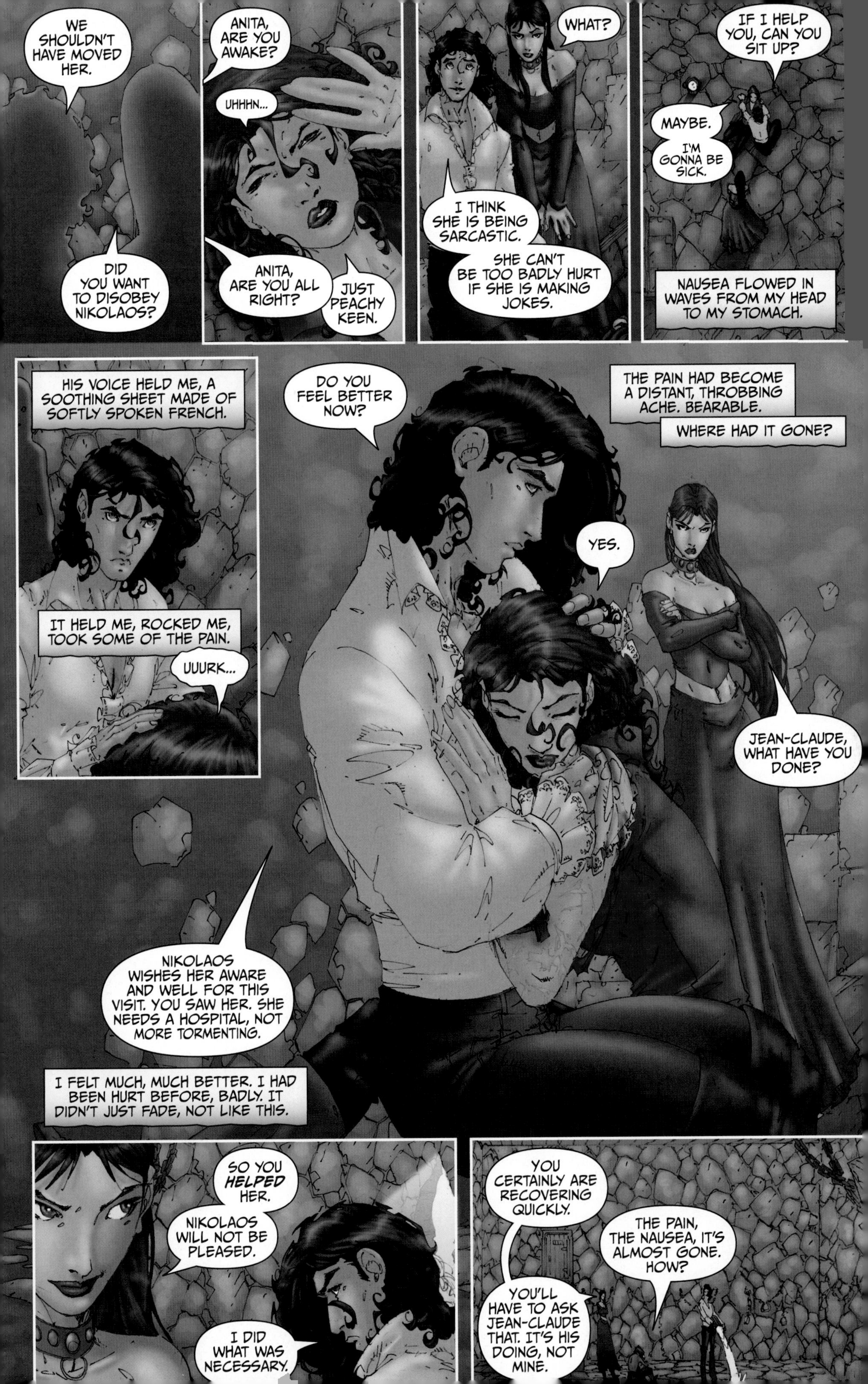
WE SHOULDN'T HAVE MOVED HER.
DID YOU WANT TO DISOBEY NIKOLAOS?
ANITA, ARE YOU AWAKE?
UHHHN...
ANITA, ARE YOU ALL RIGHT?
JUST PEACHY KEEN.
WHAT?
I THINK SHE IS BEING SARCASTIC.
SHE CAN'T BE TOO BADLY HURT IF SHE IS MAKING JOKES.
IF I HELP YOU, CAN YOU SIT UP?
MAYBE.
I'M GONNA BE SICK.
NAUSEA FLOWED IN WAVES FROM MY HEAD TO MY STOMACH.
HIS VOICE HELD ME, A SOOTHING SHEET MADE OF SOFTLY SPOKEN FRENCH.
IT HELD ME, ROCKED ME, TOOK SOME OF THE PAIN.
UUURK...
DO YOU FEEL BETTER NOW?
THE PAIN HAD BECOME A DISTANT, THROBBING ACHE. BEARABLE.
WHERE HAD IT GONE?
YES.
JEAN-CLAUDE, WHAT HAVE YOU DONE?
NIKOLAOS WISHES HER AWARE AND WELL FOR THIS VISIT. YOU SAW HER. SHE NEEDS A HOSPITAL, NOT MORE TORMENTING.
I FELT MUCH, MUCH BETTER. I HAD BEEN HURT BEFORE, BADLY. IT DIDN'T JUST FADE, NOT LIKE THIS.
SO YOU HELPED HER.
NIKOLAOS WILL NOT BE PLEASED.
I DID WHAT WAS NECESSARY.
YOU CERTAINLY ARE RECOVERING QUICKLY.
THE PAIN, THE NAUSEA, IT'S ALMOST GONE. HOW?
YOU'LL HAVE TO ASK JEAN-CLAUDE THAT. IT'S HIS DOING, NOT MINE.

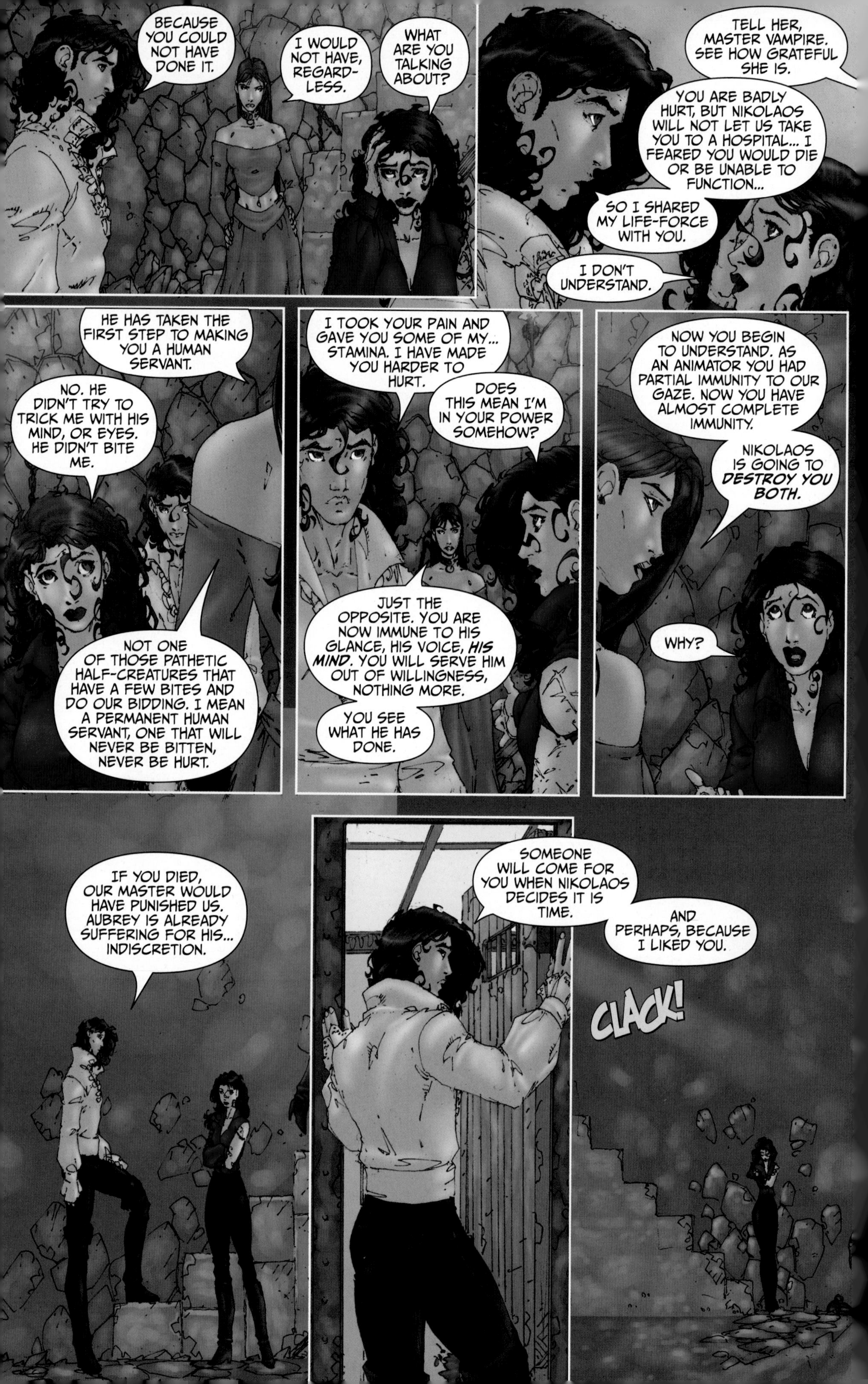
BECAUSE YOU COULD NOT HAVE DONE IT.
I WOULD NOT HAVE, REGARDLESS.
WHAT ARE YOU TALKING ABOUT?
TELL HER, MASTER VAMPIRE. SEE HOW GRATEFUL SHE IS.
YOU ARE BADLY HURT, BUT NIKOLAOS WILL NOT LET US TAKE YOU TO A HOSPITAL... I FEARED YOU WOULD DIE OR BE UNABLE TO FUNCTION...
SO I SHARED MY LIFE-FORCE WITH YOU.
I DON'T UNDERSTAND.
HE HAS TAKEN THE FIRST STEP TO MAKING YOU A HUMAN SERVANT.
NO. HE DIDN'T TRY TO TRICK ME WITH HIS MIND, OR EYES. HE DIDN'T BITE ME.
NOT ONE OF THOSE PATHETIC HALF-CREATURES THAT HAVE A FEW BITES AND DO OUR BIDDING. I MEAN A PERMANENT HUMAN SERVANT, ONE THAT WILL NEVER BE BITTEN, NEVER BE HURT.
I TOOK YOUR PAIN AND GAVE YOU SOME OF MY... STAMINA. I HAVE MADE YOU HARDER TO HURT.
DOES THIS MEAN I'M IN YOUR POWER SOMEHOW?
JUST THE OPPOSITE. YOU ARE NOW IMMUNE TO HIS GLANCE, HIS VOICE, *HIS MIND*. YOU WILL SERVE HIM OUT OF WILLINGNESS, NOTHING MORE.
YOU SEE WHAT HE HAS DONE.
NOW YOU BEGIN TO UNDERSTAND. AS AN ANIMATOR YOU HAD PARTIAL IMMUNITY TO OUR GAZE. NOW YOU HAVE ALMOST COMPLETE IMMUNITY.
NIKOLAOS IS GOING TO ***DESTROY YOU BOTH.***
WHY?
IF YOU DIED, OUR MASTER WOULD HAVE PUNISHED US. AUBREY IS ALREADY SUFFERING FOR HIS... INDISCRETION.
SOMEONE WILL COME FOR YOU WHEN NIKOLAOS DECIDES IT IS TIME.
AND PERHAPS, BECAUSE I LIKED YOU.
CLACK!

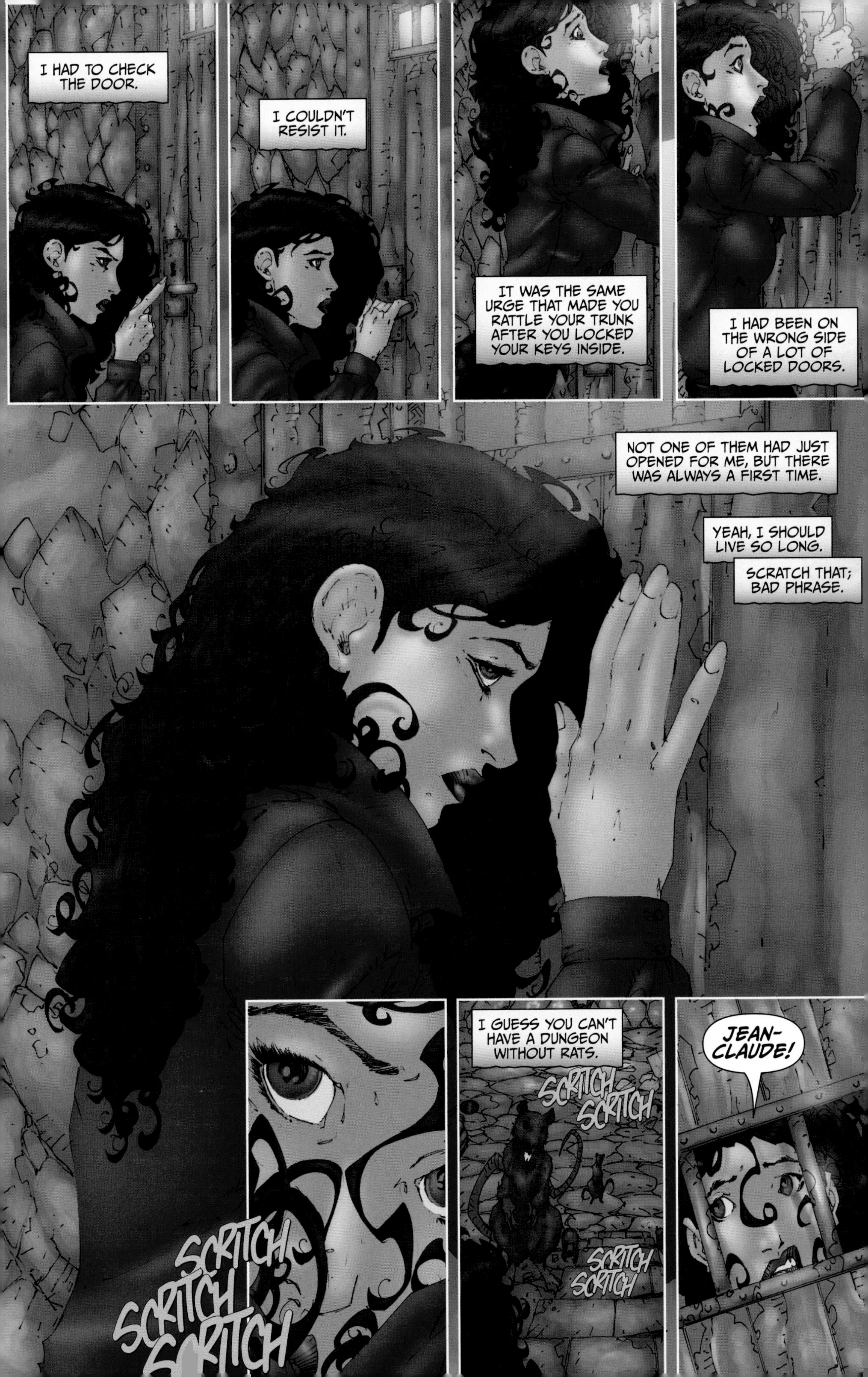
I HAD TO CHECK THE DOOR.
I COULDN'T RESIST IT.
IT WAS THE SAME URGE THAT MADE YOU RATTLE YOUR TRUNK AFTER YOU LOCKED YOUR KEYS INSIDE.
I HAD BEEN ON THE WRONG SIDE OF A LOT OF LOCKED DOORS.
NOT ONE OF THEM HAD JUST OPENED FOR ME, BUT THERE WAS ALWAYS A FIRST TIME.
YEAH, I SHOULD LIVE SO LONG.
SCRATCH THAT; BAD PHRASE.
SCRITCH! SCRITCH SCRITCH
I GUESS YOU CAN'T HAVE A DUNGEON WITHOUT RATS.
SCRITCH SCRITCH
SCRITCH SCRITCH
JEAN-CLAUDE!

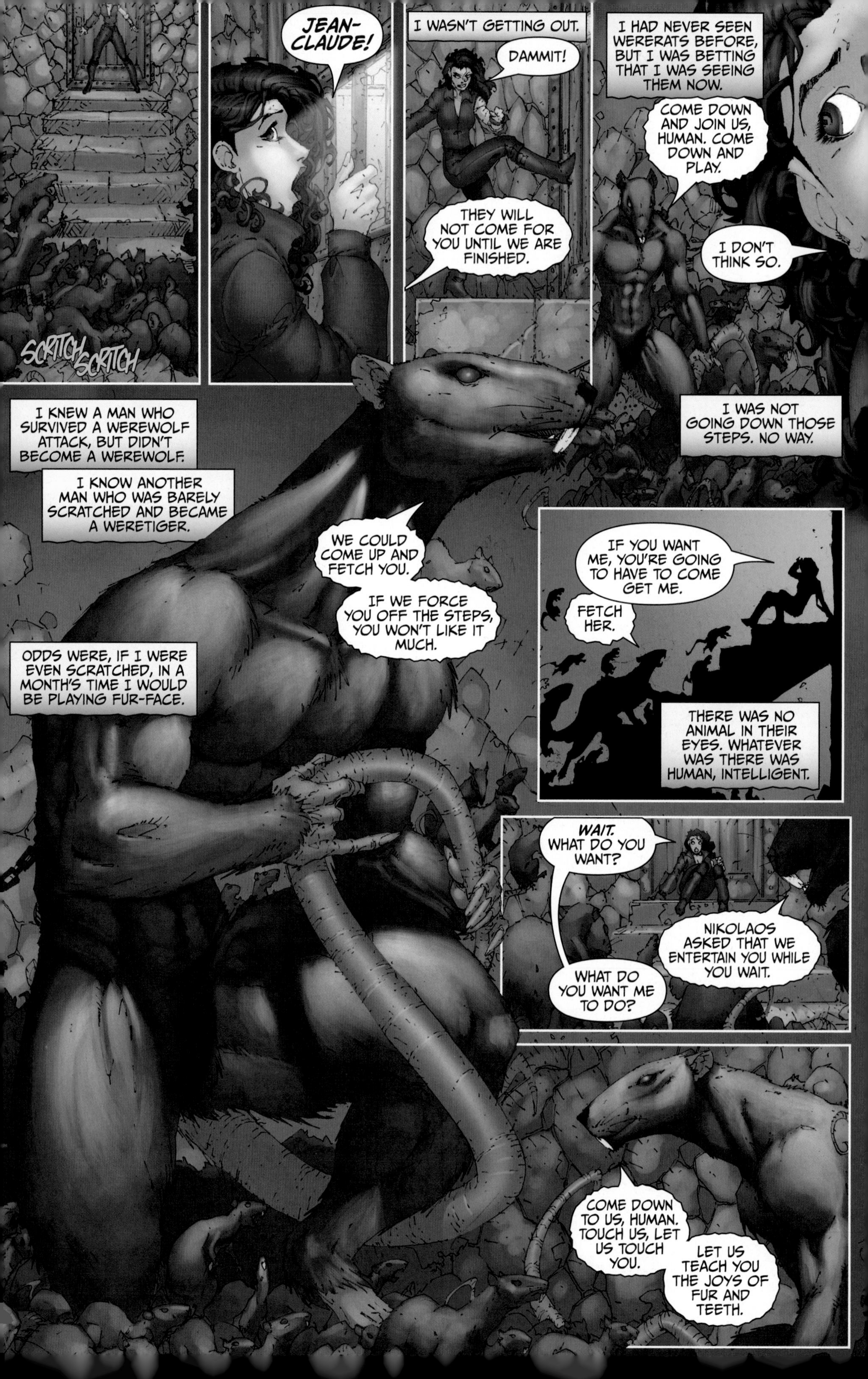
SCRITCH SCRITCH
JEAN-CLAUDE!
I WASN'T GETTING OUT.
DAMMIT!
THEY WILL NOT COME FOR YOU UNTIL WE ARE FINISHED.
I HAD NEVER SEEN WERERATS BEFORE, BUT I WAS BETTING THAT I WAS SEEING THEM NOW.
COME DOWN AND JOIN US, HUMAN. COME DOWN AND PLAY.
I DON'T THINK SO.
I WAS NOT GOING DOWN THOSE STEPS. NO WAY.
I KNEW A MAN WHO SURVIVED A WEREWOLF ATTACK, BUT DIDN'T BECOME A WEREWOLF.
I KNOW ANOTHER MAN WHO WAS BARELY SCRATCHED AND BECAME A WERETIGER.
WE COULD COME UP AND FETCH YOU.
IF WE FORCE YOU OFF THE STEPS, YOU WON'T LIKE IT MUCH.
ODDS WERE, IF I WERE EVEN SCRATCHED, IN A MONTH'S TIME I WOULD BE PLAYING FUR-FACE.
IF YOU WANT ME, YOU'RE GOING TO HAVE TO COME GET ME.
FETCH HER.
THERE WAS NO ANIMAL IN THEIR EYES. WHATEVER WAS THERE WAS HUMAN, INTELLIGENT.
WAIT. WHAT DO YOU WANT?
NIKOLAOS ASKED THAT WE ENTERTAIN YOU WHILE YOU WAIT.
WHAT DO YOU WANT ME TO DO?
COME DOWN TO US, HUMAN. TOUCH US, LET US TOUCH YOU.
LET US TEACH YOU THE JOYS OF FUR AND TEETH.

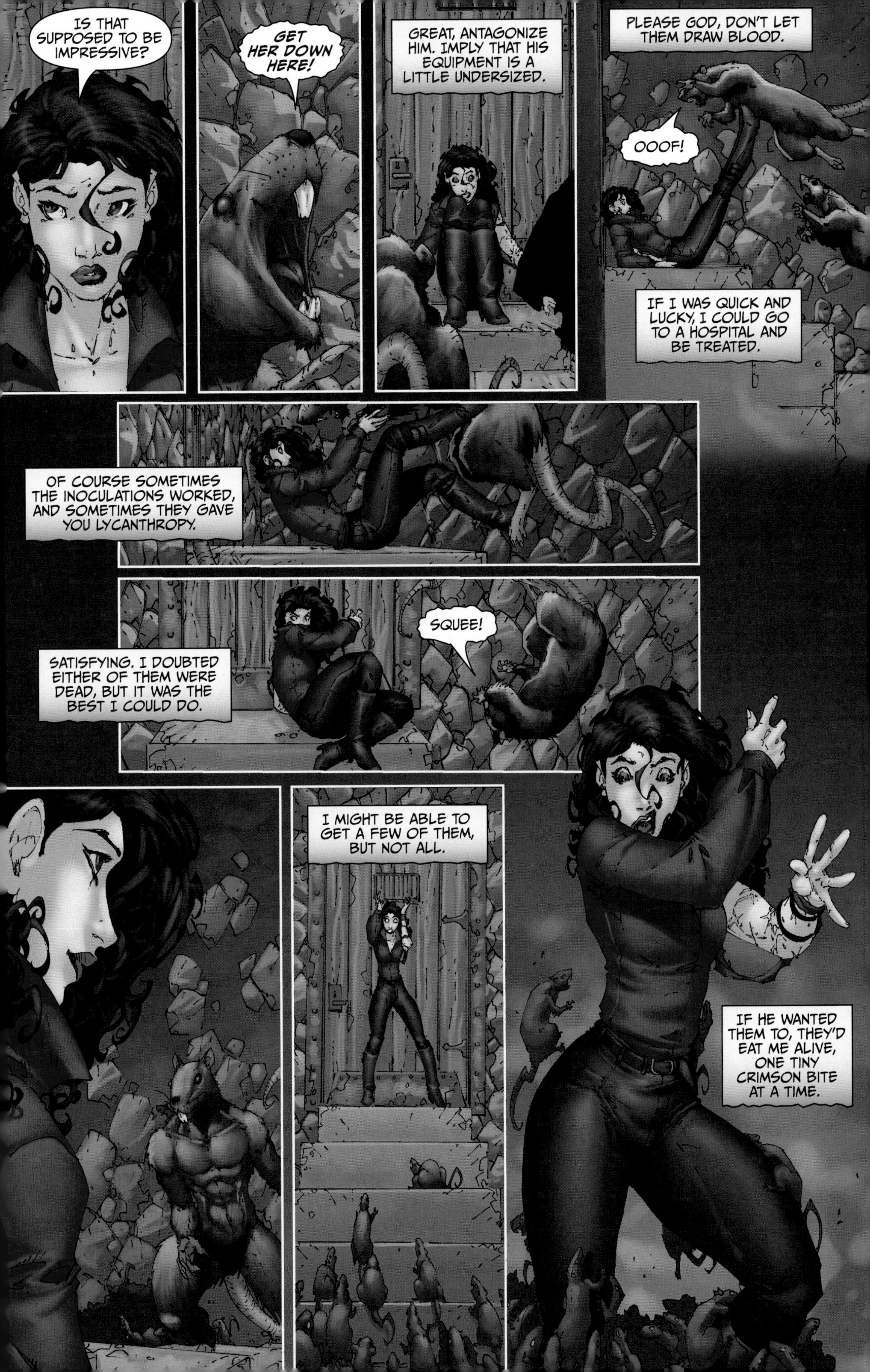

IS THAT SUPPOSED TO BE IMPRESSIVE?
GET HER DOWN HERE!
GREAT, ANTAGONIZE HIM. IMPLY THAT HIS EQUIPMENT IS A LITTLE UNDERSIZED.
PLEASE GOD, DON'T LET THEM DRAW BLOOD.
OOOF!
IF I WAS QUICK AND LUCKY, I COULD GO TO A HOSPITAL AND BE TREATED.
OF COURSE SOMETIMES THE INOCULATIONS WORKED, AND SOMETIMES THEY GAVE YOU LYCANTHROPY.
SATISFYING. I DOUBTED EITHER OF THEM WERE DEAD, BUT IT WAS THE BEST I COULD DO.
SQUEE!
I MIGHT BE ABLE TO GET A FEW OF THEM, BUT NOT ALL.
IF HE WANTED THEM TO, THEY'D EAT ME ALIVE, ONE TINY CRIMSON BITE AT A TIME.

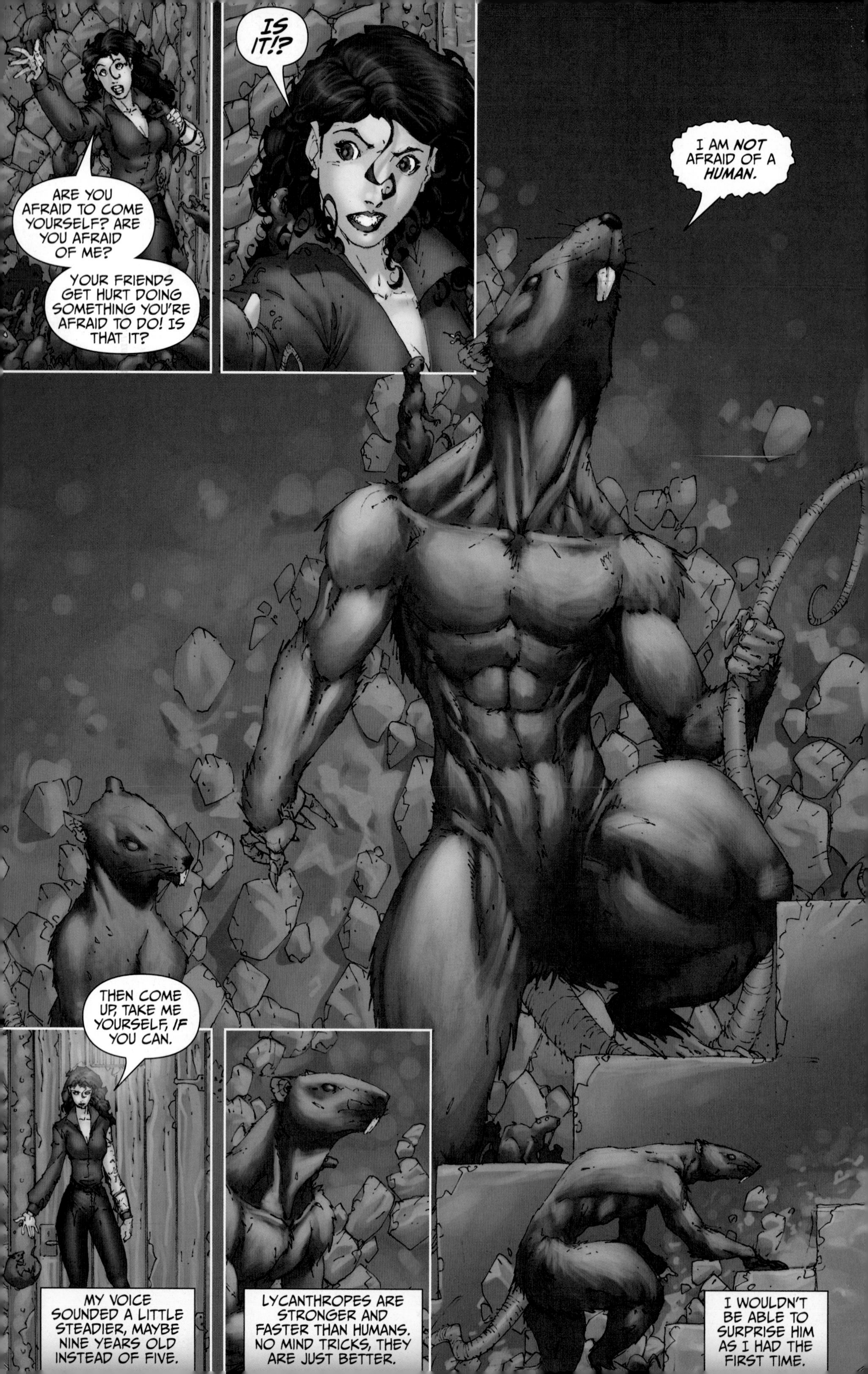

ARE YOU AFRAID TO COME YOURSELF? ARE YOU AFRAID OF ME?
YOUR FRIENDS GET HURT DOING SOMETHING YOU'RE AFRAID TO DO! IS THAT IT?
IS IT!?
I AM NOT AFRAID OF A HUMAN.
THEN COME UP, TAKE ME YOURSELF, IF YOU CAN.
MY VOICE SOUNDED A LITTLE STEADIER, MAYBE NINE YEARS OLD INSTEAD OF FIVE.
LYCANTHROPES ARE STRONGER AND FASTER THAN HUMANS. NO MIND TRICKS, THEY ARE JUST BETTER.
I WOULDN'T BE ABLE TO SURPRISE HIM AS I HAD THE FIRST TIME.

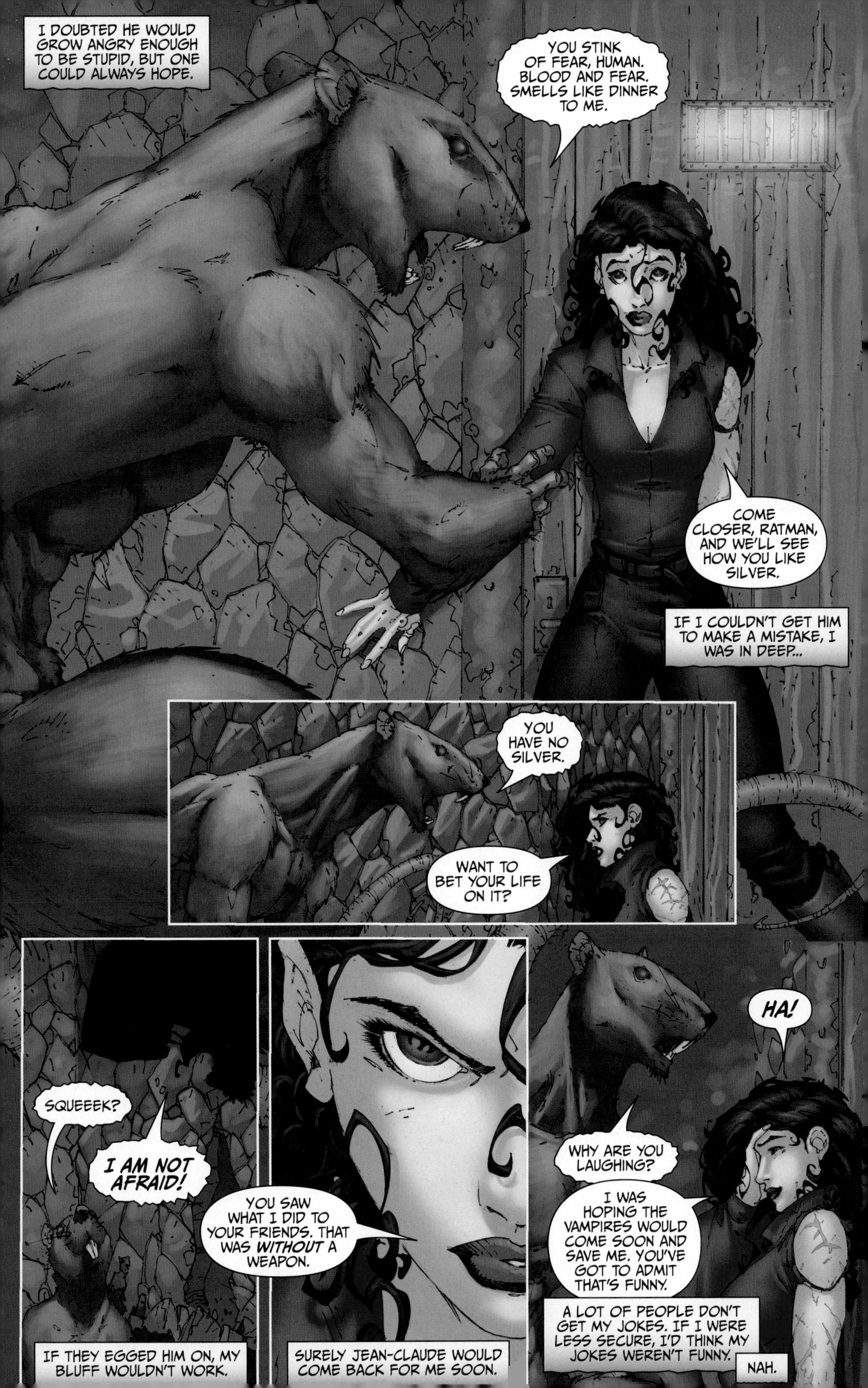
I DOUBTED HE WOULD GROW ANGRY ENOUGH TO BE STUPID, BUT ONE COULD ALWAYS HOPE.
YOU STINK OF FEAR, HUMAN. BLOOD AND FEAR. SMELLS LIKE DINNER TO ME.
COME CLOSER, RATMAN, AND WE'LL SEE HOW YOU LIKE SILVER.
IF I COULDN'T GET HIM TO MAKE A MISTAKE, I WAS IN DEEP...
YOU HAVE NO SILVER.
WANT TO BET YOUR LIFE ON IT?
SQUEEEK?
I AM NOT AFRAID!
IF THEY EGGED HIM ON, MY BLUFF WOULDN'T WORK.
YOU SAW WHAT I DID TO YOUR FRIENDS. THAT WAS WITHOUT A WEAPON.
SURELY JEAN-CLAUDE WOULD COME BACK FOR ME SOON.
HA!
WHY ARE YOU LAUGHING?
I WAS HOPING THE VAMPIRES WOULD COME SOON AND SAVE ME. YOU'VE GOT TO ADMIT THAT'S FUNNY.
A LOT OF PEOPLE DON'T GET MY JOKES. IF I WERE LESS SECURE, I'D THINK MY JOKES WEREN'T FUNNY.
NAH.

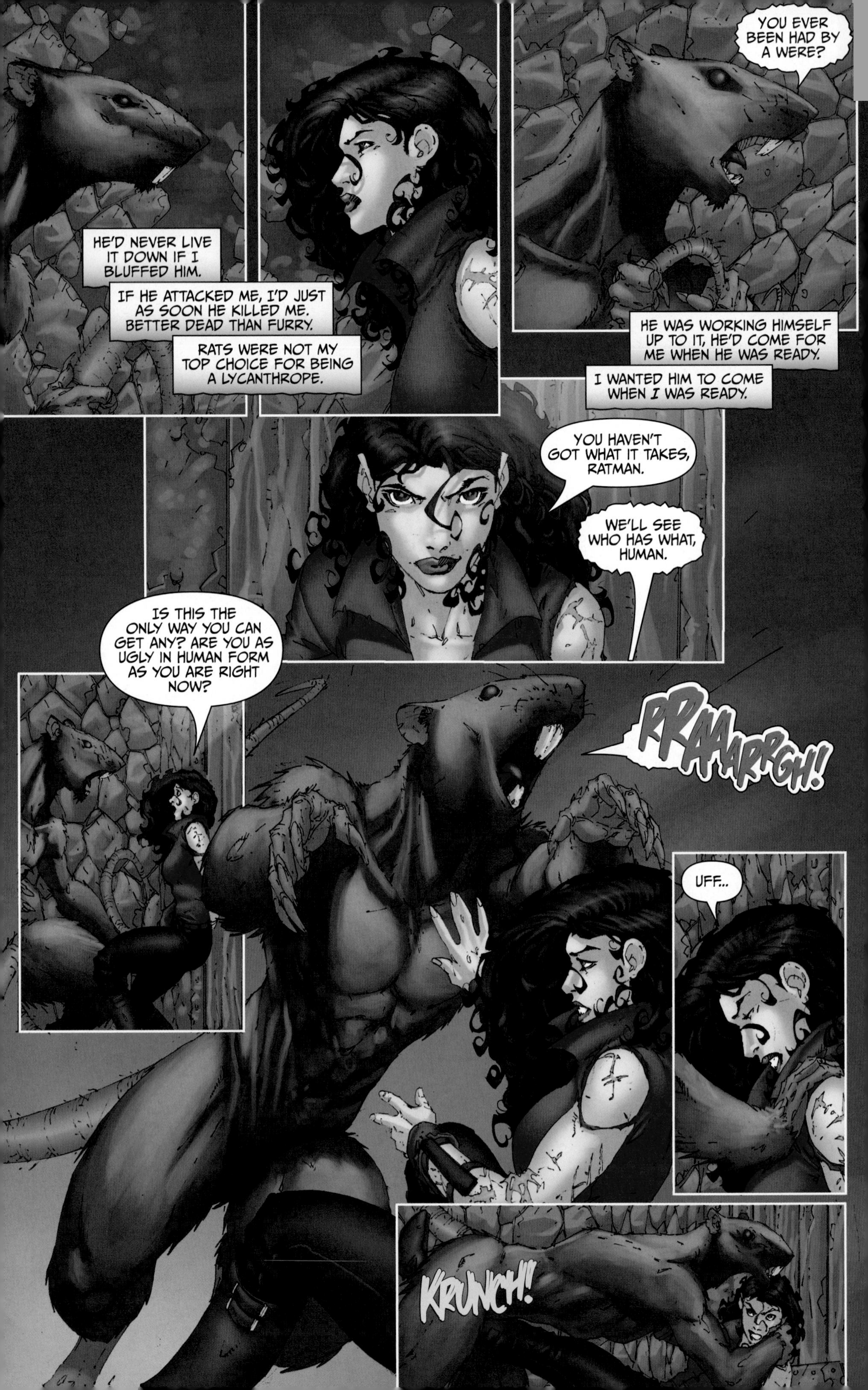
HE'D NEVER LIVE IT DOWN IF I BLUFFED HIM.
IF HE ATTACKED ME, I'D JUST AS SOON HE KILLED ME. BETTER DEAD THAN FURRY.
RATS WERE NOT MY TOP CHOICE FOR BEING A LYCANTHROPE.
YOU EVER BEEN HAD BY A WERE?
HE WAS WORKING HIMSELF UP TO IT, HE'D COME FOR ME WHEN HE WAS READY.
I WANTED HIM TO COME WHEN I WAS READY.
YOU HAVEN'T GOT WHAT IT TAKES, RATMAN.
WE'LL SEE WHO HAS WHAT, HUMAN.
IS THIS THE ONLY WAY YOU CAN GET ANY? ARE YOU AS UGLY IN HUMAN FORM AS YOU ARE RIGHT NOW?
RRAAAARRGH!
UFF...
KRUNCH!

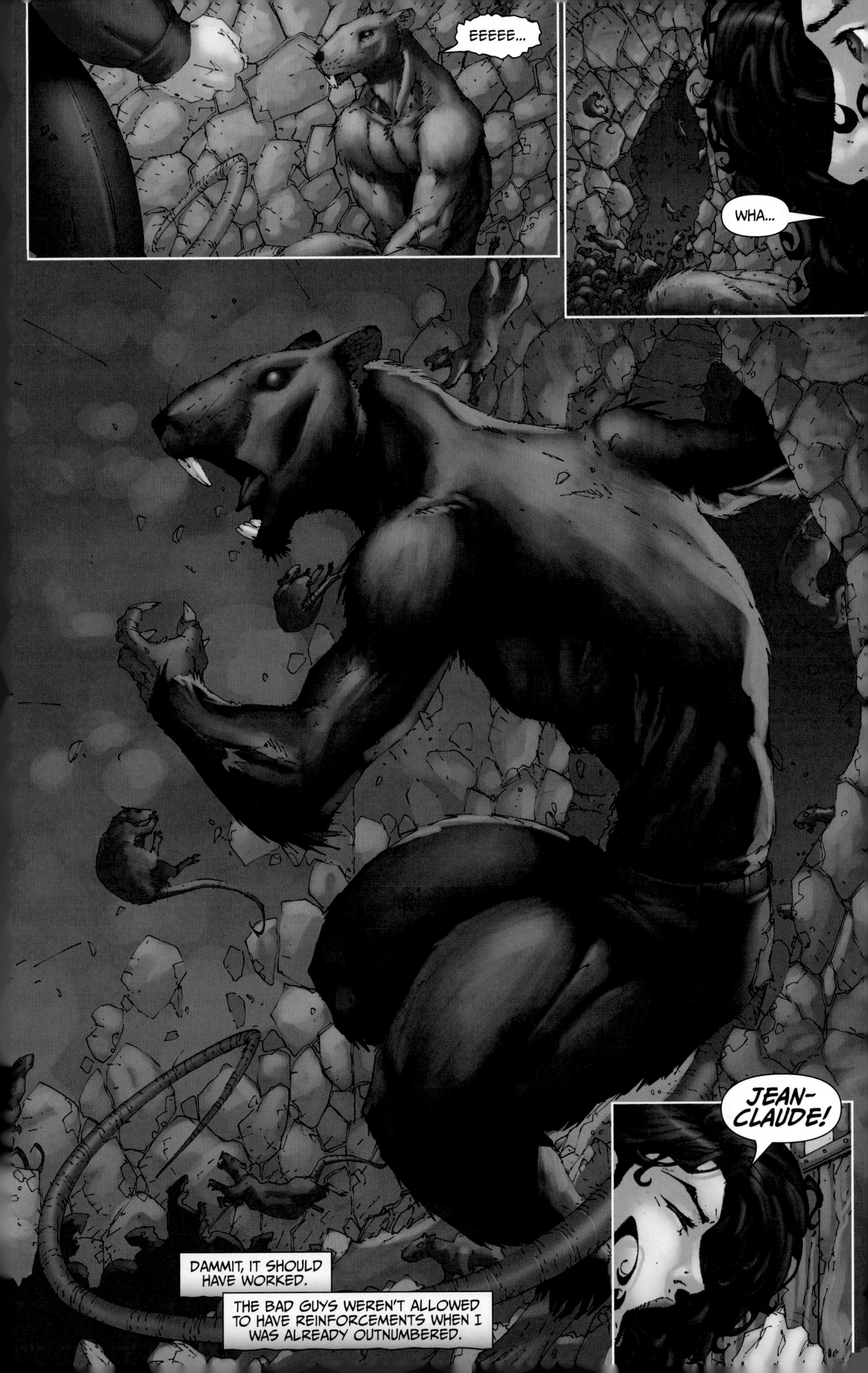
EEEEE...
WHA...
JEAN-CLAUDE!
DAMMIT, IT SHOULD HAVE WORKED.
THE BAD GUYS WEREN'T ALLOWED TO HAVE REINFORCEMENTS WHEN I WAS ALREADY OUTNUMBERED.

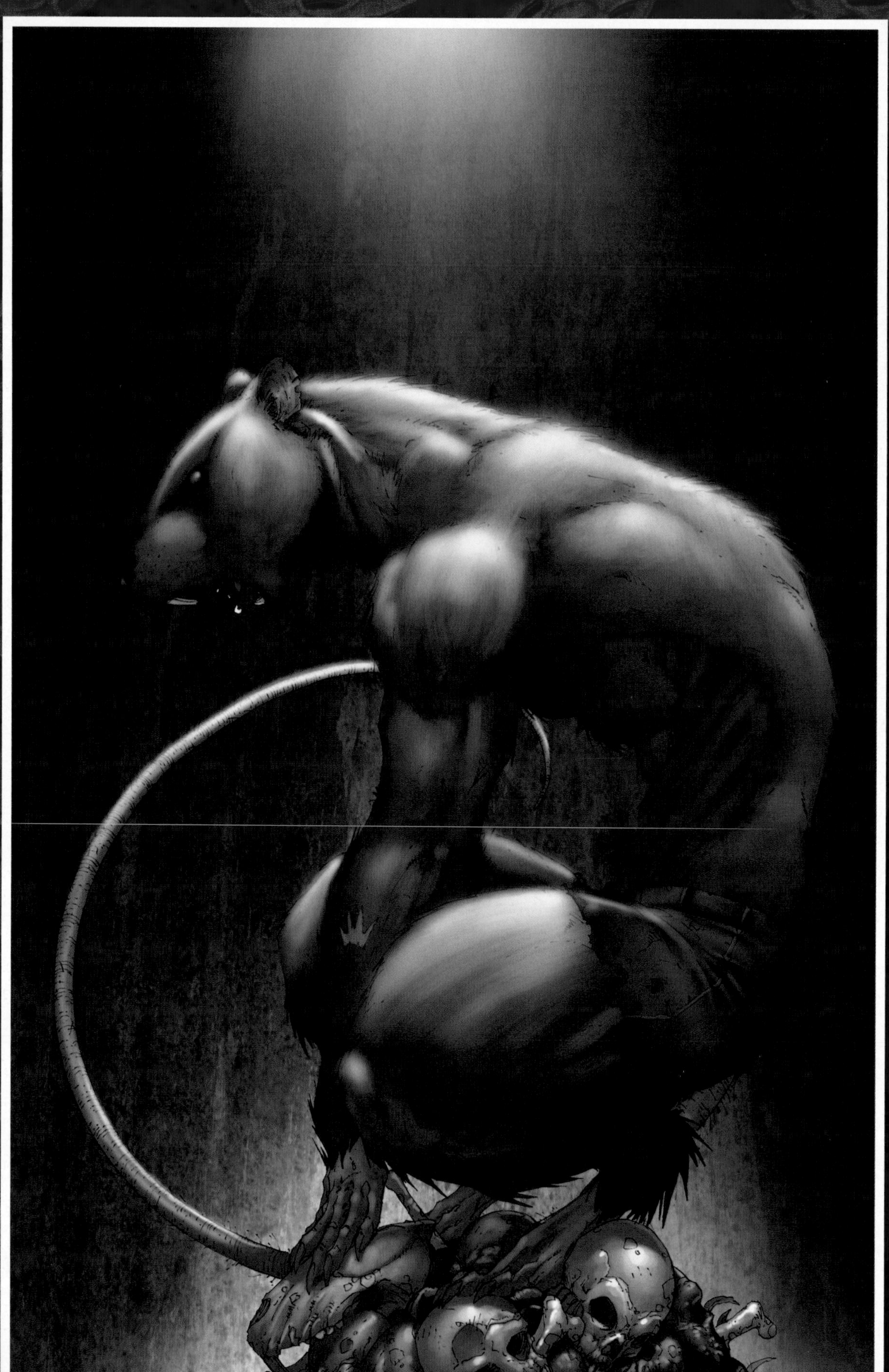

THREE

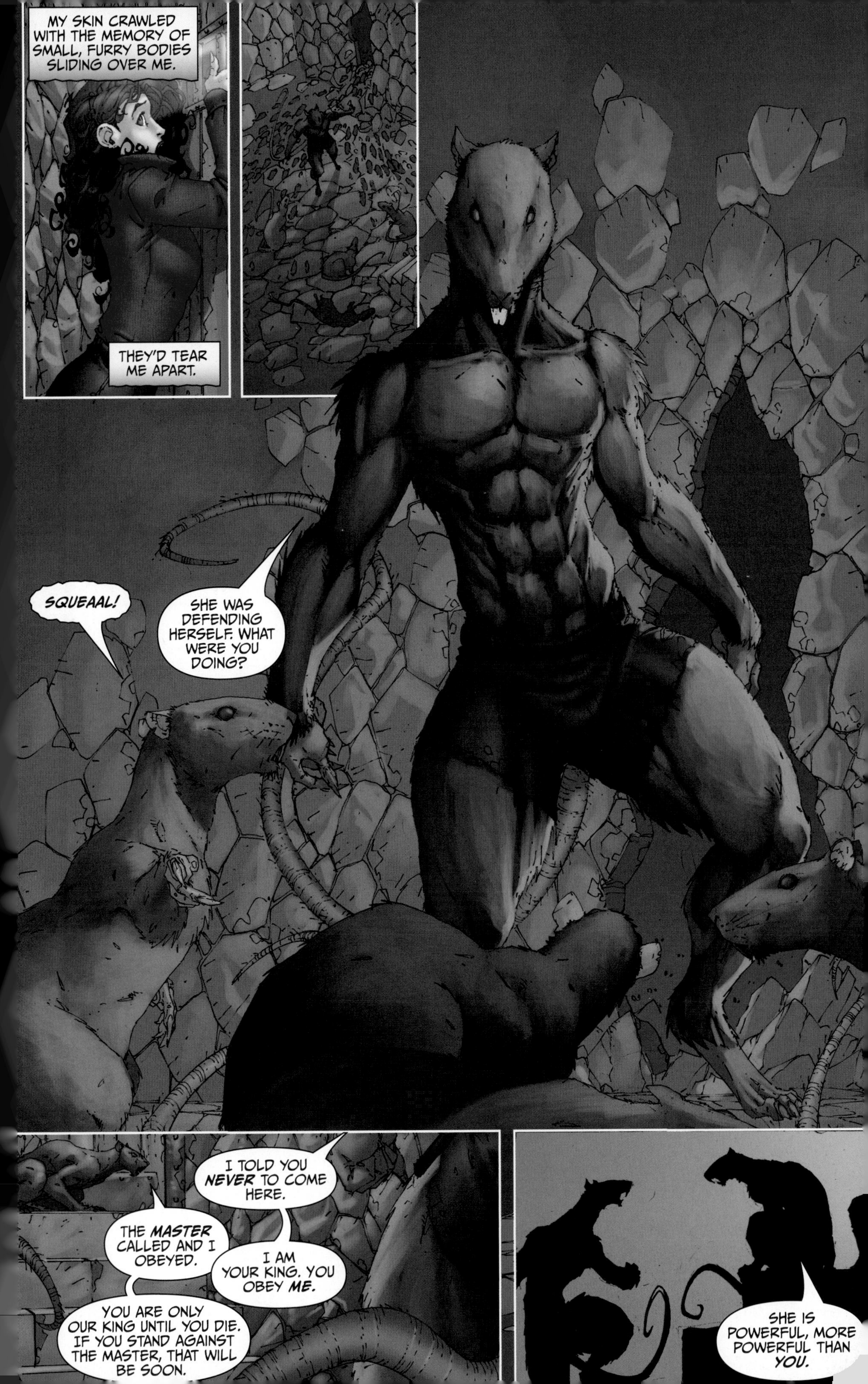

MY SKIN CRAWLED WITH THE MEMORY OF SMALL, FURRY BODIES SLIDING OVER ME.
THEY'D TEAR ME APART.
SQUEAAL!
SHE WAS DEFENDING HERSELF. WHAT WERE YOU DOING?
I TOLD YOU NEVER TO COME HERE.
THE MASTER CALLED AND I OBEYED.
I AM YOUR KING. YOU OBEY ME.
YOU ARE ONLY OUR KING UNTIL YOU DIE. IF YOU STAND AGAINST THE MASTER, THAT WILL BE SOON.
SHE IS POWERFUL, MORE POWERFUL THAN YOU.

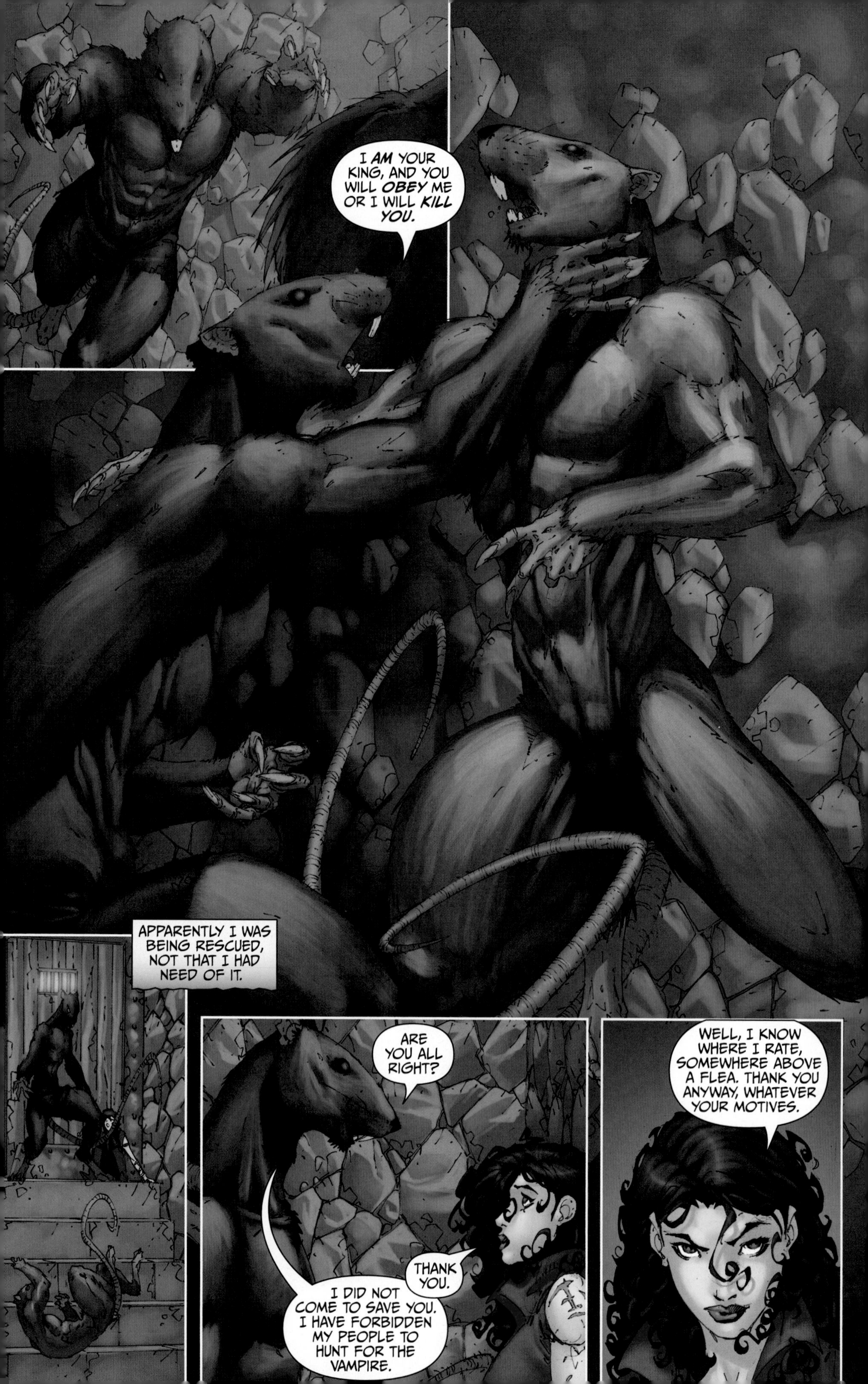
I AM YOUR KING, AND YOU WILL OBEY ME OR I WILL KILL YOU.
APPARENTLY I WAS BEING RESCUED, NOT THAT I HAD NEED OF IT.
ARE YOU ALL RIGHT?
THANK YOU.
I DID NOT COME TO SAVE YOU. I HAVE FORBIDDEN MY PEOPLE TO HUNT FOR THE VAMPIRE.
WELL, I KNOW WHERE I RATE, SOMEWHERE ABOVE A FLEA. THANK YOU ANYWAY, WHATEVER YOUR MOTIVES.

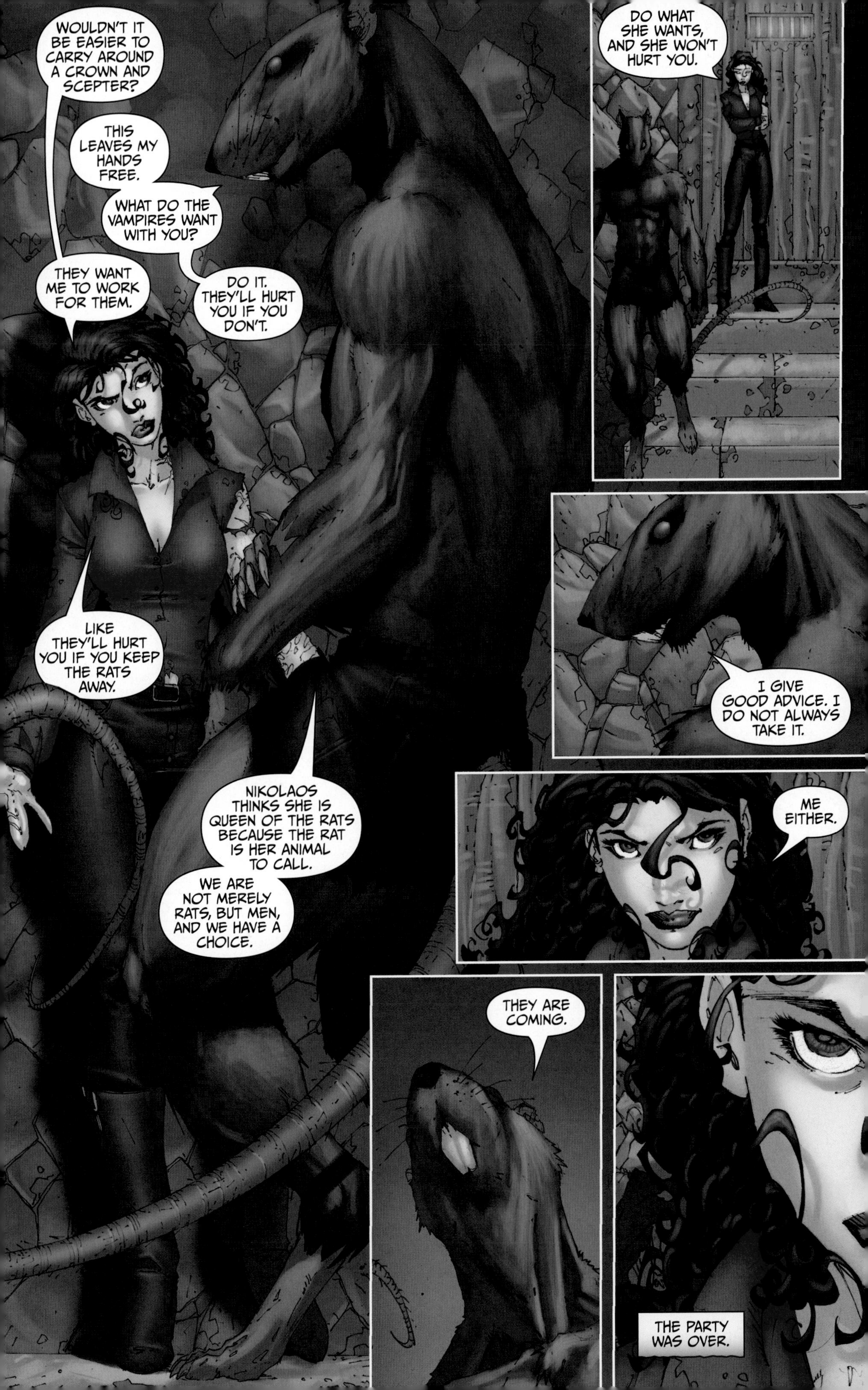
WOULDN'T IT BE EASIER TO CARRY AROUND A CROWN AND SCEPTER?
THIS LEAVES MY HANDS FREE.
WHAT DO THE VAMPIRES WANT WITH YOU?
THEY WANT ME TO WORK FOR THEM.
DO IT. THEY'LL HURT YOU IF YOU DON'T.
LIKE THEY'LL HURT YOU IF YOU KEEP THE RATS AWAY.
NIKOLAOS THINKS SHE IS QUEEN OF THE RATS BECAUSE THE RAT IS HER ANIMAL TO CALL.
WE ARE NOT MERELY RATS, BUT MEN, AND WE HAVE A CHOICE.
DO WHAT SHE WANTS, AND SHE WON'T HURT YOU.
I GIVE GOOD ADVICE. I DO NOT ALWAYS TAKE IT.
ME EITHER.
THEY ARE COMING.
THE PARTY WAS OVER.

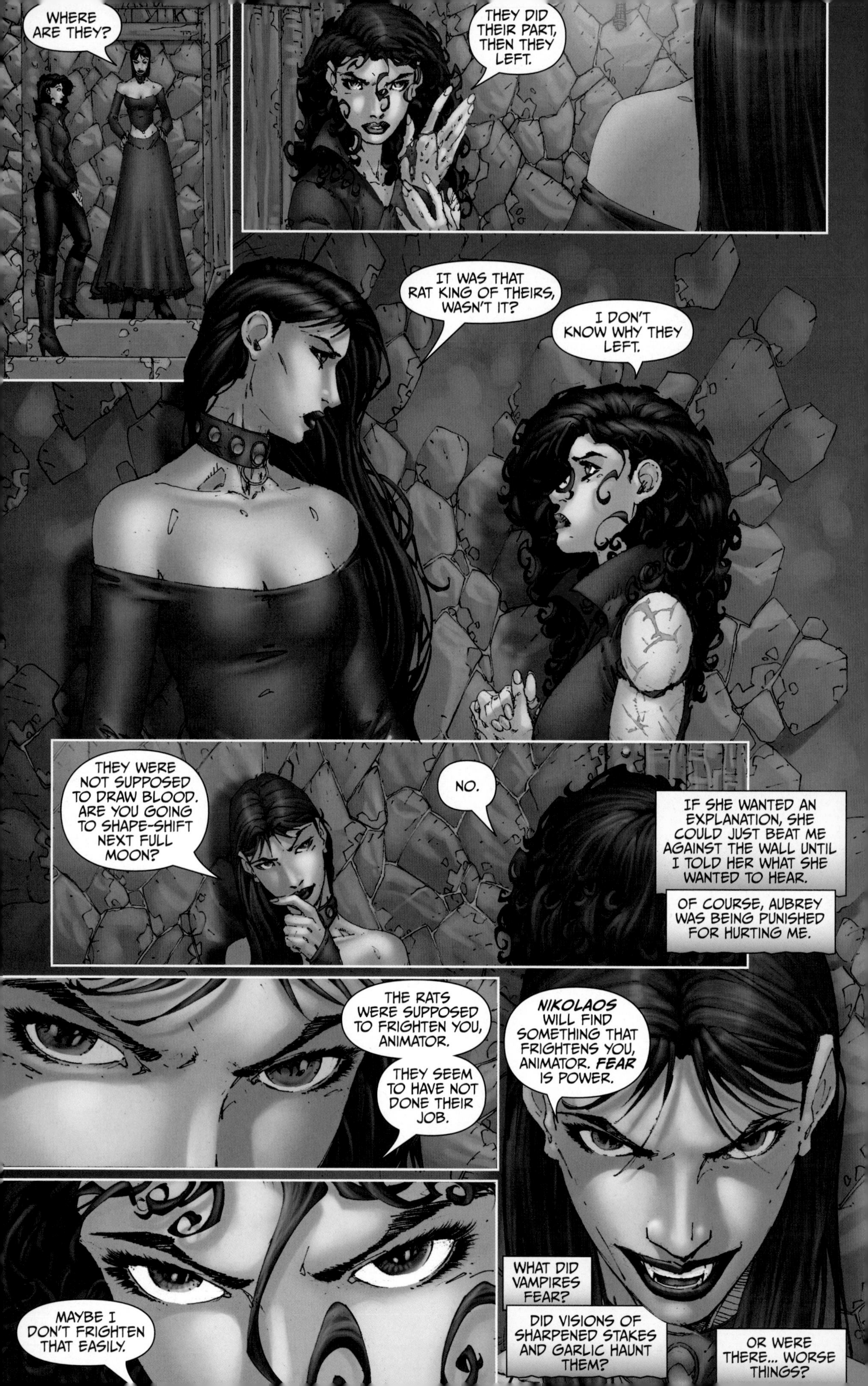
WHERE ARE THEY?
THEY DID THEIR PART, THEN THEY LEFT.
IT WAS THAT RAT KING OF THEIRS, WASN'T IT?
I DON'T KNOW WHY THEY LEFT.
THEY WERE NOT SUPPOSED TO DRAW BLOOD. ARE YOU GOING TO SHAPE-SHIFT NEXT FULL MOON?
NO.
IF SHE WANTED AN EXPLANATION, SHE COULD JUST BEAT ME AGAINST THE WALL UNTIL I TOLD HER WHAT SHE WANTED TO HEAR.
OF COURSE, AUBREY WAS BEING PUNISHED FOR HURTING ME.
THE RATS WERE SUPPOSED TO FRIGHTEN YOU, ANIMATOR.
THEY SEEM TO HAVE NOT DONE THEIR JOB.
MAYBE I DON'T FRIGHTEN THAT EASILY.
NIKOLAOS WILL FIND SOMETHING THAT FRIGHTENS YOU, ANIMATOR. *FEAR* IS POWER.
WHAT DID VAMPIRES FEAR?
DID VISIONS OF SHARPENED STAKES AND GARLIC HAUNT THEM?
OR WERE THERE... WORSE THINGS?

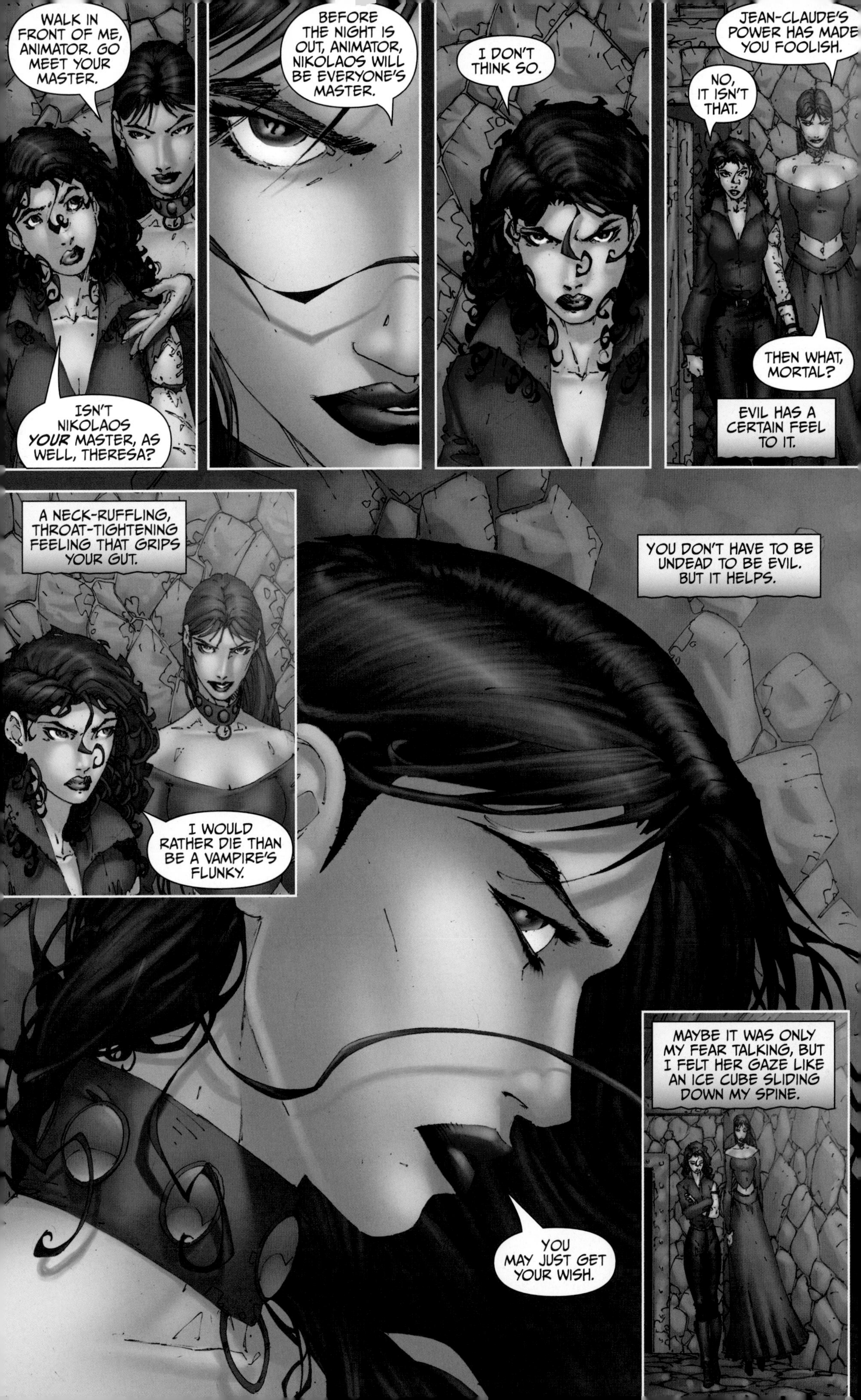
WALK IN FRONT OF ME, ANIMATOR. GO MEET YOUR MASTER.
ISN'T NIKOLAOS YOUR MASTER, AS WELL, THERESA?
BEFORE THE NIGHT IS OUT, ANIMATOR, NIKOLAOS WILL BE EVERYONE'S MASTER.
I DON'T THINK SO.
JEAN-CLAUDE'S POWER HAS MADE YOU FOOLISH.
NO, IT ISN'T THAT.
THEN WHAT, MORTAL?
EVIL HAS A CERTAIN FEEL TO IT.
A NECK-RUFFLING, THROAT-TIGHTENING FEELING THAT GRIPS YOUR GUT.
YOU DON'T HAVE TO BE UNDEAD TO BE EVIL. BUT IT HELPS.
I WOULD RATHER DIE THAN BE A VAMPIRE'S FLUNKY.
MAYBE IT WAS ONLY MY FEAR TALKING, BUT I FELT HER GAZE LIKE AN ICE CUBE SLIDING DOWN MY SPINE.
YOU MAY JUST GET YOUR WISH.

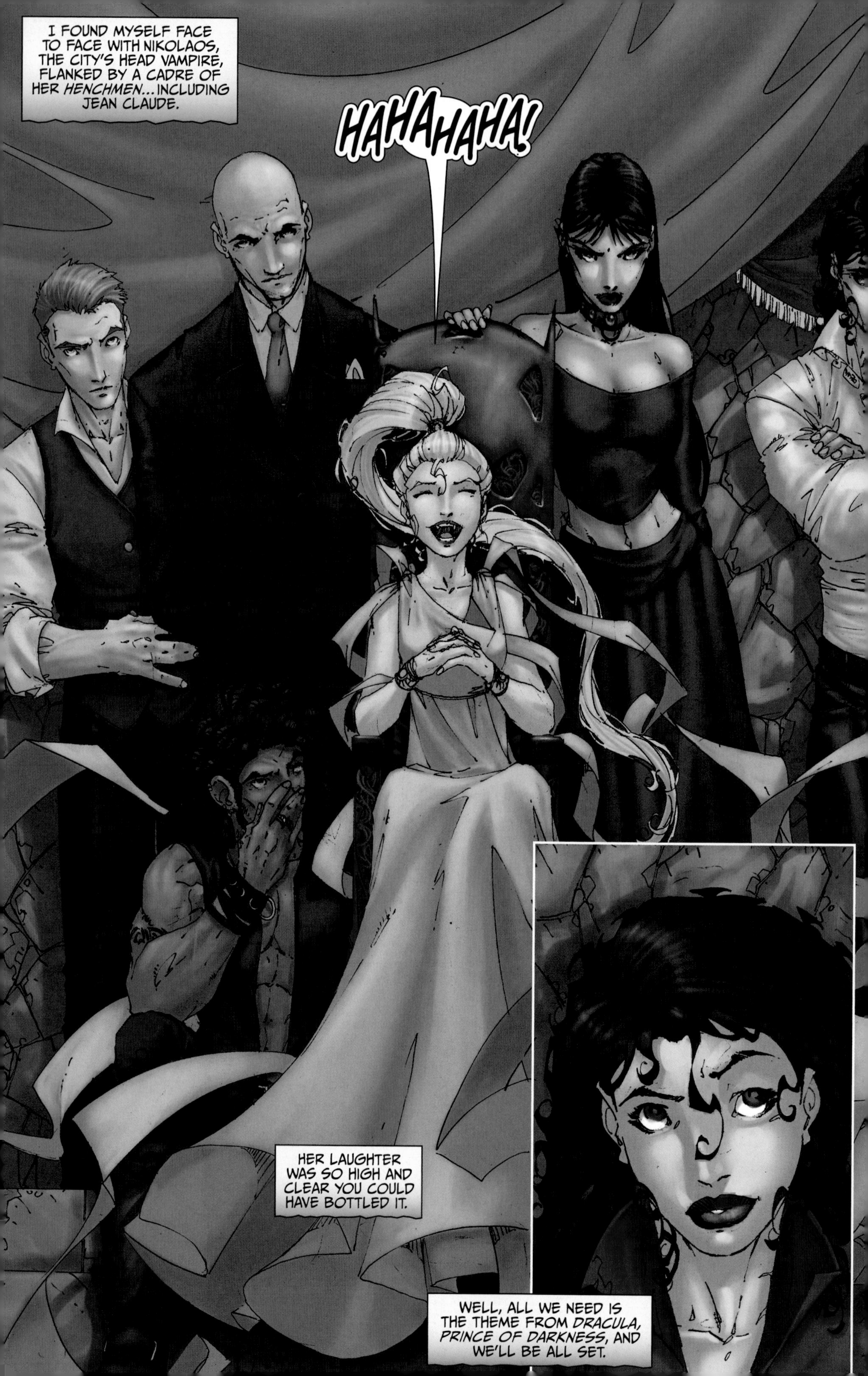
I FOUND MYSELF FACE TO FACE WITH NIKOLAOS, THE CITY'S HEAD VAMPIRE, FLANKED BY A CADRE OF HER *HENCHMEN*... INCLUDING JEAN CLAUDE.
HAHAHAHAHA!
HER LAUGHTER WAS SO HIGH AND CLEAR YOU COULD HAVE BOTTLED IT.
WELL, ALL WE NEED IS THE THEME FROM *DRACULA, PRINCE OF DARKNESS*, AND WE'LL BE ALL SET.

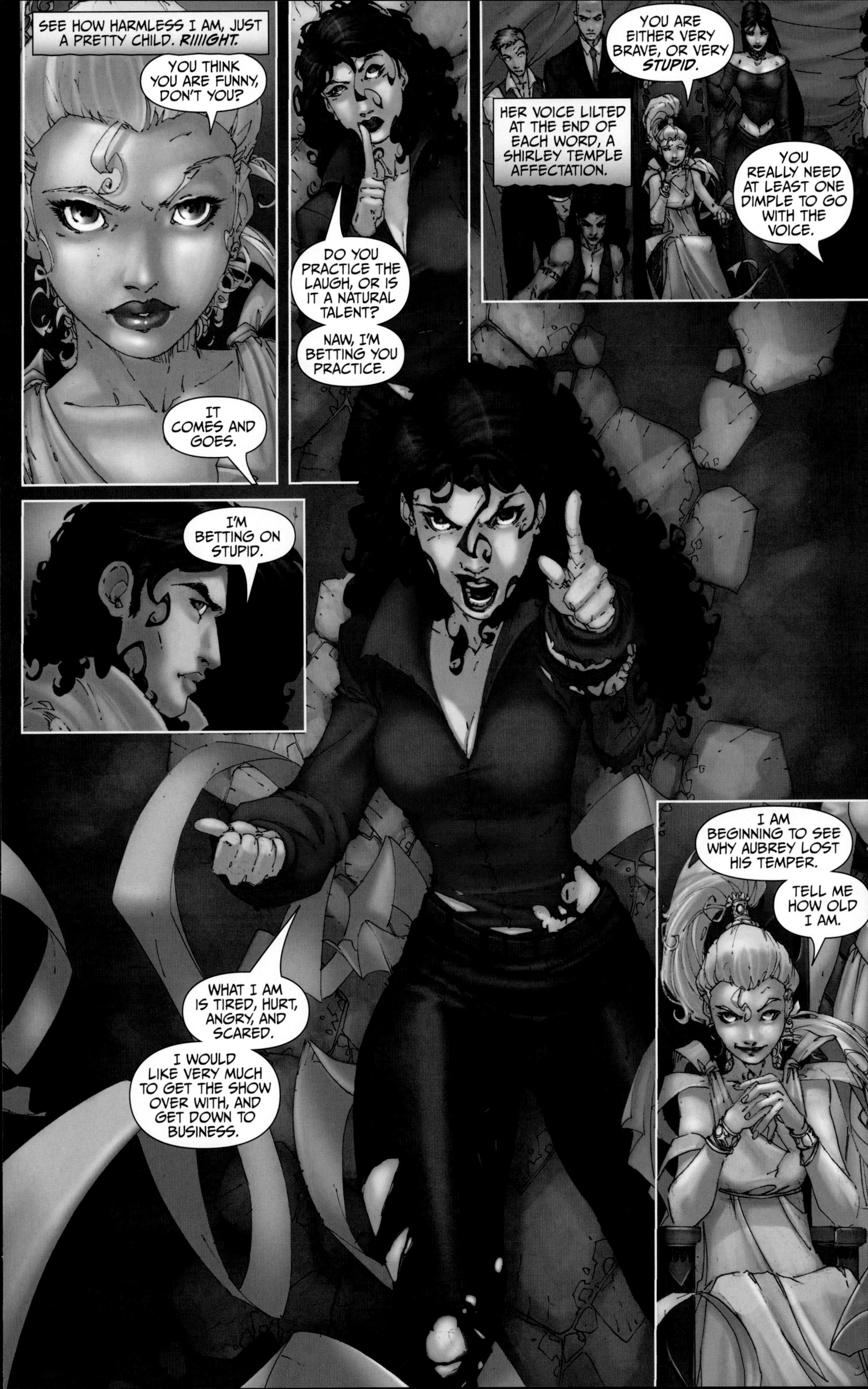

SEE HOW HARMLESS I AM, JUST A PRETTY CHILD. RIIIIGHT.
YOU THINK YOU ARE FUNNY, DON'T YOU?
IT COMES AND GOES.
DO YOU PRACTICE THE LAUGH, OR IS IT A NATURAL TALENT?
NAW, I'M BETTING YOU PRACTICE.
YOU ARE EITHER VERY BRAVE, OR VERY STUPID.
HER VOICE LILTED AT THE END OF EACH WORD, A SHIRLEY TEMPLE AFFECTATION.
YOU REALLY NEED AT LEAST ONE DIMPLE TO GO WITH THE VOICE.
I'M BETTING ON STUPID.
WHAT I AM IS TIRED, HURT, ANGRY, AND SCARED.
I WOULD LIKE VERY MUCH TO GET THE SHOW OVER WITH, AND GET DOWN TO BUSINESS.
I AM BEGINNING TO SEE WHY AUBREY LOST HIS TEMPER.
TELL ME HOW OLD I AM.

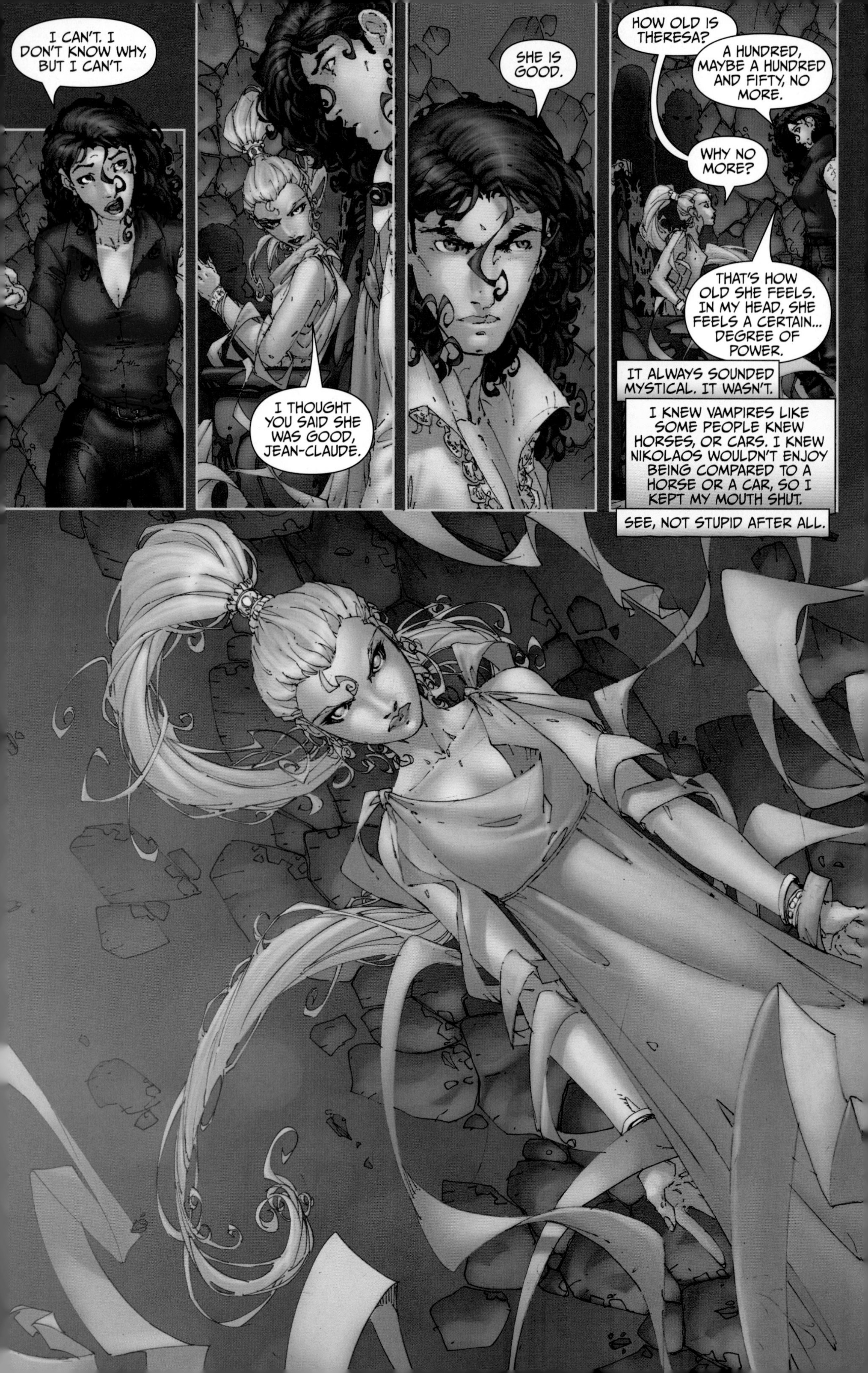
I CAN'T. I DON'T KNOW WHY, BUT I CAN'T.
I THOUGHT YOU SAID SHE WAS GOOD, JEAN-CLAUDE.
SHE IS GOOD.
HOW OLD IS THERESA?
A HUNDRED, MAYBE A HUNDRED AND FIFTY, NO MORE.
WHY NO MORE?
THAT'S HOW OLD SHE FEELS. IN MY HEAD, SHE FEELS A CERTAIN... DEGREE OF POWER.
IT ALWAYS SOUNDED MYSTICAL. IT WASN'T.
I KNEW VAMPIRES LIKE SOME PEOPLE KNEW HORSES, OR CARS. I KNEW NIKOLAOS WOULDN'T ENJOY BEING COMPARED TO A HORSE OR A CAR, SO I KEPT MY MOUTH SHUT.
SEE, NOT STUPID AFTER ALL.

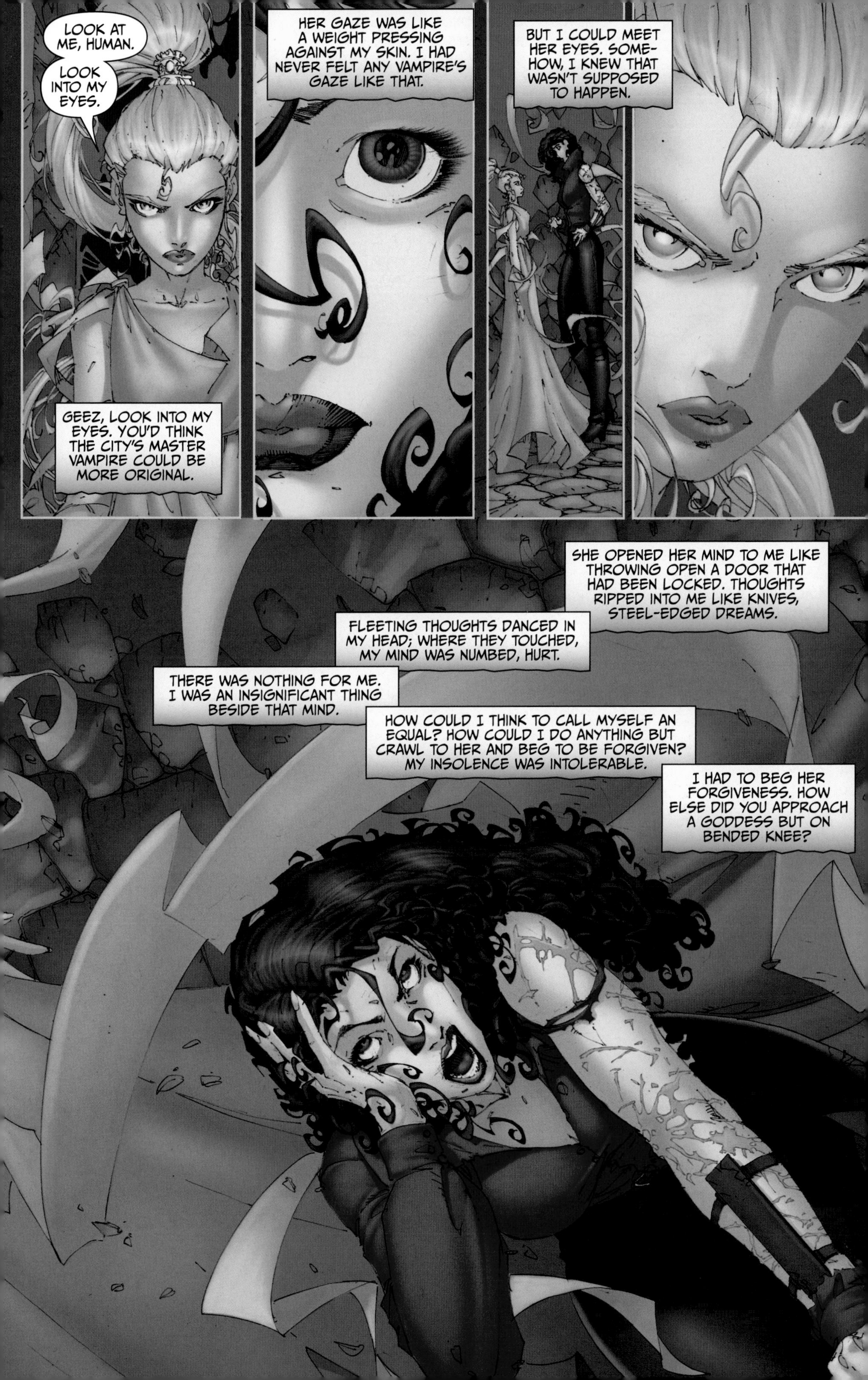
LOOK AT ME, HUMAN.
LOOK INTO MY EYES.
GEEZ, LOOK INTO MY EYES. YOU'D THINK THE CITY'S MASTER VAMPIRE COULD BE MORE ORIGINAL.
HER GAZE WAS LIKE A WEIGHT PRESSING AGAINST MY SKIN. I HAD NEVER FELT ANY VAMPIRE'S GAZE LIKE THAT.
BUT I COULD MEET HER EYES. SOME-HOW, I KNEW THAT WASN'T SUPPOSED TO HAPPEN.
SHE OPENED HER MIND TO ME LIKE THROWING OPEN A DOOR THAT HAD BEEN LOCKED. THOUGHTS RIPPED INTO ME LIKE KNIVES, STEEL-EDGED DREAMS.
FLEETING THOUGHTS DANCED IN MY HEAD; WHERE THEY TOUCHED, MY MIND WAS NUMBED, HURT.
THERE WAS NOTHING FOR ME. I WAS AN INSIGNIFICANT THING BESIDE THAT MIND.
HOW COULD I THINK TO CALL MYSELF AN EQUAL? HOW COULD I DO ANYTHING BUT CRAWL TO HER AND BEG TO BE FORGIVEN? MY INSOLENCE WAS INTOLERABLE.
I HAD TO BEG HER FORGIVENESS. HOW ELSE DID YOU APPROACH A GODDESS BUT ON BENDED KNEE?

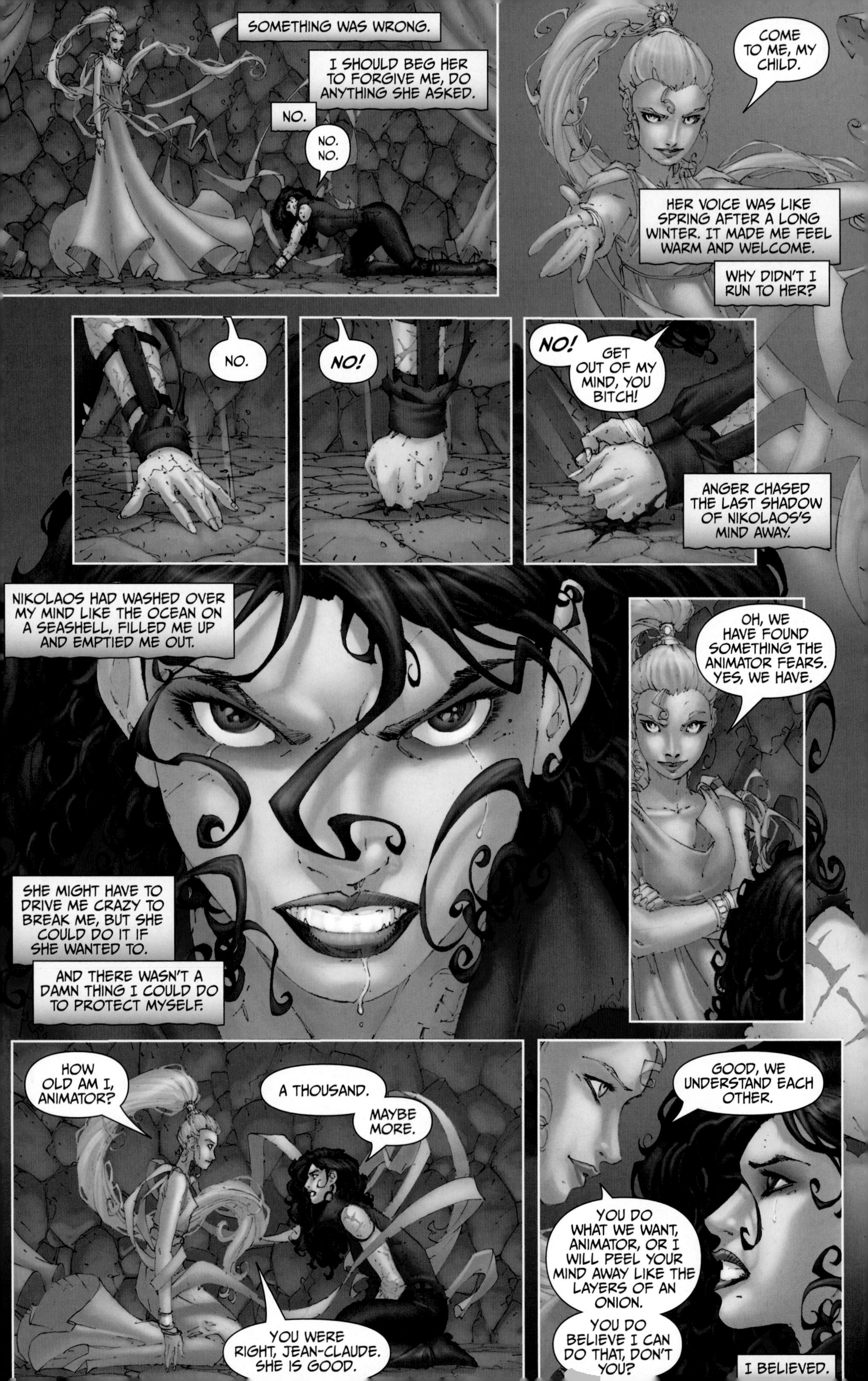
SOMETHING WAS WRONG.
I SHOULD BEG HER TO FORGIVE ME, DO ANYTHING SHE ASKED.
NO.
NO. NO.
COME TO ME, MY CHILD.
HER VOICE WAS LIKE SPRING AFTER A LONG WINTER. IT MADE ME FEEL WARM AND WELCOME.
WHY DIDN'T I RUN TO HER?
NO.
NO!
NO!
GET OUT OF MY MIND, YOU BITCH!
ANGER CHASED THE LAST SHADOW OF NIKOLAOS'S MIND AWAY.
NIKOLAOS HAD WASHED OVER MY MIND LIKE THE OCEAN ON A SEASHELL, FILLED ME UP AND EMPTIED ME OUT.
OH, WE HAVE FOUND SOMETHING THE ANIMATOR FEARS. YES, WE HAVE.
SHE MIGHT HAVE TO DRIVE ME CRAZY TO BREAK ME, BUT SHE COULD DO IT IF SHE WANTED TO.
AND THERE WASN'T A DAMN THING I COULD DO TO PROTECT MYSELF.
HOW OLD AM I, ANIMATOR?
A THOUSAND.
MAYBE MORE.
YOU WERE RIGHT, JEAN-CLAUDE. SHE IS GOOD.
GOOD, WE UNDERSTAND EACH OTHER.
YOU DO WHAT WE WANT, ANIMATOR, OR I WILL PEEL YOUR MIND AWAY LIKE THE LAYERS OF AN ONION.
YOU DO BELIEVE I CAN DO THAT, DON'T YOU?
I BELIEVED.

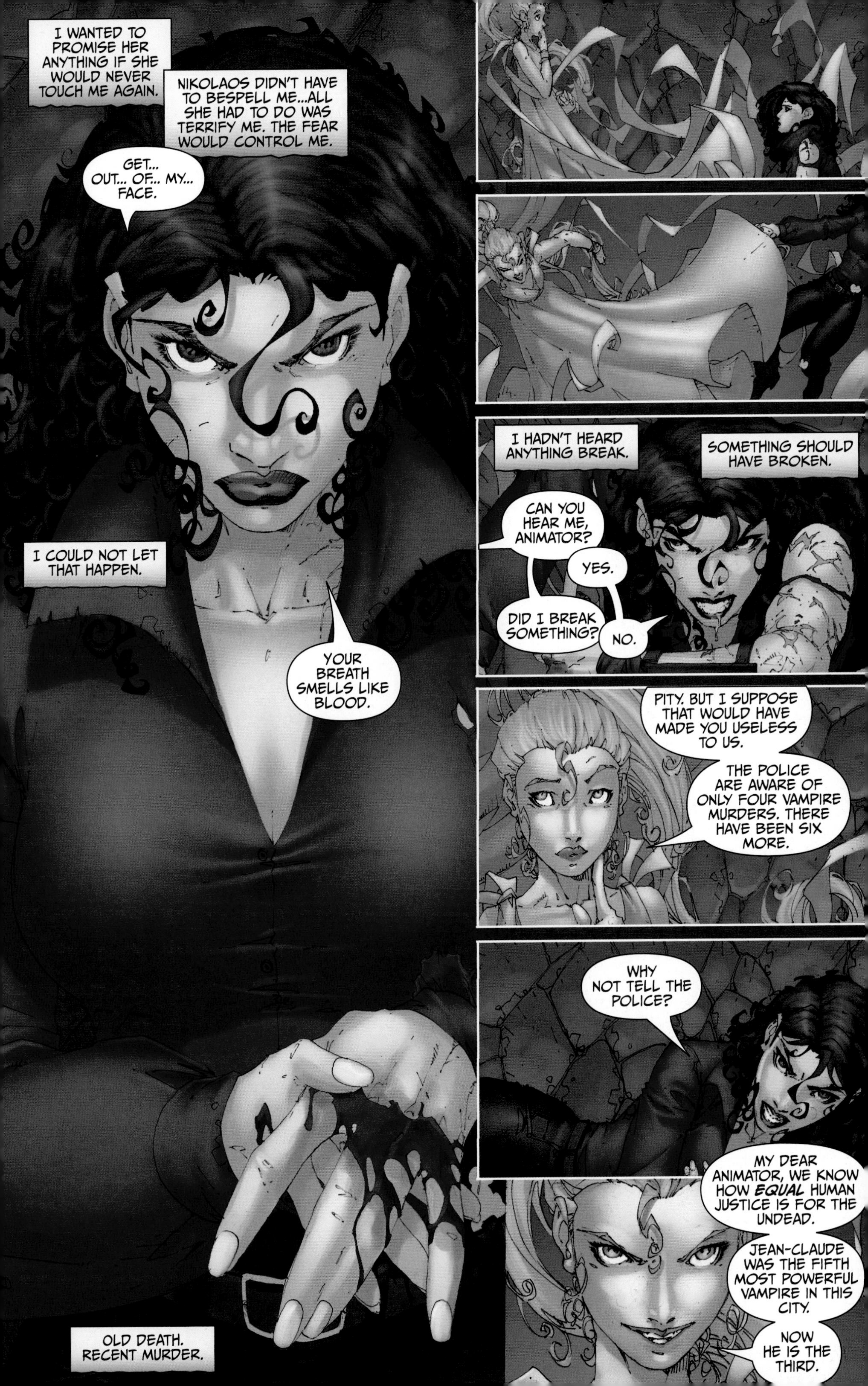
I WANTED TO PROMISE HER ANYTHING IF SHE WOULD NEVER TOUCH ME AGAIN.
NIKOLAOS DIDN'T HAVE TO BESPELL ME...ALL SHE HAD TO DO WAS TERRIFY ME. THE FEAR WOULD CONTROL ME.
GET... OUT... OF... MY... FACE.
I COULD NOT LET THAT HAPPEN.
YOUR BREATH SMELLS LIKE BLOOD.
OLD DEATH. RECENT MURDER.
I HADN'T HEARD ANYTHING BREAK.
SOMETHING SHOULD HAVE BROKEN.
CAN YOU HEAR ME, ANIMATOR?
YES.
DID I BREAK SOMETHING?
NO.
PITY. BUT I SUPPOSE THAT WOULD HAVE MADE YOU USELESS TO US.
THE POLICE ARE AWARE OF ONLY FOUR VAMPIRE MURDERS. THERE HAVE BEEN SIX MORE.
WHY NOT TELL THE POLICE?
MY DEAR ANIMATOR, WE KNOW HOW EQUAL HUMAN JUSTICE IS FOR THE UNDEAD.
JEAN-CLAUDE WAS THE FIFTH MOST POWERFUL VAMPIRE IN THIS CITY.
NOW HE IS THE THIRD.

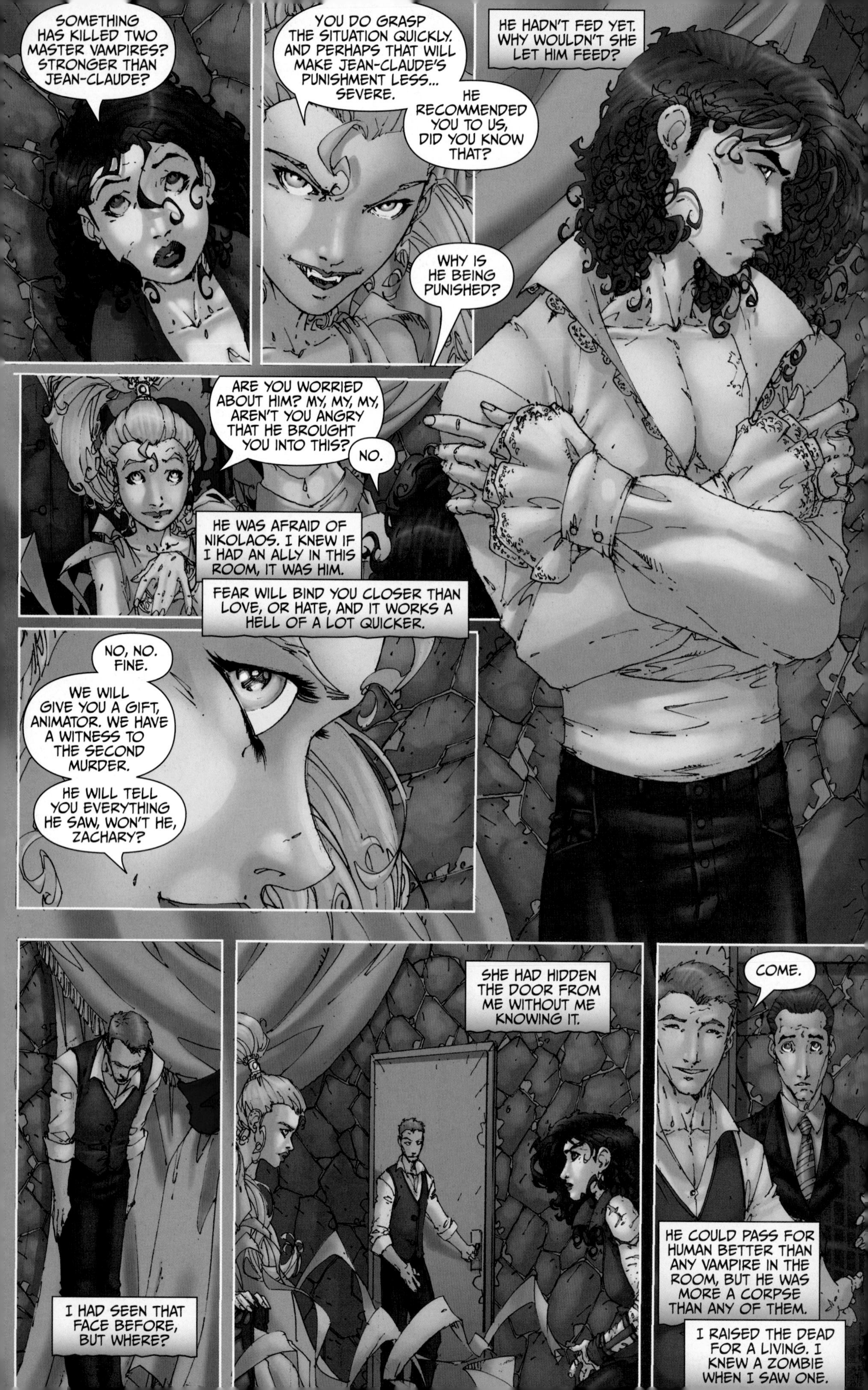
SOMETHING HAS KILLED TWO MASTER VAMPIRES? STRONGER THAN JEAN-CLAUDE?
YOU DO GRASP THE SITUATION QUICKLY. AND PERHAPS THAT WILL MAKE JEAN-CLAUDE'S PUNISHMENT LESS... SEVERE.
HE RECOMMENDED YOU TO US, DID YOU KNOW THAT?
WHY IS HE BEING PUNISHED?
HE HADN'T FED YET. WHY WOULDN'T SHE LET HIM FEED?
ARE YOU WORRIED ABOUT HIM? MY, MY, MY, AREN'T YOU ANGRY THAT HE BROUGHT YOU INTO THIS?
NO.
HE WAS AFRAID OF NIKOLAOS. I KNEW IF I HAD AN ALLY IN THIS ROOM, IT WAS HIM.
FEAR WILL BIND YOU CLOSER THAN LOVE, OR HATE, AND IT WORKS A HELL OF A LOT QUICKER.
NO, NO. FINE.
WE WILL GIVE YOU A GIFT, ANIMATOR. WE HAVE A WITNESS TO THE SECOND MURDER.
HE WILL TELL YOU EVERYTHING HE SAW, WON'T HE, ZACHARY?
I HAD SEEN THAT FACE BEFORE, BUT WHERE?
SHE HAD HIDDEN THE DOOR FROM ME WITHOUT ME KNOWING IT.
COME.
HE COULD PASS FOR HUMAN BETTER THAN ANY VAMPIRE IN THE ROOM, BUT HE WAS MORE A CORPSE THAN ANY OF THEM.
I RAISED THE DEAD FOR A LIVING. I KNEW A ZOMBIE WHEN I SAW ONE.

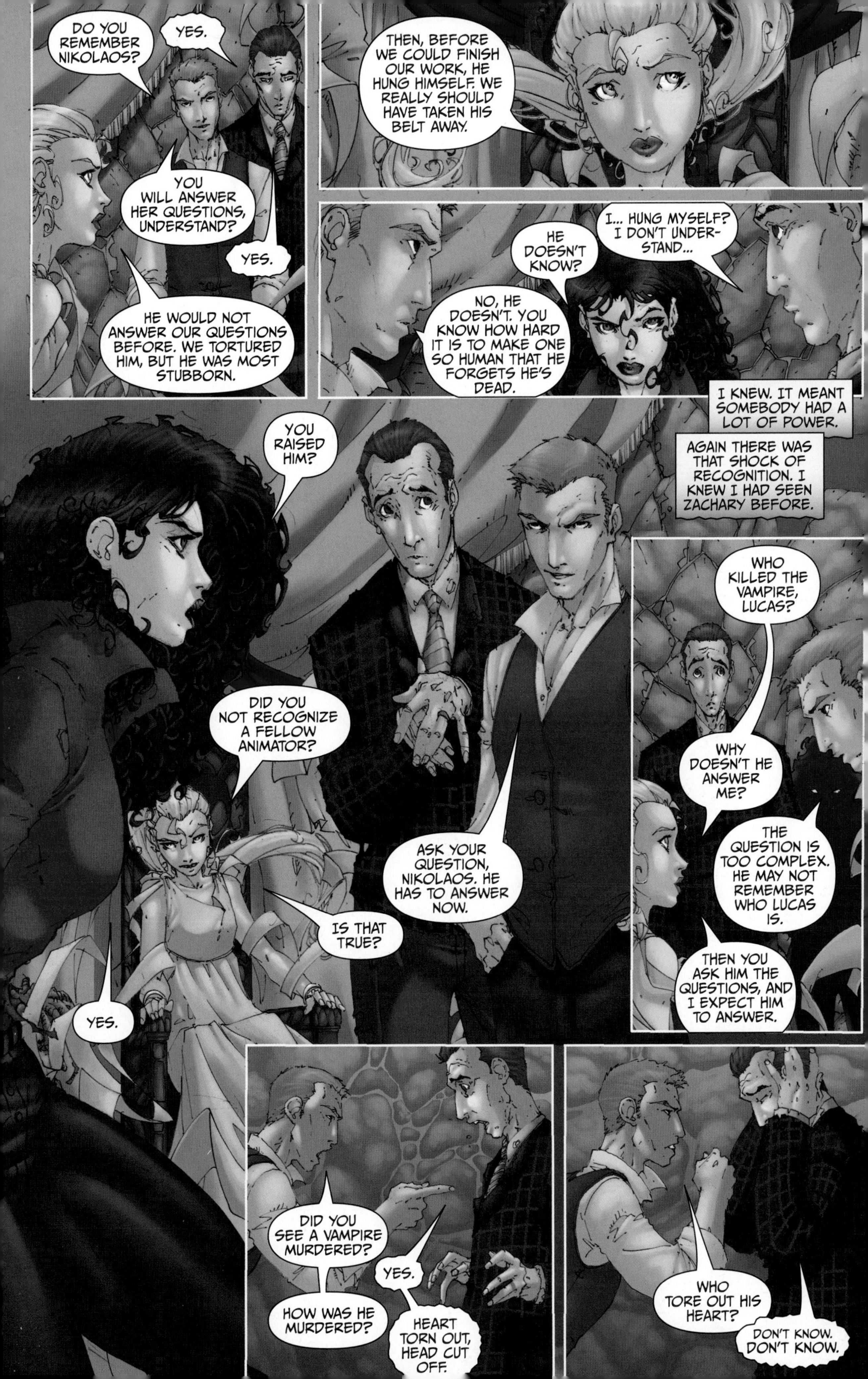

DO YOU REMEMBER NIKOLAOS?
YES.
YOU WILL ANSWER HER QUESTIONS, UNDERSTAND?
YES.
HE WOULD NOT ANSWER OUR QUESTIONS BEFORE. WE TORTURED HIM, BUT HE WAS MOST STUBBORN.
THEN, BEFORE WE COULD FINISH OUR WORK, HE HUNG HIMSELF. WE REALLY SHOULD HAVE TAKEN HIS BELT AWAY.
HE DOESN'T KNOW?
I... HUNG MYSELF? I DON'T UNDER-STAND...
NO, HE DOESN'T. YOU KNOW HOW HARD IT IS TO MAKE ONE SO HUMAN THAT HE FORGETS HE'S DEAD.
I KNEW. IT MEANT SOMEBODY HAD A LOT OF POWER.
YOU RAISED HIM?
AGAIN THERE WAS THAT SHOCK OF RECOGNITION. I KNEW I HAD SEEN ZACHARY BEFORE.
DID YOU NOT RECOGNIZE A FELLOW ANIMATOR?
ASK YOUR QUESTION, NIKOLAOS. HE HAS TO ANSWER NOW.
IS THAT TRUE?
YES.
WHO KILLED THE VAMPIRE, LUCAS?
WHY DOESN'T HE ANSWER ME?
THE QUESTION IS TOO COMPLEX. HE MAY NOT REMEMBER WHO LUCAS IS.
THEN YOU ASK HIM THE QUESTIONS, AND I EXPECT HIM TO ANSWER.
DID YOU SEE A VAMPIRE MURDERED?
YES.
HOW WAS HE MURDERED?
HEART TORN OUT, HEAD CUT OFF.
WHO TORE OUT HIS HEART?
DON'T KNOW. DON'T KNOW.

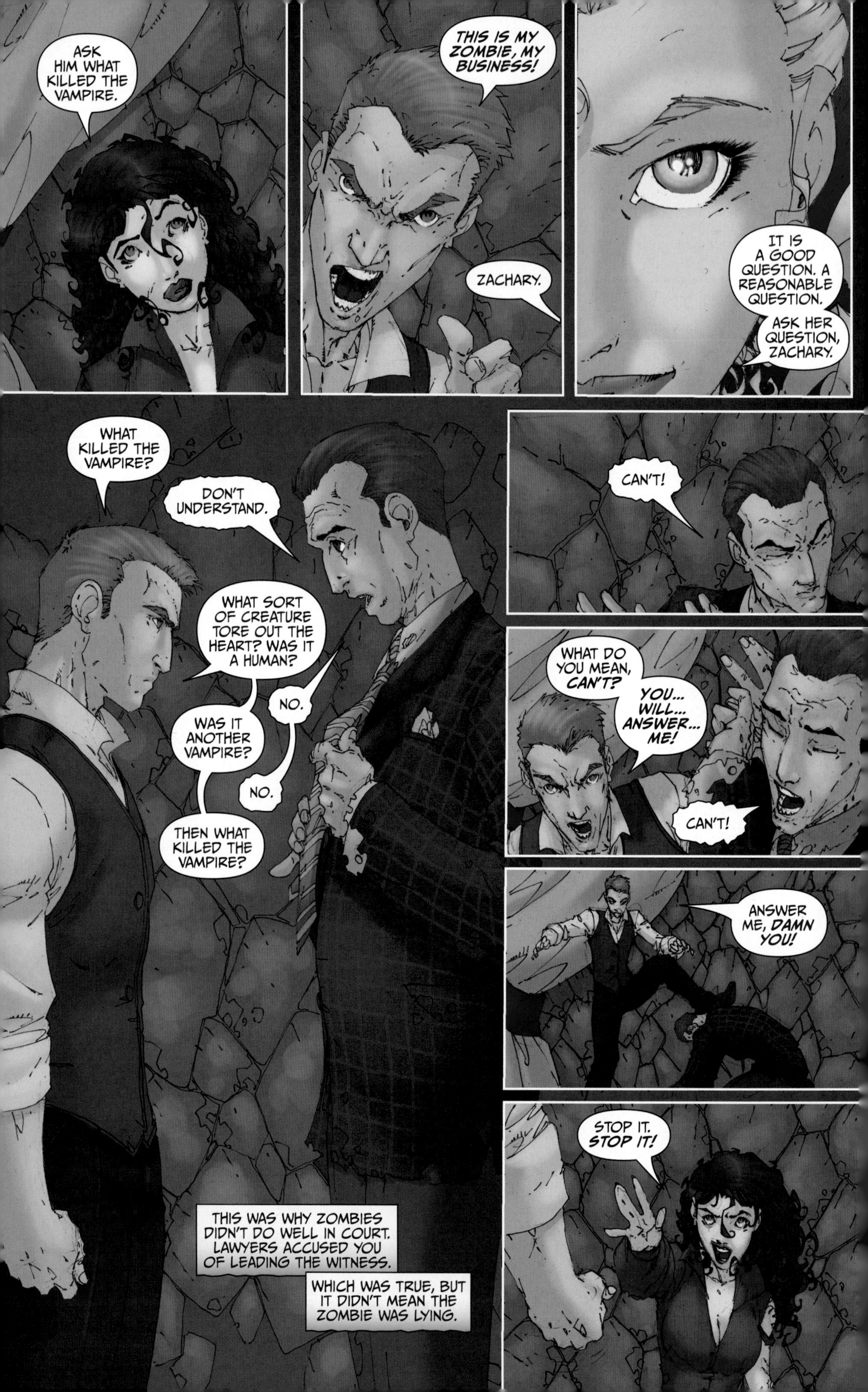
ASK HIM WHAT KILLED THE VAMPIRE.
THIS IS MY ZOMBIE, MY BUSINESS!
ZACHARY.
IT IS A GOOD QUESTION. A REASONABLE QUESTION.
ASK HER QUESTION, ZACHARY.
WHAT KILLED THE VAMPIRE?
DON'T UNDERSTAND.
WHAT SORT OF CREATURE TORE OUT THE HEART? WAS IT A HUMAN?
NO.
WAS IT ANOTHER VAMPIRE?
NO.
THEN WHAT KILLED THE VAMPIRE?
THIS WAS WHY ZOMBIES DIDN'T DO WELL IN COURT. LAWYERS ACCUSED YOU OF LEADING THE WITNESS.
WHICH WAS TRUE, BUT IT DIDN'T MEAN THE ZOMBIE WAS LYING.
CAN'T!
WHAT DO YOU MEAN, CAN'T?
YOU... WILL... ANSWER... ME!
CAN'T!
ANSWER ME, DAMN YOU!
STOP IT. STOP IT!

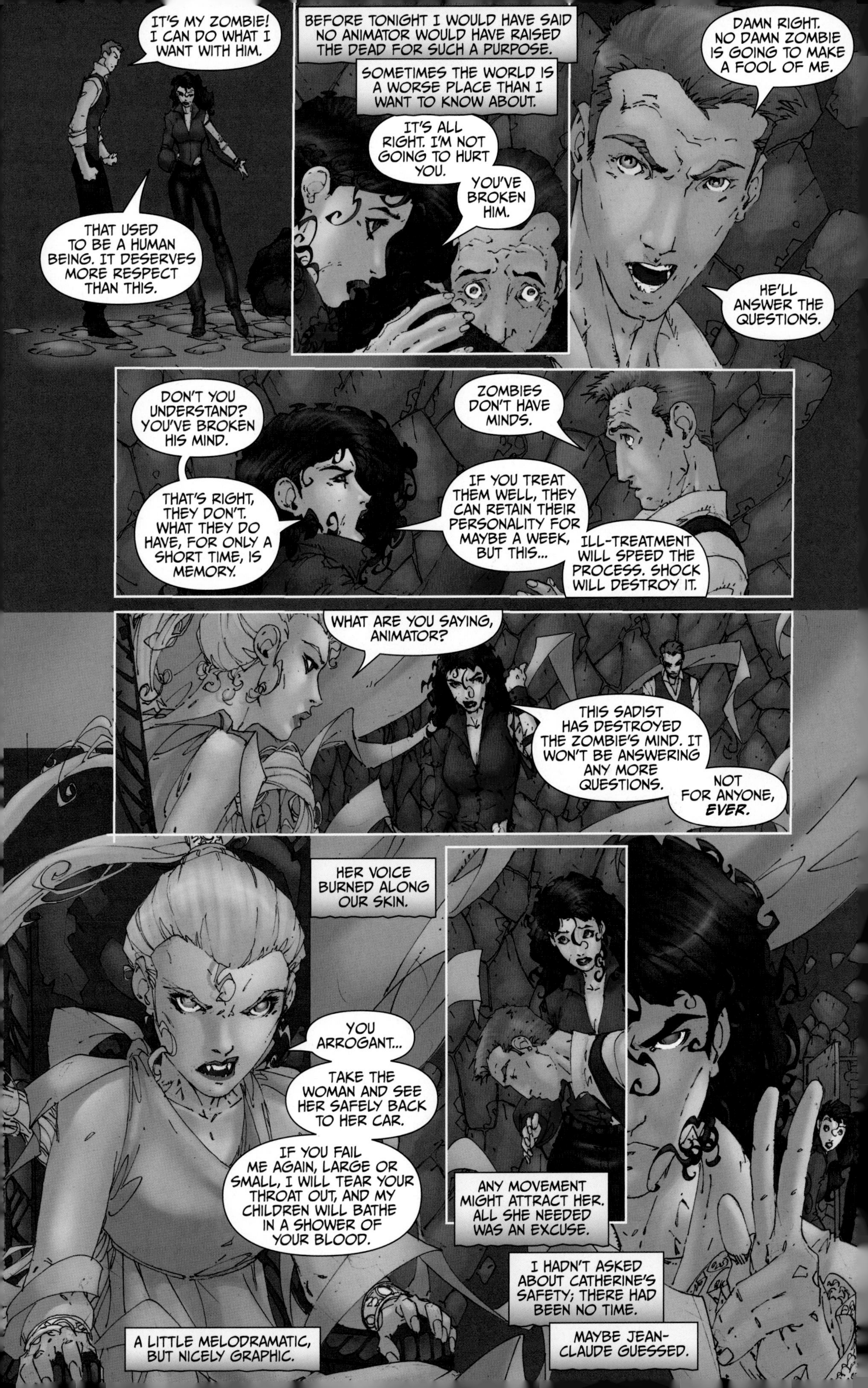
IT'S MY ZOMBIE! I CAN DO WHAT I WANT WITH HIM.
THAT USED TO BE A HUMAN BEING. IT DESERVES MORE RESPECT THAN THIS.
BEFORE TONIGHT I WOULD HAVE SAID NO ANIMATOR WOULD HAVE RAISED THE DEAD FOR SUCH A PURPOSE.
SOMETIMES THE WORLD IS A WORSE PLACE THAN I WANT TO KNOW ABOUT.
IT'S ALL RIGHT. I'M NOT GOING TO HURT YOU.
YOU'VE BROKEN HIM.
DAMN RIGHT. NO DAMN ZOMBIE IS GOING TO MAKE A FOOL OF ME.
HE'LL ANSWER THE QUESTIONS.
DON'T YOU UNDERSTAND? YOU'VE BROKEN HIS MIND.
ZOMBIES DON'T HAVE MINDS.
THAT'S RIGHT, THEY DON'T. WHAT THEY DO HAVE, FOR ONLY A SHORT TIME, IS MEMORY.
IF YOU TREAT THEM WELL, THEY CAN RETAIN THEIR PERSONALITY FOR MAYBE A WEEK, BUT THIS...
ILL-TREATMENT WILL SPEED THE PROCESS. SHOCK WILL DESTROY IT.
WHAT ARE YOU SAYING, ANIMATOR?
THIS SADIST HAS DESTROYED THE ZOMBIE'S MIND. IT WON'T BE ANSWERING ANY MORE QUESTIONS.
NOT FOR ANYONE, ***EVER.***
HER VOICE BURNED ALONG OUR SKIN.
YOU ARROGANT...
TAKE THE WOMAN AND SEE HER SAFELY BACK TO HER CAR.
IF YOU FAIL ME AGAIN, LARGE OR SMALL, I WILL TEAR YOUR THROAT OUT, AND MY CHILDREN WILL BATHE IN A SHOWER OF YOUR BLOOD.
A LITTLE MELODRAMATIC, BUT NICELY GRAPHIC.
ANY MOVEMENT MIGHT ATTRACT HER. ALL SHE NEEDED WAS AN EXCUSE.
I HADN'T ASKED ABOUT CATHERINE'S SAFETY; THERE HAD BEEN NO TIME.
MAYBE JEAN-CLAUDE GUESSED.

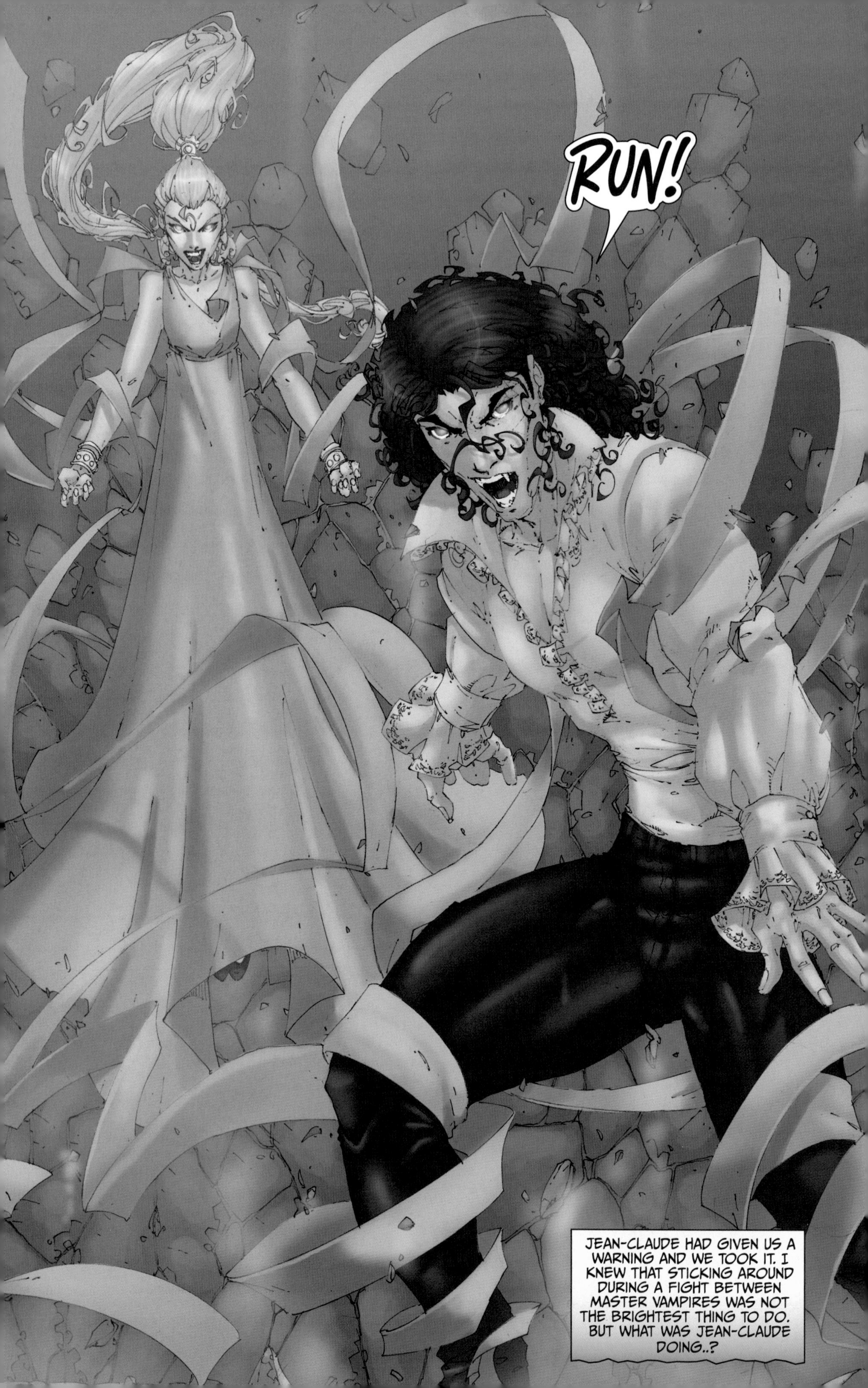
RUN!
JEAN-CLAUDE HAD GIVEN US A WARNING AND WE TOOK IT. I KNEW THAT STICKING AROUND DURING A FIGHT BETWEEN MASTER VAMPIRES WAS NOT THE BRIGHTEST THING TO DO. BUT WHAT WAS JEAN-CLAUDE DOING..?

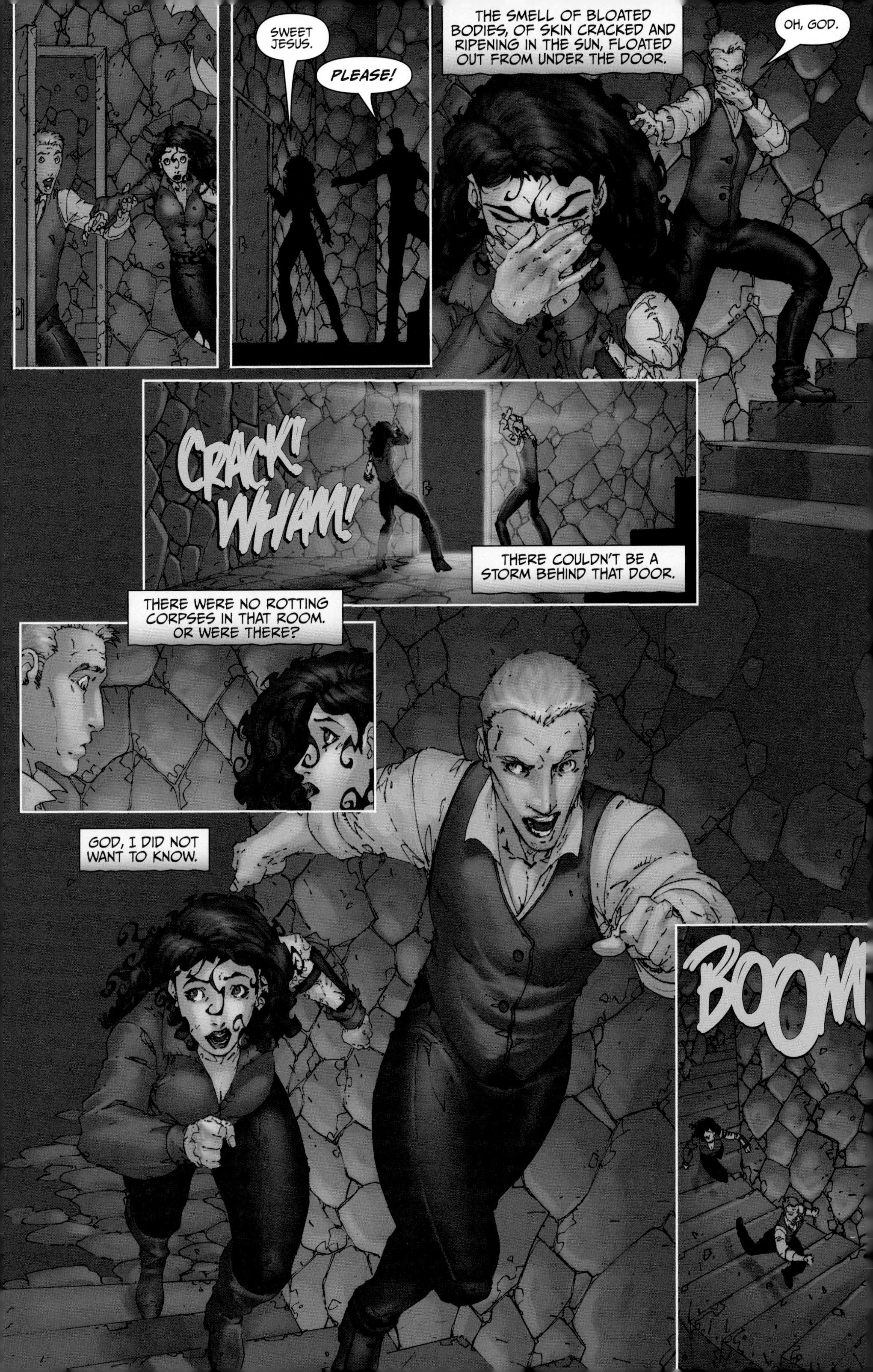

SWEET JESUS.
PLEASE!
THE SMELL OF BLOATED BODIES, OF SKIN CRACKED AND RIPENING IN THE SUN, FLOATED OUT FROM UNDER THE DOOR.
OH, GOD.
CRACK! WHAM!
THERE COULDN'T BE A STORM BEHIND THAT DOOR.
THERE WERE NO ROTTING CORPSES IN THAT ROOM. OR WERE THERE?
GOD, I DID NOT WANT TO KNOW.
BOOM

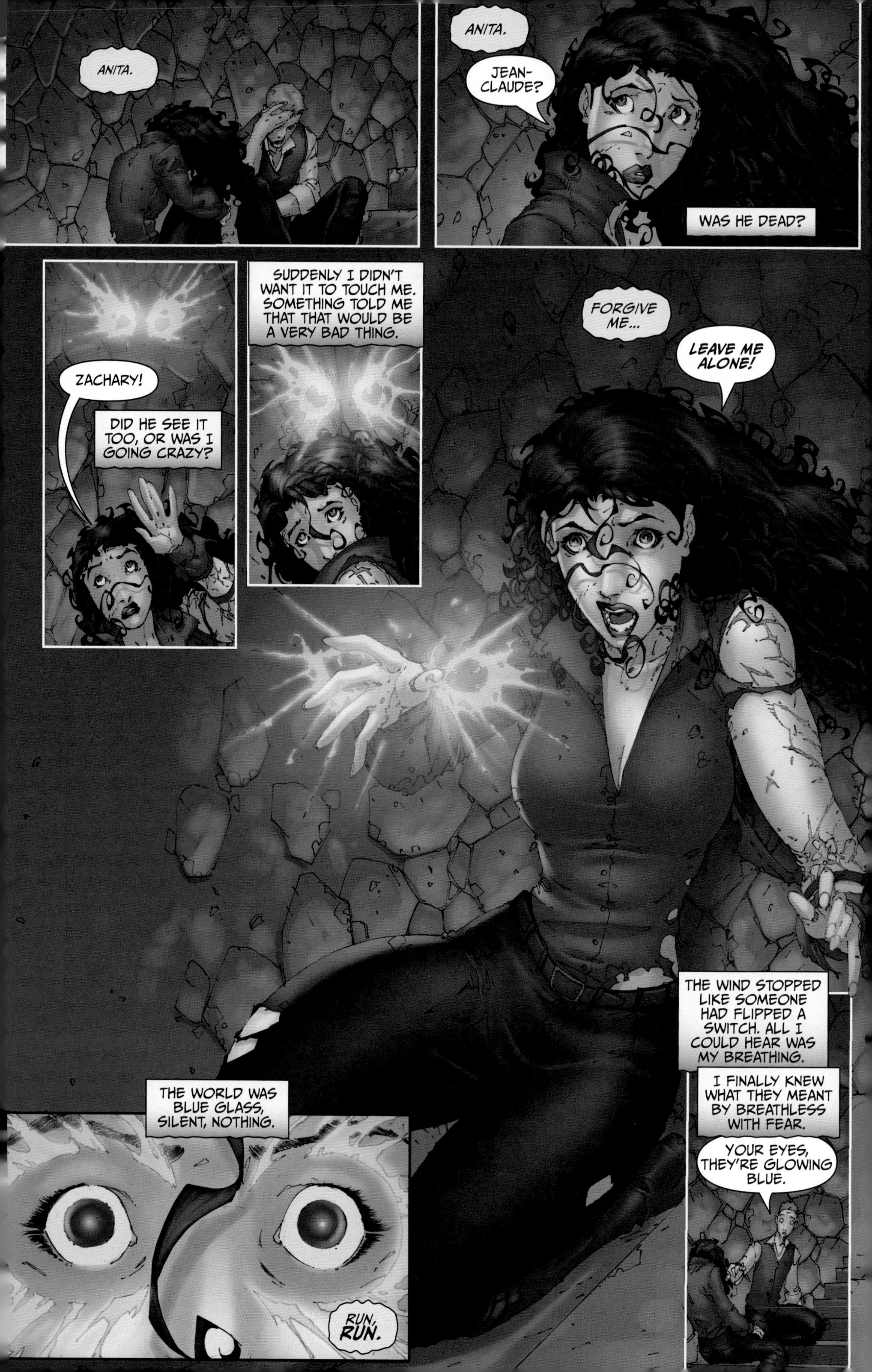
ANITA.
ANITA.
JEAN-CLAUDE?
WAS HE DEAD?
ZACHARY!
DID HE SEE IT TOO, OR WAS I GOING CRAZY?
SUDDENLY I DIDN'T WANT IT TO TOUCH ME. SOMETHING TOLD ME THAT THAT WOULD BE A VERY BAD THING.
FORGIVE ME...
LEAVE ME ALONE!
THE WIND STOPPED LIKE SOMEONE HAD FLIPPED A SWITCH. ALL I COULD HEAR WAS MY BREATHING.
I FINALLY KNEW WHAT THEY MEANT BY BREATHLESS WITH FEAR.
YOUR EYES, THEY'RE GLOWING BLUE.
THE WORLD WAS BLUE GLASS, SILENT, NOTHING.
RUN, RUN.

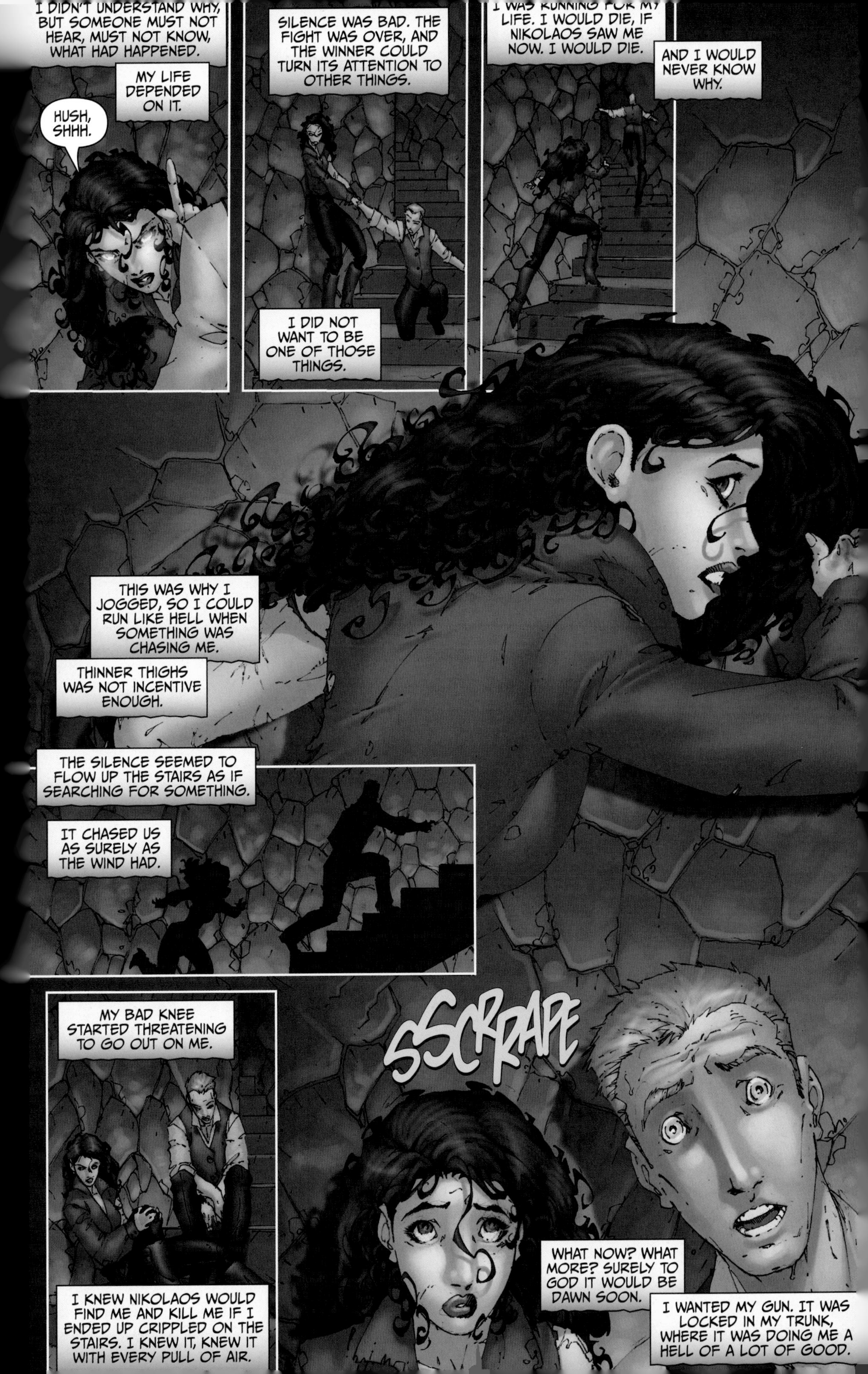
I DIDN'T UNDERSTAND WHY, BUT SOMEONE MUST NOT HEAR, MUST NOT KNOW, WHAT HAD HAPPENED.
MY LIFE DEPENDED ON IT.
HUSH, SHHH.
SILENCE WAS BAD. THE FIGHT WAS OVER, AND THE WINNER COULD TURN ITS ATTENTION TO OTHER THINGS.
I DID NOT WANT TO BE ONE OF THOSE THINGS.
I WAS RUNNING FOR MY LIFE. I WOULD DIE, IF NIKOLAOS SAW ME NOW. I WOULD DIE.
AND I WOULD NEVER KNOW WHY.
THIS WAS WHY I JOGGED, SO I COULD RUN LIKE HELL WHEN SOMETHING WAS CHASING ME.
THINNER THIGHS WAS NOT INCENTIVE ENOUGH.
THE SILENCE SEEMED TO FLOW UP THE STAIRS AS IF SEARCHING FOR SOMETHING.
IT CHASED US AS SURELY AS THE WIND HAD.
MY BAD KNEE STARTED THREATENING TO GO OUT ON ME.
I KNEW NIKOLAOS WOULD FIND ME AND KILL ME IF I ENDED UP CRIPPLED ON THE STAIRS. I KNEW IT, KNEW IT WITH EVERY PULL OF AIR.
SSCRAPE
WHAT NOW? WHAT MORE? SURELY TO GOD IT WOULD BE DAWN SOON.
I WANTED MY GUN. IT WAS LOCKED IN MY TRUNK, WHERE IT WAS DOING ME A HELL OF A LOT OF GOOD.

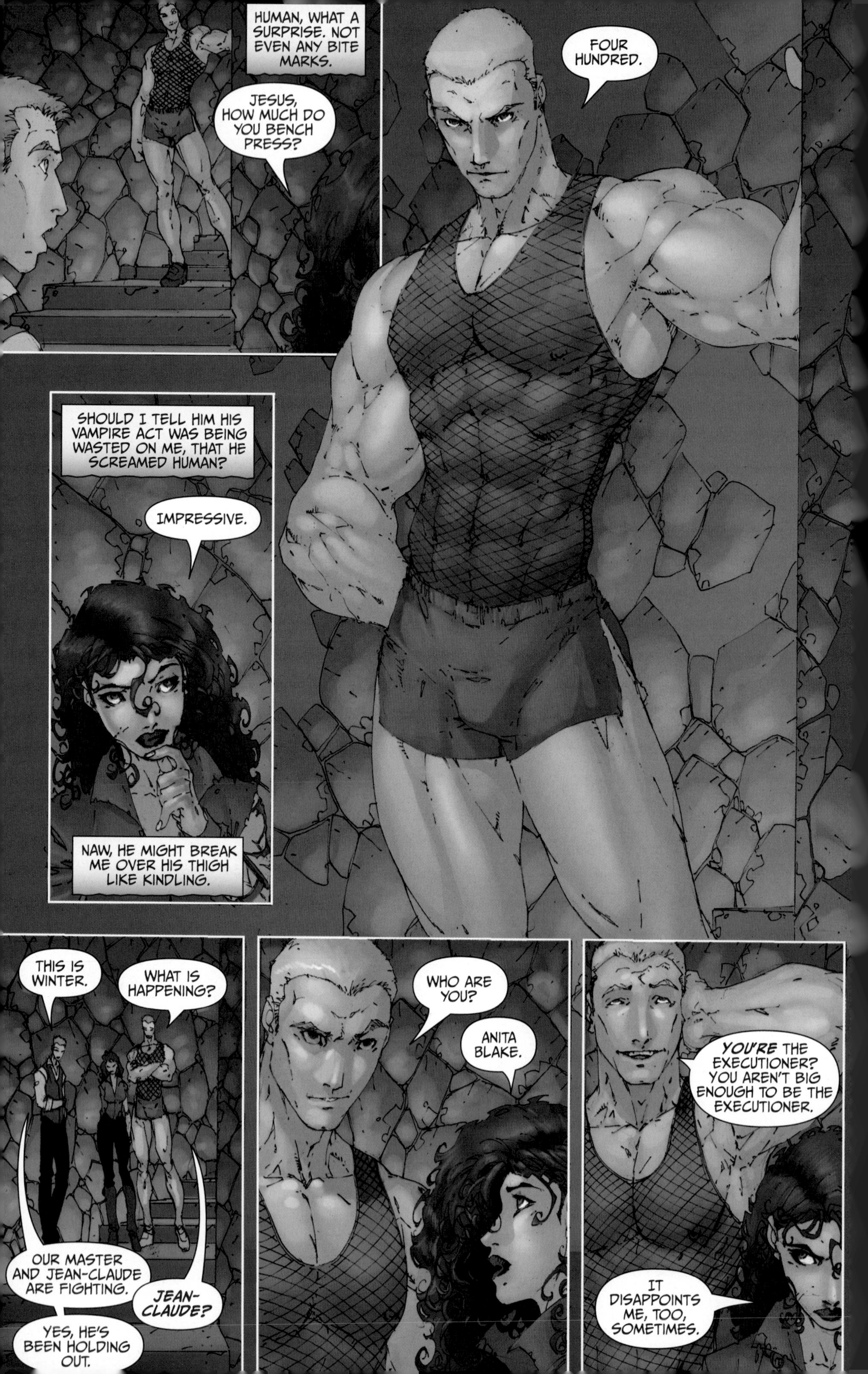
HUMAN, WHAT A SURPRISE. NOT EVEN ANY BITE MARKS.
JESUS, HOW MUCH DO YOU BENCH PRESS?
FOUR HUNDRED.
SHOULD I TELL HIM HIS VAMPIRE ACT WAS BEING WASTED ON ME, THAT HE SCREAMED HUMAN?
IMPRESSIVE.
NAW, HE MIGHT BREAK ME OVER HIS THIGH LIKE KINDLING.
THIS IS WINTER.
WHAT IS HAPPENING?
OUR MASTER AND JEAN-CLAUDE ARE FIGHTING.
JEAN-CLAUDE?
YES, HE'S BEEN HOLDING OUT.
WHO ARE YOU?
ANITA BLAKE.
YOU'RE THE EXECUTIONER? YOU AREN'T BIG ENOUGH TO BE THE EXECUTIONER.
IT DISAPPOINTS ME, TOO, SOMETIMES.

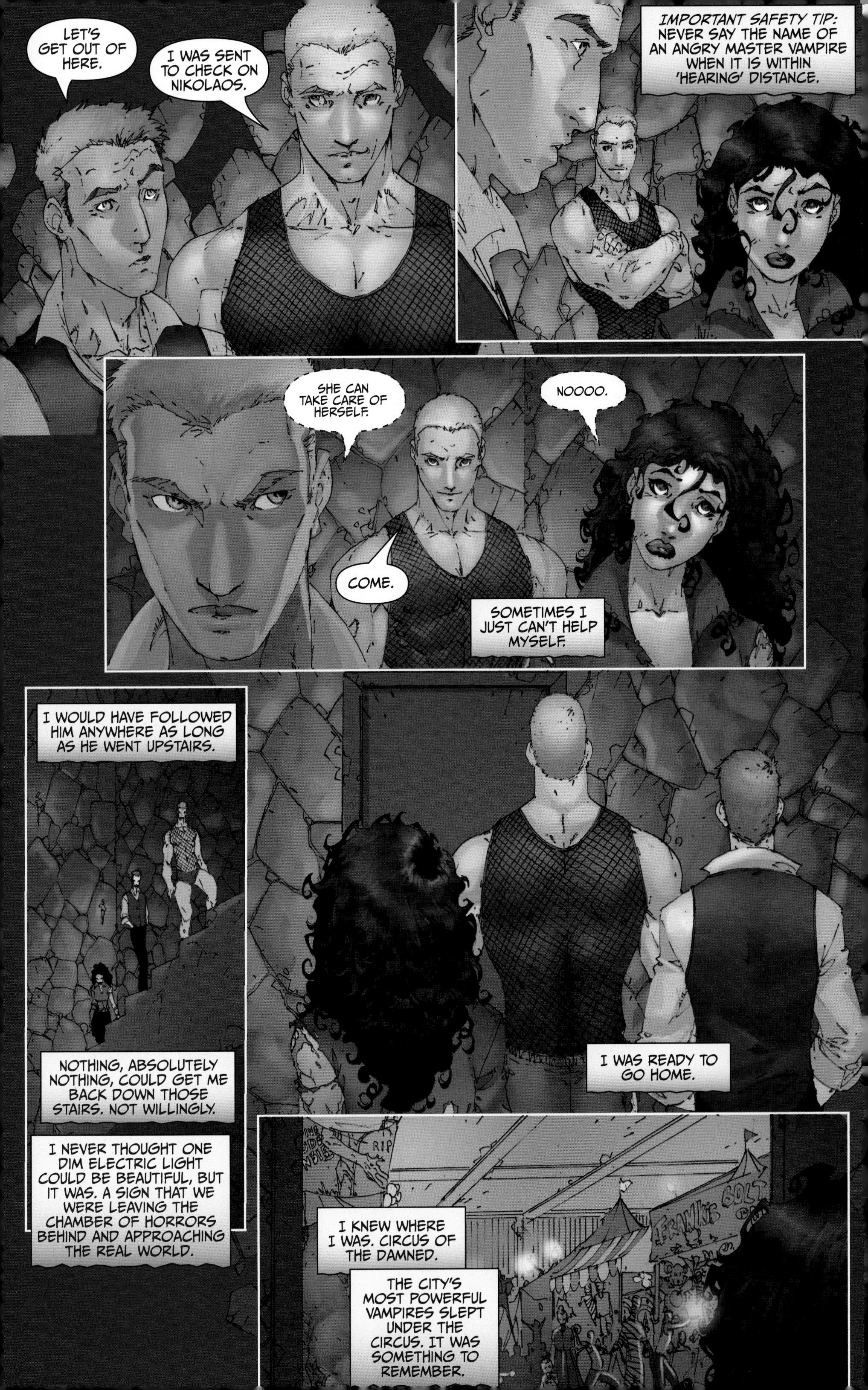
LET'S GET OUT OF HERE.
I WAS SENT TO CHECK ON NIKOLAOS.
IMPORTANT SAFETY TIP: NEVER SAY THE NAME OF AN ANGRY MASTER VAMPIRE WHEN IT IS WITHIN 'HEARING' DISTANCE.
SHE CAN TAKE CARE OF HERSELF.
NOOOO.
COME.
SOMETIMES I JUST CAN'T HELP MYSELF.
I WOULD HAVE FOLLOWED HIM ANYWHERE AS LONG AS HE WENT UPSTAIRS.
NOTHING, ABSOLUTELY NOTHING, COULD GET ME BACK DOWN THOSE STAIRS. NOT WILLINGLY.
I NEVER THOUGHT ONE DIM ELECTRIC LIGHT COULD BE BEAUTIFUL, BUT IT WAS. A SIGN THAT WE WERE LEAVING THE CHAMBER OF HORRORS BEHIND AND APPROACHING THE REAL WORLD.
I WAS READY TO GO HOME.
I KNEW WHERE I WAS. CIRCUS OF THE DAMNED.
THE CITY'S MOST POWERFUL VAMPIRES SLEPT UNDER THE CIRCUS. IT WAS SOMETHING TO REMEMBER.

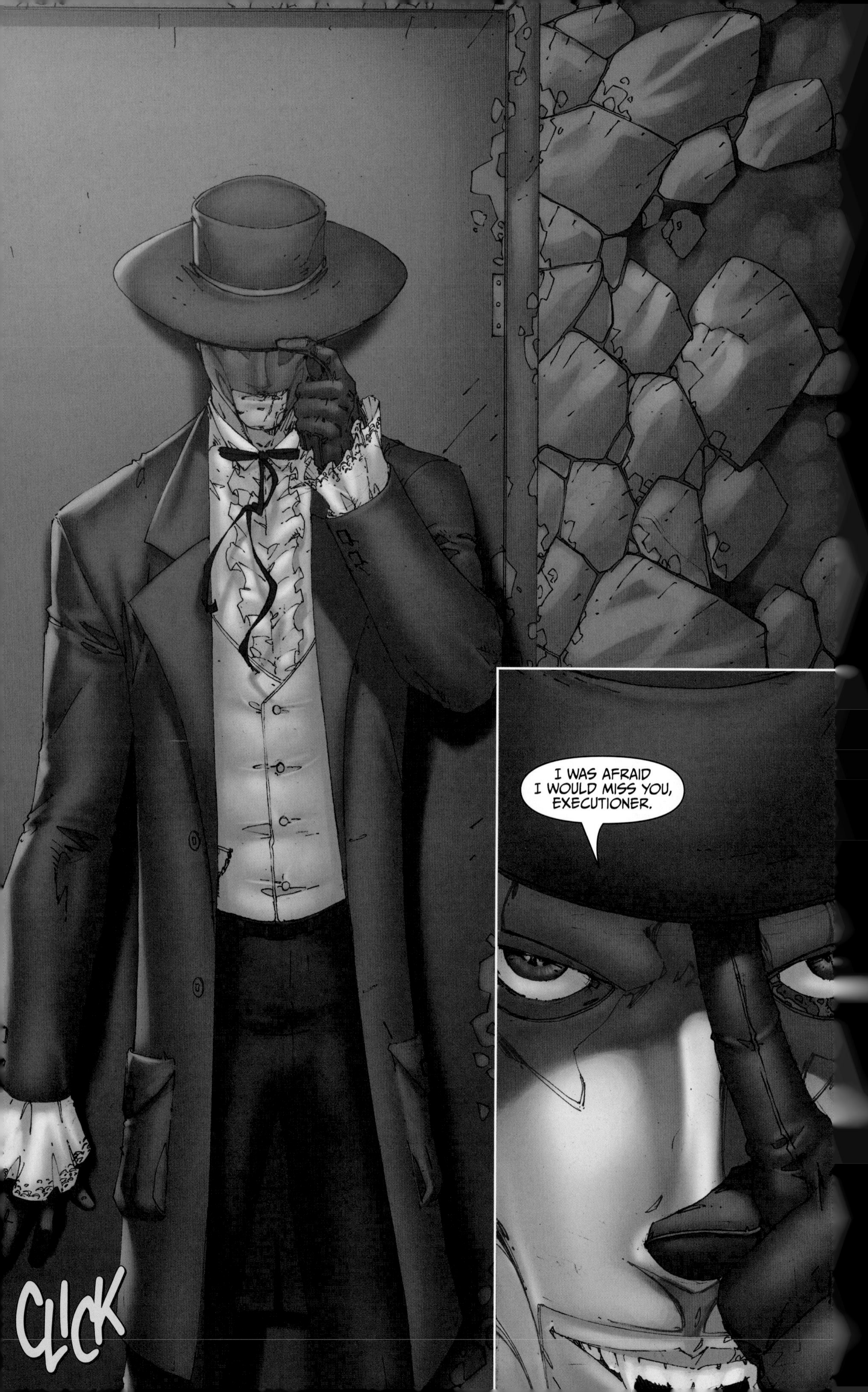
I WAS AFRAID I WOULD MISS YOU, EXECUTIONER.
CLICK

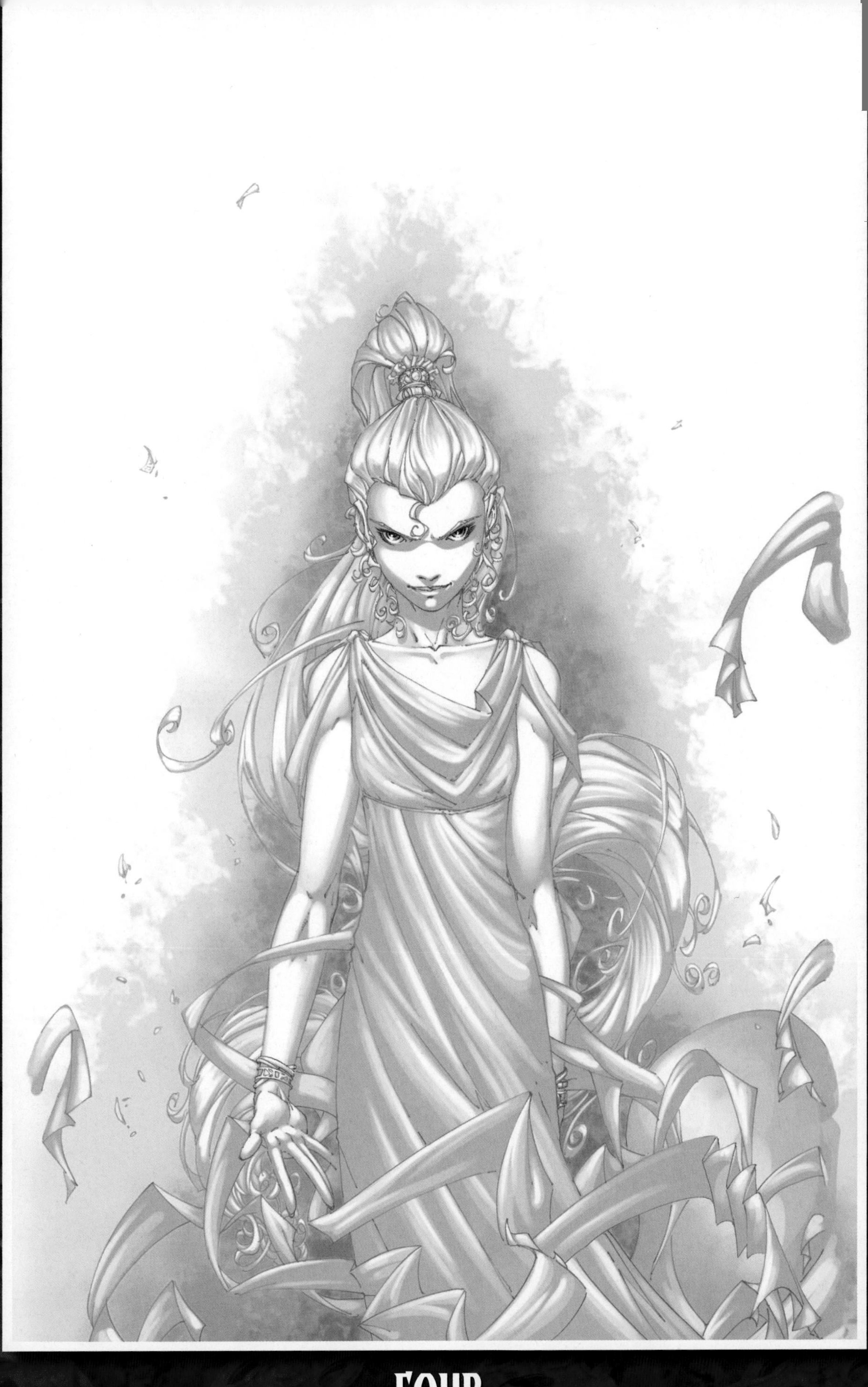

FOUR

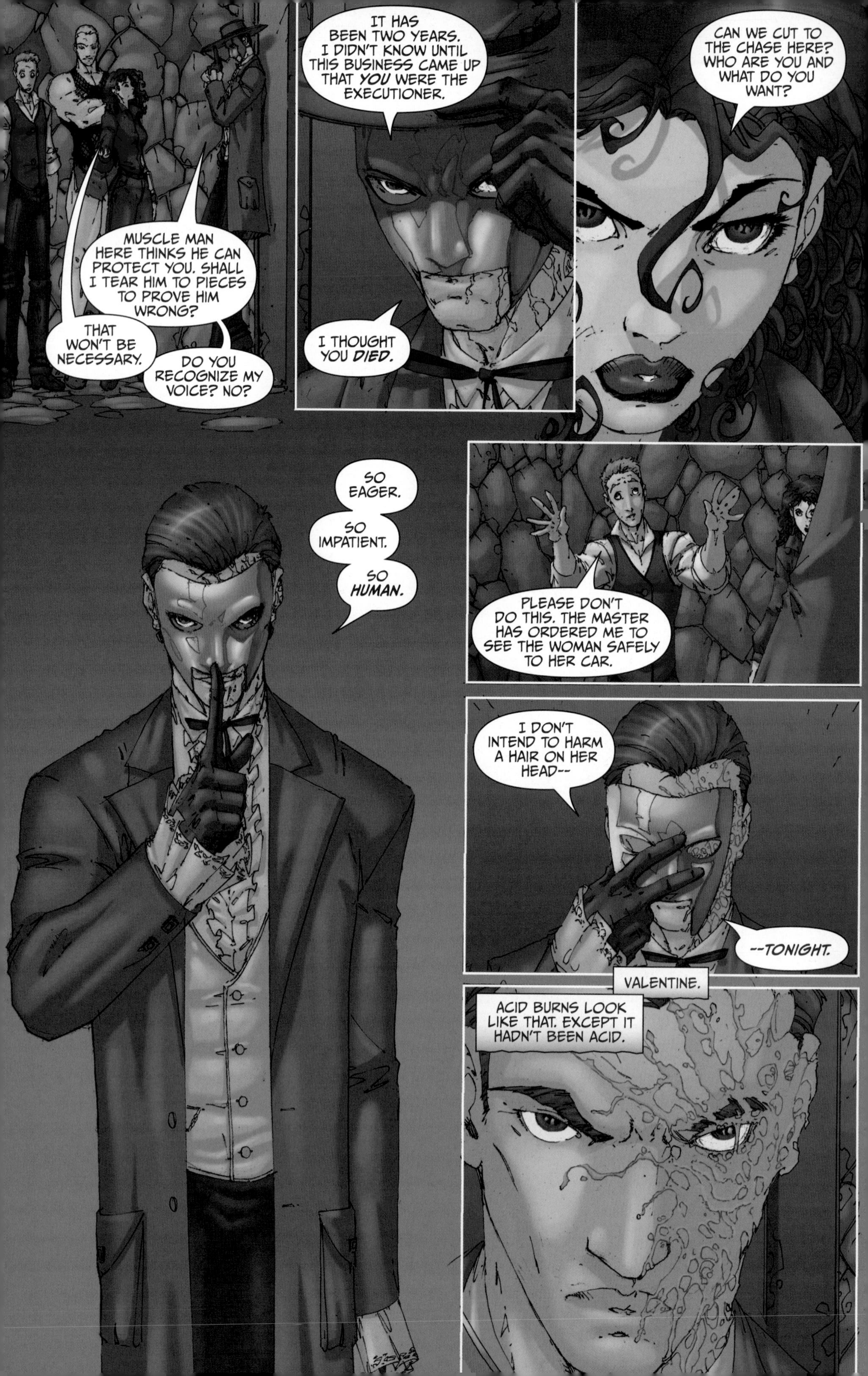
MUSCLE MAN HERE THINKS HE CAN PROTECT YOU. SHALL I TEAR HIM TO PIECES TO PROVE HIM WRONG?
THAT WON'T BE NECESSARY.
DO YOU RECOGNIZE MY VOICE? NO?
IT HAS BEEN TWO YEARS. I DIDN'T KNOW UNTIL THIS BUSINESS CAME UP THAT YOU WERE THE EXECUTIONER.
I THOUGHT YOU DIED.
CAN WE CUT TO THE CHASE HERE? WHO ARE YOU AND WHAT DO YOU WANT?
SO EAGER.
SO IMPATIENT.
SO HUMAN.
PLEASE DON'T DO THIS. THE MASTER HAS ORDERED ME TO SEE THE WOMAN SAFELY TO HER CAR.
I DON'T INTEND TO HARM A HAIR ON HER HEAD--
--TONIGHT.
VALENTINE.
ACID BURNS LOOK LIKE THAT. EXCEPT IT HADN'T BEEN ACID.

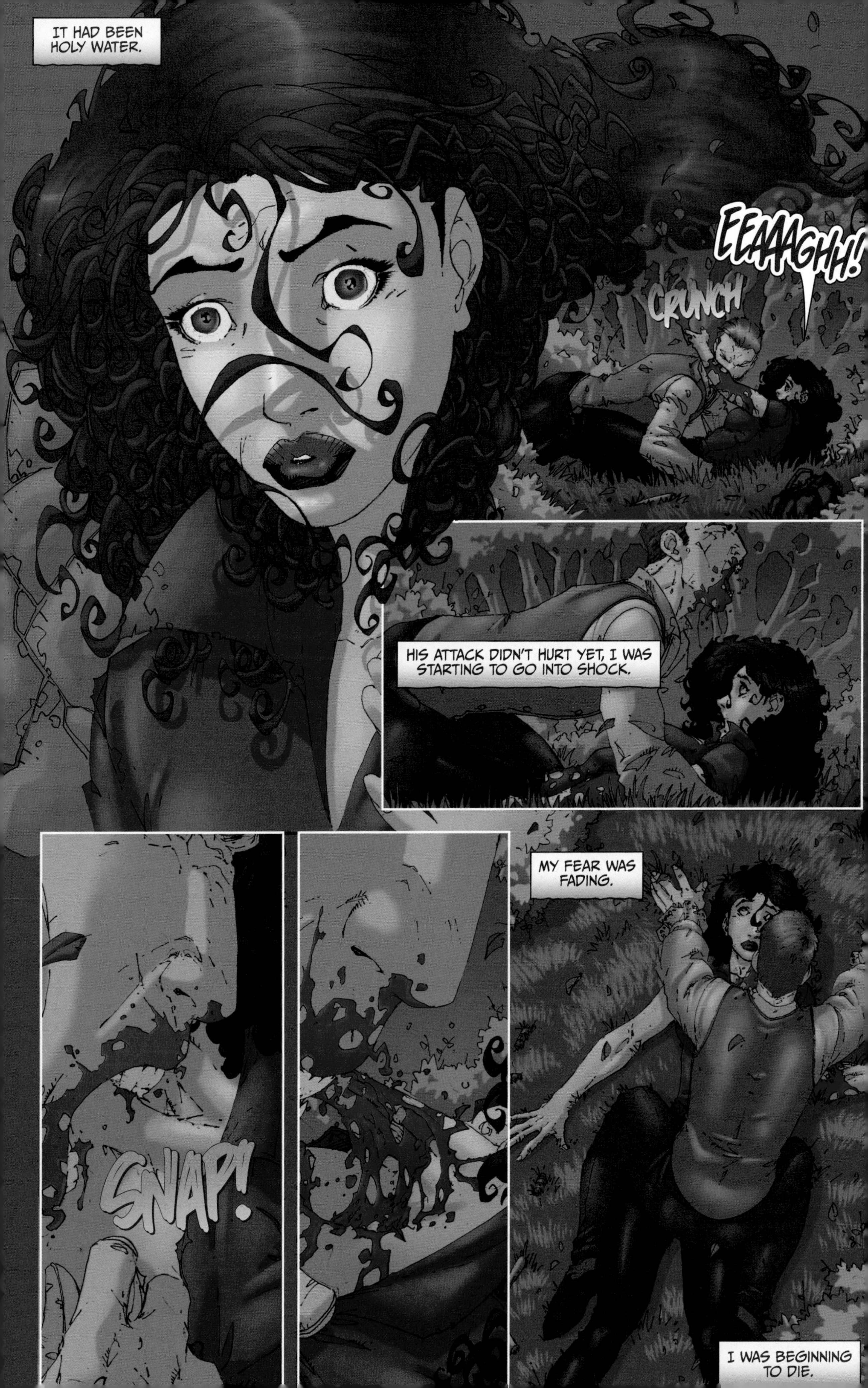
IT HAD BEEN HOLY WATER.
EEAAAGHH!
CRUNCH
HIS ATTACK DIDN'T HURT YET, I WAS STARTING TO GO INTO SHOCK.
SNAP!
MY FEAR WAS FADING.
I WAS BEGINNING TO DIE.

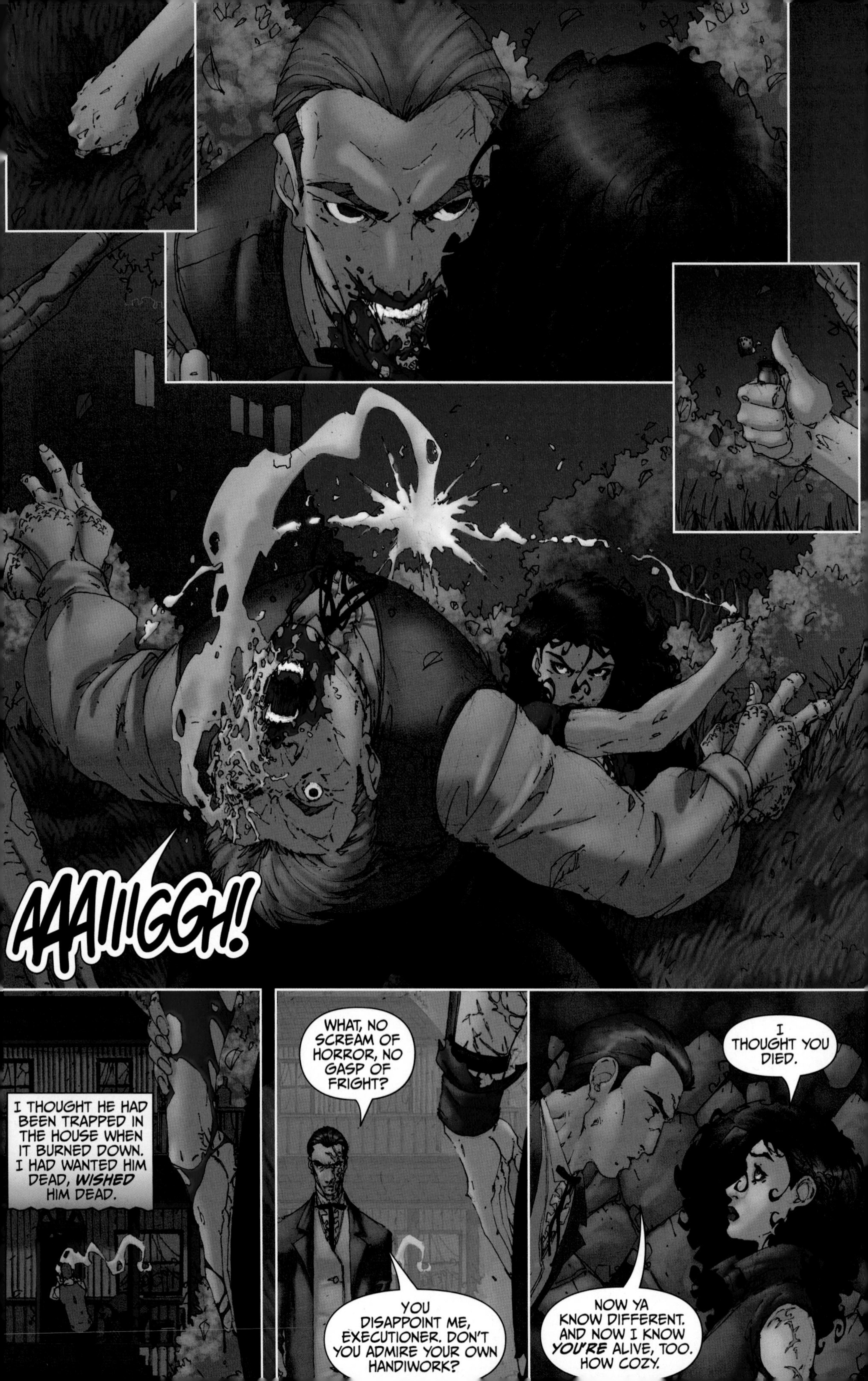
AAAIIIGGH!
I THOUGHT HE HAD BEEN TRAPPED IN THE HOUSE WHEN IT BURNED DOWN. I HAD WANTED HIM DEAD, *WISHED* HIM DEAD.
WHAT, NO SCREAM OF HORROR, NO GASP OF FRIGHT?
YOU DISAPPOINT ME, EXECUTIONER. DON'T YOU ADMIRE YOUR OWN HANDIWORK?
I THOUGHT YOU DIED.
NOW YA KNOW DIFFERENT. AND NOW I KNOW *YOU'RE* ALIVE, TOO. HOW COZY.

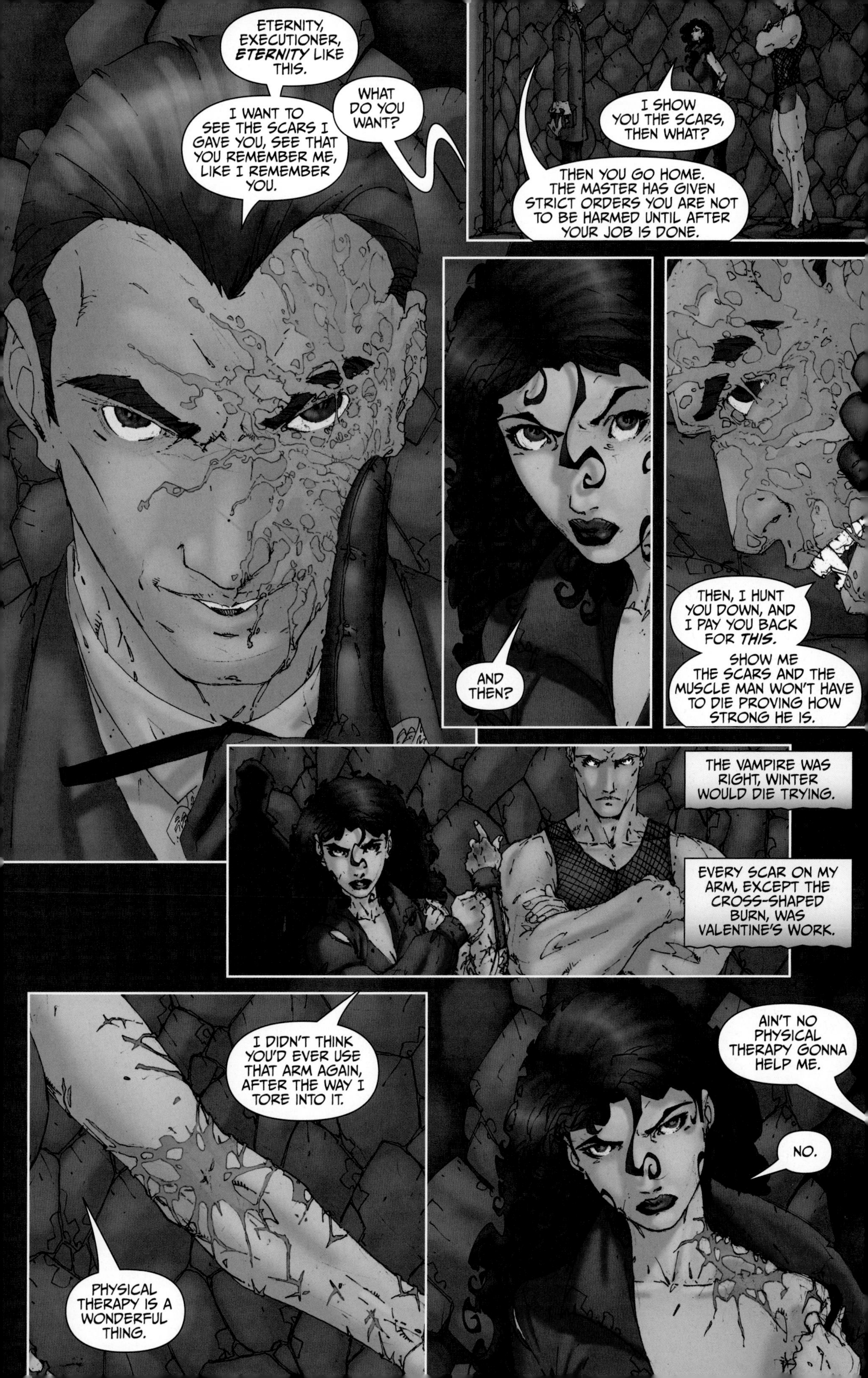
ETERNITY, EXECUTIONER, *ETERNITY* LIKE THIS.
I WANT TO SEE THE SCARS I GAVE YOU, SEE THAT YOU REMEMBER ME, LIKE I REMEMBER YOU.
WHAT DO YOU WANT?
I SHOW YOU THE SCARS, THEN WHAT?
THEN YOU GO HOME. THE MASTER HAS GIVEN STRICT ORDERS YOU ARE NOT TO BE HARMED UNTIL AFTER YOUR JOB IS DONE.
AND THEN?
THEN, I HUNT YOU DOWN, AND I PAY YOU BACK FOR *THIS.*
SHOW ME THE SCARS AND THE MUSCLE MAN WON'T HAVE TO DIE PROVING HOW STRONG HE IS.
THE VAMPIRE WAS RIGHT, WINTER WOULD DIE TRYING.
EVERY SCAR ON MY ARM, EXCEPT THE CROSS-SHAPED BURN, WAS VALENTINE'S WORK.
I DIDN'T THINK YOU'D EVER USE THAT ARM AGAIN, AFTER THE WAY I TORE INTO IT.
PHYSICAL THERAPY IS A WONDERFUL THING.
AIN'T NO PHYSICAL THERAPY GONNA HELP ME.
NO.

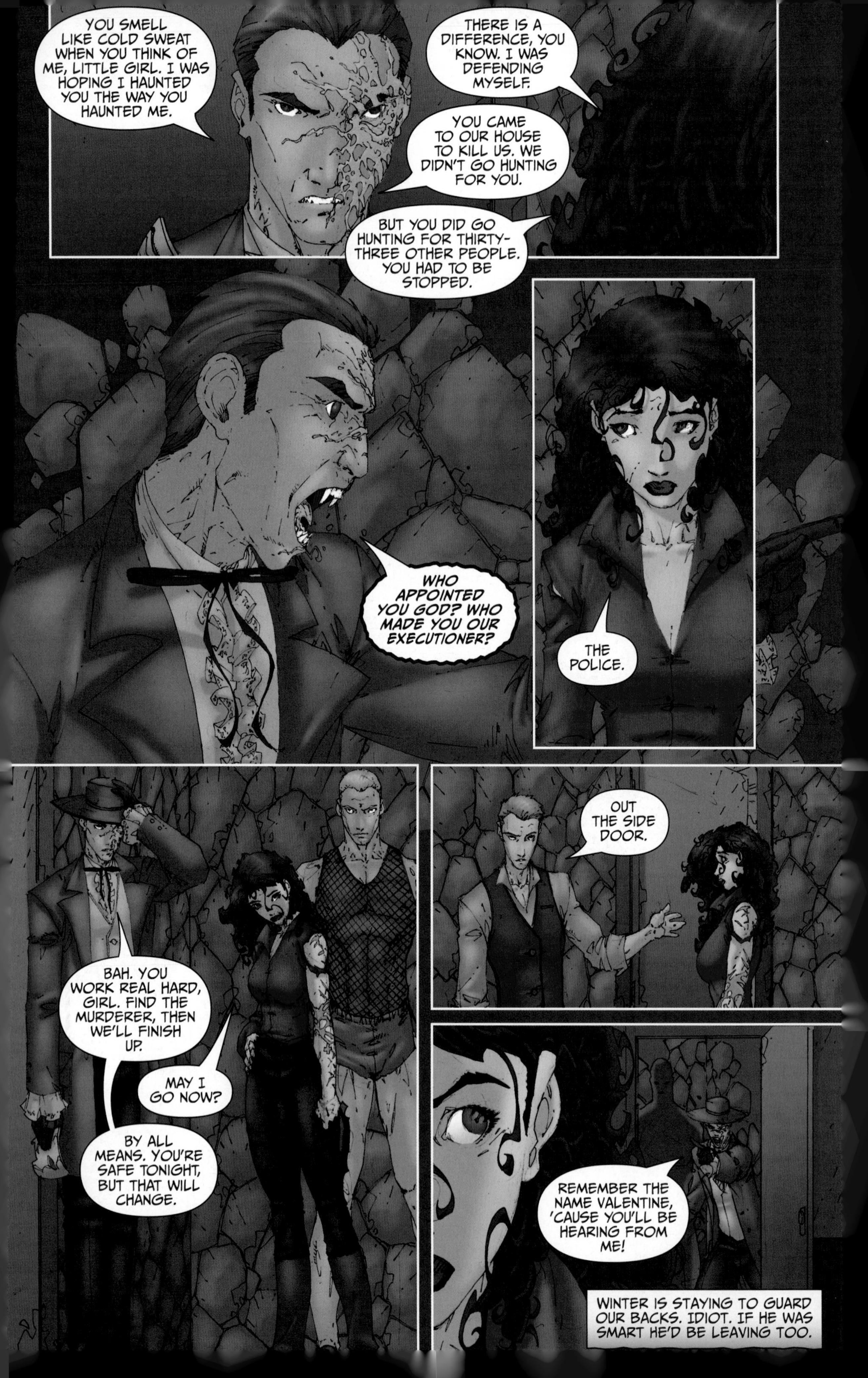
YOU SMELL LIKE COLD SWEAT WHEN YOU THINK OF ME, LITTLE GIRL. I WAS HOPING I HAUNTED YOU THE WAY YOU HAUNTED ME.
THERE IS A DIFFERENCE, YOU KNOW. I WAS DEFENDING MYSELF.
YOU CAME TO OUR HOUSE TO KILL US. WE DIDN'T GO HUNTING FOR YOU.
BUT YOU DID GO HUNTING FOR THIRTY-THREE OTHER PEOPLE. YOU HAD TO BE STOPPED.
WHO APPOINTED YOU GOD? WHO MADE YOU OUR EXECUTIONER?
THE POLICE.
BAH. YOU WORK REAL HARD, GIRL. FIND THE MURDERER, THEN WE'LL FINISH UP.
MAY I GO NOW?
BY ALL MEANS. YOU'RE SAFE TONIGHT, BUT THAT WILL CHANGE.
OUT THE SIDE DOOR.
REMEMBER THE NAME VALENTINE, 'CAUSE YOU'LL BE HEARING FROM ME!
WINTER IS STAYING TO GUARD OUR BACKS. IDIOT. IF HE WAS SMART HE'D BE LEAVING TOO.

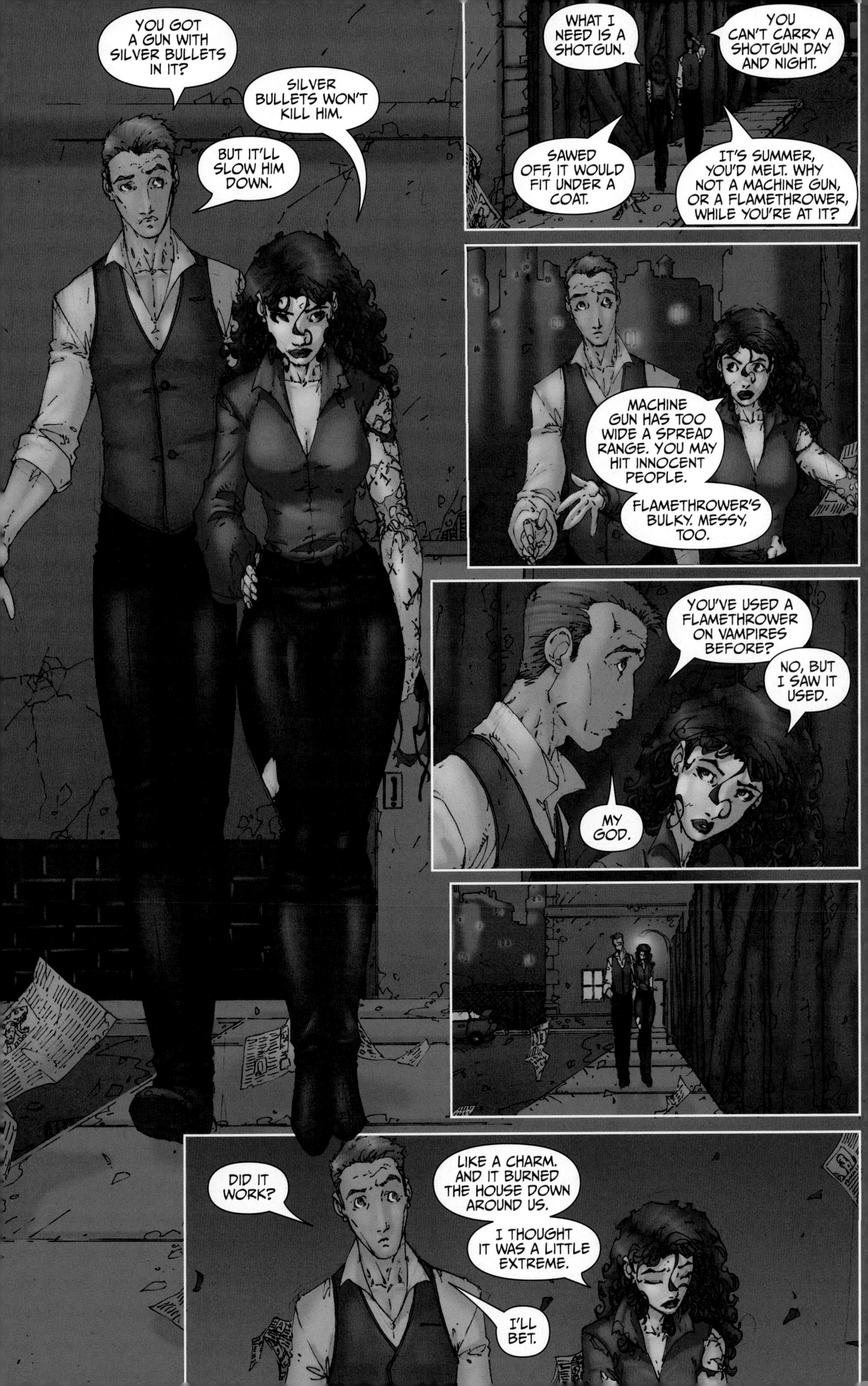
YOU GOT A GUN WITH SILVER BULLETS IN IT?
SILVER BULLETS WON'T KILL HIM.
BUT IT'LL SLOW HIM DOWN.
WHAT I NEED IS A SHOTGUN.
YOU CAN'T CARRY A SHOTGUN DAY AND NIGHT.
SAWED OFF, IT WOULD FIT UNDER A COAT.
IT'S SUMMER, YOU'D MELT. WHY NOT A MACHINE GUN, OR A FLAMETHROWER, WHILE YOU'RE AT IT?
MACHINE GUN HAS TOO WIDE A SPREAD RANGE. YOU MAY HIT INNOCENT PEOPLE.
FLAMETHROWER'S BULKY. MESSY, TOO.
YOU'VE USED A FLAMETHROWER ON VAMPIRES BEFORE?
NO, BUT I SAW IT USED.
MY GOD.
DID IT WORK?
LIKE A CHARM. AND IT BURNED THE HOUSE DOWN AROUND US.
I THOUGHT IT WAS A LITTLE EXTREME.
I'LL BET.

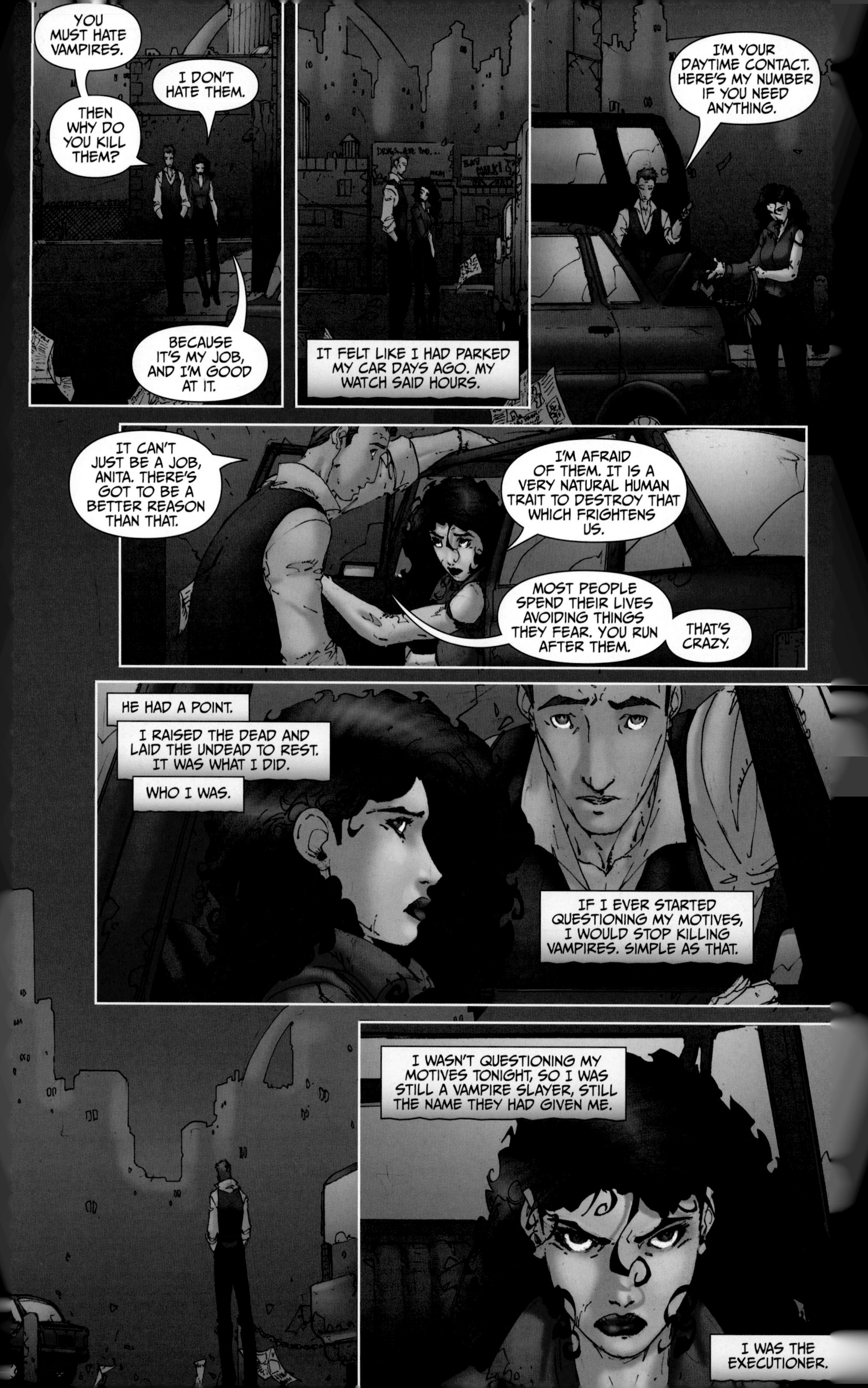
YOU MUST HATE VAMPIRES.
I DON'T HATE THEM.
THEN WHY DO YOU KILL THEM?
BECAUSE IT'S MY JOB, AND I'M GOOD AT IT.
IT FELT LIKE I HAD PARKED MY CAR DAYS AGO. MY WATCH SAID HOURS.
I'M YOUR DAYTIME CONTACT. HERE'S MY NUMBER IF YOU NEED ANYTHING.
IT CAN'T JUST BE A JOB, ANITA. THERE'S GOT TO BE A BETTER REASON THAN THAT.
I'M AFRAID OF THEM. IT IS A VERY NATURAL HUMAN TRAIT TO DESTROY THAT WHICH FRIGHTENS US.
MOST PEOPLE SPEND THEIR LIVES AVOIDING THINGS THEY FEAR. YOU RUN AFTER THEM.
THAT'S CRAZY.
HE HAD A POINT.
I RAISED THE DEAD AND LAID THE UNDEAD TO REST. IT WAS WHAT I DID.
WHO I WAS.
IF I EVER STARTED QUESTIONING MY MOTIVES, I WOULD STOP KILLING VAMPIRES. SIMPLE AS THAT.
I WASN'T QUESTIONING MY MOTIVES TONIGHT, SO I WAS STILL A VAMPIRE SLAYER, STILL THE NAME THEY HAD GIVEN ME.
I WAS THE EXECUTIONER.

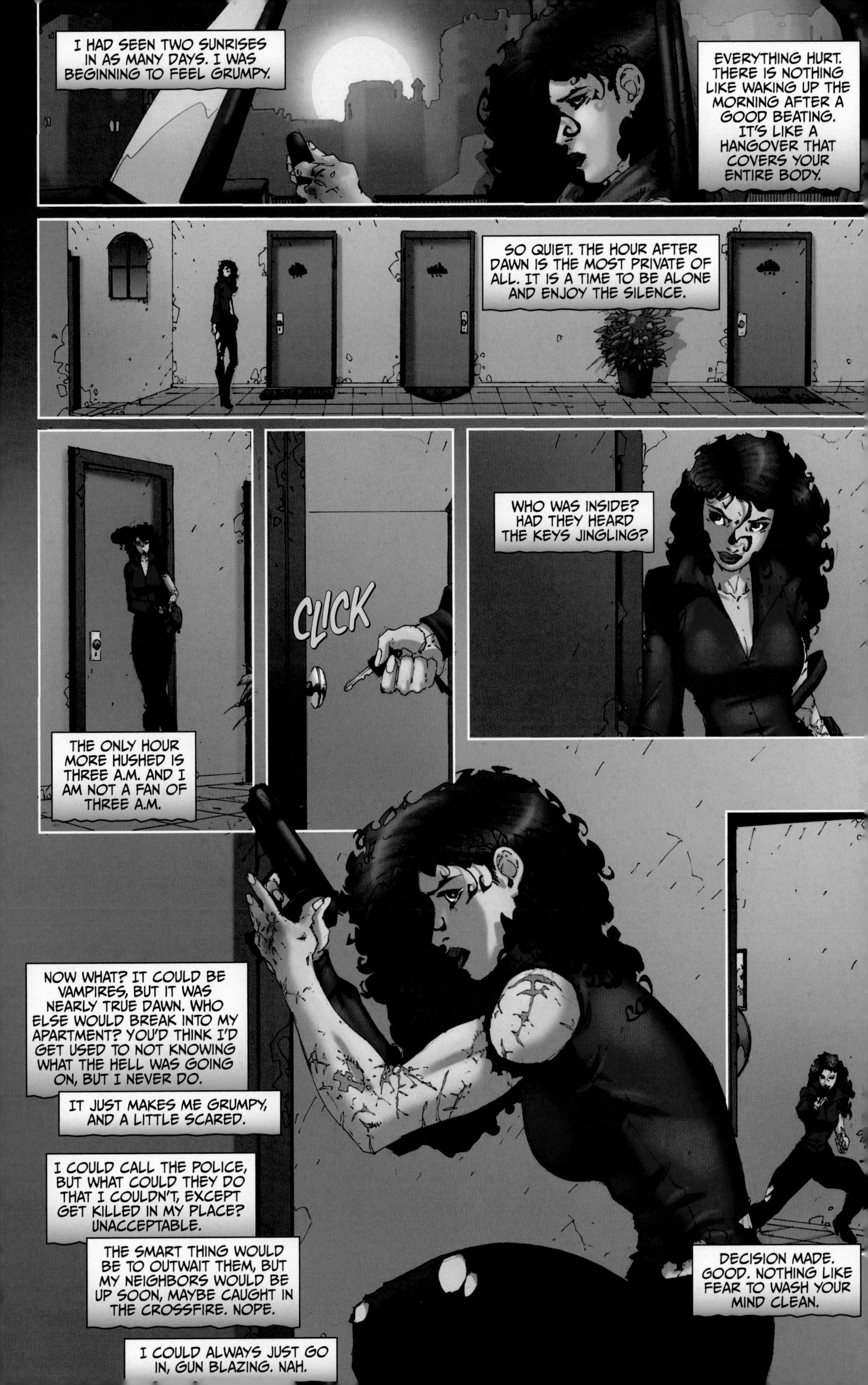
I HAD SEEN TWO SUNRISES IN AS MANY DAYS. I WAS BEGINNING TO FEEL GRUMPY.
EVERYTHING HURT. THERE IS NOTHING LIKE WAKING UP THE MORNING AFTER A GOOD BEATING. IT'S LIKE A HANGOVER THAT COVERS YOUR ENTIRE BODY.
SO QUIET. THE HOUR AFTER DAWN IS THE MOST PRIVATE OF ALL. IT IS A TIME TO BE ALONE AND ENJOY THE SILENCE.
THE ONLY HOUR MORE HUSHED IS THREE A.M. AND I AM NOT A FAN OF THREE A.M.
CLICK
WHO WAS INSIDE? HAD THEY HEARD THE KEYS JINGLING?
NOW WHAT? IT COULD BE VAMPIRES, BUT IT WAS NEARLY TRUE DAWN. WHO ELSE WOULD BREAK INTO MY APARTMENT? YOU'D THINK I'D GET USED TO NOT KNOWING WHAT THE HELL WAS GOING ON, BUT I NEVER DO.
IT JUST MAKES ME GRUMPY, AND A LITTLE SCARED.
I COULD CALL THE POLICE, BUT WHAT COULD THEY DO THAT I COULDN'T, EXCEPT GET KILLED IN MY PLACE? UNACCEPTABLE.
THE SMART THING WOULD BE TO OUTWAIT THEM, BUT MY NEIGHBORS WOULD BE UP SOON, MAYBE CAUGHT IN THE CROSSFIRE. NOPE.
I COULD ALWAYS JUST GO IN, GUN BLAZING. NAH.
DECISION MADE. GOOD. NOTHING LIKE FEAR TO WASH YOUR MIND CLEAN.

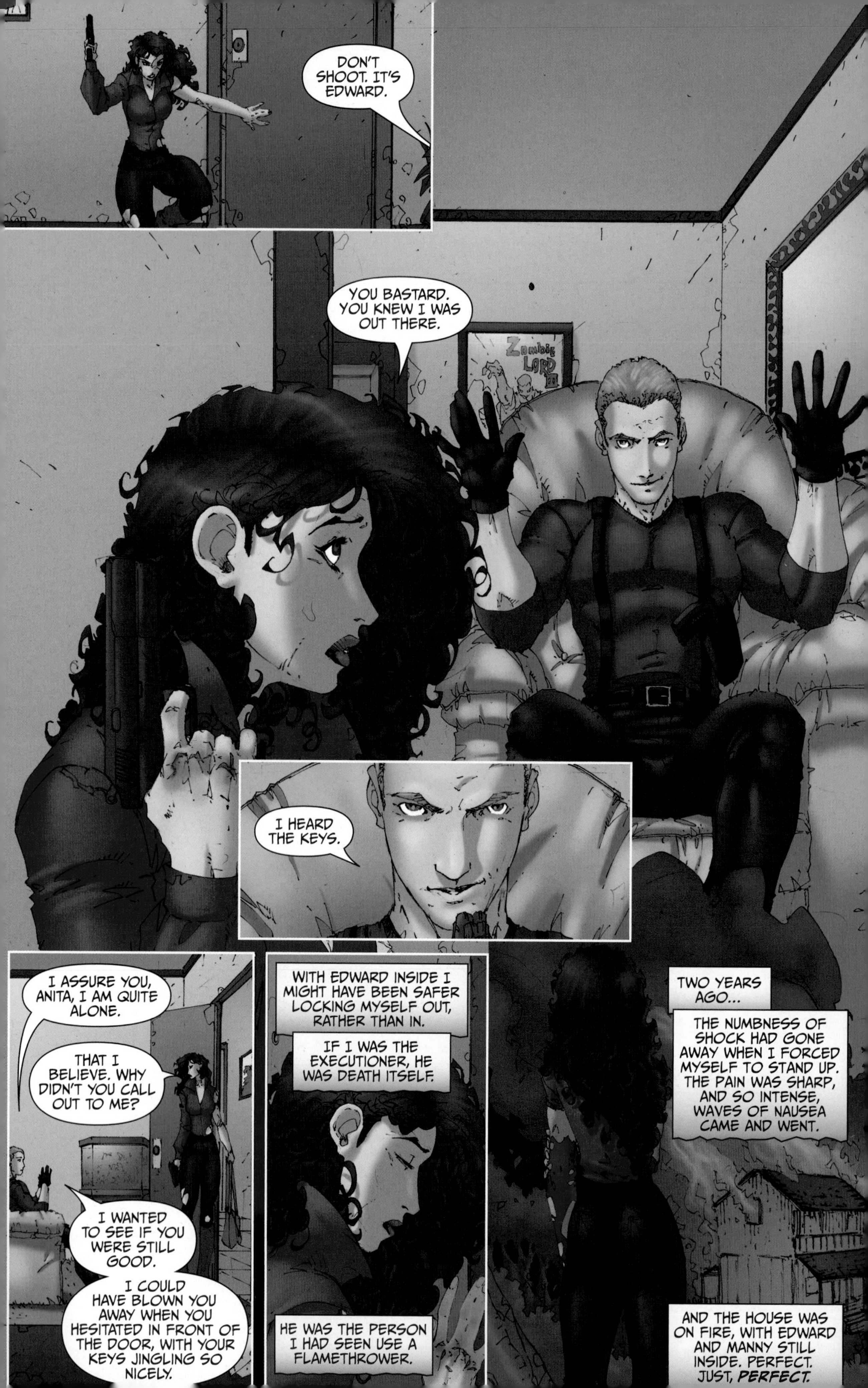
DON'T SHOOT. IT'S EDWARD.
YOU BASTARD. YOU KNEW I WAS OUT THERE.
Zombie LORD III
I HEARD THE KEYS.
I ASSURE YOU, ANITA, I AM QUITE ALONE.
THAT I BELIEVE. WHY DIDN'T YOU CALL OUT TO ME?
I WANTED TO SEE IF YOU WERE STILL GOOD.
I COULD HAVE BLOWN YOU AWAY WHEN YOU HESITATED IN FRONT OF THE DOOR, WITH YOUR KEYS JINGLING SO NICELY.
WITH EDWARD INSIDE I MIGHT HAVE BEEN SAFER LOCKING MYSELF OUT, RATHER THAN IN.
IF I WAS THE EXECUTIONER, HE WAS DEATH ITSELF.
HE WAS THE PERSON I HAD SEEN USE A FLAMETHROWER.
TWO YEARS AGO...
THE NUMBNESS OF SHOCK HAD GONE AWAY WHEN I FORCED MYSELF TO STAND UP. THE PAIN WAS SHARP, AND SO INTENSE, WAVES OF NAUSEA CAME AND WENT.
AND THE HOUSE WAS ON FIRE, WITH EDWARD AND MANNY STILL INSIDE. PERFECT. JUST, *PERFECT.*

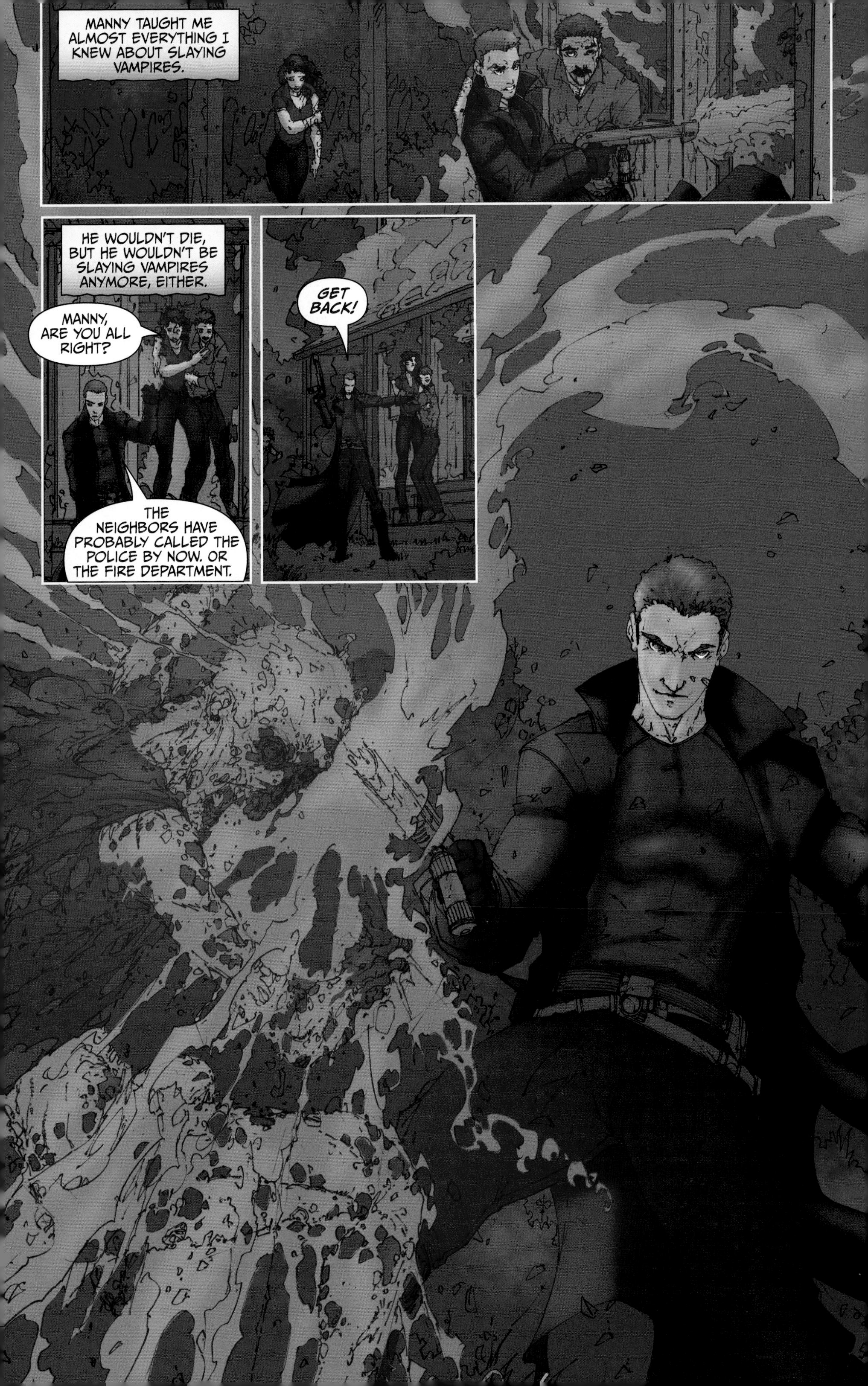
MANNY TAUGHT ME ALMOST EVERYTHING I KNEW ABOUT SLAYING VAMPIRES.
HE WOULDN'T DIE, BUT HE WOULDN'T BE SLAYING VAMPIRES ANYMORE, EITHER.
MANNY, ARE YOU ALL RIGHT?
THE NEIGHBORS HAVE PROBABLY CALLED THE POLICE BY NOW. OR THE FIRE DEPARTMENT.
GET BACK!

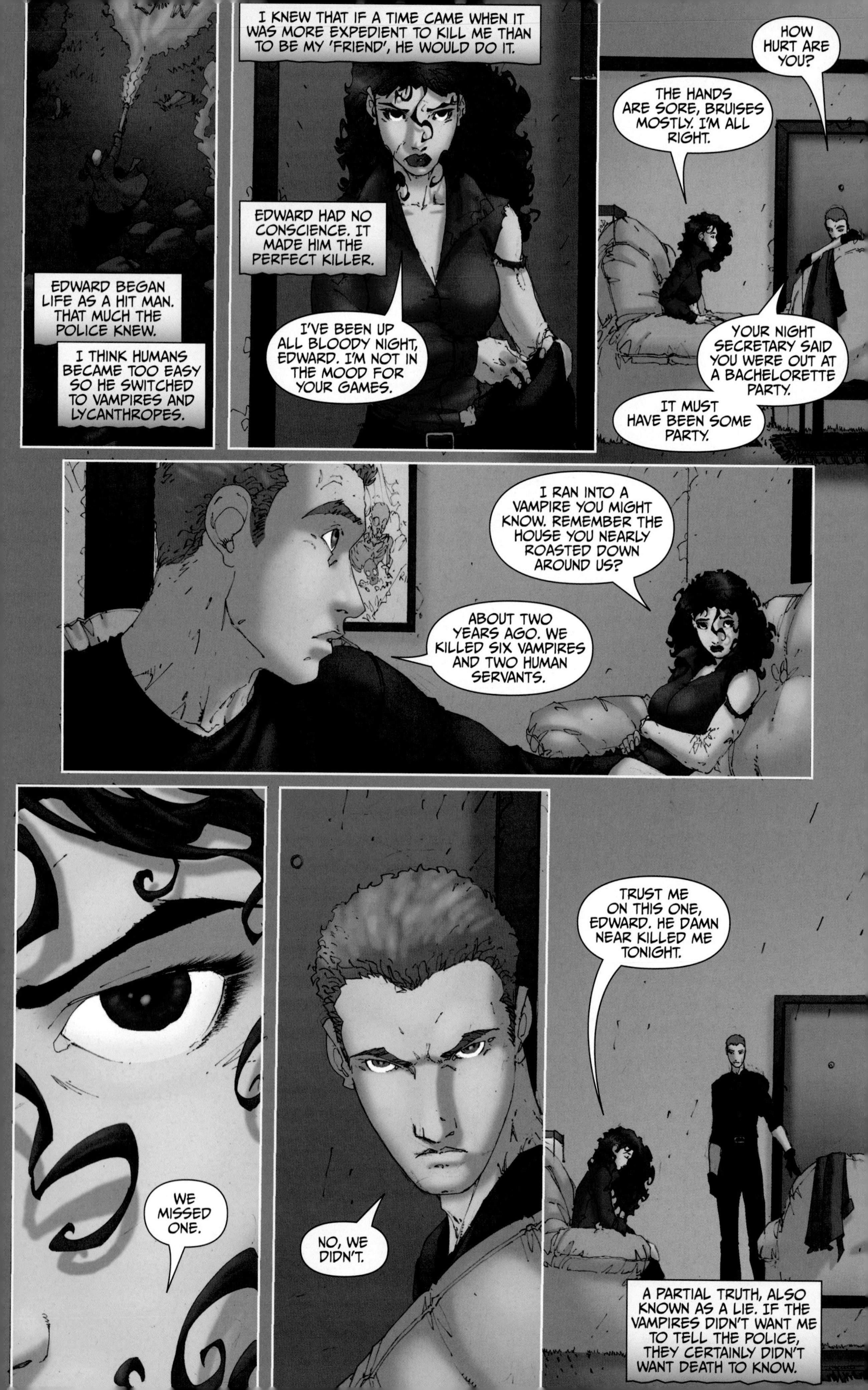
EDWARD BEGAN LIFE AS A HIT MAN. THAT MUCH THE POLICE KNEW.
I THINK HUMANS BECAME TOO EASY SO HE SWITCHED TO VAMPIRES AND LYCANTHROPES.
I KNEW THAT IF A TIME CAME WHEN IT WAS MORE EXPEDIENT TO KILL ME THAN TO BE MY 'FRIEND', HE WOULD DO IT.
EDWARD HAD NO CONSCIENCE. IT MADE HIM THE PERFECT KILLER.
I'VE BEEN UP ALL BLOODY NIGHT, EDWARD. I'M NOT IN THE MOOD FOR YOUR GAMES.
HOW HURT ARE YOU?
THE HANDS ARE SORE, BRUISES MOSTLY. I'M ALL RIGHT.
YOUR NIGHT SECRETARY SAID YOU WERE OUT AT A BACHELORETTE PARTY.
IT MUST HAVE BEEN SOME PARTY.
I RAN INTO A VAMPIRE YOU MIGHT KNOW. REMEMBER THE HOUSE YOU NEARLY ROASTED DOWN AROUND US?
ABOUT TWO YEARS AGO. WE KILLED SIX VAMPIRES AND TWO HUMAN SERVANTS.
WE MISSED ONE.
NO, WE DIDN'T.
TRUST ME ON THIS ONE, EDWARD. HE DAMN NEAR KILLED ME TONIGHT.
A PARTIAL TRUTH, ALSO KNOWN AS A LIE. IF THE VAMPIRES DIDN'T WANT ME TO TELL THE POLICE, THEY CERTAINLY DIDN'T WANT DEATH TO KNOW.

WHICH ONE?

THE ONE WHO NEARLY TORE ME TO PIECES. HE CALLS HIMSELF VALENTINE.

HE'S STILL WEARING THE HOLY WATER SCARS I GAVE HIM.

TELL ME.

THERE ISN'T MUCH TO TELL.

YOU'RE LYING, ANITA. WHY?

I HATE BEING CAUGHT IN A LIE.

THERE HAVE BEEN SOME VAMPIRES MURDERED DOWN ALONG THE RIVER. HOW LONG HAVE *YOU* BEEN IN TOWN, EDWARD?

NOT LONG.

I HEARD A RUMOR THAT YOU GOT TO MEET THE CITY'S HEAD VAMPIRE TONIGHT.

HOW THE HELL DO YOU KNOW THAT?

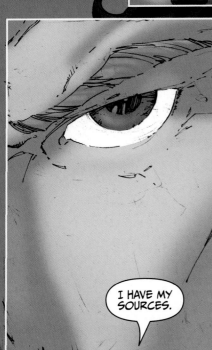

I HAVE MY SOURCES.

NO VAMPIRE WOULD TALK TO YOU, NOT WILLINGLY.

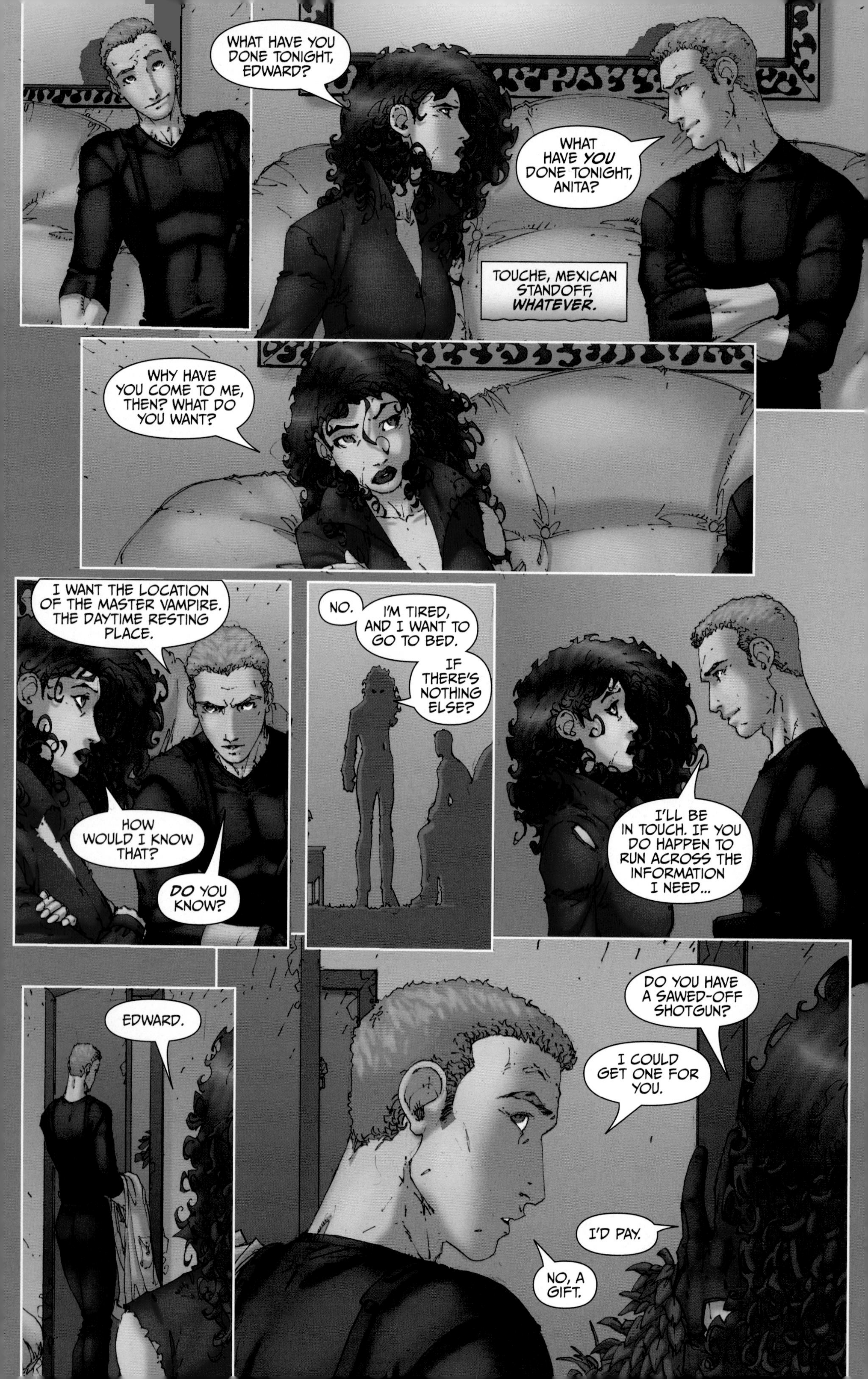
WHAT HAVE YOU DONE TONIGHT, EDWARD?
WHAT HAVE *YOU* DONE TONIGHT, ANITA?
TOUCHE, MEXICAN STANDOFF, *WHATEVER.*
WHY HAVE YOU COME TO ME, THEN? WHAT DO YOU WANT?
I WANT THE LOCATION OF THE MASTER VAMPIRE. THE DAYTIME RESTING PLACE.
HOW WOULD I KNOW THAT?
DO YOU KNOW?
NO.
I'M TIRED, AND I WANT TO GO TO BED.
IF THERE'S NOTHING ELSE?
I'LL BE IN TOUCH. IF YOU DO HAPPEN TO RUN ACROSS THE INFORMATION I NEED...
EDWARD.
DO YOU HAVE A SAWED-OFF SHOTGUN?
I COULD GET ONE FOR YOU.
I'D PAY.
NO, A GIFT.

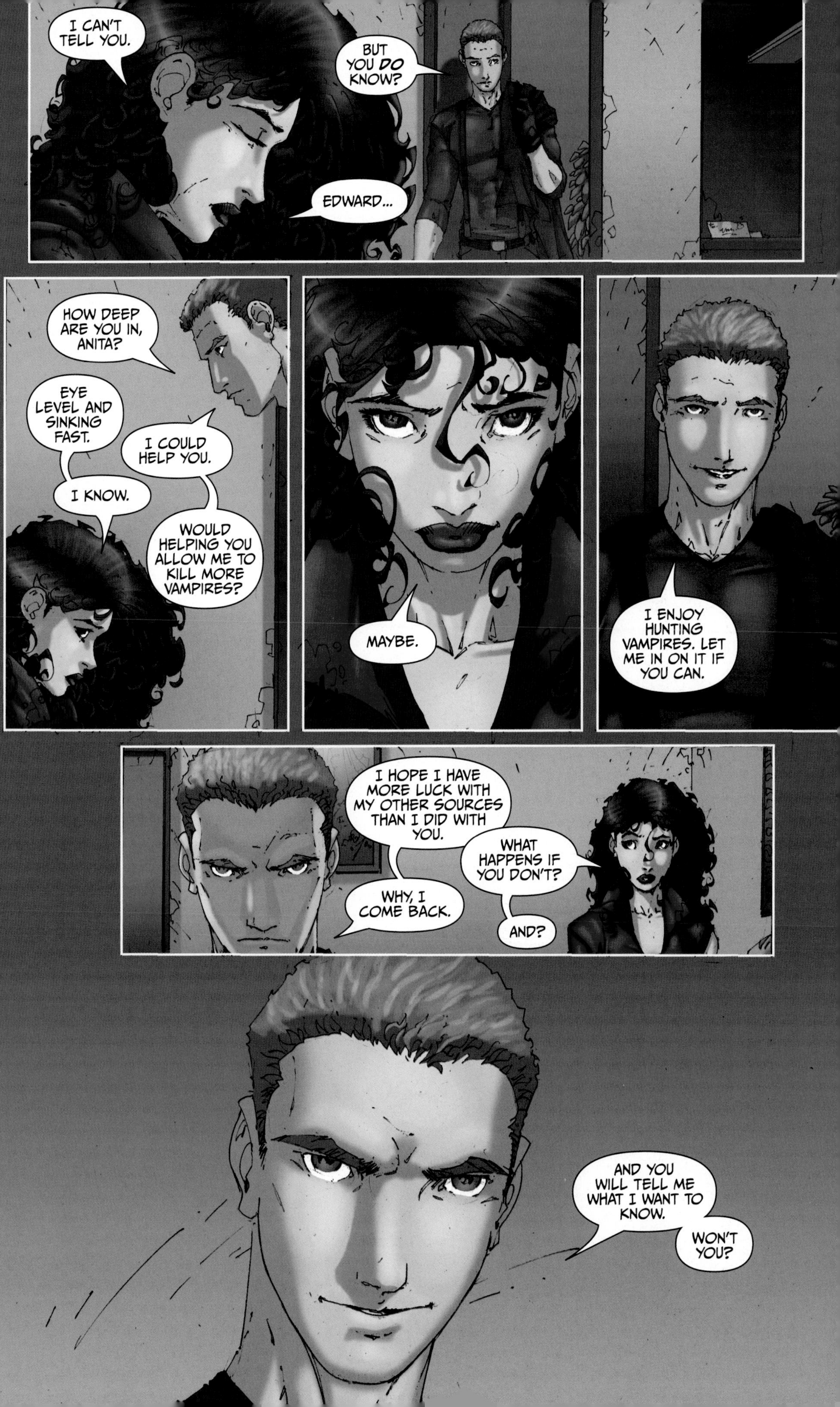
I CAN'T TELL YOU.
BUT YOU DO KNOW?
EDWARD...
HOW DEEP ARE YOU IN, ANITA?
EYE LEVEL AND SINKING FAST.
I COULD HELP YOU.
I KNOW.
WOULD HELPING YOU ALLOW ME TO KILL MORE VAMPIRES?
MAYBE.
I ENJOY HUNTING VAMPIRES. LET ME IN ON IT IF YOU CAN.
I HOPE I HAVE MORE LUCK WITH MY OTHER SOURCES THAN I DID WITH YOU.
WHAT HAPPENS IF YOU DON'T?
WHY, I COME BACK.
AND?
AND YOU WILL TELL ME WHAT I WANT TO KNOW.
WON'T YOU?

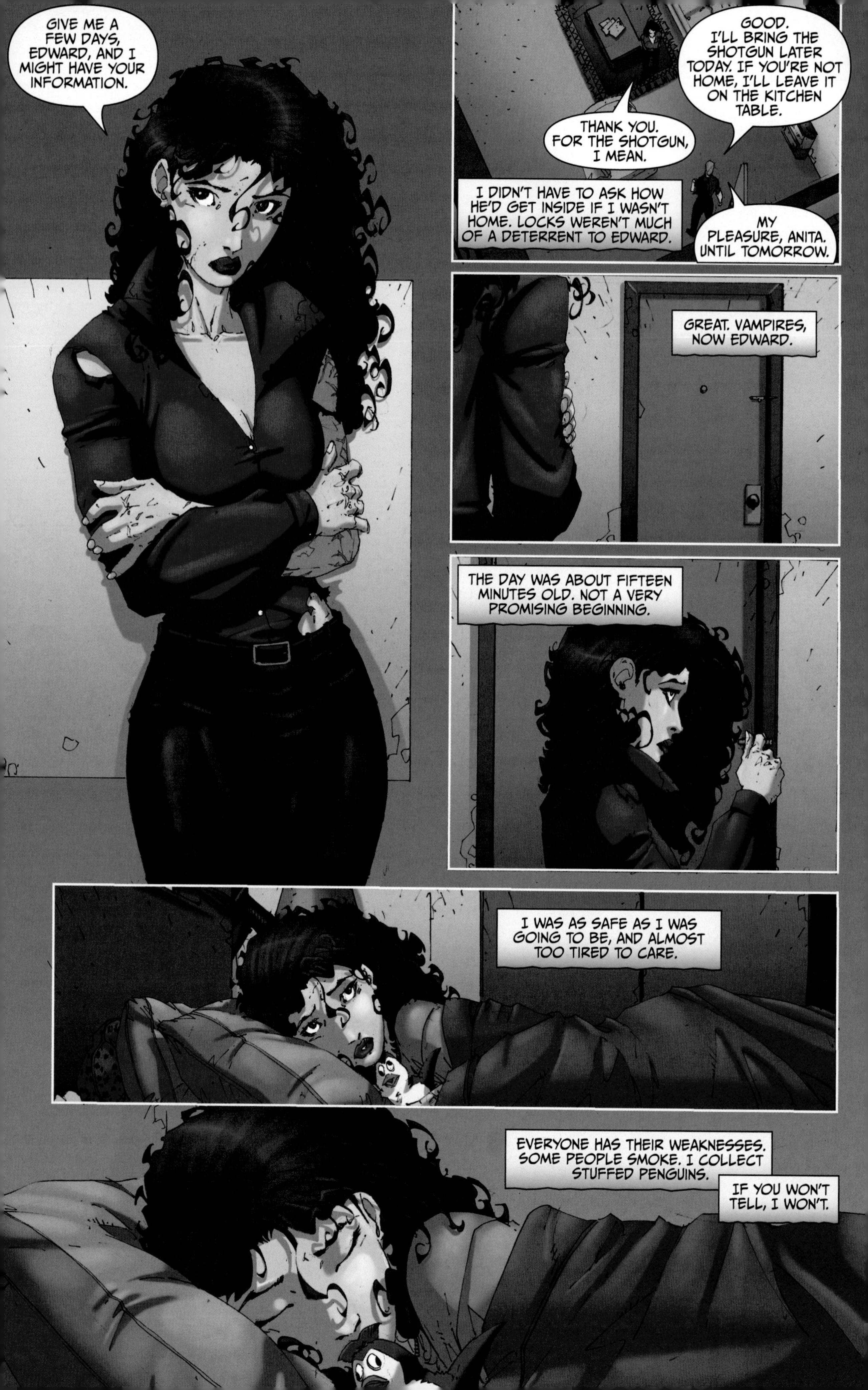
GIVE ME A FEW DAYS, EDWARD, AND I MIGHT HAVE YOUR INFORMATION.
THANK YOU. FOR THE SHOTGUN, I MEAN.
GOOD. I'LL BRING THE SHOTGUN LATER TODAY. IF YOU'RE NOT HOME, I'LL LEAVE IT ON THE KITCHEN TABLE.
I DIDN'T HAVE TO ASK HOW HE'D GET INSIDE IF I WASN'T HOME. LOCKS WEREN'T MUCH OF A DETERRENT TO EDWARD.
MY PLEASURE, ANITA. UNTIL TOMORROW.
GREAT. VAMPIRES, NOW EDWARD.
THE DAY WAS ABOUT FIFTEEN MINUTES OLD. NOT A VERY PROMISING BEGINNING.
I WAS AS SAFE AS I WAS GOING TO BE, AND ALMOST TOO TIRED TO CARE.
EVERYONE HAS THEIR WEAKNESSES. SOME PEOPLE SMOKE. I COLLECT STUFFED PENGUINS.
IF YOU WON'T TELL, I WON'T.

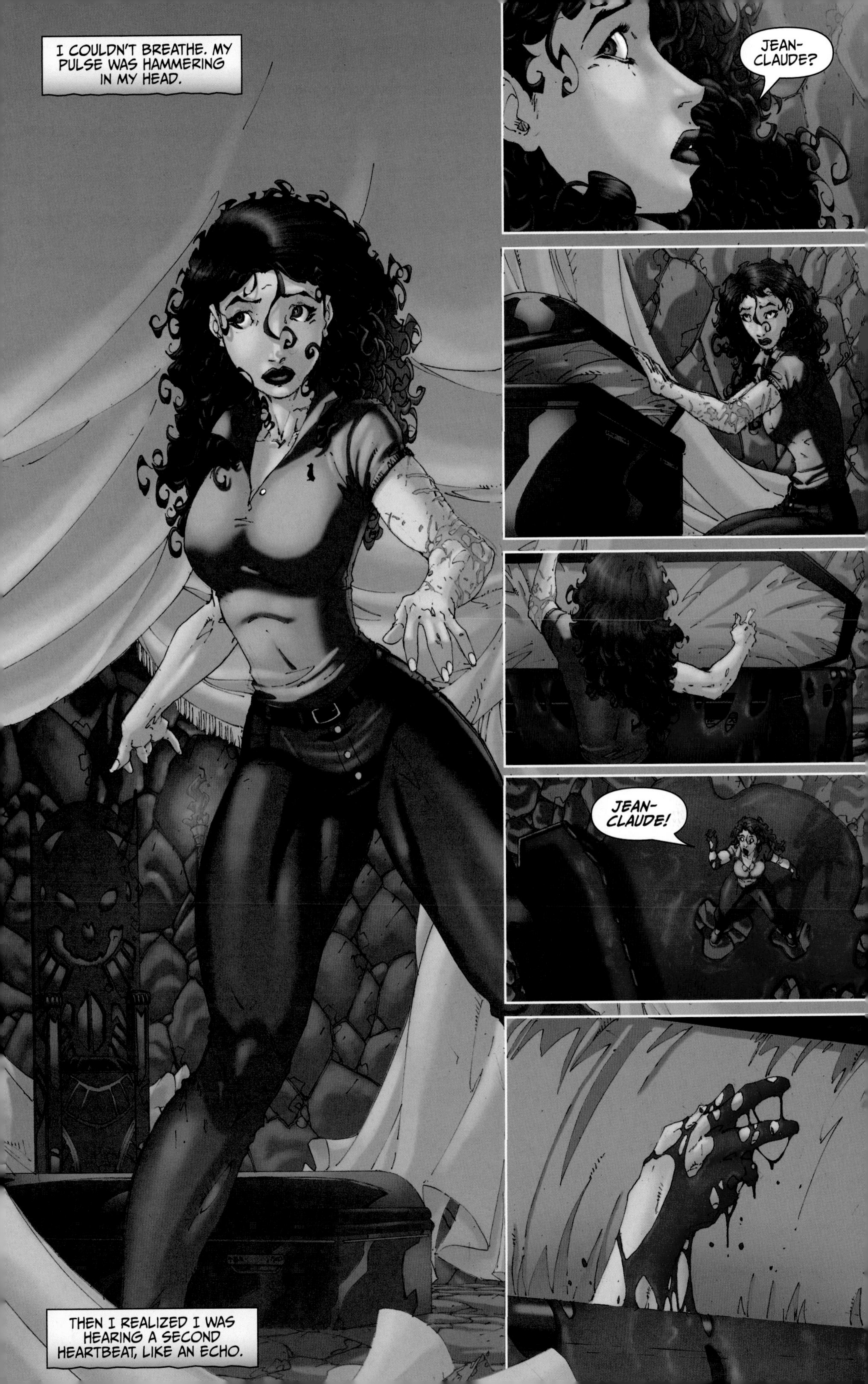
I COULDN'T BREATHE. MY PULSE WAS HAMMERING IN MY HEAD.
THEN I REALIZED I WAS HEARING A SECOND HEARTBEAT, LIKE AN ECHO.
JEAN-CLAUDE?
JEAN-CLAUDE!

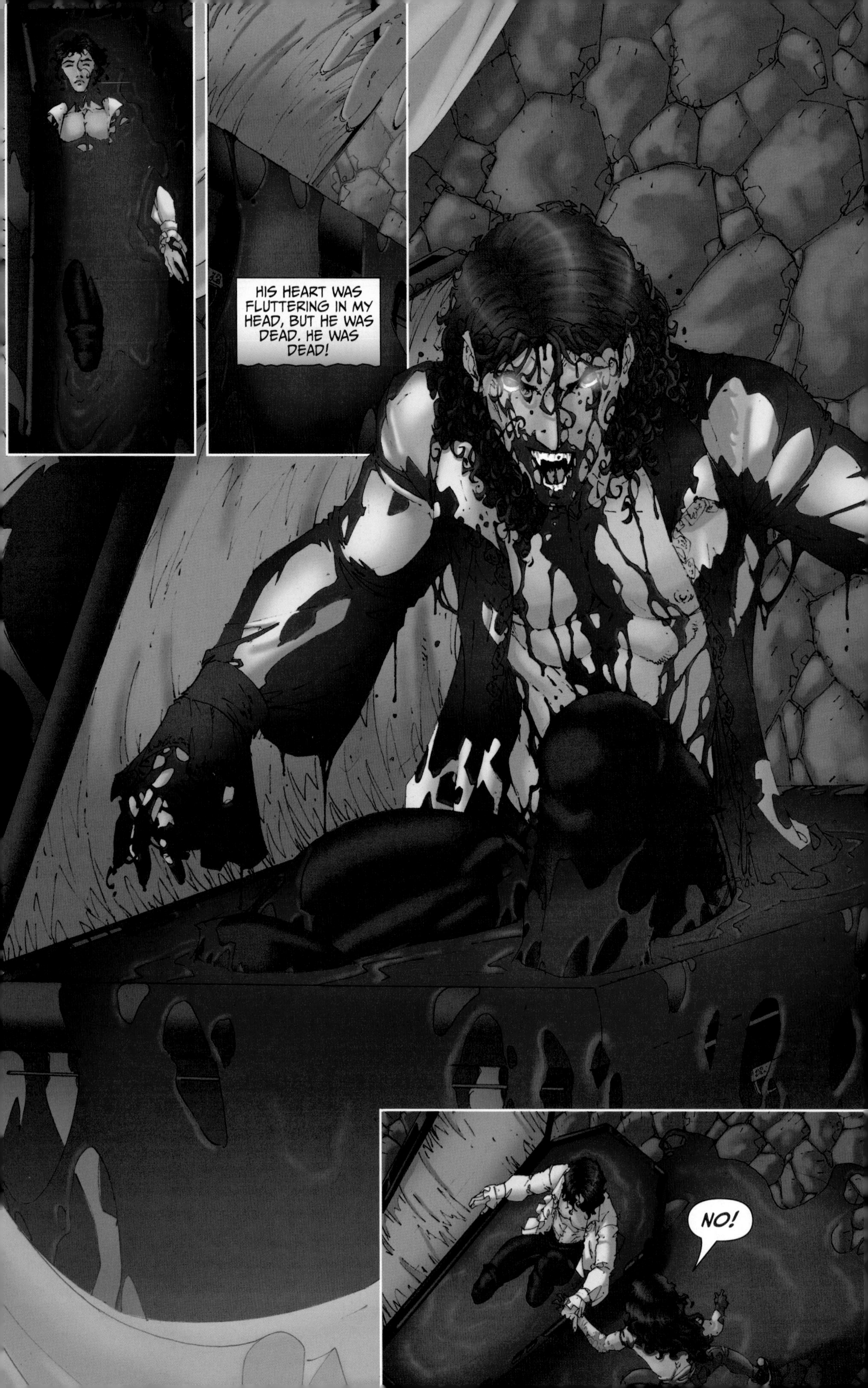
HIS HEART WAS FLUTTERING IN MY HEAD, BUT HE WAS DEAD. HE WAS DEAD!
NO!

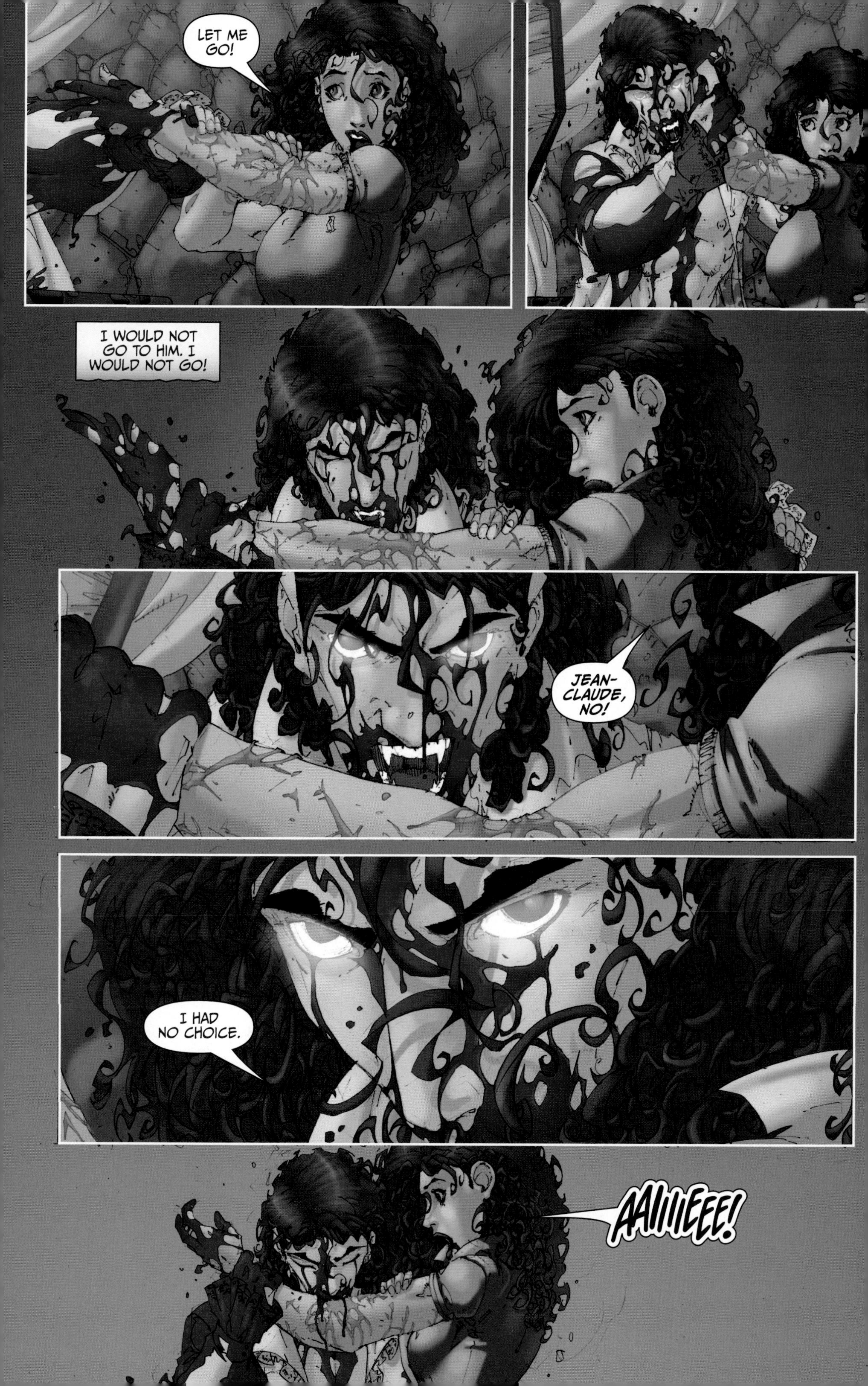
LET ME GO!
I WOULD NOT GO TO HIM. I WOULD NOT GO!
JEAN-CLAUDE, NO!
I HAD NO CHOICE.
AAIIIIEEE!

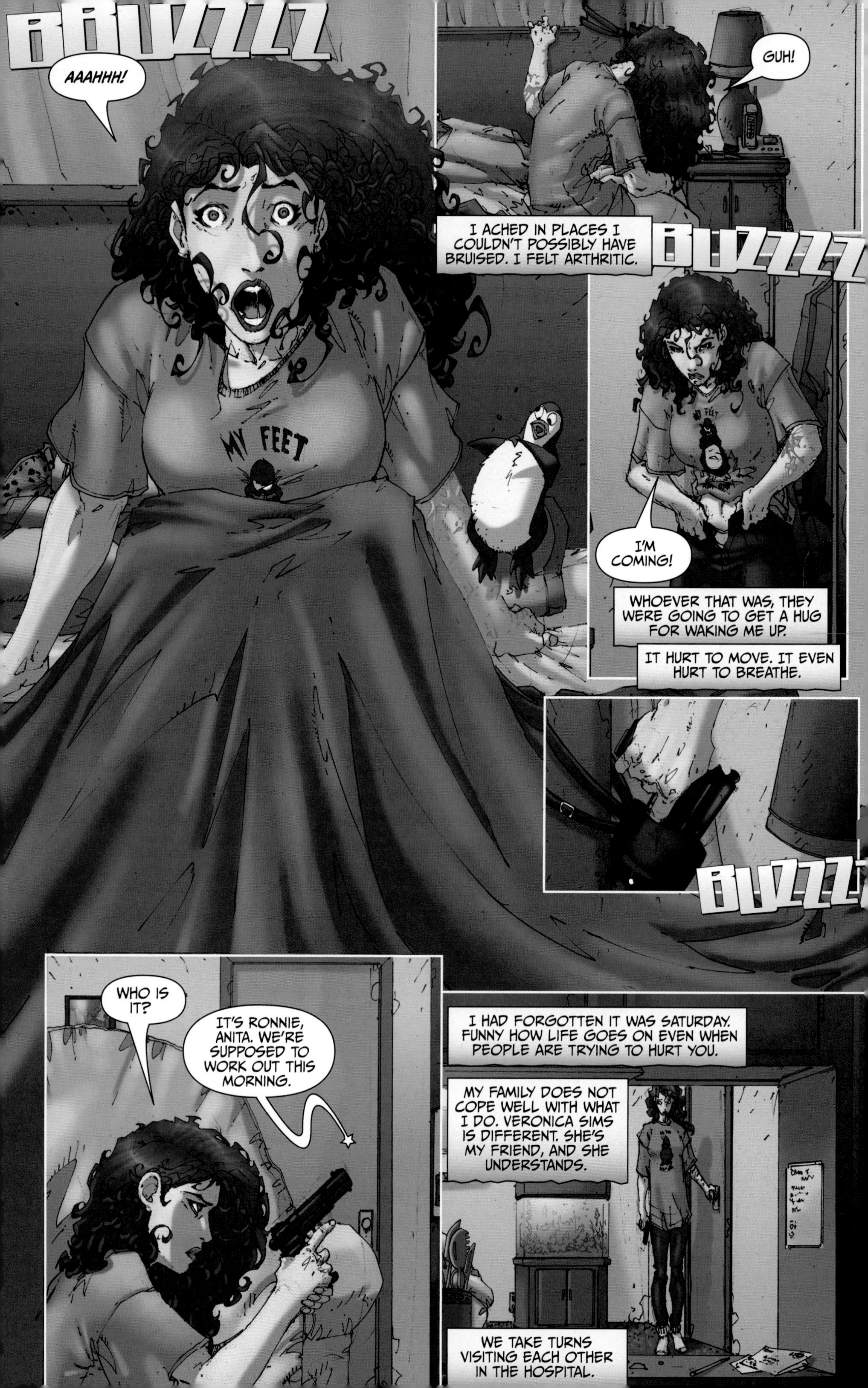
BBUZZZZ
AAAHHH!
MY FEET
GUH!
I ACHED IN PLACES I COULDN'T POSSIBLY HAVE BRUISED. I FELT ARTHRITIC.
BUZZZZ
MY FEET
I'M COMING!
WHOEVER THAT WAS, THEY WERE GOING TO GET A HUG FOR WAKING ME UP.
IT HURT TO MOVE. IT EVEN HURT TO BREATHE.
BUZZZZ
WHO IS IT?
IT'S RONNIE, ANITA. WE'RE SUPPOSED TO WORK OUT THIS MORNING.
I HAD FORGOTTEN IT WAS SATURDAY. FUNNY HOW LIFE GOES ON EVEN WHEN PEOPLE ARE TRYING TO HURT YOU.
MY FAMILY DOES NOT COPE WELL WITH WHAT I DO. VERONICA SIMS IS DIFFERENT. SHE'S MY FRIEND, AND SHE UNDERSTANDS.
WE TAKE TURNS VISITING EACH OTHER IN THE HOSPITAL.

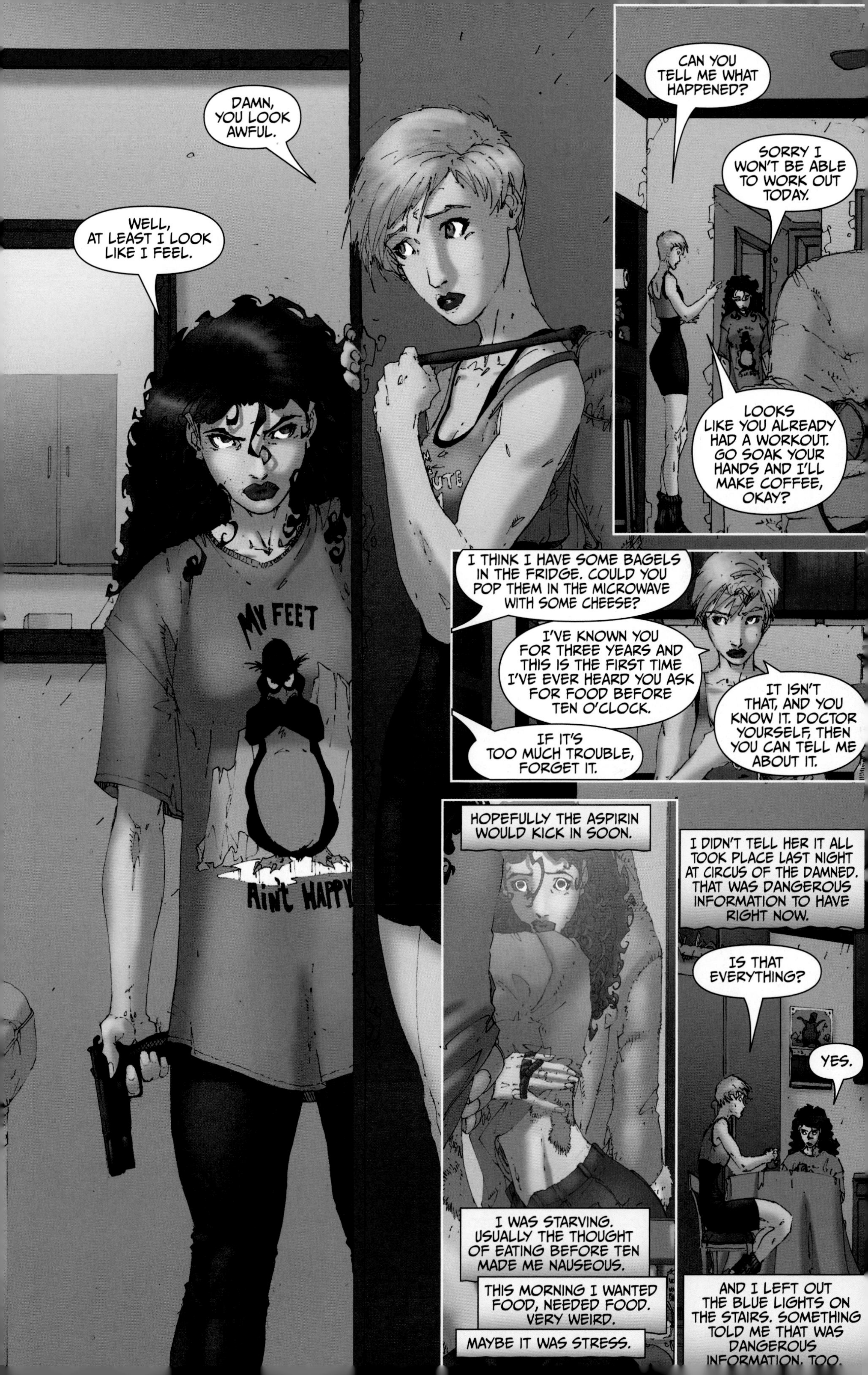

DAMN, YOU LOOK AWFUL.
WELL, AT LEAST I LOOK LIKE I FEEL.
MY FEET AIN'T HAPPY
CAN YOU TELL ME WHAT HAPPENED?
SORRY I WON'T BE ABLE TO WORK OUT TODAY.
LOOKS LIKE YOU ALREADY HAD A WORKOUT. GO SOAK YOUR HANDS AND I'LL MAKE COFFEE, OKAY?
I THINK I HAVE SOME BAGELS IN THE FRIDGE. COULD YOU POP THEM IN THE MICROWAVE WITH SOME CHEESE?
I'VE KNOWN YOU FOR THREE YEARS AND THIS IS THE FIRST TIME I'VE EVER HEARD YOU ASK FOR FOOD BEFORE TEN O'CLOCK.
IF IT'S TOO MUCH TROUBLE, FORGET IT.
IT ISN'T THAT, AND YOU KNOW IT. DOCTOR YOURSELF, THEN YOU CAN TELL ME ABOUT IT.
HOPEFULLY THE ASPIRIN WOULD KICK IN SOON.
I WAS STARVING. USUALLY THE THOUGHT OF EATING BEFORE TEN MADE ME NAUSEOUS.
THIS MORNING I WANTED FOOD, NEEDED FOOD. VERY WEIRD.
MAYBE IT WAS STRESS.
I DIDN'T TELL HER IT ALL TOOK PLACE LAST NIGHT AT CIRCUS OF THE DAMNED. THAT WAS DANGEROUS INFORMATION TO HAVE RIGHT NOW.
IS THAT EVERYTHING?
YES.
AND I LEFT OUT THE BLUE LIGHTS ON THE STAIRS. SOMETHING TOLD ME THAT WAS DANGEROUS INFORMATION, TOO.

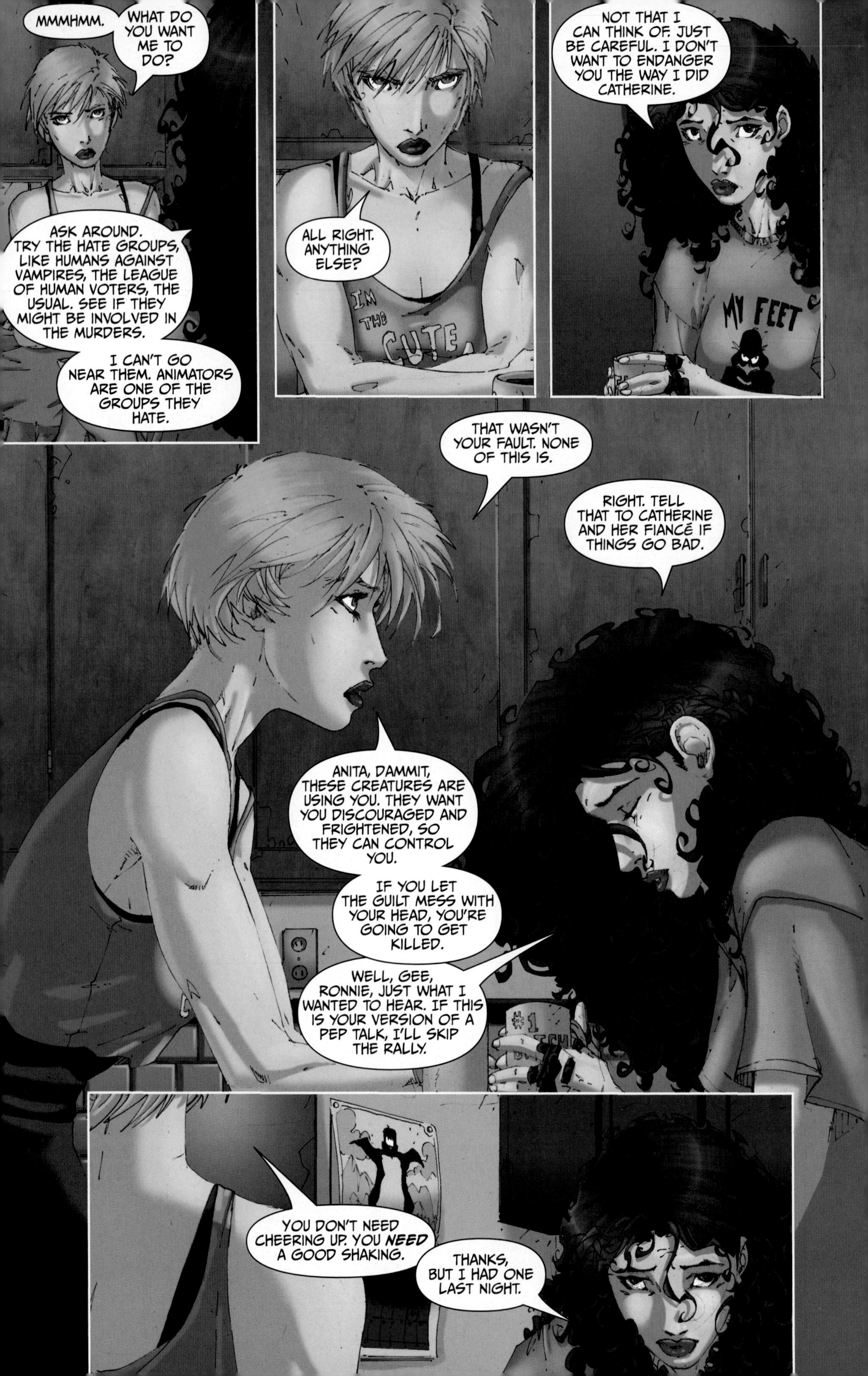
MMMHMM.
WHAT DO YOU WANT ME TO DO?
ASK AROUND. TRY THE HATE GROUPS, LIKE HUMANS AGAINST VAMPIRES, THE LEAGUE OF HUMAN VOTERS, THE USUAL. SEE IF THEY MIGHT BE INVOLVED IN THE MURDERS.
I CAN'T GO NEAR THEM. ANIMATORS ARE ONE OF THE GROUPS THEY HATE.
ALL RIGHT. ANYTHING ELSE?
I'M THE CUTE
NOT THAT I CAN THINK OF. JUST BE CAREFUL. I DON'T WANT TO ENDANGER YOU THE WAY I DID CATHERINE.
MY FEET
THAT WASN'T YOUR FAULT. NONE OF THIS IS.
RIGHT. TELL THAT TO CATHERINE AND HER FIANCÉ IF THINGS GO BAD.
ANITA, DAMMIT, THESE CREATURES ARE USING YOU. THEY WANT YOU DISCOURAGED AND FRIGHTENED, SO THEY CAN CONTROL YOU.
IF YOU LET THE GUILT MESS WITH YOUR HEAD, YOU'RE GOING TO GET KILLED.
WELL, GEE, RONNIE, JUST WHAT I WANTED TO HEAR. IF THIS IS YOUR VERSION OF A PEP TALK, I'LL SKIP THE RALLY.
YOU DON'T NEED CHEERING UP. YOU ***NEED*** A GOOD SHAKING.
THANKS, BUT I HAD ONE LAST NIGHT.

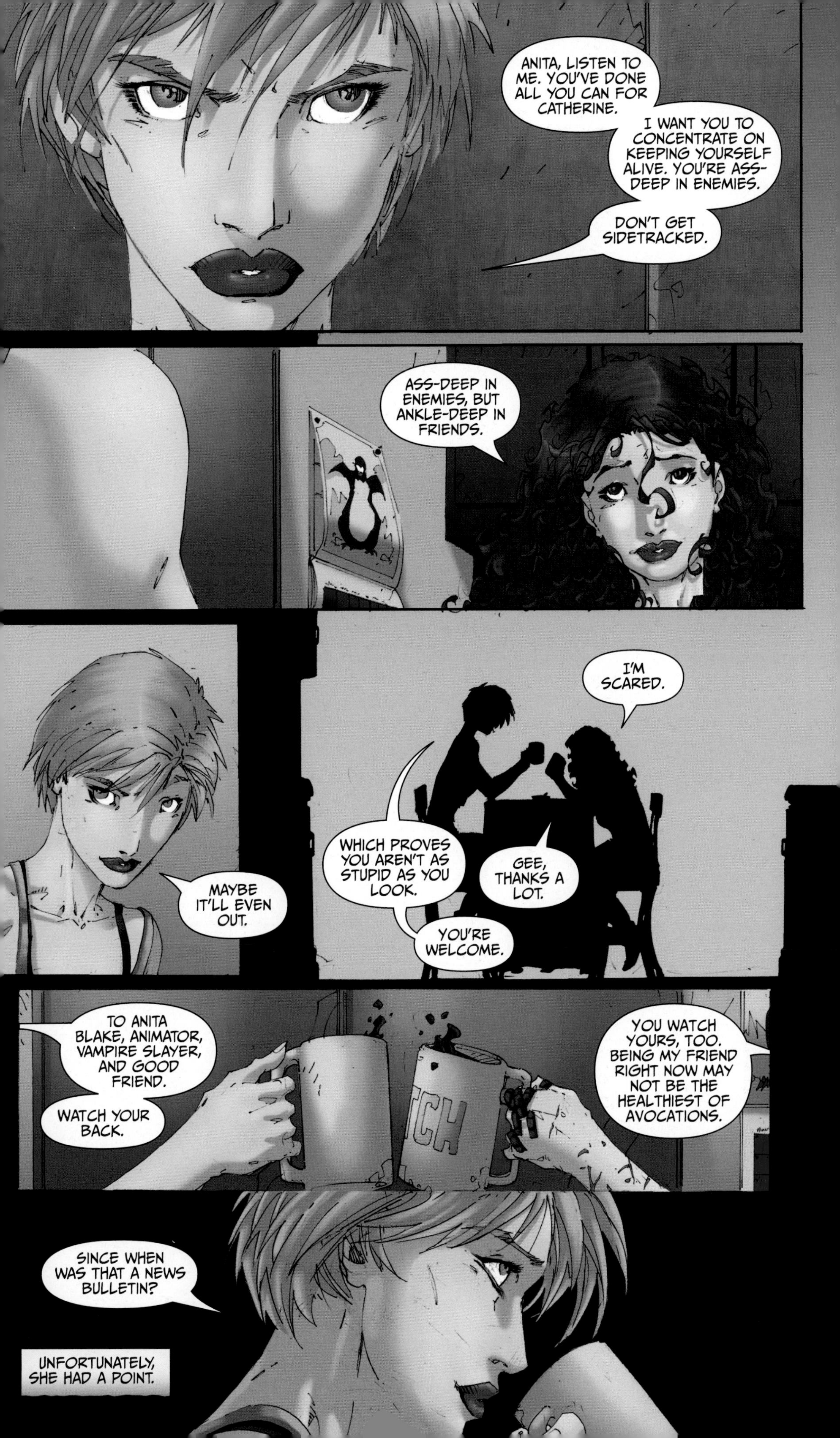
ANITA, LISTEN TO ME. YOU'VE DONE ALL YOU CAN FOR CATHERINE.
I WANT YOU TO CONCENTRATE ON KEEPING YOURSELF ALIVE. YOU'RE ASS-DEEP IN ENEMIES.
DON'T GET SIDETRACKED.
ASS-DEEP IN ENEMIES, BUT ANKLE-DEEP IN FRIENDS.
MAYBE IT'LL EVEN OUT.
I'M SCARED.
WHICH PROVES YOU AREN'T AS STUPID AS YOU LOOK.
GEE, THANKS A LOT.
YOU'RE WELCOME.
TO ANITA BLAKE, ANIMATOR, VAMPIRE SLAYER, AND GOOD FRIEND.
WATCH YOUR BACK.
YOU WATCH YOURS, TOO. BEING MY FRIEND RIGHT NOW MAY NOT BE THE HEALTHIEST OF AVOCATIONS.
SINCE WHEN WAS THAT A NEWS BULLETIN?
UNFORTUNATELY, SHE HAD A POINT.

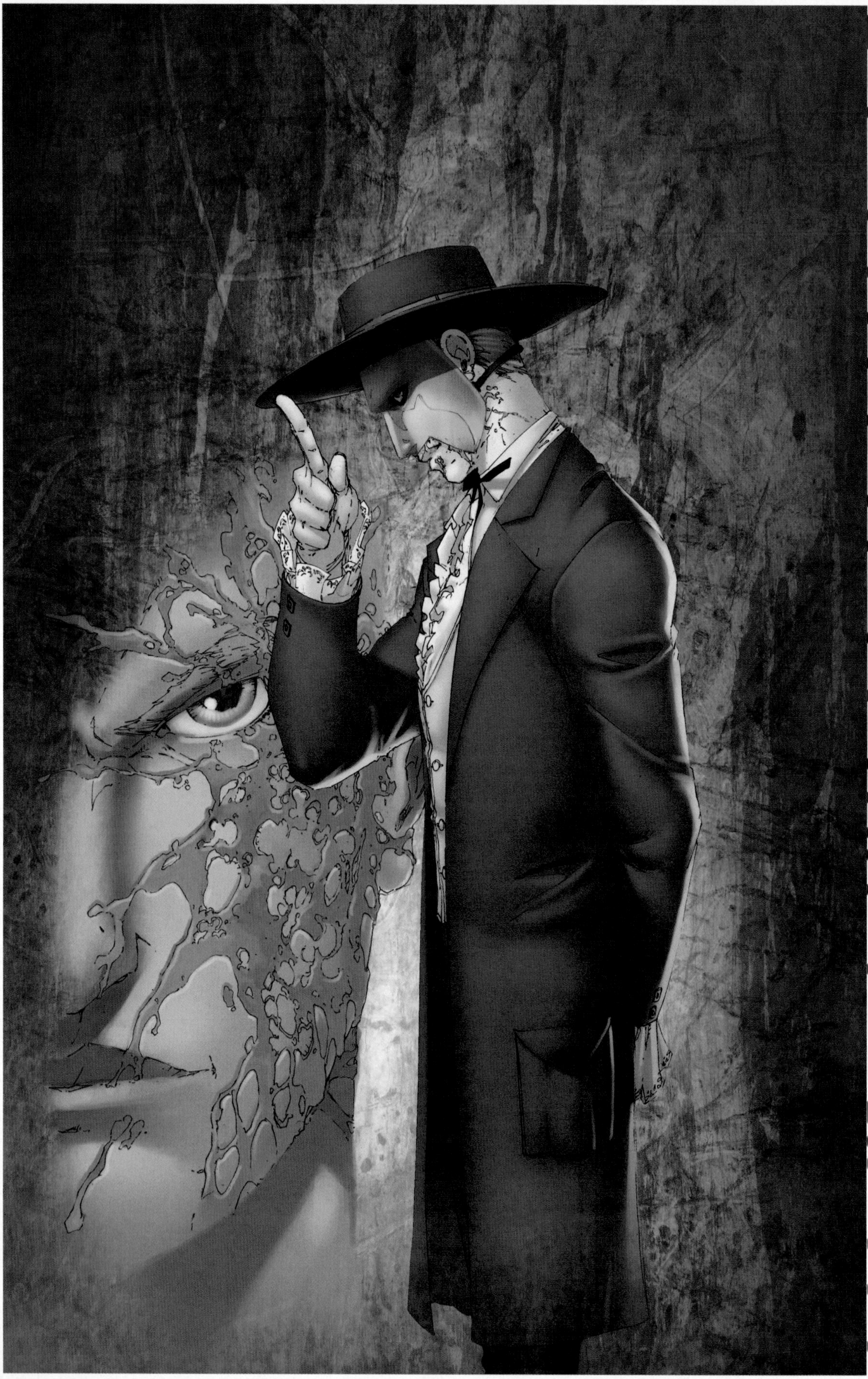

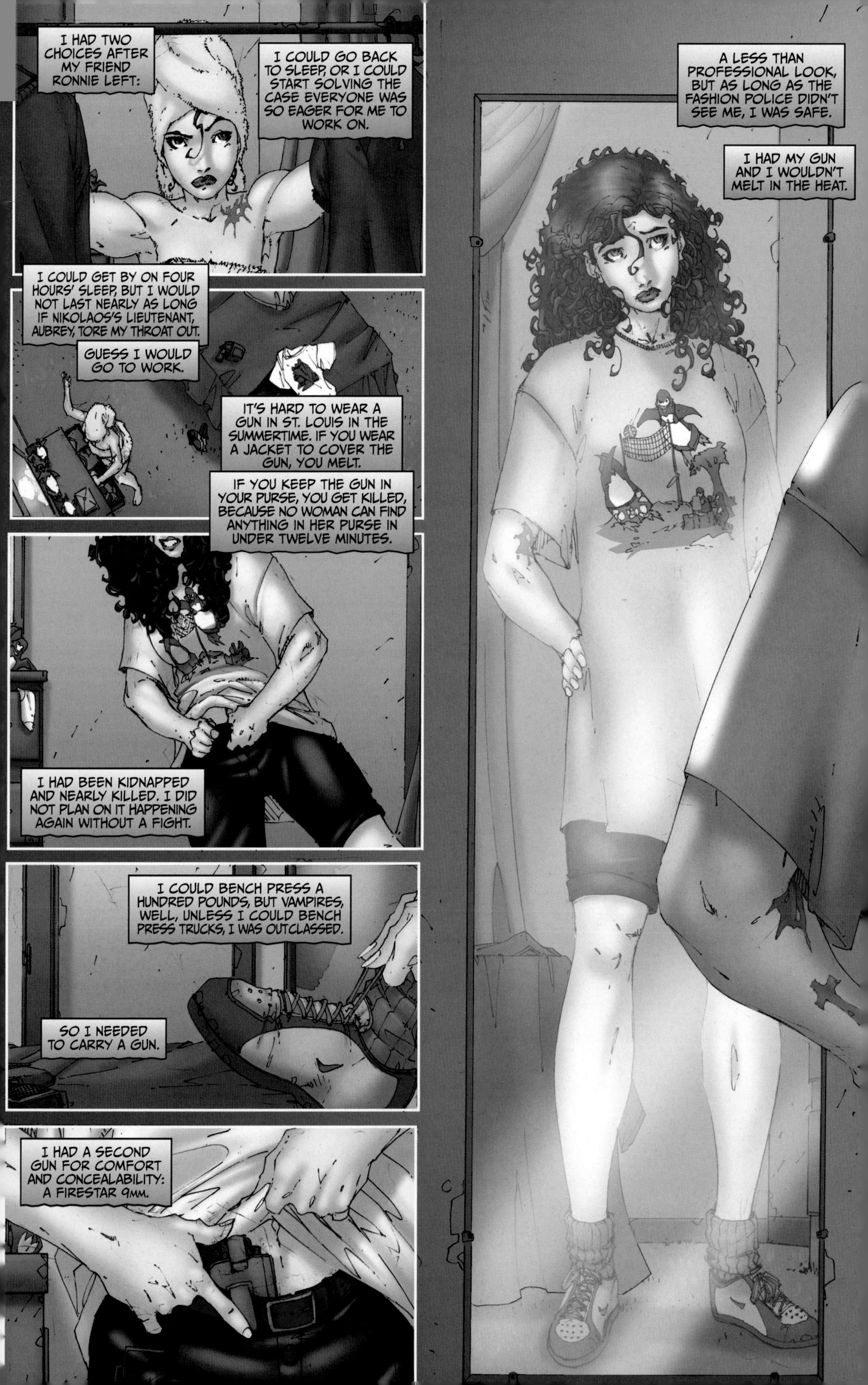
I HAD TWO CHOICES AFTER MY FRIEND RONNIE LEFT:
I COULD GO BACK TO SLEEP, OR I COULD START SOLVING THE CASE EVERYONE WAS SO EAGER FOR ME TO WORK ON.
I COULD GET BY ON FOUR HOURS' SLEEP, BUT I WOULD NOT LAST NEARLY AS LONG IF NIKOLAOS'S LIEUTENANT, AUBREY, TORE MY THROAT OUT.
GUESS I WOULD GO TO WORK.
IT'S HARD TO WEAR A GUN IN ST. LOUIS IN THE SUMMERTIME. IF YOU WEAR A JACKET TO COVER THE GUN, YOU MELT.
IF YOU KEEP THE GUN IN YOUR PURSE, YOU GET KILLED, BECAUSE NO WOMAN CAN FIND ANYTHING IN HER PURSE IN UNDER TWELVE MINUTES.
I HAD BEEN KIDNAPPED AND NEARLY KILLED. I DID NOT PLAN ON IT HAPPENING AGAIN WITHOUT A FIGHT.
I COULD BENCH PRESS A HUNDRED POUNDS, BUT VAMPIRES, WELL, UNLESS I COULD BENCH PRESS TRUCKS, I WAS OUTCLASSED.
SO I NEEDED TO CARRY A GUN.
I HAD A SECOND GUN FOR COMFORT AND CONCEALABILITY: A FIRESTAR 9MM.
A LESS THAN PROFESSIONAL LOOK, BUT AS LONG AS THE FASHION POLICE DIDN'T SEE ME, I WAS SAFE.
I HAD MY GUN AND I WOULDN'T MELT IN THE HEAT.

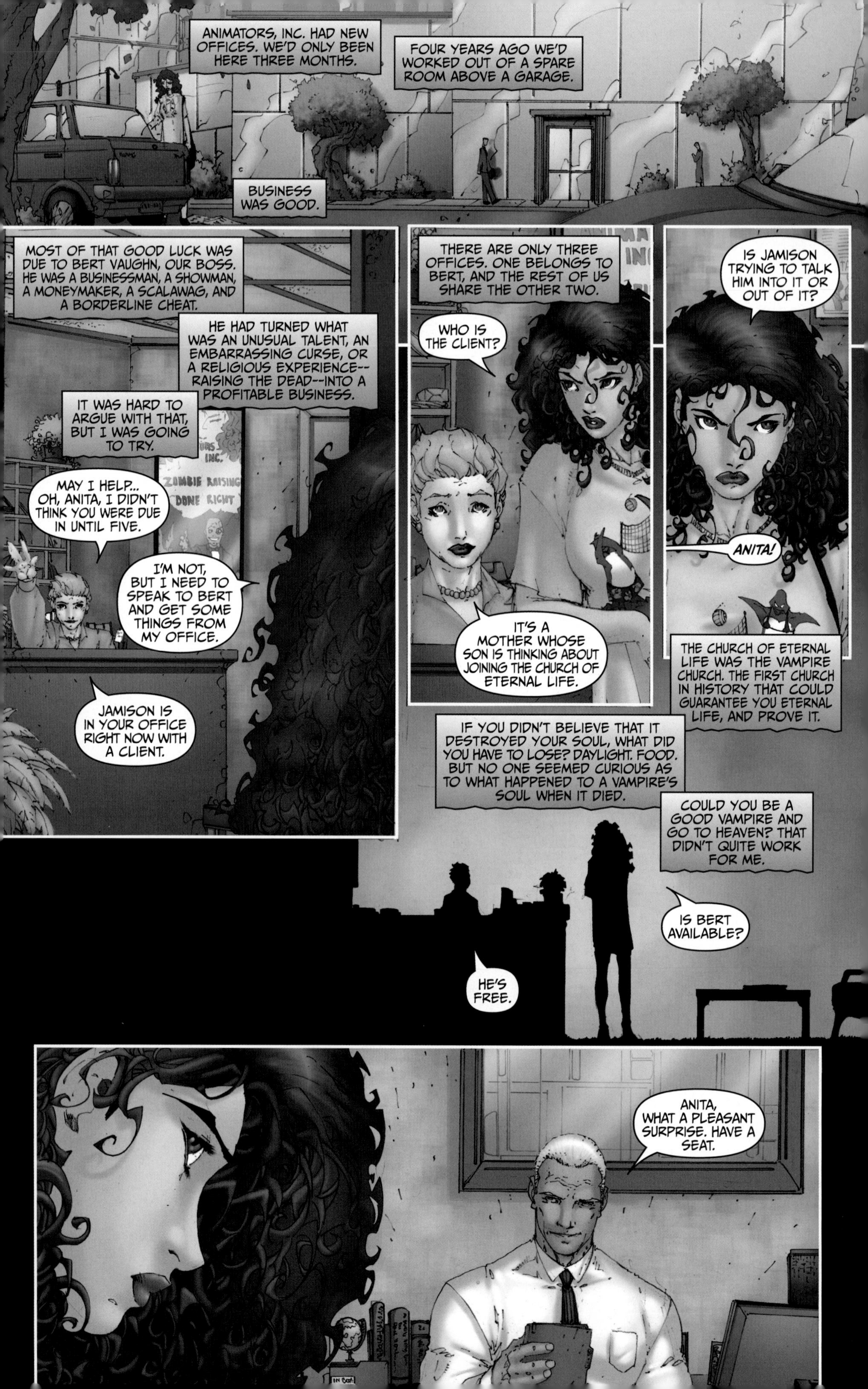
ANIMATORS, INC. HAD NEW OFFICES. WE'D ONLY BEEN HERE THREE MONTHS.
FOUR YEARS AGO WE'D WORKED OUT OF A SPARE ROOM ABOVE A GARAGE.
BUSINESS WAS GOOD.
MOST OF THAT GOOD LUCK WAS DUE TO BERT VAUGHN, OUR BOSS. HE WAS A BUSINESSMAN, A SHOWMAN, A MONEYMAKER, A SCALAWAG, AND A BORDERLINE CHEAT.
HE HAD TURNED WHAT WAS AN UNUSUAL TALENT, AN EMBARRASSING CURSE, OR A RELIGIOUS EXPERIENCE--RAISING THE DEAD--INTO A PROFITABLE BUSINESS.
IT WAS HARD TO ARGUE WITH THAT, BUT I WAS GOING TO TRY.
ZOMBIE RAISING DONE RIGHT
MAY I HELP... OH, ANITA, I DIDN'T THINK YOU WERE DUE IN UNTIL FIVE.
I'M NOT, BUT I NEED TO SPEAK TO BERT AND GET SOME THINGS FROM MY OFFICE.
JAMISON IS IN YOUR OFFICE RIGHT NOW WITH A CLIENT.
THERE ARE ONLY THREE OFFICES. ONE BELONGS TO BERT, AND THE REST OF US SHARE THE OTHER TWO.
WHO IS THE CLIENT?
IT'S A MOTHER WHOSE SON IS THINKING ABOUT JOINING THE CHURCH OF ETERNAL LIFE.
IS JAMISON TRYING TO TALK HIM INTO IT OR OUT OF IT?
ANITA!
THE CHURCH OF ETERNAL LIFE WAS THE VAMPIRE CHURCH. THE FIRST CHURCH IN HISTORY THAT COULD GUARANTEE YOU ETERNAL LIFE, AND PROVE IT.
IF YOU DIDN'T BELIEVE THAT IT DESTROYED YOUR SOUL, WHAT DID YOU HAVE TO LOSE? DAYLIGHT. FOOD. BUT NO ONE SEEMED CURIOUS AS TO WHAT HAPPENED TO A VAMPIRE'S SOUL WHEN IT DIED.
COULD YOU BE A GOOD VAMPIRE AND GO TO HEAVEN? THAT DIDN'T QUITE WORK FOR ME.
IS BERT AVAILABLE?
HE'S FREE.
ANITA, WHAT A PLEASANT SURPRISE. HAVE A SEAT.

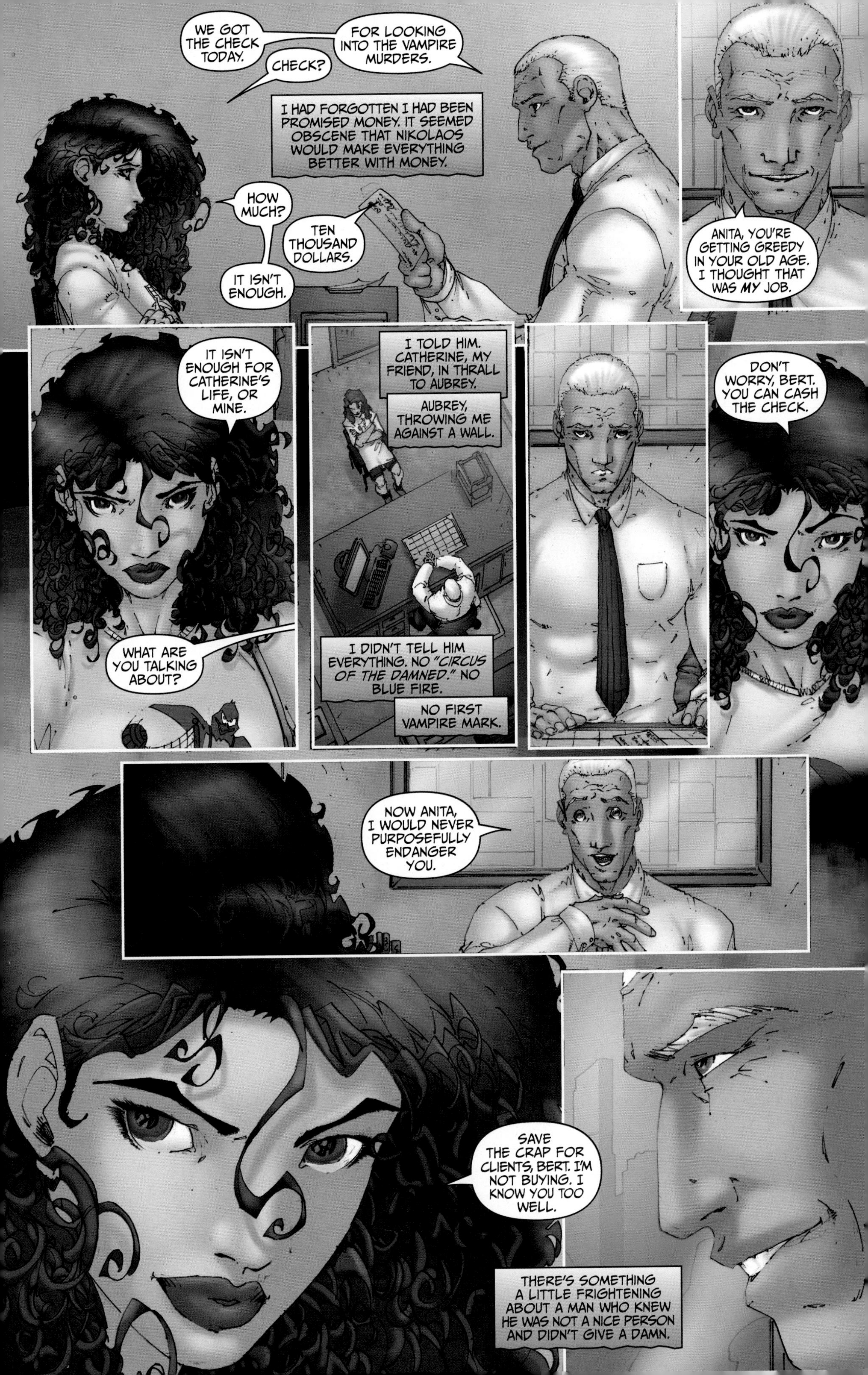
WE GOT THE CHECK TODAY.
FOR LOOKING INTO THE VAMPIRE MURDERS.
CHECK?
I HAD FORGOTTEN I HAD BEEN PROMISED MONEY. IT SEEMED OBSCENE THAT NIKOLAOS WOULD MAKE EVERYTHING BETTER WITH MONEY.
HOW MUCH?
TEN THOUSAND DOLLARS.
IT ISN'T ENOUGH.
ANITA, YOU'RE GETTING GREEDY IN YOUR OLD AGE. I THOUGHT THAT WAS *MY* JOB.
IT ISN'T ENOUGH FOR CATHERINE'S LIFE, OR MINE.
WHAT ARE YOU TALKING ABOUT?
I TOLD HIM. CATHERINE, MY FRIEND, IN THRALL TO AUBREY.
AUBREY, THROWING ME AGAINST A WALL.
I DIDN'T TELL HIM EVERYTHING. NO "*CIRCUS OF THE DAMNED*." NO BLUE FIRE.
NO FIRST VAMPIRE MARK.
DON'T WORRY, BERT. YOU CAN CASH THE CHECK.
NOW ANITA, I WOULD NEVER PURPOSEFULLY ENDANGER YOU.
SAVE THE CRAP FOR CLIENTS, BERT. I'M NOT BUYING. I KNOW YOU TOO WELL.
THERE'S SOMETHING A LITTLE FRIGHTENING ABOUT A MAN WHO KNEW HE WAS NOT A NICE PERSON AND DIDN'T GIVE A DAMN.

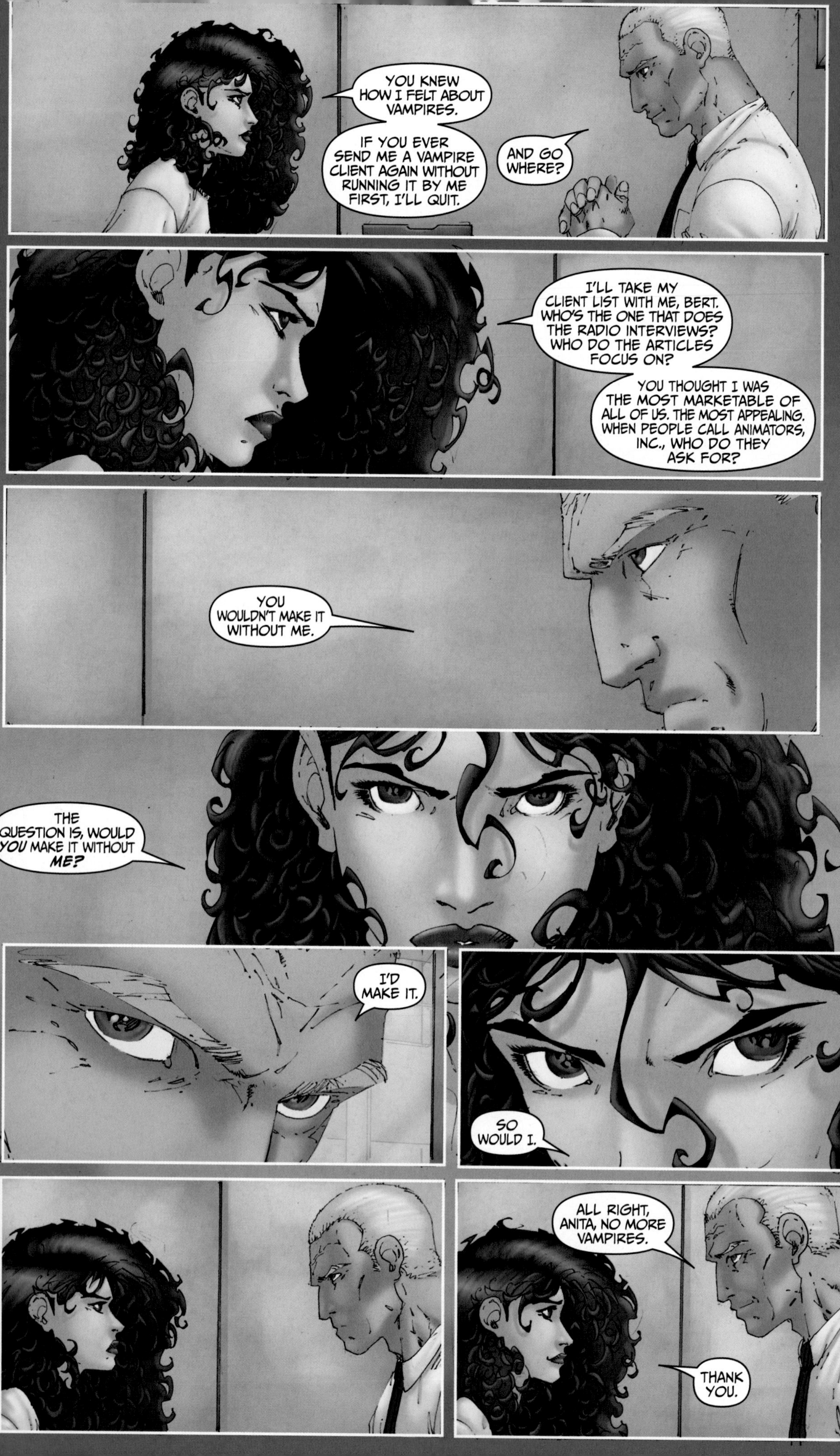
YOU KNEW HOW I FELT ABOUT VAMPIRES.
IF YOU EVER SEND ME A VAMPIRE CLIENT AGAIN WITHOUT RUNNING IT BY ME FIRST, I'LL QUIT.
AND GO WHERE?
I'LL TAKE MY CLIENT LIST WITH ME, BERT. WHO'S THE ONE THAT DOES THE RADIO INTERVIEWS? WHO DO THE ARTICLES FOCUS ON?
YOU THOUGHT I WAS THE MOST MARKETABLE OF ALL OF US. THE MOST APPEALING. WHEN PEOPLE CALL ANIMATORS, INC., WHO DO THEY ASK FOR?
YOU WOULDN'T MAKE IT WITHOUT ME.
THE QUESTION IS, WOULD *YOU* MAKE IT WITHOUT ***ME?***
I'D MAKE IT.
SO WOULD I.
ALL RIGHT, ANITA, NO MORE VAMPIRES.
THANK YOU.

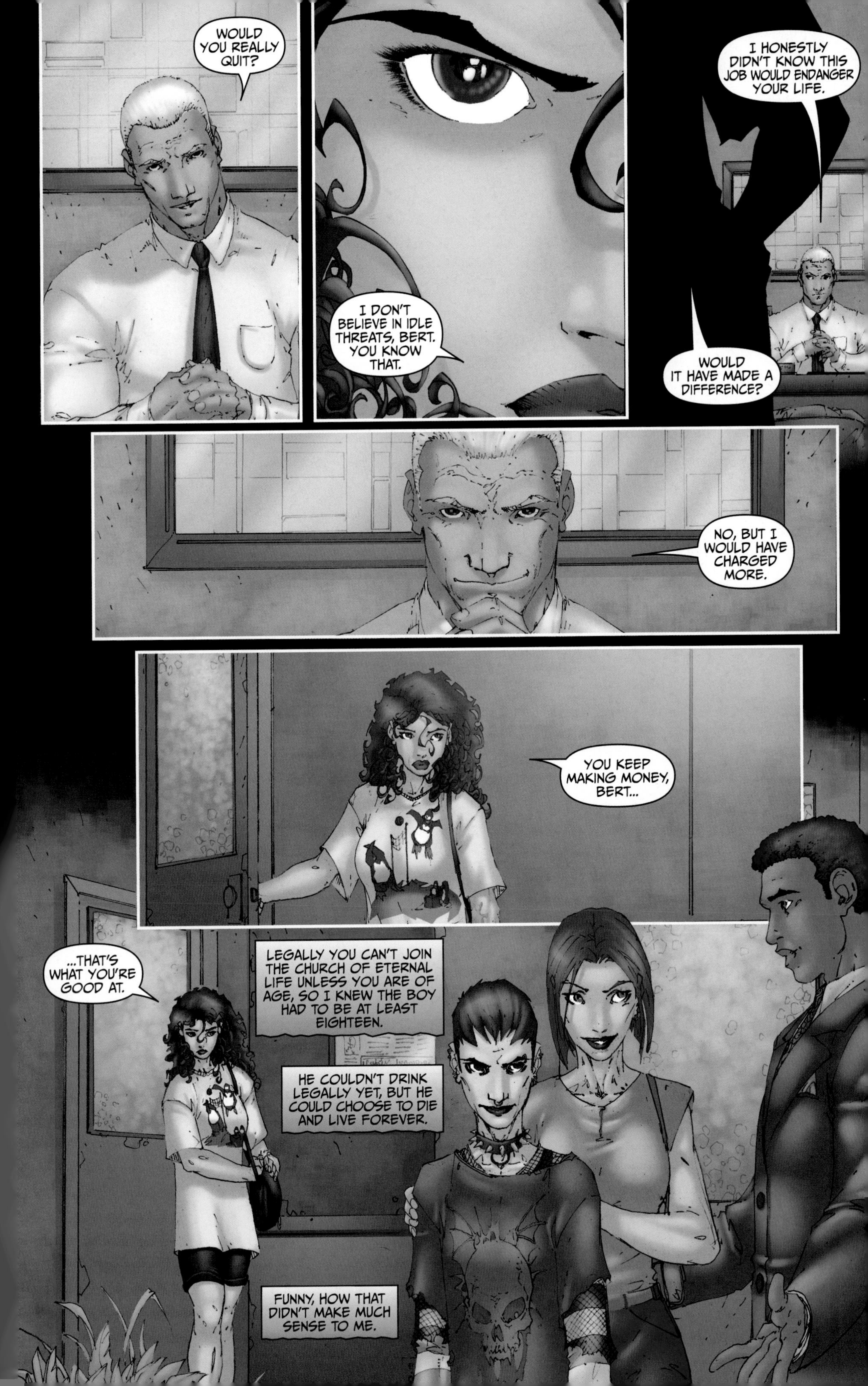
WOULD YOU REALLY QUIT?
I DON'T BELIEVE IN IDLE THREATS, BERT. YOU KNOW THAT.
I HONESTLY DIDN'T KNOW THIS JOB WOULD ENDANGER YOUR LIFE.
WOULD IT HAVE MADE A DIFFERENCE?
NO, BUT I WOULD HAVE CHARGED MORE.
YOU KEEP MAKING MONEY, BERT...
...THAT'S WHAT YOU'RE GOOD AT.
LEGALLY YOU CAN'T JOIN THE CHURCH OF ETERNAL LIFE UNLESS YOU ARE OF AGE, SO I KNEW THE BOY HAD TO BE AT LEAST EIGHTEEN.
HE COULDN'T DRINK LEGALLY YET, BUT HE COULD CHOOSE TO DIE AND LIVE FOREVER.
FUNNY, HOW THAT DIDN'T MAKE MUCH SENSE TO ME.

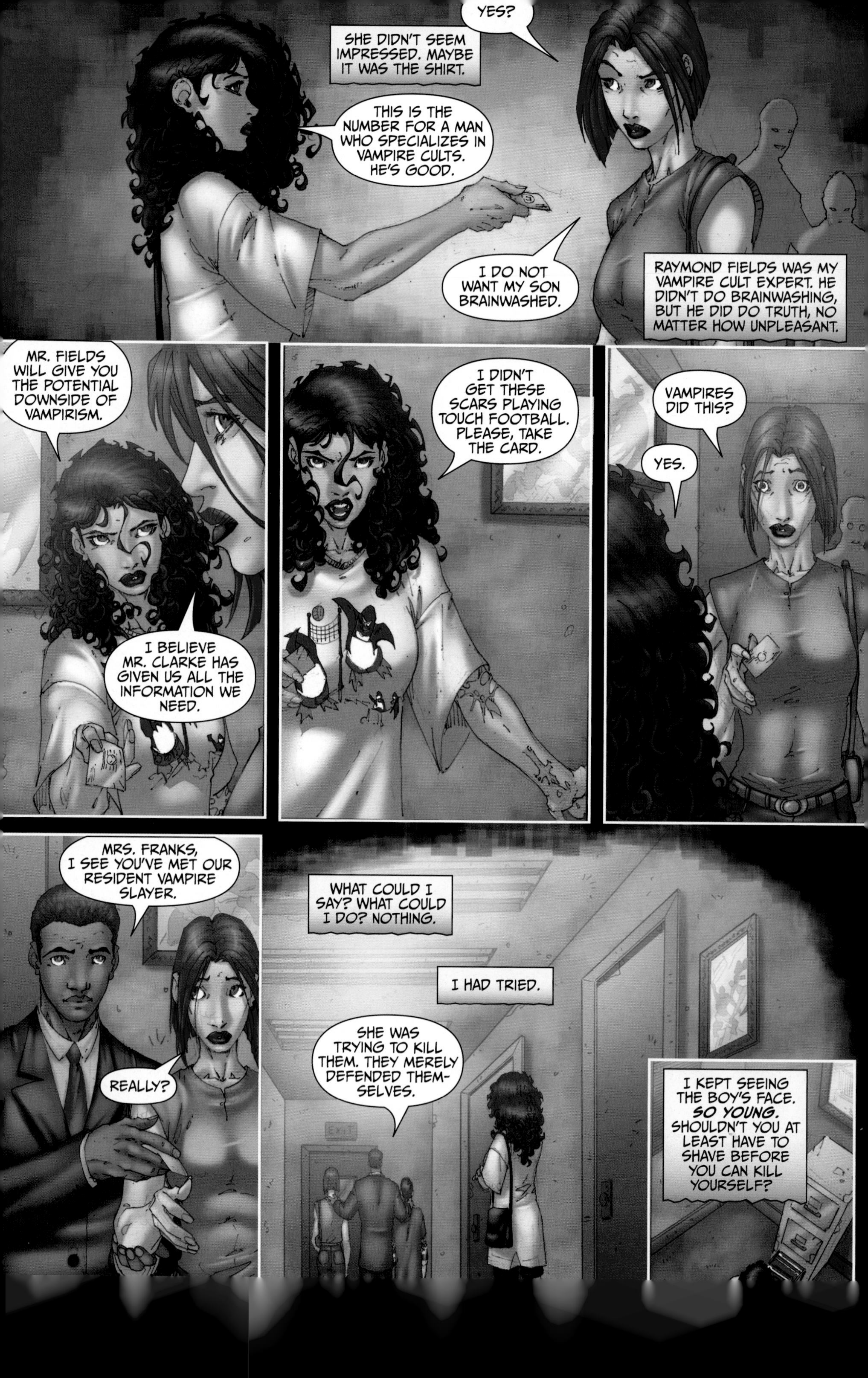
YES?
SHE DIDN'T SEEM IMPRESSED. MAYBE IT WAS THE SHIRT.
THIS IS THE NUMBER FOR A MAN WHO SPECIALIZES IN VAMPIRE CULTS. HE'S GOOD.
I DO NOT WANT MY SON BRAINWASHED.
RAYMOND FIELDS WAS MY VAMPIRE CULT EXPERT. HE DIDN'T DO BRAINWASHING, BUT HE DID DO TRUTH, NO MATTER HOW UNPLEASANT.
MR. FIELDS WILL GIVE YOU THE POTENTIAL DOWNSIDE OF VAMPIRISM.
I BELIEVE MR. CLARKE HAS GIVEN US ALL THE INFORMATION WE NEED.
I DIDN'T GET THESE SCARS PLAYING TOUCH FOOTBALL. PLEASE, TAKE THE CARD.
VAMPIRES DID THIS?
YES.
MRS. FRANKS, I SEE YOU'VE MET OUR RESIDENT VAMPIRE SLAYER.
REALLY?
WHAT COULD I SAY? WHAT COULD I DO? NOTHING.
I HAD TRIED.
SHE WAS TRYING TO KILL THEM. THEY MERELY DEFENDED THEM-SELVES.
EXIT
I KEPT SEEING THE BOY'S FACE. SO YOUNG. SHOULDN'T YOU AT LEAST HAVE TO SHAVE BEFORE YOU CAN KILL YOURSELF?

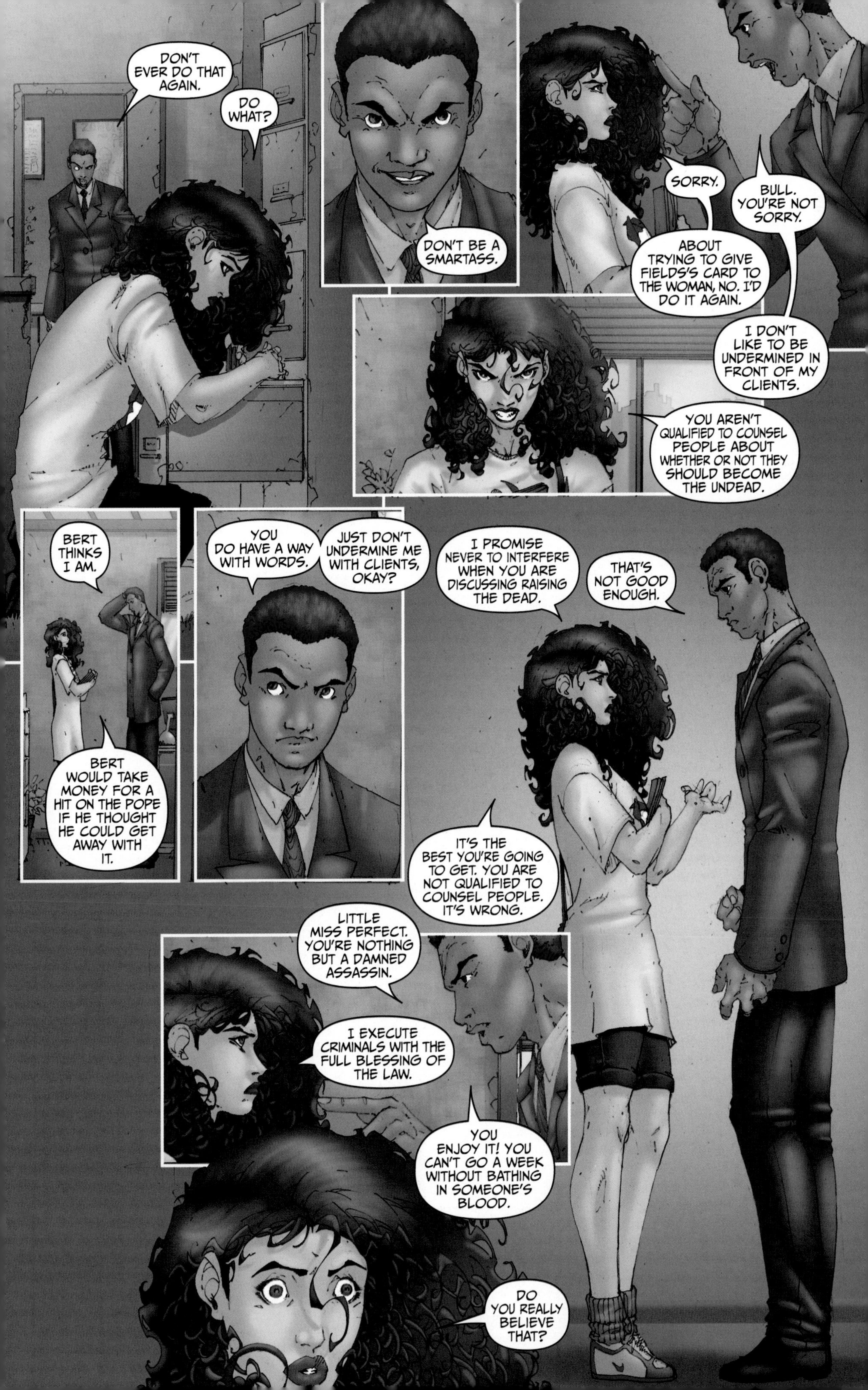
DON'T EVER DO THAT AGAIN.
DO WHAT?
DON'T BE A SMARTASS.
SORRY.
BULL. YOU'RE NOT SORRY.
ABOUT TRYING TO GIVE FIELDS'S CARD TO THE WOMAN, NO. I'D DO IT AGAIN.
I DON'T LIKE TO BE UNDERMINED IN FRONT OF MY CLIENTS.
YOU AREN'T QUALIFIED TO COUNSEL PEOPLE ABOUT WHETHER OR NOT THEY SHOULD BECOME THE UNDEAD.
BERT THINKS I AM.
BERT WOULD TAKE MONEY FOR A HIT ON THE POPE IF HE THOUGHT HE COULD GET AWAY WITH IT.
YOU DO HAVE A WAY WITH WORDS.
JUST DON'T UNDERMINE ME WITH CLIENTS, OKAY?
I PROMISE NEVER TO INTERFERE WHEN YOU ARE DISCUSSING RAISING THE DEAD.
THAT'S NOT GOOD ENOUGH.
IT'S THE BEST YOU'RE GOING TO GET. YOU ARE NOT QUALIFIED TO COUNSEL PEOPLE. IT'S WRONG.
LITTLE MISS PERFECT. YOU'RE NOTHING BUT A DAMNED ASSASSIN.
I EXECUTE CRIMINALS WITH THE FULL BLESSING OF THE LAW.
YOU ENJOY IT! YOU CAN'T GO A WEEK WITHOUT BATHING IN SOMEONE'S BLOOD.
DO YOU REALLY BELIEVE THAT?

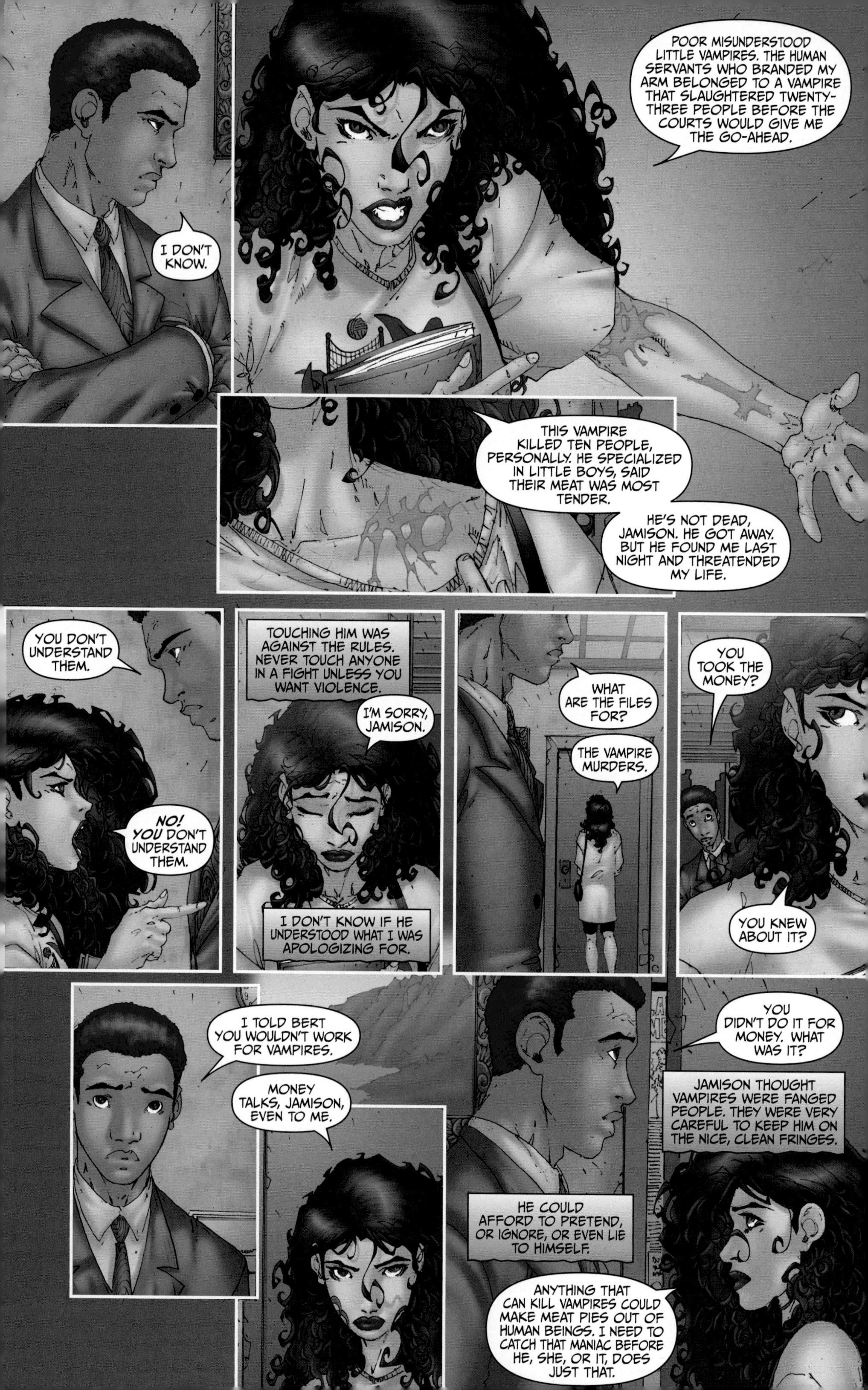
POOR MISUNDERSTOOD LITTLE VAMPIRES. THE HUMAN SERVANTS WHO BRANDED MY ARM BELONGED TO A VAMPIRE THAT SLAUGHTERED TWENTY-THREE PEOPLE BEFORE THE COURTS WOULD GIVE ME THE GO-AHEAD.
I DON'T KNOW.
THIS VAMPIRE KILLED TEN PEOPLE, PERSONALLY. HE SPECIALIZED IN LITTLE BOYS, SAID THEIR MEAT WAS MOST TENDER.
HE'S NOT DEAD, JAMISON. HE GOT AWAY. BUT HE FOUND ME LAST NIGHT AND THREATENDED MY LIFE.
YOU DON'T UNDERSTAND THEM.
NO! YOU DON'T UNDERSTAND THEM.
TOUCHING HIM WAS AGAINST THE RULES. NEVER TOUCH ANYONE IN A FIGHT UNLESS YOU WANT VIOLENCE.
I'M SORRY, JAMISON.
I DON'T KNOW IF HE UNDERSTOOD WHAT I WAS APOLOGIZING FOR.
WHAT ARE THE FILES FOR?
THE VAMPIRE MURDERS.
YOU TOOK THE MONEY?
YOU KNEW ABOUT IT?
I TOLD BERT YOU WOULDN'T WORK FOR VAMPIRES.
MONEY TALKS, JAMISON, EVEN TO ME.
YOU DIDN'T DO IT FOR MONEY. WHAT WAS IT?
JAMISON THOUGHT VAMPIRES WERE FANGED PEOPLE. THEY WERE VERY CAREFUL TO KEEP HIM ON THE NICE, CLEAN FRINGES.
HE COULD AFFORD TO PRETEND, OR IGNORE, OR EVEN LIE TO HIMSELF.
ANYTHING THAT CAN KILL VAMPIRES COULD MAKE MEAT PIES OUT OF HUMAN BEINGS. I NEED TO CATCH THAT MANIAC BEFORE HE, SHE, OR IT, DOES JUST THAT.

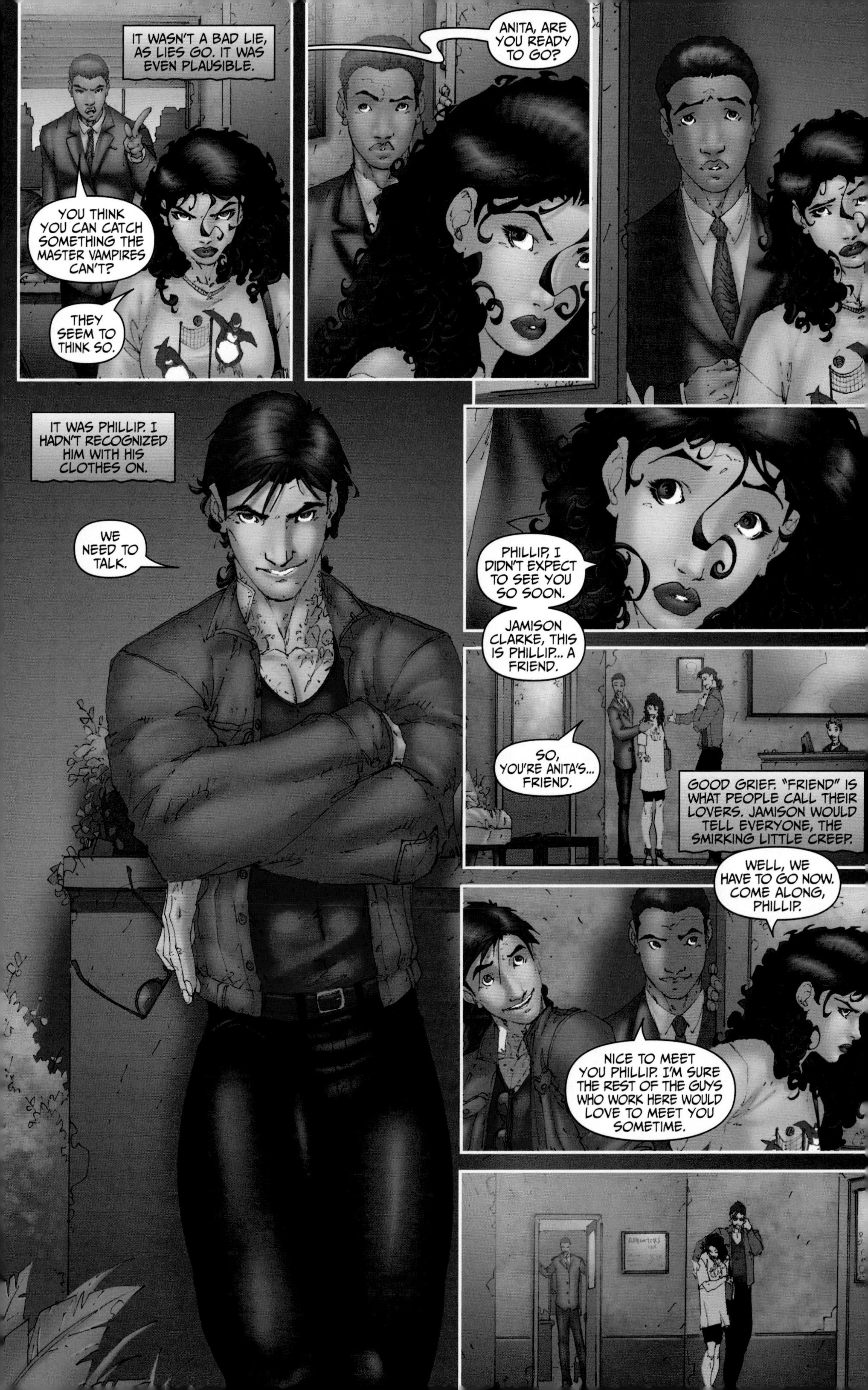
IT WASN'T A BAD LIE, AS LIES GO. IT WAS EVEN PLAUSIBLE.
YOU THINK YOU CAN CATCH SOMETHING THE MASTER VAMPIRES CAN'T?
THEY SEEM TO THINK SO.
ANITA, ARE YOU READY TO GO?
IT WAS PHILLIP. I HADN'T RECOGNIZED HIM WITH HIS CLOTHES ON.
WE NEED TO TALK.
PHILLIP, I DIDN'T EXPECT TO SEE YOU SO SOON.
JAMISON CLARKE, THIS IS PHILLIP... A FRIEND.
SO, YOU'RE ANITA'S... FRIEND.
GOOD GRIEF. "FRIEND" IS WHAT PEOPLE CALL THEIR LOVERS. JAMISON WOULD TELL EVERYONE, THE SMIRKING LITTLE CREEP.
WELL, WE HAVE TO GO NOW. COME ALONG, PHILLIP.
NICE TO MEET YOU PHILLIP. I'M SURE THE REST OF THE GUYS WHO WORK HERE WOULD LOVE TO MEET YOU SOMETIME.

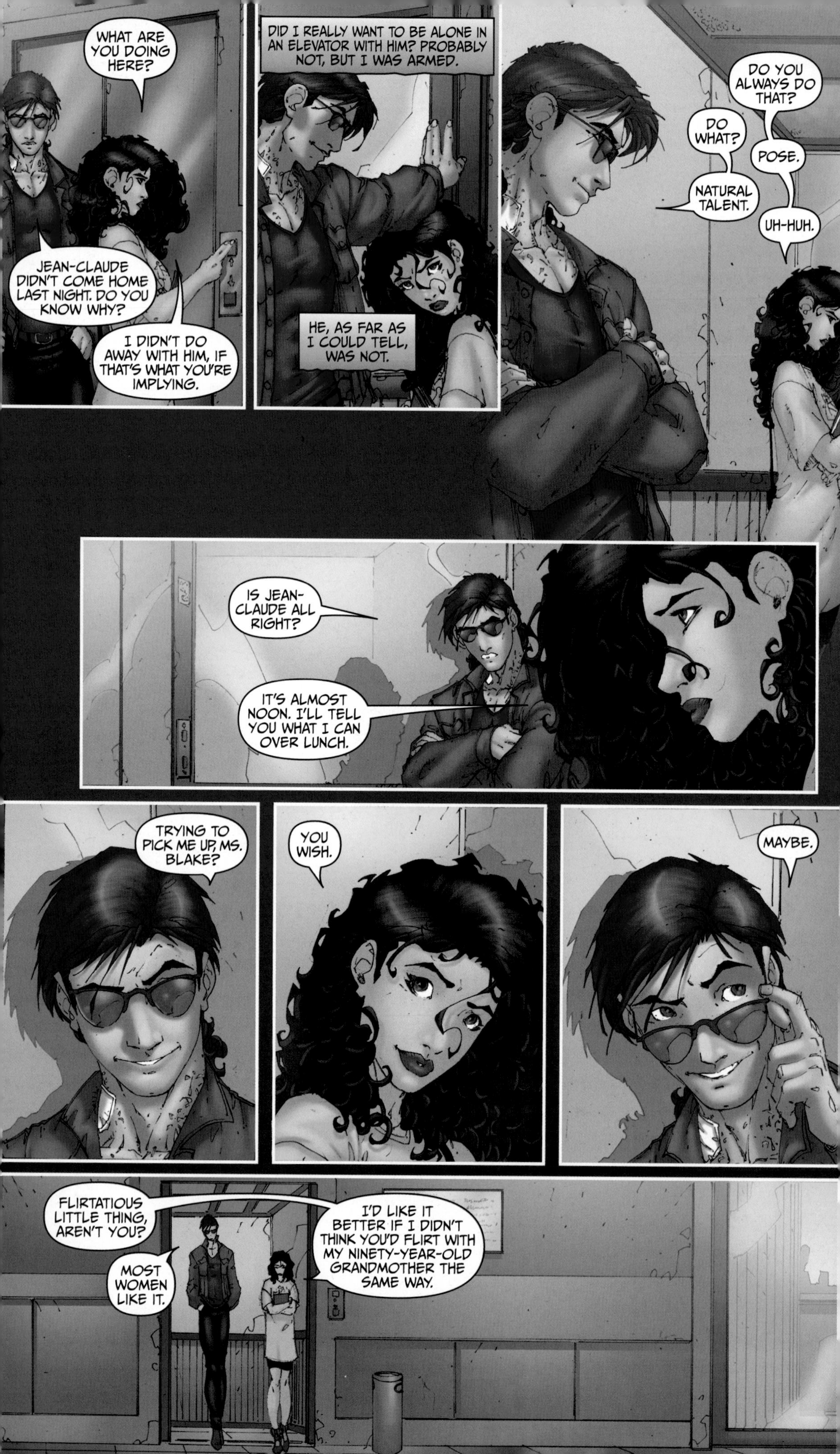
WHAT ARE YOU DOING HERE?
JEAN-CLAUDE DIDN'T COME HOME LAST NIGHT. DO YOU KNOW WHY?
I DIDN'T DO AWAY WITH HIM, IF THAT'S WHAT YOU'RE IMPLYING.
DID I REALLY WANT TO BE ALONE IN AN ELEVATOR WITH HIM? PROBABLY NOT, BUT I WAS ARMED.
HE, AS FAR AS I COULD TELL, WAS NOT.
DO YOU ALWAYS DO THAT?
DO WHAT?
POSE.
NATURAL TALENT.
UH-HUH.
IS JEAN-CLAUDE ALL RIGHT?
IT'S ALMOST NOON. I'LL TELL YOU WHAT I CAN OVER LUNCH.
TRYING TO PICK ME UP, MS. BLAKE?
YOU WISH.
MAYBE.
FLIRTATIOUS LITTLE THING, AREN'T YOU?
MOST WOMEN LIKE IT.
I'D LIKE IT BETTER IF I DIDN'T THINK YOU'D FLIRT WITH MY NINETY-YEAR-OLD GRANDMOTHER THE SAME WAY.

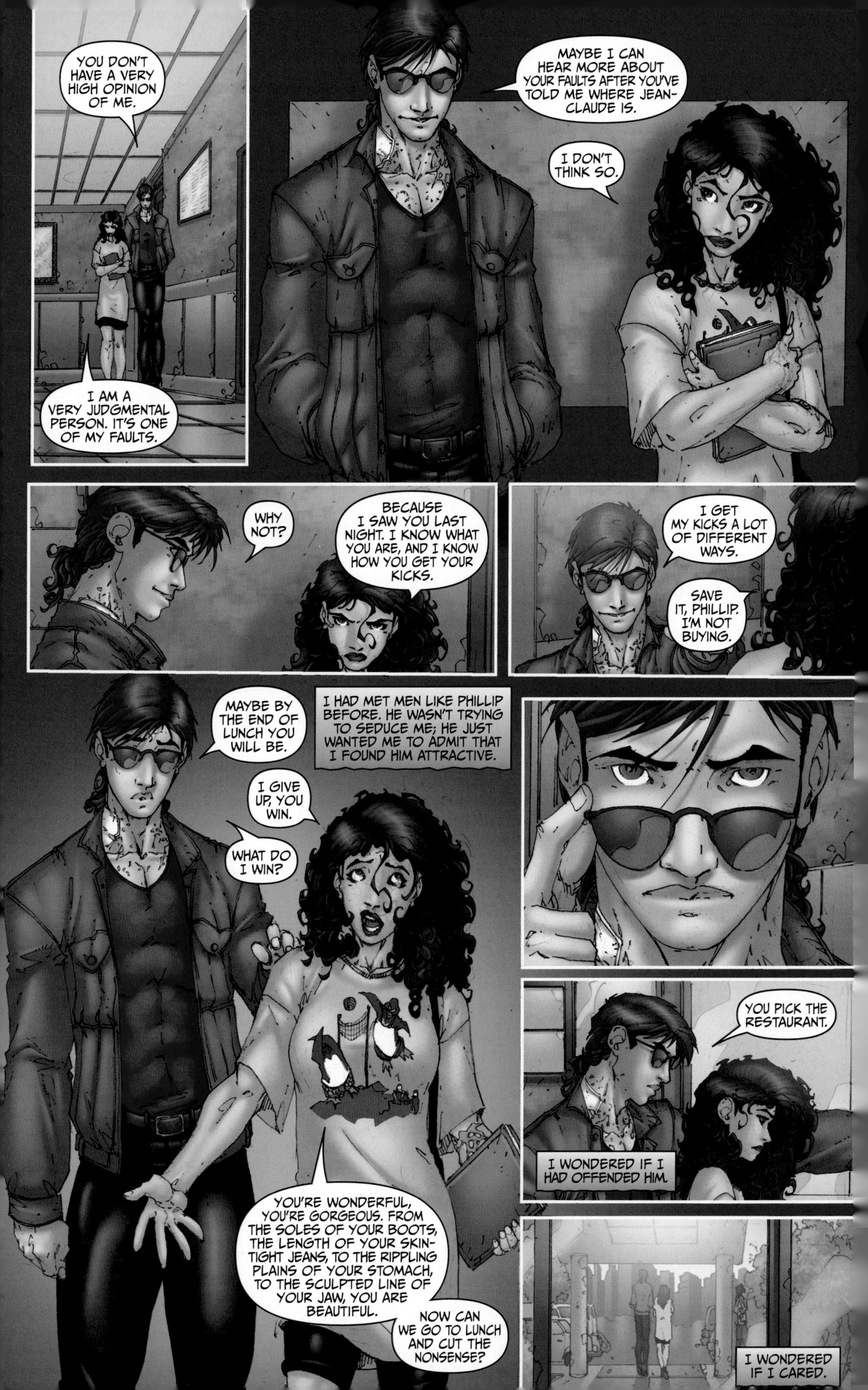
YOU DON'T HAVE A VERY HIGH OPINION OF ME.
I AM A VERY JUDGMENTAL PERSON. IT'S ONE OF MY FAULTS.
MAYBE I CAN HEAR MORE ABOUT YOUR FAULTS AFTER YOU'VE TOLD ME WHERE JEAN-CLAUDE IS.
I DON'T THINK SO.
WHY NOT?
BECAUSE I SAW YOU LAST NIGHT. I KNOW WHAT YOU ARE, AND I KNOW HOW YOU GET YOUR KICKS.
I GET MY KICKS A LOT OF DIFFERENT WAYS.
SAVE IT, PHILLIP. I'M NOT BUYING.
MAYBE BY THE END OF LUNCH YOU WILL BE.
I HAD MET MEN LIKE PHILLIP BEFORE. HE WASN'T TRYING TO SEDUCE ME; HE JUST WANTED ME TO ADMIT THAT I FOUND HIM ATTRACTIVE.
I GIVE UP, YOU WIN.
WHAT DO I WIN?
YOU'RE WONDERFUL, YOU'RE GORGEOUS. FROM THE SOLES OF YOUR BOOTS, THE LENGTH OF YOUR SKIN-TIGHT JEANS, TO THE RIPPLING PLAINS OF YOUR STOMACH, TO THE SCULPTED LINE OF YOUR JAW, YOU ARE BEAUTIFUL.
NOW CAN WE GO TO LUNCH AND CUT THE NONSENSE?
YOU PICK THE RESTAURANT.
I WONDERED IF I HAD OFFENDED HIM.
I WONDERED IF I CARED.

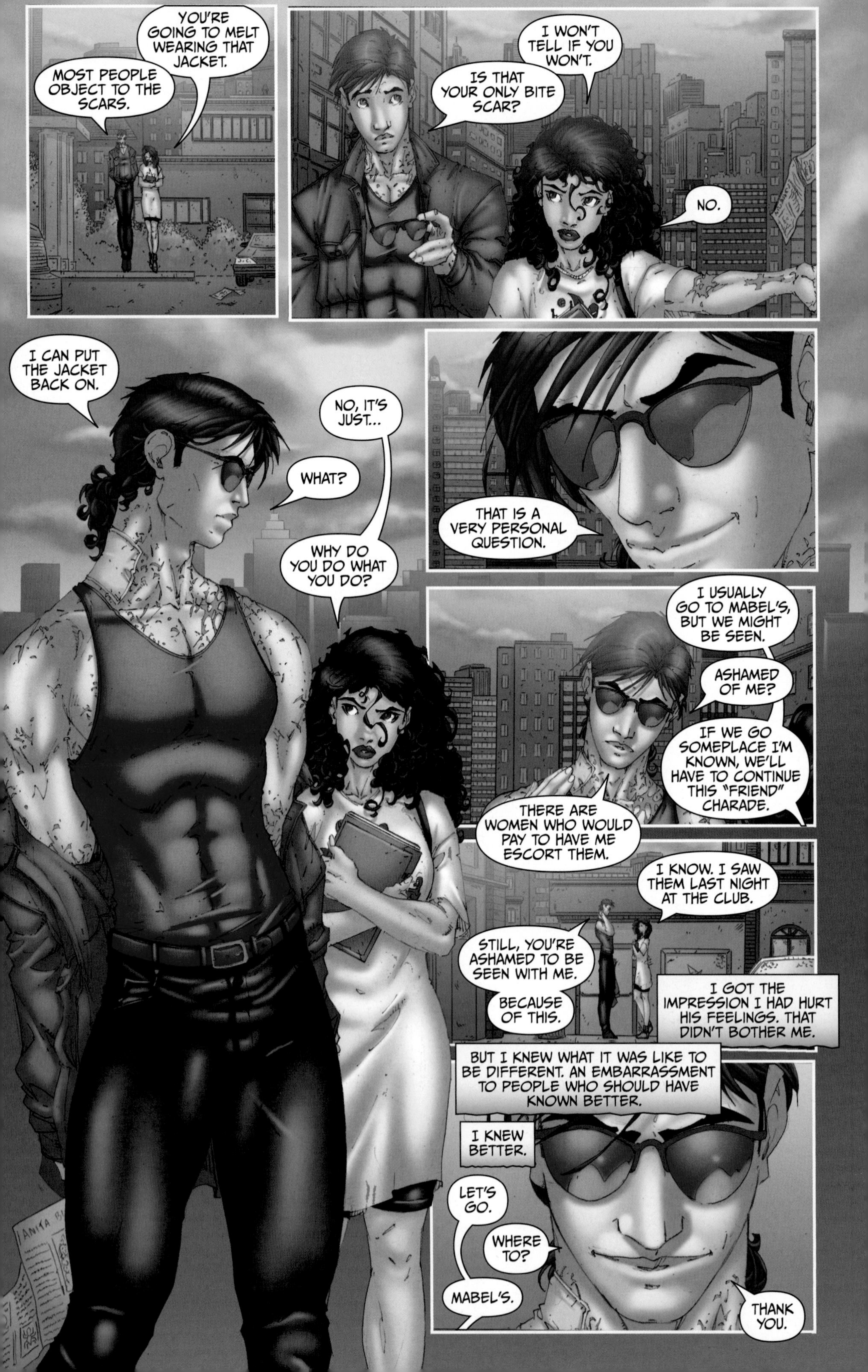
MOST PEOPLE OBJECT TO THE SCARS.
YOU'RE GOING TO MELT WEARING THAT JACKET.
IS THAT YOUR ONLY BITE SCAR?
I WON'T TELL IF YOU WON'T.
NO.
I CAN PUT THE JACKET BACK ON.
NO, IT'S JUST...
WHAT?
WHY DO YOU DO WHAT YOU DO?
THAT IS A VERY PERSONAL QUESTION.
I USUALLY GO TO MABEL'S, BUT WE MIGHT BE SEEN.
ASHAMED OF ME?
IF WE GO SOMEPLACE I'M KNOWN, WE'LL HAVE TO CONTINUE THIS "FRIEND" CHARADE.
THERE ARE WOMEN WHO WOULD PAY TO HAVE ME ESCORT THEM.
I KNOW. I SAW THEM LAST NIGHT AT THE CLUB.
STILL, YOU'RE ASHAMED TO BE SEEN WITH ME.
BECAUSE OF THIS.
I GOT THE IMPRESSION I HAD HURT HIS FEELINGS. THAT DIDN'T BOTHER ME.
BUT I KNEW WHAT IT WAS LIKE TO BE DIFFERENT. AN EMBARRASSMENT TO PEOPLE WHO SHOULD HAVE KNOWN BETTER.
I KNEW BETTER.
LET'S GO.
WHERE TO?
MABEL'S.
THANK YOU.

MABEL'S IS A CAFETERIA, BUT THE FOOD IS WONDERFUL.

ON SATURDAYS IT WAS NEARLY DESERTED.

HI, BEATRICE. THIS IS PHILLIP.

HI, PHILLIP.

DID SHE NOTICE THE SCARS? DID IT MATTER TO HER?

I GAVE HIM AN EDITED VERSION OF LAST NIGHT.

MOSTLY, I TOLD HIM ABOUT JEAN-CLAUDE AND NIKOLAOS AND THE PUNISHMENT.

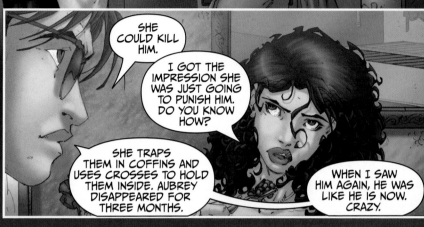

SHE COULD KILL HIM.

I GOT THE IMPRESSION SHE WAS JUST GOING TO PUNISH HIM. DO YOU KNOW HOW?

SHE TRAPS THEM IN COFFINS AND USES CROSSES TO HOLD THEM INSIDE. AUBREY DISAPPEARED FOR THREE MONTHS.

WHEN I SAW HIM AGAIN, HE WAS LIKE HE IS NOW. CRAZY.

WOULD JEAN-CLAUDE GO CRAZY?

BLACKBERRIES, YUCK. I GOT THE WRONG PIE. WHAT WAS THE MATTER WITH ME?

WHAT ARE YOU GOING TO DO NOW?

PHILLIP WAS THE DAYTIME EYES-AND-EARS OF THE UNDEAD. I DIDN'T WANT TO SHARE INFORMATION WITH HIM.

YET WHEN I TALKED WITH THE VICTIM'S NEAREST AND DEAREST IN THE COMPANY OF THE POLICE, SHE TOLD US ZIP.

I NEEDED INFORMATION, AND FAST.

I'M GOING TO TALK TO REBECCA MILES.

I KNOW HER. SHE WAS MAURICE'S... PROPERTY.

I MIGHT BE ABLE TO HELP.

I DON'T WANT A CIVILIAN ALONG WHILE I WORK.

HOW ARE YOU GOING TO CONVINCE REBECCA THAT YOU WORK FOR THE MASTER VAMPIRE OF THE CITY? THE EXECUTIONER WORKING FOR VAMPIRES?

I DON'T KNOW.

I'LL COME ALONG AND HELP SMOOTH THE WATERS.

IF PHILLIP COULD HELP ME, I SAW NO HARM IN IT.

AS LONG AS HE DIDN'T FLASH THAT SMILE AT THE WRONG TIME AND GET MOLESTED BY NUNS, WE WOULD BE SAFE.

ALL RIGHT. LET'S GO.

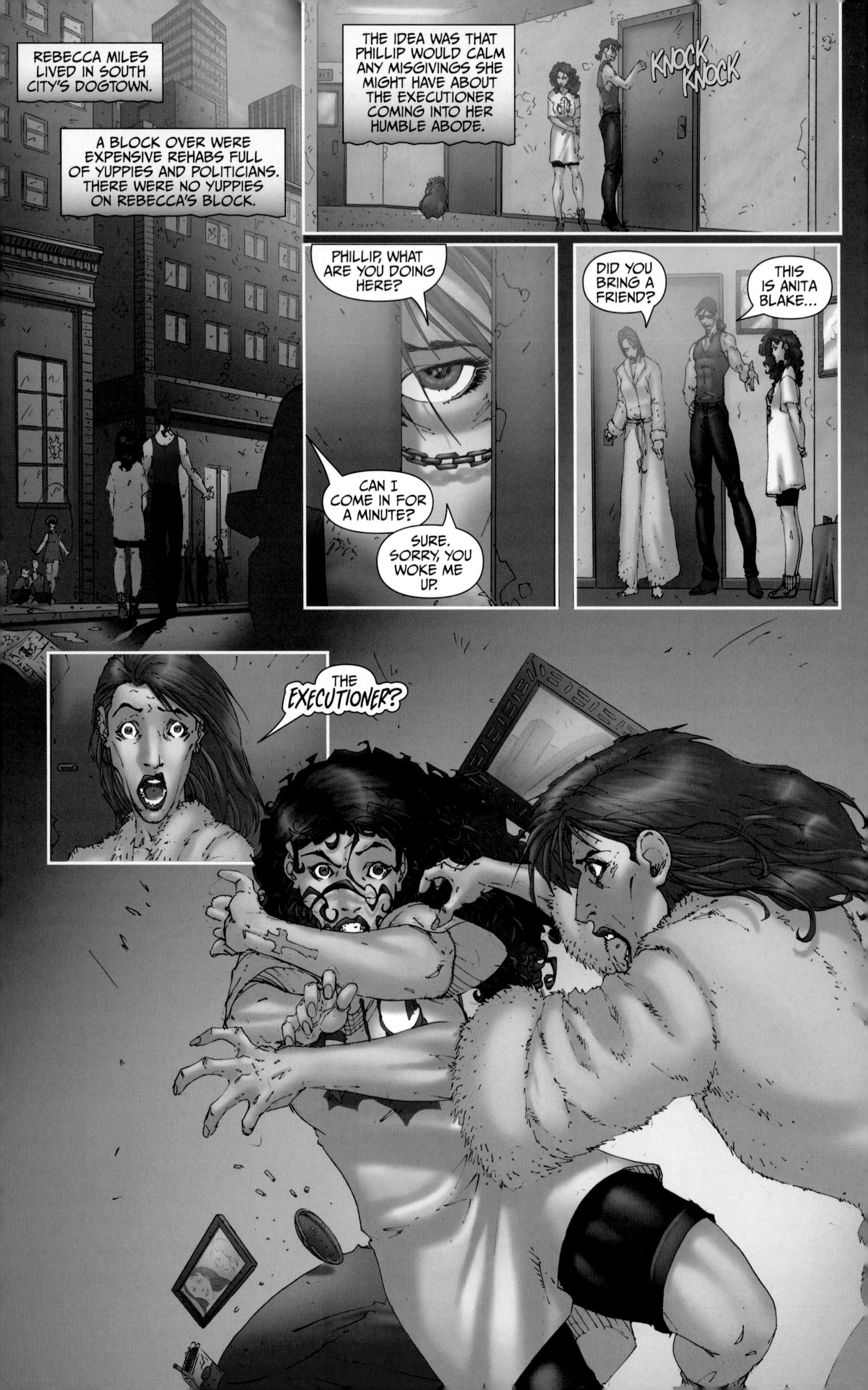
REBECCA MILES LIVED IN SOUTH CITY'S DOGTOWN.
A BLOCK OVER WERE EXPENSIVE REHABS FULL OF YUPPIES AND POLITICIANS. THERE WERE NO YUPPIES ON REBECCA'S BLOCK.
THE IDEA WAS THAT PHILLIP WOULD CALM ANY MISGIVINGS SHE MIGHT HAVE ABOUT THE EXECUTIONER COMING INTO HER HUMBLE ABODE.
KNOCK KNOCK
PHILLIP, WHAT ARE YOU DOING HERE?
CAN I COME IN FOR A MINUTE?
SURE. SORRY, YOU WOKE ME UP.
DID YOU BRING A FRIEND?
THIS IS ANITA BLAKE...
THE EXECUTIONER?

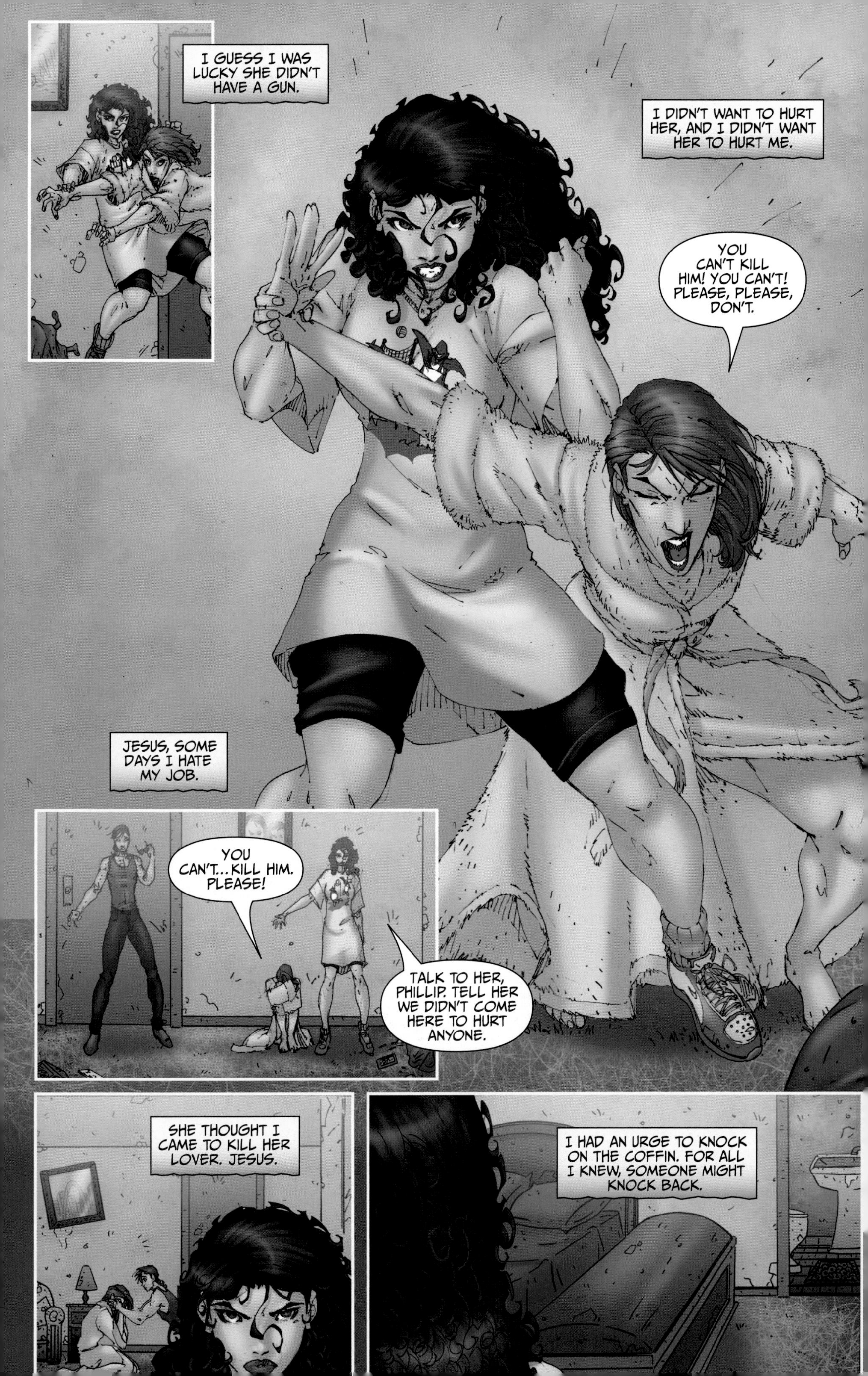
I GUESS I WAS LUCKY SHE DIDN'T HAVE A GUN.
I DIDN'T WANT TO HURT HER, AND I DIDN'T WANT HER TO HURT ME.
YOU CAN'T KILL HIM! YOU CAN'T! PLEASE, PLEASE, DON'T.
JESUS, SOME DAYS I HATE MY JOB.
YOU CAN'T... KILL HIM. PLEASE!
TALK TO HER, PHILLIP. TELL HER WE DIDN'T COME HERE TO HURT ANYONE.
SHE THOUGHT I CAME TO KILL HER LOVER. JESUS.
I HAD AN URGE TO KNOCK ON THE COFFIN. FOR ALL I KNEW, SOMEONE MIGHT KNOCK BACK.

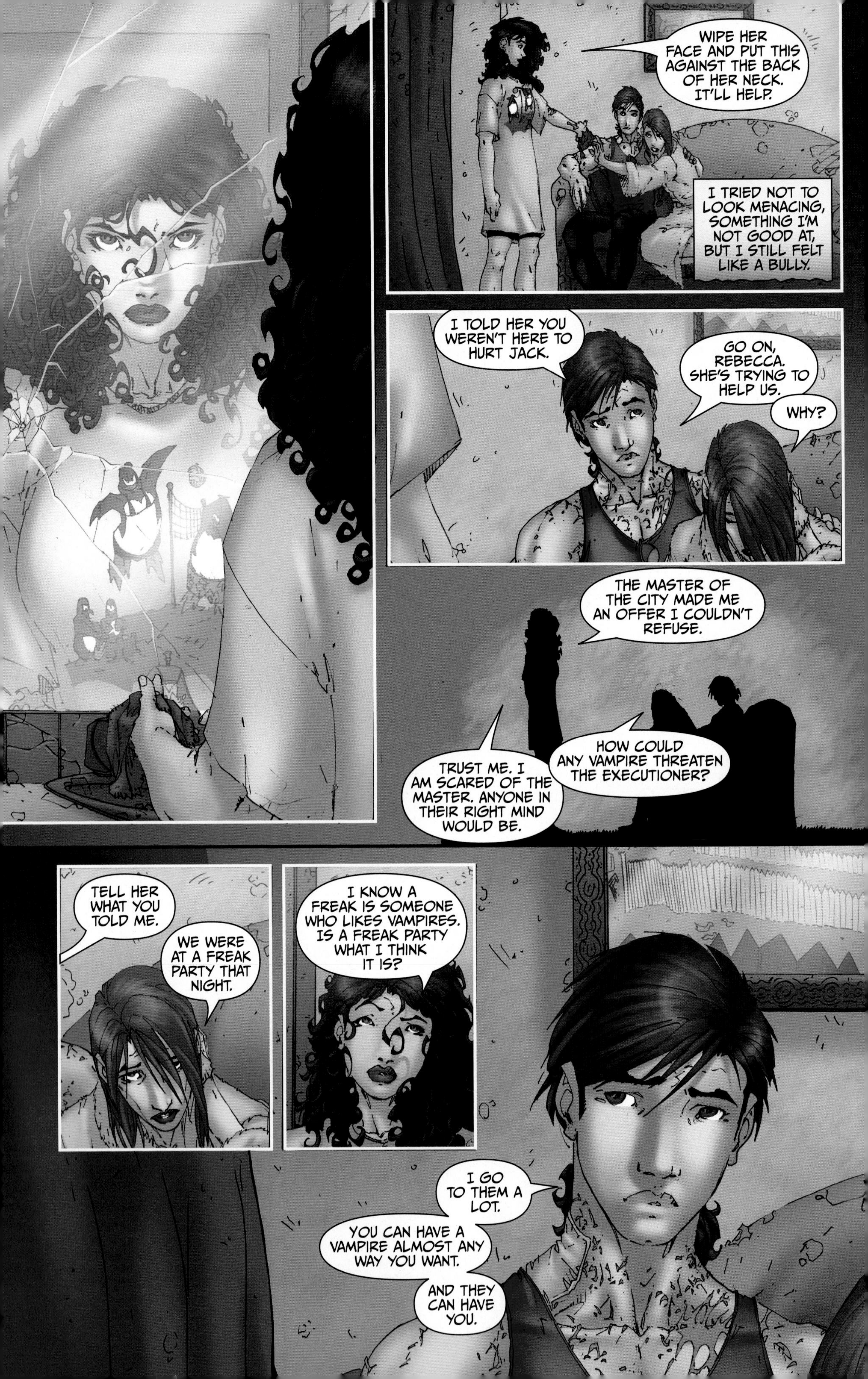
WIPE HER FACE AND PUT THIS AGAINST THE BACK OF HER NECK. IT'LL HELP.
I TRIED NOT TO LOOK MENACING, SOMETHING I'M NOT GOOD AT, BUT I STILL FELT LIKE A BULLY.
I TOLD HER YOU WEREN'T HERE TO HURT JACK.
GO ON, REBECCA. SHE'S TRYING TO HELP US.
WHY?
THE MASTER OF THE CITY MADE ME AN OFFER I COULDN'T REFUSE.
HOW COULD ANY VAMPIRE THREATEN THE EXECUTIONER?
TRUST ME. I AM SCARED OF THE MASTER. ANYONE IN THEIR RIGHT MIND WOULD BE.
TELL HER WHAT YOU TOLD ME.
WE WERE AT A FREAK PARTY THAT NIGHT.
I KNOW A FREAK IS SOMEONE WHO LIKES VAMPIRES. IS A FREAK PARTY WHAT I THINK IT IS?
I GO TO THEM A LOT.
YOU CAN HAVE A VAMPIRE ALMOST ANY WAY YOU WANT.
AND THEY CAN HAVE YOU.

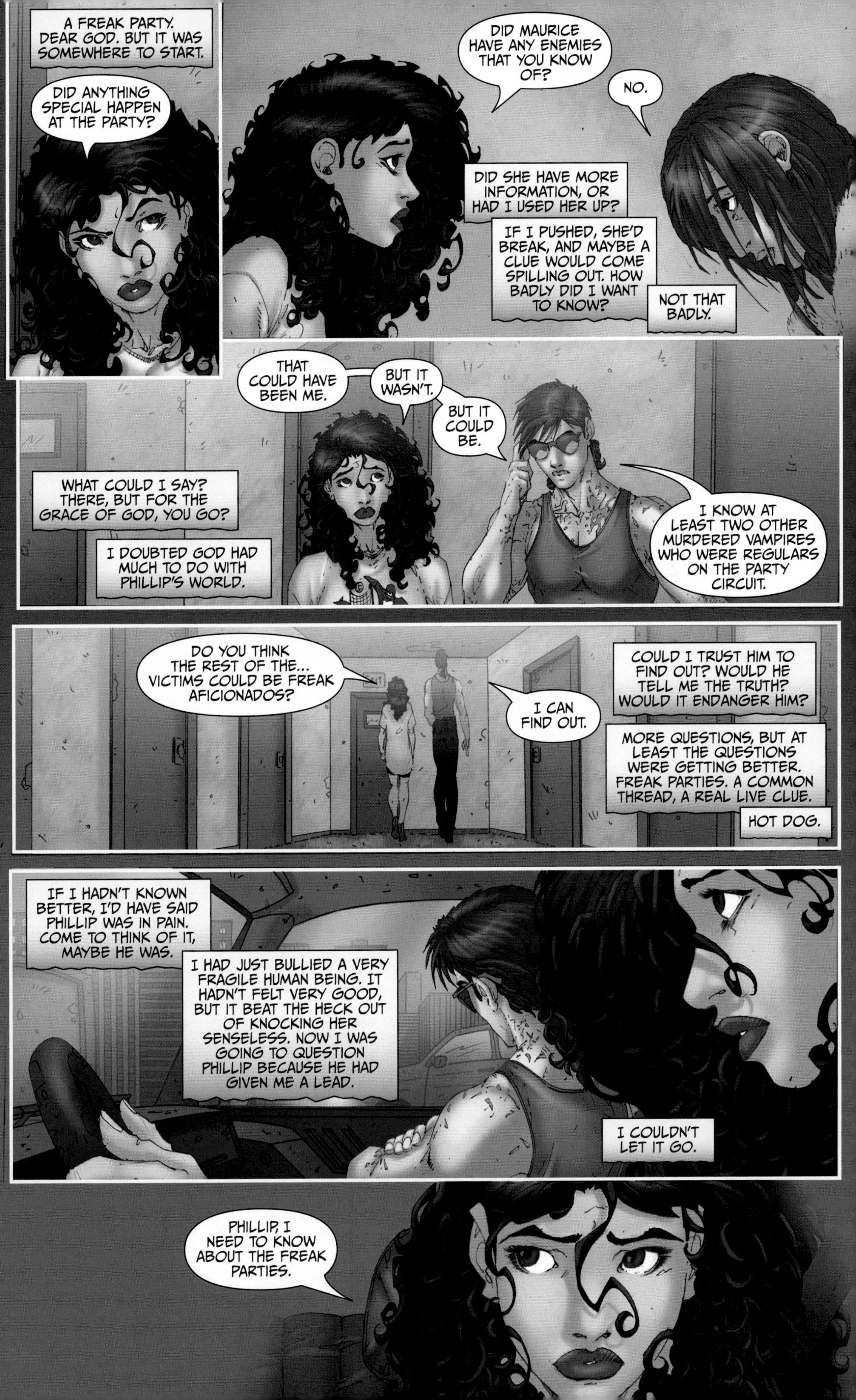
A FREAK PARTY. DEAR GOD. BUT IT WAS SOMEWHERE TO START.
DID ANYTHING SPECIAL HAPPEN AT THE PARTY?
DID MAURICE HAVE ANY ENEMIES THAT YOU KNOW OF?
NO.
DID SHE HAVE MORE INFORMATION, OR HAD I USED HER UP?
IF I PUSHED, SHE'D BREAK, AND MAYBE A CLUE WOULD COME SPILLING OUT. HOW BADLY DID I WANT TO KNOW?
NOT THAT BADLY.
THAT COULD HAVE BEEN ME.
BUT IT WASN'T.
BUT IT COULD BE.
WHAT COULD I SAY? THERE, BUT FOR THE GRACE OF GOD, YOU GO?
I DOUBTED GOD HAD MUCH TO DO WITH PHILLIP'S WORLD.
I KNOW AT LEAST TWO OTHER MURDERED VAMPIRES WHO WERE REGULARS ON THE PARTY CIRCUIT.
DO YOU THINK THE REST OF THE... VICTIMS COULD BE FREAK AFICIONADOS?
I CAN FIND OUT.
COULD I TRUST HIM TO FIND OUT? WOULD HE TELL ME THE TRUTH? WOULD IT ENDANGER HIM?
MORE QUESTIONS, BUT AT LEAST THE QUESTIONS WERE GETTING BETTER. FREAK PARTIES. A COMMON THREAD, A REAL LIVE CLUE.
HOT DOG.
IF I HADN'T KNOWN BETTER, I'D HAVE SAID PHILLIP WAS IN PAIN. COME TO THINK OF IT, MAYBE HE WAS.
I HAD JUST BULLIED A VERY FRAGILE HUMAN BEING. IT HADN'T FELT VERY GOOD, BUT IT BEAT THE HECK OUT OF KNOCKING HER SENSELESS. NOW I WAS GOING TO QUESTION PHILLIP BECAUSE HE HAD GIVEN ME A LEAD.
I COULDN'T LET IT GO.
PHILLIP, I NEED TO KNOW ABOUT THE FREAK PARTIES.

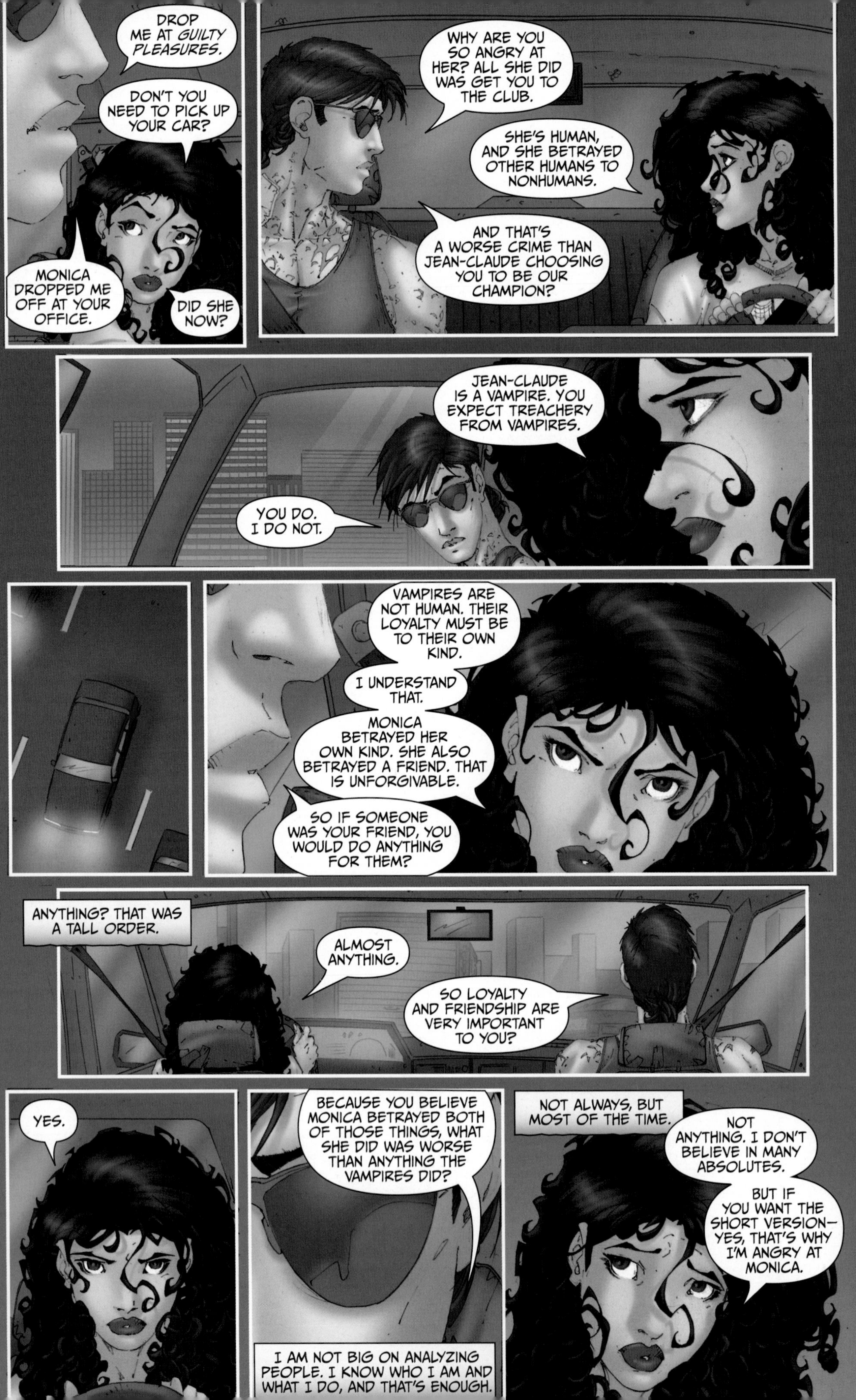
DROP ME AT *GUILTY PLEASURES.*
DON'T YOU NEED TO PICK UP YOUR CAR?
MONICA DROPPED ME OFF AT YOUR OFFICE.
DID SHE NOW?
WHY ARE YOU SO ANGRY AT HER? ALL SHE DID WAS GET YOU TO THE CLUB.
SHE'S HUMAN, AND SHE BETRAYED OTHER HUMANS TO NONHUMANS.
AND THAT'S A WORSE CRIME THAN JEAN-CLAUDE CHOOSING YOU TO BE OUR CHAMPION?
JEAN-CLAUDE IS A VAMPIRE. YOU EXPECT TREACHERY FROM VAMPIRES.
YOU DO. I DO NOT.
VAMPIRES ARE NOT HUMAN. THEIR LOYALTY MUST BE TO THEIR OWN KIND.
I UNDERSTAND THAT.
MONICA BETRAYED HER OWN KIND. SHE ALSO BETRAYED A FRIEND. THAT IS UNFORGIVABLE.
SO IF SOMEONE WAS YOUR FRIEND, YOU WOULD DO ANYTHING FOR THEM?
ANYTHING? THAT WAS A TALL ORDER.
ALMOST ANYTHING.
SO LOYALTY AND FRIENDSHIP ARE VERY IMPORTANT TO YOU?
YES.
BECAUSE YOU BELIEVE MONICA BETRAYED BOTH OF THOSE THINGS, WHAT SHE DID WAS WORSE THAN ANYTHING THE VAMPIRES DID?
I AM NOT BIG ON ANALYZING PEOPLE. I KNOW WHO I AM AND WHAT I DO, AND THAT'S ENOUGH.
NOT ALWAYS, BUT MOST OF THE TIME.
NOT ANYTHING. I DON'T BELIEVE IN MANY ABSOLUTES.
BUT IF YOU WANT THE SHORT VERSION— YES, THAT'S WHY I'M ANGRY AT MONICA.

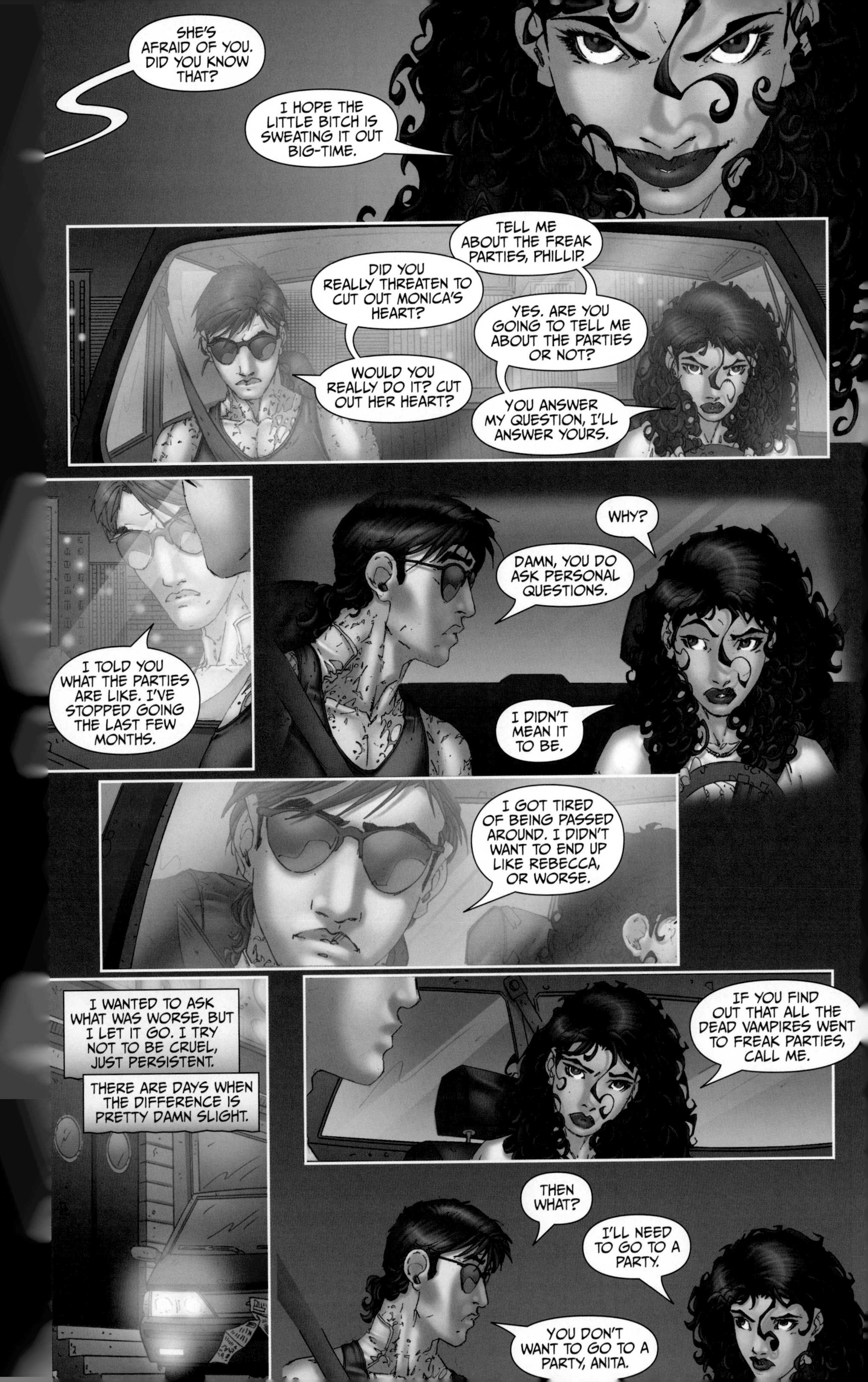
SHE'S AFRAID OF YOU. DID YOU KNOW THAT?
I HOPE THE LITTLE BITCH IS SWEATING IT OUT BIG-TIME.
TELL ME ABOUT THE FREAK PARTIES, PHILLIP.
DID YOU REALLY THREATEN TO CUT OUT MONICA'S HEART?
YES. ARE YOU GOING TO TELL ME ABOUT THE PARTIES OR NOT?
WOULD YOU REALLY DO IT? CUT OUT HER HEART?
YOU ANSWER MY QUESTION, I'LL ANSWER YOURS.
I TOLD YOU WHAT THE PARTIES ARE LIKE. I'VE STOPPED GOING THE LAST FEW MONTHS.
WHY?
DAMN, YOU DO ASK PERSONAL QUESTIONS.
I DIDN'T MEAN IT TO BE.
I GOT TIRED OF BEING PASSED AROUND. I DIDN'T WANT TO END UP LIKE REBECCA, OR WORSE.
I WANTED TO ASK WHAT WAS WORSE, BUT I LET IT GO. I TRY NOT TO BE CRUEL, JUST PERSISTENT.
THERE ARE DAYS WHEN THE DIFFERENCE IS PRETTY DAMN SLIGHT.
IF YOU FIND OUT THAT ALL THE DEAD VAMPIRES WENT TO FREAK PARTIES, CALL ME.
THEN WHAT?
I'LL NEED TO GO TO A PARTY.
YOU DON'T WANT TO GO TO A PARTY, ANITA.

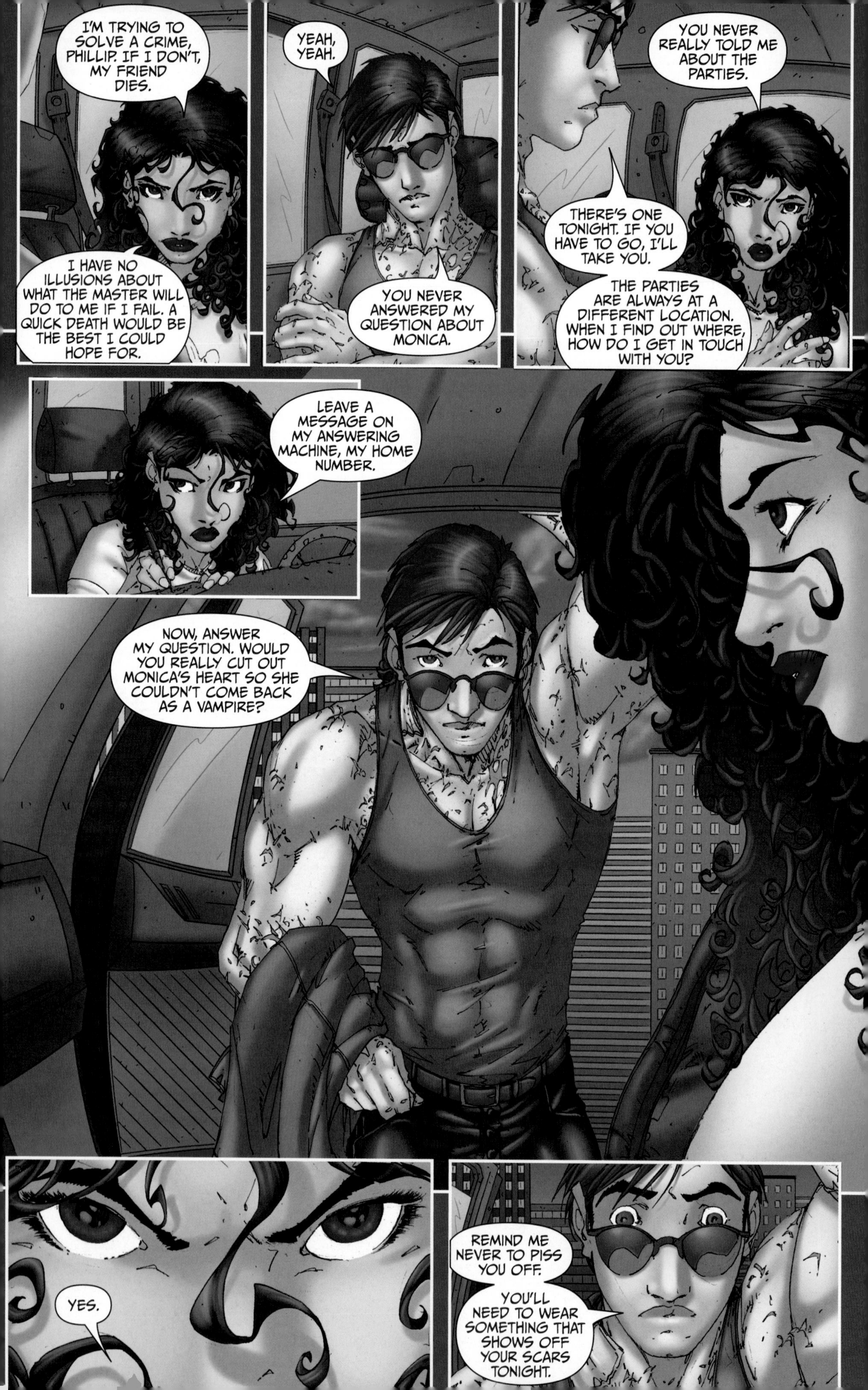
I'M TRYING TO SOLVE A CRIME, PHILLIP. IF I DON'T, MY FRIEND DIES.
I HAVE NO ILLUSIONS ABOUT WHAT THE MASTER WILL DO TO ME IF I FAIL. A QUICK DEATH WOULD BE THE BEST I COULD HOPE FOR.
YEAH, YEAH.
YOU NEVER ANSWERED MY QUESTION ABOUT MONICA.
YOU NEVER REALLY TOLD ME ABOUT THE PARTIES.
THERE'S ONE TONIGHT. IF YOU HAVE TO GO, I'LL TAKE YOU.
THE PARTIES ARE ALWAYS AT A DIFFERENT LOCATION. WHEN I FIND OUT WHERE, HOW DO I GET IN TOUCH WITH YOU?
LEAVE A MESSAGE ON MY ANSWERING MACHINE, MY HOME NUMBER.
NOW, ANSWER MY QUESTION. WOULD YOU REALLY CUT OUT MONICA'S HEART SO SHE COULDN'T COME BACK AS A VAMPIRE?
YES.
REMIND ME NEVER TO PISS YOU OFF.
YOU'LL NEED TO WEAR SOMETHING THAT SHOWS OFF YOUR SCARS TONIGHT.

ARE YOU AS GOOD AT BEING A FRIEND AS YOU ARE AN ENEMY?

WHAT COULD I SAY?

YOU DON'T WANT ME FOR AN ENEMY, PHILLIP. I MAKE A MUCH BETTER FRIEND.

YEAH, I'LL BET YOU DO.

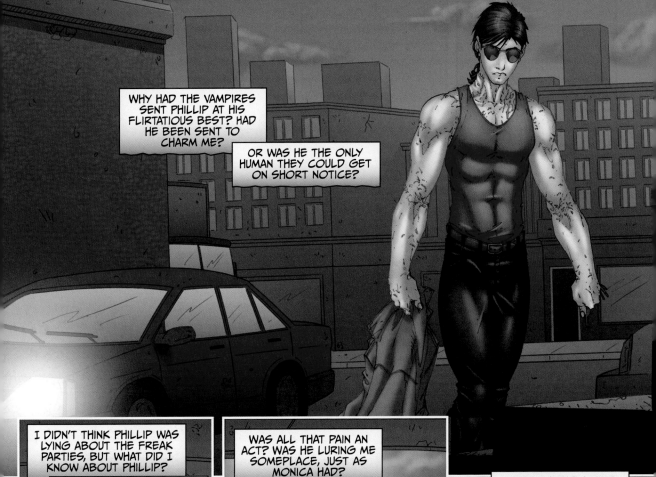

WHY HAD THE VAMPIRES SENT PHILLIP AT HIS FLIRTATIOUS BEST? HAD HE BEEN SENT TO CHARM ME?

OR WAS HE THE ONLY HUMAN THEY COULD GET ON SHORT NOTICE?

I DIDN'T THINK PHILLIP WAS LYING ABOUT THE FREAK PARTIES, BUT WHAT DID I KNOW ABOUT PHILLIP?

HE STRIPPED AT *GUILTY PLEASURES*, NOT EXACTLY A CHARACTER REFERENCE. EVEN WORSE, HE WAS A VAMPIRE JUNKIE.

WAS ALL THAT PAIN AN ACT? WAS HE LURING ME SOMEPLACE, JUST AS MONICA HAD?

I NEEDED TO KNOW. THERE WAS ONE PLACE I COULD GO THAT MIGHT HAVE THE ANSWERS, THE ONLY PLACE IN THE DISTRICT I WAS TRULY WELCOME.

DEAD DAVE'S, A NICE BAR THAT SERVED A MEAN HAMBURGER. THE PROPRIETOR WAS AN EX-COP WHO HAD BEEN KICKED OFF THE FORCE FOR BEING DEAD. PICKY, PICKY.

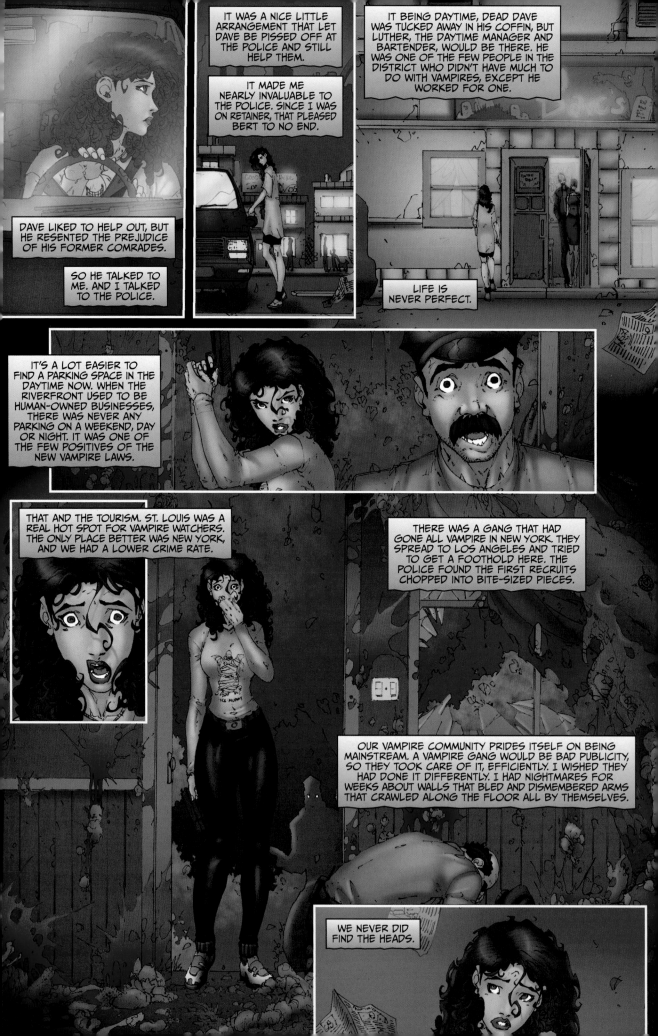

IT WAS A NICE LITTLE ARRANGEMENT THAT LET DAVE BE PISSED OFF AT THE POLICE AND STILL HELP THEM.

IT MADE ME NEARLY INVALUABLE TO THE POLICE. SINCE I WAS ON RETAINER, THAT PLEASED BERT TO NO END.

IT BEING DAYTIME, DEAD DAVE WAS TUCKED AWAY IN HIS COFFIN, BUT LUTHER, THE DAYTIME MANAGER AND BARTENDER, WOULD BE THERE. HE WAS ONE OF THE FEW PEOPLE IN THE DISTRICT WHO DIDN'T HAVE MUCH TO DO WITH VAMPIRES, EXCEPT HE WORKED FOR ONE.

DAVE LIKED TO HELP OUT, BUT HE RESENTED THE PREJUDICE OF HIS FORMER COMRADES.

SO HE TALKED TO ME. AND I TALKED TO THE POLICE.

LIFE IS NEVER PERFECT.

IT'S A LOT EASIER TO FIND A PARKING SPACE IN THE DAYTIME NOW. WHEN THE RIVERFRONT USED TO BE HUMAN-OWNED BUSINESSES, THERE WAS NEVER ANY PARKING ON A WEEKEND, DAY OR NIGHT. IT WAS ONE OF THE FEW POSITIVES OF THE NEW VAMPIRE LAWS.

THAT AND THE TOURISM. ST. LOUIS WAS A REAL HOT SPOT FOR VAMPIRE WATCHERS. THE ONLY PLACE BETTER WAS NEW YORK, AND WE HAD A LOWER CRIME RATE.

THERE WAS A GANG THAT HAD GONE ALL VAMPIRE IN NEW YORK. THEY SPREAD TO LOS ANGELES AND TRIED TO GET A FOOTHOLD HERE. THE POLICE FOUND THE FIRST RECRUITS CHOPPED INTO BITE-SIZED PIECES.

OUR VAMPIRE COMMUNITY PRIDES ITSELF ON BEING MAINSTREAM. A VAMPIRE GANG WOULD BE BAD PUBLICITY, SO THEY TOOK CARE OF IT, EFFICIENTLY. I WISHED THEY HAD DONE IT DIFFERENTLY. I HAD NIGHTMARES FOR WEEKS ABOUT WALLS THAT BLED AND DISMEMBERED ARMS THAT CRAWLED ALONG THE FLOOR ALL BY THEMSELVES.

WE NEVER DID FIND THE HEADS.

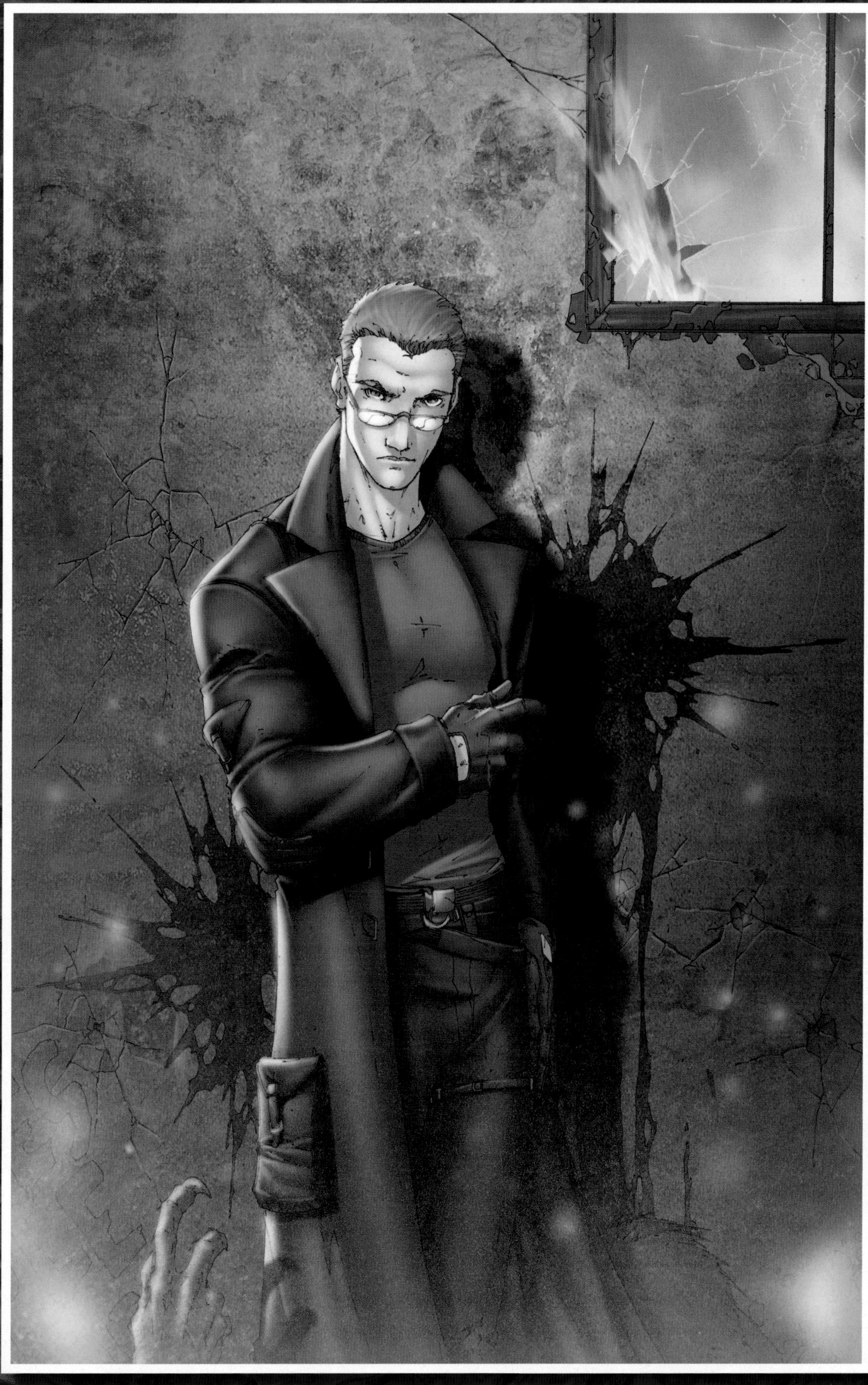

SIX

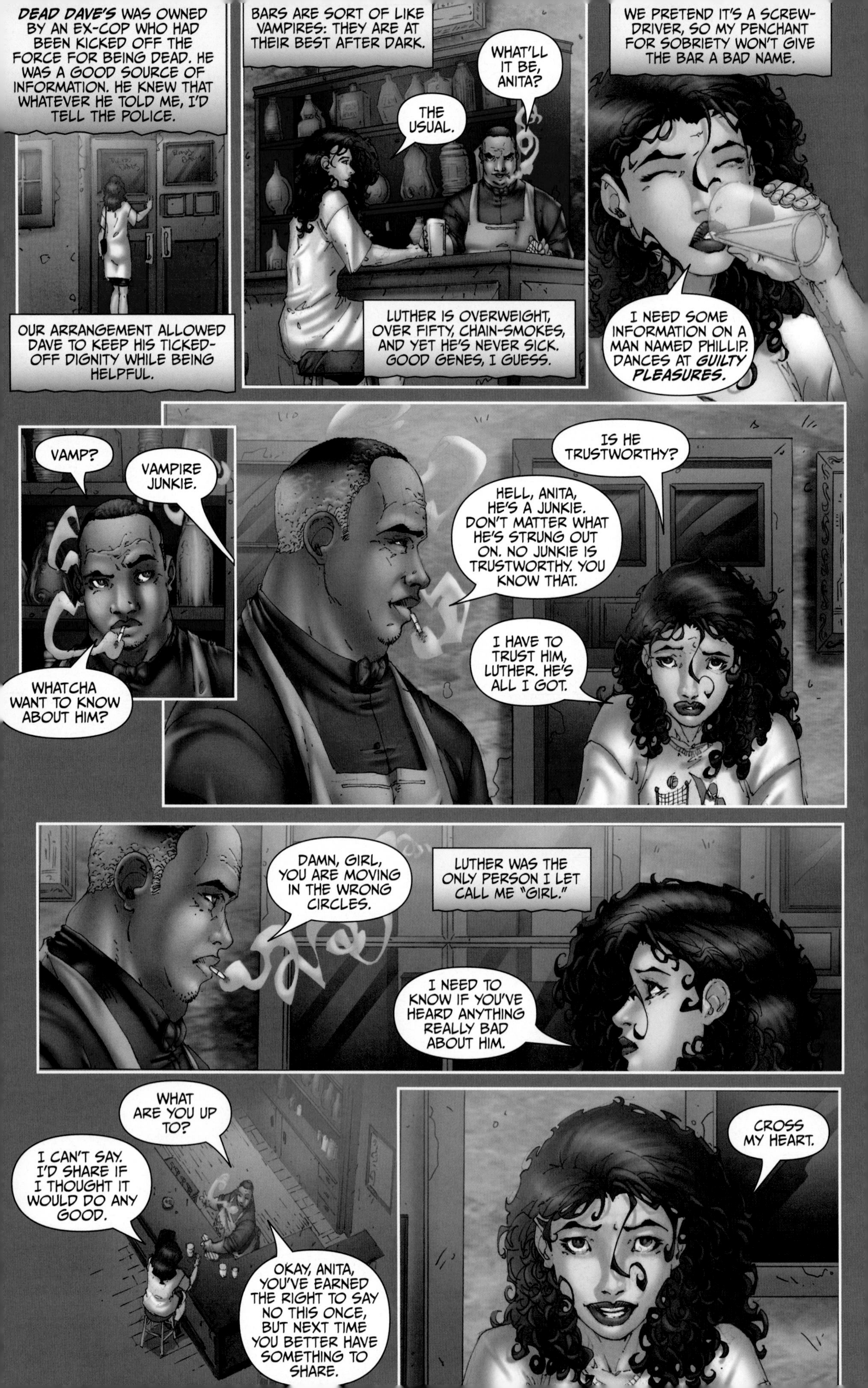
DEAD DAVE'S WAS OWNED BY AN EX-COP WHO HAD BEEN KICKED OFF THE FORCE FOR BEING DEAD. HE WAS A GOOD SOURCE OF INFORMATION. HE KNEW THAT WHATEVER HE TOLD ME, I'D TELL THE POLICE.
OUR ARRANGEMENT ALLOWED DAVE TO KEEP HIS TICKED-OFF DIGNITY WHILE BEING HELPFUL.
BARS ARE SORT OF LIKE VAMPIRES: THEY ARE AT THEIR BEST AFTER DARK.
WHAT'LL IT BE, ANITA?
THE USUAL.
LUTHER IS OVERWEIGHT, OVER FIFTY, CHAIN-SMOKES, AND YET HE'S NEVER SICK. GOOD GENES, I GUESS.
WE PRETEND IT'S A SCREW-DRIVER, SO MY PENCHANT FOR SOBRIETY WON'T GIVE THE BAR A BAD NAME.
I NEED SOME INFORMATION ON A MAN NAMED PHILLIP. DANCES AT GUILTY PLEASURES.
VAMP?
VAMPIRE JUNKIE.
WHATCHA WANT TO KNOW ABOUT HIM?
IS HE TRUSTWORTHY?
HELL, ANITA, HE'S A JUNKIE. DON'T MATTER WHAT HE'S STRUNG OUT ON. NO JUNKIE IS TRUSTWORTHY. YOU KNOW THAT.
I HAVE TO TRUST HIM, LUTHER. HE'S ALL I GOT.
DAMN, GIRL, YOU ARE MOVING IN THE WRONG CIRCLES.
LUTHER WAS THE ONLY PERSON I LET CALL ME "GIRL."
I NEED TO KNOW IF YOU'VE HEARD ANYTHING REALLY BAD ABOUT HIM.
WHAT ARE YOU UP TO?
I CAN'T SAY. I'D SHARE IF I THOUGHT IT WOULD DO ANY GOOD.
OKAY, ANITA, YOU'VE EARNED THE RIGHT TO SAY NO THIS ONCE, BUT NEXT TIME YOU BETTER HAVE SOMETHING TO SHARE.
CROSS MY HEART.

WE DON'T HAVE NO DIRT ON HIM, 'CEPT HE'S A JUNKIE AND HE DOES THE FREAK CIRCUIT.

YOU HAVEN'T HEARD ANYTHING ELSE ABOUT HIM?

CRAP, ANITA, THAT'S BAD ENOUGH.

HE'S A PROFESSIONAL VICTIM. MOST OF THE TALK AROUND HERE IS ABOUT THE PREDATORS, NOT THE SHEEP.

WAIT, I GOT SOMETHING. VAMP CALLS HIMSELF VALENTINE, WEARS A MASK. HE'S BEEN BRAGGING HE DID OL' PHILLIP THE FIRST TIME.

SO?

VALENTINE CLAIMS HE JUMPED THE BOY WHEN HE WAS SMALL. CLAIMS PHILLIP LIKED IT SO MUCH AND THAT'S WHY HE'S A JUNKIE.

DEAR GOD. HE EVER SAY HOW OLD PHILLIP WAS WHEN HE WAS ATTACKED?

WORD IS ANYTHING OVER TWELVE IS TOO OLD FOR VALENTINE, 'LESS IT'S REVENGE. WORD IS IF THE MASTER DIDN'T KEEP HIM IN LINE, HE'D BE DAMN DANGEROUS.

YOU BET HE'S DANGEROUS.

YOU KNOW HIM?

I NEED TO KNOW WHERE VALENTINE STAYS DURING THE DAY.

THAT'S TWO BITS OF INFORMATION FOR NOTHING. I DON'T THINK SO.

HE WEARS A MASK BECAUSE I DOUSED HIM WITH HOLY WATER ABOUT TWO YEARS AGO. UNTIL LAST NIGHT, I THOUGHT HE WAS DEAD.

HE'S GOING TO KILL ME, IF HE CAN.

YOU'RE AWFUL HARD TO KILL, ANITA.

THERE'S A FIRST TIME, LUTHER, AND THAT'S ALL IT TAKES.

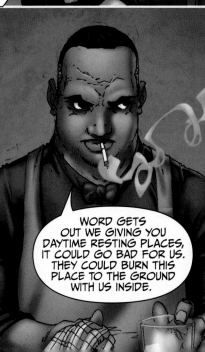

WORD GETS OUT WE GIVING YOU DAYTIME RESTING PLACES, IT COULD GO BAD FOR US. THEY COULD BURN THIS PLACE TO THE GROUND WITH US INSIDE.

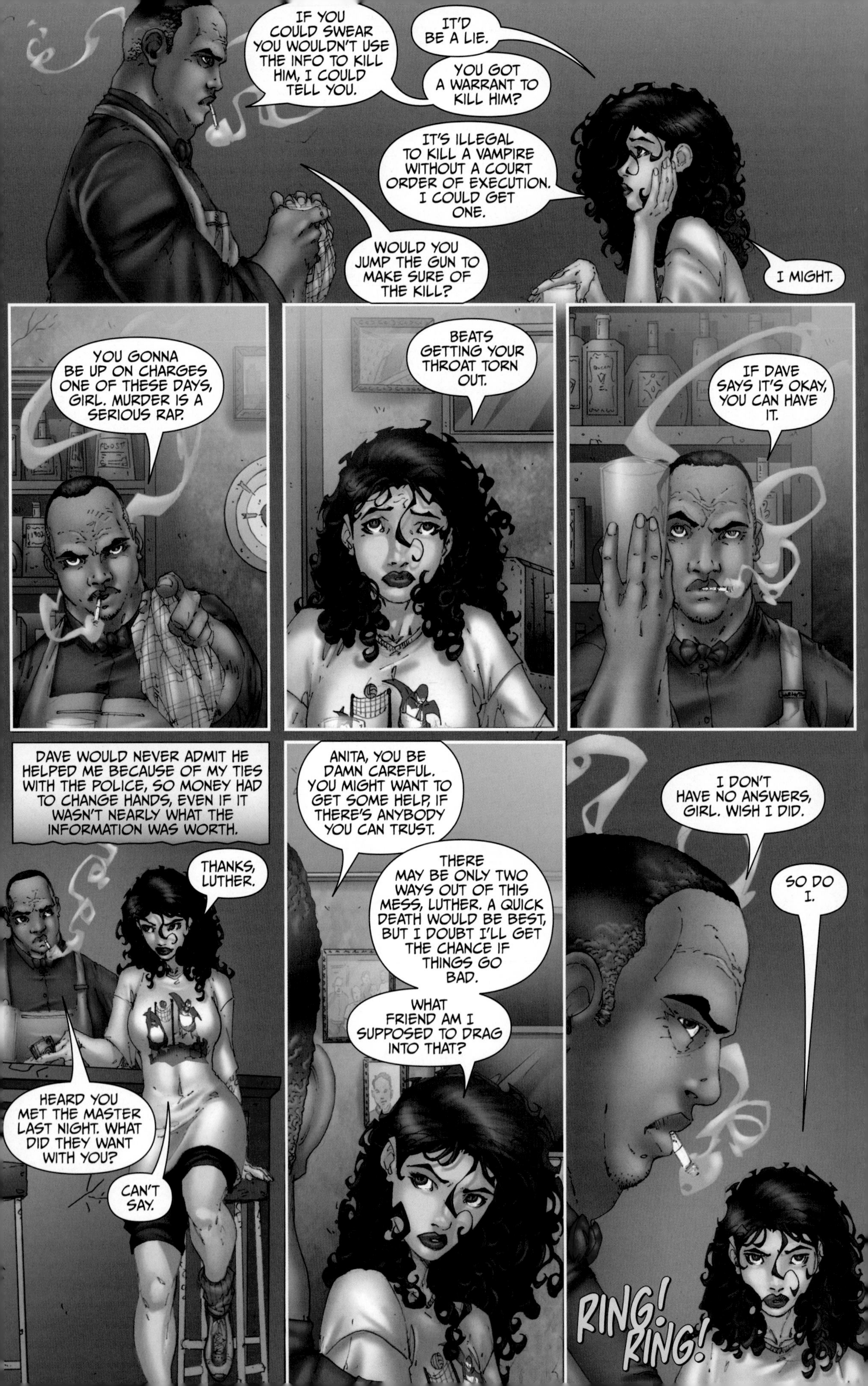
IF YOU COULD SWEAR YOU WOULDN'T USE THE INFO TO KILL HIM, I COULD TELL YOU.
IT'D BE A LIE.
YOU GOT A WARRANT TO KILL HIM?
IT'S ILLEGAL TO KILL A VAMPIRE WITHOUT A COURT ORDER OF EXECUTION. I COULD GET ONE.
WOULD YOU JUMP THE GUN TO MAKE SURE OF THE KILL?
I MIGHT.
YOU GONNA BE UP ON CHARGES ONE OF THESE DAYS, GIRL. MURDER IS A SERIOUS RAP.
BEATS GETTING YOUR THROAT TORN OUT.
IF DAVE SAYS IT'S OKAY, YOU CAN HAVE IT.
DAVE WOULD NEVER ADMIT HE HELPED ME BECAUSE OF MY TIES WITH THE POLICE, SO MONEY HAD TO CHANGE HANDS, EVEN IF IT WASN'T NEARLY WHAT THE INFORMATION WAS WORTH.
THANKS, LUTHER.
HEARD YOU MET THE MASTER LAST NIGHT. WHAT DID THEY WANT WITH YOU?
CAN'T SAY.
ANITA, YOU BE DAMN CAREFUL. YOU MIGHT WANT TO GET SOME HELP, IF THERE'S ANYBODY YOU CAN TRUST.
THERE MAY BE ONLY TWO WAYS OUT OF THIS MESS, LUTHER. A QUICK DEATH WOULD BE BEST, BUT I DOUBT I'LL GET THE CHANCE IF THINGS GO BAD.
WHAT FRIEND AM I SUPPOSED TO DRAG INTO THAT?
I DON'T HAVE NO ANSWERS, GIRL. WISH I DID.
SO DO I.
RING! RING!

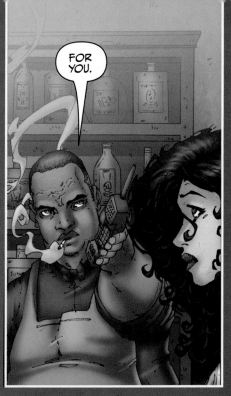

FOR YOU.

YES.

IT'S RONNIE.

YOU HAVE SOMETHING?

THERE'S A RUMOR GOING AROUND -- HUMANS AGAINST VAMPIRES. A DEATH SQUAD DESIGNED TO WIPE THE VAMPIRES OFF THE FACE OF THE EARTH.

YOU HAVE PROOF, A WITNESS?

NOT YET.

RONNIE...

COME ON, ANITA. THIS IS GOOD NEWS.

I CAN'T TAKE A RUMOR ABOUT H.A.V. TO THE MASTER. THE VAMPIRES WOULD SLAUGHTER THEM. WE'RE NOT EVEN SURE THAT H.A.V. IS REALLY BEHIND THE MURDERS.

ALL RIGHT, ALL RIGHT. I'LL HAVE SOMETHING MORE CONCRETE BY TOMORROW, I PROMISE.

THANKS, RONNIE.

WHAT ARE FRIENDS FOR? BESIDES, BERT'S GOING TO HAVE TO PAY FOR OVERTIME AND BRIBES.

EITHER WAY, I LOVE THE LOOK OF PAIN WHEN HE HAS TO PART WITH MONEY.

ME, TOO.

WHAT ARE YOU DOING TONIGHT?

GOING TO A PARTY.

WHAT?

IT'S YOUR BASIC TRADE BODILY FLUIDS TYPE PARTY, EXCEPT WITH VAMPIRES. I'LL BE UNDERCOVER.

THAT IS VERY FREAKY.

YOU'RE GOING IN WITHOUT BACKUP, AREN'T YOU?

YOU'RE ALONE.

BUT I'M NOT SURROUNDED BY VAMPIRES AND FREAKAZOIDS.

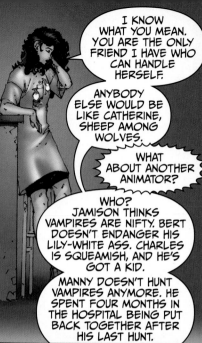

I KNOW WHAT YOU MEAN. YOU ARE THE ONLY FRIEND I HAVE WHO CAN HANDLE HERSELF.

ANYBODY ELSE WOULD BE LIKE CATHERINE, SHEEP AMONG WOLVES.

WHAT ABOUT ANOTHER ANIMATOR?

WHO? JAMISON THINKS VAMPIRES ARE NIFTY. BERT DOESN'T ENDANGER HIS LILY-WHITE ASS. CHARLES IS SQUEAMISH, AND HE'S GOT A KID.

MANNY DOESN'T HUNT VAMPIRES ANYMORE. HE SPENT FOUR MONTHS IN THE HOSPITAL BEING PUT BACK TOGETHER AFTER HIS LAST HUNT.

YOU WERE IN THE HOSPITAL, TOO.

A BROKEN ARM AND BUSTED COLLARBONE WERE MY WORST INJURIES, RONNIE. MANNY ALMOST DIED.

BESIDES, HE'S GOT A WIFE AND FOUR KIDS.

IF YOU'RE AT *HAV* HEADQUARTERS, THAT LAST PART IS DEBATABLE.

DON'T BE CUTE, YOU KNOW WHAT I MEAN.

MANNY WAS THE ANIMATOR WHO TRAINED ME. HE WAS A TRADITIONALIST, A STAKE-AND-GARLIC MAN. TWO YEARS AGO, ROSITA, MANNY'S WIFE, HAD BEGGED ME NOT TO ENDANGER HER HUSBAND ANYMORE.

FIFTY-TWO WAS TOO OLD TO HUNT VAMPIRES, SHE HAD SAID. WHAT WOULD HAPPEN TO HER AND THE CHILDREN? SOMEHOW I HAD GOTTEN ALL THE BLAME. SHE MADE ME SWEAR BEFORE GOD THAT I WOULD NEVER AGAIN ASK MANNY TO JOIN ME ON A HUNT.

IF SHE HADN'T CRIED, I WOULD HAVE HELD OUT. CRYING WAS DAMNED UNFAIR IN A FIGHT. YOU'LL PROMISE ANYTHING JUST TO STOP THE TEARS.

ALL RIGHT, BUT YOU BE CAREFUL.

CAREFUL AS A VIRGIN ON HER WEDDING NIGHT.

YOU ARE INCORRIGIBLE. WATCH YOUR BACK.

YOU DO THE SAME.

GOOD NEWS?

YEAH.

HUMANS AGAINST VAMPIRES HAD A DEATH SQUAD. MAYBE. BUT MAYBE WAS BETTER THAN WHAT I'D HAD BEFORE.

IF I WAS ON THE RIGHT TRACK, I'D ATTRACT ATTENTION SOON. WHICH MEANT SOMEONE MIGHT TRY TO KILL ME. WOULDN'T THAT BE FUN?

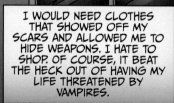

I WOULD NEED CLOTHES THAT SHOWED OFF MY SCARS AND ALLOWED ME TO HIDE WEAPONS. I HATE TO SHOP. OF COURSE, IT BEAT THE HECK OUT OF HAVING MY LIFE THREATENED BY VAMPIRES.

I COULD GO SHOPPING NOW AND BE THREATENED BY VAMPIRES IN THE EVENING. A PERFECT WAY TO SPEND A SATURDAY NIGHT.

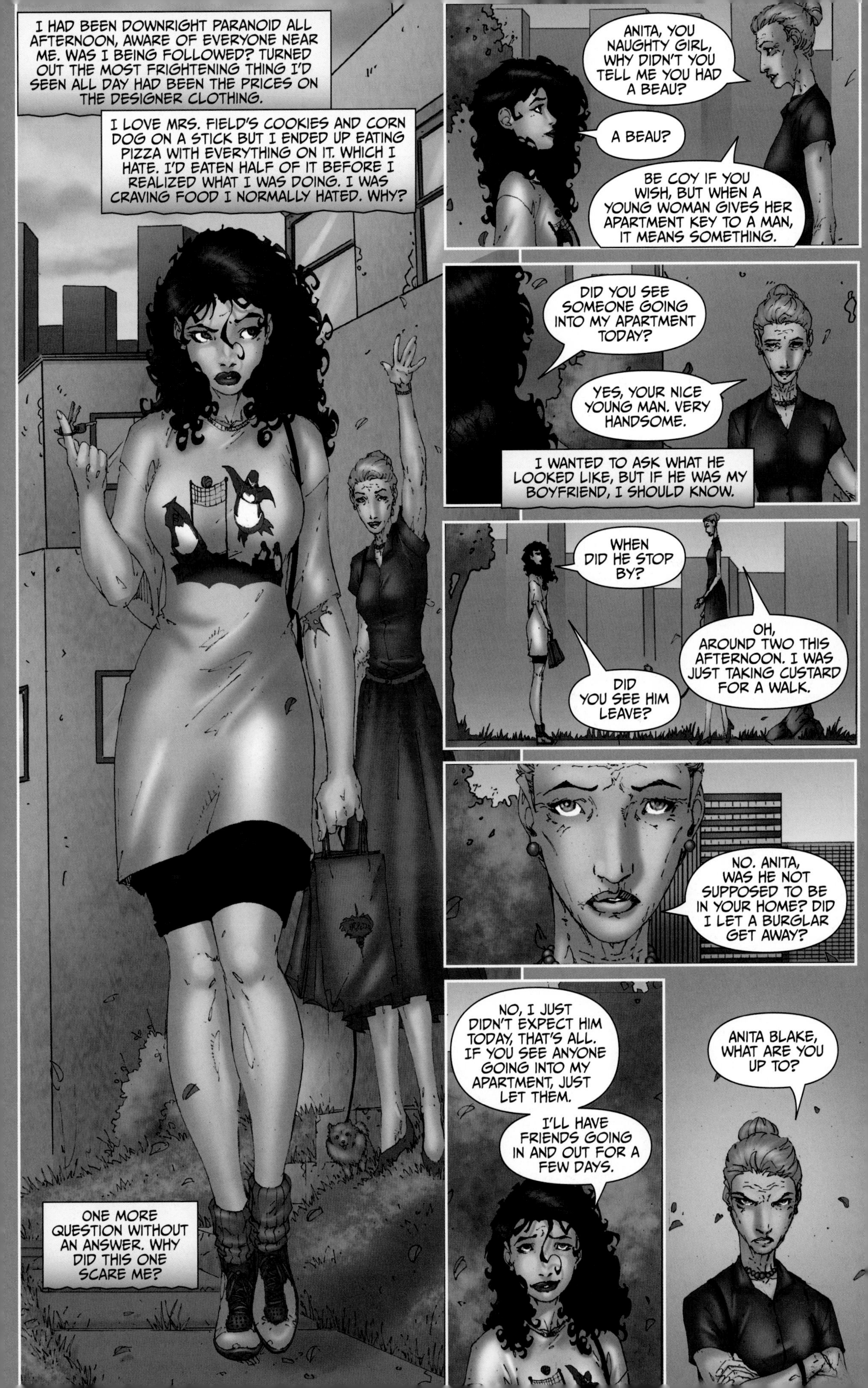
I HAD BEEN DOWNRIGHT PARANOID ALL AFTERNOON, AWARE OF EVERYONE NEAR ME. WAS I BEING FOLLOWED? TURNED OUT THE MOST FRIGHTENING THING I'D SEEN ALL DAY HAD BEEN THE PRICES ON THE DESIGNER CLOTHING.
I LOVE MRS. FIELD'S COOKIES AND CORN DOG ON A STICK BUT I ENDED UP EATING PIZZA WITH EVERYTHING ON IT. WHICH I HATE. I'D EATEN HALF OF IT BEFORE I REALIZED WHAT I WAS DOING. I WAS CRAVING FOOD I NORMALLY HATED. WHY?
ONE MORE QUESTION WITHOUT AN ANSWER. WHY DID THIS ONE SCARE ME?
ANITA, YOU NAUGHTY GIRL, WHY DIDN'T YOU TELL ME YOU HAD A BEAU?
A BEAU?
BE COY IF YOU WISH, BUT WHEN A YOUNG WOMAN GIVES HER APARTMENT KEY TO A MAN, IT MEANS SOMETHING.
DID YOU SEE SOMEONE GOING INTO MY APARTMENT TODAY?
YES, YOUR NICE YOUNG MAN. VERY HANDSOME.
I WANTED TO ASK WHAT HE LOOKED LIKE, BUT IF HE WAS MY BOYFRIEND, I SHOULD KNOW.
WHEN DID HE STOP BY?
OH, AROUND TWO THIS AFTERNOON. I WAS JUST TAKING CUSTARD FOR A WALK.
DID YOU SEE HIM LEAVE?
NO. ANITA, WAS HE NOT SUPPOSED TO BE IN YOUR HOME? DID I LET A BURGLAR GET AWAY?
NO, I JUST DIDN'T EXPECT HIM TODAY, THAT'S ALL. IF YOU SEE ANYONE GOING INTO MY APARTMENT, JUST LET THEM.
I'LL HAVE FRIENDS GOING IN AND OUT FOR A FEW DAYS.
ANITA BLAKE, WHAT ARE YOU UP TO?

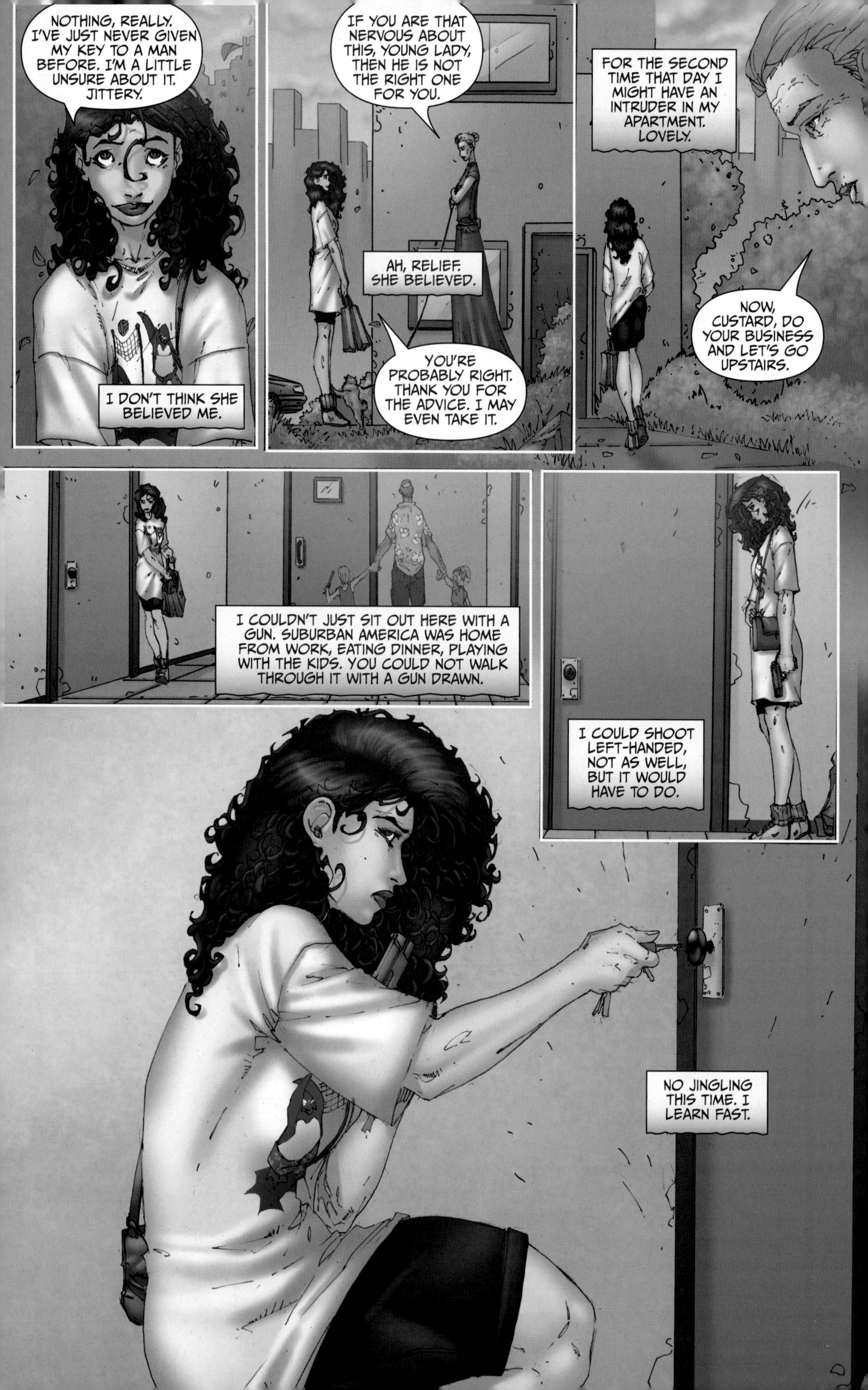
NOTHING, REALLY. I'VE JUST NEVER GIVEN MY KEY TO A MAN BEFORE. I'M A LITTLE UNSURE ABOUT IT. JITTERY.
I DON'T THINK SHE BELIEVED ME.
IF YOU ARE THAT NERVOUS ABOUT THIS, YOUNG LADY, THEN HE IS NOT THE RIGHT ONE FOR YOU.
AH, RELIEF. SHE BELIEVED.
YOU'RE PROBABLY RIGHT. THANK YOU FOR THE ADVICE. I MAY EVEN TAKE IT.
FOR THE SECOND TIME THAT DAY I MIGHT HAVE AN INTRUDER IN MY APARTMENT. LOVELY.
NOW, CUSTARD, DO YOUR BUSINESS AND LET'S GO UPSTAIRS.
I COULDN'T JUST SIT OUT HERE WITH A GUN. SUBURBAN AMERICA WAS HOME FROM WORK, EATING DINNER, PLAYING WITH THE KIDS. YOU COULD NOT WALK THROUGH IT WITH A GUN DRAWN.
I COULD SHOOT LEFT-HANDED, NOT AS WELL, BUT IT WOULD HAVE TO DO.
NO JINGLING THIS TIME. I LEARN FAST.

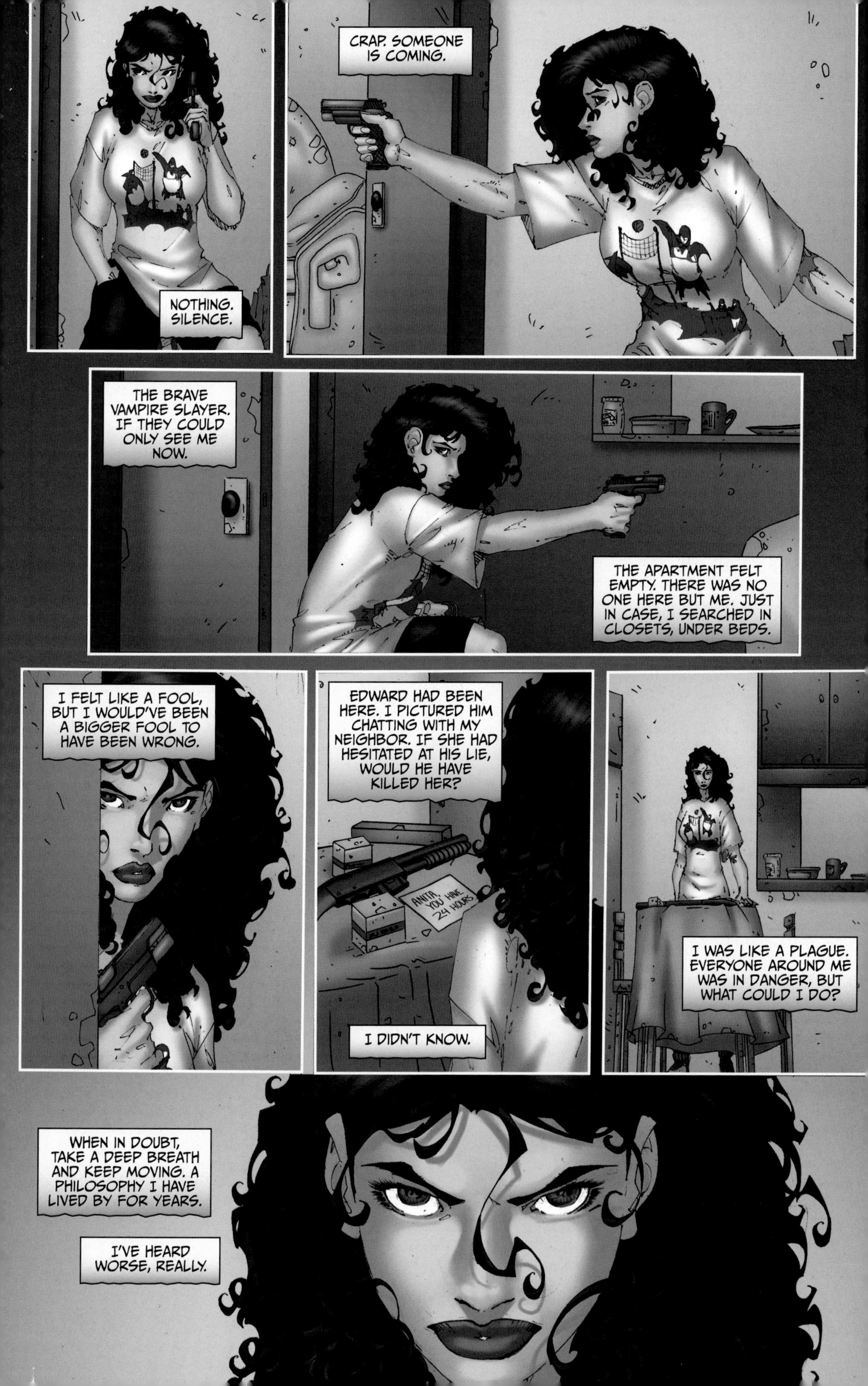
NOTHING. SILENCE.
CRAP. SOMEONE IS COMING.
THE BRAVE VAMPIRE SLAYER. IF THEY COULD ONLY SEE ME NOW.
THE APARTMENT FELT EMPTY. THERE WAS NO ONE HERE BUT ME. JUST IN CASE, I SEARCHED IN CLOSETS, UNDER BEDS.
I FELT LIKE A FOOL, BUT I WOULD'VE BEEN A BIGGER FOOL TO HAVE BEEN WRONG.
EDWARD HAD BEEN HERE. I PICTURED HIM CHATTING WITH MY NEIGHBOR. IF SHE HAD HESITATED AT HIS LIE, WOULD HE HAVE KILLED HER?
ANITA, YOU HAVE 24 HOURS.
I DIDN'T KNOW.
I WAS LIKE A PLAGUE. EVERYONE AROUND ME WAS IN DANGER, BUT WHAT COULD I DO?
WHEN IN DOUBT, TAKE A DEEP BREATH AND KEEP MOVING. A PHILOSOPHY I HAVE LIVED BY FOR YEARS.
I'VE HEARD WORSE, REALLY.

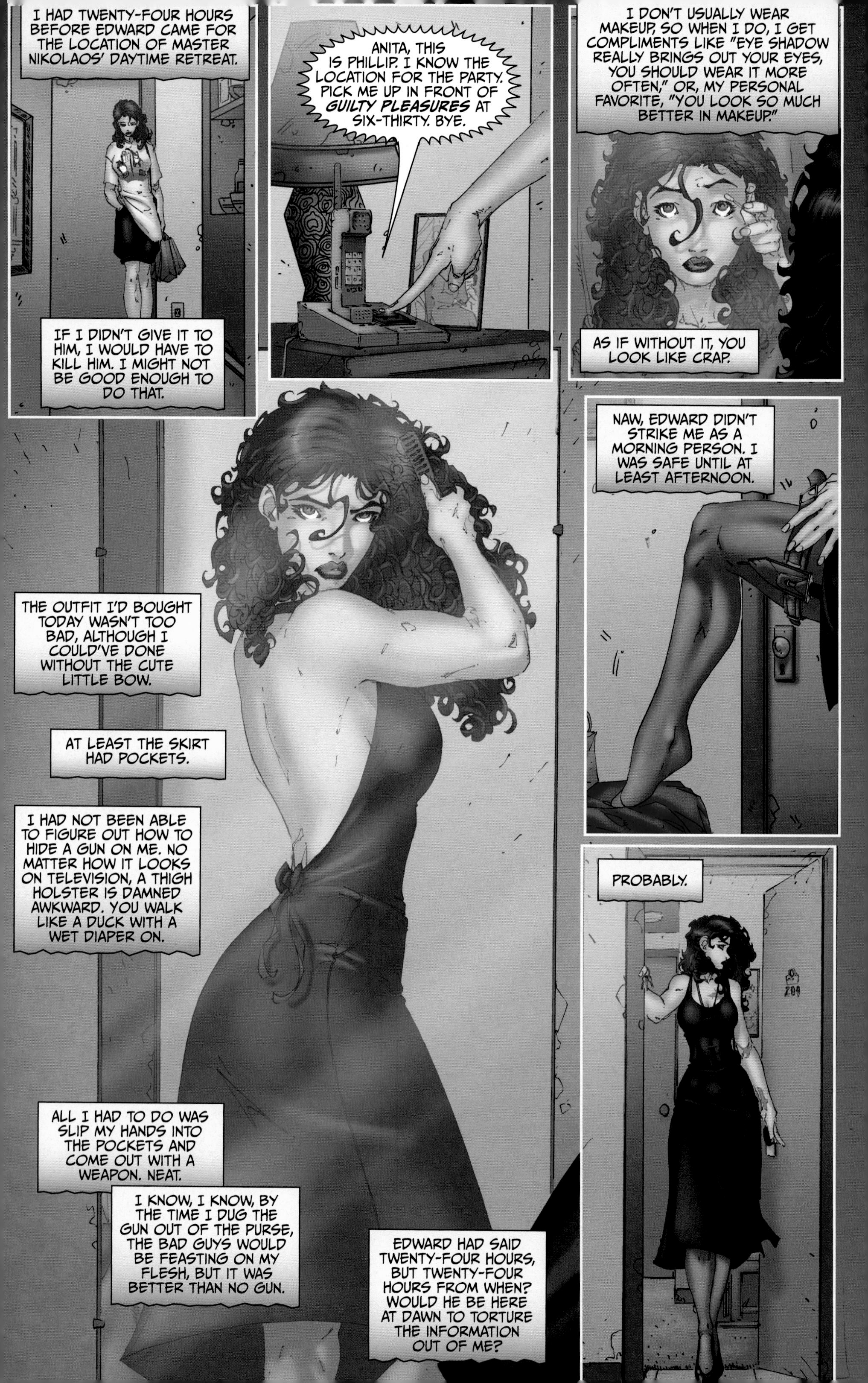
I HAD TWENTY-FOUR HOURS BEFORE EDWARD CAME FOR THE LOCATION OF MASTER NIKOLAOS' DAYTIME RETREAT.
IF I DIDN'T GIVE IT TO HIM, I WOULD HAVE TO KILL HIM. I MIGHT NOT BE GOOD ENOUGH TO DO THAT.
ANITA, THIS IS PHILLIP. I KNOW THE LOCATION FOR THE PARTY. PICK ME UP IN FRONT OF GUILTY PLEASURES AT SIX-THIRTY. BYE.
I DON'T USUALLY WEAR MAKEUP, SO WHEN I DO, I GET COMPLIMENTS LIKE "EYE SHADOW REALLY BRINGS OUT YOUR EYES, YOU SHOULD WEAR IT MORE OFTEN," OR, MY PERSONAL FAVORITE, "YOU LOOK SO MUCH BETTER IN MAKEUP."
AS IF WITHOUT IT, YOU LOOK LIKE CRAP.
THE OUTFIT I'D BOUGHT TODAY WASN'T TOO BAD, ALTHOUGH I COULD'VE DONE WITHOUT THE CUTE LITTLE BOW.
AT LEAST THE SKIRT HAD POCKETS.
I HAD NOT BEEN ABLE TO FIGURE OUT HOW TO HIDE A GUN ON ME. NO MATTER HOW IT LOOKS ON TELEVISION, A THIGH HOLSTER IS DAMNED AWKWARD. YOU WALK LIKE A DUCK WITH A WET DIAPER ON.
ALL I HAD TO DO WAS SLIP MY HANDS INTO THE POCKETS AND COME OUT WITH A WEAPON. NEAT.
I KNOW, I KNOW, BY THE TIME I DUG THE GUN OUT OF THE PURSE, THE BAD GUYS WOULD BE FEASTING ON MY FLESH, BUT IT WAS BETTER THAN NO GUN.
EDWARD HAD SAID TWENTY-FOUR HOURS, BUT TWENTY-FOUR HOURS FROM WHEN? WOULD HE BE HERE AT DAWN TO TORTURE THE INFORMATION OUT OF ME?
NAW, EDWARD DIDN'T STRIKE ME AS A MORNING PERSON. I WAS SAFE UNTIL AT LEAST AFTERNOON.
PROBABLY.
204

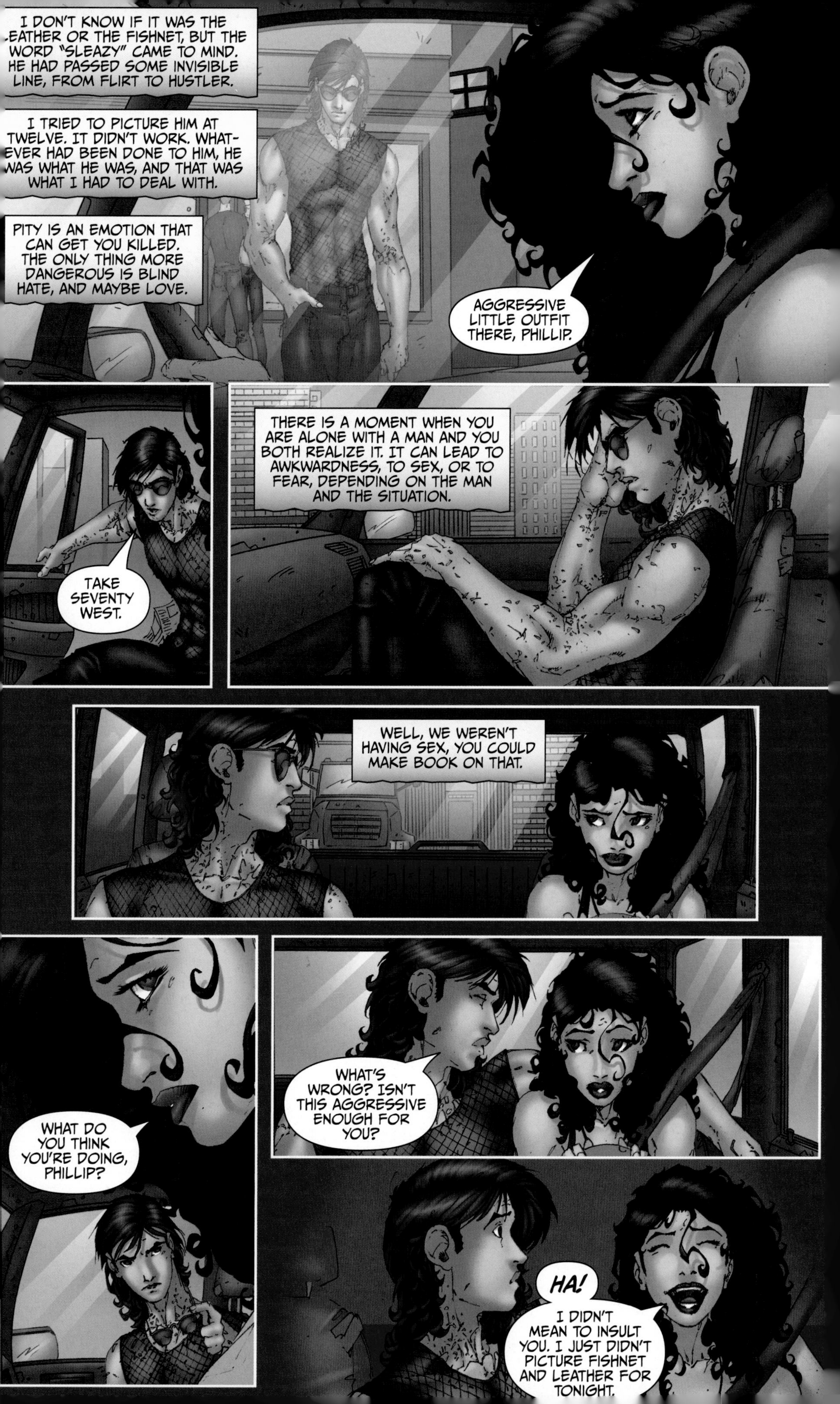
I DON'T KNOW IF IT WAS THE LEATHER OR THE FISHNET, BUT THE WORD "SLEAZY" CAME TO MIND. HE HAD PASSED SOME INVISIBLE LINE, FROM FLIRT TO HUSTLER.
I TRIED TO PICTURE HIM AT TWELVE. IT DIDN'T WORK. WHATEVER HAD BEEN DONE TO HIM, HE WAS WHAT HE WAS, AND THAT WAS WHAT I HAD TO DEAL WITH.
PITY IS AN EMOTION THAT CAN GET YOU KILLED. THE ONLY THING MORE DANGEROUS IS BLIND HATE, AND MAYBE LOVE.
AGGRESSIVE LITTLE OUTFIT THERE, PHILLIP.
TAKE SEVENTY WEST.
THERE IS A MOMENT WHEN YOU ARE ALONE WITH A MAN AND YOU BOTH REALIZE IT. IT CAN LEAD TO AWKWARDNESS, TO SEX, OR TO FEAR, DEPENDING ON THE MAN AND THE SITUATION.
WELL, WE WEREN'T HAVING SEX, YOU COULD MAKE BOOK ON THAT.
WHAT DO YOU THINK YOU'RE DOING, PHILLIP?
WHAT'S WRONG? ISN'T THIS AGGRESSIVE ENOUGH FOR YOU?
HA!
I DIDN'T MEAN TO INSULT YOU. I JUST DIDN'T PICTURE FISHNET AND LEATHER FOR TONIGHT.

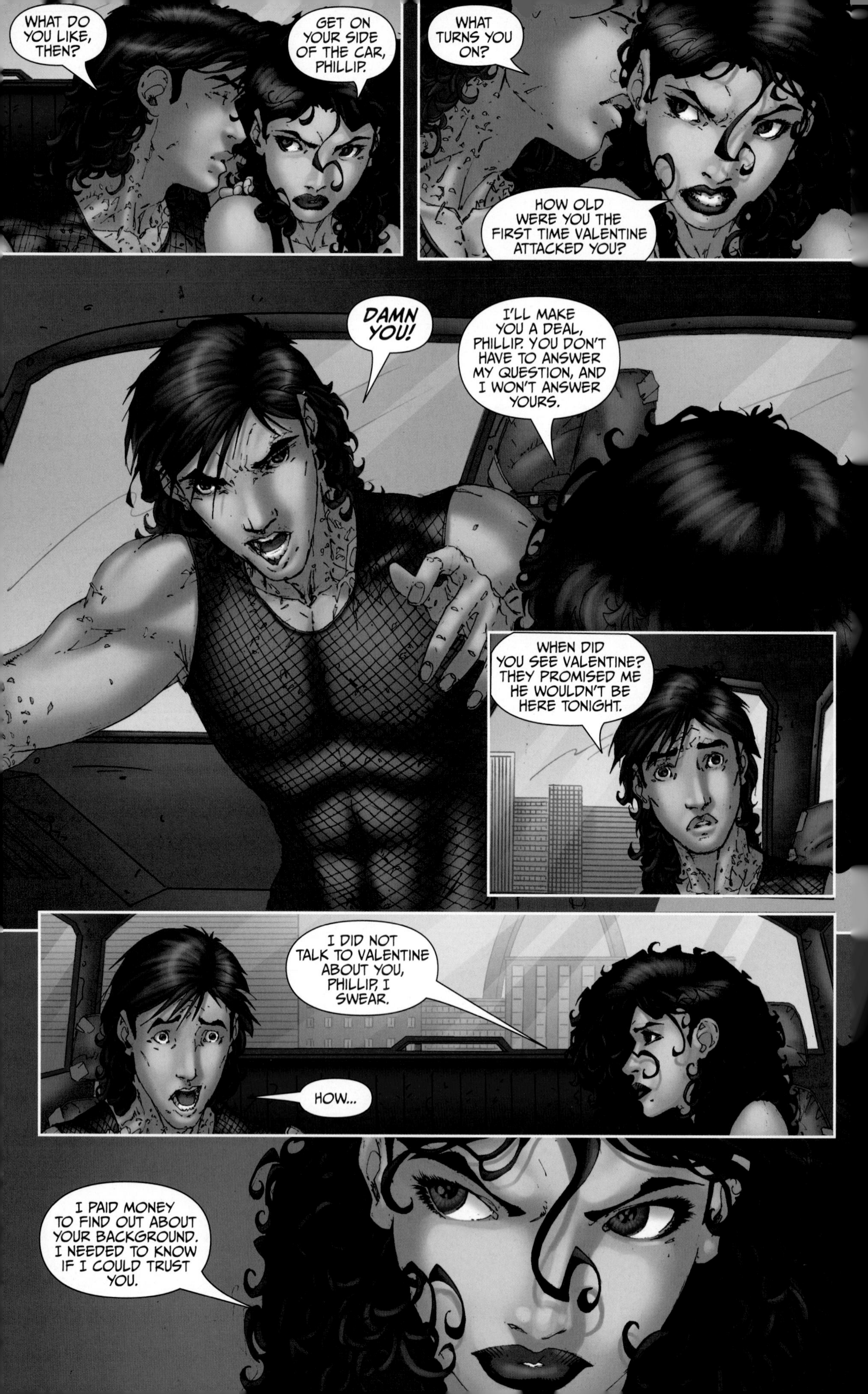
WHAT DO YOU LIKE, THEN?
GET ON YOUR SIDE OF THE CAR, PHILLIP.
WHAT TURNS YOU ON?
HOW OLD WERE YOU THE FIRST TIME VALENTINE ATTACKED YOU?
DAMN YOU!
I'LL MAKE YOU A DEAL, PHILLIP. YOU DON'T HAVE TO ANSWER MY QUESTION, AND I WON'T ANSWER YOURS.
WHEN DID YOU SEE VALENTINE? THEY PROMISED ME HE WOULDN'T BE HERE TONIGHT.
I DID NOT TALK TO VALENTINE ABOUT YOU, PHILLIP, I SWEAR.
HOW...
I PAID MONEY TO FIND OUT ABOUT YOUR BACKGROUND. I NEEDED TO KNOW IF I COULD TRUST YOU.

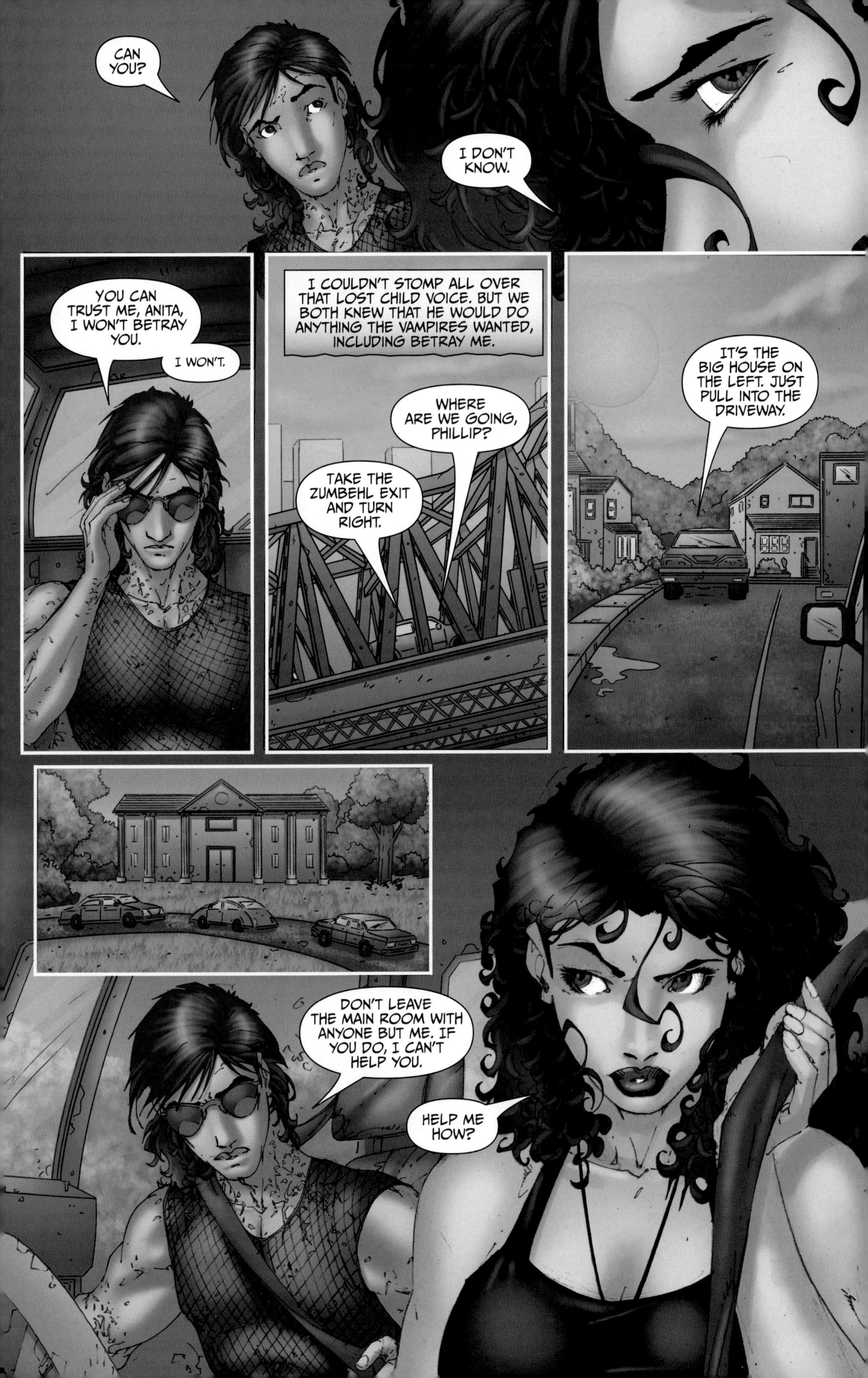
CAN YOU?
I DON'T KNOW.
YOU CAN TRUST ME, ANITA, I WON'T BETRAY YOU.
I WON'T.
I COULDN'T STOMP ALL OVER THAT LOST CHILD VOICE. BUT WE BOTH KNEW THAT HE WOULD DO ANYTHING THE VAMPIRES WANTED, INCLUDING BETRAY ME.
WHERE ARE WE GOING, PHILLIP?
TAKE THE ZUMBEHL EXIT AND TURN RIGHT.
IT'S THE BIG HOUSE ON THE LEFT. JUST PULL INTO THE DRIVEWAY.
DON'T LEAVE THE MAIN ROOM WITH ANYONE BUT ME. IF YOU DO, I CAN'T HELP YOU.
HELP ME HOW?

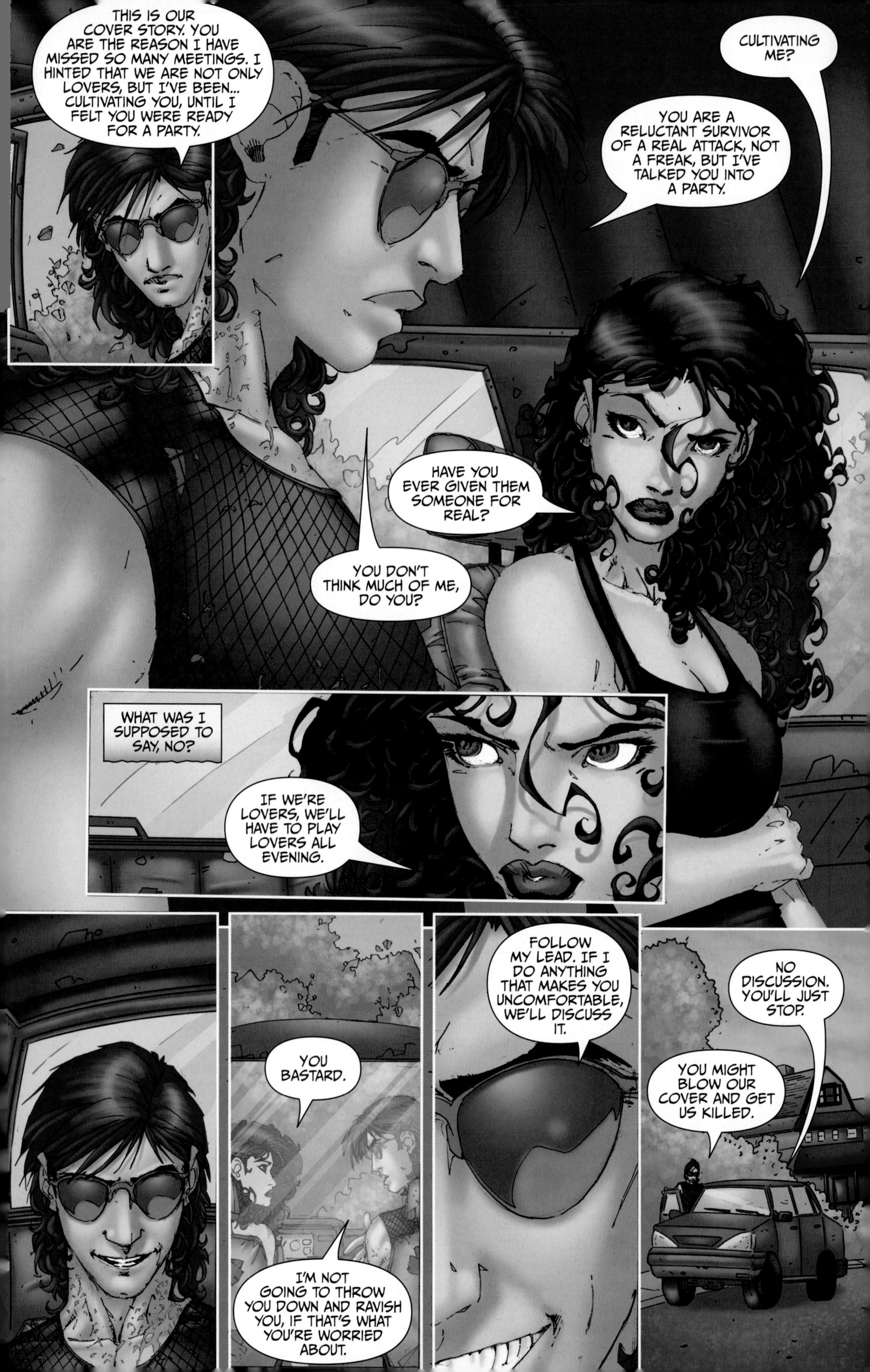
THIS IS OUR COVER STORY. YOU ARE THE REASON I HAVE MISSED SO MANY MEETINGS. I HINTED THAT WE ARE NOT ONLY LOVERS, BUT I'VE BEEN... CULTIVATING YOU, UNTIL I FELT YOU WERE READY FOR A PARTY.
CULTIVATING ME?
YOU ARE A RELUCTANT SURVIVOR OF A REAL ATTACK, NOT A FREAK, BUT I'VE TALKED YOU INTO A PARTY.
HAVE YOU EVER GIVEN THEM SOMEONE FOR REAL?
YOU DON'T THINK MUCH OF ME, DO YOU?
WHAT WAS I SUPPOSED TO SAY, NO?
IF WE'RE LOVERS, WE'LL HAVE TO PLAY LOVERS ALL EVENING.
YOU BASTARD.
I'M NOT GOING TO THROW YOU DOWN AND RAVISH YOU, IF THAT'S WHAT YOU'RE WORRIED ABOUT.
FOLLOW MY LEAD. IF I DO ANYTHING THAT MAKES YOU UNCOMFORTABLE, WE'LL DISCUSS IT.
NO DISCUSSION. YOU'LL JUST STOP.
YOU MIGHT BLOW OUR COVER AND GET US KILLED.

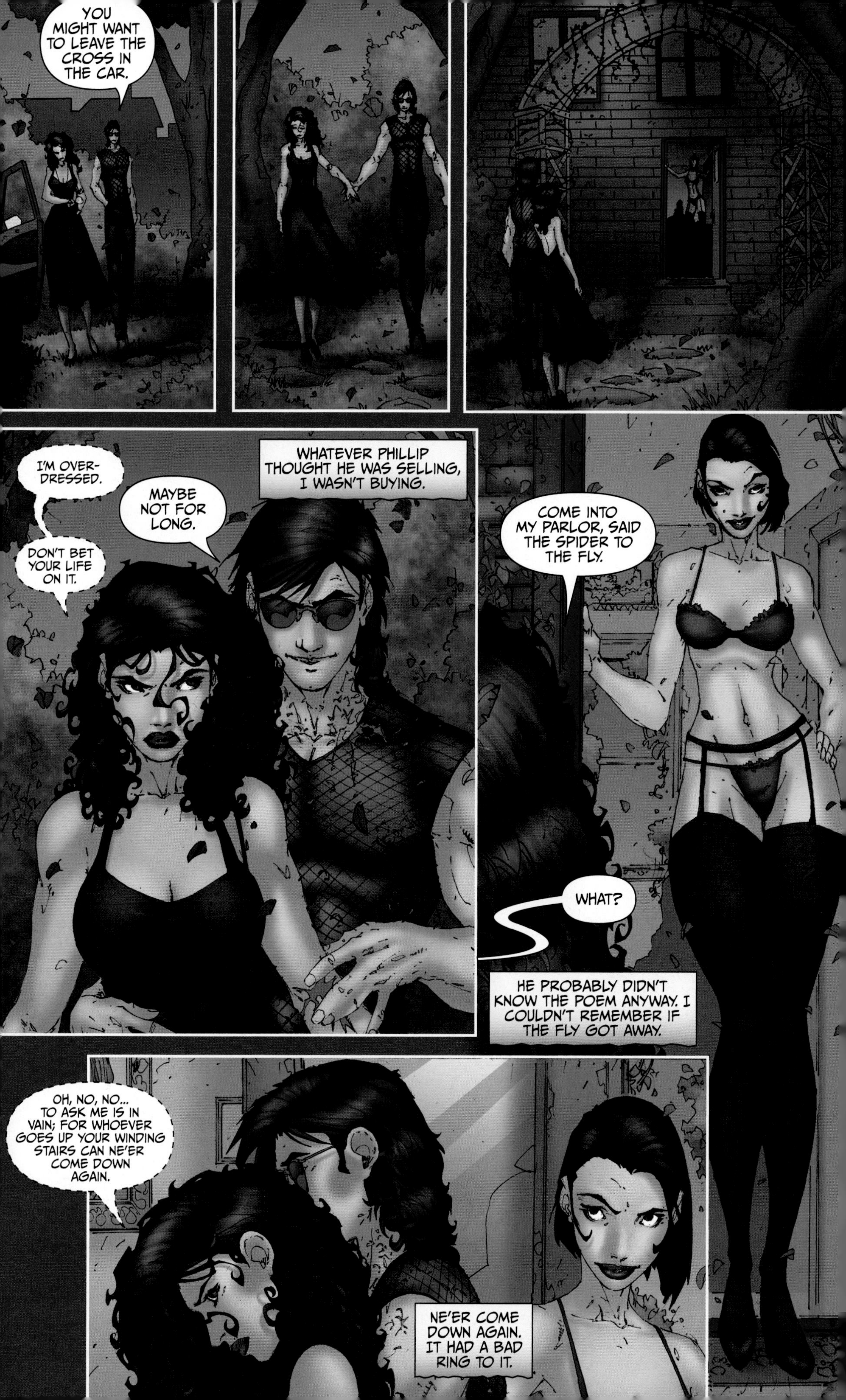
YOU MIGHT WANT TO LEAVE THE CROSS IN THE CAR.
I'M OVER-DRESSED.
WHATEVER PHILLIP THOUGHT HE WAS SELLING, I WASN'T BUYING.
MAYBE NOT FOR LONG.
DON'T BET YOUR LIFE ON IT.
COME INTO MY PARLOR, SAID THE SPIDER TO THE FLY.
WHAT?
HE PROBABLY DIDN'T KNOW THE POEM ANYWAY. I COULDN'T REMEMBER IF THE FLY GOT AWAY.
OH, NO, NO... TO ASK ME IS IN VAIN; FOR WHOEVER GOES UP YOUR WINDING STAIRS CAN NE'ER COME DOWN AGAIN.
NE'ER COME DOWN AGAIN. IT HAD A BAD RING TO IT.

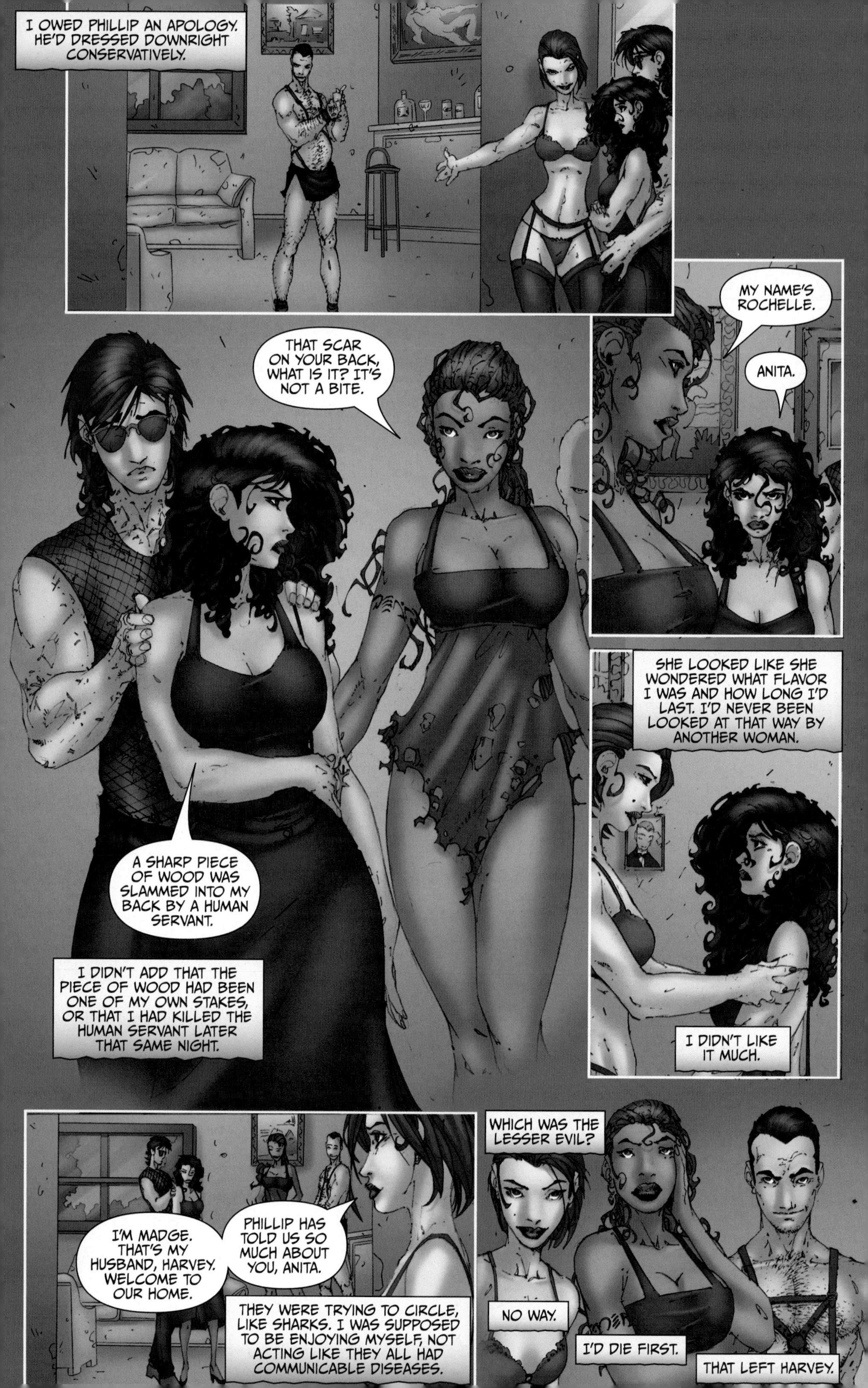

I OWED PHILLIP AN APOLOGY. HE'D DRESSED DOWNRIGHT CONSERVATIVELY.
THAT SCAR ON YOUR BACK, WHAT IS IT? IT'S NOT A BITE.
A SHARP PIECE OF WOOD WAS SLAMMED INTO MY BACK BY A HUMAN SERVANT.
I DIDN'T ADD THAT THE PIECE OF WOOD HAD BEEN ONE OF MY OWN STAKES, OR THAT I HAD KILLED THE HUMAN SERVANT LATER THAT SAME NIGHT.
MY NAME'S ROCHELLE.
ANITA.
SHE LOOKED LIKE SHE WONDERED WHAT FLAVOR I WAS AND HOW LONG I'D LAST. I'D NEVER BEEN LOOKED AT THAT WAY BY ANOTHER WOMAN.
I DIDN'T LIKE IT MUCH.
I'M MADGE. THAT'S MY HUSBAND, HARVEY. WELCOME TO OUR HOME.
PHILLIP HAS TOLD US SO MUCH ABOUT YOU, ANITA.
THEY WERE TRYING TO CIRCLE, LIKE SHARKS. I WAS SUPPOSED TO BE ENJOYING MYSELF, NOT ACTING LIKE THEY ALL HAD COMMUNICABLE DISEASES.
WHICH WAS THE LESSER EVIL?
NO WAY.
I'D DIE FIRST.
THAT LEFT HARVEY.

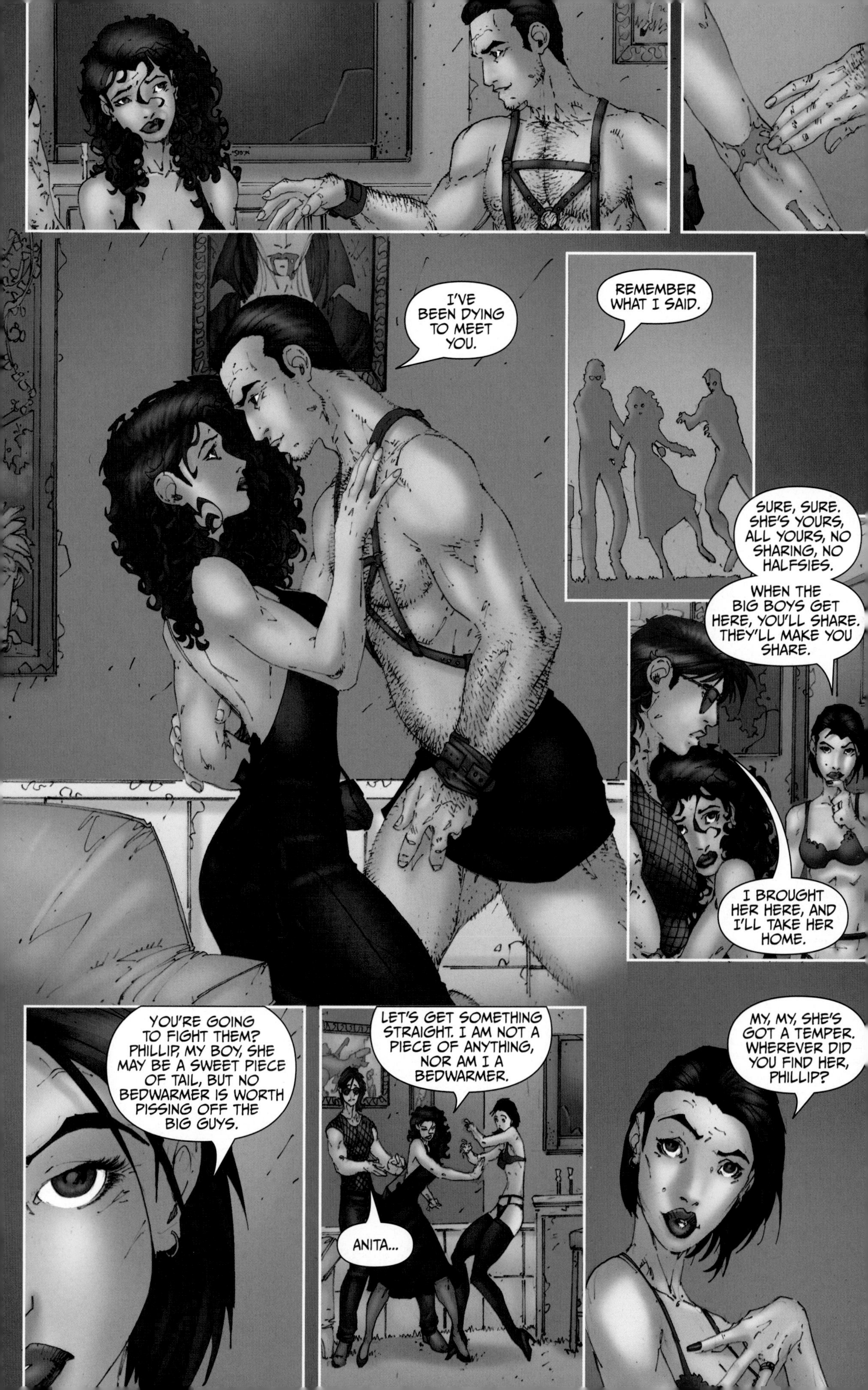
I'VE BEEN DYING TO MEET YOU.
REMEMBER WHAT I SAID.
SURE, SURE. SHE'S YOURS, ALL YOURS, NO SHARING, NO HALFSIES.
WHEN THE BIG BOYS GET HERE, YOU'LL SHARE. THEY'LL MAKE YOU SHARE.
I BROUGHT HER HERE, AND I'LL TAKE HER HOME.
YOU'RE GOING TO FIGHT THEM? PHILLIP, MY BOY, SHE MAY BE A SWEET PIECE OF TAIL, BUT NO BEDWARMER IS WORTH PISSING OFF THE BIG GUYS.
LET'S GET SOMETHING STRAIGHT. I AM NOT A PIECE OF ANYTHING, NOR AM I A BEDWARMER.
ANITA...
MY, MY, SHE'S GOT A TEMPER. WHEREVER DID YOU FIND HER, PHILLIP?

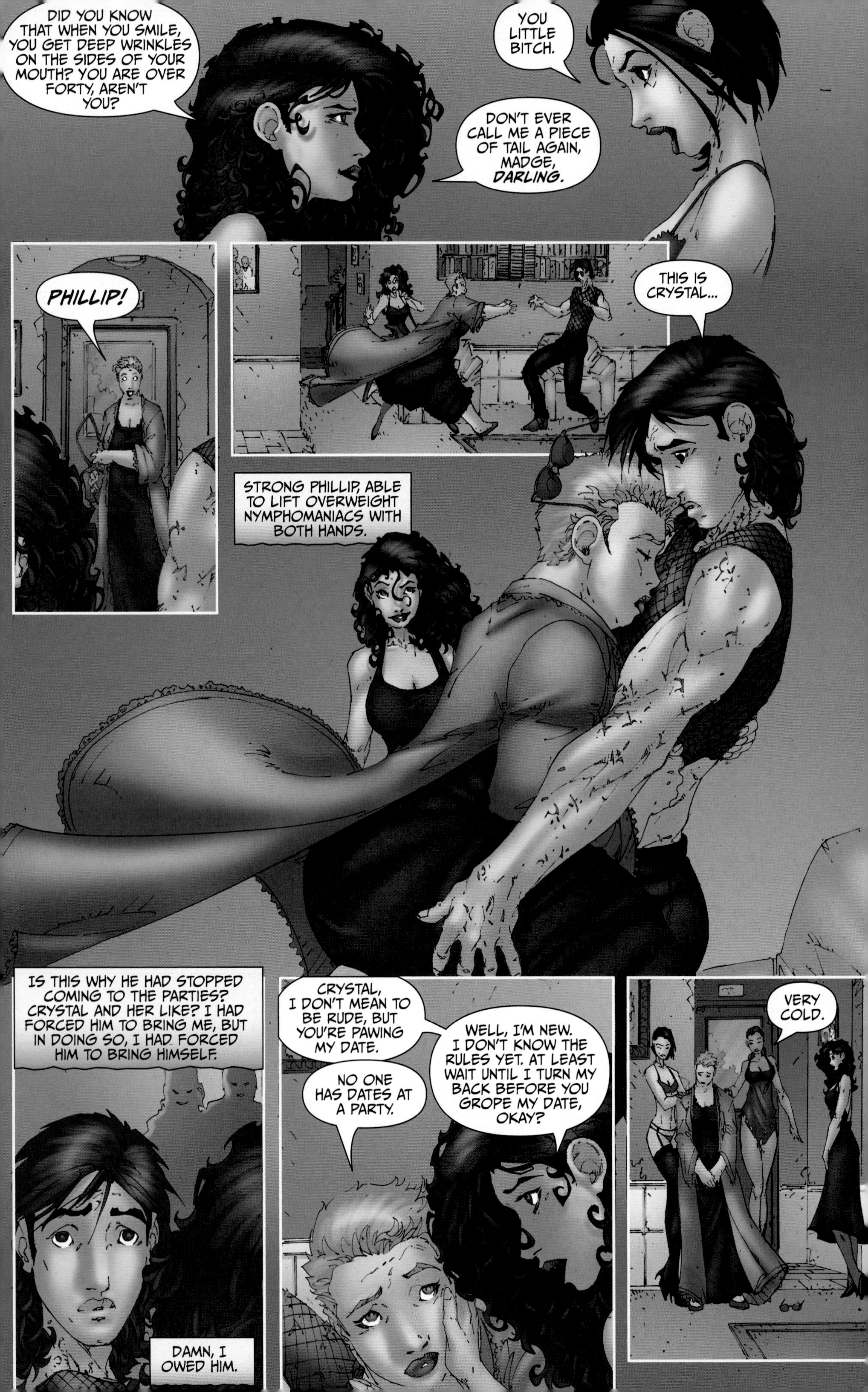
DID YOU KNOW THAT WHEN YOU SMILE, YOU GET DEEP WRINKLES ON THE SIDES OF YOUR MOUTH? YOU ARE OVER FORTY, AREN'T YOU?
YOU LITTLE BITCH.
DON'T EVER CALL ME A PIECE OF TAIL AGAIN, MADGE, DARLING.
PHILLIP!
THIS IS CRYSTAL...
STRONG PHILLIP, ABLE TO LIFT OVERWEIGHT NYMPHOMANIACS WITH BOTH HANDS.
IS THIS WHY HE HAD STOPPED COMING TO THE PARTIES? CRYSTAL AND HER LIKE? I HAD FORCED HIM TO BRING ME, BUT IN DOING SO, I HAD FORCED HIM TO BRING HIMSELF.
DAMN, I OWED HIM.
CRYSTAL, I DON'T MEAN TO BE RUDE, BUT YOU'RE PAWING MY DATE.
NO ONE HAS DATES AT A PARTY.
WELL, I'M NEW. I DON'T KNOW THE RULES YET. AT LEAST WAIT UNTIL I TURN MY BACK BEFORE YOU GROPE MY DATE, OKAY?
VERY COLD.

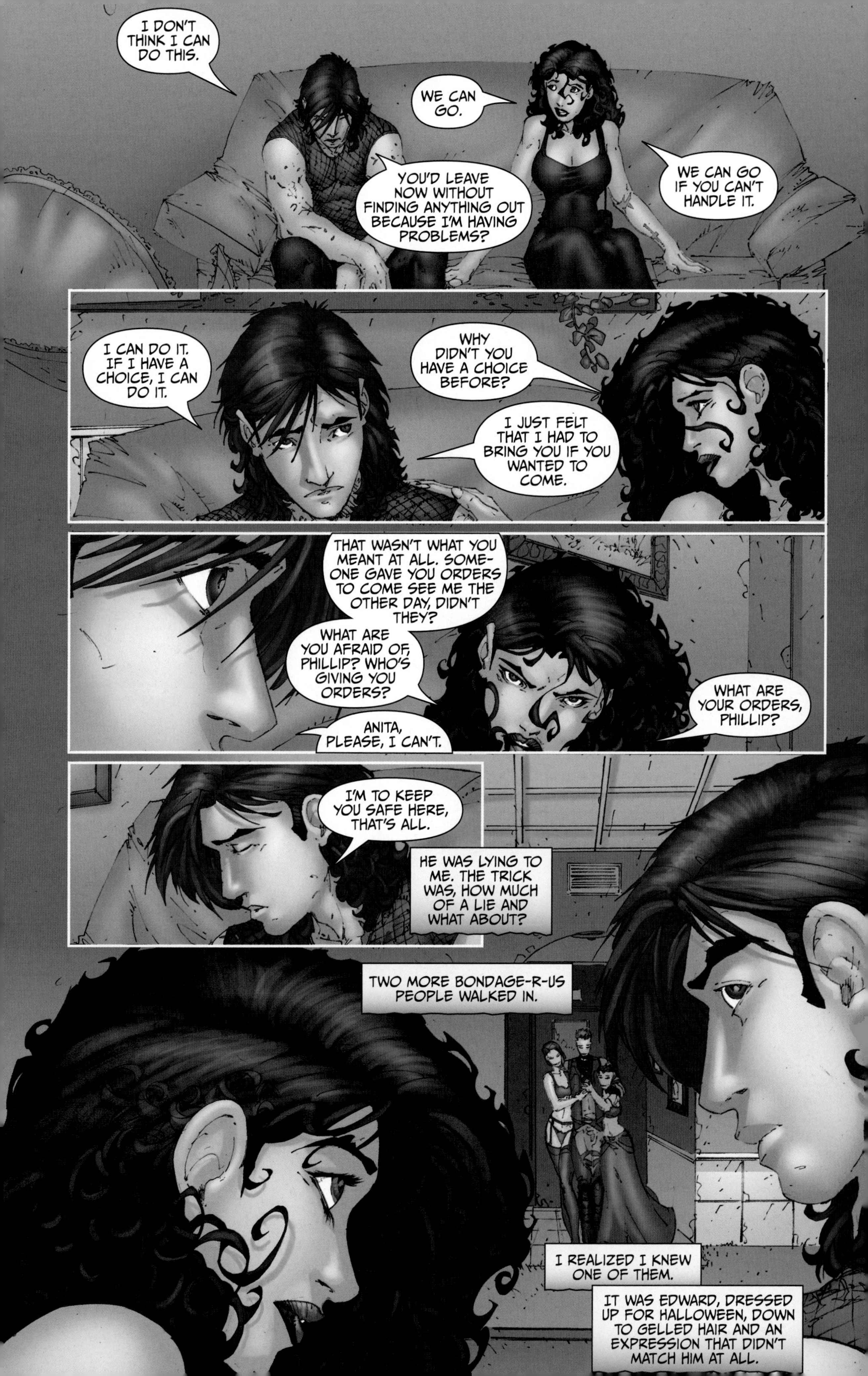

I DON'T THINK I CAN DO THIS.
WE CAN GO.
YOU'D LEAVE NOW WITHOUT FINDING ANYTHING OUT BECAUSE I'M HAVING PROBLEMS?
WE CAN GO IF YOU CAN'T HANDLE IT.
I CAN DO IT. IF I HAVE A CHOICE, I CAN DO IT.
WHY DIDN'T YOU HAVE A CHOICE BEFORE?
I JUST FELT THAT I HAD TO BRING YOU IF YOU WANTED TO COME.
THAT WASN'T WHAT YOU MEANT AT ALL. SOME-ONE GAVE YOU ORDERS TO COME SEE ME THE OTHER DAY, DIDN'T THEY?
WHAT ARE YOU AFRAID OF, PHILLIP? WHO'S GIVING YOU ORDERS?
ANITA, PLEASE, I CAN'T.
WHAT ARE YOUR ORDERS, PHILLIP?
I'M TO KEEP YOU SAFE HERE, THAT'S ALL.
HE WAS LYING TO ME. THE TRICK WAS, HOW MUCH OF A LIE AND WHAT ABOUT?
TWO MORE BONDAGE-R-US PEOPLE WALKED IN.
I REALIZED I KNEW ONE OF THEM.
IT WAS EDWARD, DRESSED UP FOR HALLOWEEN, DOWN TO GELLED HAIR AND AN EXPRESSION THAT DIDN'T MATCH HIM AT ALL.

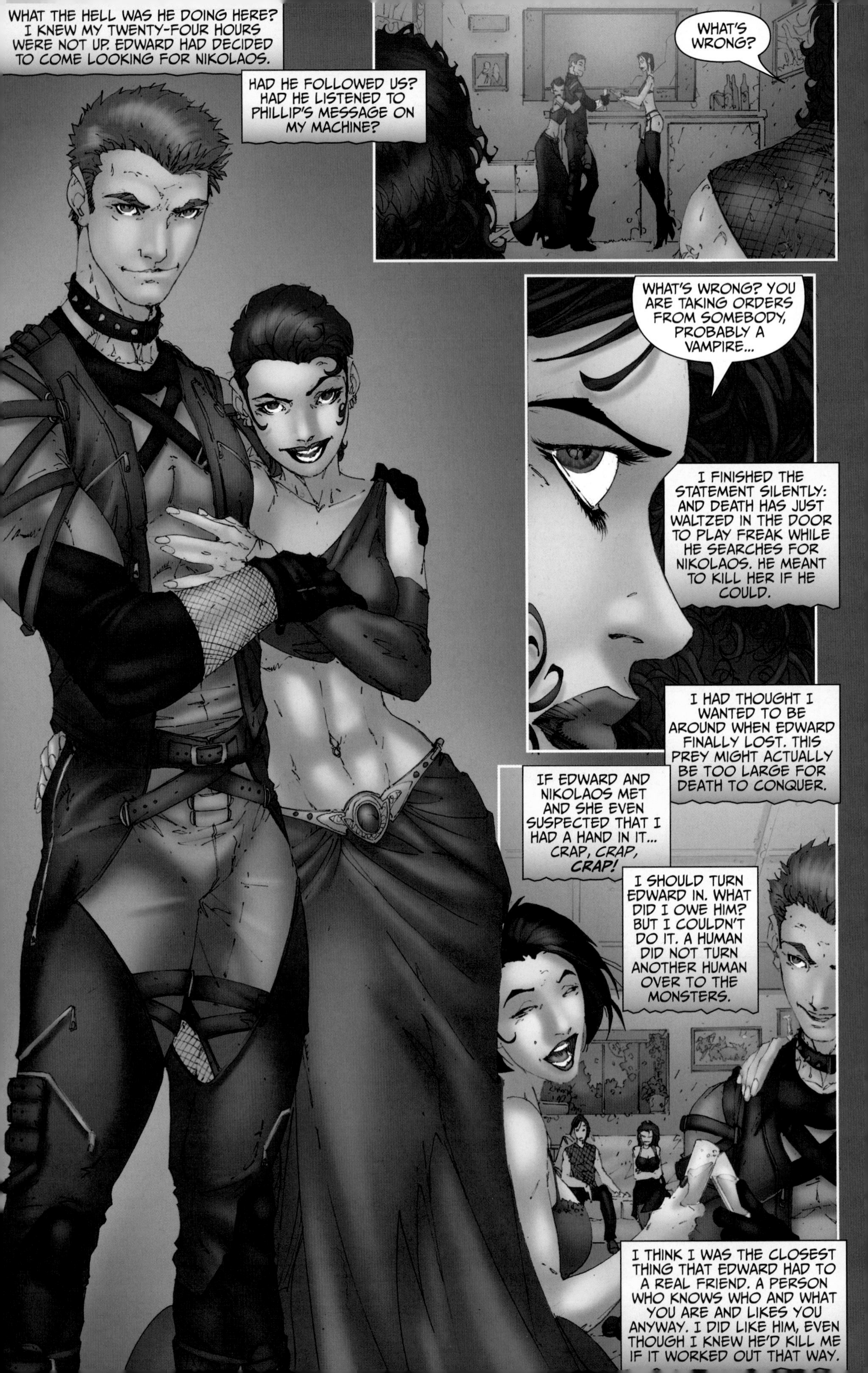
WHAT THE HELL WAS HE DOING HERE? I KNEW MY TWENTY-FOUR HOURS WERE NOT UP. EDWARD HAD DECIDED TO COME LOOKING FOR NIKOLAOS.
HAD HE FOLLOWED US? HAD HE LISTENED TO PHILLIP'S MESSAGE ON MY MACHINE?
WHAT'S WRONG?
WHAT'S WRONG? YOU ARE TAKING ORDERS FROM SOMEBODY, PROBABLY A VAMPIRE...
I FINISHED THE STATEMENT SILENTLY: AND DEATH HAS JUST WALTZED IN THE DOOR TO PLAY FREAK WHILE HE SEARCHES FOR NIKOLAOS. HE MEANT TO KILL HER IF HE COULD.
I HAD THOUGHT I WANTED TO BE AROUND WHEN EDWARD FINALLY LOST. THIS PREY MIGHT ACTUALLY BE TOO LARGE FOR DEATH TO CONQUER.
IF EDWARD AND NIKOLAOS MET AND SHE EVEN SUSPECTED THAT I HAD A HAND IN IT... CRAP, CRAP, CRAP!
I SHOULD TURN EDWARD IN. WHAT DID I OWE HIM? BUT I COULDN'T DO IT. A HUMAN DID NOT TURN ANOTHER HUMAN OVER TO THE MONSTERS.
I THINK I WAS THE CLOSEST THING THAT EDWARD HAD TO A REAL FRIEND. A PERSON WHO KNOWS WHO AND WHAT YOU ARE AND LIKES YOU ANYWAY. I DID LIKE HIM, EVEN THOUGH I KNEW HE'D KILL ME IF IT WORKED OUT THAT WAY.

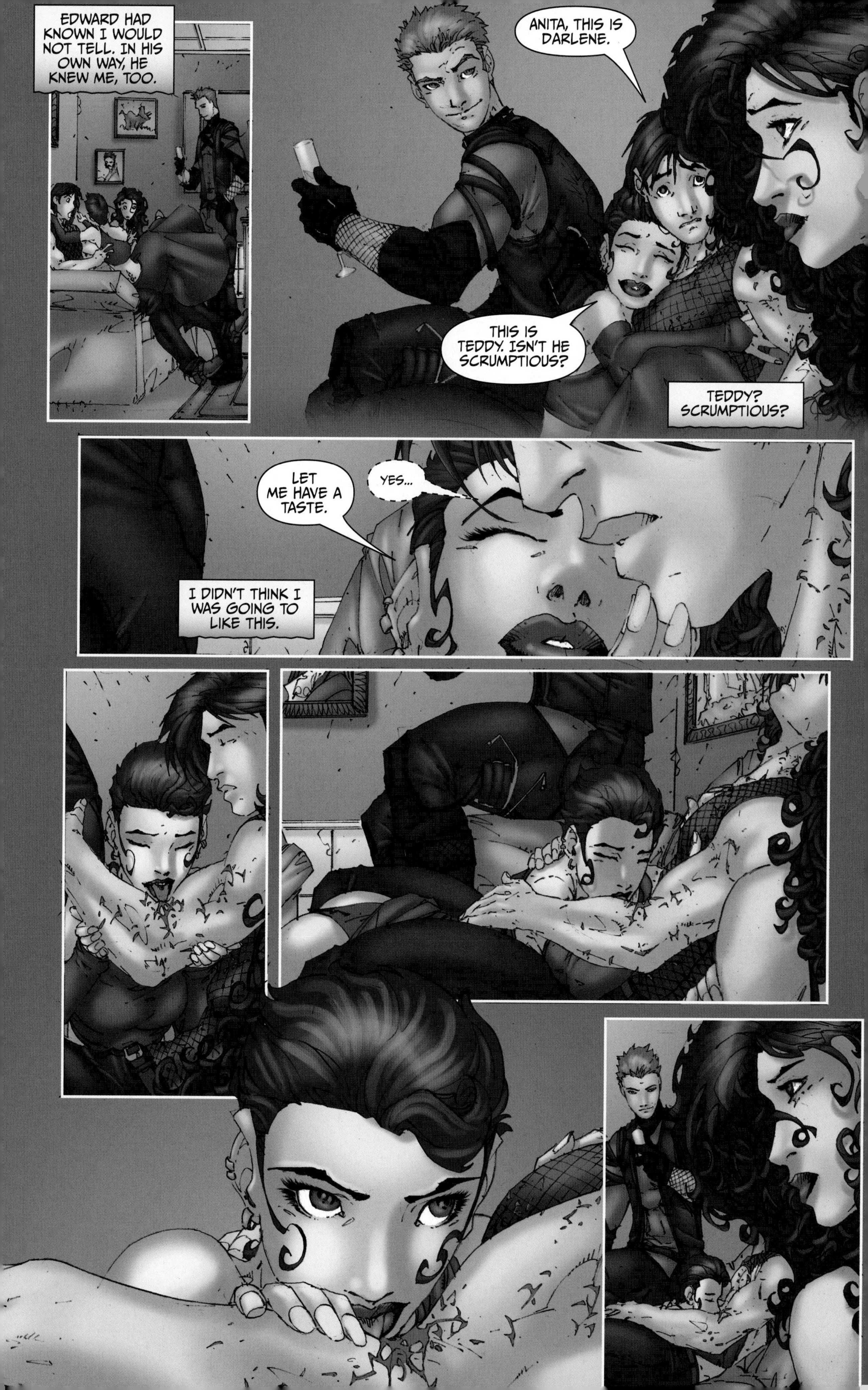
EDWARD HAD KNOWN I WOULD NOT TELL. IN HIS OWN WAY, HE KNEW ME, TOO.
ANITA, THIS IS DARLENE.
THIS IS TEDDY. ISN'T HE SCRUMPTIOUS?
TEDDY? SCRUMPTIOUS?
LET ME HAVE A TASTE.
YES...
I DIDN'T THINK I WAS GOING TO LIKE THIS.

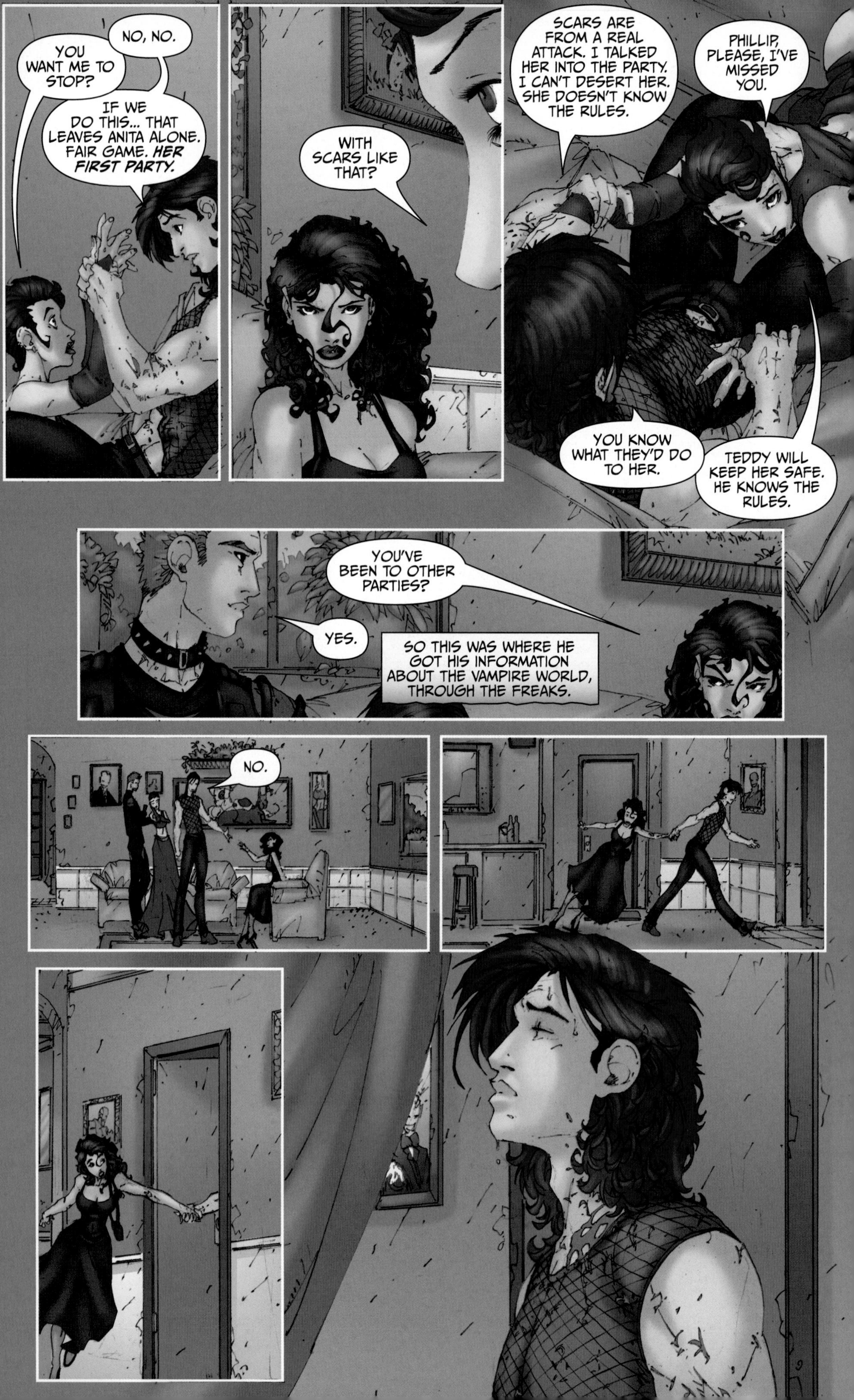
YOU WANT ME TO STOP?
NO, NO.
IF WE DO THIS... THAT LEAVES ANITA ALONE. FAIR GAME. *HER FIRST PARTY.*
WITH SCARS LIKE THAT?
SCARS ARE FROM A REAL ATTACK. I TALKED HER INTO THE PARTY. I CAN'T DESERT HER. SHE DOESN'T KNOW THE RULES.
PHILLIP, PLEASE, I'VE MISSED YOU.
YOU KNOW WHAT THEY'D DO TO HER.
TEDDY WILL KEEP HER SAFE. HE KNOWS THE RULES.
YOU'VE BEEN TO OTHER PARTIES?
YES.
SO THIS WAS WHERE HE GOT HIS INFORMATION ABOUT THE VAMPIRE WORLD, THROUGH THE FREAKS.
NO.

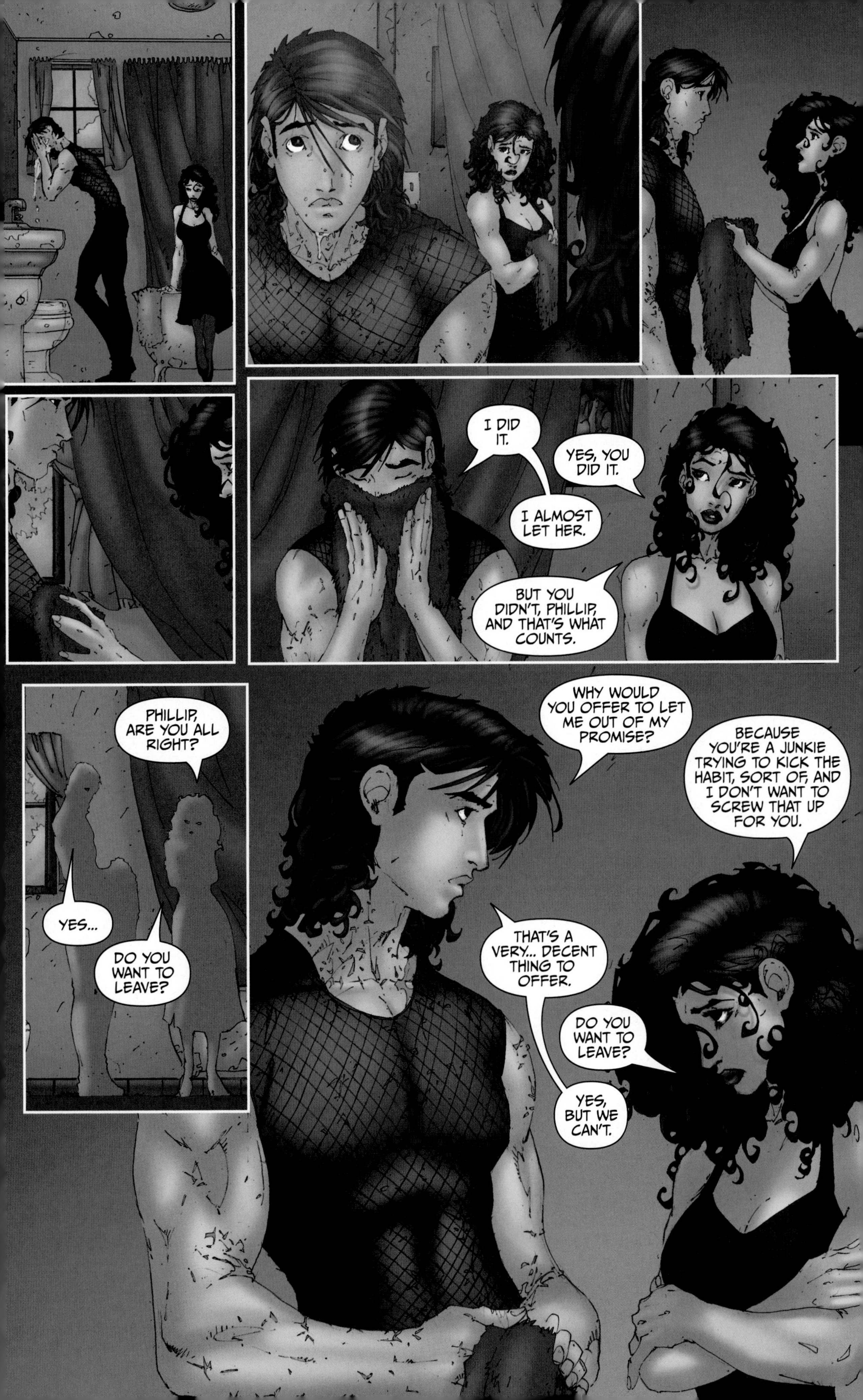
I DID IT.
YES, YOU DID IT.
I ALMOST LET HER.
BUT YOU DIDN'T, PHILLIP, AND THAT'S WHAT COUNTS.
PHILLIP, ARE YOU ALL RIGHT?
YES...
DO YOU WANT TO LEAVE?
WHY WOULD YOU OFFER TO LET ME OUT OF MY PROMISE?
BECAUSE YOU'RE A JUNKIE TRYING TO KICK THE HABIT, SORT OF, AND I DON'T WANT TO SCREW THAT UP FOR YOU.
THAT'S A VERY... DECENT THING TO OFFER.
DO YOU WANT TO LEAVE?
YES, BUT WE CAN'T.

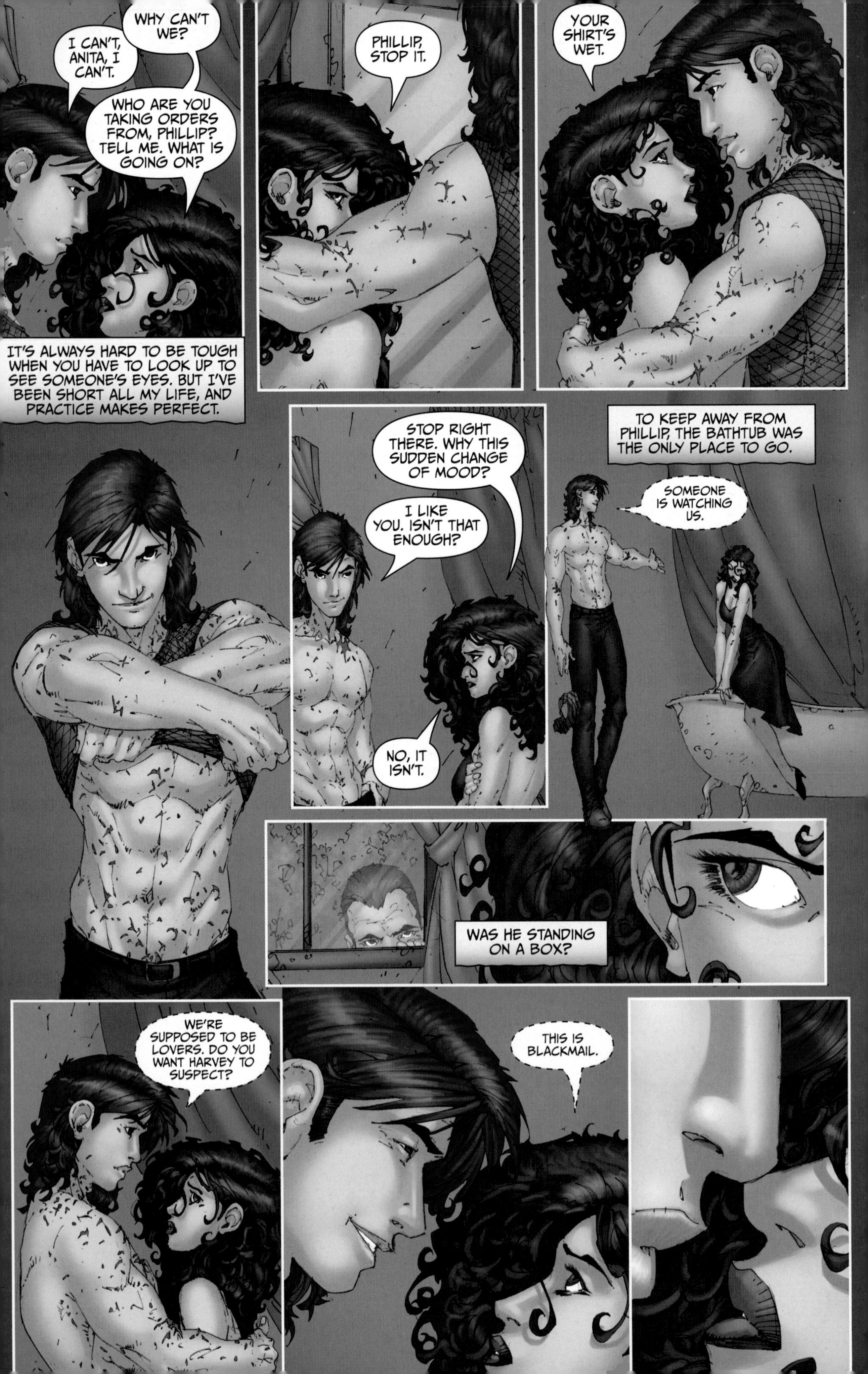
I CAN'T, ANITA, I CAN'T.
WHY CAN'T WE?
WHO ARE YOU TAKING ORDERS FROM, PHILLIP? TELL ME. WHAT IS GOING ON?
IT'S ALWAYS HARD TO BE TOUGH WHEN YOU HAVE TO LOOK UP TO SEE SOMEONE'S EYES. BUT I'VE BEEN SHORT ALL MY LIFE, AND PRACTICE MAKES PERFECT.
PHILLIP, STOP IT.
YOUR SHIRT'S WET.
STOP RIGHT THERE. WHY THIS SUDDEN CHANGE OF MOOD?
I LIKE YOU. ISN'T THAT ENOUGH?
NO, IT ISN'T.
TO KEEP AWAY FROM PHILLIP, THE BATHTUB WAS THE ONLY PLACE TO GO.
SOMEONE IS WATCHING US.
WAS HE STANDING ON A BOX?
WE'RE SUPPOSED TO BE LOVERS. DO YOU WANT HARVEY TO SUSPECT?
THIS IS BLACKMAIL.

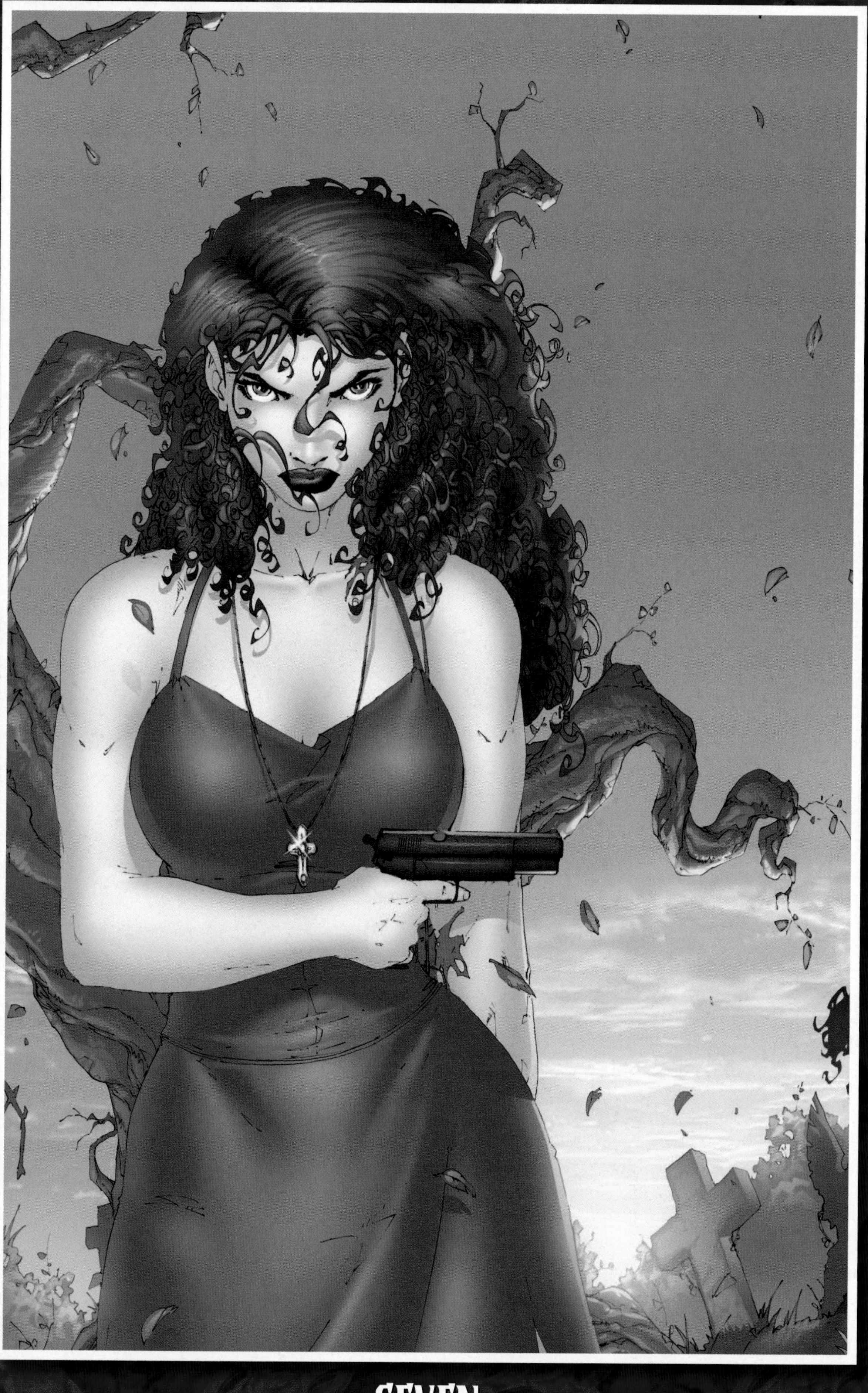

SEVEN

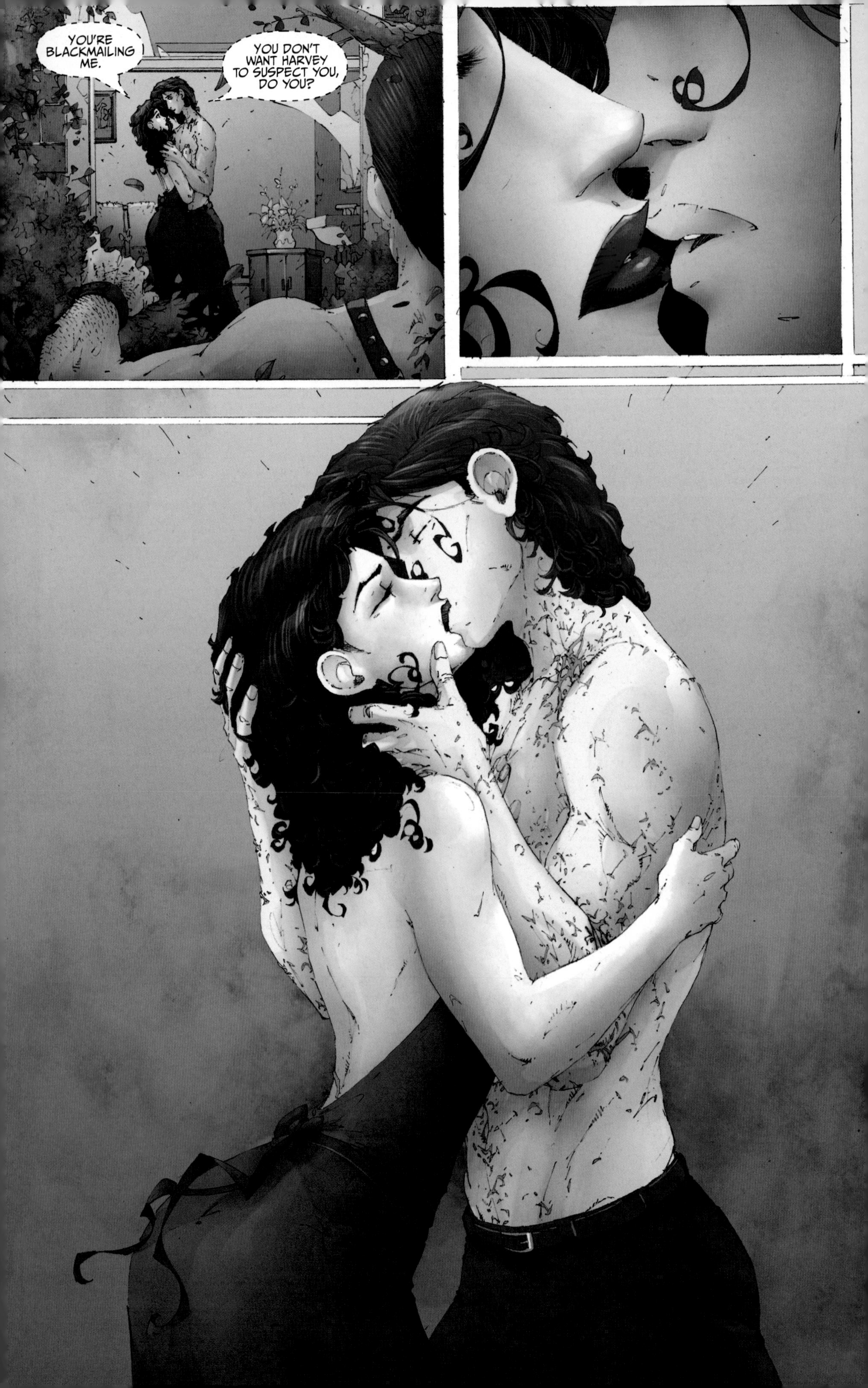
YOU'RE BLACKMAILING ME.
YOU DON'T WANT HARVEY TO SUSPECT YOU, DO YOU?

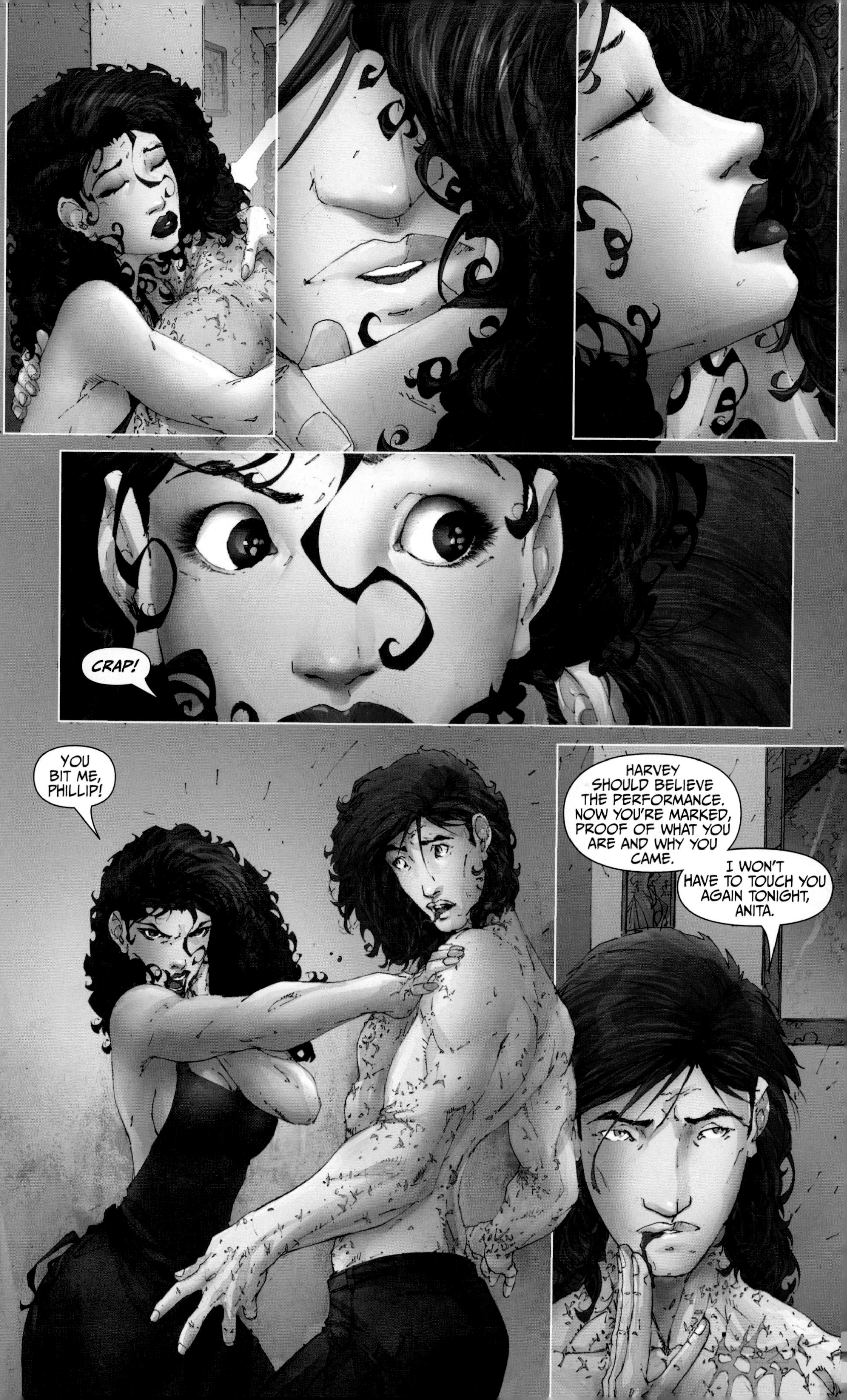
CRAP!
YOU BIT ME, PHILLIP!
HARVEY SHOULD BELIEVE THE PERFORMANCE. NOW YOU'RE MARKED, PROOF OF WHAT YOU ARE AND WHY YOU CAME.
I WON'T HAVE TO TOUCH YOU AGAIN TONIGHT, ANITA.

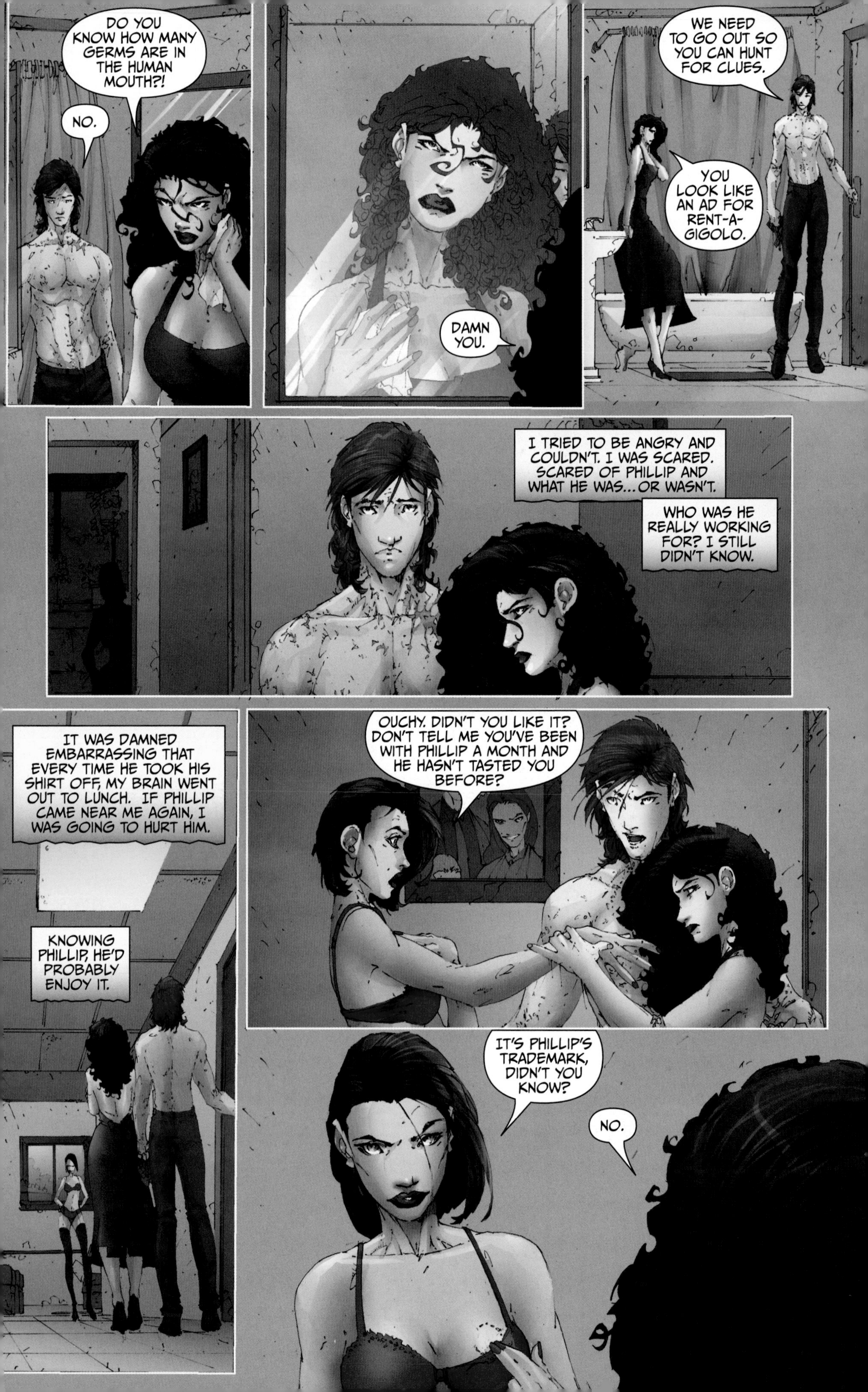
DO YOU KNOW HOW MANY GERMS ARE IN THE HUMAN MOUTH?!
NO.
DAMN YOU.
WE NEED TO GO OUT SO YOU CAN HUNT FOR CLUES.
YOU LOOK LIKE AN AD FOR RENT-A-GIGOLO.
I TRIED TO BE ANGRY AND COULDN'T. I WAS SCARED. SCARED OF PHILLIP AND WHAT HE WAS...OR WASN'T.
WHO WAS HE REALLY WORKING FOR? I STILL DIDN'T KNOW.
IT WAS DAMNED EMBARRASSING THAT EVERY TIME HE TOOK HIS SHIRT OFF, MY BRAIN WENT OUT TO LUNCH. IF PHILLIP CAME NEAR ME AGAIN, I WAS GOING TO HURT HIM.
KNOWING PHILLIP, HE'D PROBABLY ENJOY IT.
OUCHY. DIDN'T YOU LIKE IT? DON'T TELL ME YOU'VE BEEN WITH PHILLIP A MONTH AND HE HASN'T TASTED YOU BEFORE?
IT'S PHILLIP'S TRADEMARK, DIDN'T YOU KNOW?
NO.

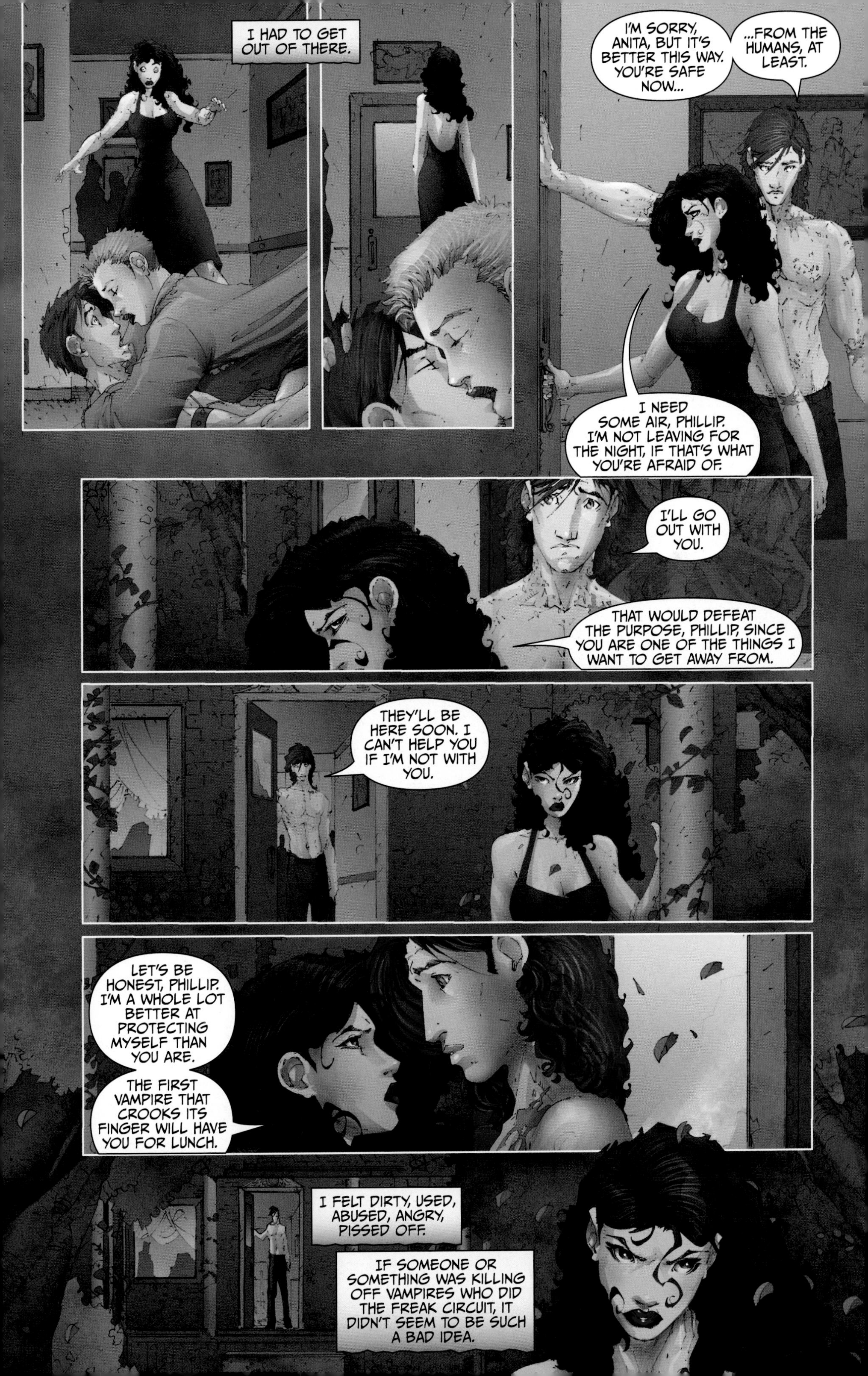
I HAD TO GET OUT OF THERE.
I'M SORRY, ANITA, BUT IT'S BETTER THIS WAY. YOU'RE SAFE NOW...
...FROM THE HUMANS, AT LEAST.
I NEED SOME AIR, PHILLIP. I'M NOT LEAVING FOR THE NIGHT, IF THAT'S WHAT YOU'RE AFRAID OF.
I'LL GO OUT WITH YOU.
THAT WOULD DEFEAT THE PURPOSE, PHILLIP, SINCE YOU ARE ONE OF THE THINGS I WANT TO GET AWAY FROM.
THEY'LL BE HERE SOON. I CAN'T HELP YOU IF I'M NOT WITH YOU.
LET'S BE HONEST, PHILLIP. I'M A WHOLE LOT BETTER AT PROTECTING MYSELF THAN YOU ARE.
THE FIRST VAMPIRE THAT CROOKS ITS FINGER WILL HAVE YOU FOR LUNCH.
I FELT DIRTY, USED, ABUSED, ANGRY, PISSED OFF.
IF SOMEONE OR SOMETHING WAS KILLING OFF VAMPIRES WHO DID THE FREAK CIRCUIT, IT DIDN'T SEEM TO BE SUCH A BAD IDEA.

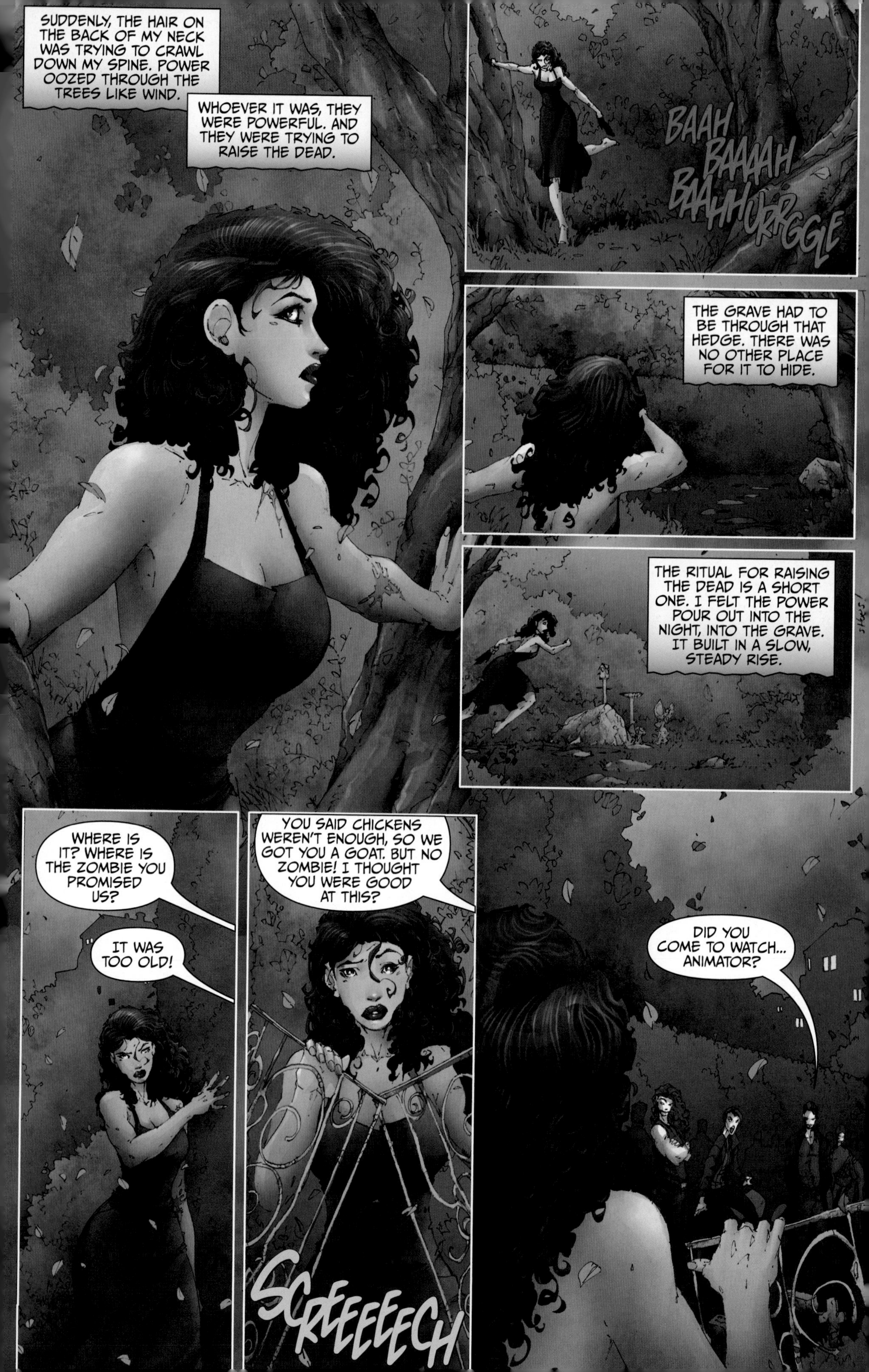
SUDDENLY, THE HAIR ON THE BACK OF MY NECK WAS TRYING TO CRAWL DOWN MY SPINE. POWER OOZED THROUGH THE TREES LIKE WIND.
WHOEVER IT WAS, THEY WERE POWERFUL. AND THEY WERE TRYING TO RAISE THE DEAD.
BAAH BAAAAH BAAHHURRGGLE
THE GRAVE HAD TO BE THROUGH THAT HEDGE. THERE WAS NO OTHER PLACE FOR IT TO HIDE.
THE RITUAL FOR RAISING THE DEAD IS A SHORT ONE. I FELT THE POWER POUR OUT INTO THE NIGHT, INTO THE GRAVE. IT BUILT IN A SLOW, STEADY RISE.
WHERE IS IT? WHERE IS THE ZOMBIE YOU PROMISED US?
IT WAS TOO OLD!
YOU SAID CHICKENS WEREN'T ENOUGH, SO WE GOT YOU A GOAT. BUT NO ZOMBIE! I THOUGHT YOU WERE GOOD AT THIS?
SCREEEEECH
DID YOU COME TO WATCH... ANIMATOR?

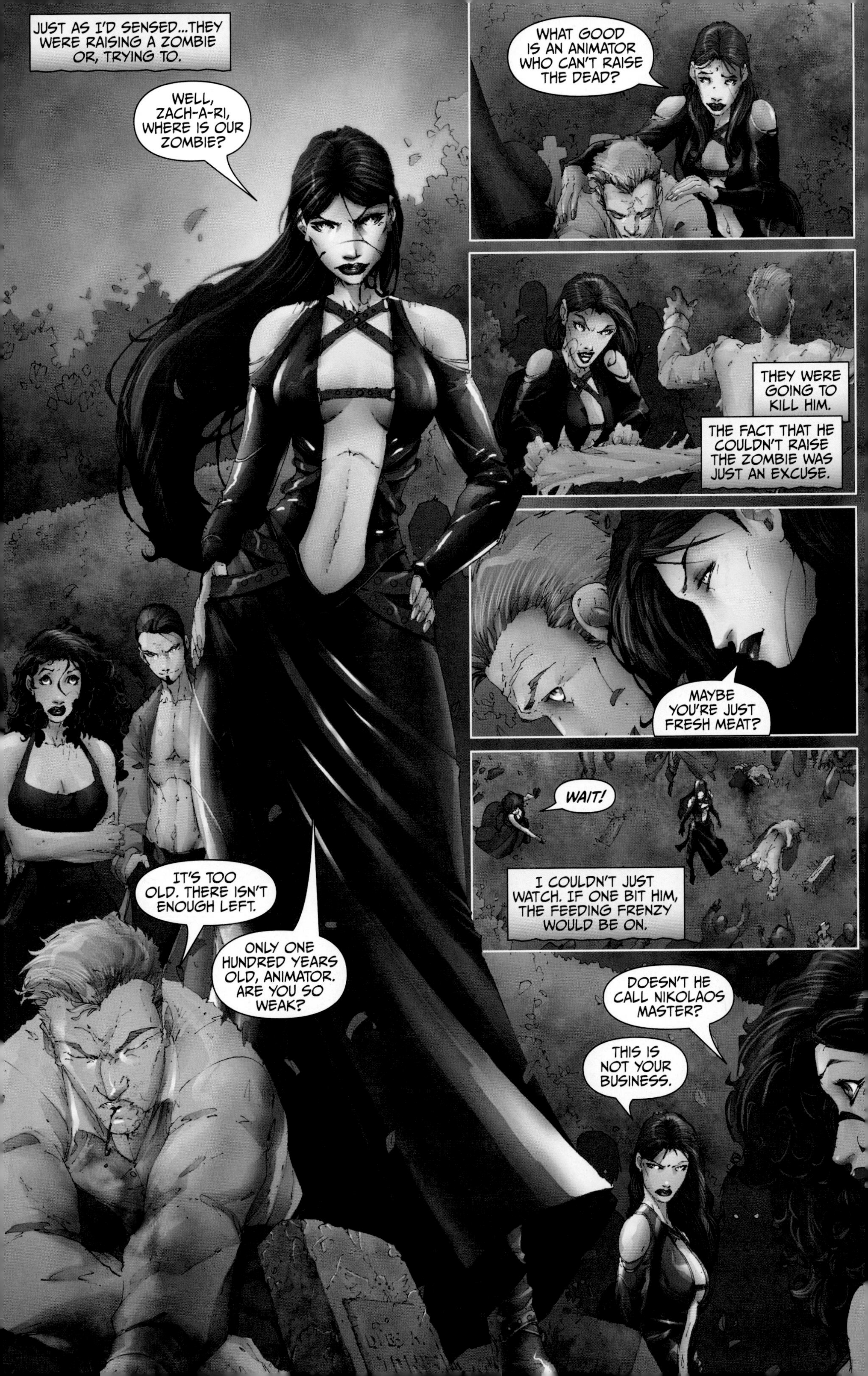
JUST AS I'D SENSED...THEY WERE RAISING A ZOMBIE OR, TRYING TO.
WELL, ZACH-A-RI, WHERE IS OUR ZOMBIE?
IT'S TOO OLD. THERE ISN'T ENOUGH LEFT.
ONLY ONE HUNDRED YEARS OLD, ANIMATOR. ARE YOU SO WEAK?
WHAT GOOD IS AN ANIMATOR WHO CAN'T RAISE THE DEAD?
THEY WERE GOING TO KILL HIM.
THE FACT THAT HE COULDN'T RAISE THE ZOMBIE WAS JUST AN EXCUSE.
MAYBE YOU'RE JUST FRESH MEAT?
WAIT!
I COULDN'T JUST WATCH. IF ONE BIT HIM, THE FEEDING FRENZY WOULD BE ON.
DOESN'T HE CALL NIKOLAOS MASTER?
THIS IS NOT YOUR BUSINESS.

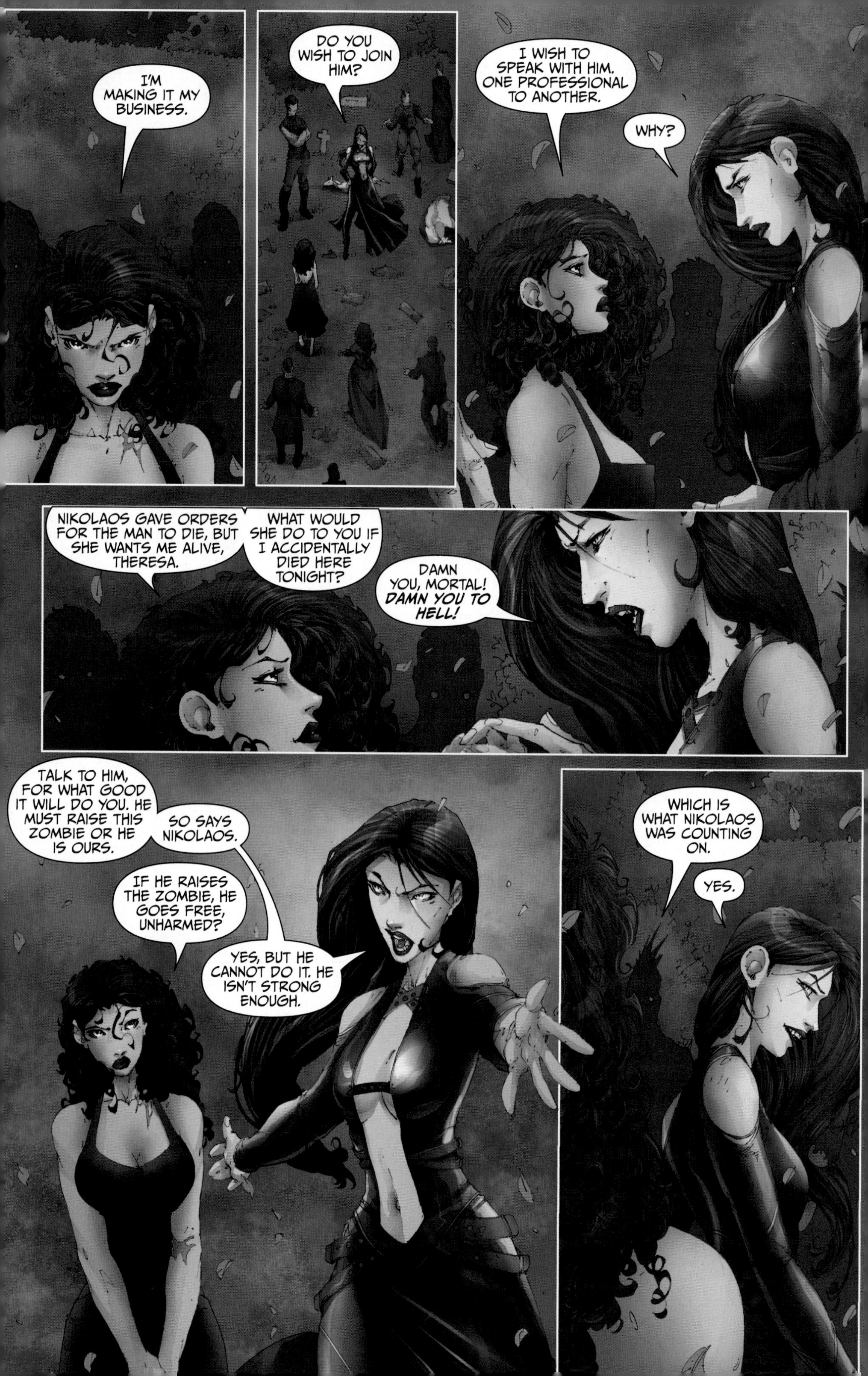
I'M MAKING IT MY BUSINESS.
DO YOU WISH TO JOIN HIM?
I WISH TO SPEAK WITH HIM. ONE PROFESSIONAL TO ANOTHER.
WHY?
NIKOLAOS GAVE ORDERS FOR THE MAN TO DIE, BUT SHE WANTS ME ALIVE, THERESA.
WHAT WOULD SHE DO TO YOU IF I ACCIDENTALLY DIED HERE TONIGHT?
DAMN YOU, MORTAL! *DAMN YOU TO HELL!*
TALK TO HIM, FOR WHAT GOOD IT WILL DO YOU. HE MUST RAISE THIS ZOMBIE OR HE IS OURS.
SO SAYS NIKOLAOS.
IF HE RAISES THE ZOMBIE, HE GOES FREE, UNHARMED?
YES, BUT HE CANNOT DO IT. HE ISN'T STRONG ENOUGH.
WHICH IS WHAT NIKOLAOS WAS COUNTING ON.
YES.

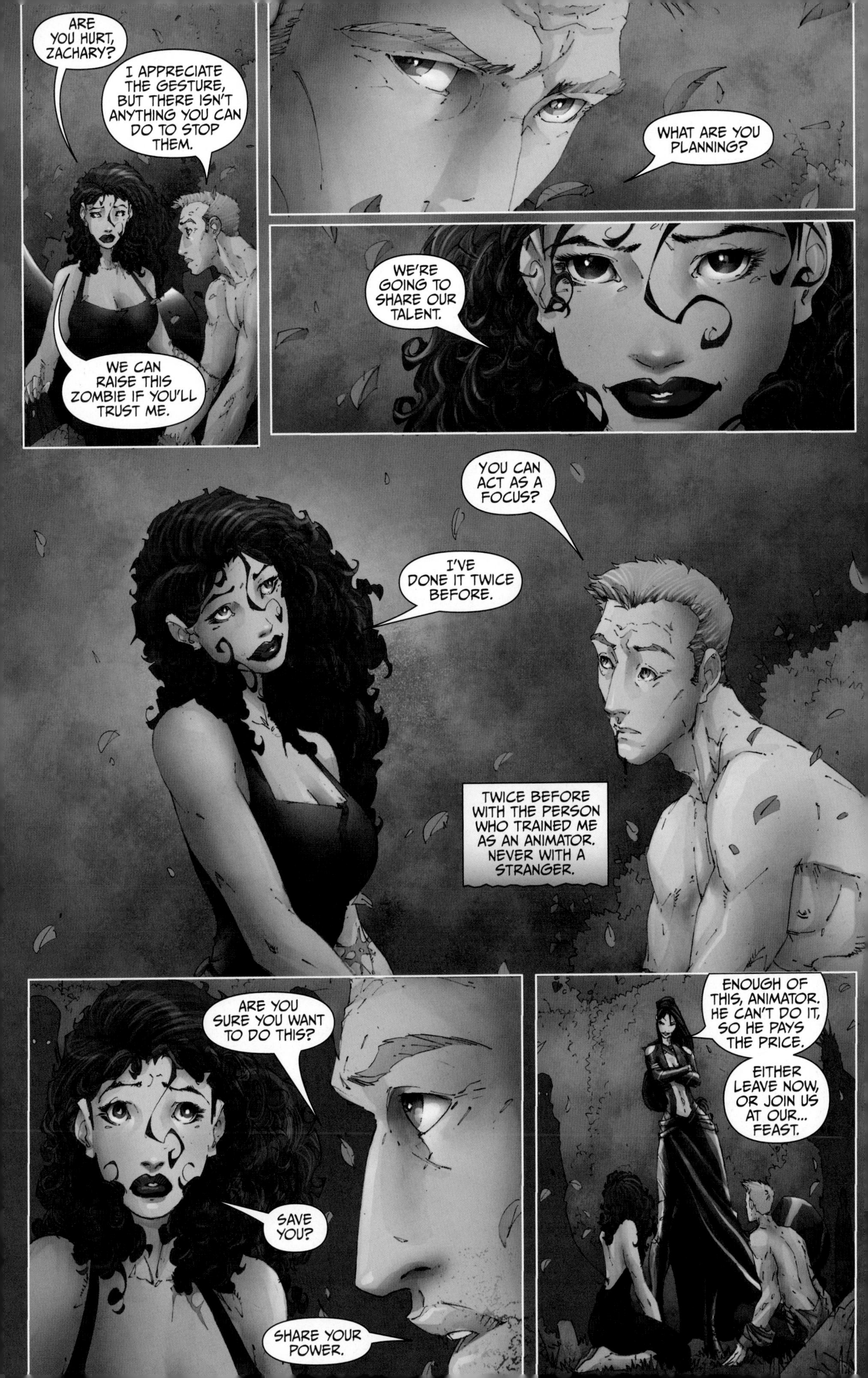

ARE YOU HURT, ZACHARY?
I APPRECIATE THE GESTURE, BUT THERE ISN'T ANYTHING YOU CAN DO TO STOP THEM.
WE CAN RAISE THIS ZOMBIE IF YOU'LL TRUST ME.
WHAT ARE YOU PLANNING?
WE'RE GOING TO SHARE OUR TALENT.
YOU CAN ACT AS A FOCUS?
I'VE DONE IT TWICE BEFORE.
TWICE BEFORE WITH THE PERSON WHO TRAINED ME AS AN ANIMATOR. NEVER WITH A STRANGER.
ARE YOU SURE YOU WANT TO DO THIS?
SAVE YOU?
SHARE YOUR POWER.
ENOUGH OF THIS, ANIMATOR. HE CAN'T DO IT, SO HE PAYS THE PRICE.
EITHER LEAVE NOW, OR JOIN US AT OUR... FEAST.

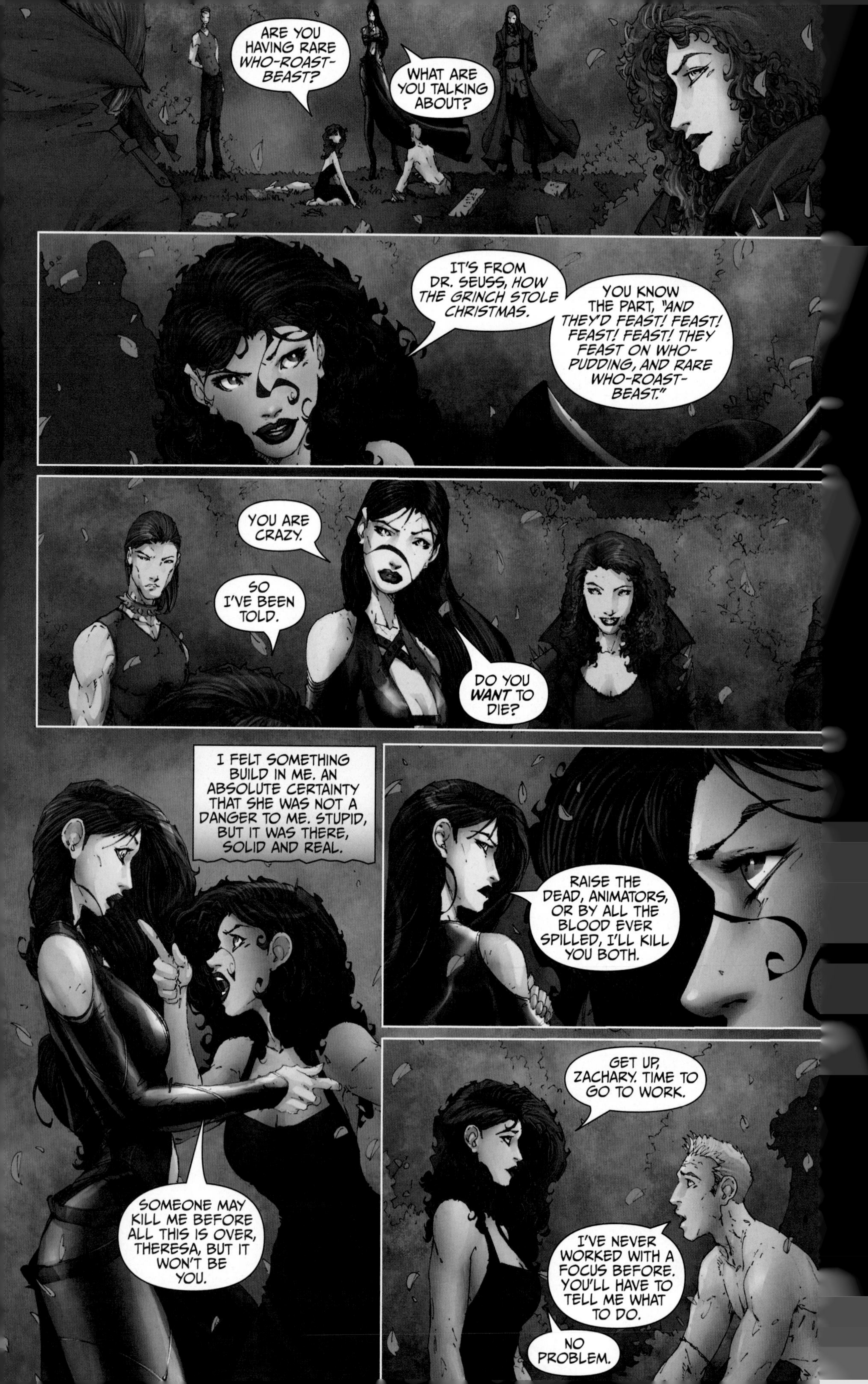
ARE YOU HAVING RARE *WHO-ROAST-BEAST?*
WHAT ARE YOU TALKING ABOUT?
IT'S FROM DR. SEUSS, *HOW THE GRINCH STOLE CHRISTMAS.*
YOU KNOW THE PART, *"AND THEY'D FEAST! FEAST! FEAST! FEAST! THEY FEAST ON WHO-PUDDING, AND RARE WHO-ROAST-BEAST."*
YOU ARE CRAZY.
SO I'VE BEEN TOLD.
DO YOU *WANT* TO DIE?
I FELT SOMETHING BUILD IN ME. AN ABSOLUTE CERTAINTY THAT SHE WAS NOT A DANGER TO ME. STUPID, BUT IT WAS THERE, SOLID AND REAL.
SOMEONE MAY KILL ME BEFORE ALL THIS IS OVER, THERESA, BUT IT WON'T BE YOU.
RAISE THE DEAD, ANIMATORS, OR BY ALL THE BLOOD EVER SPILLED, I'LL KILL YOU BOTH.
GET UP, ZACHARY. TIME TO GO TO WORK.
I'VE NEVER WORKED WITH A FOCUS BEFORE. YOU'LL HAVE TO TELL ME WHAT TO DO.
NO PROBLEM.

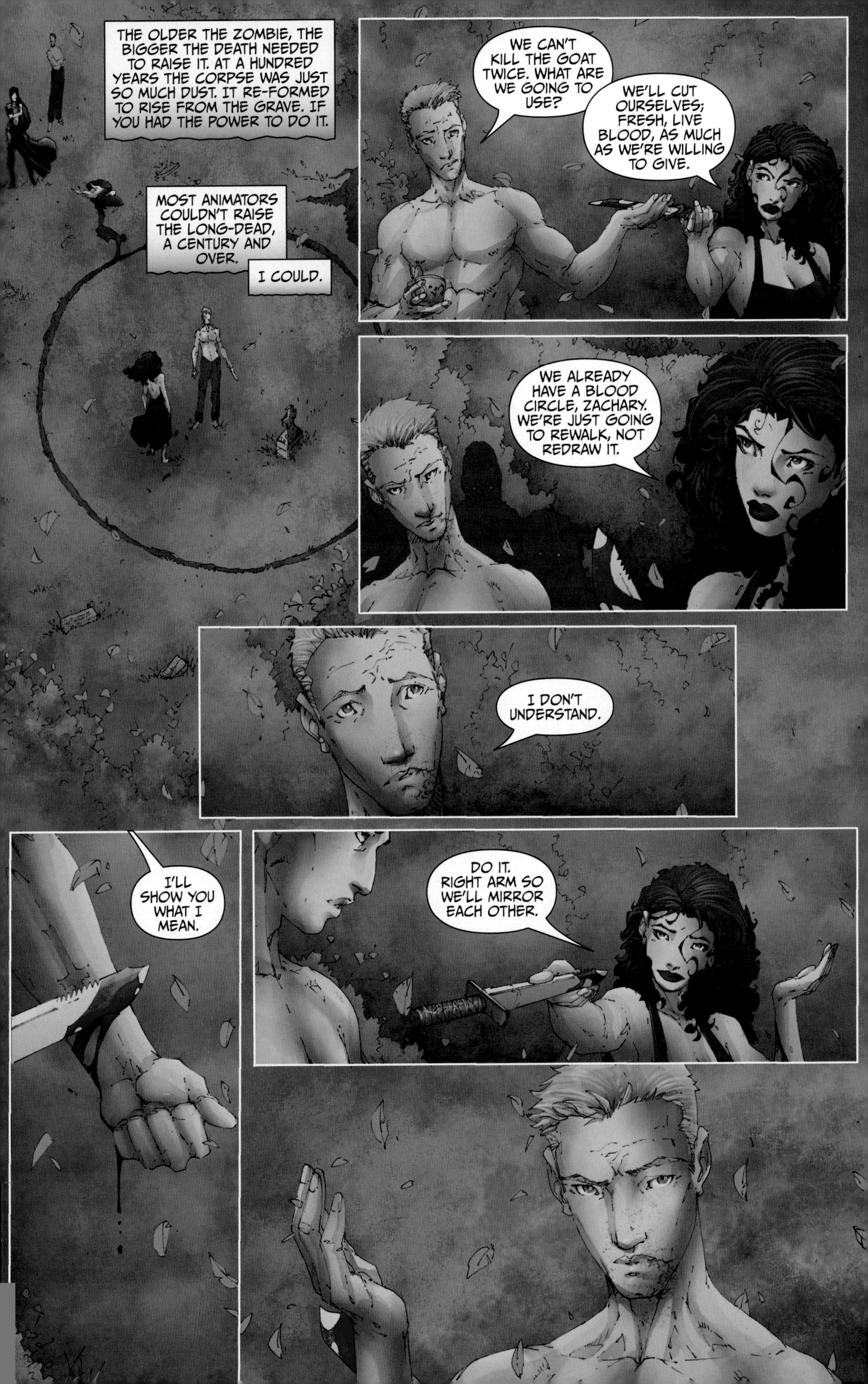
THE OLDER THE ZOMBIE, THE BIGGER THE DEATH NEEDED TO RAISE IT. AT A HUNDRED YEARS THE CORPSE WAS JUST SO MUCH DUST. IT RE-FORMED TO RISE FROM THE GRAVE. IF YOU HAD THE POWER TO DO IT.
MOST ANIMATORS COULDN'T RAISE THE LONG-DEAD, A CENTURY AND OVER.
I COULD.
WE CAN'T KILL THE GOAT TWICE. WHAT ARE WE GOING TO USE?
WE'LL CUT OURSELVES; FRESH, LIVE BLOOD, AS MUCH AS WE'RE WILLING TO GIVE.
WE ALREADY HAVE A BLOOD CIRCLE, ZACHARY. WE'RE JUST GOING TO REWALK, NOT REDRAW IT.
I DON'T UNDERSTAND.
I'LL SHOW YOU WHAT I MEAN.
DO IT. RIGHT ARM SO WE'LL MIRROR EACH OTHER.

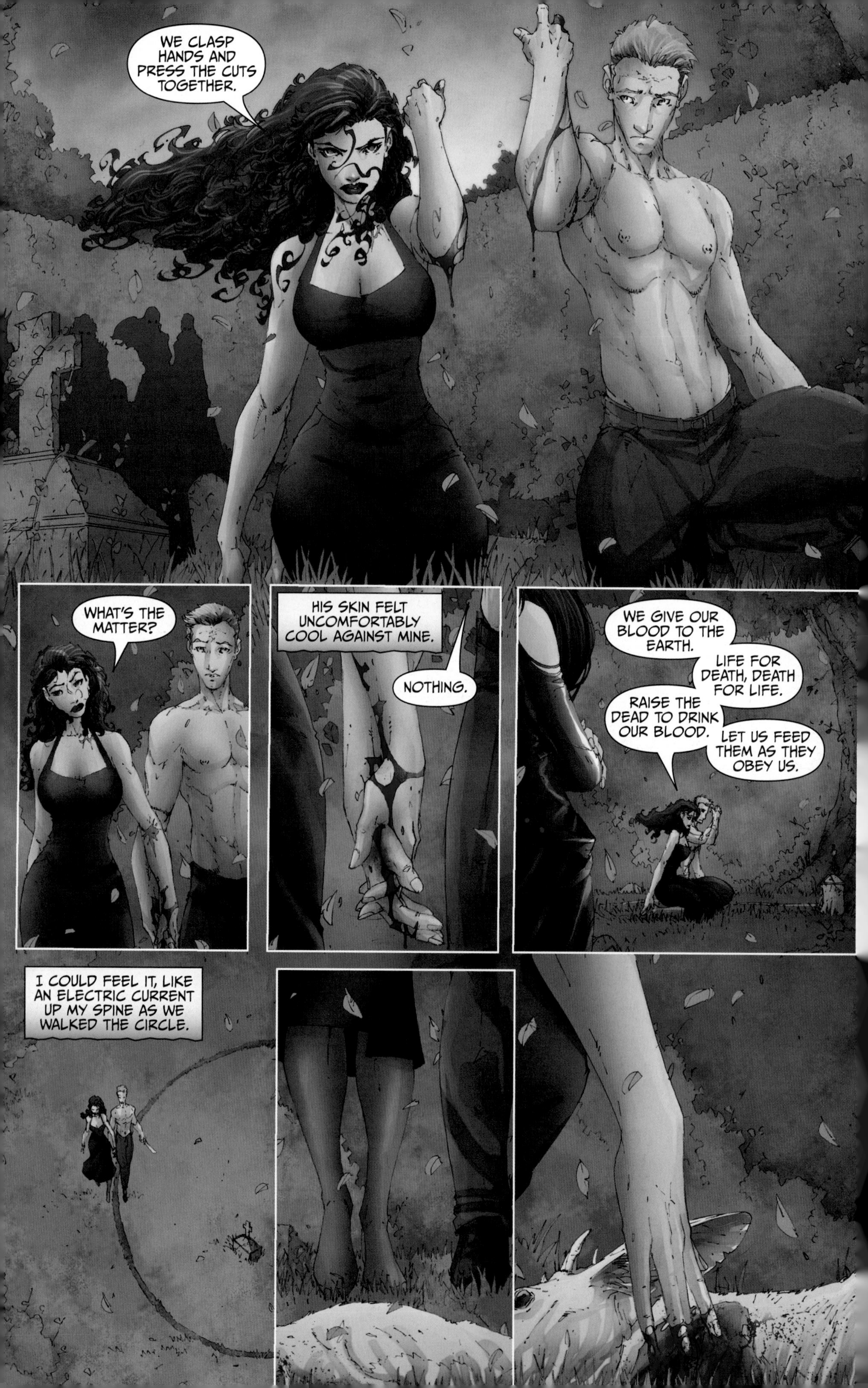
WE CLASP HANDS AND PRESS THE CUTS TOGETHER.
WHAT'S THE MATTER?
HIS SKIN FELT UNCOMFORTABLY COOL AGAINST MINE.
NOTHING.
WE GIVE OUR BLOOD TO THE EARTH.
LIFE FOR DEATH, DEATH FOR LIFE.
RAISE THE DEAD TO DRINK OUR BLOOD.
LET US FEED THEM AS THEY OBEY US.
I COULD FEEL IT, LIKE AN ELECTRIC CURRENT UP MY SPINE AS WE WALKED THE CIRCLE.

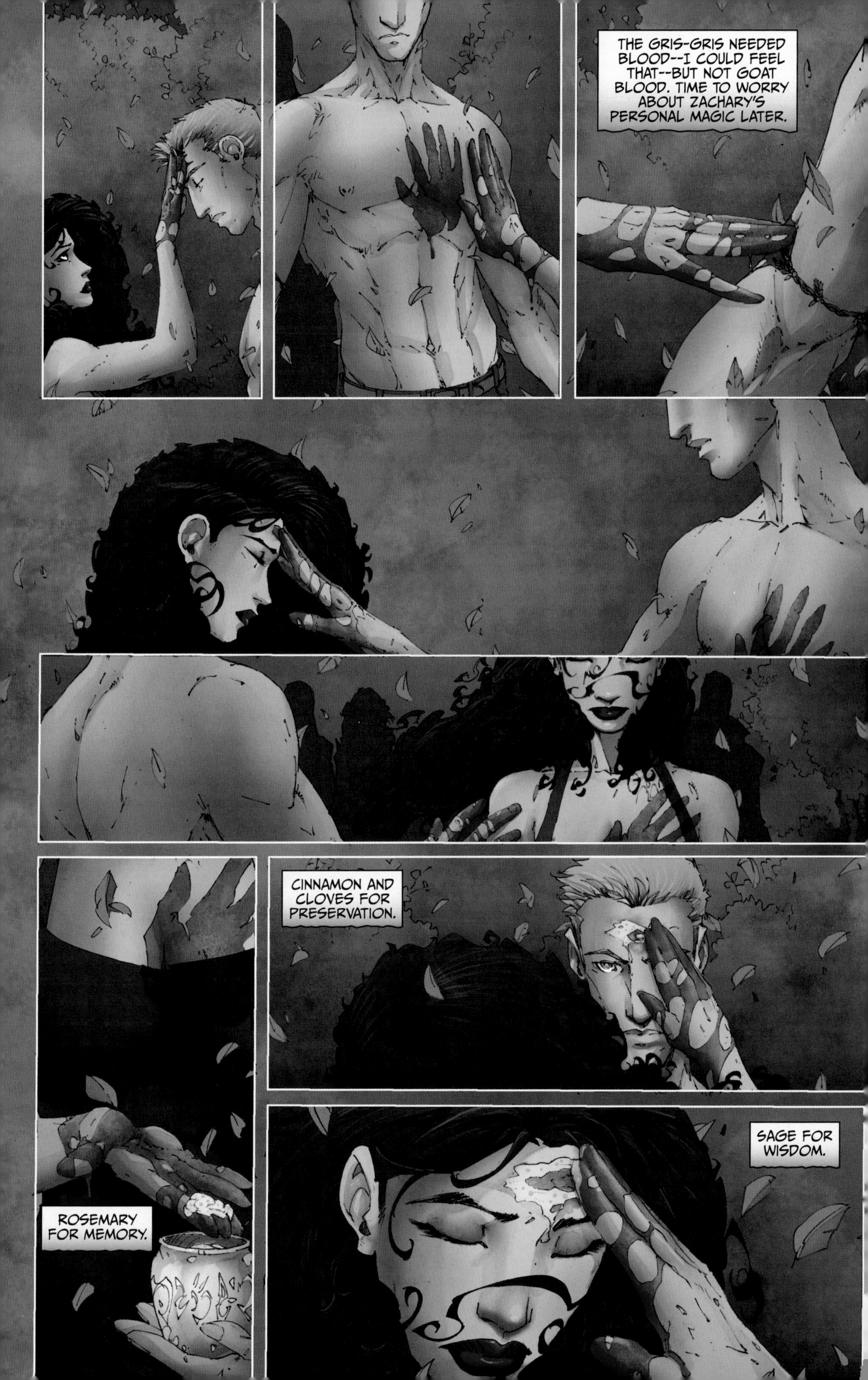
THE GRIS-GRIS NEEDED BLOOD--I COULD FEEL THAT--BUT NOT GOAT BLOOD. TIME TO WORRY ABOUT ZACHARY'S PERSONAL MAGIC LATER.
CINNAMON AND CLOVES FOR PRESERVATION.
ROSEMARY FOR MEMORY.
SAGE FOR WISDOM.

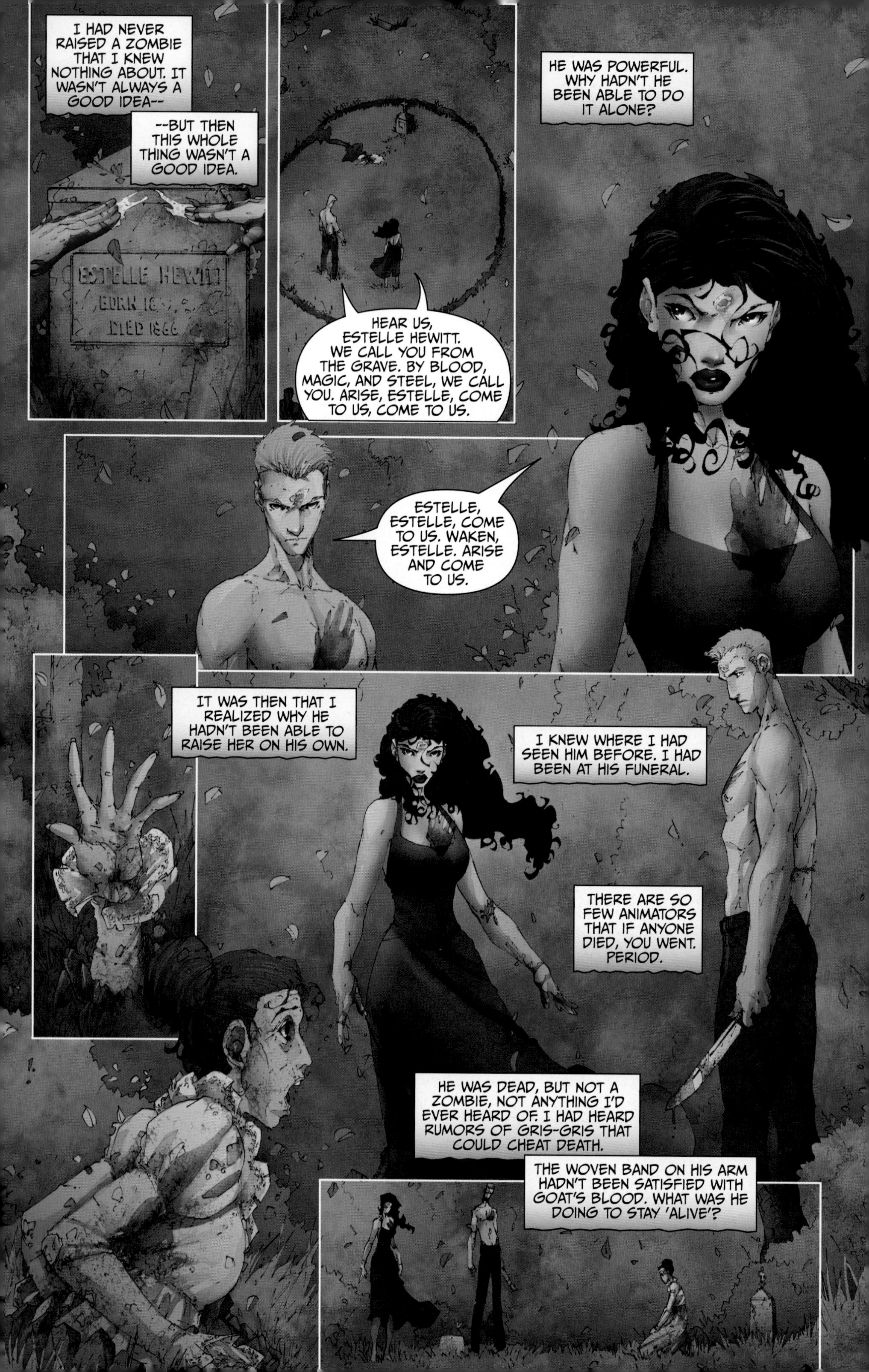

I HAD NEVER RAISED A ZOMBIE THAT I KNEW NOTHING ABOUT. IT WASN'T ALWAYS A GOOD IDEA--
--BUT THEN THIS WHOLE THING WASN'T A GOOD IDEA.
ESTELLE HEWITT
BORN 18
DIED 1866
HEAR US, ESTELLE HEWITT. WE CALL YOU FROM THE GRAVE. BY BLOOD, MAGIC, AND STEEL, WE CALL YOU. ARISE, ESTELLE, COME TO US, COME TO US.
HE WAS POWERFUL. WHY HADN'T HE BEEN ABLE TO DO IT ALONE?
ESTELLE, ESTELLE, COME TO US. WAKEN, ESTELLE. ARISE AND COME TO US.
IT WAS THEN THAT I REALIZED WHY HE HADN'T BEEN ABLE TO RAISE HER ON HIS OWN.
I KNEW WHERE I HAD SEEN HIM BEFORE. I HAD BEEN AT HIS FUNERAL.
THERE ARE SO FEW ANIMATORS THAT IF ANYONE DIED, YOU WENT. PERIOD.
HE WAS DEAD, BUT NOT A ZOMBIE, NOT ANYTHING I'D EVER HEARD OF. I HAD HEARD RUMORS OF GRIS-GRIS THAT COULD CHEAT DEATH.
THE WOVEN BAND ON HIS ARM HADN'T BEEN SATISFIED WITH GOAT'S BLOOD. WHAT WAS HE DOING TO STAY 'ALIVE'?

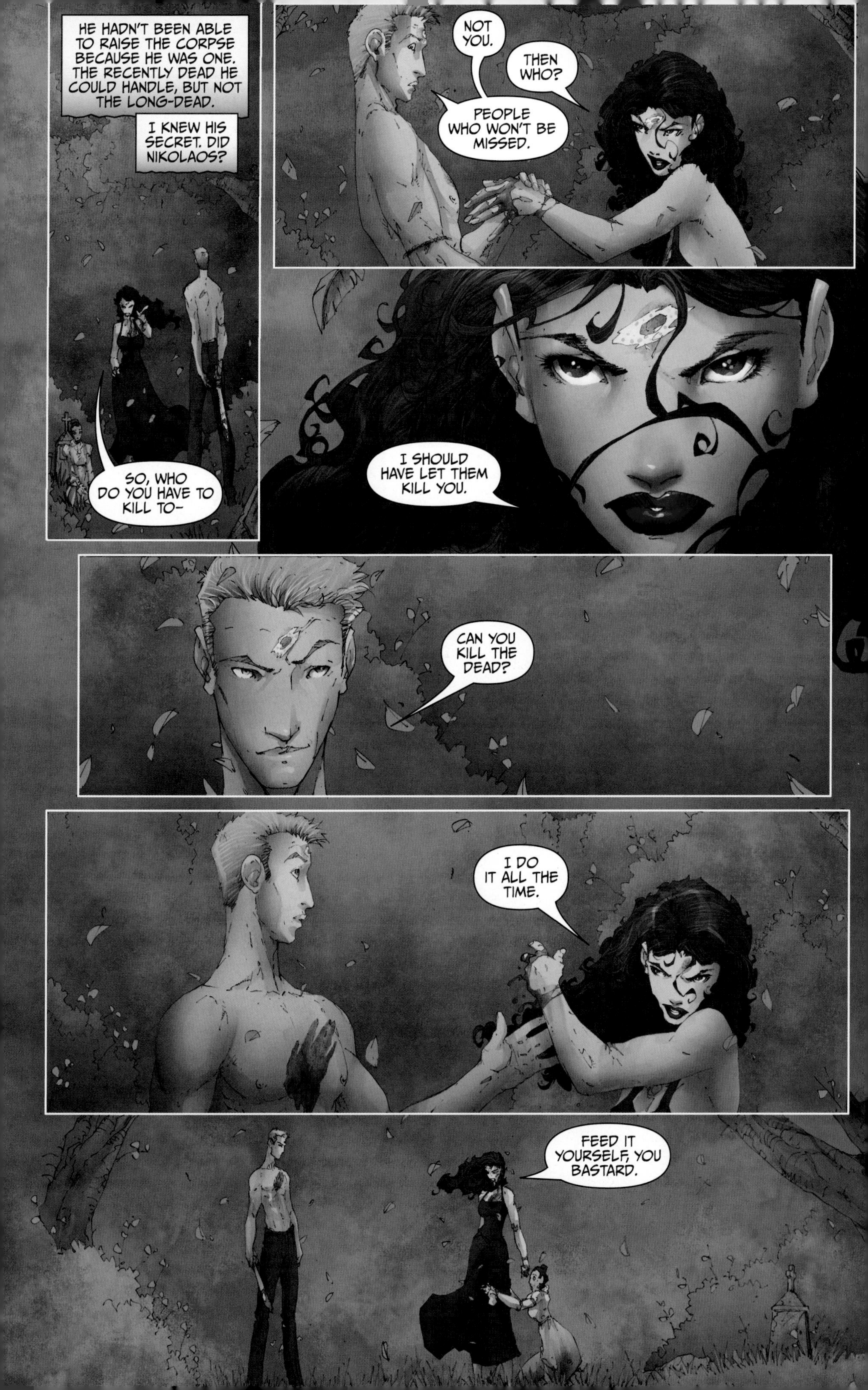
HE HADN'T BEEN ABLE TO RAISE THE CORPSE BECAUSE HE WAS ONE. THE RECENTLY DEAD HE COULD HANDLE, BUT NOT THE LONG-DEAD.
I KNEW HIS SECRET. DID NIKOLAOS?
SO, WHO DO YOU HAVE TO KILL TO-
NOT YOU.
THEN WHO?
PEOPLE WHO WON'T BE MISSED.
I SHOULD HAVE LET THEM KILL YOU.
CAN YOU KILL THE DEAD?
I DO IT ALL THE TIME.
FEED IT YOURSELF, YOU BASTARD.

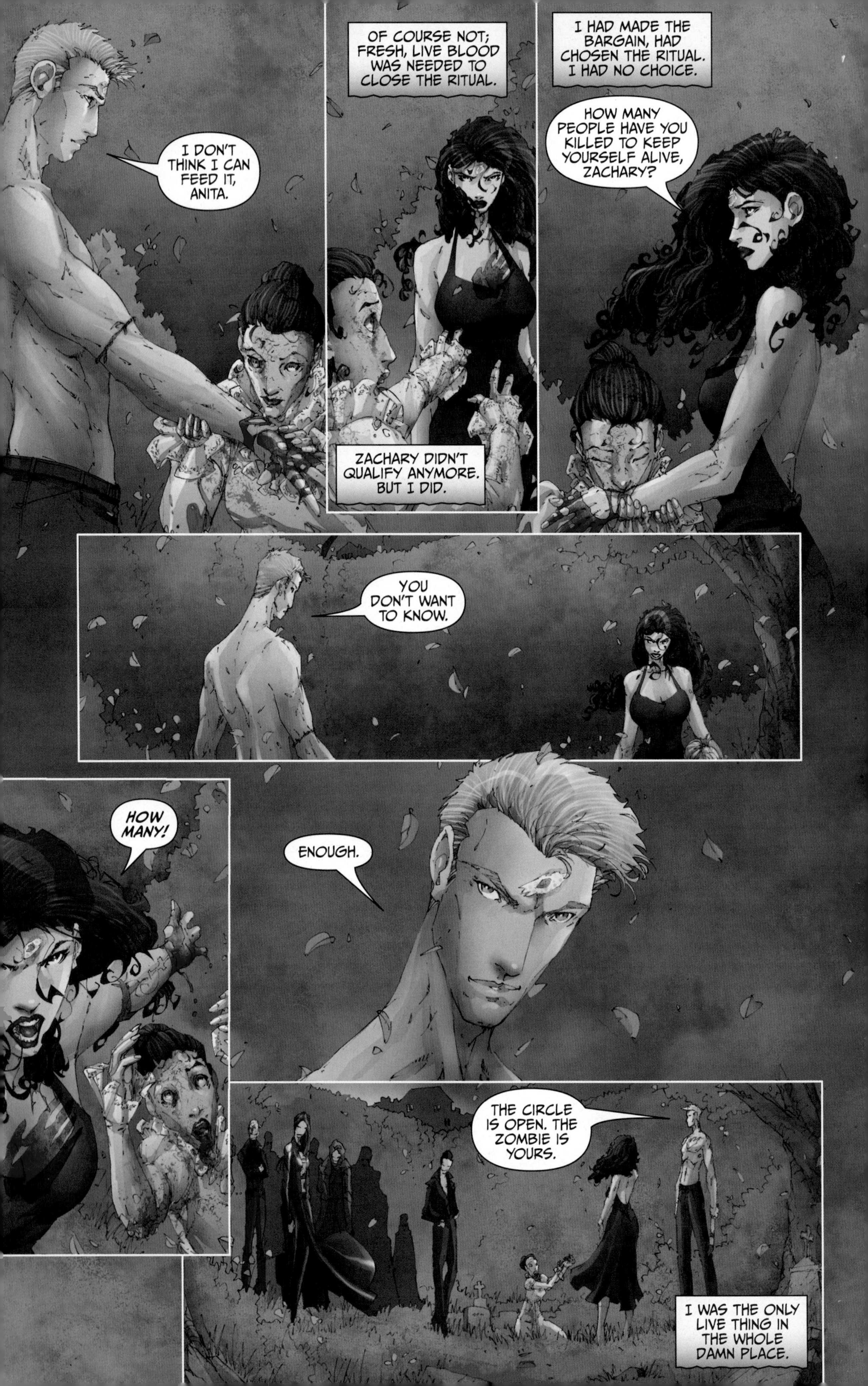
I DON'T THINK I CAN FEED IT, ANITA.
OF COURSE NOT; FRESH, LIVE BLOOD WAS NEEDED TO CLOSE THE RITUAL.
ZACHARY DIDN'T QUALIFY ANYMORE. BUT I DID.
I HAD MADE THE BARGAIN, HAD CHOSEN THE RITUAL. I HAD NO CHOICE.
HOW MANY PEOPLE HAVE YOU KILLED TO KEEP YOURSELF ALIVE, ZACHARY?
YOU DON'T WANT TO KNOW.
HOW MANY!
ENOUGH.
THE CIRCLE IS OPEN. THE ZOMBIE IS YOURS.
I WAS THE ONLY LIVE THING IN THE WHOLE DAMN PLACE.

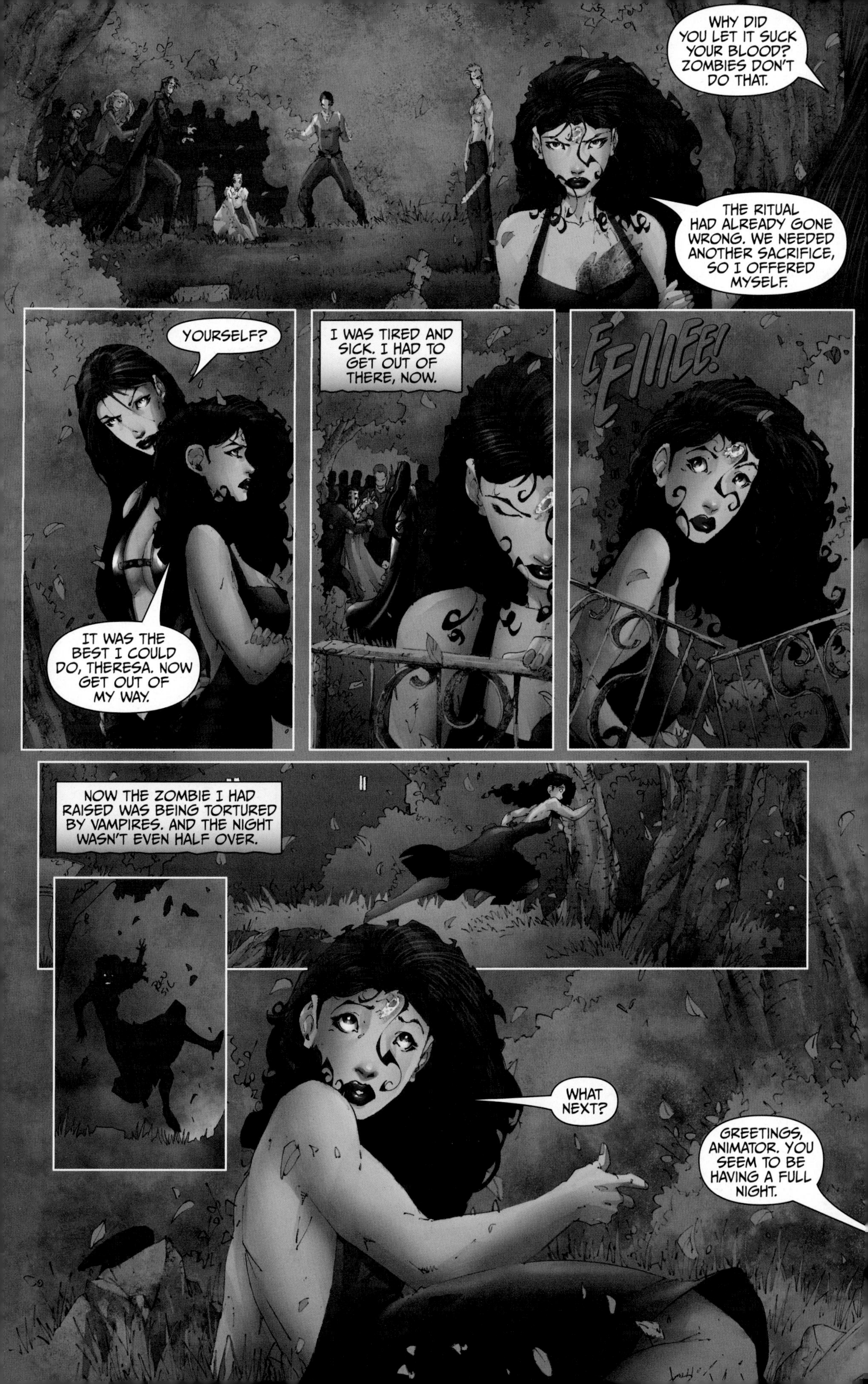
WHY DID YOU LET IT SUCK YOUR BLOOD? ZOMBIES DON'T DO THAT.
THE RITUAL HAD ALREADY GONE WRONG. WE NEEDED ANOTHER SACRIFICE, SO I OFFERED MYSELF.
YOURSELF?
IT WAS THE BEST I COULD DO, THERESA. NOW GET OUT OF MY WAY.
I WAS TIRED AND SICK. I HAD TO GET OUT OF THERE, NOW.
EEIIIIEE!
NOW THE ZOMBIE I HAD RAISED WAS BEING TORTURED BY VAMPIRES. AND THE NIGHT WASN'T EVEN HALF OVER.
WHAT NEXT?
GREETINGS, ANIMATOR. YOU SEEM TO BE HAVING A FULL NIGHT.

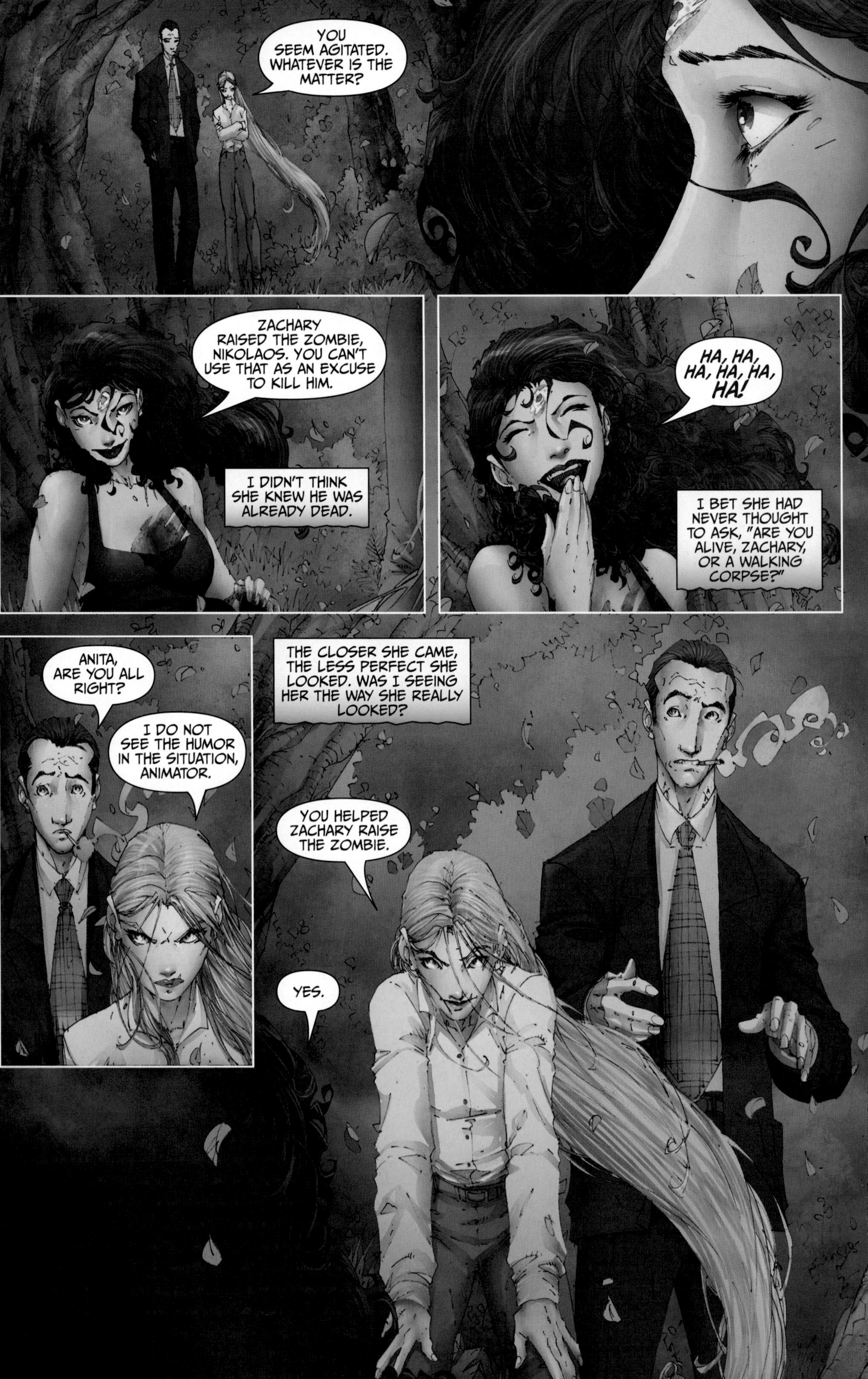
YOU SEEM AGITATED. WHATEVER IS THE MATTER?
ZACHARY RAISED THE ZOMBIE, NIKOLAOS. YOU CAN'T USE THAT AS AN EXCUSE TO KILL HIM.
I DIDN'T THINK SHE KNEW HE WAS ALREADY DEAD.
HA, HA, HA, HA, HA, HA!
I BET SHE HAD NEVER THOUGHT TO ASK, "ARE YOU ALIVE, ZACHARY, OR A WALKING CORPSE?"
ANITA, ARE YOU ALL RIGHT?
I DO NOT SEE THE HUMOR IN THE SITUATION, ANIMATOR.
THE CLOSER SHE CAME, THE LESS PERFECT SHE LOOKED. WAS I SEEING HER THE WAY SHE REALLY LOOKED?
YOU HELPED ZACHARY RAISE THE ZOMBIE.
YES.

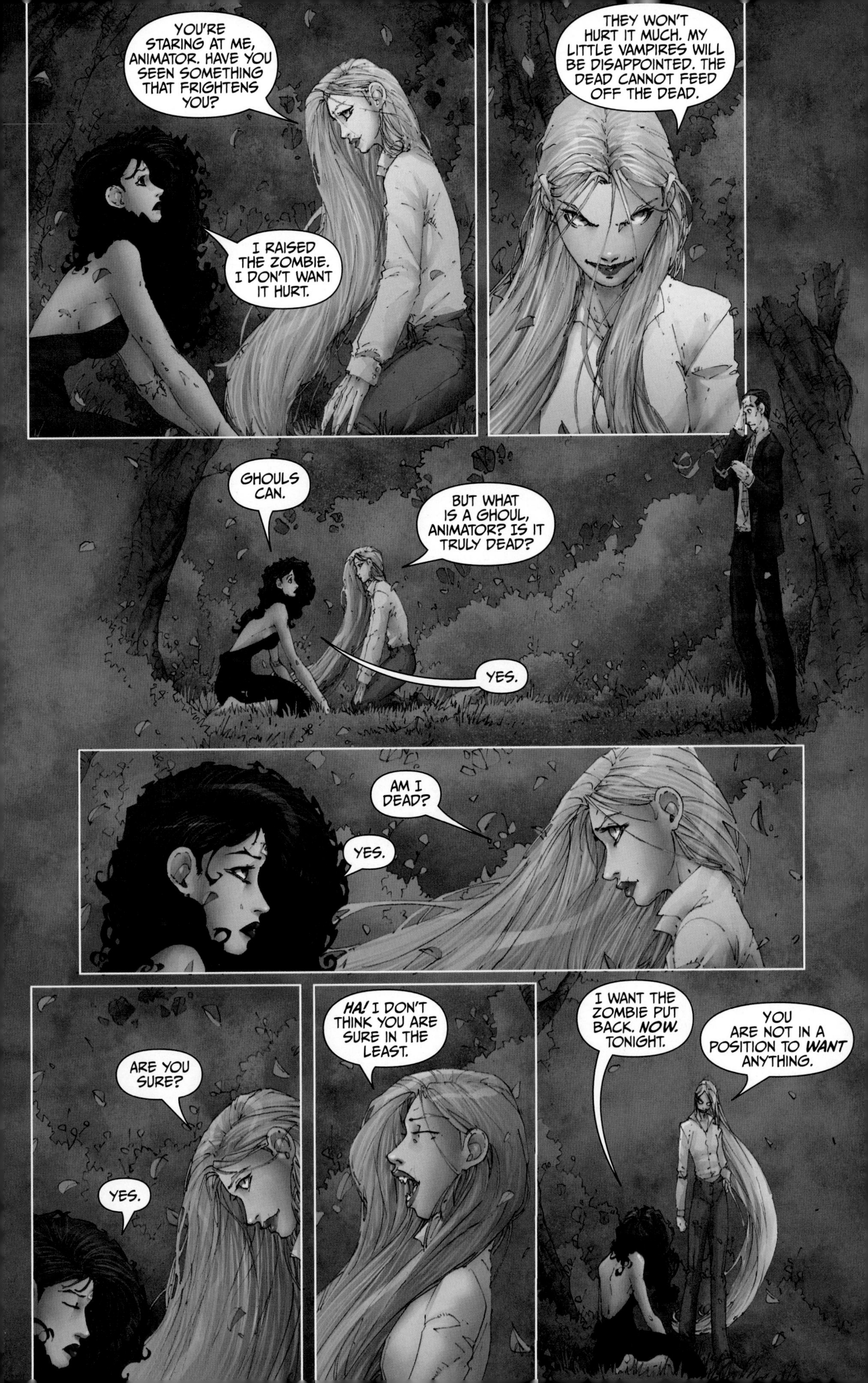
YOU'RE STARING AT ME, ANIMATOR. HAVE YOU SEEN SOMETHING THAT FRIGHTENS YOU?
I RAISED THE ZOMBIE. I DON'T WANT IT HURT.
THEY WON'T HURT IT MUCH. MY LITTLE VAMPIRES WILL BE DISAPPOINTED. THE DEAD CANNOT FEED OFF THE DEAD.
GHOULS CAN.
BUT WHAT IS A GHOUL, ANIMATOR? IS IT TRULY DEAD?
YES.
AM I DEAD?
YES.
ARE YOU SURE?
YES.
HA! I DON'T THINK YOU ARE SURE IN THE LEAST.
I WANT THE ZOMBIE PUT BACK. NOW. TONIGHT.
YOU ARE NOT IN A POSITION TO WANT ANYTHING.

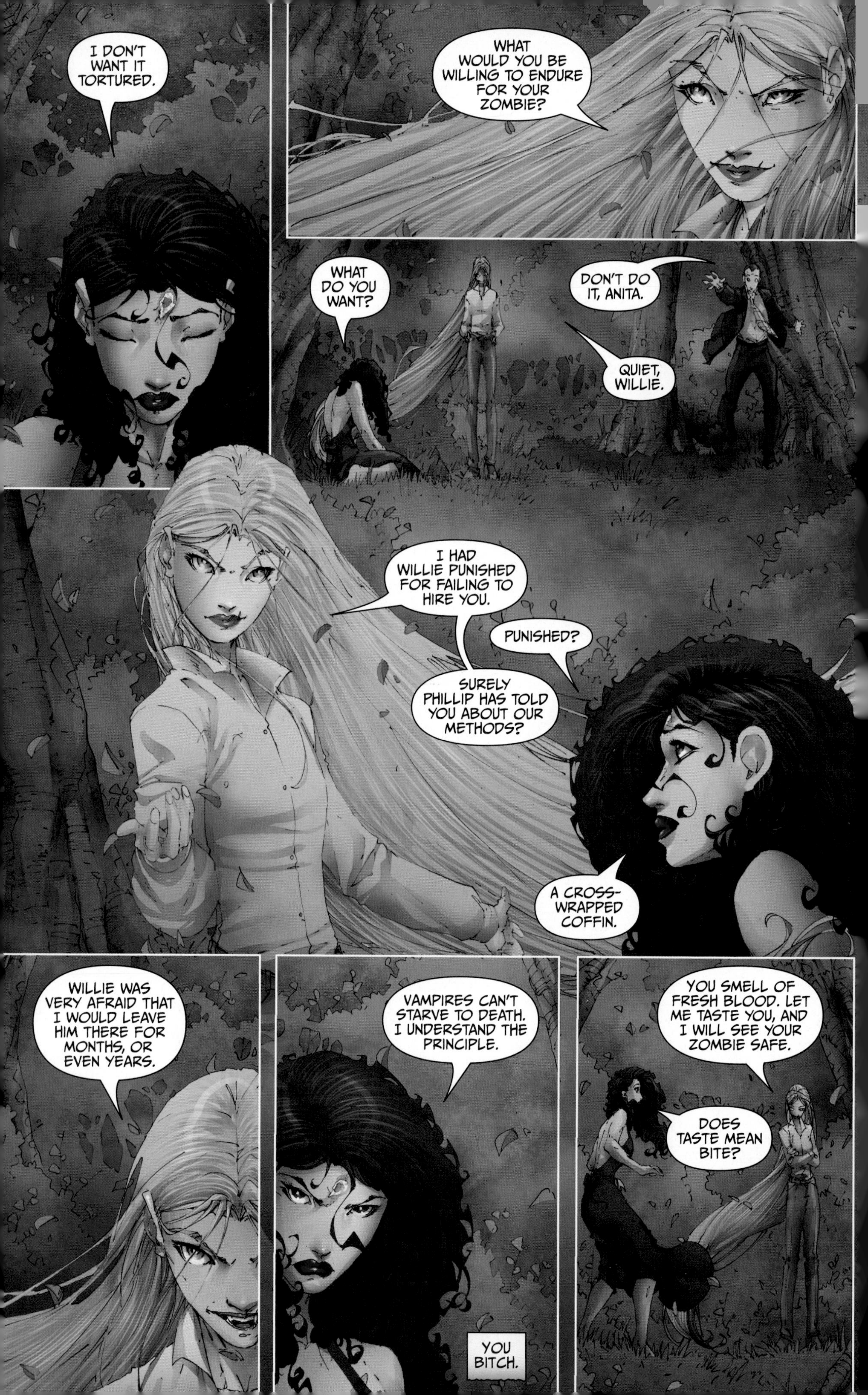
I DON'T WANT IT TORTURED.
WHAT WOULD YOU BE WILLING TO ENDURE FOR YOUR ZOMBIE?
WHAT DO YOU WANT?
DON'T DO IT, ANITA.
QUIET, WILLIE.
I HAD WILLIE PUNISHED FOR FAILING TO HIRE YOU.
PUNISHED?
SURELY PHILLIP HAS TOLD YOU ABOUT OUR METHODS?
A CROSS-WRAPPED COFFIN.
WILLIE WAS VERY AFRAID THAT I WOULD LEAVE HIM THERE FOR MONTHS, OR EVEN YEARS.
VAMPIRES CAN'T STARVE TO DEATH. I UNDERSTAND THE PRINCIPLE.
YOU BITCH.
YOU SMELL OF FRESH BLOOD. LET ME TASTE YOU, AND I WILL SEE YOUR ZOMBIE SAFE.
DOES TASTE MEAN BITE?

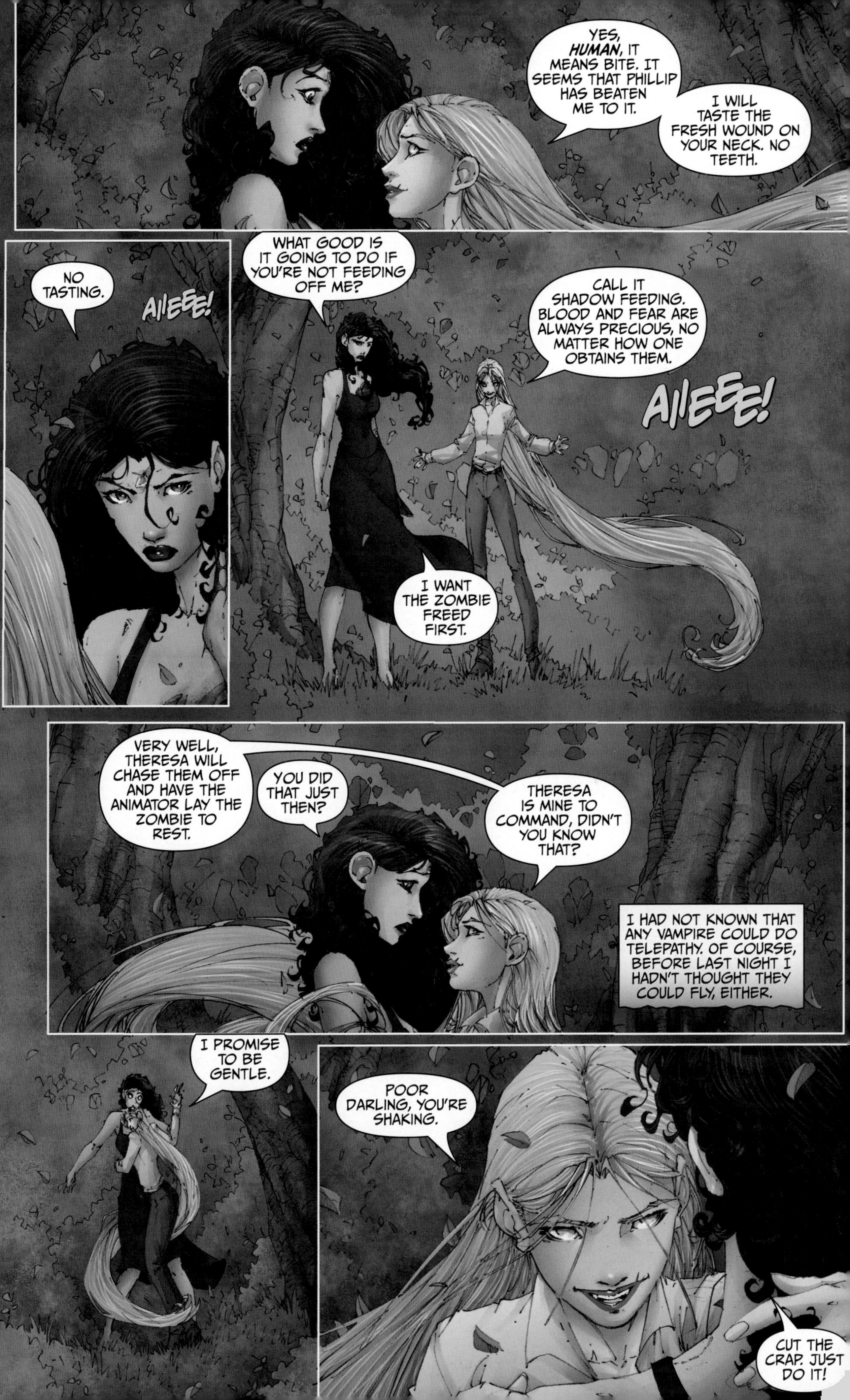

YES, HUMAN, IT MEANS BITE. IT SEEMS THAT PHILLIP HAS BEATEN ME TO IT.
I WILL TASTE THE FRESH WOUND ON YOUR NECK. NO TEETH.
NO TASTING.
AIIEEE!
WHAT GOOD IS IT GOING TO DO IF YOU'RE NOT FEEDING OFF ME?
CALL IT SHADOW FEEDING. BLOOD AND FEAR ARE ALWAYS PRECIOUS, NO MATTER HOW ONE OBTAINS THEM.
AIIEEE!
I WANT THE ZOMBIE FREED FIRST.
VERY WELL, THERESA WILL CHASE THEM OFF AND HAVE THE ANIMATOR LAY THE ZOMBIE TO REST.
YOU DID THAT JUST THEN?
THERESA IS MINE TO COMMAND, DIDN'T YOU KNOW THAT?
I HAD NOT KNOWN THAT ANY VAMPIRE COULD DO TELEPATHY. OF COURSE, BEFORE LAST NIGHT I HADN'T THOUGHT THEY COULD FLY, EITHER.
I PROMISE TO BE GENTLE.
POOR DARLING, YOU'RE SHAKING.
CUT THE CRAP. JUST DO IT!

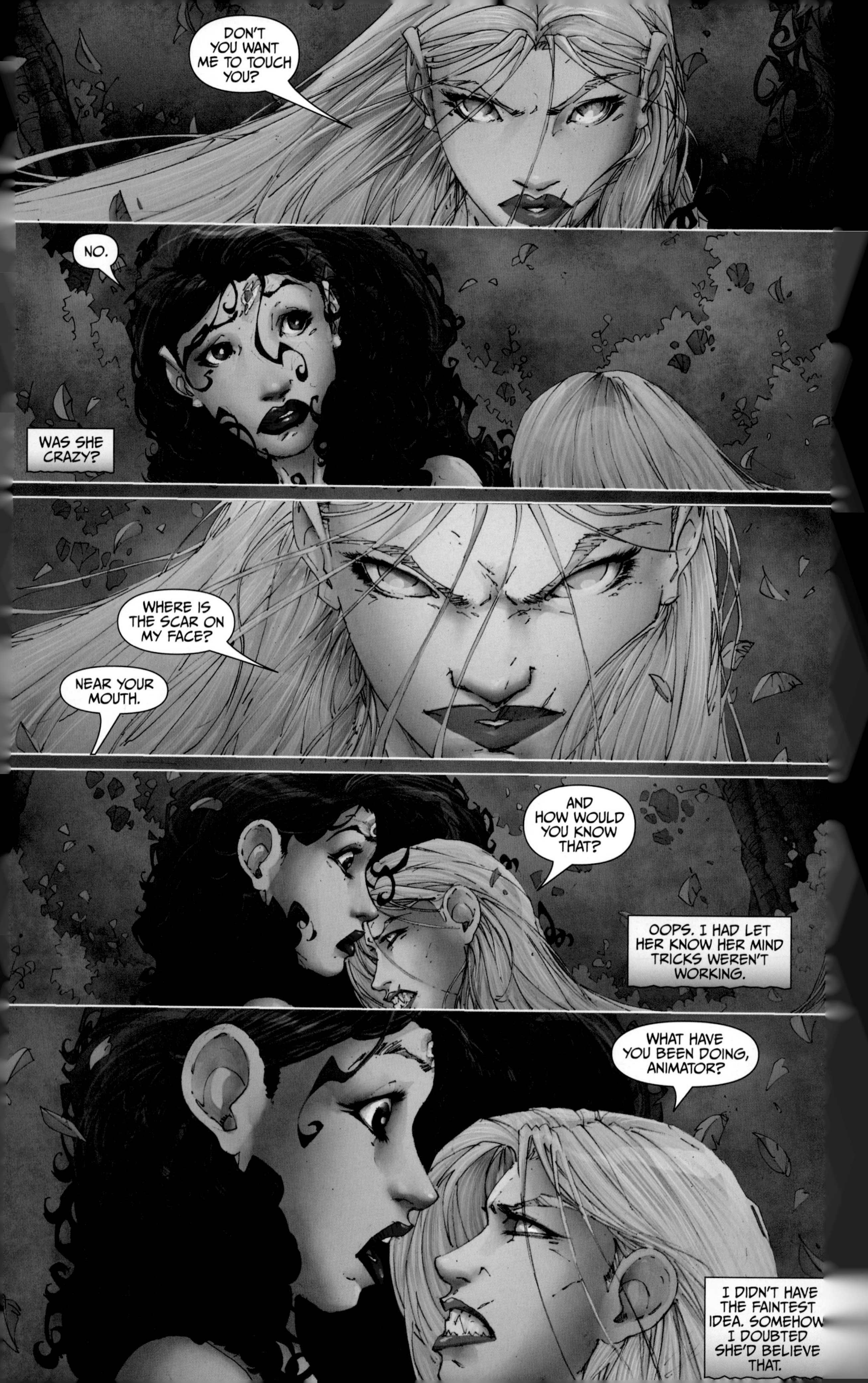

DON'T YOU WANT ME TO TOUCH YOU?
NO.
WAS SHE CRAZY?
WHERE IS THE SCAR ON MY FACE?
NEAR YOUR MOUTH.
AND HOW WOULD YOU KNOW THAT?
OOPS. I HAD LET HER KNOW HER MIND TRICKS WEREN'T WORKING.
WHAT HAVE YOU BEEN DOING, ANIMATOR?
I DIDN'T HAVE THE FAINTEST IDEA. SOMEHOW I DOUBTED SHE'D BELIEVE THAT.

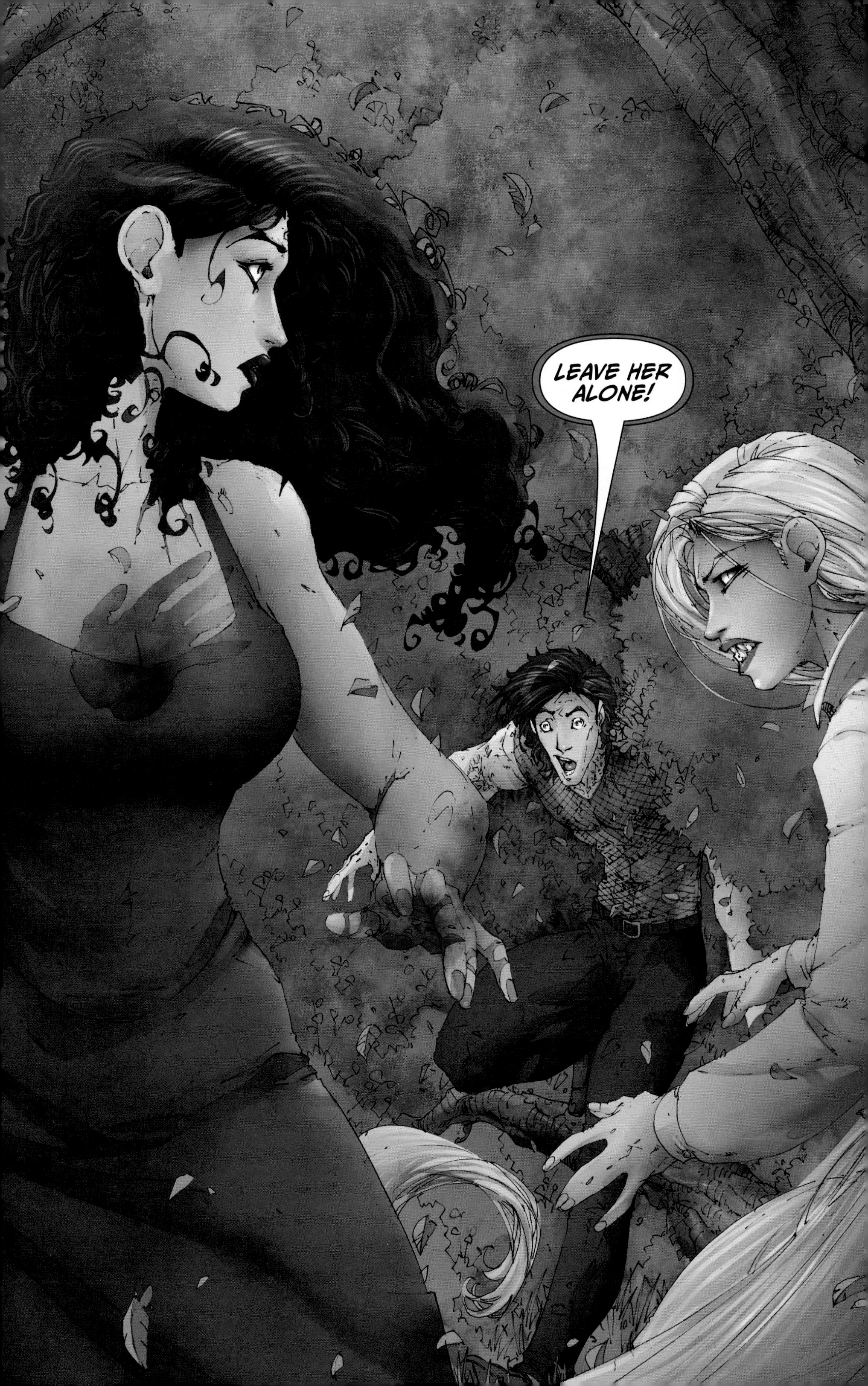
LEAVE HER ALONE!

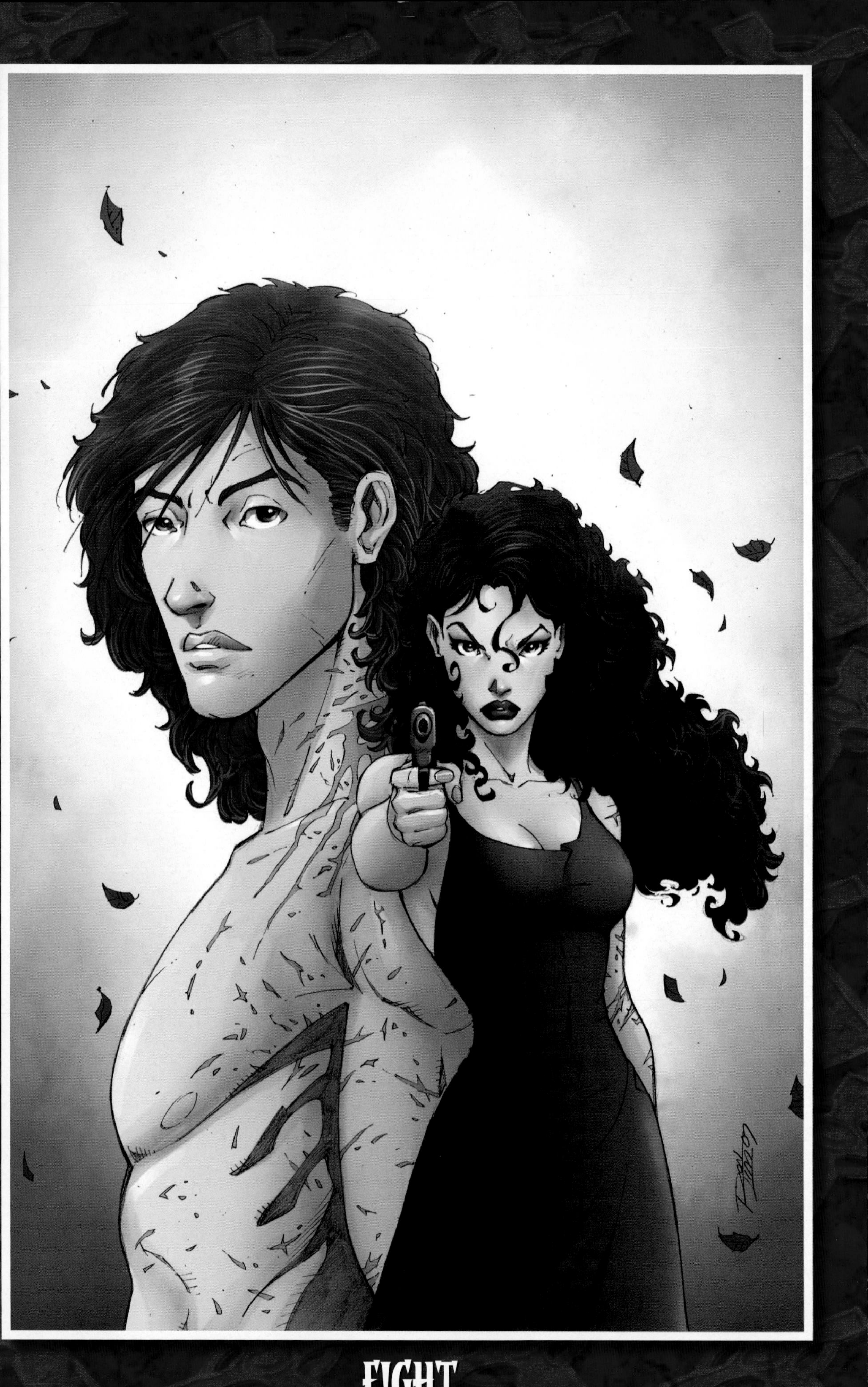

EIGHT

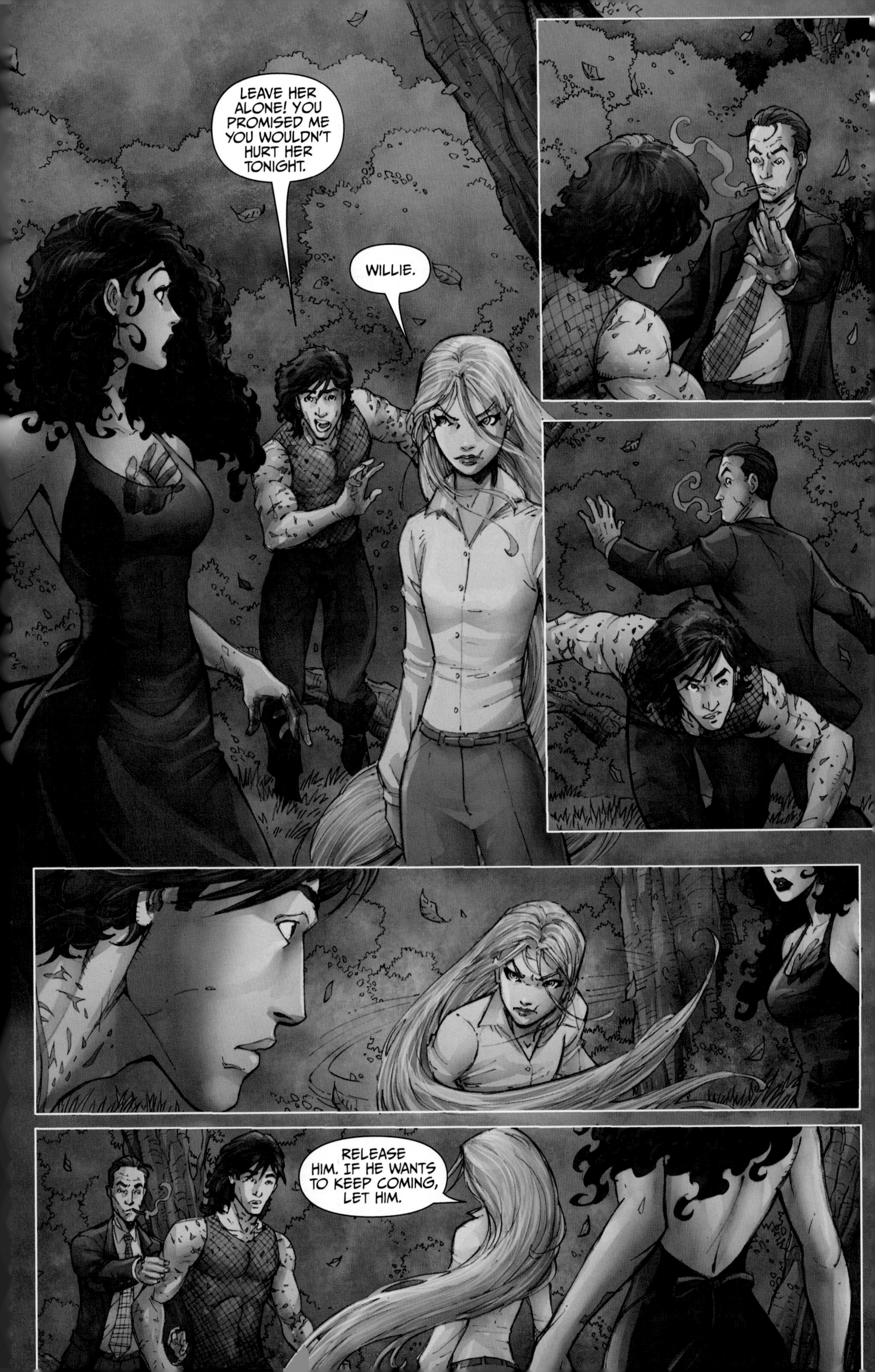
LEAVE HER ALONE! YOU PROMISED ME YOU WOULDN'T HURT HER TONIGHT.
WILLIE.
RELEASE HIM. IF HE WANTS TO KEEP COMING, LET HIM.

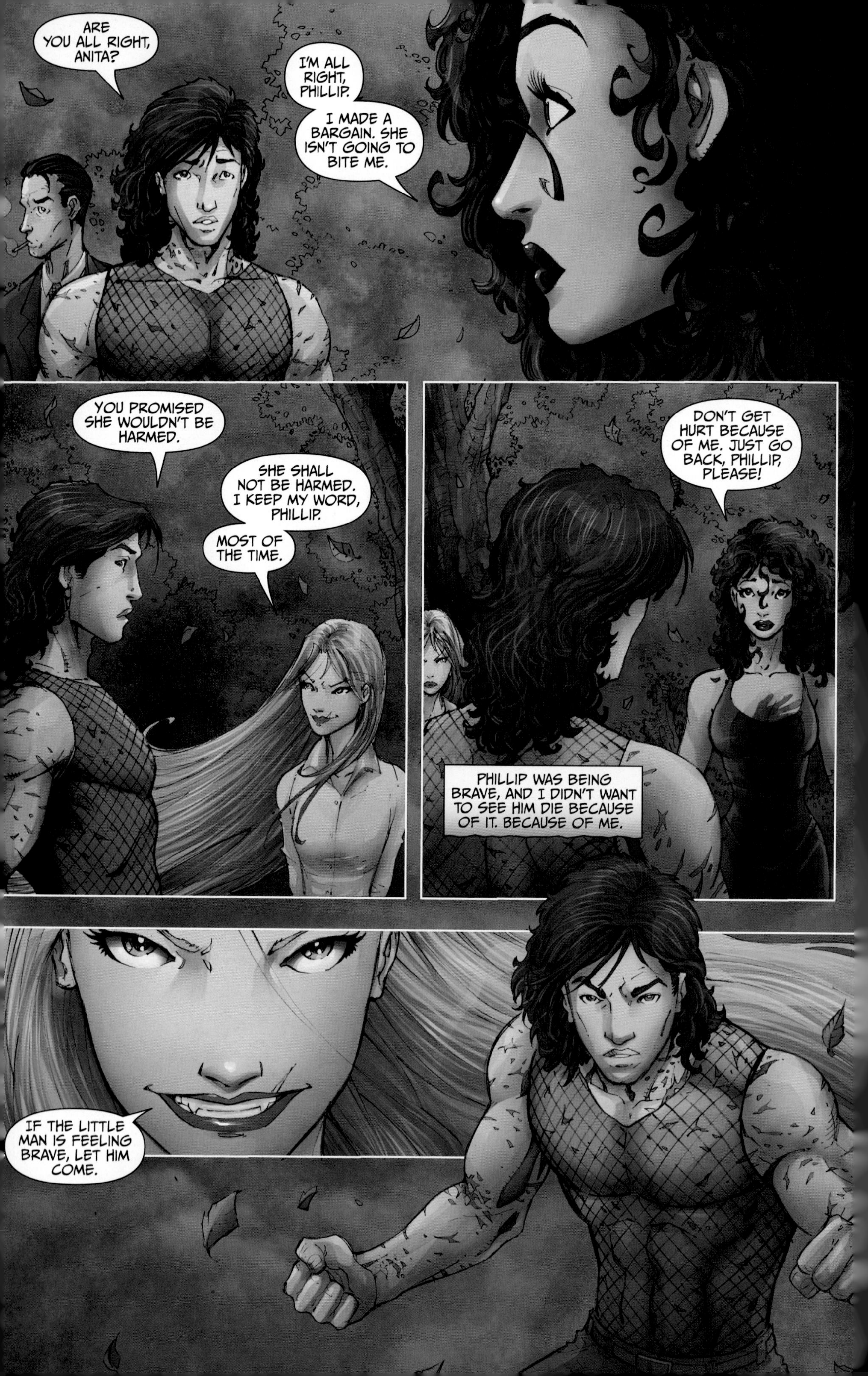
ARE YOU ALL RIGHT, ANITA?
I'M ALL RIGHT, PHILLIP.
I MADE A BARGAIN. SHE ISN'T GOING TO BITE ME.
YOU PROMISED SHE WOULDN'T BE HARMED.
SHE SHALL NOT BE HARMED. I KEEP MY WORD, PHILLIP.
MOST OF THE TIME.
DON'T GET HURT BECAUSE OF ME. JUST GO BACK, PHILLIP, PLEASE!
PHILLIP WAS BEING BRAVE, AND I DIDN'T WANT TO SEE HIM DIE BECAUSE OF IT. BECAUSE OF ME.
IF THE LITTLE MAN IS FEELING BRAVE, LET HIM COME.

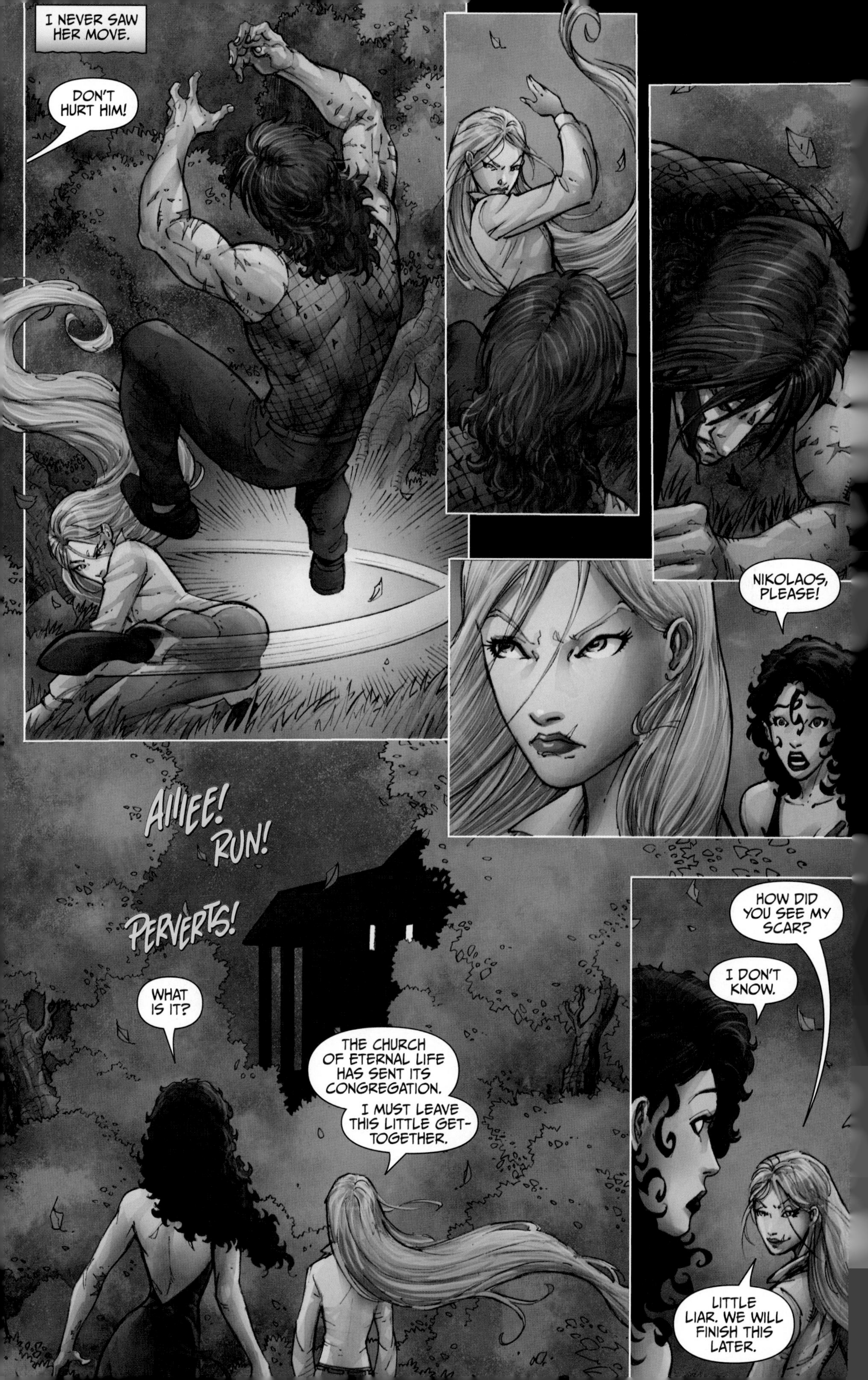
I NEVER SAW HER MOVE.
DON'T HURT HIM!
NIKOLAOS, PLEASE!
AIIIEE!
RUN!
PERVERTS!
WHAT IS IT?
THE CHURCH OF ETERNAL LIFE HAS SENT ITS CONGREGATION.
I MUST LEAVE THIS LITTLE GET-TOGETHER.
HOW DID YOU SEE MY SCAR?
I DON'T KNOW.
LITTLE LIAR. WE WILL FINISH THIS LATER.

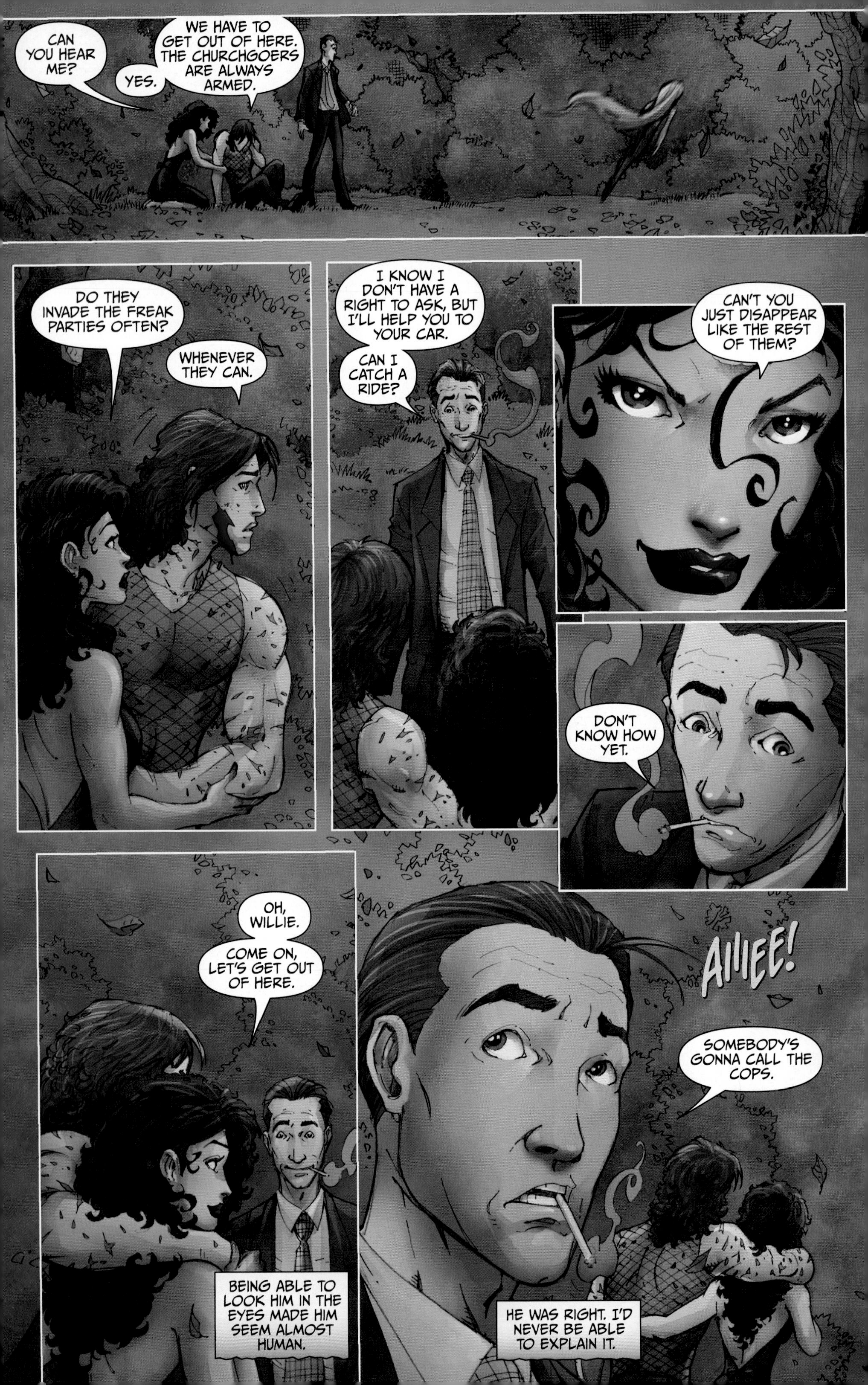
CAN YOU HEAR ME?
YES.
WE HAVE TO GET OUT OF HERE. THE CHURCHGOERS ARE ALWAYS ARMED.
DO THEY INVADE THE FREAK PARTIES OFTEN?
WHENEVER THEY CAN.
I KNOW I DON'T HAVE A RIGHT TO ASK, BUT I'LL HELP YOU TO YOUR CAR.
CAN I CATCH A RIDE?
CAN'T YOU JUST DISAPPEAR LIKE THE REST OF THEM?
DON'T KNOW HOW YET.
OH, WILLIE.
COME ON, LET'S GET OUT OF HERE.
BEING ABLE TO LOOK HIM IN THE EYES MADE HIM SEEM ALMOST HUMAN.
AIIEE!
SOMEBODY'S GONNA CALL THE COPS.
HE WAS RIGHT. I'D NEVER BE ABLE TO EXPLAIN IT.

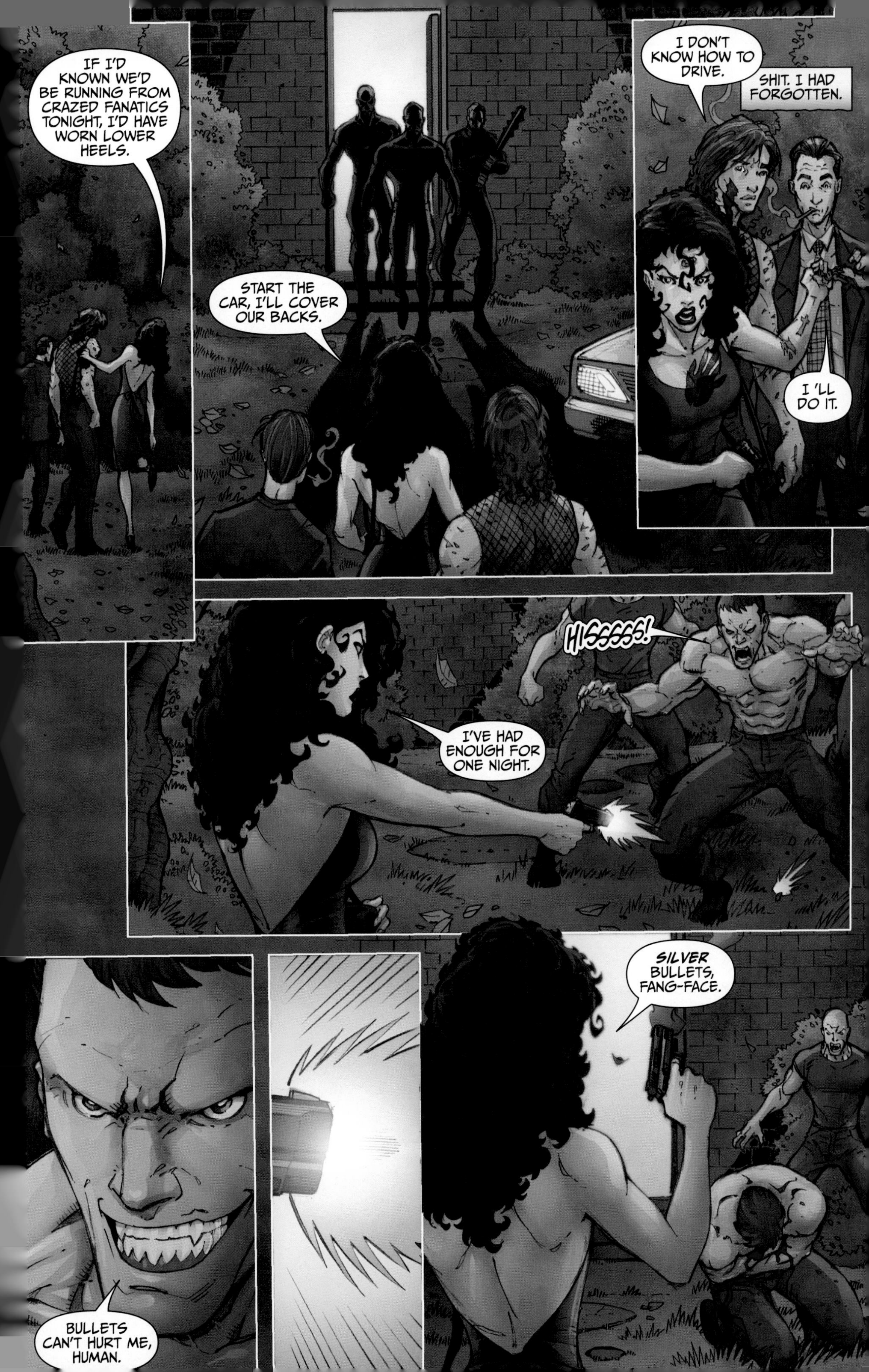
IF I'D KNOWN WE'D BE RUNNING FROM CRAZED FANATICS TONIGHT, I'D HAVE WORN LOWER HEELS.
START THE CAR, I'LL COVER OUR BACKS.
I DON'T KNOW HOW TO DRIVE.
SHIT. I HAD FORGOTTEN.
I 'LL DO IT.
HISSSSS!
I'VE HAD ENOUGH FOR ONE NIGHT.
BULLETS CAN'T HURT ME, HUMAN.
SILVER BULLETS, FANG-FACE.

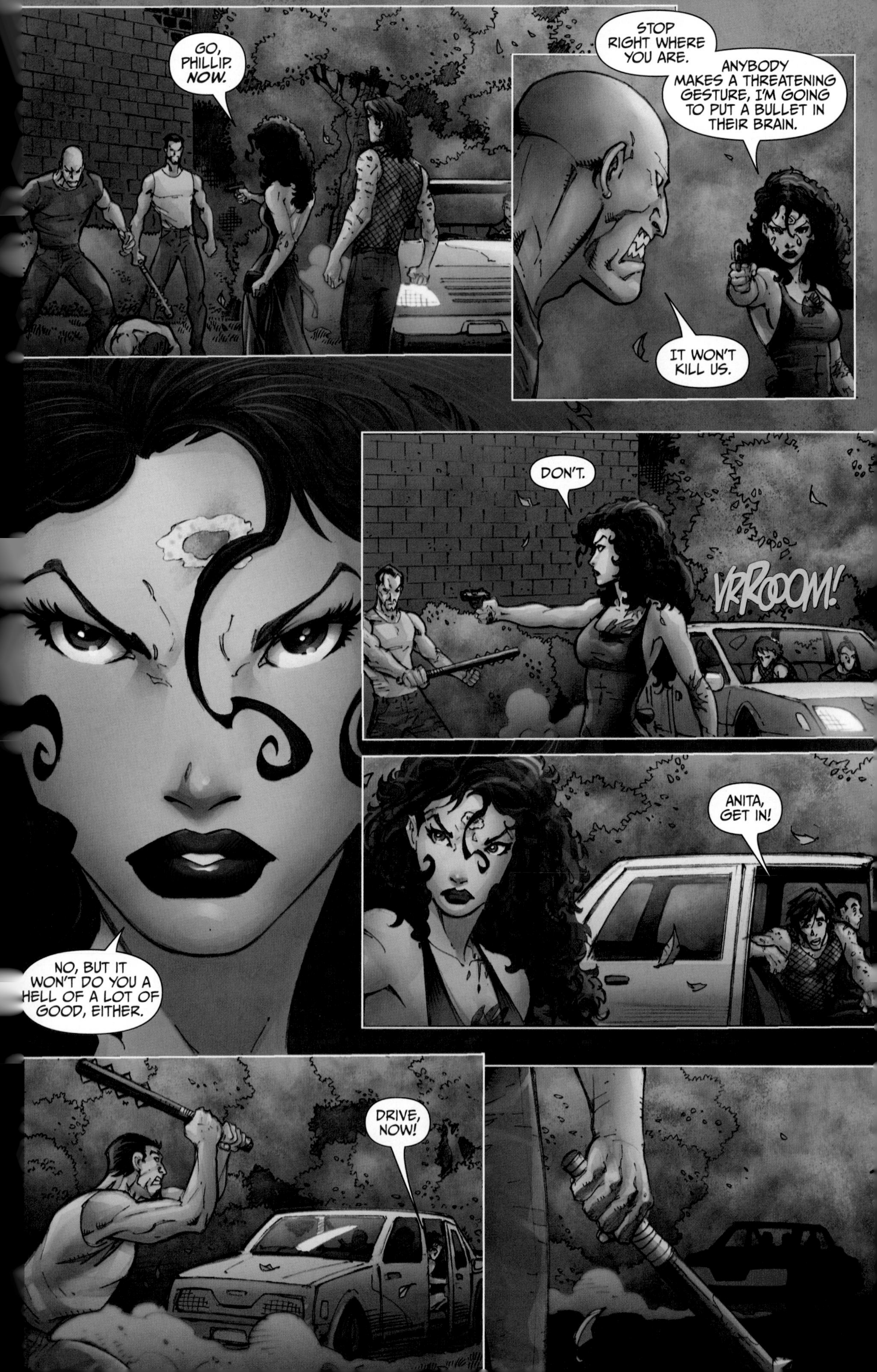
GO, PHILLIP. NOW.
STOP RIGHT WHERE YOU ARE.
ANYBODY MAKES A THREATENING GESTURE, I'M GOING TO PUT A BULLET IN THEIR BRAIN.
IT WON'T KILL US.
NO, BUT IT WON'T DO YOU A HELL OF A LOT OF GOOD, EITHER.
DON'T.
VRROOM!
ANITA, GET IN!
DRIVE, NOW!

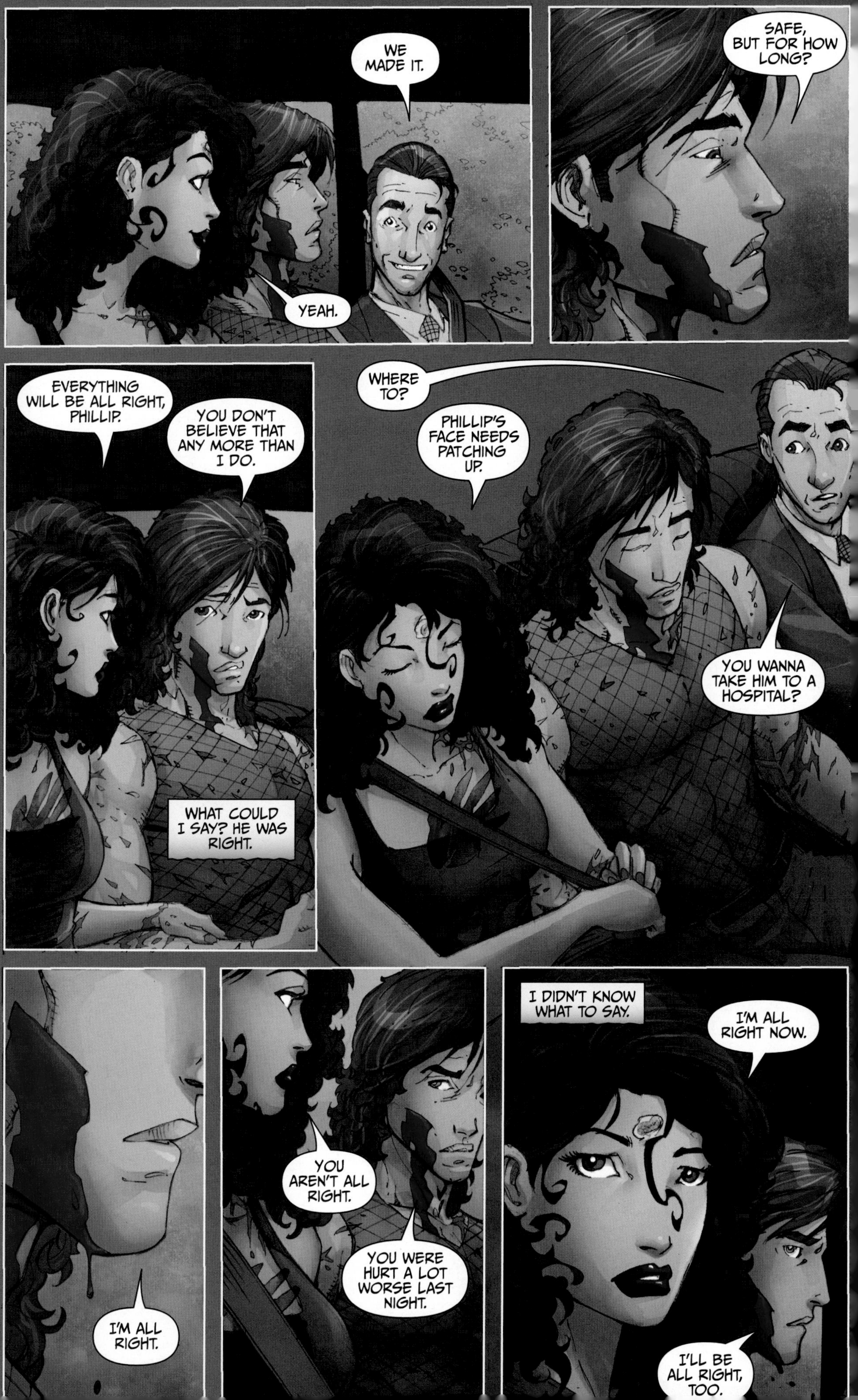
WE MADE IT.
YEAH.
SAFE, BUT FOR HOW LONG?
EVERYTHING WILL BE ALL RIGHT, PHILLIP.
YOU DON'T BELIEVE THAT ANY MORE THAN I DO.
WHAT COULD I SAY? HE WAS RIGHT.
WHERE TO?
PHILLIP'S FACE NEEDS PATCHING UP.
YOU WANNA TAKE HIM TO A HOSPITAL?
I'M ALL RIGHT.
YOU AREN'T ALL RIGHT.
YOU WERE HURT A LOT WORSE LAST NIGHT.
I DIDN'T KNOW WHAT TO SAY.
I'M ALL RIGHT NOW.
I'LL BE ALL RIGHT, TOO.

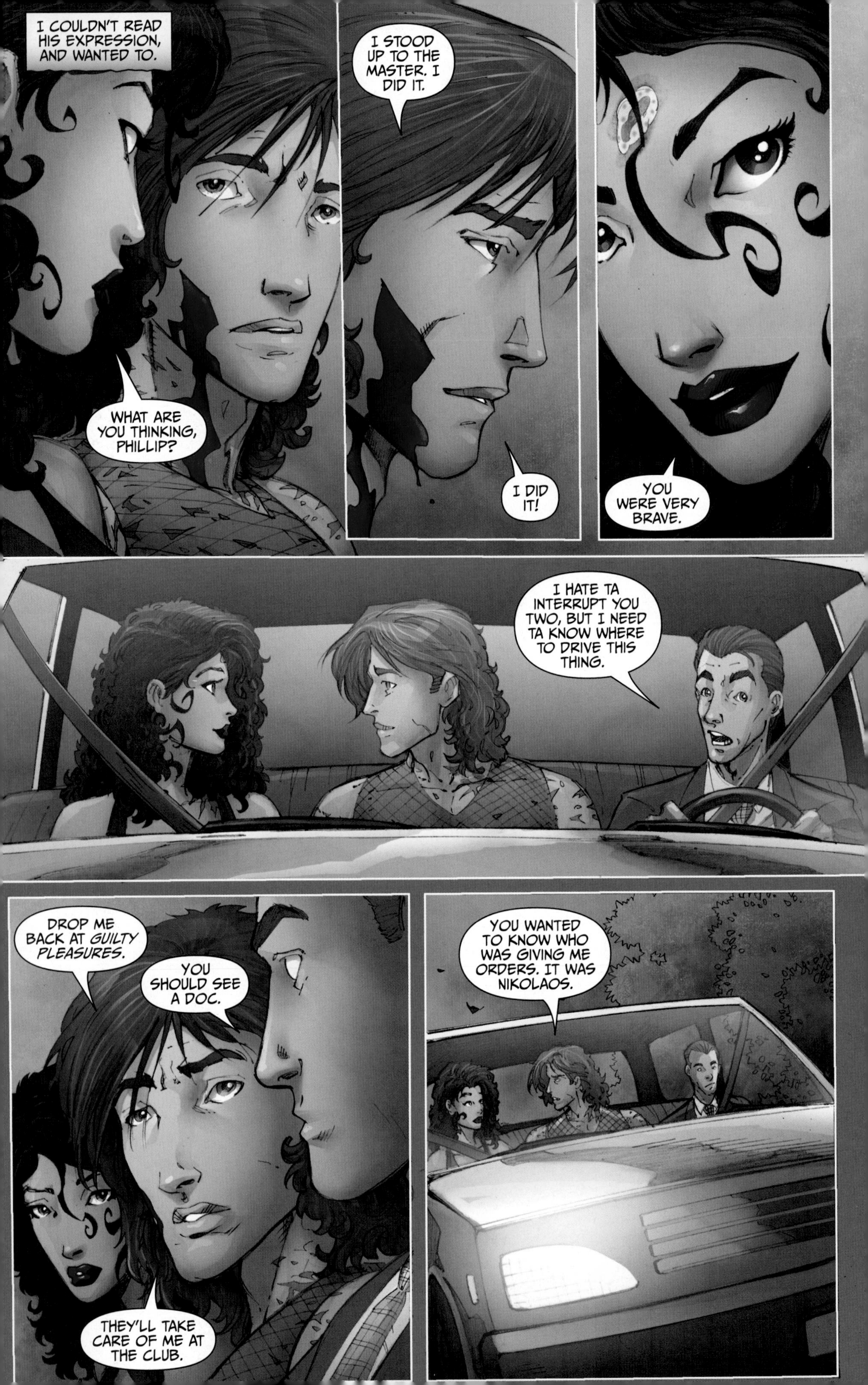
I COULDN'T READ HIS EXPRESSION, AND WANTED TO.
WHAT ARE YOU THINKING, PHILLIP?
I STOOD UP TO THE MASTER. I DID IT.
I DID IT!
YOU WERE VERY BRAVE.
I HATE TA INTERRUPT YOU TWO, BUT I NEED TA KNOW WHERE TO DRIVE THIS THING.
DROP ME BACK AT *GUILTY PLEASURES*.
YOU SHOULD SEE A DOC.
THEY'LL TAKE CARE OF ME AT THE CLUB.
YOU WANTED TO KNOW WHO WAS GIVING ME ORDERS. IT WAS NIKOLAOS.

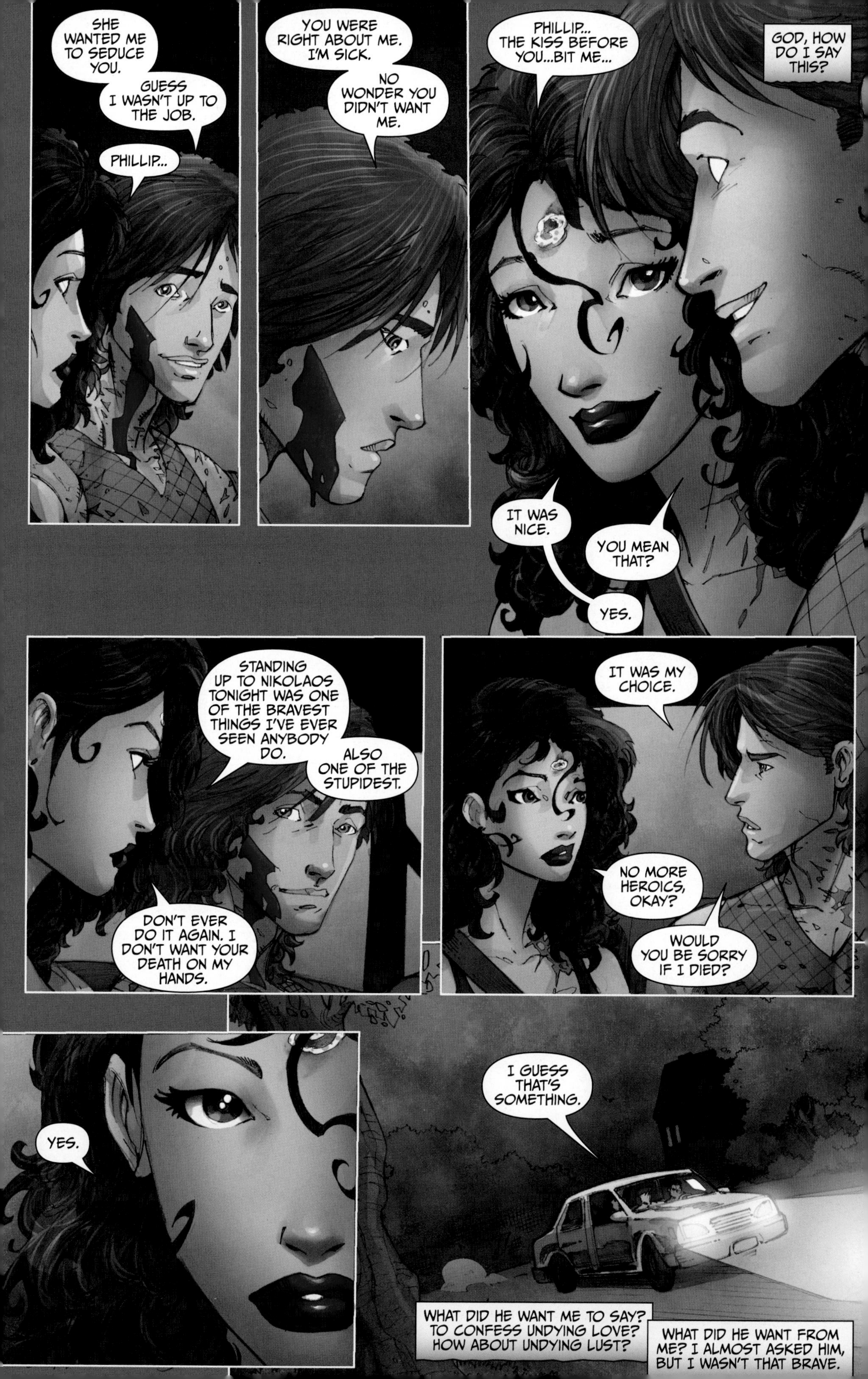
SHE WANTED ME TO SEDUCE YOU.
GUESS I WASN'T UP TO THE JOB.
PHILLIP...
YOU WERE RIGHT ABOUT ME. I'M SICK.
NO WONDER YOU DIDN'T WANT ME.
PHILLIP... THE KISS BEFORE YOU...BIT ME...
GOD, HOW DO I SAY THIS?
IT WAS NICE.
YOU MEAN THAT?
YES.
STANDING UP TO NIKOLAOS TONIGHT WAS ONE OF THE BRAVEST THINGS I'VE EVER SEEN ANYBODY DO.
ALSO ONE OF THE STUPIDEST.
DON'T EVER DO IT AGAIN. I DON'T WANT YOUR DEATH ON MY HANDS.
IT WAS MY CHOICE.
NO MORE HEROICS, OKAY?
WOULD YOU BE SORRY IF I DIED?
YES.
I GUESS THAT'S SOMETHING.
WHAT DID HE WANT ME TO SAY? TO CONFESS UNDYING LOVE? HOW ABOUT UNDYING LUST?
WHAT DID HE WANT FROM ME? I ALMOST ASKED HIM, BUT I WASN'T THAT BRAVE.

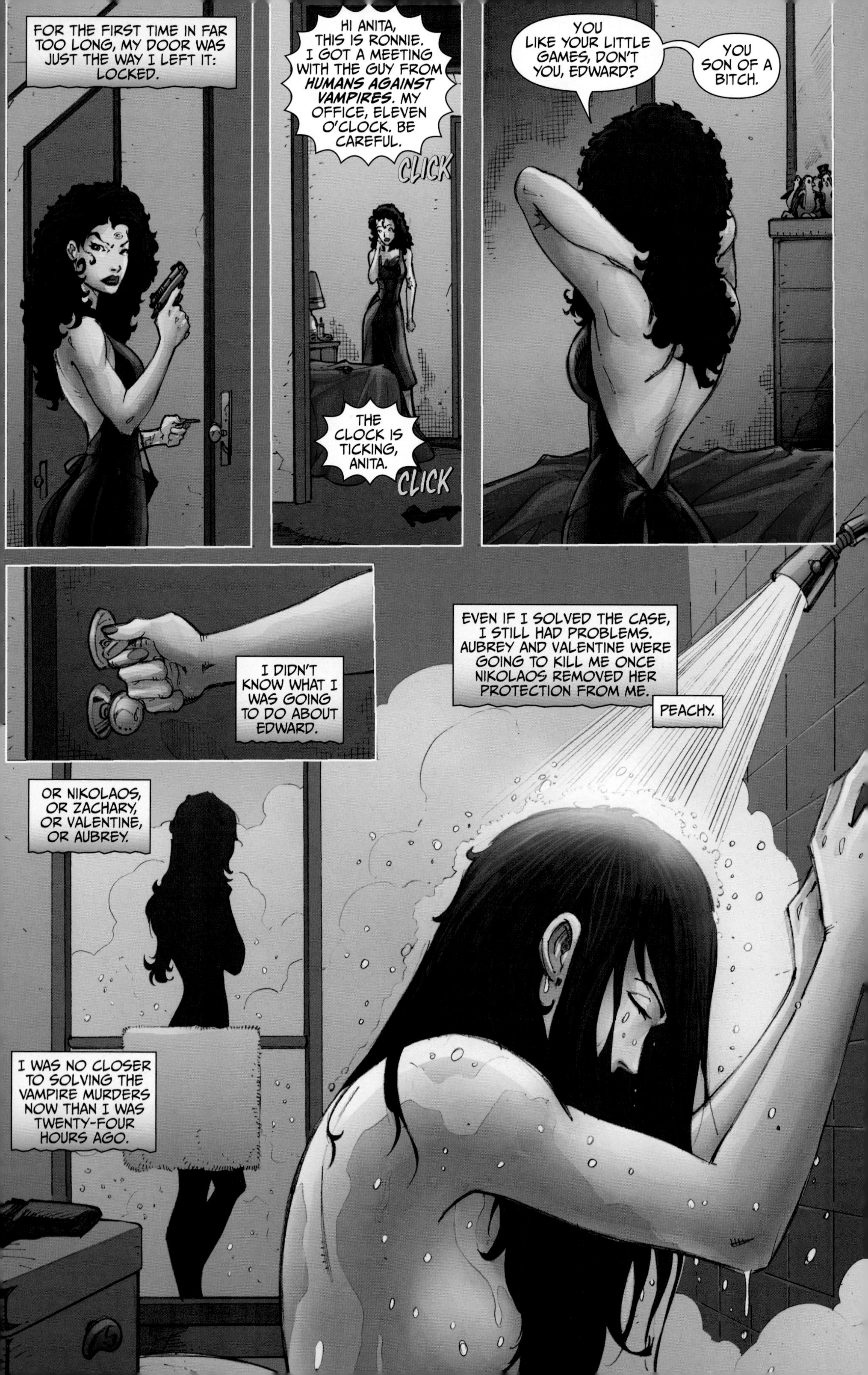
FOR THE FIRST TIME IN FAR TOO LONG, MY DOOR WAS JUST THE WAY I LEFT IT: LOCKED.
HI ANITA, THIS IS RONNIE. I GOT A MEETING WITH THE GUY FROM HUMANS AGAINST VAMPIRES. MY OFFICE, ELEVEN O'CLOCK. BE CAREFUL.
CLICK
THE CLOCK IS TICKING, ANITA.
CLICK
YOU LIKE YOUR LITTLE GAMES, DON'T YOU, EDWARD?
YOU SON OF A BITCH.
I DIDN'T KNOW WHAT I WAS GOING TO DO ABOUT EDWARD.
EVEN IF I SOLVED THE CASE, I STILL HAD PROBLEMS. AUBREY AND VALENTINE WERE GOING TO KILL ME ONCE NIKOLAOS REMOVED HER PROTECTION FROM ME.
PEACHY.
OR NIKOLAOS, OR ZACHARY, OR VALENTINE, OR AUBREY.
I WAS NO CLOSER TO SOLVING THE VAMPIRE MURDERS NOW THAN I WAS TWENTY-FOUR HOURS AGO.

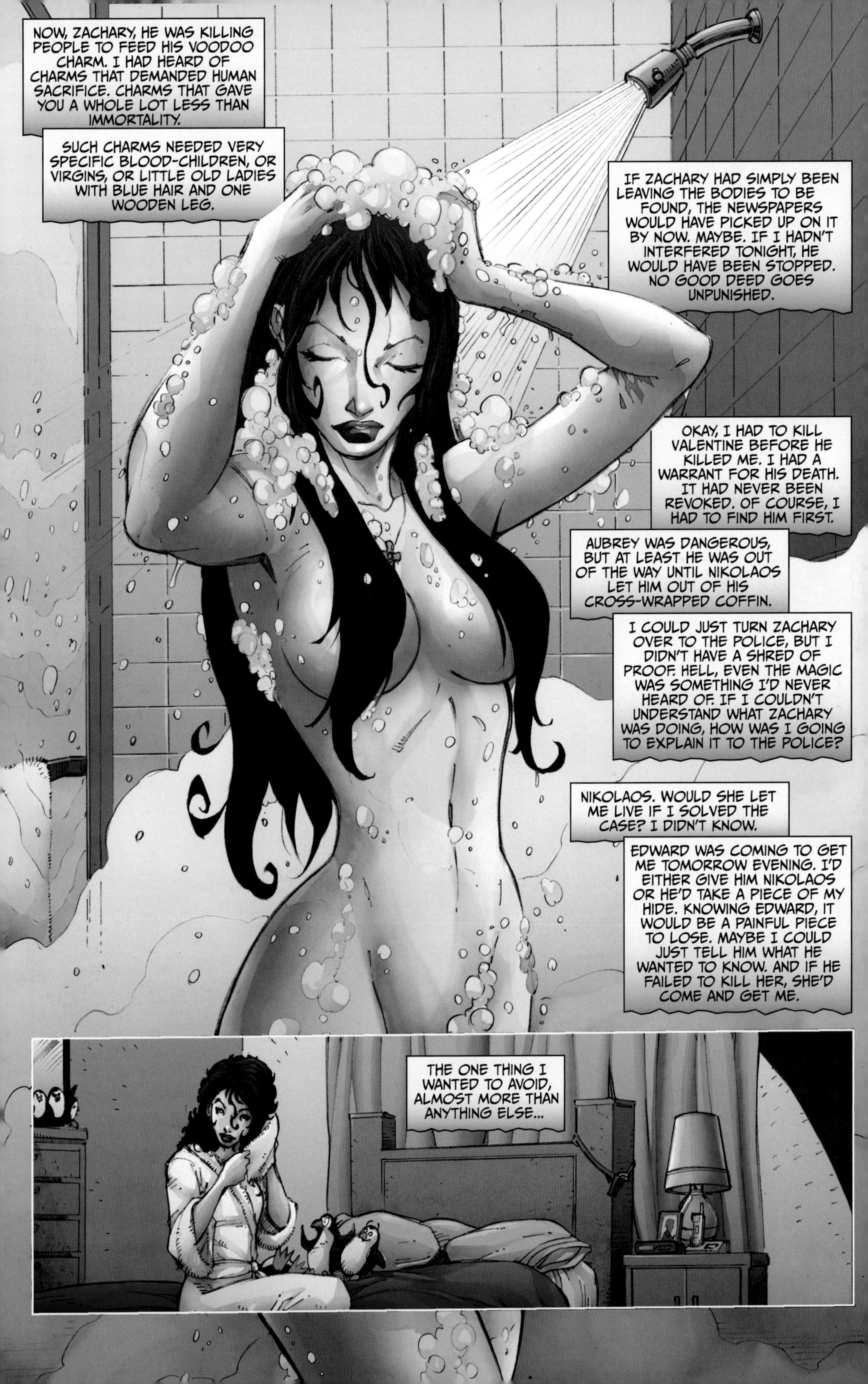
NOW, ZACHARY, HE WAS KILLING PEOPLE TO FEED HIS VOODOO CHARM. I HAD HEARD OF CHARMS THAT DEMANDED HUMAN SACRIFICE. CHARMS THAT GAVE YOU A WHOLE LOT LESS THAN IMMORTALITY.
SUCH CHARMS NEEDED VERY SPECIFIC BLOOD–CHILDREN, OR VIRGINS, OR LITTLE OLD LADIES WITH BLUE HAIR AND ONE WOODEN LEG.
IF ZACHARY HAD SIMPLY BEEN LEAVING THE BODIES TO BE FOUND, THE NEWSPAPERS WOULD HAVE PICKED UP ON IT BY NOW. MAYBE. IF I HADN'T INTERFERED TONIGHT, HE WOULD HAVE BEEN STOPPED. NO GOOD DEED GOES UNPUNISHED.
OKAY, I HAD TO KILL VALENTINE BEFORE HE KILLED ME. I HAD A WARRANT FOR HIS DEATH. IT HAD NEVER BEEN REVOKED. OF COURSE, I HAD TO FIND HIM FIRST.
AUBREY WAS DANGEROUS, BUT AT LEAST HE WAS OUT OF THE WAY UNTIL NIKOLAOS LET HIM OUT OF HIS CROSS-WRAPPED COFFIN.
I COULD JUST TURN ZACHARY OVER TO THE POLICE, BUT I DIDN'T HAVE A SHRED OF PROOF. HELL, EVEN THE MAGIC WAS SOMETHING I'D NEVER HEARD OF. IF I COULDN'T UNDERSTAND WHAT ZACHARY WAS DOING, HOW WAS I GOING TO EXPLAIN IT TO THE POLICE?
NIKOLAOS. WOULD SHE LET ME LIVE IF I SOLVED THE CASE? I DIDN'T KNOW.
EDWARD WAS COMING TO GET ME TOMORROW EVENING. I'D EITHER GIVE HIM NIKOLAOS OR HE'D TAKE A PIECE OF MY HIDE. KNOWING EDWARD, IT WOULD BE A PAINFUL PIECE TO LOSE. MAYBE I COULD JUST TELL HIM WHAT HE WANTED TO KNOW. AND IF HE FAILED TO KILL HER, SHE'D COME AND GET ME.
THE ONE THING I WANTED TO AVOID, ALMOST MORE THAN ANYTHING ELSE...

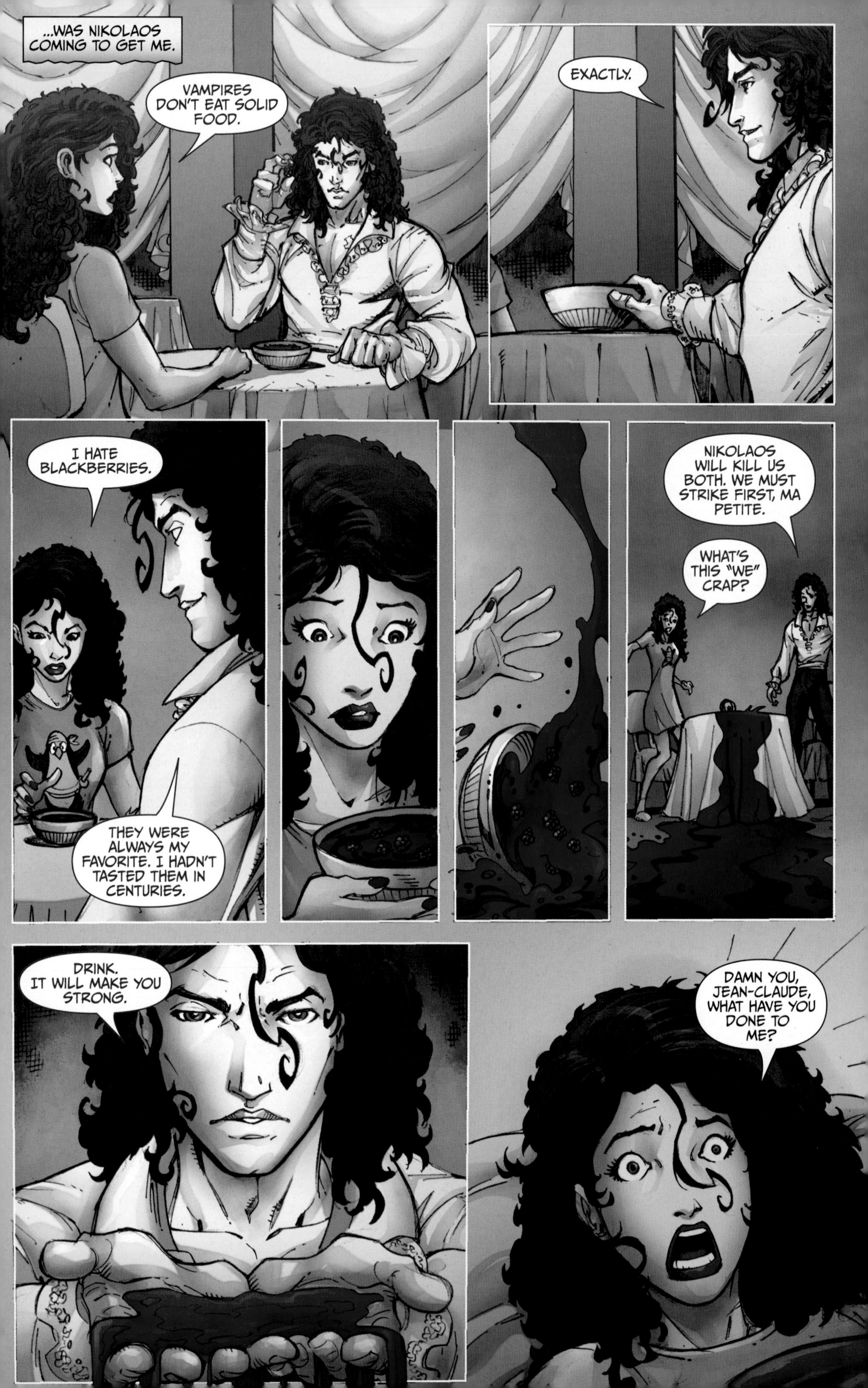
...WAS NIKOLAOS COMING TO GET ME.
VAMPIRES DON'T EAT SOLID FOOD.
EXACTLY.
I HATE BLACKBERRIES.
THEY WERE ALWAYS MY FAVORITE. I HADN'T TASTED THEM IN CENTURIES.
NIKOLAOS WILL KILL US BOTH. WE MUST STRIKE FIRST, MA PETITE.
WHAT'S THIS "WE" CRAP?
DRINK. IT WILL MAKE YOU STRONG.
DAMN YOU, JEAN-CLAUDE, WHAT HAVE YOU DONE TO ME?

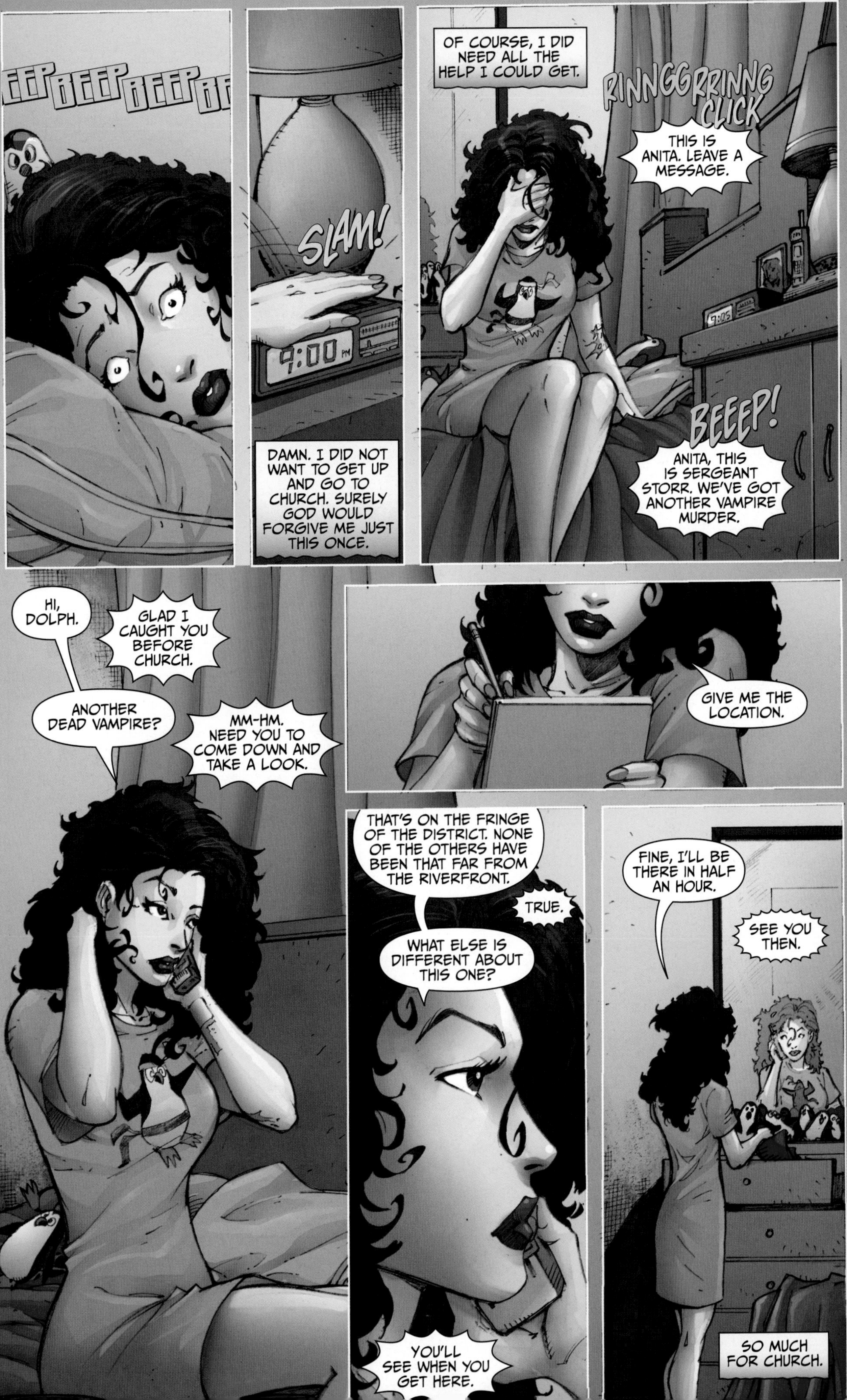

BEEP BEEP BEEP
SLAM!
DAMN. I DID NOT WANT TO GET UP AND GO TO CHURCH. SURELY GOD WOULD FORGIVE ME JUST THIS ONCE.
OF COURSE, I DID NEED ALL THE HELP I COULD GET.
RINNGGRRINNG
CLICK
THIS IS ANITA. LEAVE A MESSAGE.
BEEEP!
ANITA, THIS IS SERGEANT STORR. WE'VE GOT ANOTHER VAMPIRE MURDER.
HI, DOLPH.
GLAD I CAUGHT YOU BEFORE CHURCH.
ANOTHER DEAD VAMPIRE?
MM-HM. NEED YOU TO COME DOWN AND TAKE A LOOK.
GIVE ME THE LOCATION.
THAT'S ON THE FRINGE OF THE DISTRICT. NONE OF THE OTHERS HAVE BEEN THAT FAR FROM THE RIVERFRONT.
TRUE.
WHAT ELSE IS DIFFERENT ABOUT THIS ONE?
YOU'LL SEE WHEN YOU GET HERE.
FINE, I'LL BE THERE IN HALF AN HOUR.
SEE YOU THEN.
SO MUCH FOR CHURCH.

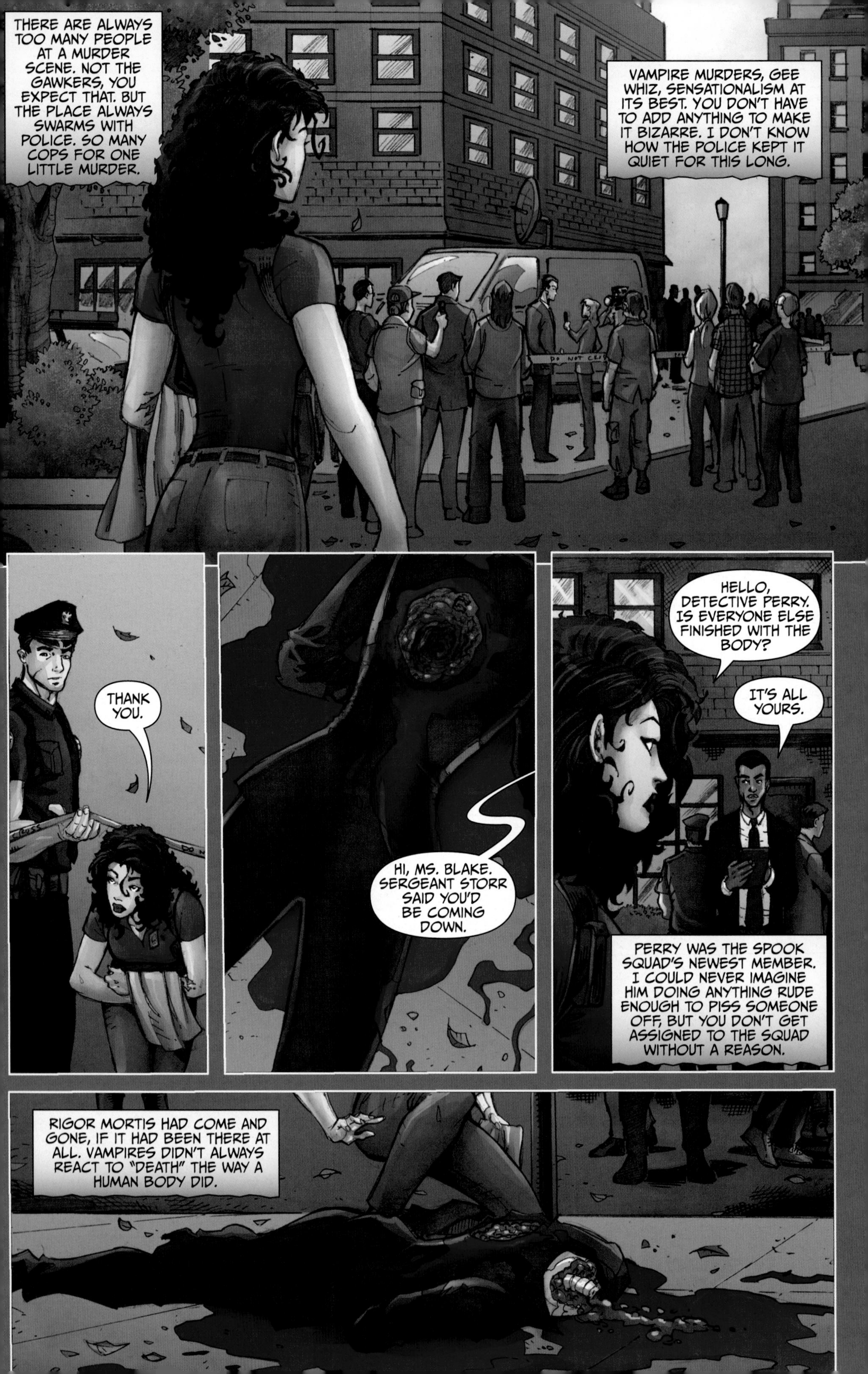
THERE ARE ALWAYS TOO MANY PEOPLE AT A MURDER SCENE. NOT THE GAWKERS, YOU EXPECT THAT. BUT THE PLACE ALWAYS SWARMS WITH POLICE. SO MANY COPS FOR ONE LITTLE MURDER.
VAMPIRE MURDERS, GEE WHIZ, SENSATIONALISM AT ITS BEST. YOU DON'T HAVE TO ADD ANYTHING TO MAKE IT BIZARRE. I DON'T KNOW HOW THE POLICE KEPT IT QUIET FOR THIS LONG.
THANK YOU.
HI, MS. BLAKE. SERGEANT STORR SAID YOU'D BE COMING DOWN.
HELLO, DETECTIVE PERRY. IS EVERYONE ELSE FINISHED WITH THE BODY?
IT'S ALL YOURS.
PERRY WAS THE SPOOK SQUAD'S NEWEST MEMBER. I COULD NEVER IMAGINE HIM DOING ANYTHING RUDE ENOUGH TO PISS SOMEONE OFF, BUT YOU DON'T GET ASSIGNED TO THE SQUAD WITHOUT A REASON.
RIGOR MORTIS HAD COME AND GONE, IF IT HAD BEEN THERE AT ALL. VAMPIRES DIDN'T ALWAYS REACT TO "DEATH" THE WAY A HUMAN BODY DID.

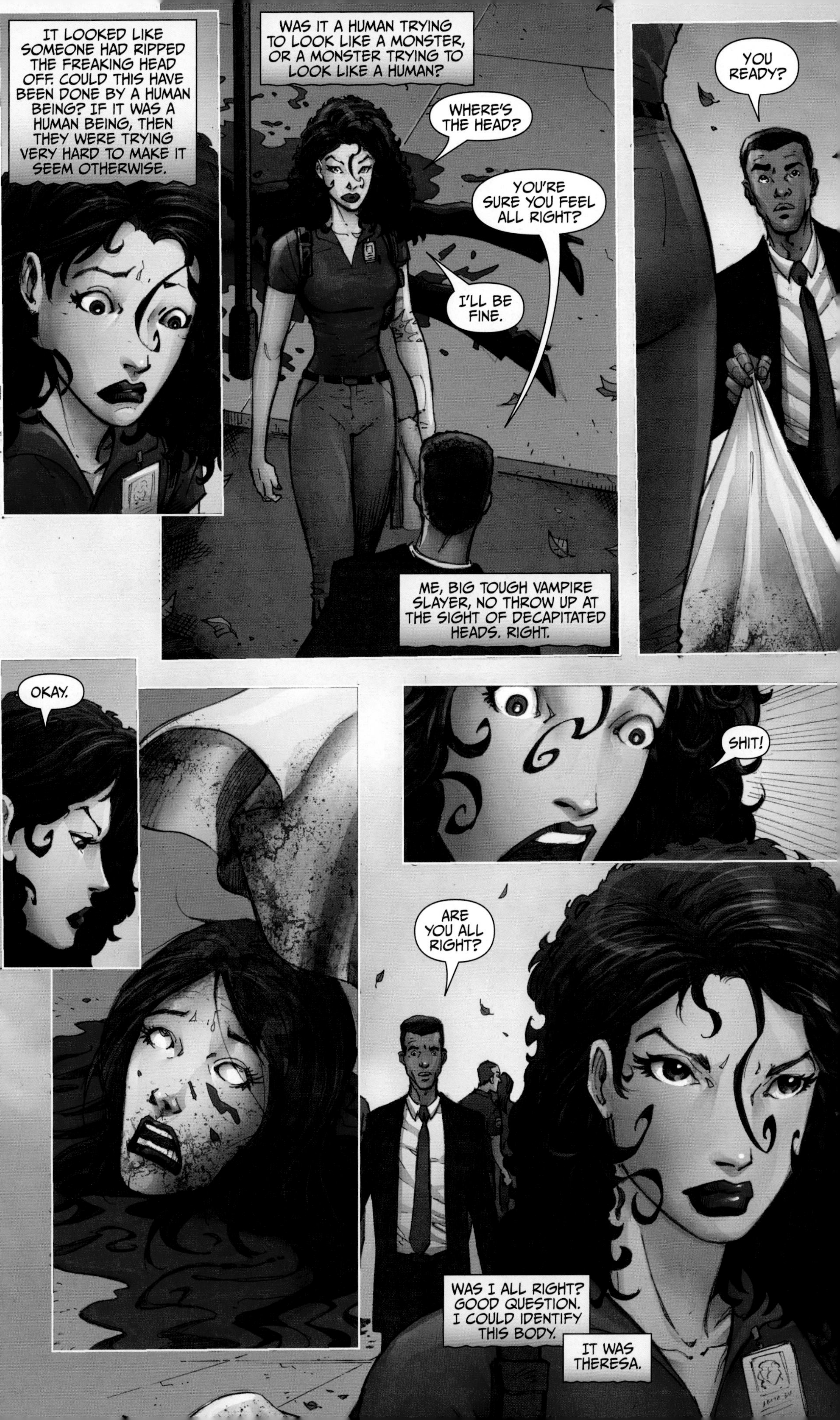
IT LOOKED LIKE SOMEONE HAD RIPPED THE FREAKING HEAD OFF. COULD THIS HAVE BEEN DONE BY A HUMAN BEING? IF IT WAS A HUMAN BEING, THEN THEY WERE TRYING VERY HARD TO MAKE IT SEEM OTHERWISE.
WAS IT A HUMAN TRYING TO LOOK LIKE A MONSTER, OR A MONSTER TRYING TO LOOK LIKE A HUMAN?
WHERE'S THE HEAD?
YOU'RE SURE YOU FEEL ALL RIGHT?
I'LL BE FINE.
ME, BIG TOUGH VAMPIRE SLAYER, NO THROW UP AT THE SIGHT OF DECAPITATED HEADS. RIGHT.
YOU READY?
OKAY.
SHIT!
ARE YOU ALL RIGHT?
WAS I ALL RIGHT? GOOD QUESTION. I COULD IDENTIFY THIS BODY.
IT WAS THERESA.

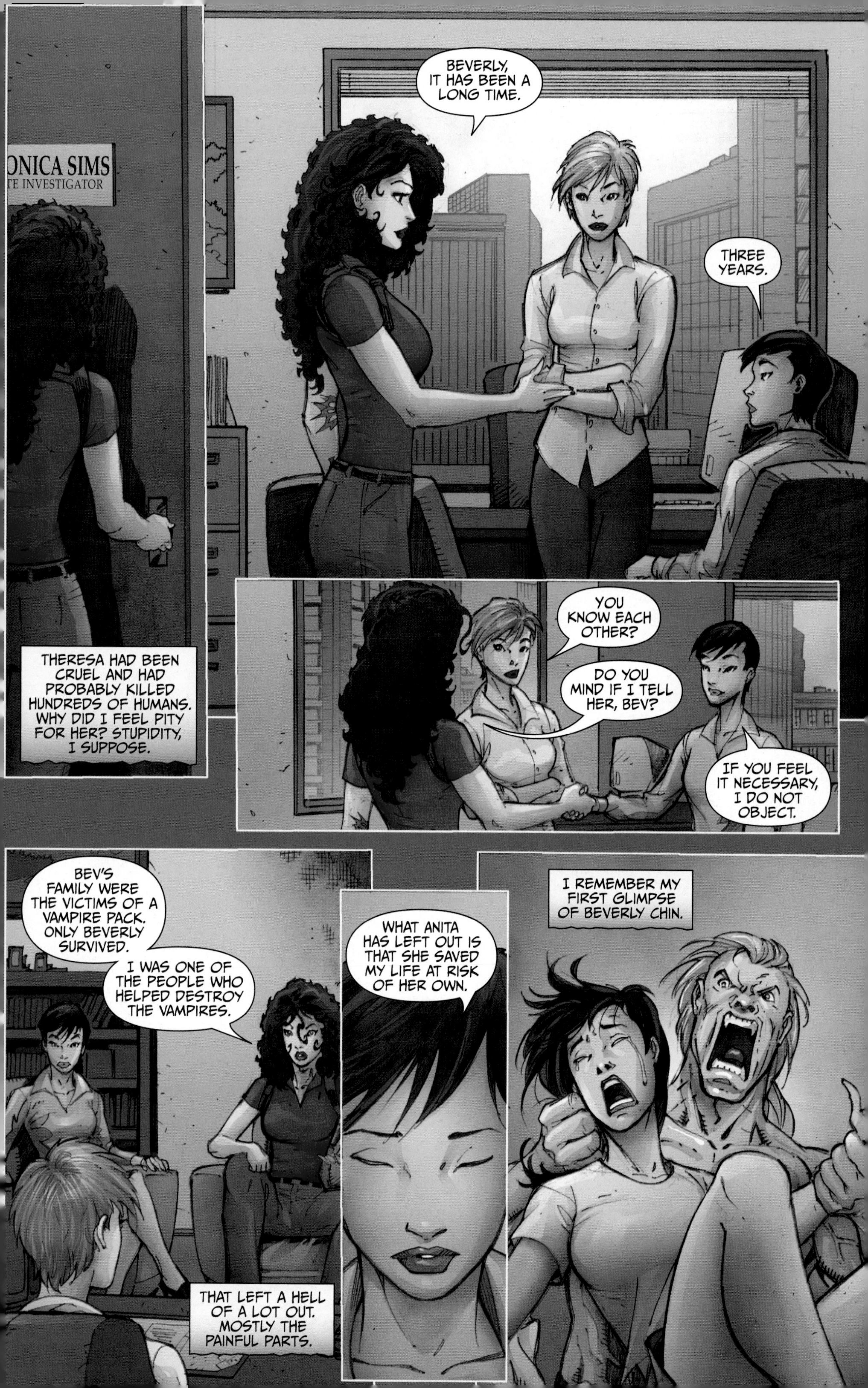
ONICA SIMS
TE INVESTIGATOR
BEVERLY, IT HAS BEEN A LONG TIME.
THREE YEARS.
THERESA HAD BEEN CRUEL AND HAD PROBABLY KILLED HUNDREDS OF HUMANS. WHY DID I FEEL PITY FOR HER? STUPIDITY, I SUPPOSE.
YOU KNOW EACH OTHER?
DO YOU MIND IF I TELL HER, BEV?
IF YOU FEEL IT NECESSARY, I DO NOT OBJECT.
BEV'S FAMILY WERE THE VICTIMS OF A VAMPIRE PACK. ONLY BEVERLY SURVIVED.
I WAS ONE OF THE PEOPLE WHO HELPED DESTROY THE VAMPIRES.
THAT LEFT A HELL OF A LOT OUT. MOSTLY THE PAINFUL PARTS.
WHAT ANITA HAS LEFT OUT IS THAT SHE SAVED MY LIFE AT RISK OF HER OWN.
I REMEMBER MY FIRST GLIMPSE OF BEVERLY CHIN.

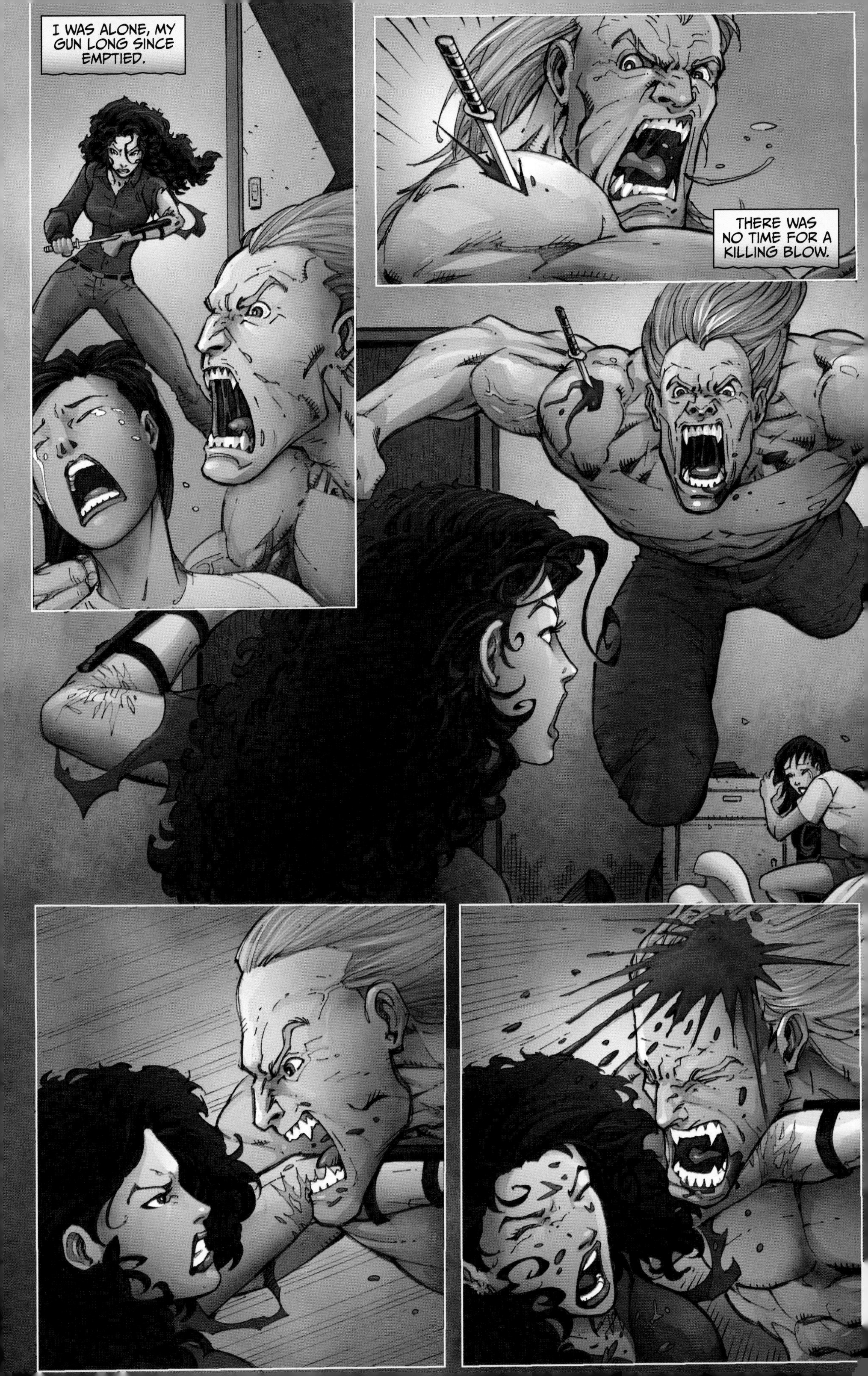
I WAS ALONE, MY GUN LONG SINCE EMPTIED.
THERE WAS NO TIME FOR A KILLING BLOW.

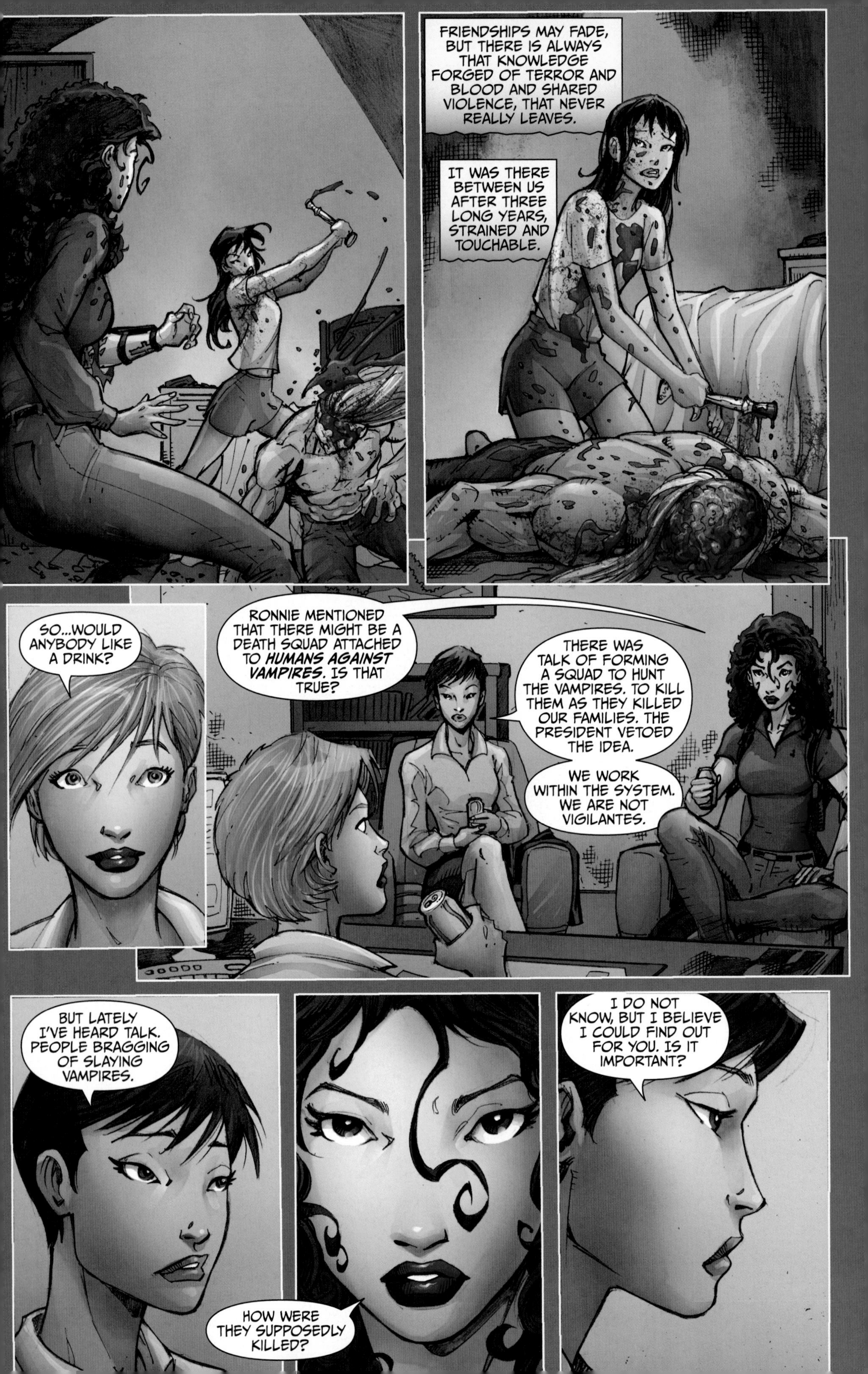
FRIENDSHIPS MAY FADE, BUT THERE IS ALWAYS THAT KNOWLEDGE FORGED OF TERROR AND BLOOD AND SHARED VIOLENCE, THAT NEVER REALLY LEAVES.
IT WAS THERE BETWEEN US AFTER THREE LONG YEARS, STRAINED AND TOUCHABLE.
SO...WOULD ANYBODY LIKE A DRINK?
RONNIE MENTIONED THAT THERE MIGHT BE A DEATH SQUAD ATTACHED TO HUMANS AGAINST VAMPIRES. IS THAT TRUE?
THERE WAS TALK OF FORMING A SQUAD TO HUNT THE VAMPIRES. TO KILL THEM AS THEY KILLED OUR FAMILIES. THE PRESIDENT VETOED THE IDEA.
WE WORK WITHIN THE SYSTEM. WE ARE NOT VIGILANTES.
BUT LATELY I'VE HEARD TALK. PEOPLE BRAGGING OF SLAYING VAMPIRES.
HOW WERE THEY SUPPOSEDLY KILLED?
I DO NOT KNOW, BUT I BELIEVE I COULD FIND OUT FOR YOU. IS IT IMPORTANT?

THE POLICE HAVE HIDDEN CERTAIN DETAILS FROM THE GENERAL PUBLIC. THINGS ONLY THE MURDERER WOULD KNOW.

I SEE.

I DO NOT BELIEVE IT IS MURDER, EVEN IF MY PEOPLE HAVE DONE WHAT THE PAPERS SAY. KILLING DANGEROUS ANIMALS SHOULD NOT BE A CRIME.

IN PART, I AGREED WITH HER. ONCE I WOULD HAVE AGREED WHOLE-HEARTEDLY.

THEN WHY TELL US?

I OWE YOU.

YOU SAVED MY LIFE AS WELL. YOU OWE ME NOTHING.

THERE WILL ALWAYS BE A DEBT BETWEEN US, ALWAYS.

BEV HAD BEGGED ME NOT TO TELL THE POLICE SHE HAD KILLED THE VAMPIRE. THAT SHE WAS CAPABLE OF SUCH VIOLENCE HORRIFIED HER.

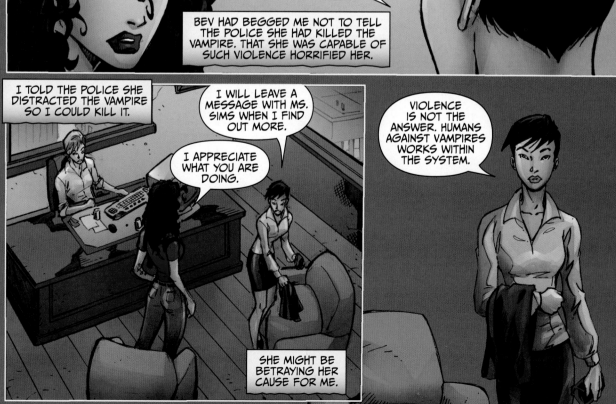

I TOLD THE POLICE SHE DISTRACTED THE VAMPIRE SO I COULD KILL IT.

I WILL LEAVE A MESSAGE WITH MS. SIMS WHEN I FIND OUT MORE.

I APPRECIATE WHAT YOU ARE DOING.

VIOLENCE IS NOT THE ANSWER. HUMANS AGAINST VAMPIRES WORKS WITHIN THE SYSTEM.

SHE MIGHT BE BETRAYING HER CAUSE FOR ME.

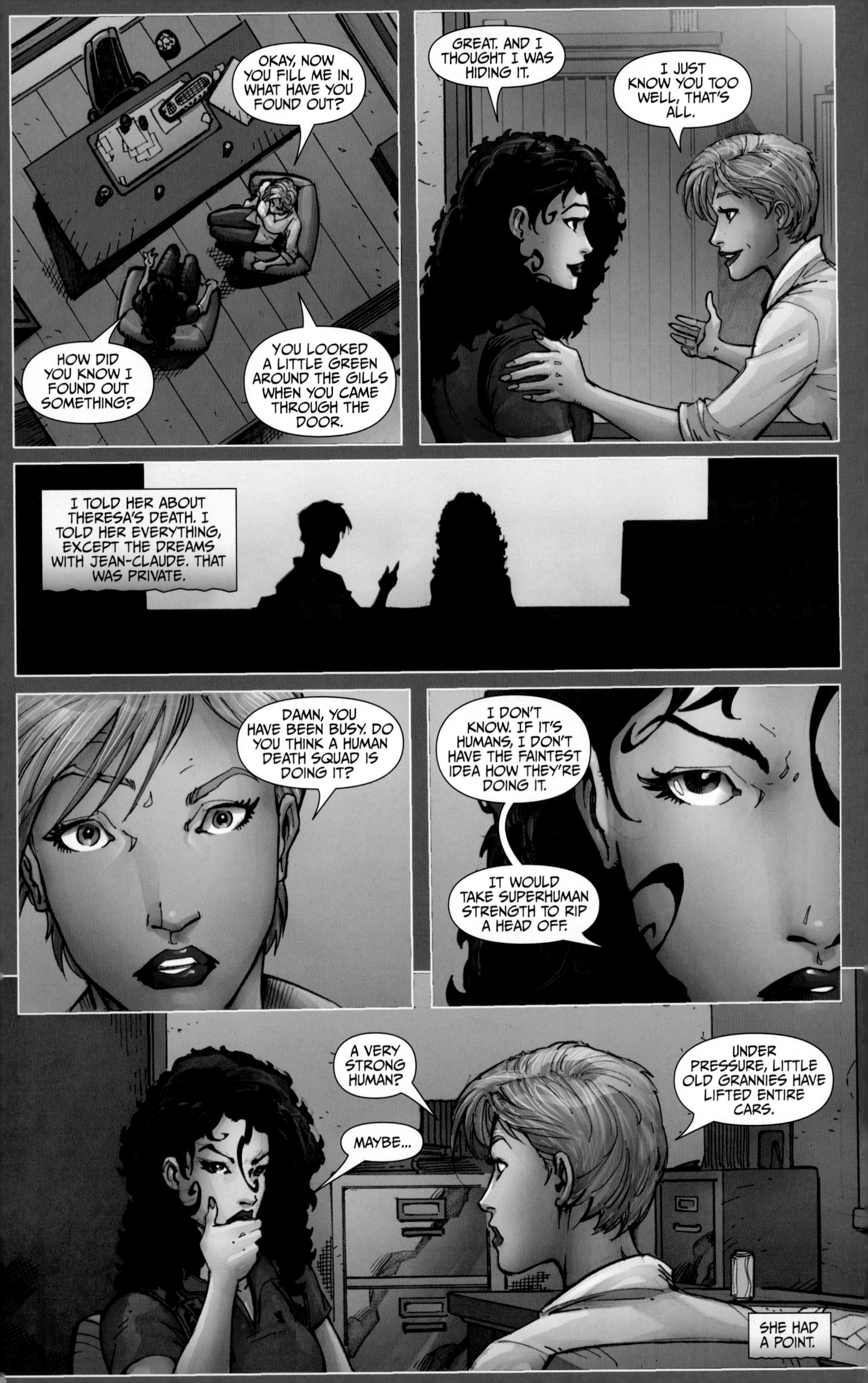
OKAY, NOW YOU FILL ME IN. WHAT HAVE YOU FOUND OUT?
HOW DID YOU KNOW I FOUND OUT SOMETHING?
YOU LOOKED A LITTLE GREEN AROUND THE GILLS WHEN YOU CAME THROUGH THE DOOR.
GREAT. AND I THOUGHT I WAS HIDING IT.
I JUST KNOW YOU TOO WELL, THAT'S ALL.
I TOLD HER ABOUT THERESA'S DEATH. I TOLD HER EVERYTHING, EXCEPT THE DREAMS WITH JEAN-CLAUDE. THAT WAS PRIVATE.
DAMN, YOU HAVE BEEN BUSY. DO YOU THINK A HUMAN DEATH SQUAD IS DOING IT?
I DON'T KNOW. IF IT'S HUMANS, I DON'T HAVE THE FAINTEST IDEA HOW THEY'RE DOING IT.
IT WOULD TAKE SUPERHUMAN STRENGTH TO RIP A HEAD OFF.
A VERY STRONG HUMAN?
MAYBE...
UNDER PRESSURE, LITTLE OLD GRANNIES HAVE LIFTED ENTIRE CARS.
SHE HAD A POINT.

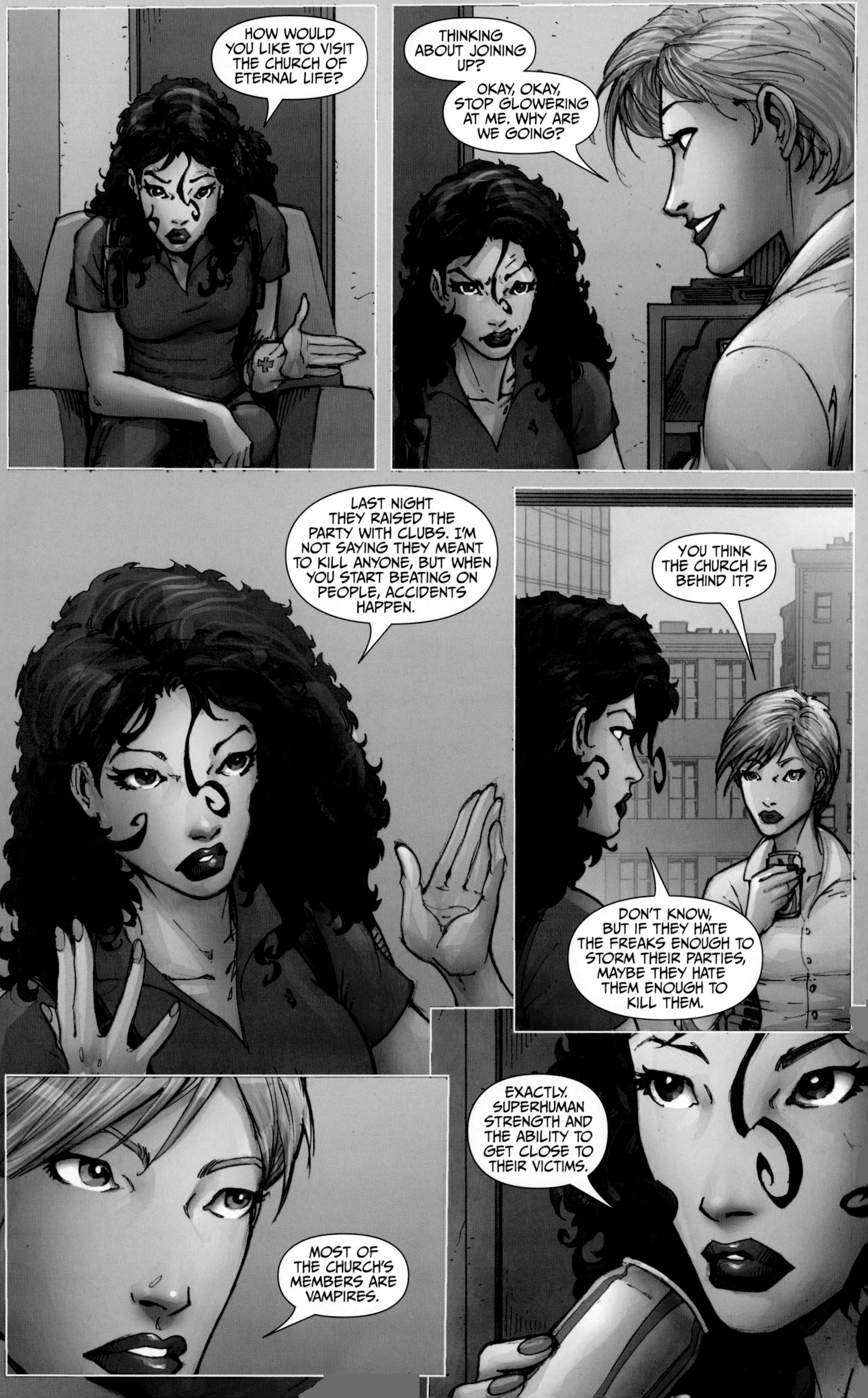
HOW WOULD YOU LIKE TO VISIT THE CHURCH OF ETERNAL LIFE?
THINKING ABOUT JOINING UP?
OKAY, OKAY, STOP GLOWERING AT ME. WHY ARE WE GOING?
LAST NIGHT THEY RAISED THE PARTY WITH CLUBS. I'M NOT SAYING THEY MEANT TO KILL ANYONE, BUT WHEN YOU START BEATING ON PEOPLE, ACCIDENTS HAPPEN.
YOU THINK THE CHURCH IS BEHIND IT?
DON'T KNOW, BUT IF THEY HATE THE FREAKS ENOUGH TO STORM THEIR PARTIES, MAYBE THEY HATE THEM ENOUGH TO KILL THEM.
MOST OF THE CHURCH'S MEMBERS ARE VAMPIRES.
EXACTLY. SUPERHUMAN STRENGTH AND THE ABILITY TO GET CLOSE TO THEIR VICTIMS.

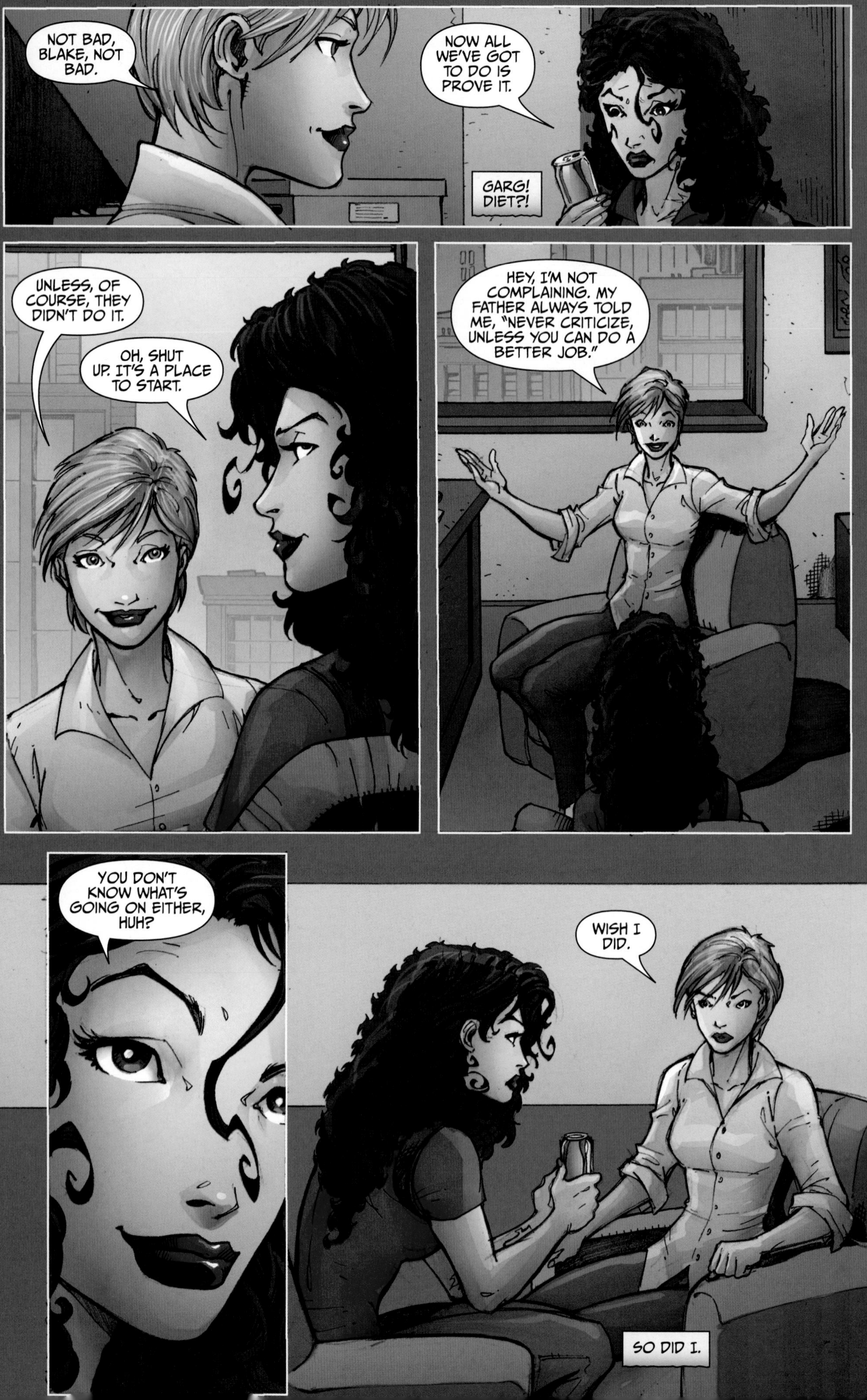
NOT BAD, BLAKE, NOT BAD.
NOW ALL WE'VE GOT TO DO IS PROVE IT.
GARG! DIET?!
UNLESS, OF COURSE, THEY DIDN'T DO IT.
OH, SHUT UP. IT'S A PLACE TO START.
HEY, I'M NOT COMPLAINING. MY FATHER ALWAYS TOLD ME, "NEVER CRITICIZE, UNLESS YOU CAN DO A BETTER JOB."
YOU DON'T KNOW WHAT'S GOING ON EITHER, HUH?
WISH I DID.
SO DID I.

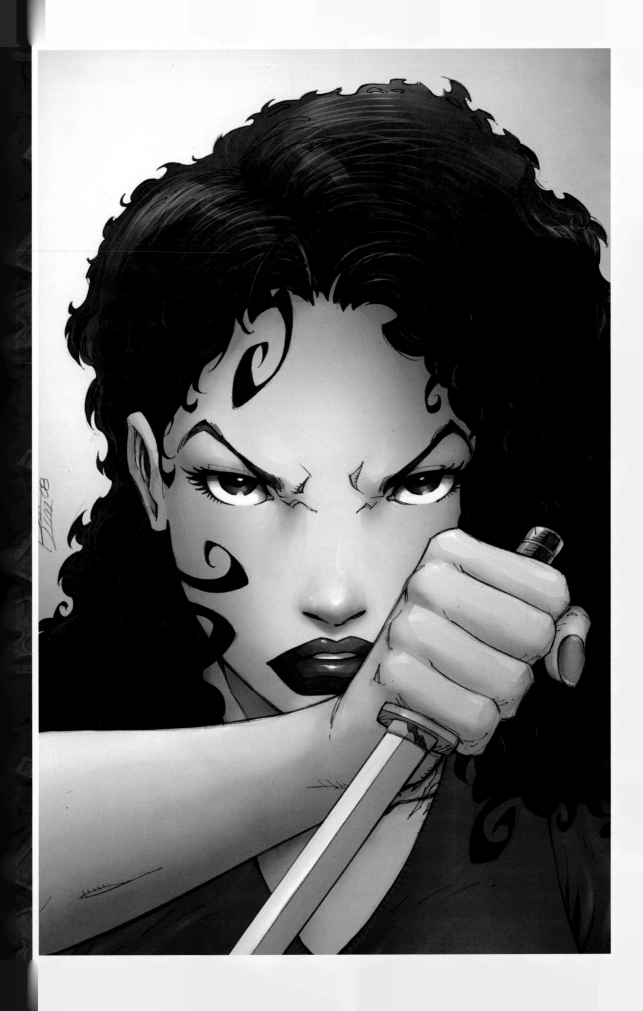

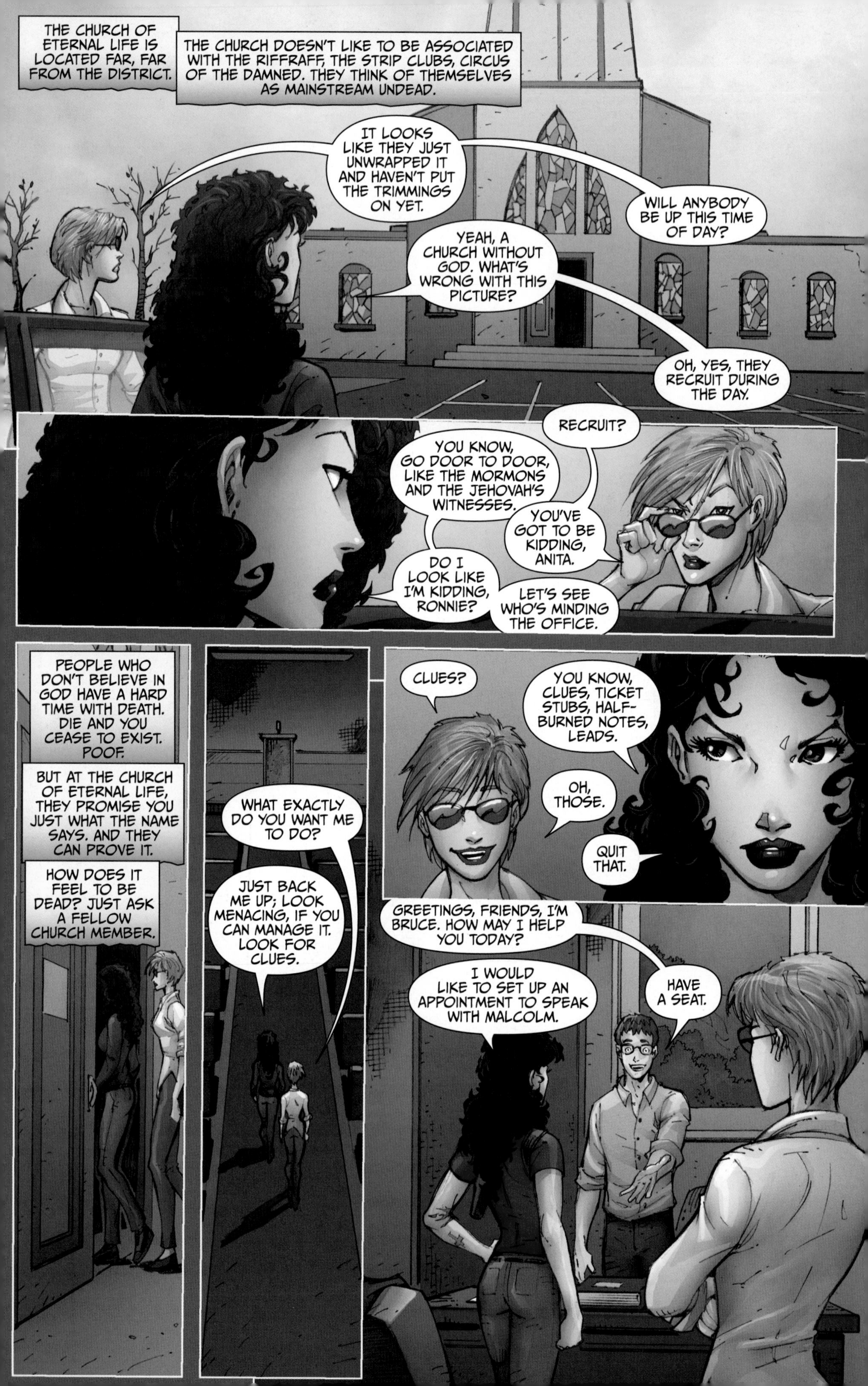
THE CHURCH OF ETERNAL LIFE IS LOCATED FAR, FAR FROM THE DISTRICT.
THE CHURCH DOESN'T LIKE TO BE ASSOCIATED WITH THE RIFFRAFF, THE STRIP CLUBS, CIRCUS OF THE DAMNED. THEY THINK OF THEMSELVES AS MAINSTREAM UNDEAD.
IT LOOKS LIKE THEY JUST UNWRAPPED IT AND HAVEN'T PUT THE TRIMMINGS ON YET.
WILL ANYBODY BE UP THIS TIME OF DAY?
YEAH, A CHURCH WITHOUT GOD. WHAT'S WRONG WITH THIS PICTURE?
OH, YES, THEY RECRUIT DURING THE DAY.
RECRUIT?
YOU KNOW, GO DOOR TO DOOR, LIKE THE MORMONS AND THE JEHOVAH'S WITNESSES.
YOU'VE GOT TO BE KIDDING, ANITA.
DO I LOOK LIKE I'M KIDDING, RONNIE?
LET'S SEE WHO'S MINDING THE OFFICE.
PEOPLE WHO DON'T BELIEVE IN GOD HAVE A HARD TIME WITH DEATH. DIE AND YOU CEASE TO EXIST. POOF.
BUT AT THE CHURCH OF ETERNAL LIFE, THEY PROMISE YOU JUST WHAT THE NAME SAYS. AND THEY CAN PROVE IT.
HOW DOES IT FEEL TO BE DEAD? JUST ASK A FELLOW CHURCH MEMBER.
WHAT EXACTLY DO YOU WANT ME TO DO?
JUST BACK ME UP; LOOK MENACING, IF YOU CAN MANAGE IT. LOOK FOR CLUES.
CLUES?
YOU KNOW, CLUES, TICKET STUBS, HALF-BURNED NOTES, LEADS.
OH, THOSE.
QUIT THAT.
GREETINGS, FRIENDS, I'M BRUCE. HOW MAY I HELP YOU TODAY?
I WOULD LIKE TO SET UP AN APPOINTMENT TO SPEAK WITH MALCOLM.
HAVE A SEAT.

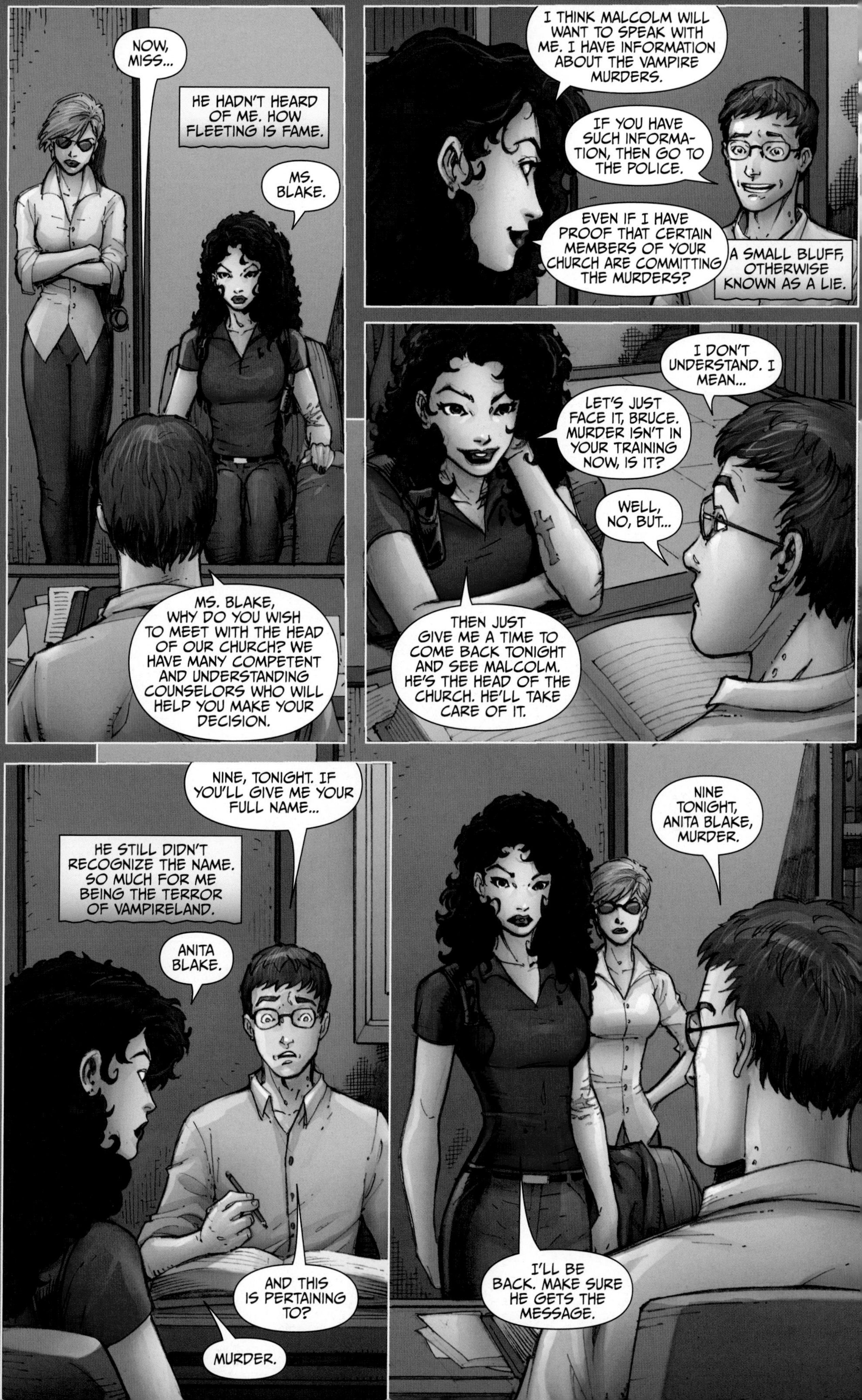

NOW, MISS...
HE HADN'T HEARD OF ME. HOW FLEETING IS FAME.
MS. BLAKE.
MS. BLAKE, WHY DO YOU WISH TO MEET WITH THE HEAD OF OUR CHURCH? WE HAVE MANY COMPETENT AND UNDERSTANDING COUNSELORS WHO WILL HELP YOU MAKE YOUR DECISION.
I THINK MALCOLM WILL WANT TO SPEAK WITH ME. I HAVE INFORMATION ABOUT THE VAMPIRE MURDERS.
IF YOU HAVE SUCH INFORMATION, THEN GO TO THE POLICE.
EVEN IF I HAVE PROOF THAT CERTAIN MEMBERS OF YOUR CHURCH ARE COMMITTING THE MURDERS?
A SMALL BLUFF, OTHERWISE KNOWN AS A LIE.
I DON'T UNDERSTAND. I MEAN...
LET'S JUST FACE IT, BRUCE. MURDER ISN'T IN YOUR TRAINING NOW, IS IT?
WELL, NO, BUT...
THEN JUST GIVE ME A TIME TO COME BACK TONIGHT AND SEE MALCOLM. HE'S THE HEAD OF THE CHURCH. HE'LL TAKE CARE OF IT.
NINE, TONIGHT. IF YOU'LL GIVE ME YOUR FULL NAME...
HE STILL DIDN'T RECOGNIZE THE NAME. SO MUCH FOR ME BEING THE TERROR OF VAMPIRELAND.
ANITA BLAKE.
AND THIS IS PERTAINING TO?
MURDER.
NINE TONIGHT, ANITA BLAKE, MURDER.
I'LL BE BACK. MAKE SURE HE GETS THE MESSAGE.

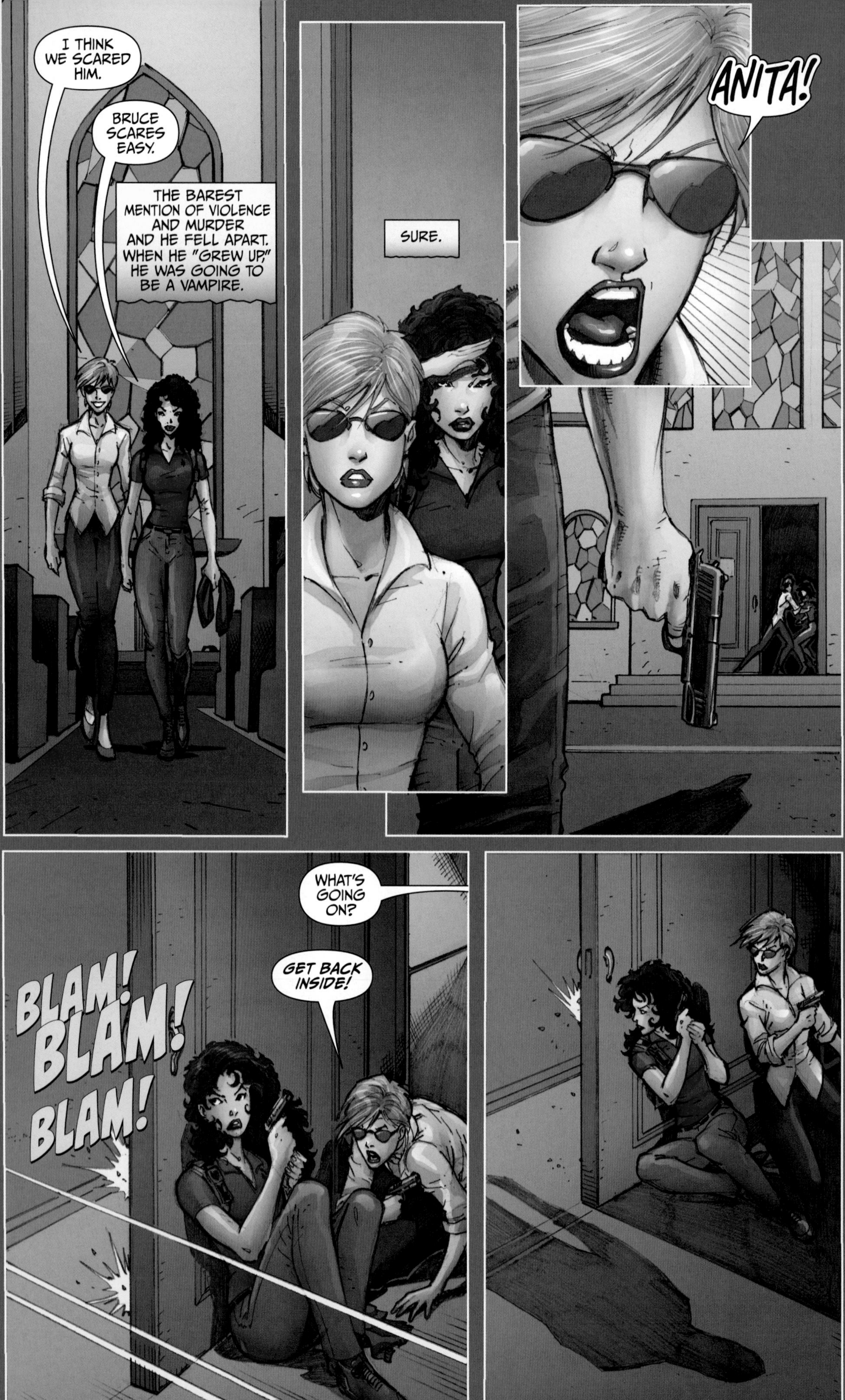
I THINK WE SCARED HIM.
BRUCE SCARES EASY.
THE BAREST MENTION OF VIOLENCE AND MURDER AND HE FELL APART. WHEN HE "GREW UP," HE WAS GOING TO BE A VAMPIRE.
SURE.
ANITA!
BLAM! BLAM! BLAM!
WHAT'S GOING ON?
GET BACK INSIDE!

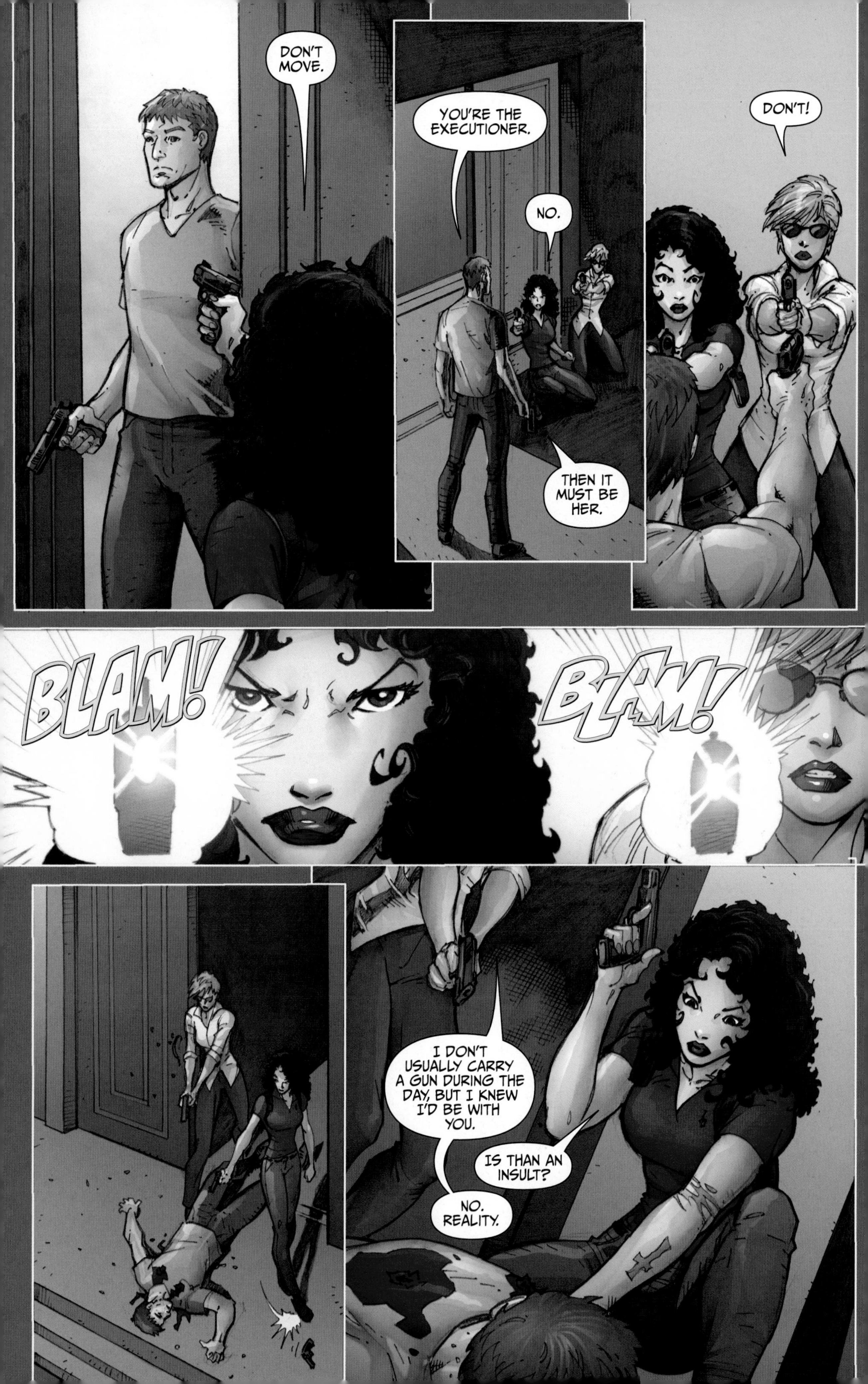

DON'T MOVE.
YOU'RE THE EXECUTIONER.
NO.
THEN IT MUST BE HER.
DON'T!
BLAM!
BLAM!
I DON'T USUALLY CARRY A GUN DURING THE DAY, BUT I KNEW I'D BE WITH YOU.
IS THAN AN INSULT?
NO. REALITY.

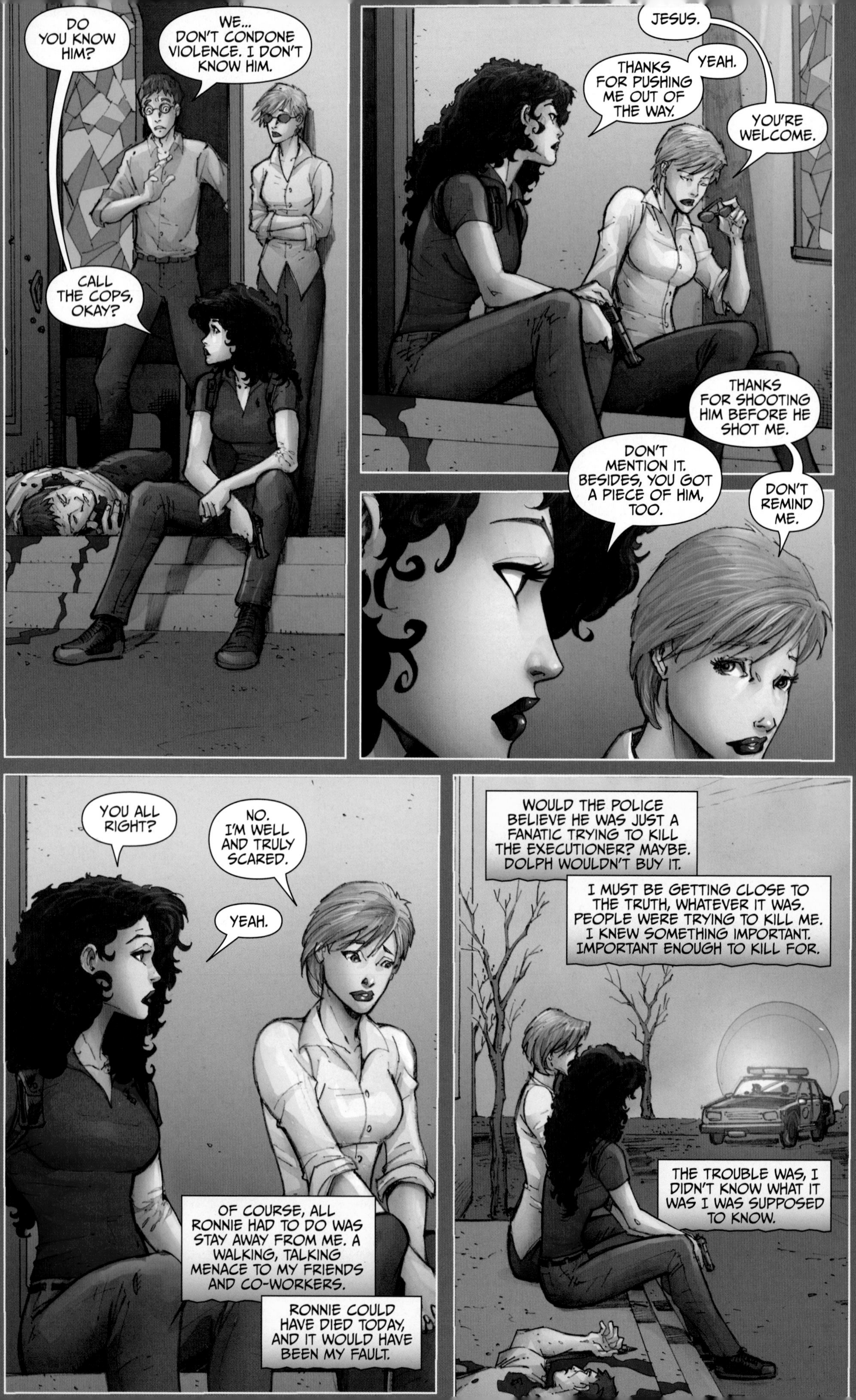
DO YOU KNOW HIM?
WE... DON'T CONDONE VIOLENCE. I DON'T KNOW HIM.
CALL THE COPS, OKAY?
JESUS.
YEAH.
THANKS FOR PUSHING ME OUT OF THE WAY.
YOU'RE WELCOME.
THANKS FOR SHOOTING HIM BEFORE HE SHOT ME.
DON'T MENTION IT. BESIDES, YOU GOT A PIECE OF HIM, TOO.
DON'T REMIND ME.
YOU ALL RIGHT?
NO. I'M WELL AND TRULY SCARED.
YEAH.
OF COURSE, ALL RONNIE HAD TO DO WAS STAY AWAY FROM ME. A WALKING, TALKING MENACE TO MY FRIENDS AND CO-WORKERS.
RONNIE COULD HAVE DIED TODAY, AND IT WOULD HAVE BEEN MY FAULT.
WOULD THE POLICE BELIEVE HE WAS JUST A FANATIC TRYING TO KILL THE EXECUTIONER? MAYBE. DOLPH WOULDN'T BUY IT.
I MUST BE GETTING CLOSE TO THE TRUTH, WHATEVER IT WAS. PEOPLE WERE TRYING TO KILL ME. I KNEW SOMETHING IMPORTANT. IMPORTANT ENOUGH TO KILL FOR.
THE TROUBLE WAS, I DIDN'T KNOW WHAT IT WAS I WAS SUPPOSED TO KNOW.

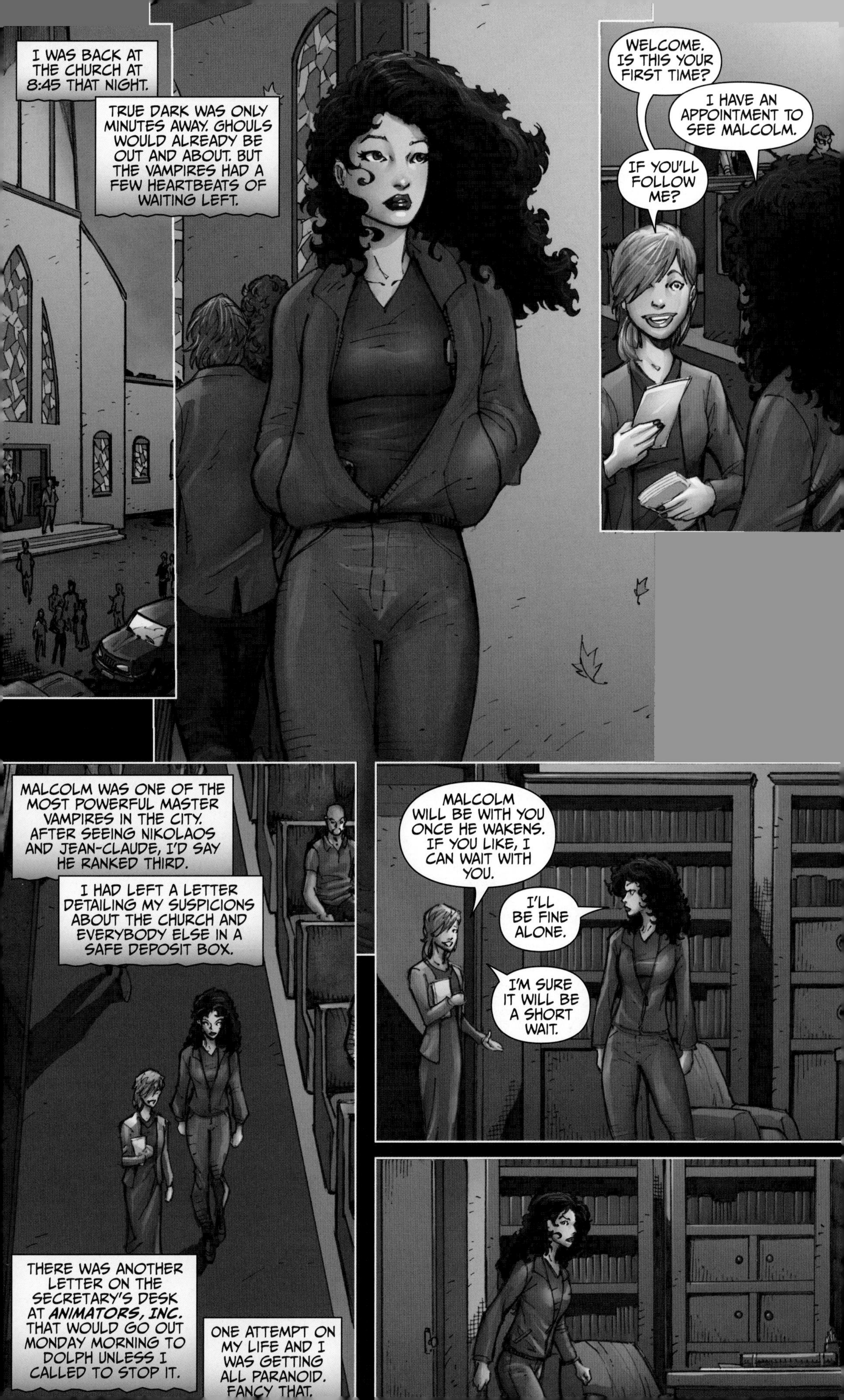
I WAS BACK AT THE CHURCH AT 8:45 THAT NIGHT.
TRUE DARK WAS ONLY MINUTES AWAY. GHOULS WOULD ALREADY BE OUT AND ABOUT. BUT THE VAMPIRES HAD A FEW HEARTBEATS OF WAITING LEFT.
WELCOME. IS THIS YOUR FIRST TIME?
I HAVE AN APPOINTMENT TO SEE MALCOLM.
IF YOU'LL FOLLOW ME?
MALCOLM WAS ONE OF THE MOST POWERFUL MASTER VAMPIRES IN THE CITY. AFTER SEEING NIKOLAOS AND JEAN-CLAUDE, I'D SAY HE RANKED THIRD.
I HAD LEFT A LETTER DETAILING MY SUSPICIONS ABOUT THE CHURCH AND EVERYBODY ELSE IN A SAFE DEPOSIT BOX.
THERE WAS ANOTHER LETTER ON THE SECRETARY'S DESK AT ANIMATORS, INC. THAT WOULD GO OUT MONDAY MORNING TO DOLPH UNLESS I CALLED TO STOP IT.
ONE ATTEMPT ON MY LIFE AND I WAS GETTING ALL PARANOID. FANCY THAT.
MALCOLM WILL BE WITH YOU ONCE HE WAKENS. IF YOU LIKE, I CAN WAIT WITH YOU.
I'LL BE FINE ALONE.
I'M SURE IT WILL BE A SHORT WAIT.

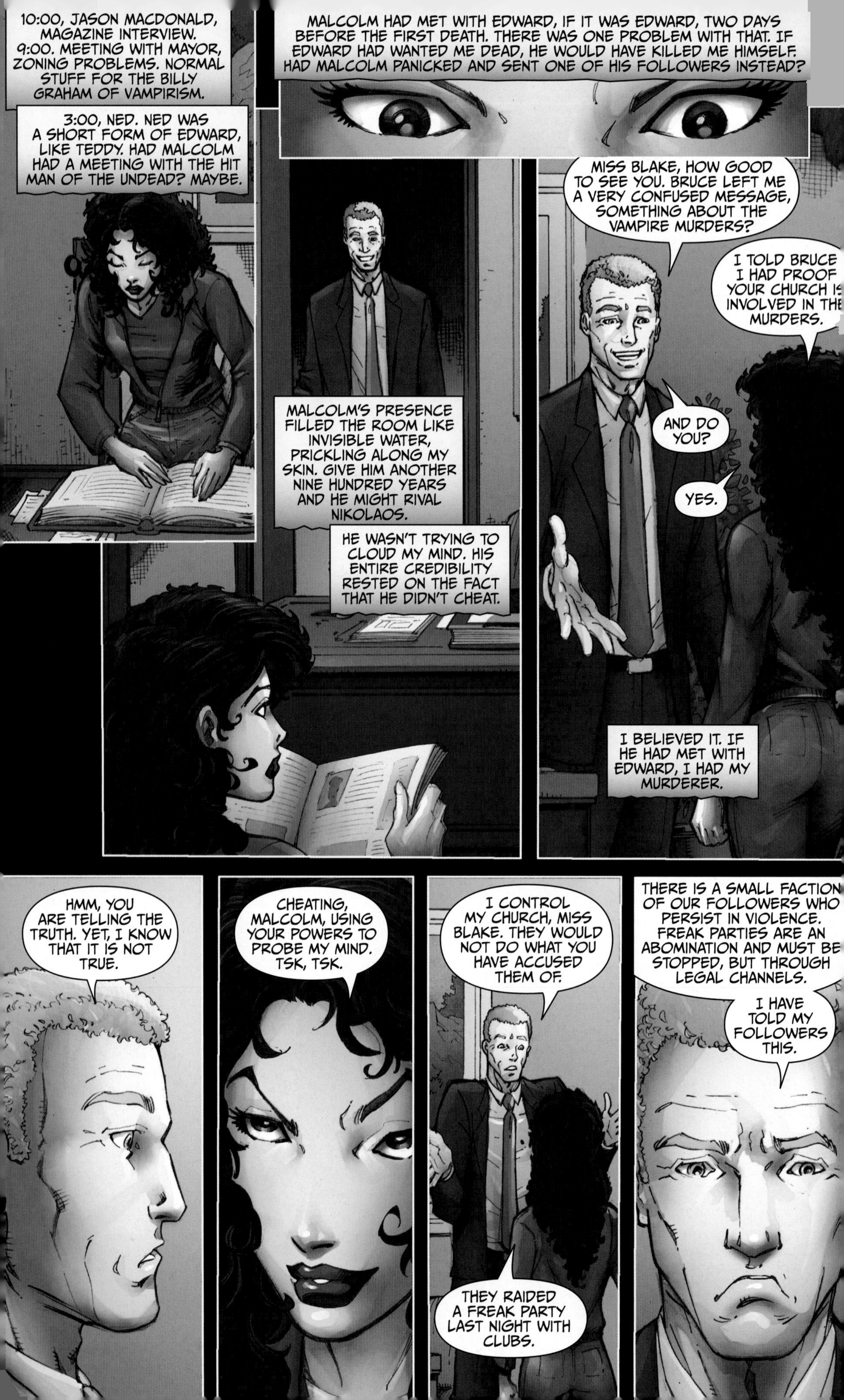
10:00, JASON MACDONALD, MAGAZINE INTERVIEW. 9:00. MEETING WITH MAYOR, ZONING PROBLEMS. NORMAL STUFF FOR THE BILLY GRAHAM OF VAMPIRISM.
MALCOLM HAD MET WITH EDWARD, IF IT WAS EDWARD, TWO DAYS BEFORE THE FIRST DEATH. THERE WAS ONE PROBLEM WITH THAT. IF EDWARD HAD WANTED ME DEAD, HE WOULD HAVE KILLED ME HIMSELF. HAD MALCOLM PANICKED AND SENT ONE OF HIS FOLLOWERS INSTEAD?
3:00, NED. NED WAS A SHORT FORM OF EDWARD, LIKE TEDDY. HAD MALCOLM HAD A MEETING WITH THE HIT MAN OF THE UNDEAD? MAYBE.
MALCOLM'S PRESENCE FILLED THE ROOM LIKE INVISIBLE WATER, PRICKLING ALONG MY SKIN. GIVE HIM ANOTHER NINE HUNDRED YEARS AND HE MIGHT RIVAL NIKOLAOS.
HE WASN'T TRYING TO CLOUD MY MIND. HIS ENTIRE CREDIBILITY RESTED ON THE FACT THAT HE DIDN'T CHEAT.
MISS BLAKE, HOW GOOD TO SEE YOU. BRUCE LEFT ME A VERY CONFUSED MESSAGE, SOMETHING ABOUT THE VAMPIRE MURDERS?
I TOLD BRUCE I HAD PROOF YOUR CHURCH IS INVOLVED IN THE MURDERS.
AND DO YOU?
YES.
I BELIEVED IT. IF HE HAD MET WITH EDWARD, I HAD MY MURDERER.
HMM, YOU ARE TELLING THE TRUTH. YET, I KNOW THAT IT IS NOT TRUE.
CHEATING, MALCOLM, USING YOUR POWERS TO PROBE MY MIND. TSK, TSK.
I CONTROL MY CHURCH, MISS BLAKE. THEY WOULD NOT DO WHAT YOU HAVE ACCUSED THEM OF.
THEY RAIDED A FREAK PARTY LAST NIGHT WITH CLUBS.
THERE IS A SMALL FACTION OF OUR FOLLOWERS WHO PERSIST IN VIOLENCE. FREAK PARTIES ARE AN ABOMINATION AND MUST BE STOPPED, BUT THROUGH LEGAL CHANNELS.
I HAVE TOLD MY FOLLOWERS THIS.

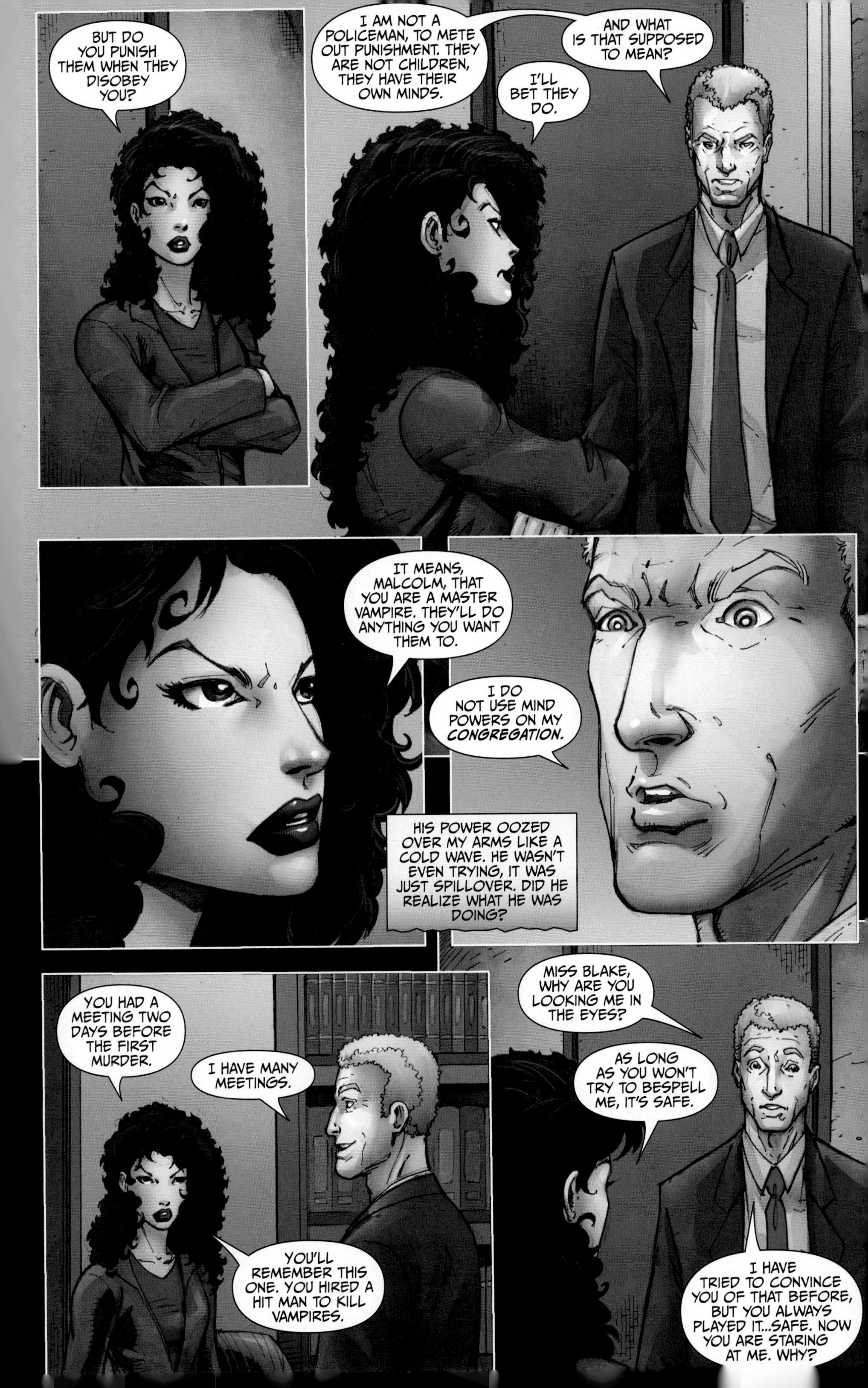
BUT DO YOU PUNISH THEM WHEN THEY DISOBEY YOU?
I AM NOT A POLICEMAN, TO METE OUT PUNISHMENT. THEY ARE NOT CHILDREN, THEY HAVE THEIR OWN MINDS.
I'LL BET THEY DO.
AND WHAT IS THAT SUPPOSED TO MEAN?
IT MEANS, MALCOLM, THAT YOU ARE A MASTER VAMPIRE. THEY'LL DO ANYTHING YOU WANT THEM TO.
I DO NOT USE MIND POWERS ON MY *CONGREGATION.*
HIS POWER OOZED OVER MY ARMS LIKE A COLD WAVE. HE WASN'T EVEN TRYING, IT WAS JUST SPILLOVER. DID HE REALIZE WHAT HE WAS DOING?
YOU HAD A MEETING TWO DAYS BEFORE THE FIRST MURDER.
I HAVE MANY MEETINGS.
YOU'LL REMEMBER THIS ONE. YOU HIRED A HIT MAN TO KILL VAMPIRES.
MISS BLAKE, WHY ARE YOU LOOKING ME IN THE EYES?
AS LONG AS YOU WON'T TRY TO BESPELL ME, IT'S SAFE.
I HAVE TRIED TO CONVINCE YOU OF THAT BEFORE, BUT YOU ALWAYS PLAYED IT...SAFE. NOW YOU ARE STARING AT ME. WHY?

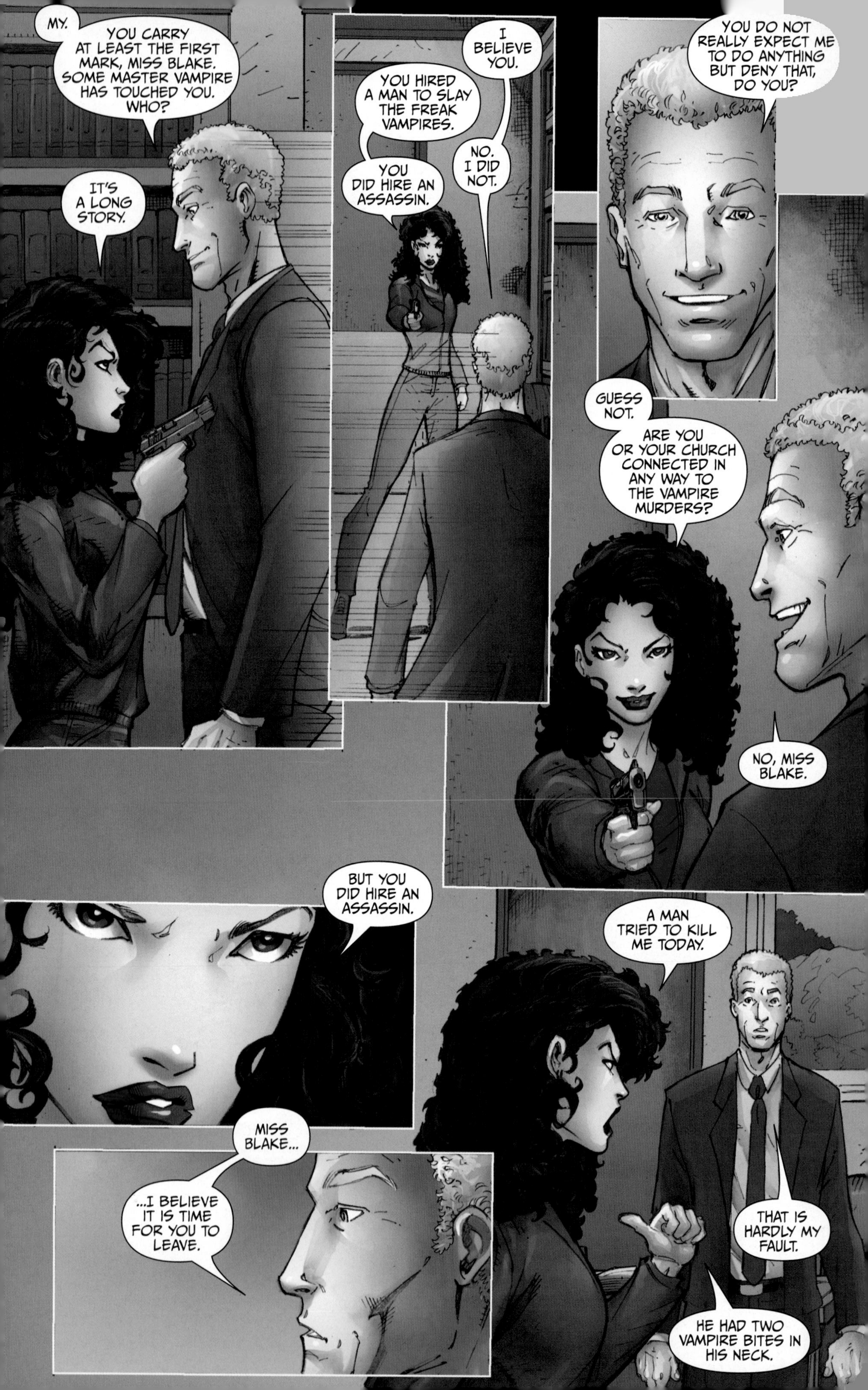
MY.
YOU CARRY AT LEAST THE FIRST MARK, MISS BLAKE. SOME MASTER VAMPIRE HAS TOUCHED YOU. WHO?
IT'S A LONG STORY.
YOU HIRED A MAN TO SLAY THE FREAK VAMPIRES.
I BELIEVE YOU.
YOU DID HIRE AN ASSASSIN.
NO. I DID NOT.
YOU DO NOT REALLY EXPECT ME TO DO ANYTHING BUT DENY THAT, DO YOU?
GUESS NOT.
ARE YOU OR YOUR CHURCH CONNECTED IN ANY WAY TO THE VAMPIRE MURDERS?
NO, MISS BLAKE.
BUT YOU DID HIRE AN ASSASSIN.
MISS BLAKE...
...I BELIEVE IT IS TIME FOR YOU TO LEAVE.
A MAN TRIED TO KILL ME TODAY.
THAT IS HARDLY MY FAULT.
HE HAD TWO VAMPIRE BITES IN HIS NECK.

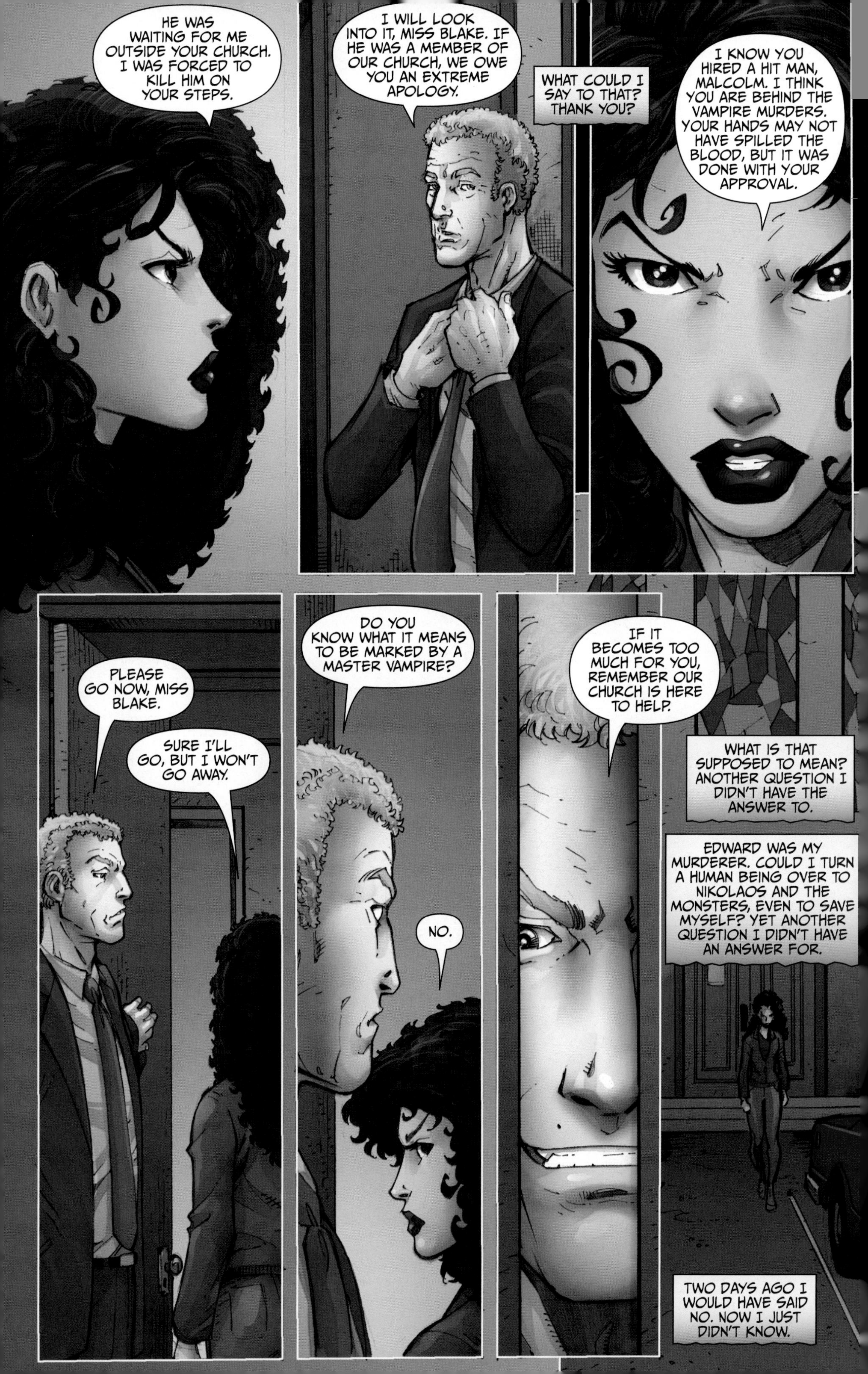
HE WAS WAITING FOR ME OUTSIDE YOUR CHURCH. I WAS FORCED TO KILL HIM ON YOUR STEPS.
I WILL LOOK INTO IT, MISS BLAKE. IF HE WAS A MEMBER OF OUR CHURCH, WE OWE YOU AN EXTREME APOLOGY.
WHAT COULD I SAY TO THAT? THANK YOU?
I KNOW YOU HIRED A HIT MAN, MALCOLM. I THINK YOU ARE BEHIND THE VAMPIRE MURDERS. YOUR HANDS MAY NOT HAVE SPILLED THE BLOOD, BUT IT WAS DONE WITH YOUR APPROVAL.
PLEASE GO NOW, MISS BLAKE.
SURE I'LL GO, BUT I WON'T GO AWAY.
DO YOU KNOW WHAT IT MEANS TO BE MARKED BY A MASTER VAMPIRE?
NO.
IF IT BECOMES TOO MUCH FOR YOU, REMEMBER OUR CHURCH IS HERE TO HELP.
WHAT IS THAT SUPPOSED TO MEAN? ANOTHER QUESTION I DIDN'T HAVE THE ANSWER TO.
EDWARD WAS MY MURDERER. COULD I TURN A HUMAN BEING OVER TO NIKOLAOS AND THE MONSTERS, EVEN TO SAVE MYSELF? YET ANOTHER QUESTION I DIDN'T HAVE AN ANSWER FOR.
TWO DAYS AGO I WOULD HAVE SAID NO. NOW I JUST DIDN'T KNOW.

I DIDN'T WANT TO GO BACK TO MY APARTMENT. EDWARD WOULD BE COMING TONIGHT. IF I DIDN'T TELL HIM WHERE NIKOLAOS SLEPT IN DAYLIGHT, HE'D FORCE THE INFORMATION FROM ME. COMPLICATED.

AND NOW I THOUGHT HE WAS MY MURDERER. VERY COMPLICATED.

THE ONLY THING I COULD DO WAS AVOID HIM. THAT WOULDN'T WORK FOREVER, BUT MAYBE I'D HAVE A BRAINSTORM AND FIGURE IT ALL OUT.

ALL RIGHT, THERE WASN'T MUCH CHANCE OF THAT, BUT ONE COULD ALWAYS HOPE.

MAYBE RONNIE WOULD HAVE A MESSAGE FOR ME. SOMETHING HELPFUL.

MAYBE I COULD AVOID EDWARD ALL NIGHT IF I SLEPT IN A HOTEL. IF I'D HAD ANY SOLID PROOF AT ALL, I'D HAVE CALLED THE POLICE.

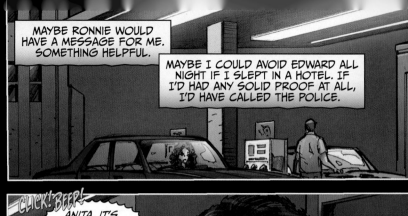

CLICK! BEEP!

ANITA, IT'S WILLIE! THEY GOT PHILLIP! THEY'RE HURTIN' HIM BAD! YOU GOTTA COME--

CLICK! BEEP!

THIS IS NIKOLAOS. YOU'VE HEARD WILLIE'S MESSAGE. COME AND GET IT, ANIMATOR. I DON'T REALLY HAVE TO THREATEN YOUR PRETTY LOVER, DO I?

CLICK!

ANITA, TELL ME WHERE YOU ARE. I CAN HELP YOU.

GOD HELP ME, THEN.

I'M THE CLOSEST THING YOU'VE GOT TO AN ALLY.

WHAM!

DAMMIT!

WHAT ARE YOU LOOKING AT?!

PHILLIP WAS BEING HURT BECAUSE OF ME. JUST LIKE CATHERINE AND RONNIE. NO MORE. NO FREAKING MORE.

I WAS GOING TO GET PHILLIP, SAVE HIM ANY WAY I COULD. THEN I WAS TURNING THE WHOLE BLASTED THING OVER TO THE POLICE. I WAS BAILING OUT BEFORE MORE PEOPLE GOT HURT.

I WAS GOING BACK DOWN THOSE STAIRS INTO THE MASTER'S LAIR, AT NIGHT. THE ANGER WAS FADING IN A WASH OF COLD, SKIN-SHIVERING FEAR. I WOULD NOT GO IN THERE AFRAID.

I HELD ONTO MY ANGER WITH EVERYTHING I HAD.

THIS WAS THE CLOSEST I'D COME TO HATE IN A LONG TIME. MOST HATRED IS BASED ON FEAR, ONE WAY OR ANOTHER.

I WRAPPED MYSELF IN ANGER WITH A DASH OF HATE... AND AT THE BOTTOM OF IT ALL WAS AN ICY CENTER OF PURE TERROR.

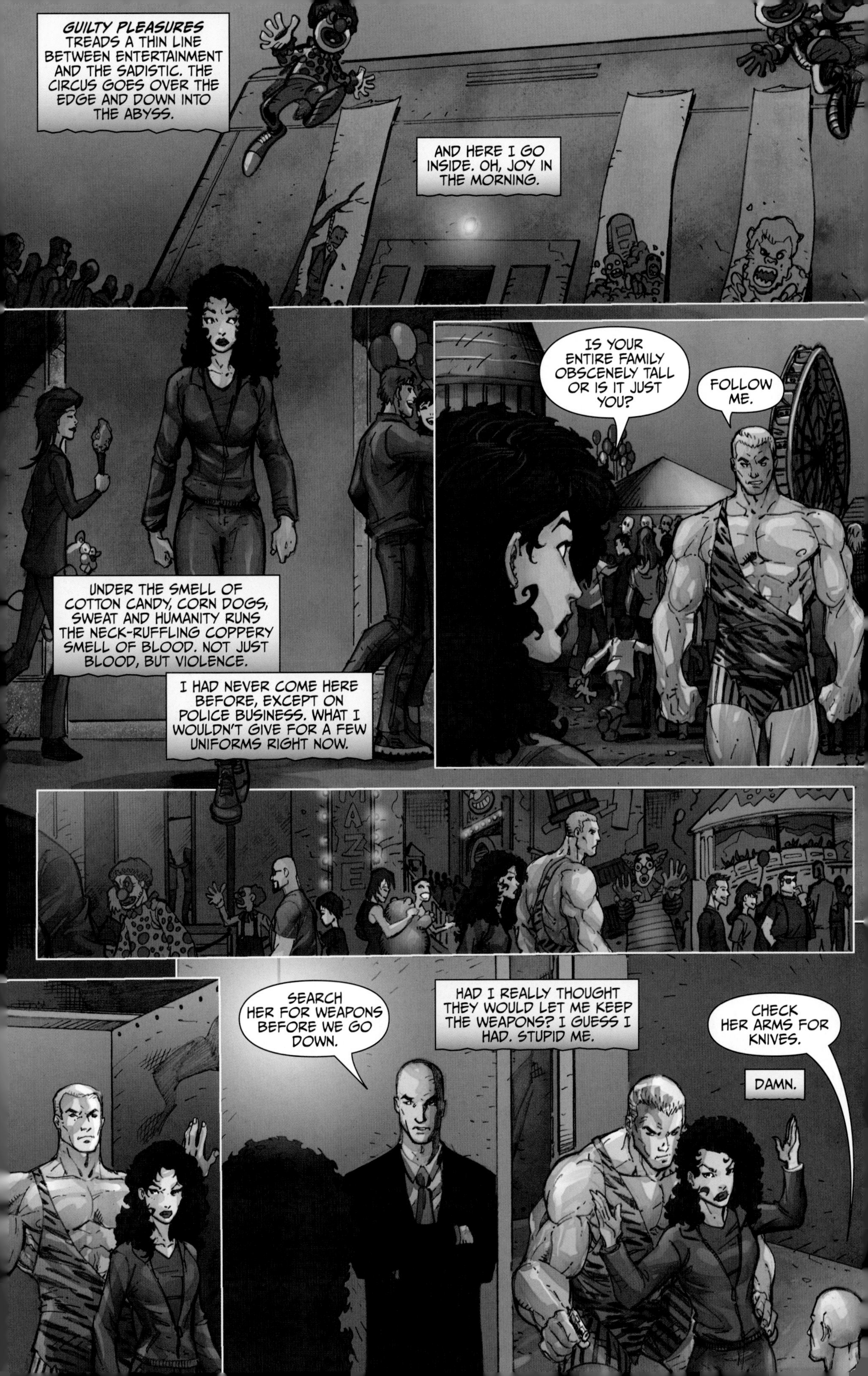
GUILTY PLEASURES TREADS A THIN LINE BETWEEN ENTERTAINMENT AND THE SADISTIC. THE CIRCUS GOES OVER THE EDGE AND DOWN INTO THE ABYSS.
AND HERE I GO INSIDE. OH, JOY IN THE MORNING.
UNDER THE SMELL OF COTTON CANDY, CORN DOGS, SWEAT AND HUMANITY RUNS THE NECK-RUFFLING COPPERY SMELL OF BLOOD. NOT JUST BLOOD, BUT VIOLENCE.
I HAD NEVER COME HERE BEFORE, EXCEPT ON POLICE BUSINESS. WHAT I WOULDN'T GIVE FOR A FEW UNIFORMS RIGHT NOW.
IS YOUR ENTIRE FAMILY OBSCENELY TALL OR IS IT JUST YOU?
FOLLOW ME.
MAZE
SEARCH HER FOR WEAPONS BEFORE WE GO DOWN.
HAD I REALLY THOUGHT THEY WOULD LET ME KEEP THE WEAPONS? I GUESS I HAD. STUPID ME.
CHECK HER ARMS FOR KNIVES.
DAMN.

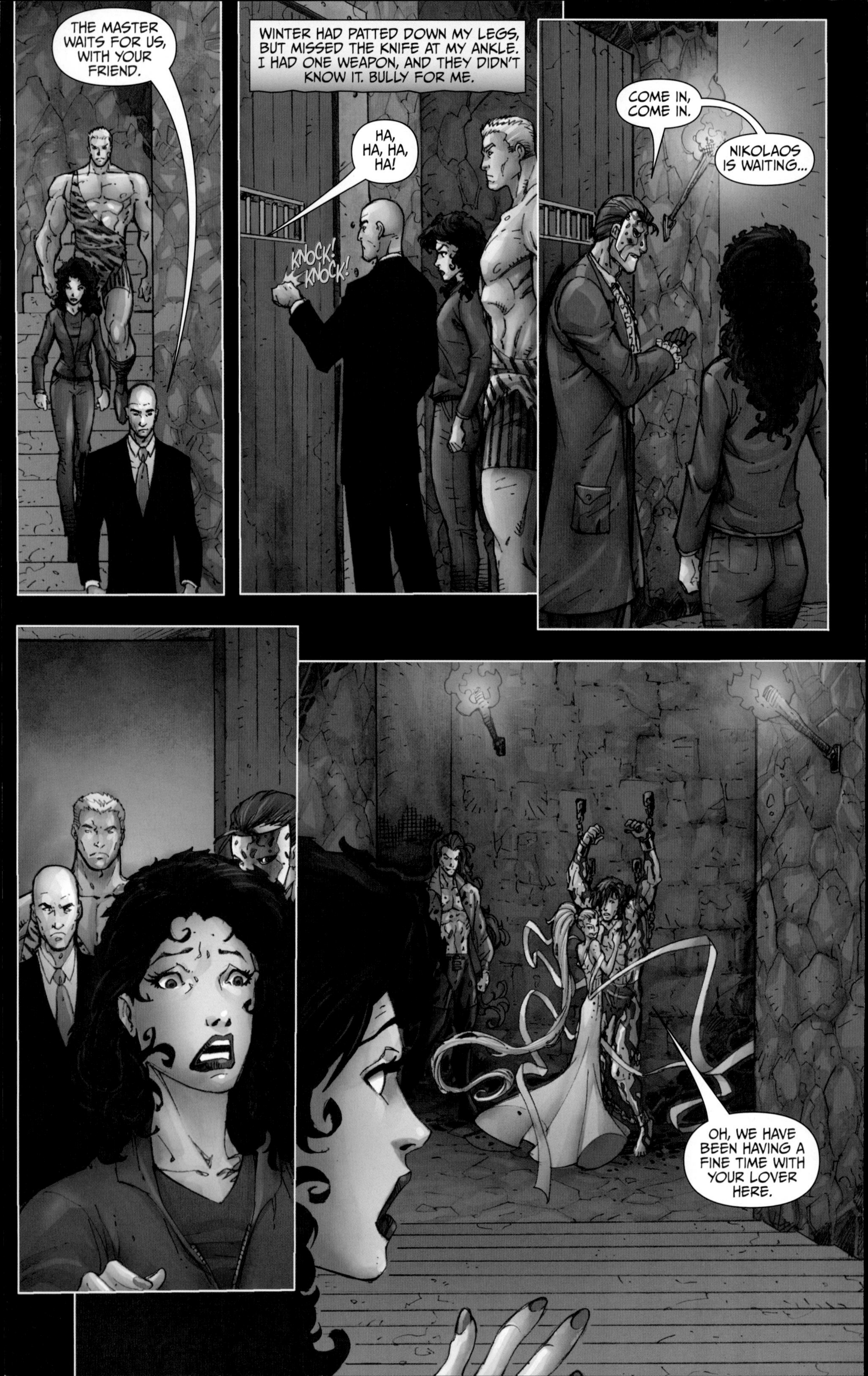
THE MASTER WAITS FOR US, WITH YOUR FRIEND.
WINTER HAD PATTED DOWN MY LEGS, BUT MISSED THE KNIFE AT MY ANKLE. I HAD ONE WEAPON, AND THEY DIDN'T KNOW IT. BULLY FOR ME.
HA, HA, HA, HA!
KNOCK! KNOCK!
COME IN, COME IN.
NIKOLAOS IS WAITING...
OH, WE HAVE BEEN HAVING A FINE TIME WITH YOUR LOVER HERE.

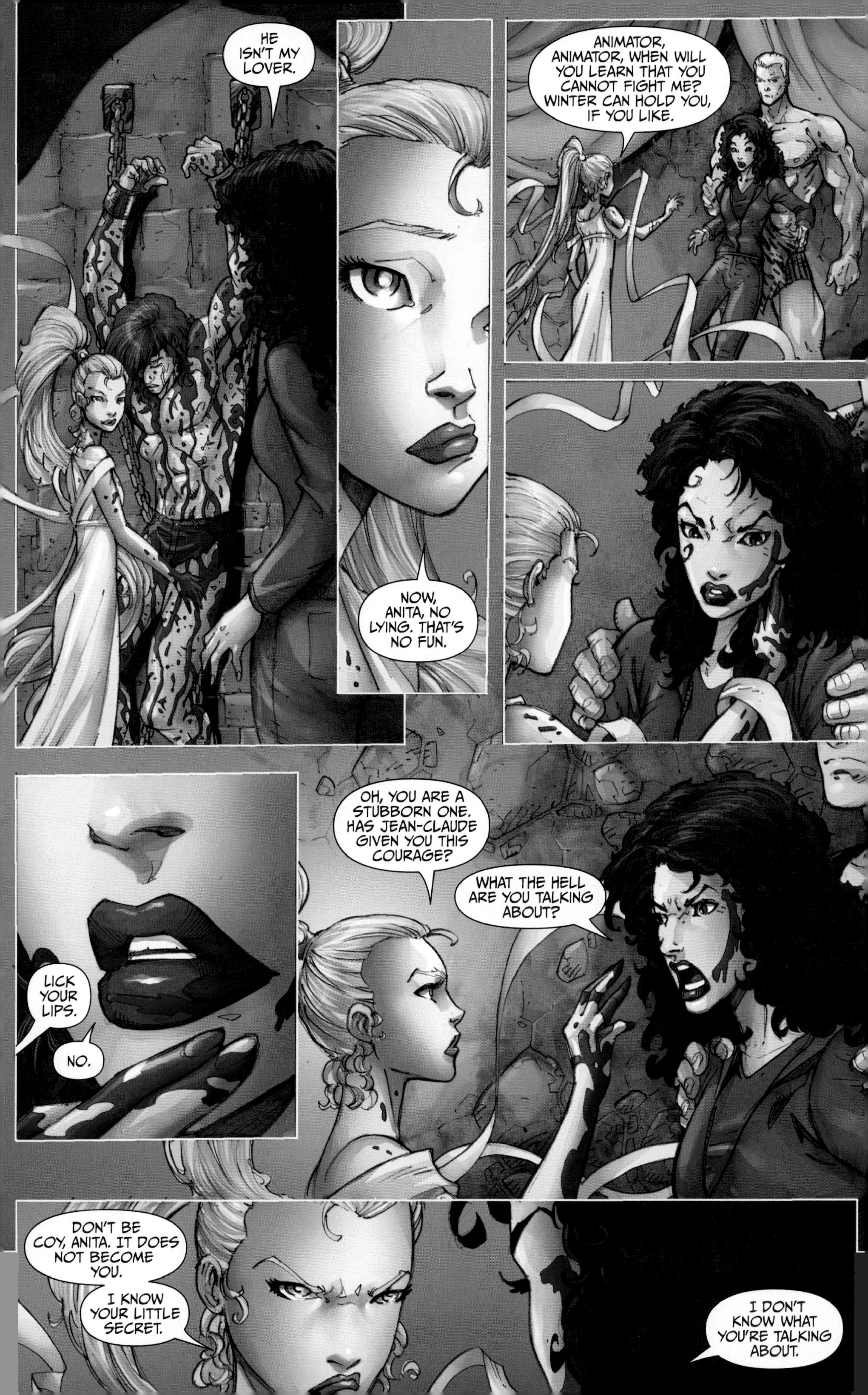
HE ISN'T MY LOVER.
NOW, ANITA, NO LYING. THAT'S NO FUN.
ANIMATOR, ANIMATOR, WHEN WILL YOU LEARN THAT YOU CANNOT FIGHT ME? WINTER CAN HOLD YOU, IF YOU LIKE.
LICK YOUR LIPS.
NO.
OH, YOU ARE A STUBBORN ONE. HAS JEAN-CLAUDE GIVEN YOU THIS COURAGE?
WHAT THE HELL ARE YOU TALKING ABOUT?
DON'T BE COY, ANITA. IT DOES NOT BECOME YOU.
I KNOW YOUR LITTLE SECRET.
I DON'T KNOW WHAT YOU'RE TALKING ABOUT.

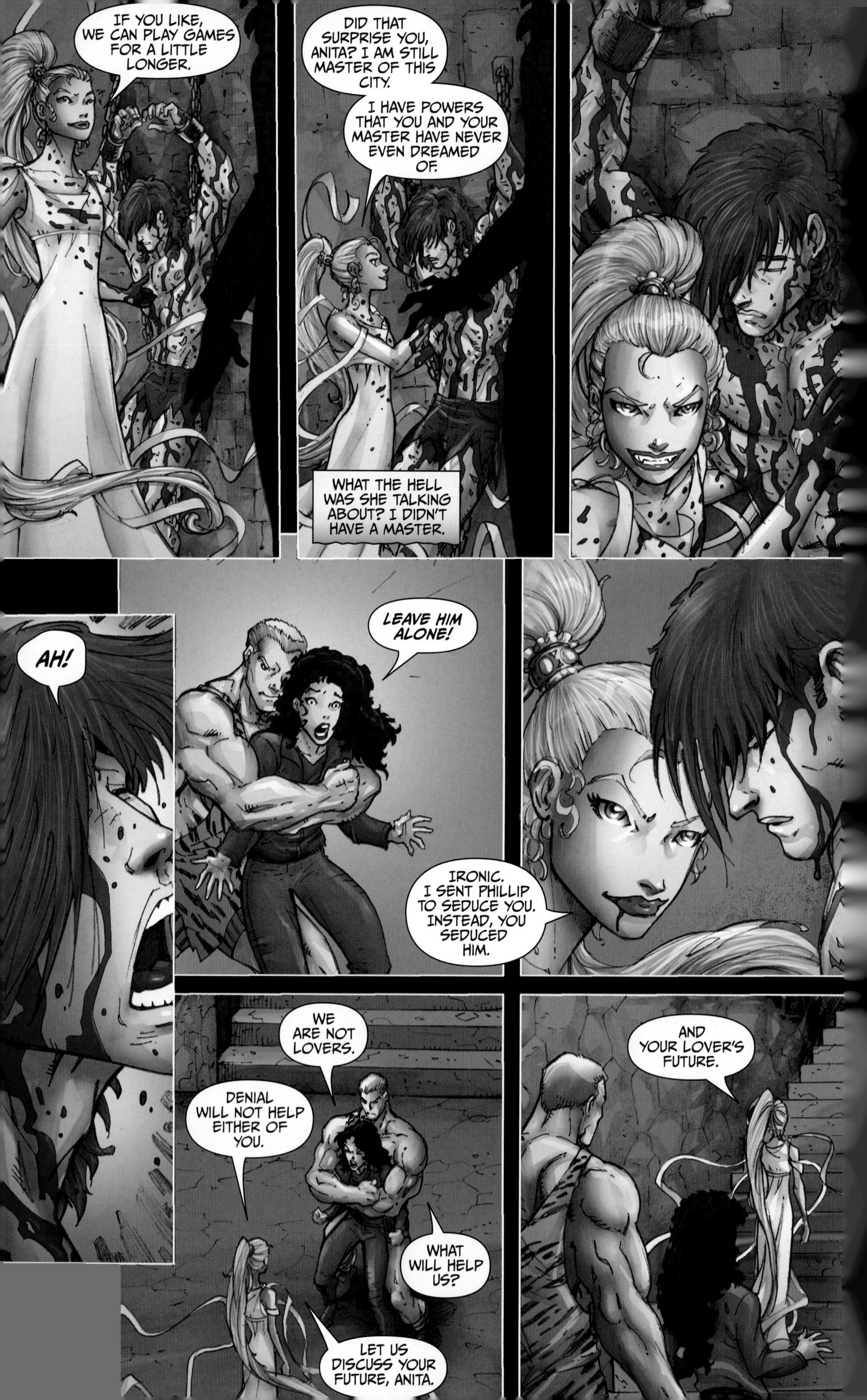
IF YOU LIKE, WE CAN PLAY GAMES FOR A LITTLE LONGER.
DID THAT SURPRISE YOU, ANITA? I AM STILL MASTER OF THIS CITY.
I HAVE POWERS THAT YOU AND YOUR MASTER HAVE NEVER EVEN DREAMED OF.
WHAT THE HELL WAS SHE TALKING ABOUT? I DIDN'T HAVE A MASTER.
AH!
LEAVE HIM ALONE!
IRONIC. I SENT PHILLIP TO SEDUCE YOU. INSTEAD, YOU SEDUCED HIM.
WE ARE NOT LOVERS.
DENIAL WILL NOT HELP EITHER OF YOU.
WHAT WILL HELP US?
LET US DISCUSS YOUR FUTURE, ANITA.
AND YOUR LOVER'S FUTURE.

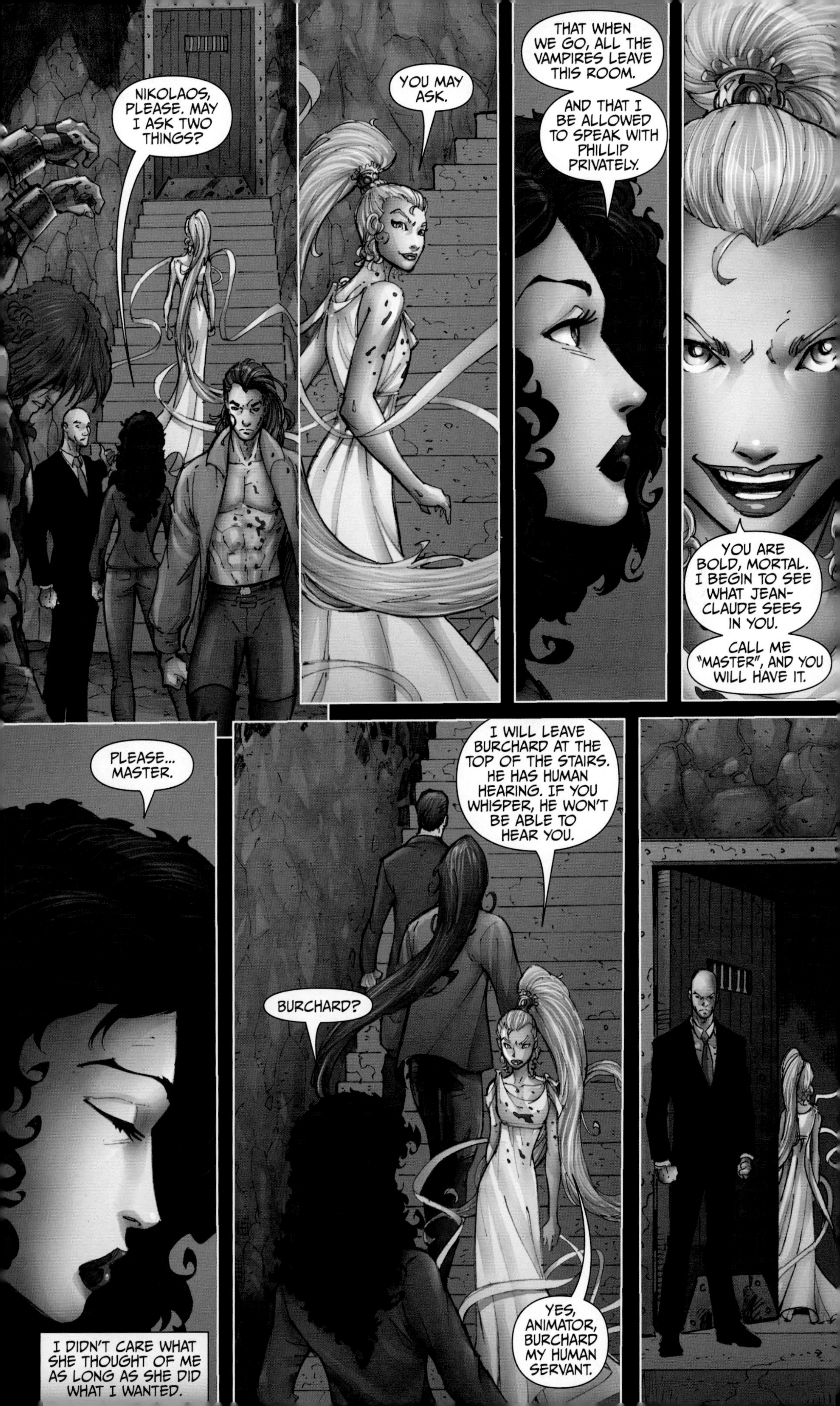
NIKOLAOS, PLEASE. MAY I ASK TWO THINGS?
YOU MAY ASK.
THAT WHEN WE GO, ALL THE VAMPIRES LEAVE THIS ROOM.
AND THAT I BE ALLOWED TO SPEAK WITH PHILLIP PRIVATELY.
YOU ARE BOLD, MORTAL. I BEGIN TO SEE WHAT JEAN-CLAUDE SEES IN YOU.
CALL ME "MASTER", AND YOU WILL HAVE IT.
PLEASE... MASTER.
I DIDN'T CARE WHAT SHE THOUGHT OF ME AS LONG AS SHE DID WHAT I WANTED.
I WILL LEAVE BURCHARD AT THE TOP OF THE STAIRS. HE HAS HUMAN HEARING. IF YOU WHISPER, HE WON'T BE ABLE TO HEAR YOU.
BURCHARD?
YES, ANIMATOR, BURCHARD MY HUMAN SERVANT.

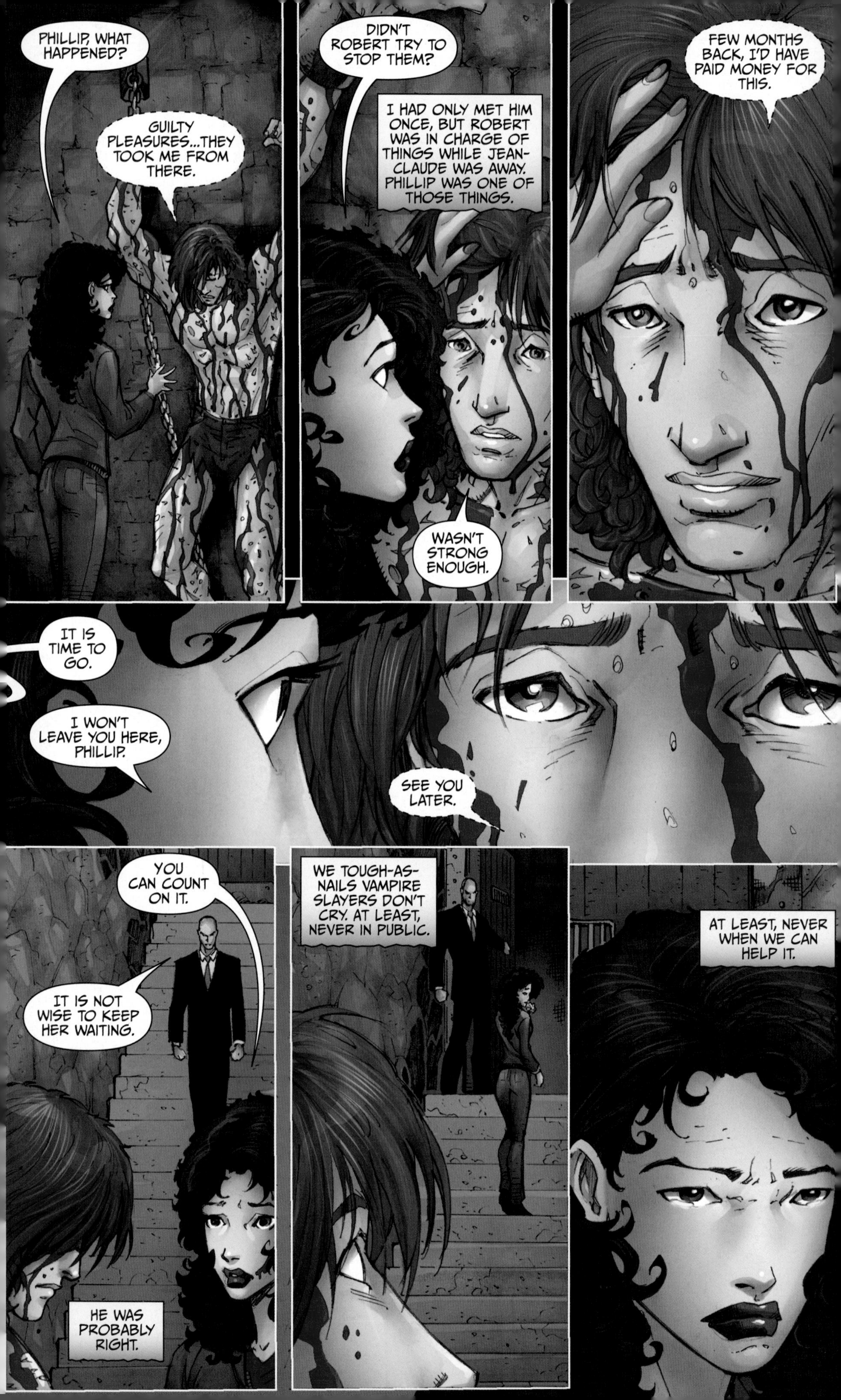
PHILLIP, WHAT HAPPENED?
GUILTY PLEASURES...THEY TOOK ME FROM THERE.
DIDN'T ROBERT TRY TO STOP THEM?
I HAD ONLY MET HIM ONCE, BUT ROBERT WAS IN CHARGE OF THINGS WHILE JEAN-CLAUDE WAS AWAY. PHILLIP WAS ONE OF THOSE THINGS.
WASN'T STRONG ENOUGH.
FEW MONTHS BACK, I'D HAVE PAID MONEY FOR THIS.
IT IS TIME TO GO.
I WON'T LEAVE YOU HERE, PHILLIP.
SEE YOU LATER.
YOU CAN COUNT ON IT.
IT IS NOT WISE TO KEEP HER WAITING.
HE WAS PROBABLY RIGHT.
WE TOUGH-AS-NAILS VAMPIRE SLAYERS DON'T CRY. AT LEAST, NEVER IN PUBLIC.
AT LEAST, NEVER WHEN WE CAN HELP IT.

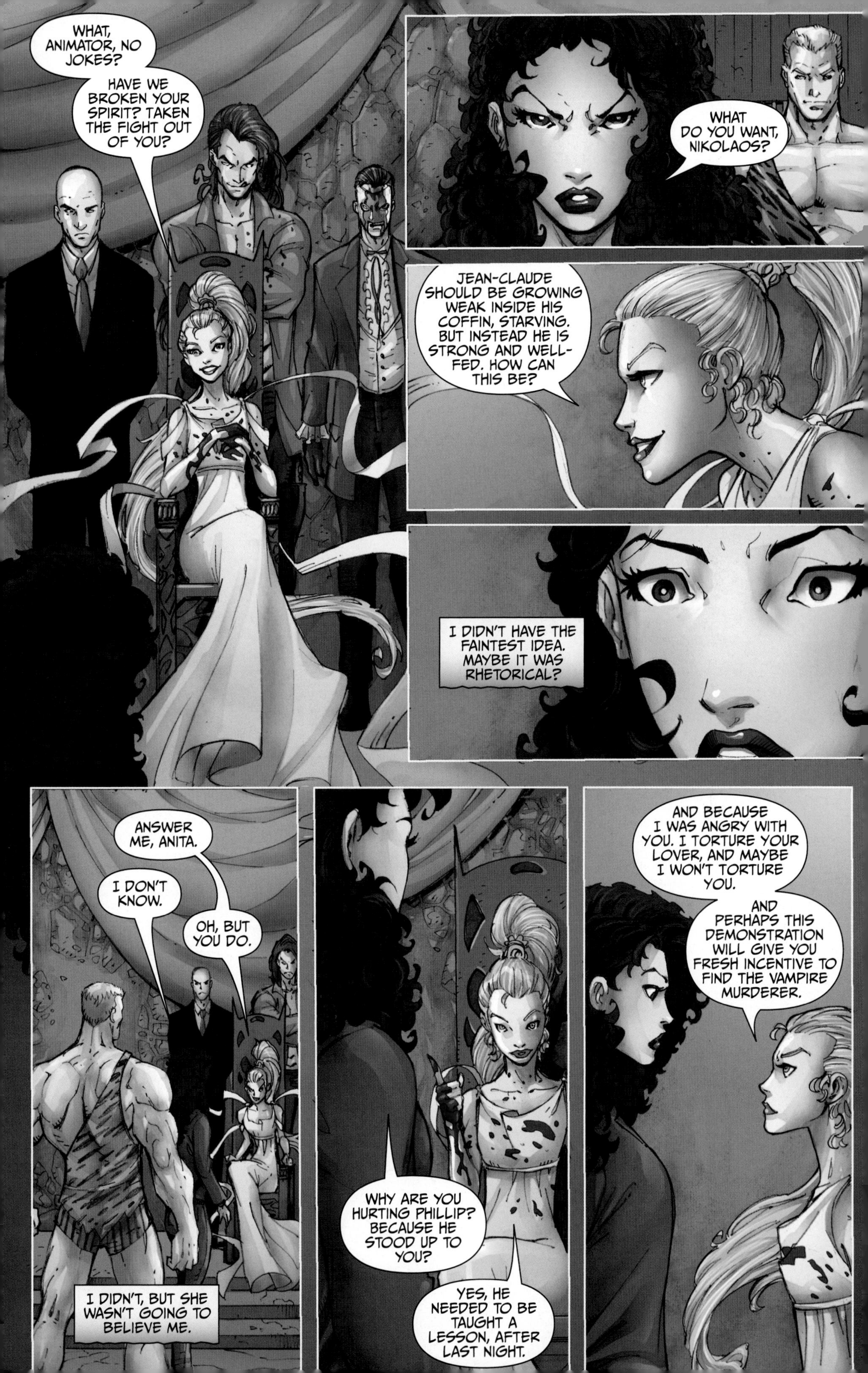

WHAT, ANIMATOR, NO JOKES?
HAVE WE BROKEN YOUR SPIRIT? TAKEN THE FIGHT OUT OF YOU?
WHAT DO YOU WANT, NIKOLAOS?
JEAN-CLAUDE SHOULD BE GROWING WEAK INSIDE HIS COFFIN, STARVING. BUT INSTEAD HE IS STRONG AND WELL-FED. HOW CAN THIS BE?
I DIDN'T HAVE THE FAINTEST IDEA. MAYBE IT WAS RHETORICAL?
ANSWER ME, ANITA.
I DON'T KNOW.
OH, BUT YOU DO.
I DIDN'T, BUT SHE WASN'T GOING TO BELIEVE ME.
WHY ARE YOU HURTING PHILLIP? BECAUSE HE STOOD UP TO YOU?
YES, HE NEEDED TO BE TAUGHT A LESSON, AFTER LAST NIGHT.
AND BECAUSE I WAS ANGRY WITH YOU. I TORTURE YOUR LOVER, AND MAYBE I WON'T TORTURE YOU.
AND PERHAPS THIS DEMONSTRATION WILL GIVE YOU FRESH INCENTIVE TO FIND THE VAMPIRE MURDERER.

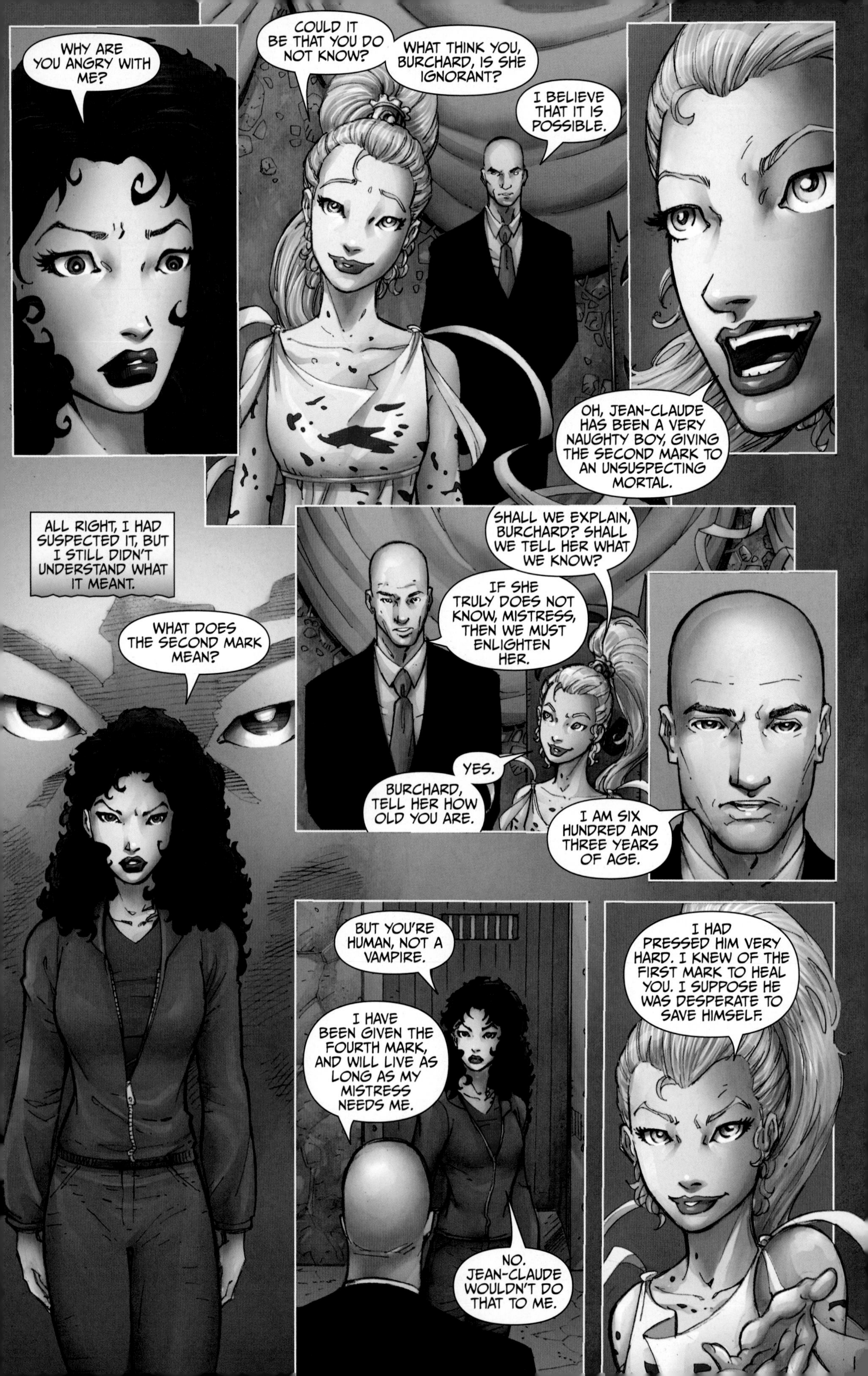
WHY ARE YOU ANGRY WITH ME?
COULD IT BE THAT YOU DO NOT KNOW?
WHAT THINK YOU, BURCHARD, IS SHE IGNORANT?
I BELIEVE THAT IT IS POSSIBLE.
OH, JEAN-CLAUDE HAS BEEN A VERY NAUGHTY BOY, GIVING THE SECOND MARK TO AN UNSUSPECTING MORTAL.
ALL RIGHT, I HAD SUSPECTED IT, BUT I STILL DIDN'T UNDERSTAND WHAT IT MEANT.
WHAT DOES THE SECOND MARK MEAN?
SHALL WE EXPLAIN, BURCHARD? SHALL WE TELL HER WHAT WE KNOW?
IF SHE TRULY DOES NOT KNOW, MISTRESS, THEN WE MUST ENLIGHTEN HER.
YES.
BURCHARD, TELL HER HOW OLD YOU ARE.
I AM SIX HUNDRED AND THREE YEARS OF AGE.
BUT YOU'RE HUMAN, NOT A VAMPIRE.
I HAVE BEEN GIVEN THE FOURTH MARK, AND WILL LIVE AS LONG AS MY MISTRESS NEEDS ME.
NO. JEAN-CLAUDE WOULDN'T DO THAT TO ME.
I HAD PRESSED HIM VERY HARD. I KNEW OF THE FIRST MARK TO HEAL YOU. I SUPPOSE HE WAS DESPERATE TO SAVE HIMSELF.

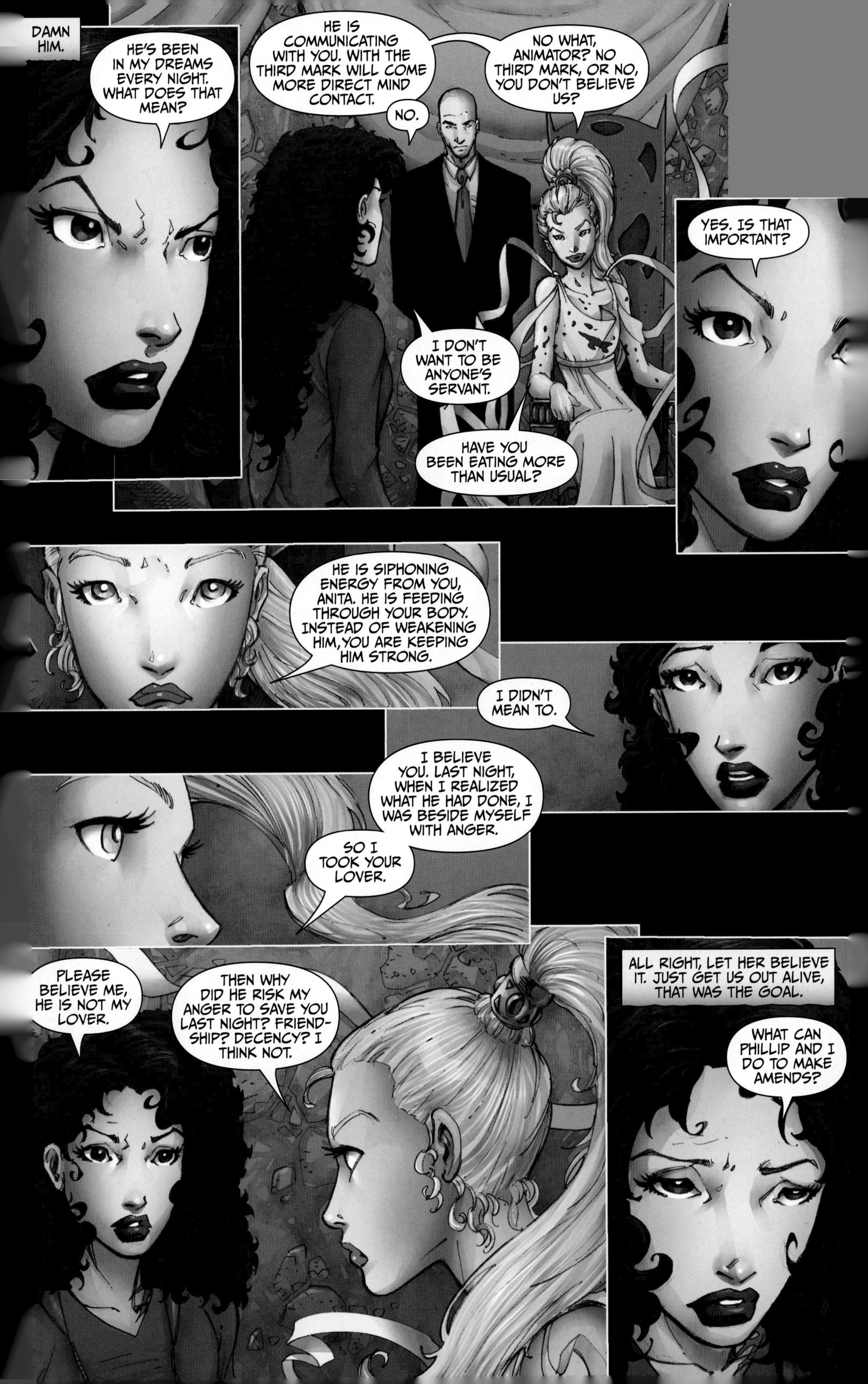
DAMN HIM.
HE'S BEEN IN MY DREAMS EVERY NIGHT. WHAT DOES THAT MEAN?
HE IS COMMUNICATING WITH YOU. WITH THE THIRD MARK WILL COME MORE DIRECT MIND CONTACT.
NO.
NO WHAT, ANIMATOR? NO THIRD MARK, OR NO, YOU DON'T BELIEVE US?
I DON'T WANT TO BE ANYONE'S SERVANT.
HAVE YOU BEEN EATING MORE THAN USUAL?
YES. IS THAT IMPORTANT?
HE IS SIPHONING ENERGY FROM YOU, ANITA. HE IS FEEDING THROUGH YOUR BODY. INSTEAD OF WEAKENING HIM, YOU ARE KEEPING HIM STRONG.
I DIDN'T MEAN TO.
I BELIEVE YOU. LAST NIGHT, WHEN I REALIZED WHAT HE HAD DONE, I WAS BESIDE MYSELF WITH ANGER.
SO I TOOK YOUR LOVER.
PLEASE BELIEVE ME, HE IS NOT MY LOVER.
THEN WHY DID HE RISK MY ANGER TO SAVE YOU LAST NIGHT? FRIENDSHIP? DECENCY? I THINK NOT.
ALL RIGHT, LET HER BELIEVE IT. JUST GET US OUT ALIVE, THAT WAS THE GOAL.
WHAT CAN PHILLIP AND I DO TO MAKE AMENDS?

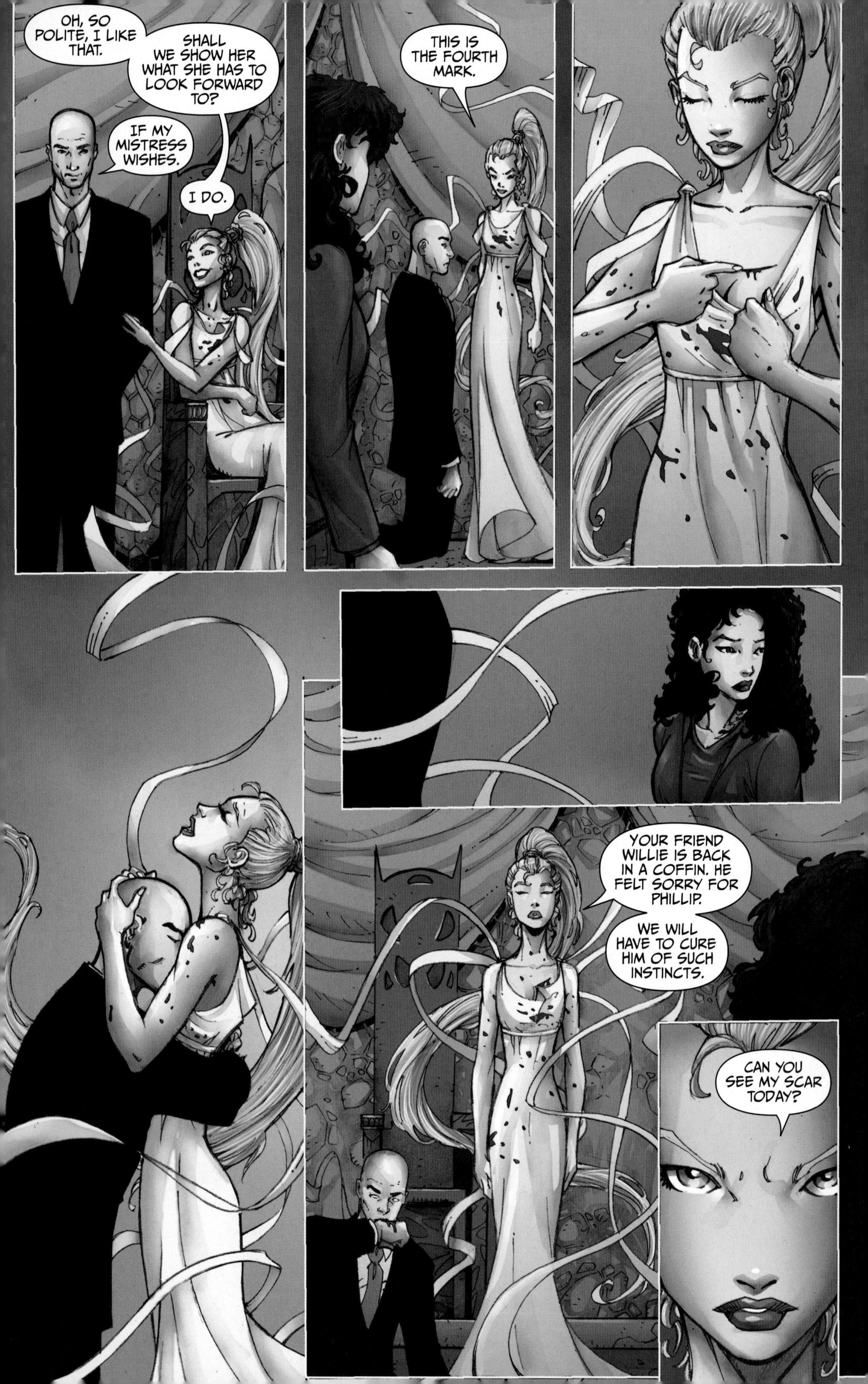

OH, SO POLITE, I LIKE THAT.
SHALL WE SHOW HER WHAT SHE HAS TO LOOK FORWARD TO?
IF MY MISTRESS WISHES.
I DO.
THIS IS THE FOURTH MARK.
YOUR FRIEND WILLIE IS BACK IN A COFFIN. HE FELT SORRY FOR PHILLIP.
WE WILL HAVE TO CURE HIM OF SUCH INSTINCTS.
CAN YOU SEE MY SCAR TODAY?

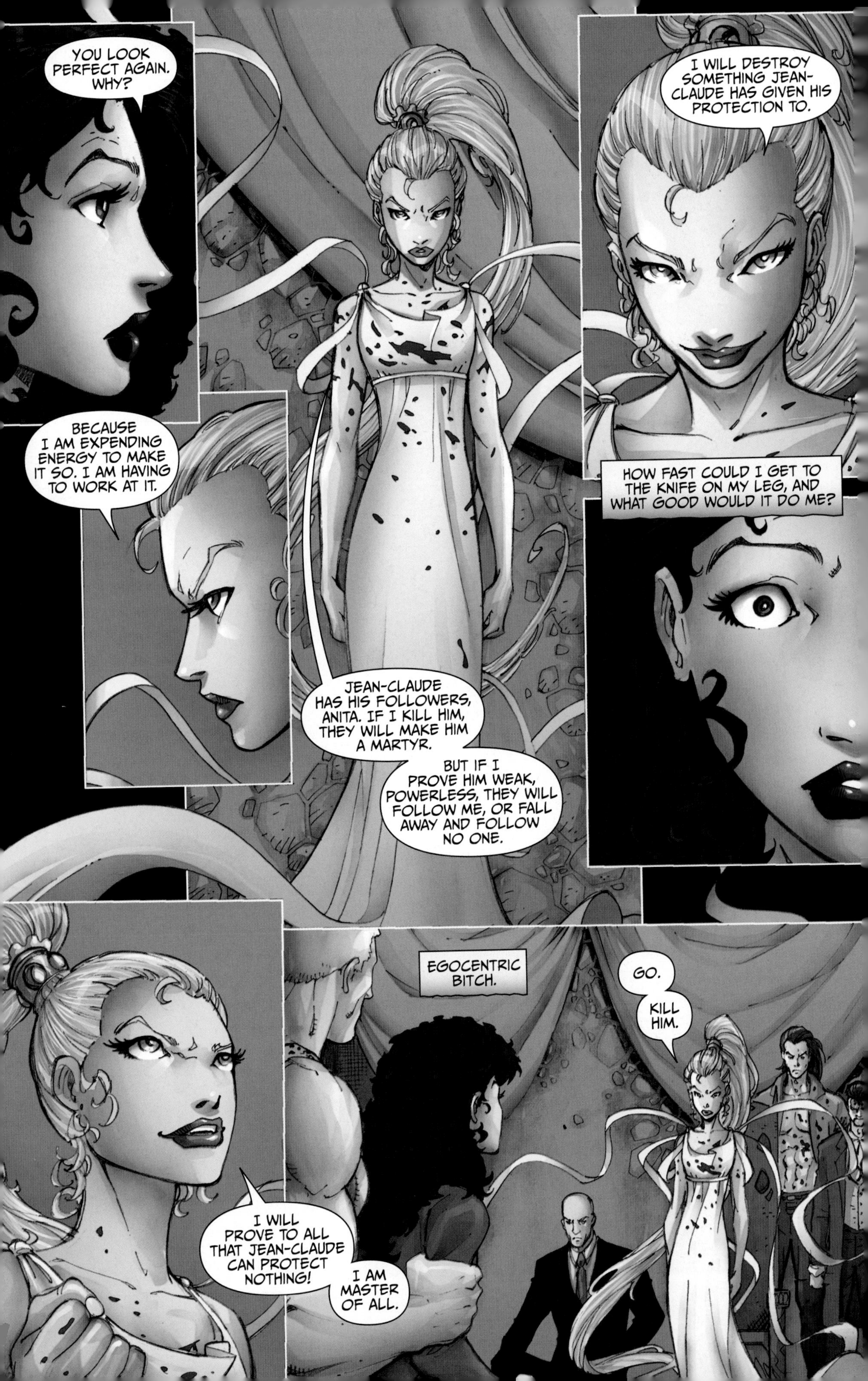
YOU LOOK PERFECT AGAIN. WHY?
I WILL DESTROY SOMETHING JEAN-CLAUDE HAS GIVEN HIS PROTECTION TO.
BECAUSE I AM EXPENDING ENERGY TO MAKE IT SO. I AM HAVING TO WORK AT IT.
JEAN-CLAUDE HAS HIS FOLLOWERS, ANITA. IF I KILL HIM, THEY WILL MAKE HIM A MARTYR.
BUT IF I PROVE HIM WEAK, POWERLESS, THEY WILL FOLLOW ME, OR FALL AWAY AND FOLLOW NO ONE.
HOW FAST COULD I GET TO THE KNIFE ON MY LEG, AND WHAT GOOD WOULD IT DO ME?
I WILL PROVE TO ALL THAT JEAN-CLAUDE CAN PROTECT NOTHING!
I AM MASTER OF ALL.
EGOCENTRIC BITCH.
GO.
KILL HIM.

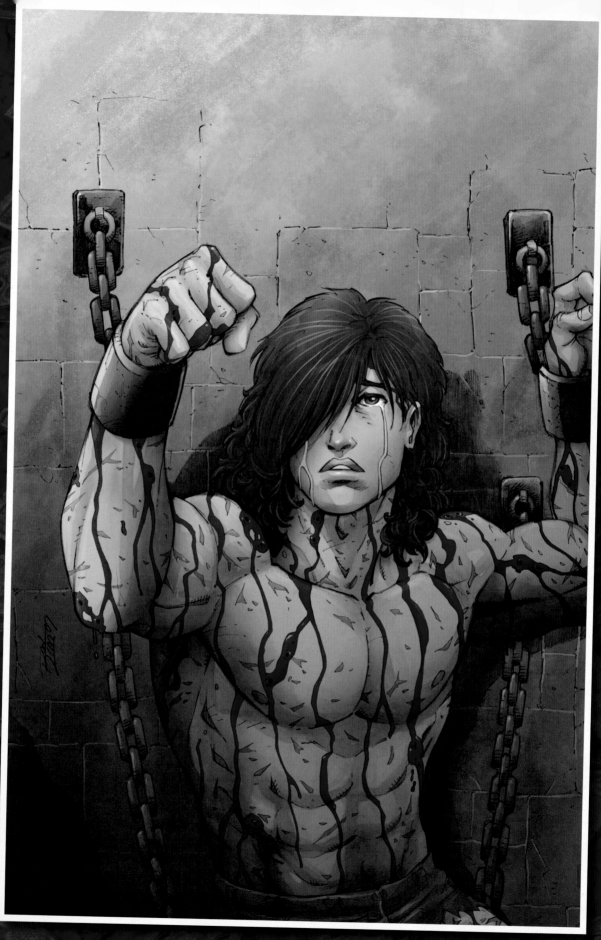

TEN

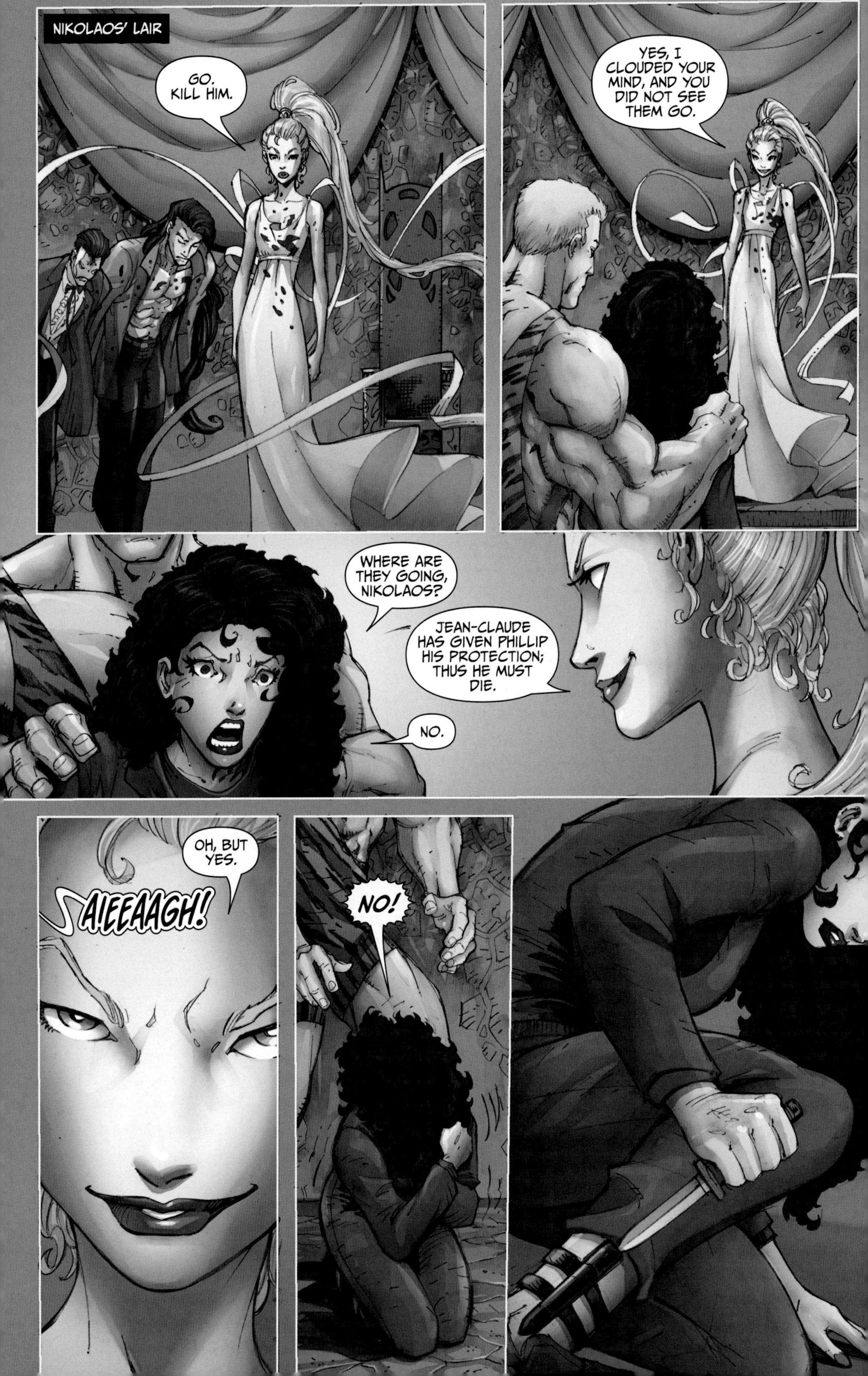
NIKOLAOS' LAIR
GO. KILL HIM.
YES, I CLOUDED YOUR MIND, AND YOU DID NOT SEE THEM GO.
WHERE ARE THEY GOING, NIKOLAOS?
JEAN-CLAUDE HAS GIVEN PHILLIP HIS PROTECTION; THUS HE MUST DIE.
NO.
OH, BUT YES.
AIEEAAGH!
NO!

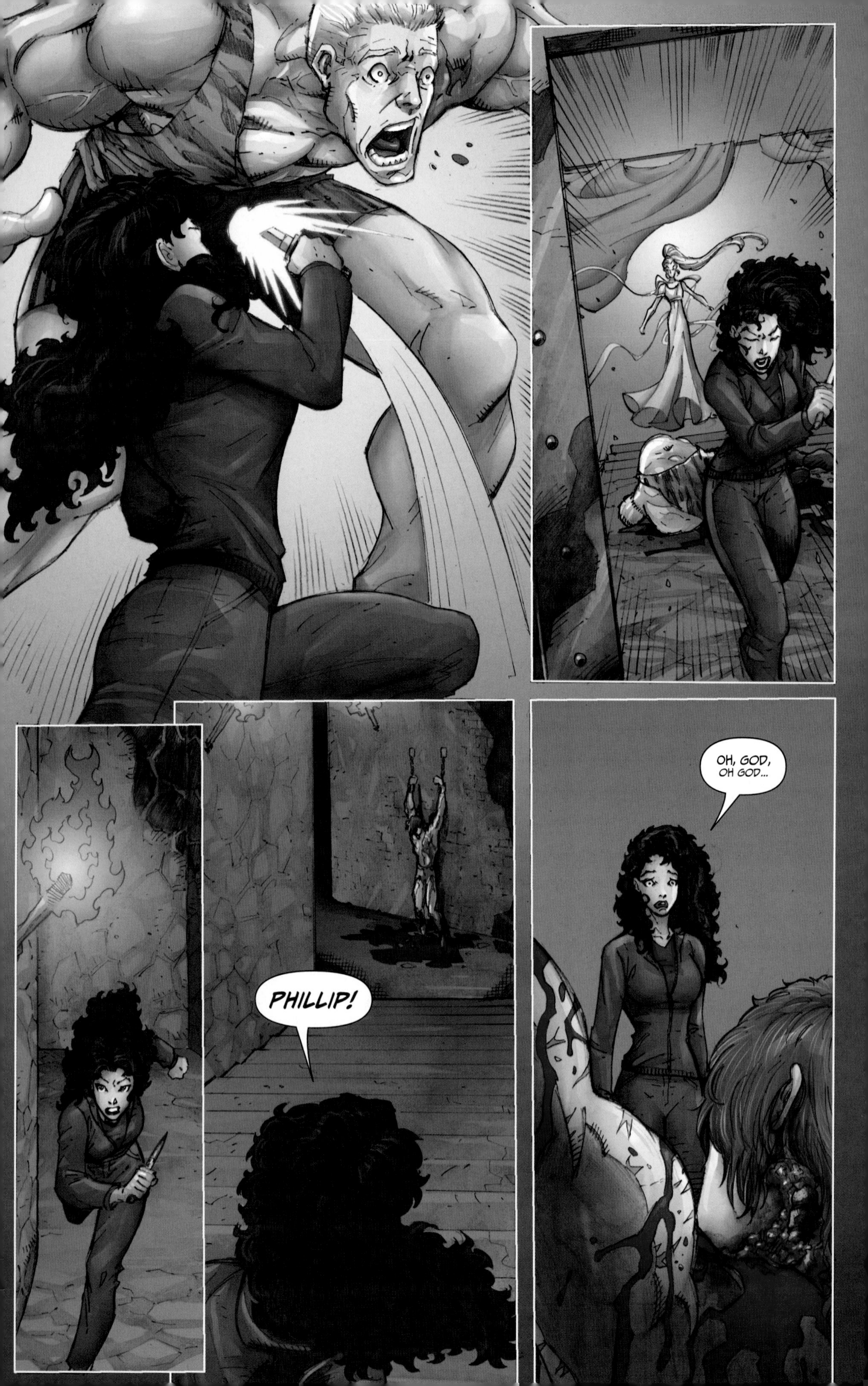
PHILLIP!
OH, GOD,
OH GOD...

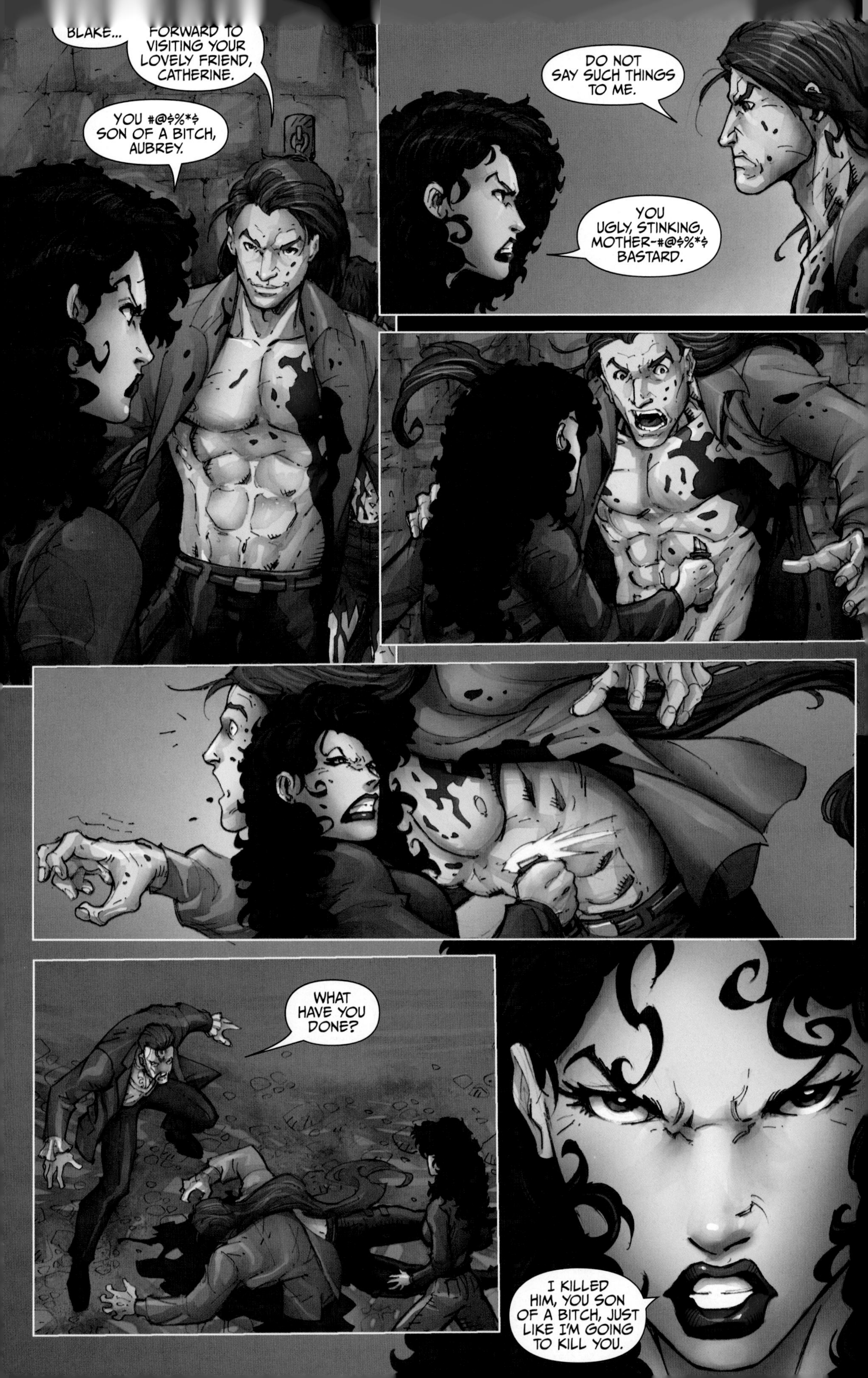
BLAKE...
FORWARD TO VISITING YOUR LOVELY FRIEND, CATHERINE.
YOU #@$%*$ SON OF A BITCH, AUBREY.
DO NOT SAY SUCH THINGS TO ME.
YOU UGLY, STINKING, MOTHER-#@$%*$ BASTARD.
WHAT HAVE YOU DONE?
I KILLED HIM, YOU SON OF A BITCH, JUST LIKE I'M GOING TO KILL YOU.

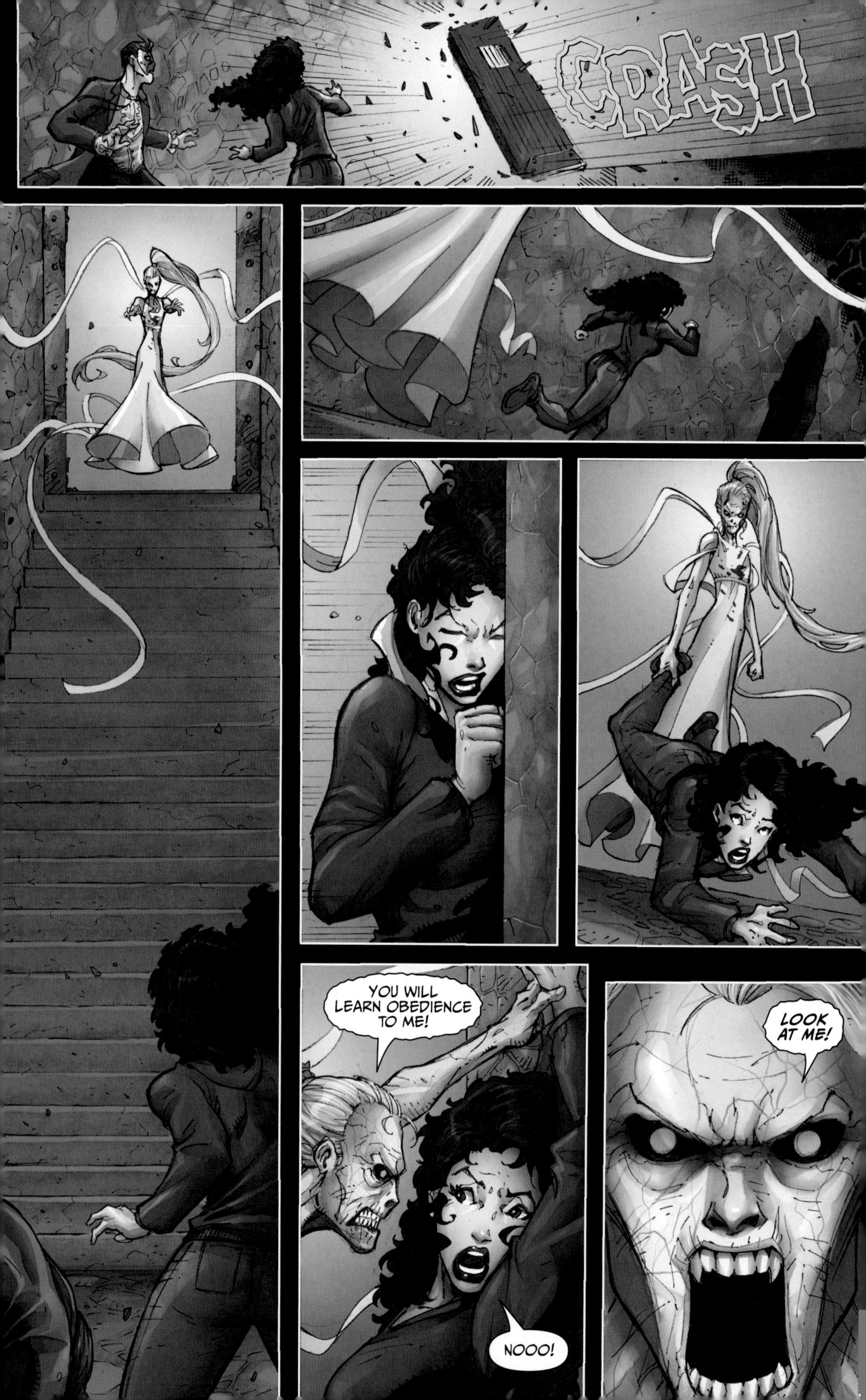
CRASH
YOU WILL LEARN OBEDIENCE TO ME!
NOOO!
LOOK AT ME!

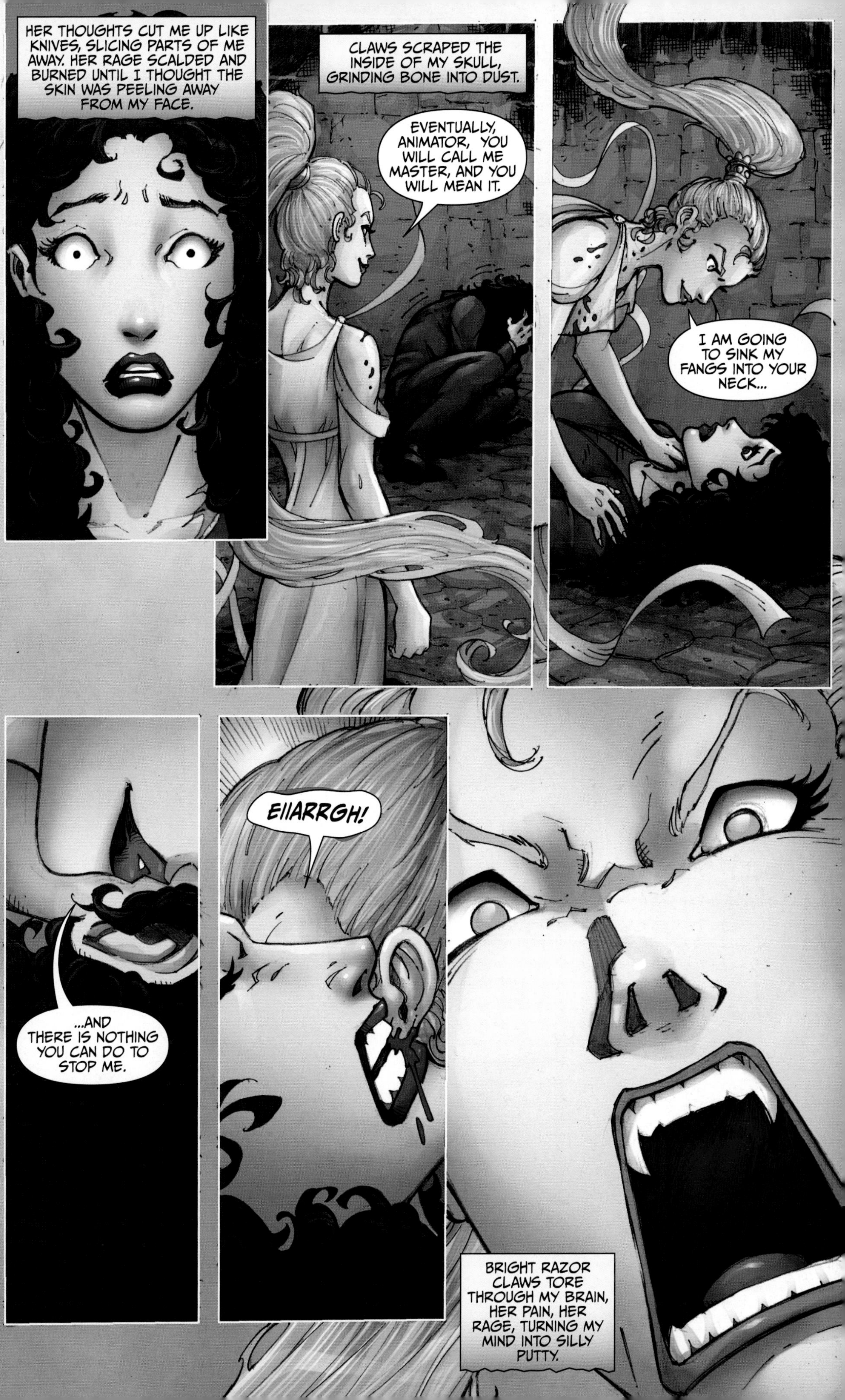
HER THOUGHTS CUT ME UP LIKE KNIVES, SLICING PARTS OF ME AWAY. HER RAGE SCALDED AND BURNED UNTIL I THOUGHT THE SKIN WAS PEELING AWAY FROM MY FACE.
CLAWS SCRAPED THE INSIDE OF MY SKULL, GRINDING BONE INTO DUST.
EVENTUALLY, ANIMATOR, YOU WILL CALL ME MASTER, AND YOU WILL MEAN IT.
I AM GOING TO SINK MY FANGS INTO YOUR NECK...
...AND THERE IS NOTHING YOU CAN DO TO STOP ME.
EIIARRGH!
BRIGHT RAZOR CLAWS TORE THROUGH MY BRAIN, HER PAIN, HER RAGE, TURNING MY MIND INTO SILLY PUTTY.

ROBERT.

I WAS AFRAID YOU WOULDN'T WAKE UP BEFORE DAWN. ARE YOU HURT?

WHERE AM I?

JEAN-CLAUDE'S OFFICE AT GUILTY PLEASURES.

HOW DID I GET HERE?

NIKOLAOS BROUGHT YOU. SHE SAID, 'HERE'S YOUR MASTER'S WHORE.'

YOU KNOW WHAT JEAN-CLAUDE HAS DONE?

MY MASTER HAS MARKED YOU TWICE. WHEN I SPEAK TO YOU, I AM SPEAKING TO HIM.

DID HE MEAN THAT FIGURATIVELY, OR LITERALLY? I REALLY DIDN'T WANT TO KNOW.

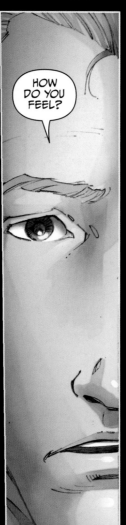

HOW DO YOU FEEL?

...

...BATHROOM?

THIS WAY.

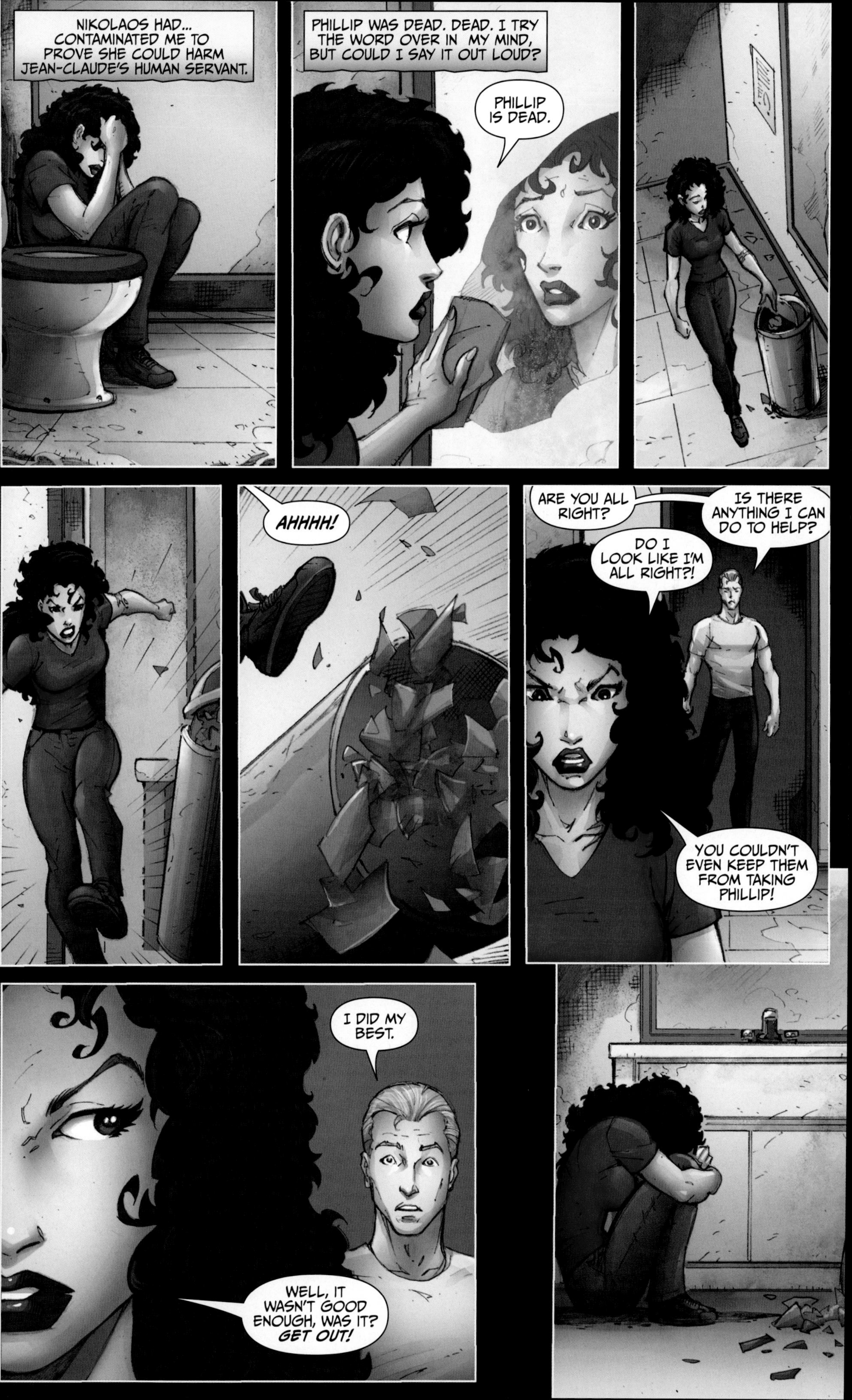
NIKOLAOS HAD... CONTAMINATED ME TO PROVE SHE COULD HARM JEAN-CLAUDE'S HUMAN SERVANT.
PHILLIP WAS DEAD. DEAD. I TRY THE WORD OVER IN MY MIND, BUT COULD I SAY IT OUT LOUD?
PHILLIP IS DEAD.
AHHHH!
ARE YOU ALL RIGHT?
IS THERE ANYTHING I CAN DO TO HELP?
DO I LOOK LIKE I'M ALL RIGHT?!
YOU COULDN'T EVEN KEEP THEM FROM TAKING PHILLIP!
I DID MY BEST.
WELL, IT WASN'T GOOD ENOUGH, WAS IT? GET OUT!

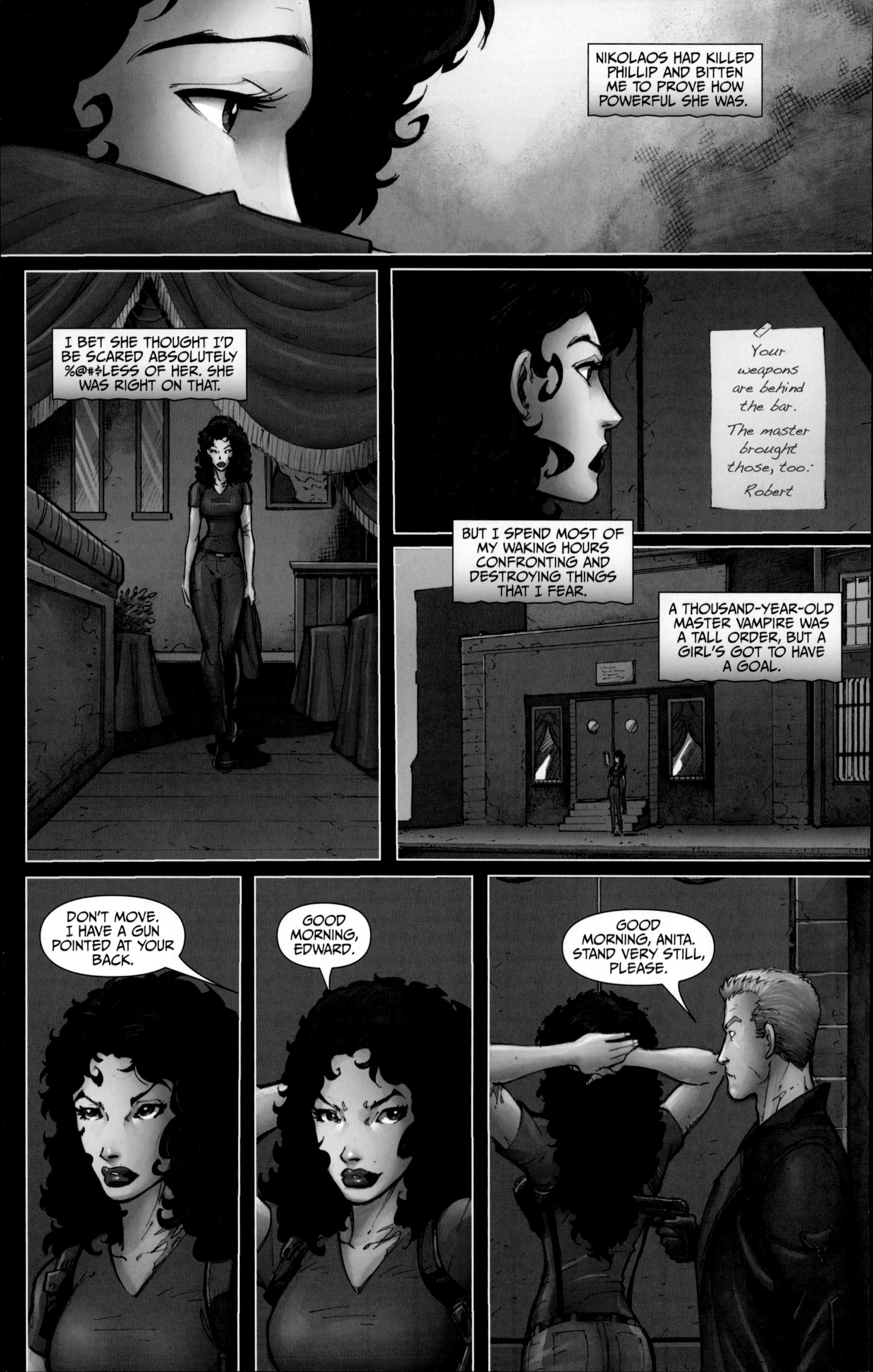
NIKOLAOS HAD KILLED PHILLIP AND BITTEN ME TO PROVE HOW POWERFUL SHE WAS.
I BET SHE THOUGHT I'D BE SCARED ABSOLUTELY %@#$LESS OF HER. SHE WAS RIGHT ON THAT.
Your weapons are behind the bar. The master brought those, too. Robert
BUT I SPEND MOST OF MY WAKING HOURS CONFRONTING AND DESTROYING THINGS THAT I FEAR.
A THOUSAND-YEAR-OLD MASTER VAMPIRE WAS A TALL ORDER, BUT A GIRL'S GOT TO HAVE A GOAL.
DON'T MOVE. I HAVE A GUN POINTED AT YOUR BACK.
GOOD MORNING, EDWARD.
GOOD MORNING, ANITA. STAND VERY STILL, PLEASE.

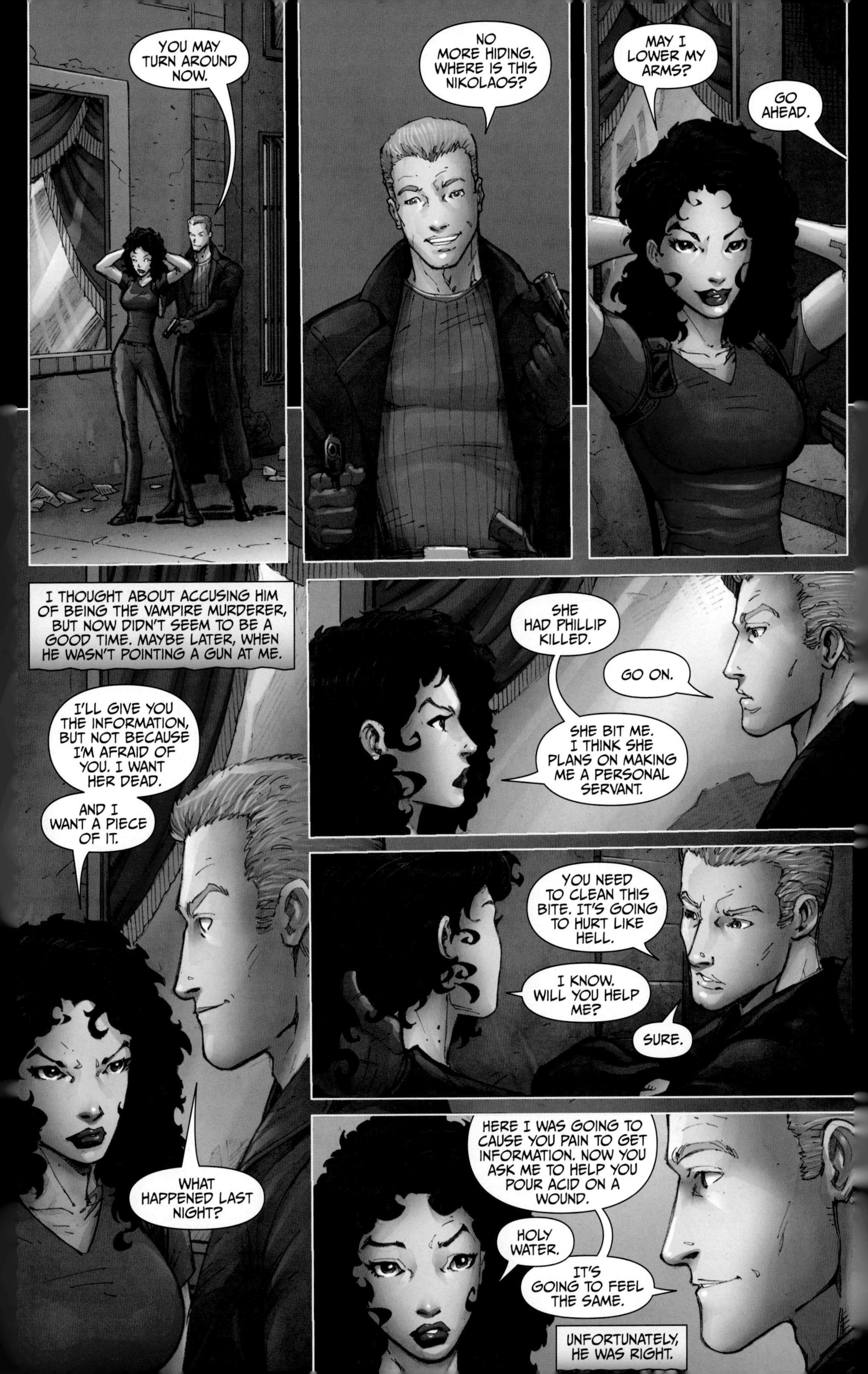
YOU MAY TURN AROUND NOW.
NO MORE HIDING. WHERE IS THIS NIKOLAOS?
MAY I LOWER MY ARMS?
GO AHEAD.
I THOUGHT ABOUT ACCUSING HIM OF BEING THE VAMPIRE MURDERER, BUT NOW DIDN'T SEEM TO BE A GOOD TIME. MAYBE LATER, WHEN HE WASN'T POINTING A GUN AT ME.
I'LL GIVE YOU THE INFORMATION, BUT NOT BECAUSE I'M AFRAID OF YOU. I WANT HER DEAD.
AND I WANT A PIECE OF IT.
WHAT HAPPENED LAST NIGHT?
SHE HAD PHILLIP KILLED.
GO ON.
SHE BIT ME. I THINK SHE PLANS ON MAKING ME A PERSONAL SERVANT.
YOU NEED TO CLEAN THIS BITE. IT'S GOING TO HURT LIKE HELL.
I KNOW. WILL YOU HELP ME?
SURE.
HERE I WAS GOING TO CAUSE YOU PAIN TO GET INFORMATION. NOW YOU ASK ME TO HELP YOU POUR ACID ON A WOUND.
HOLY WATER.
IT'S GOING TO FEEL THE SAME.
UNFORTUNATELY, HE WAS RIGHT.

AAAHHH!

YOU SON OF A BITCH!

HOW DO YOU FEEL?

LIKE SOMEONE'S BEEN SHOVING A RED HOT KNIFE AGAINST MY THROAT.

DO YOU WANT TO STOP AND REST?

NO. I WANT IT CLEAN, EDWARD. ALL THE WAY.

IT IS CUSTOMARY TO DO THIS OVER A MATTER OF DAYS, YOU KNOW.

I DON'T HAVE A FEW DAYS. I NEED THIS WOUND CLEANED BEFORE NIGHTFALL.

BECAUSE NIKOLAOS WILL HAVE A HOLD ON YOU UNLESS THE WOUND IS PURIFIED.

YES.

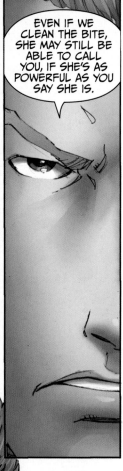

EVEN IF WE CLEAN THE BITE, SHE MAY STILL BE ABLE TO CALL YOU, IF SHE'S AS POWERFUL AS YOU SAY SHE IS.

YOU THINK NIKOLAOS CAN TURN ME AGAINST YOU, EVEN IF WE CLEAN THE BITE?

WE VAMPIRE SLAYERS TAKE OUR CHANCES.

THAT WASN'T A NO.

IT WASN'T A YES, EITHER.

OH GOODY, EDWARD DIDN'T KNOW EITHER.

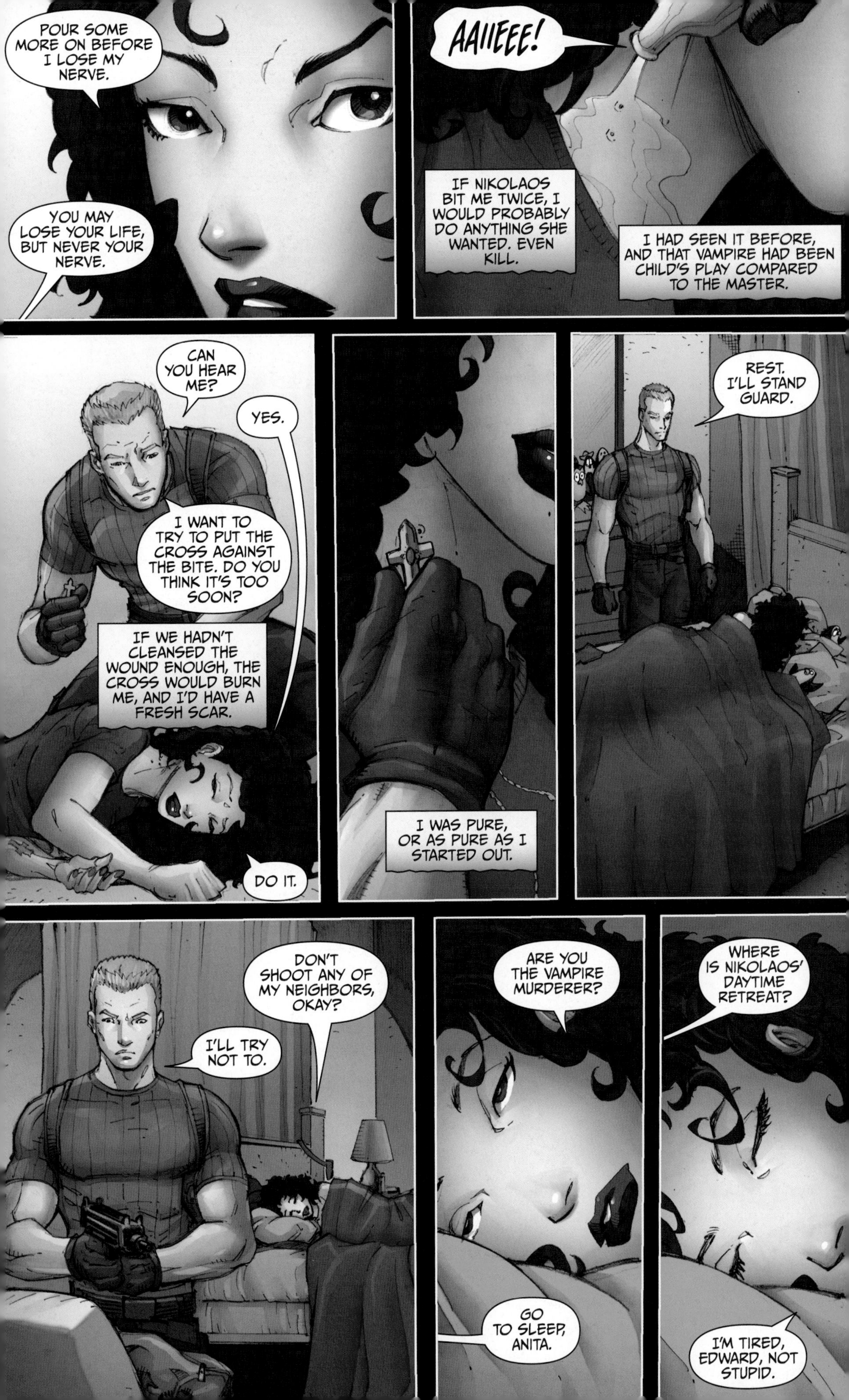
POUR SOME MORE ON BEFORE I LOSE MY NERVE.
YOU MAY LOSE YOUR LIFE, BUT NEVER YOUR NERVE.
AAIIEEE!
IF NIKOLAOS BIT ME TWICE, I WOULD PROBABLY DO ANYTHING SHE WANTED. EVEN KILL.
I HAD SEEN IT BEFORE, AND THAT VAMPIRE HAD BEEN CHILD'S PLAY COMPARED TO THE MASTER.
CAN YOU HEAR ME?
YES.
I WANT TO TRY TO PUT THE CROSS AGAINST THE BITE. DO YOU THINK IT'S TOO SOON?
IF WE HADN'T CLEANSED THE WOUND ENOUGH, THE CROSS WOULD BURN ME, AND I'D HAVE A FRESH SCAR.
DO IT.
I WAS PURE, OR AS PURE AS I STARTED OUT.
REST. I'LL STAND GUARD.
DON'T SHOOT ANY OF MY NEIGHBORS, OKAY?
I'LL TRY NOT TO.
ARE YOU THE VAMPIRE MURDERER?
GO TO SLEEP, ANITA.
WHERE IS NIKOLAOS' DAYTIME RETREAT?
I'M TIRED, EDWARD, NOT STUPID.

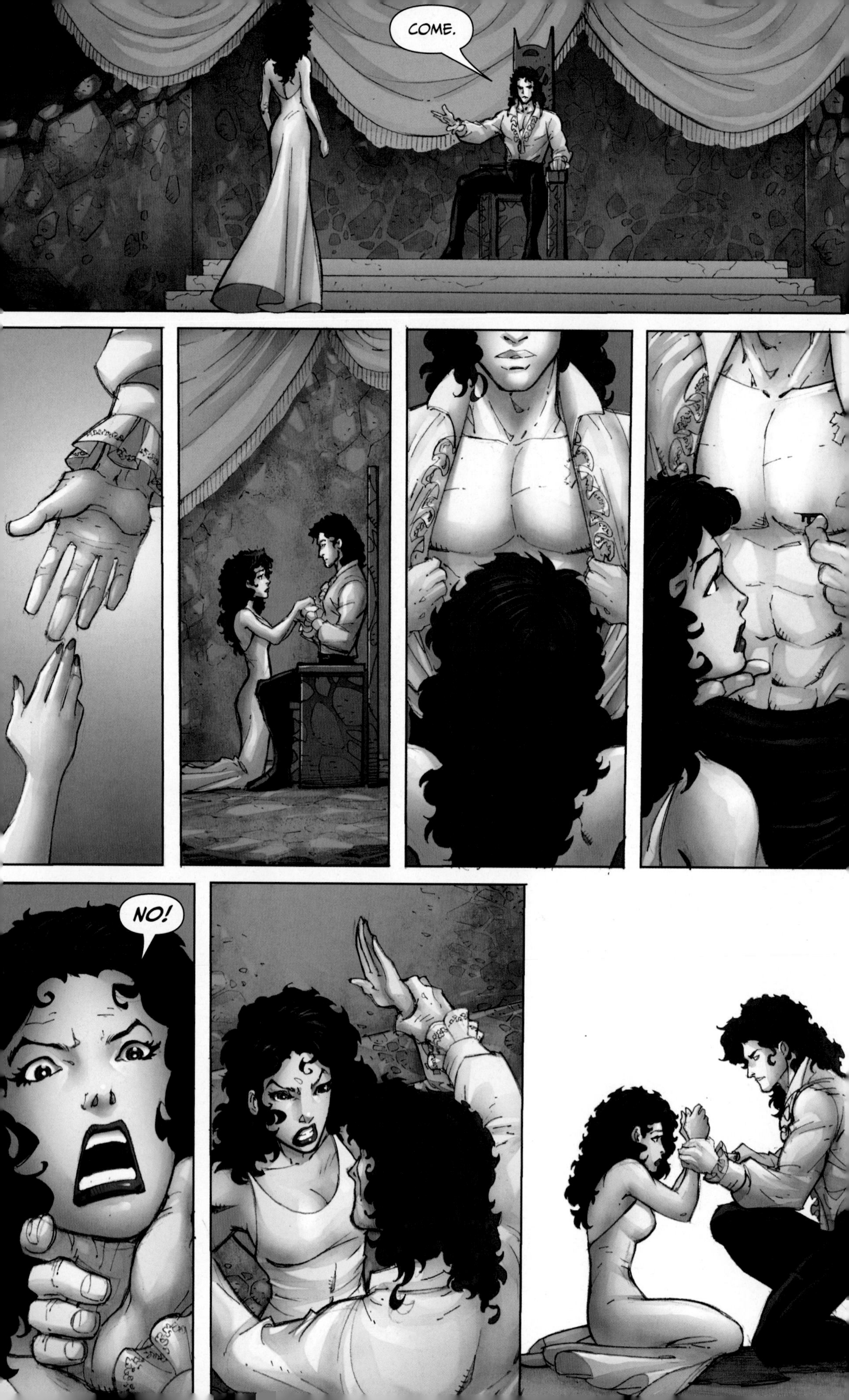
COME.
NO!

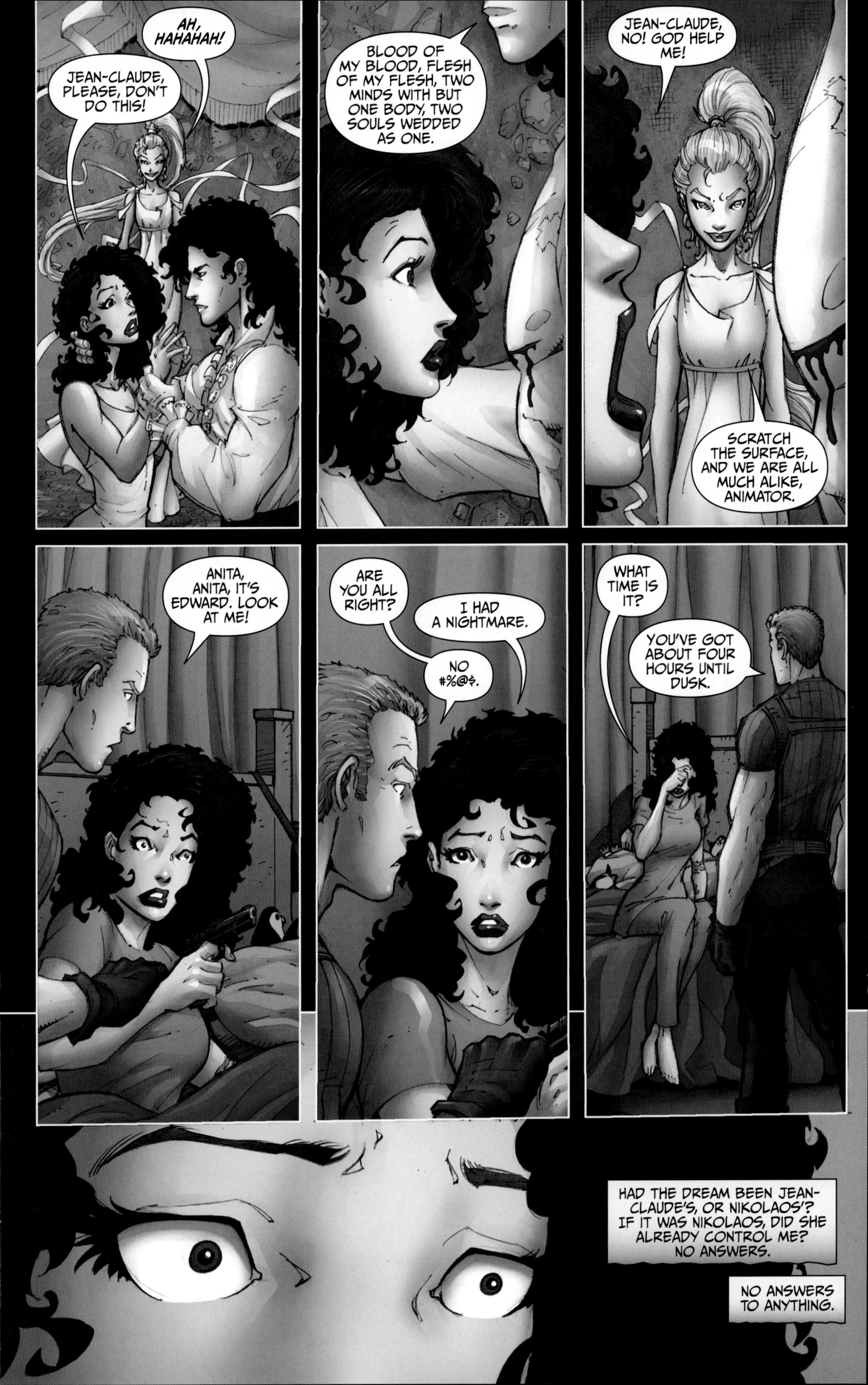
JEAN-CLAUDE, PLEASE, DON'T DO THIS!
AH, HAHAHAH!
BLOOD OF MY BLOOD, FLESH OF MY FLESH, TWO MINDS WITH BUT ONE BODY, TWO SOULS WEDDED AS ONE.
JEAN-CLAUDE, NO! GOD HELP ME!
SCRATCH THE SURFACE, AND WE ARE ALL MUCH ALIKE, ANIMATOR.
ANITA, ANITA, IT'S EDWARD. LOOK AT ME!
ARE YOU ALL RIGHT?
I HAD A NIGHTMARE.
NO #%@$.
WHAT TIME IS IT?
YOU'VE GOT ABOUT FOUR HOURS UNTIL DUSK.
HAD THE DREAM BEEN JEAN-CLAUDE'S, OR NIKOLAOS'? IF IT WAS NIKOLAOS, DID SHE ALREADY CONTROL ME? NO ANSWERS.
NO ANSWERS TO ANYTHING.

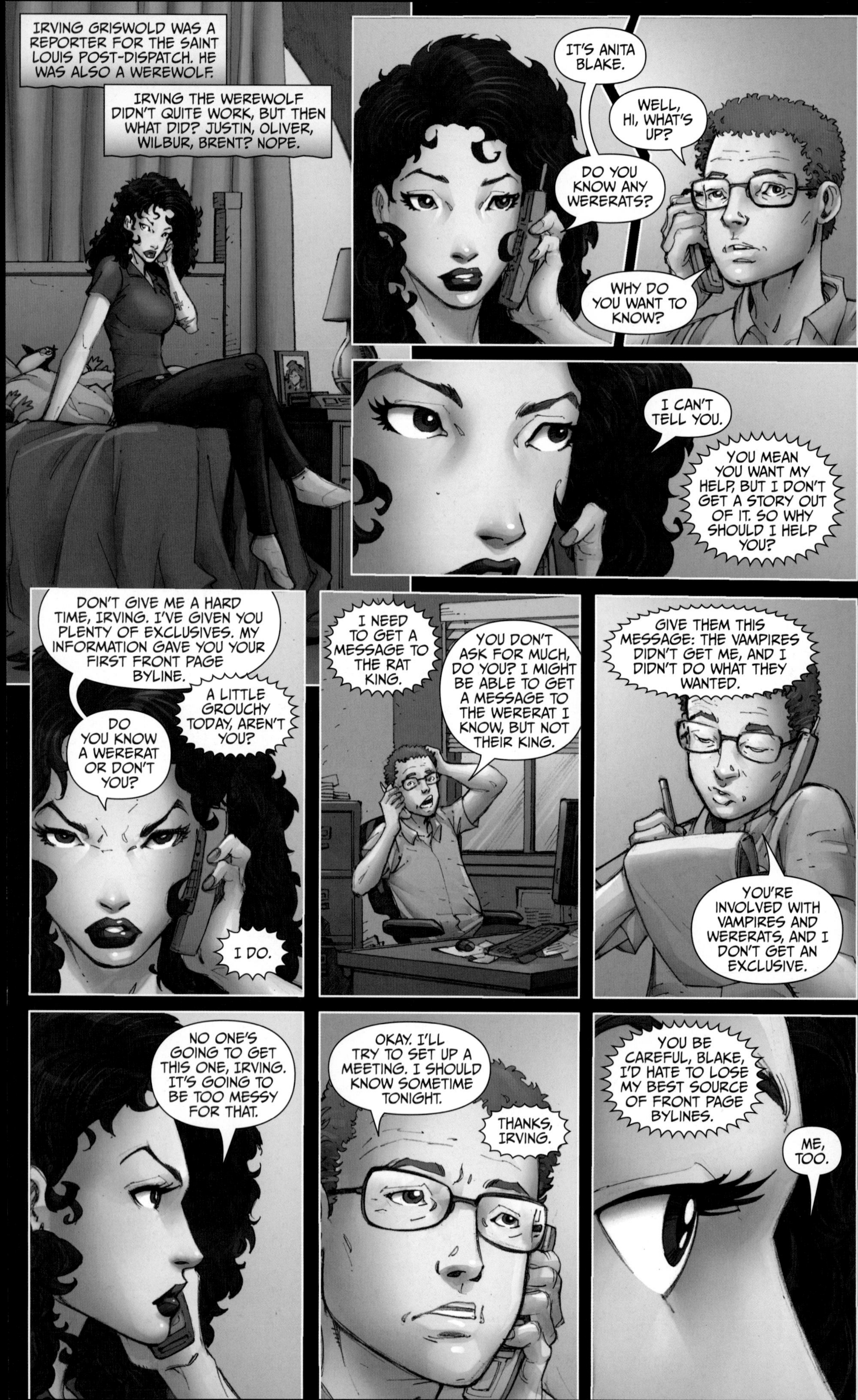
IRVING GRISWOLD WAS A REPORTER FOR THE SAINT LOUIS POST-DISPATCH. HE WAS ALSO A WEREWOLF.
IRVING THE WEREWOLF DIDN'T QUITE WORK, BUT THEN WHAT DID? JUSTIN, OLIVER, WILBUR, BRENT? NOPE.
IT'S ANITA BLAKE.
WELL, HI, WHAT'S UP?
DO YOU KNOW ANY WERERATS?
WHY DO YOU WANT TO KNOW?
I CAN'T TELL YOU.
YOU MEAN YOU WANT MY HELP, BUT I DON'T GET A STORY OUT OF IT. SO WHY SHOULD I HELP YOU?
DON'T GIVE ME A HARD TIME, IRVING. I'VE GIVEN YOU PLENTY OF EXCLUSIVES. MY INFORMATION GAVE YOU YOUR FIRST FRONT PAGE BYLINE.
A LITTLE GROUCHY TODAY, AREN'T YOU?
DO YOU KNOW A WERERAT OR DON'T YOU?
I DO.
I NEED TO GET A MESSAGE TO THE RAT KING.
YOU DON'T ASK FOR MUCH, DO YOU? I MIGHT BE ABLE TO GET A MESSAGE TO THE WERERAT I KNOW, BUT NOT THEIR KING.
GIVE THEM THIS MESSAGE: THE VAMPIRES DIDN'T GET ME, AND I DIDN'T DO WHAT THEY WANTED.
YOU'RE INVOLVED WITH VAMPIRES AND WERERATS, AND I DON'T GET AN EXCLUSIVE.
NO ONE'S GOING TO GET THIS ONE, IRVING. IT'S GOING TO BE TOO MESSY FOR THAT.
OKAY. I'LL TRY TO SET UP A MEETING. I SHOULD KNOW SOMETIME TONIGHT.
THANKS, IRVING.
YOU BE CAREFUL, BLAKE, I'D HATE TO LOSE MY BEST SOURCE OF FRONT PAGE BYLINES.
ME, TOO.

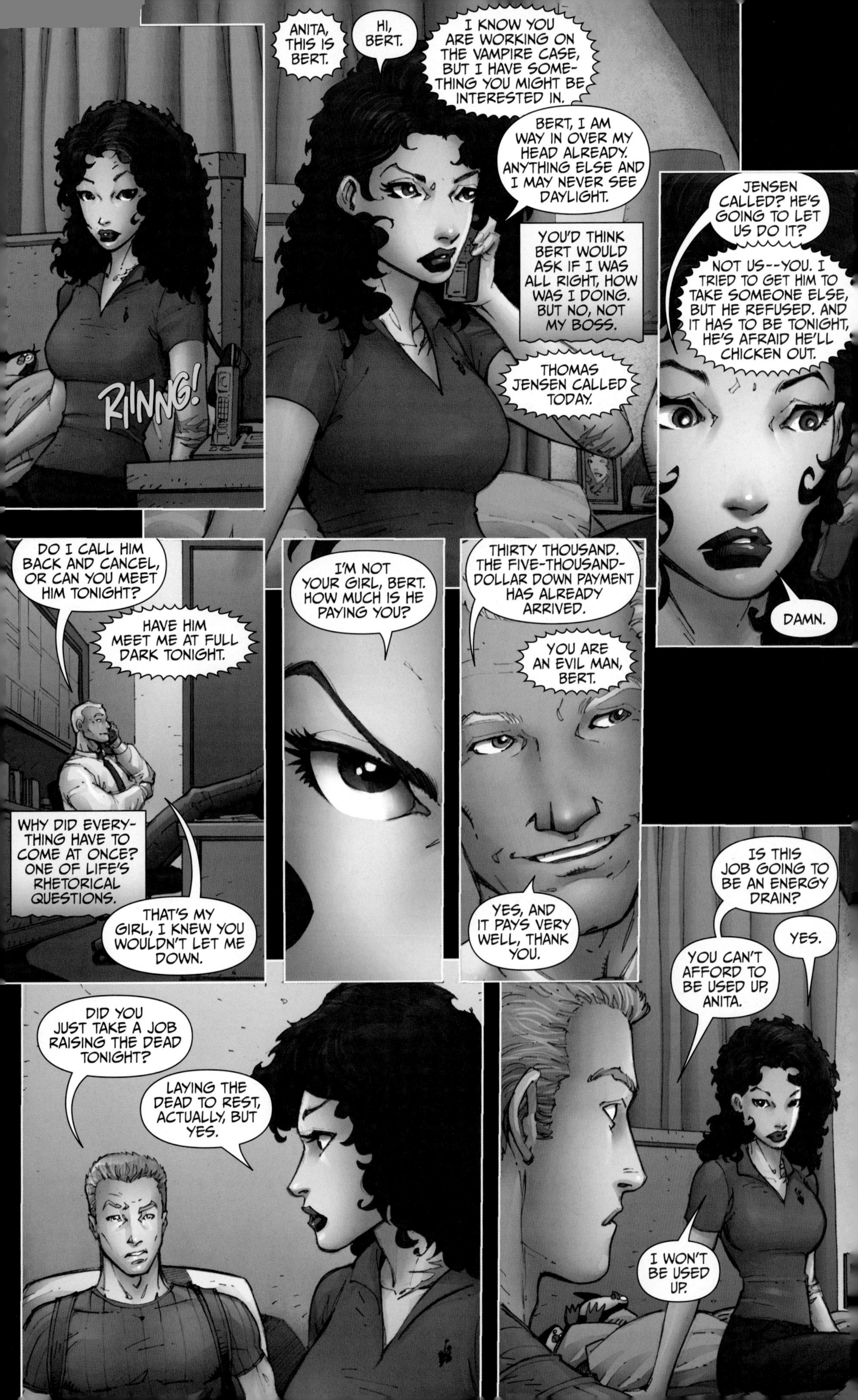

RIINNG!
ANITA, THIS IS BERT.
HI, BERT.
I KNOW YOU ARE WORKING ON THE VAMPIRE CASE, BUT I HAVE SOMETHING YOU MIGHT BE INTERESTED IN.
BERT, I AM WAY IN OVER MY HEAD ALREADY. ANYTHING ELSE AND I MAY NEVER SEE DAYLIGHT.
YOU'D THINK BERT WOULD ASK IF I WAS ALL RIGHT, HOW WAS I DOING. BUT NO, NOT MY BOSS.
THOMAS JENSEN CALLED TODAY.
JENSEN CALLED? HE'S GOING TO LET US DO IT?
NOT US--YOU. I TRIED TO GET HIM TO TAKE SOMEONE ELSE, BUT HE REFUSED. AND IT HAS TO BE TONIGHT, HE'S AFRAID HE'LL CHICKEN OUT.
DAMN.
DO I CALL HIM BACK AND CANCEL, OR CAN YOU MEET HIM TONIGHT?
HAVE HIM MEET ME AT FULL DARK TONIGHT.
WHY DID EVERYTHING HAVE TO COME AT ONCE? ONE OF LIFE'S RHETORICAL QUESTIONS.
THAT'S MY GIRL, I KNEW YOU WOULDN'T LET ME DOWN.
I'M NOT YOUR GIRL, BERT. HOW MUCH IS HE PAYING YOU?
THIRTY THOUSAND. THE FIVE-THOUSAND-DOLLAR DOWN PAYMENT HAS ALREADY ARRIVED.
YOU ARE AN EVIL MAN, BERT.
YES, AND IT PAYS VERY WELL, THANK YOU.
DID YOU JUST TAKE A JOB RAISING THE DEAD TONIGHT?
LAYING THE DEAD TO REST, ACTUALLY, BUT YES.
IS THIS JOB GOING TO BE AN ENERGY DRAIN?
YES.
YOU CAN'T AFFORD TO BE USED UP, ANITA.
I WON'T BE USED UP.

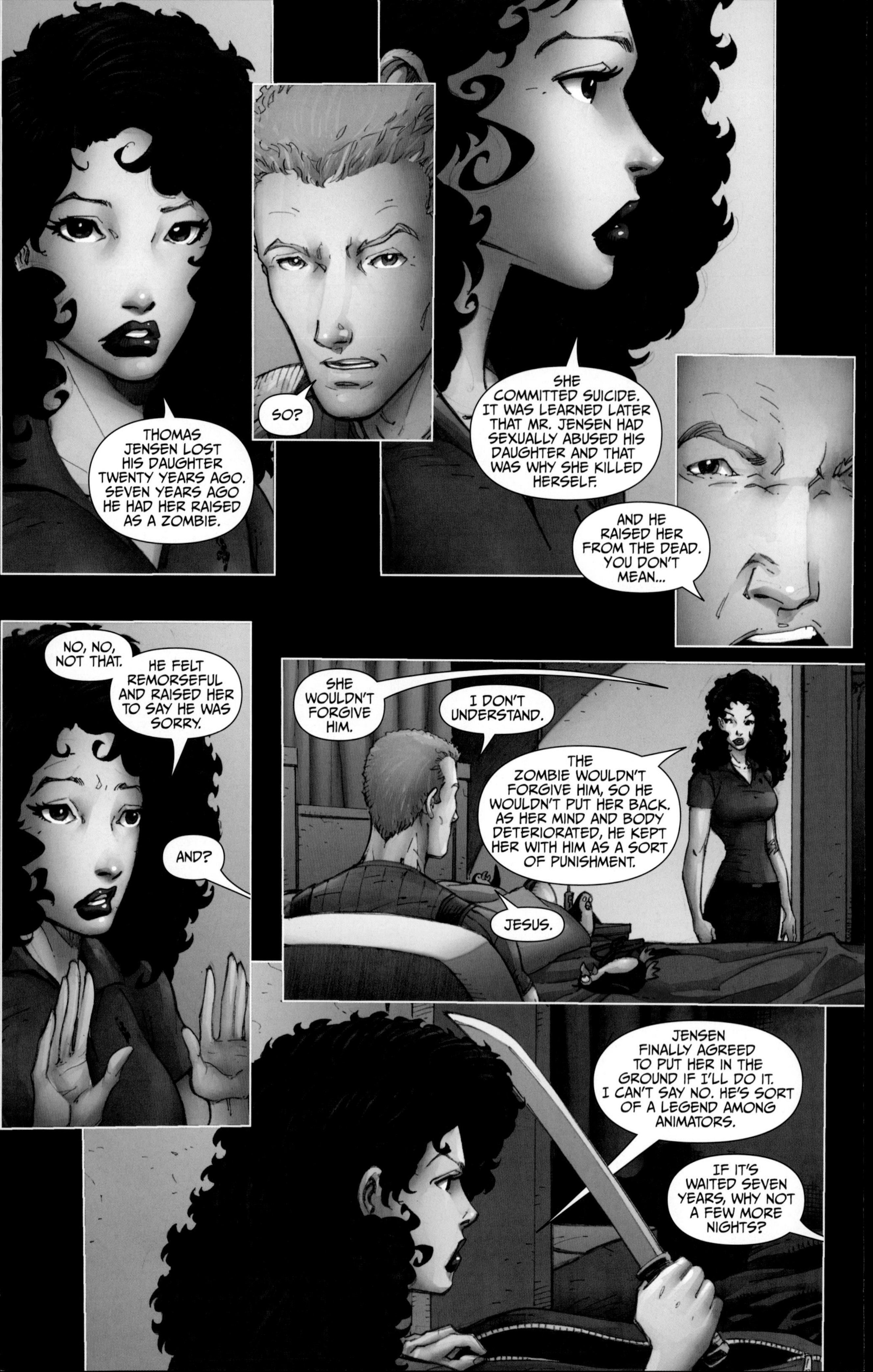
THOMAS JENSEN LOST HIS DAUGHTER TWENTY YEARS AGO. SEVEN YEARS AGO HE HAD HER RAISED AS A ZOMBIE.
SO?
SHE COMMITTED SUICIDE. IT WAS LEARNED LATER THAT MR. JENSEN HAD SEXUALLY ABUSED HIS DAUGHTER AND THAT WAS WHY SHE KILLED HERSELF.
AND HE RAISED HER FROM THE DEAD. YOU DON'T MEAN...
NO, NO, NOT THAT.
HE FELT REMORSEFUL AND RAISED HER TO SAY HE WAS SORRY.
AND?
SHE WOULDN'T FORGIVE HIM.
I DON'T UNDERSTAND.
THE ZOMBIE WOULDN'T FORGIVE HIM, SO HE WOULDN'T PUT HER BACK. AS HER MIND AND BODY DETERIORATED, HE KEPT HER WITH HIM AS A SORT OF PUNISHMENT.
JESUS.
JENSEN FINALLY AGREED TO PUT HER IN THE GROUND IF I'LL DO IT. I CAN'T SAY NO. HE'S SORT OF A LEGEND AMONG ANIMATORS.
IF IT'S WAITED SEVEN YEARS, WHY NOT A FEW MORE NIGHTS?

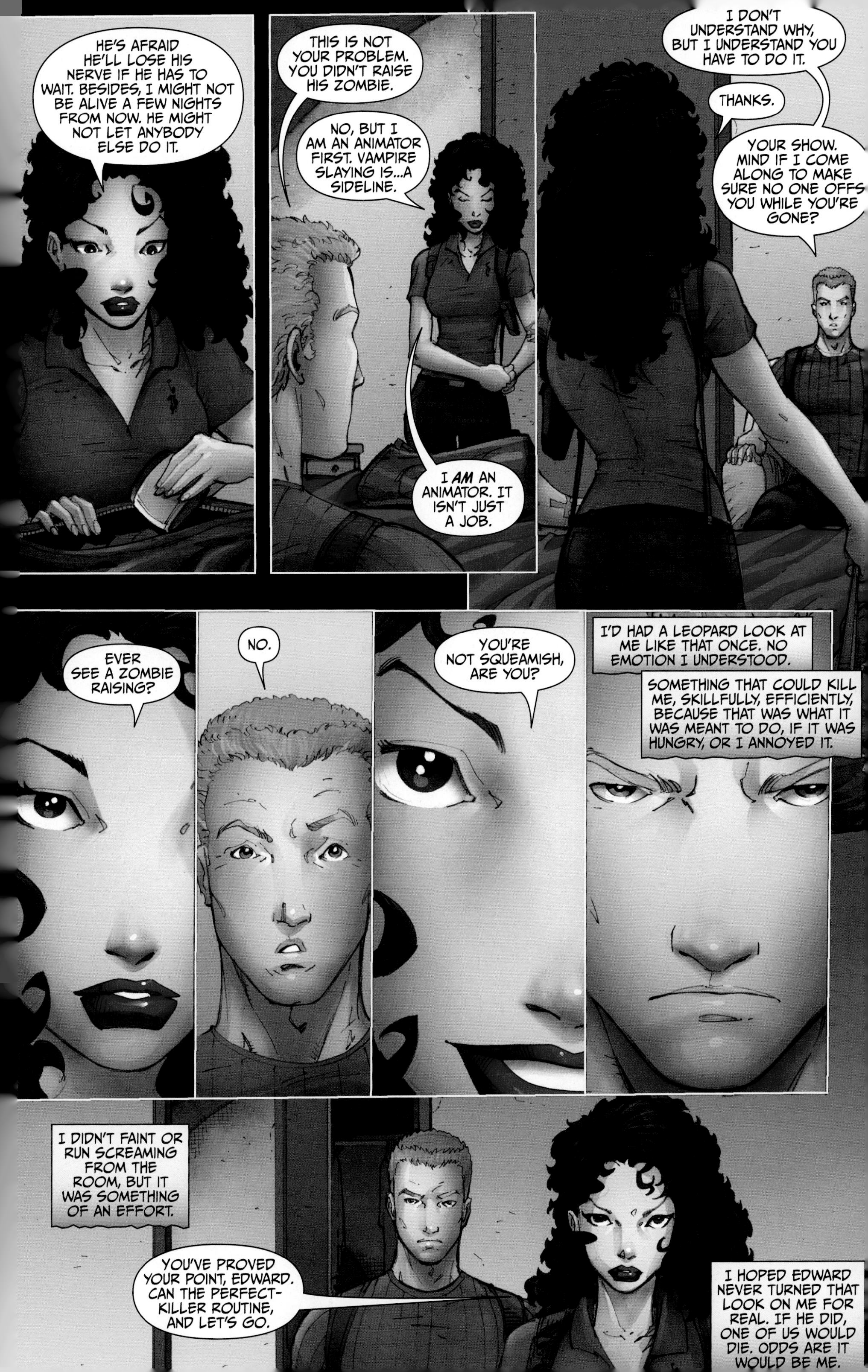
HE'S AFRAID HE'LL LOSE HIS NERVE IF HE HAS TO WAIT. BESIDES, I MIGHT NOT BE ALIVE A FEW NIGHTS FROM NOW. HE MIGHT NOT LET ANYBODY ELSE DO IT.
THIS IS NOT YOUR PROBLEM. YOU DIDN'T RAISE HIS ZOMBIE.
NO, BUT I AM AN ANIMATOR FIRST. VAMPIRE SLAYING IS...A SIDELINE.
I *AM* AN ANIMATOR. IT ISN'T JUST A JOB.
I DON'T UNDERSTAND WHY, BUT I UNDERSTAND YOU HAVE TO DO IT.
THANKS.
YOUR SHOW. MIND IF I COME ALONG TO MAKE SURE NO ONE OFFS YOU WHILE YOU'RE GONE?
EVER SEE A ZOMBIE RAISING?
NO.
YOU'RE NOT SQUEAMISH, ARE YOU?
I'D HAD A LEOPARD LOOK AT ME LIKE THAT ONCE. NO EMOTION I UNDERSTOOD.
SOMETHING THAT COULD KILL ME, SKILLFULLY, EFFICIENTLY, BECAUSE THAT WAS WHAT IT WAS MEANT TO DO, IF IT WAS HUNGRY, OR I ANNOYED IT.
I DIDN'T FAINT OR RUN SCREAMING FROM THE ROOM, BUT IT WAS SOMETHING OF AN EFFORT.
YOU'VE PROVED YOUR POINT, EDWARD. CAN THE PERFECT-KILLER ROUTINE, AND LET'S GO.
I HOPED EDWARD NEVER TURNED THAT LOOK ON ME FOR REAL. IF HE DID, ONE OF US WOULD DIE. ODDS ARE IT WOULD BE ME.

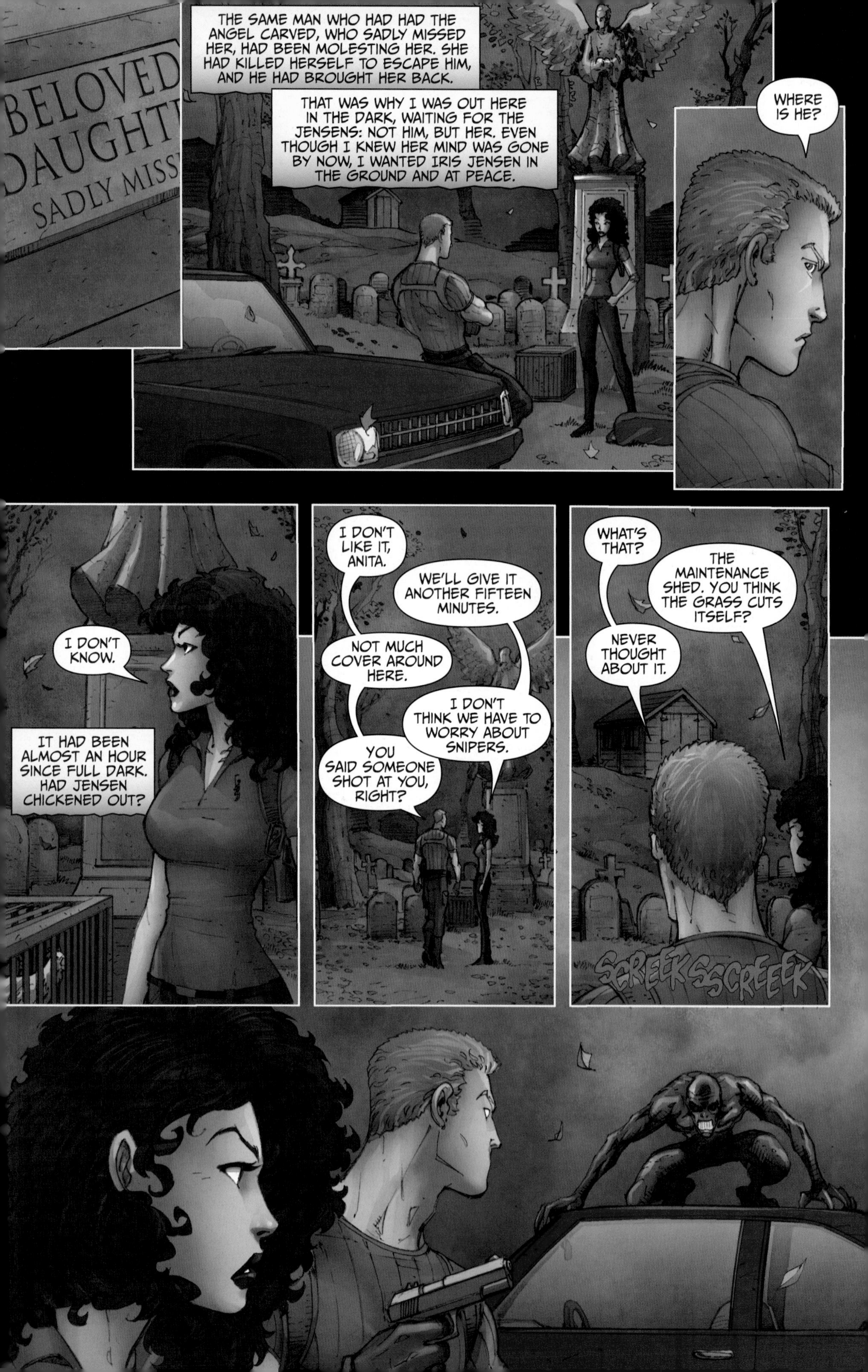
BELOVED DAUGHT
SADLY MISS
THE SAME MAN WHO HAD HAD THE ANGEL CARVED, WHO SADLY MISSED HER, HAD BEEN MOLESTING HER. SHE HAD KILLED HERSELF TO ESCAPE HIM, AND HE HAD BROUGHT HER BACK.
THAT WAS WHY I WAS OUT HERE IN THE DARK, WAITING FOR THE JENSENS: NOT HIM, BUT HER. EVEN THOUGH I KNEW HER MIND WAS GONE BY NOW, I WANTED IRIS JENSEN IN THE GROUND AND AT PEACE.
WHERE IS HE?
I DON'T KNOW.
IT HAD BEEN ALMOST AN HOUR SINCE FULL DARK. HAD JENSEN CHICKENED OUT?
I DON'T LIKE IT, ANITA.
WE'LL GIVE IT ANOTHER FIFTEEN MINUTES.
NOT MUCH COVER AROUND HERE.
I DON'T THINK WE HAVE TO WORRY ABOUT SNIPERS.
YOU SAID SOMEONE SHOT AT YOU, RIGHT?
WHAT'S THAT?
THE MAINTENANCE SHED. YOU THINK THE GRASS CUTS ITSELF?
NEVER THOUGHT ABOUT IT.
SCREEK SCREEEK

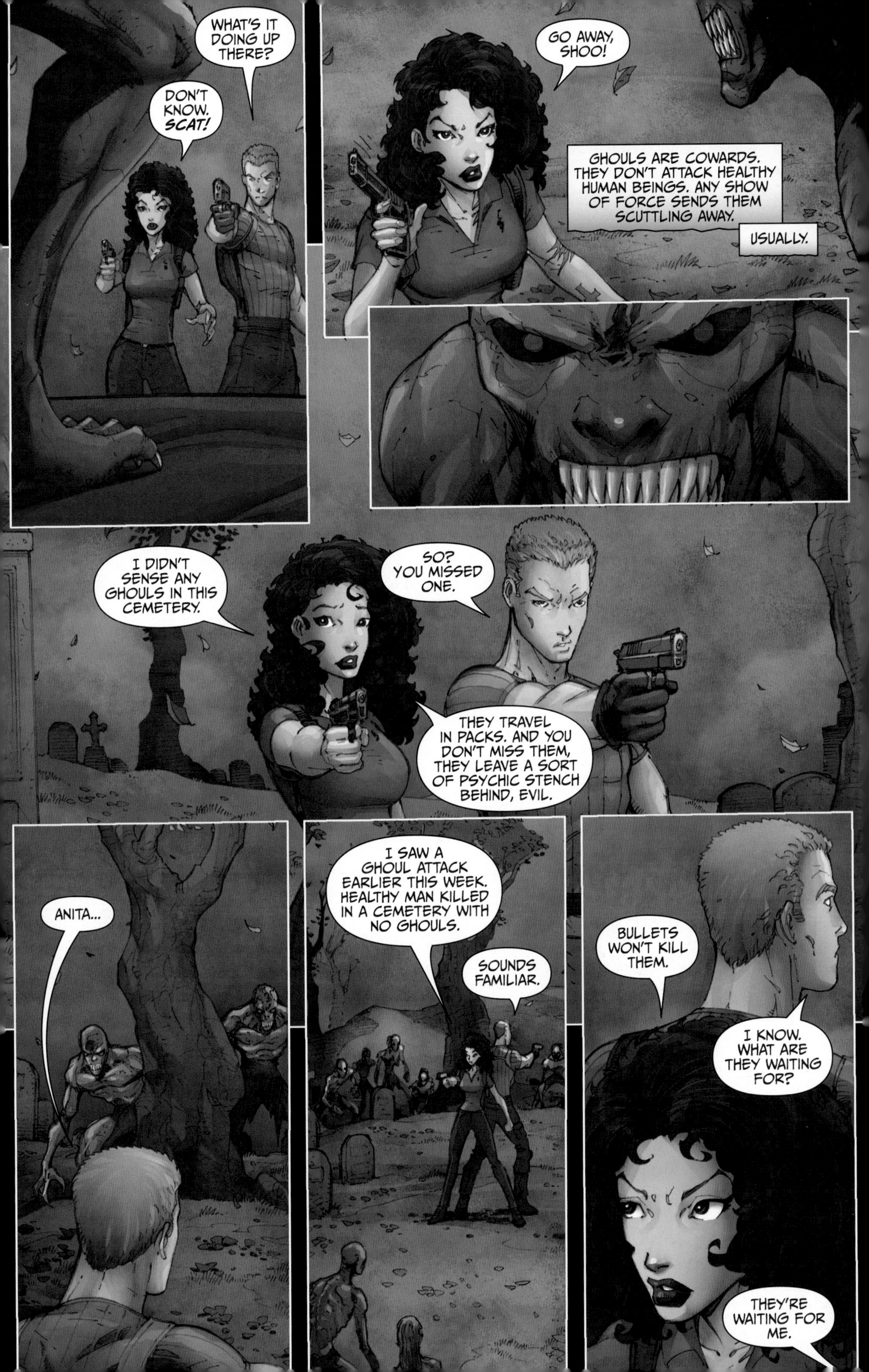
WHAT'S IT DOING UP THERE?
DON'T KNOW. SCAT!
GO AWAY, SHOO!
GHOULS ARE COWARDS. THEY DON'T ATTACK HEALTHY HUMAN BEINGS. ANY SHOW OF FORCE SENDS THEM SCUTTLING AWAY.
USUALLY.
I DIDN'T SENSE ANY GHOULS IN THIS CEMETERY.
SO? YOU MISSED ONE.
THEY TRAVEL IN PACKS. AND YOU DON'T MISS THEM, THEY LEAVE A SORT OF PSYCHIC STENCH BEHIND, EVIL.
ANITA...
I SAW A GHOUL ATTACK EARLIER THIS WEEK. HEALTHY MAN KILLED IN A CEMETERY WITH NO GHOULS.
SOUNDS FAMILIAR.
BULLETS WON'T KILL THEM.
I KNOW. WHAT ARE THEY WAITING FOR?
THEY'RE WAITING FOR ME.

WHO IS THIS?

THE VAMPIRE MURDERER, I PRESUME.

WHEN DID YOU GUESS?

JUST NOW. I'M A LITTLE SLOW THIS YEAR.

ZACHARY. HE WASN'T KILLING HUMANS TO FEED HIS GRIS-GRIS, THE MAGIC THAT KEPT HIM UNDEAD INSTEAD OF JUST PLAIN DEAD.

HE WAS KILLING VAMPIRES.

I THOUGHT YOU'D FIGURE IT OUT EVENTUALLY.

THAT'S WHY YOU DESTROYED THE ZOMBIE WITNESS'S MIND. HOW DID YOU GET THE TWO-BITER TO SHOOT ME AT THE CHURCH?

I TOLD HIM THE ORDERS CAME FROM NIKOLAOS.

HOW ARE YOU GETTING THE GHOULS OUT OF THEIR CEMETERY? HOW COME THEY OBEY YOUR ORDERS?

YOU KNOW THE THEORY THAT IF YOU BURY AN ANIMATOR IN A CEMETERY, YOU GET GHOULS?

WHEN I CAME OUT OF THE GRAVE, THEY CAME WITH ME, AND THEY WERE MINE. *MINE.*

THERE AREN'T ENOUGH ANIMATORS IN THE WORLD TO ACCOUNT FOR ALL THE GHOULS.

I'VE BEEN THINKING ABOUT THAT. I THINK THAT THE MORE ZOMBIES YOU RAISE IN A CEMETERY...

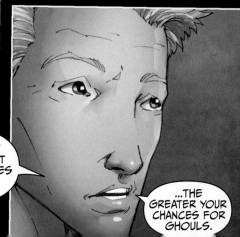

...THE GREATER YOUR CHANCES FOR GHOULS.

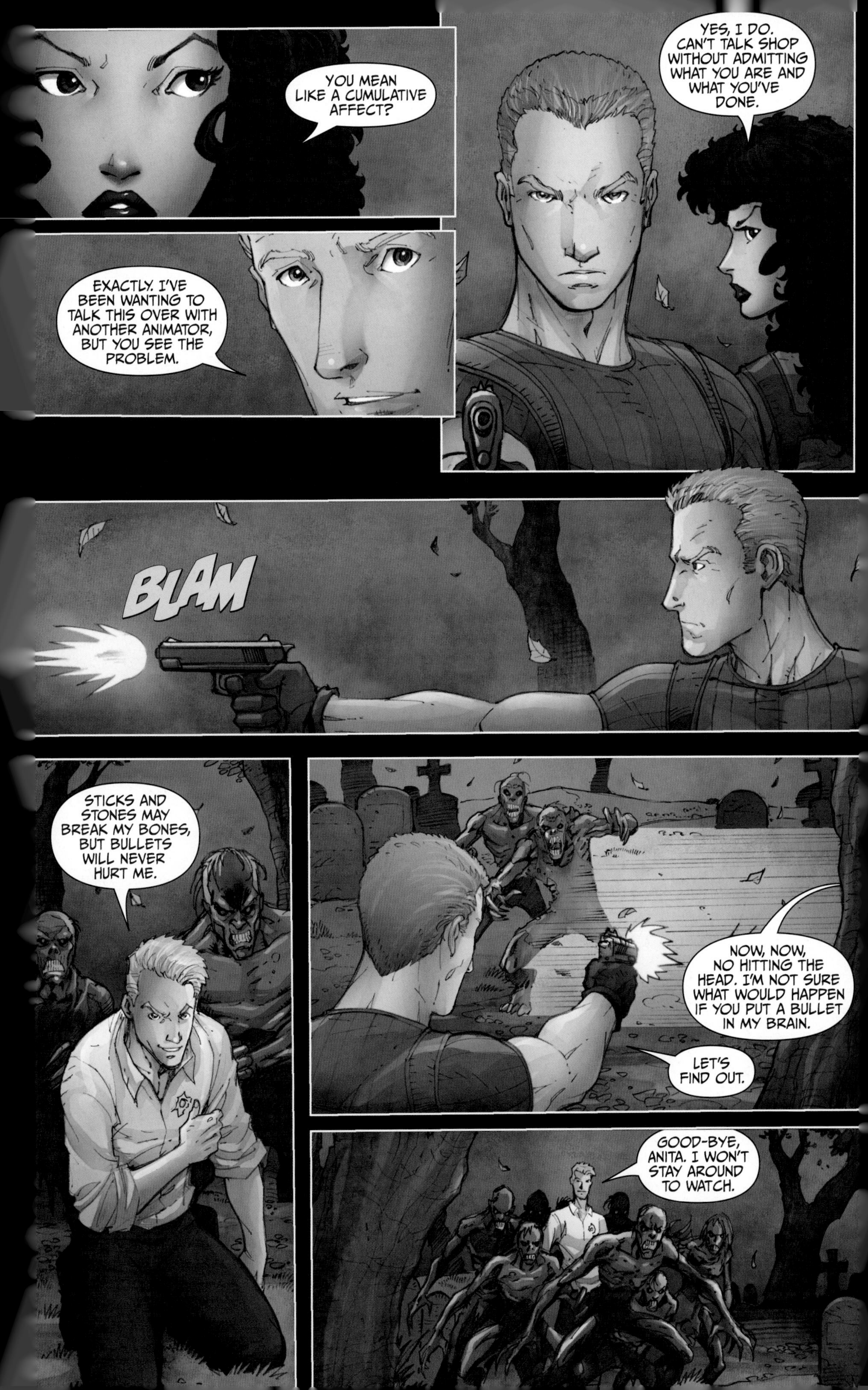
YOU MEAN LIKE A CUMULATIVE AFFECT?
YES, I DO. CAN'T TALK SHOP WITHOUT ADMITTING WHAT YOU ARE AND WHAT YOU'VE DONE.
EXACTLY. I'VE BEEN WANTING TO TALK THIS OVER WITH ANOTHER ANIMATOR, BUT YOU SEE THE PROBLEM.
BLAM
STICKS AND STONES MAY BREAK MY BONES, BUT BULLETS WILL NEVER HURT ME.
NOW, NOW, NO HITTING THE HEAD. I'M NOT SURE WHAT WOULD HAPPEN IF YOU PUT A BULLET IN MY BRAIN.
LET'S FIND OUT.
GOOD-BYE, ANITA. I WON'T STAY AROUND TO WATCH.

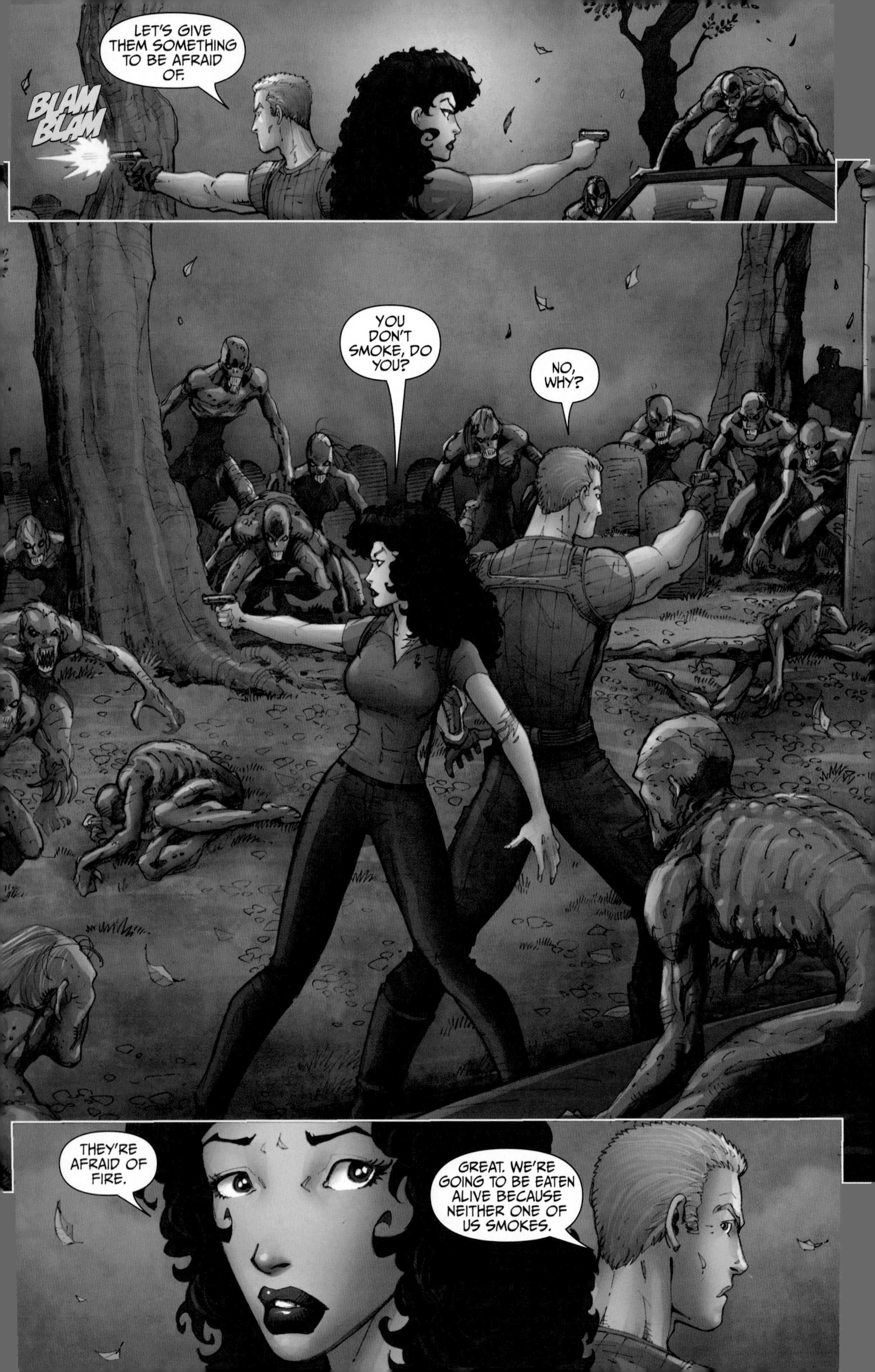
LET'S GIVE THEM SOMETHING TO BE AFRAID OF.
BLAM BLAM
YOU DON'T SMOKE, DO YOU?
NO, WHY?
THEY'RE AFRAID OF FIRE.
GREAT. WE'RE GOING TO BE EATEN ALIVE BECAUSE NEITHER ONE OF US SMOKES.

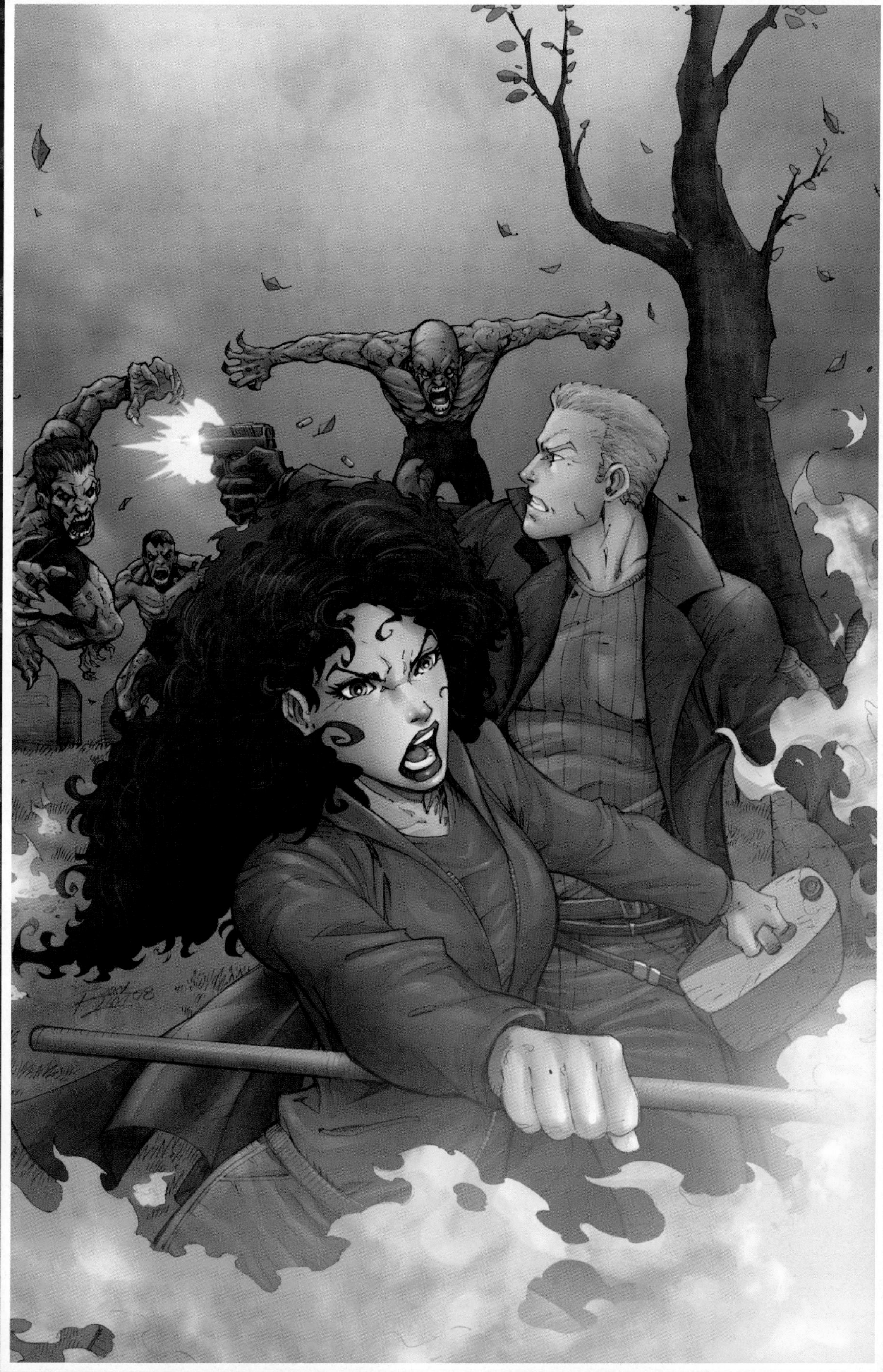

ELEVEN

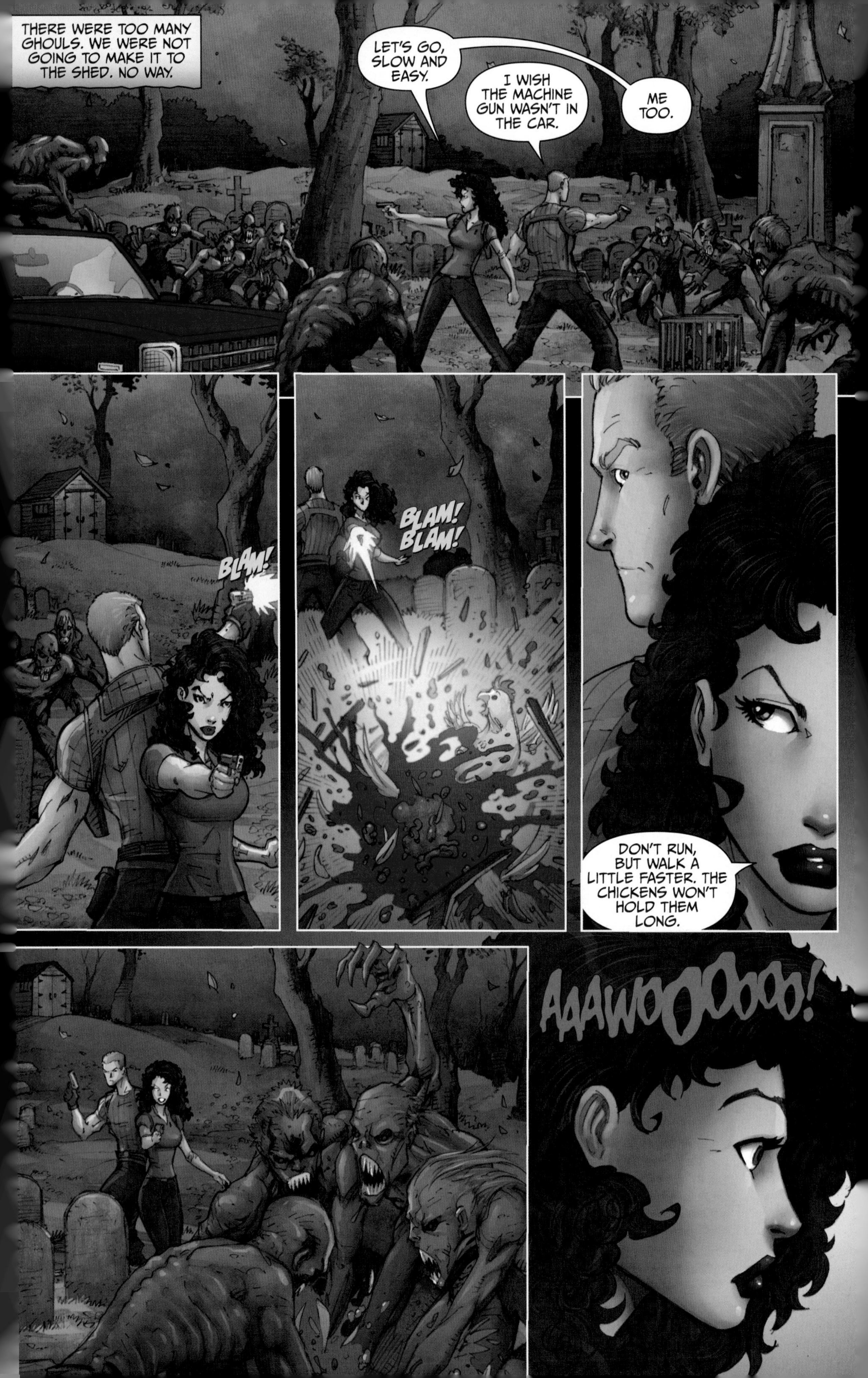
THERE WERE TOO MANY GHOULS. WE WERE NOT GOING TO MAKE IT TO THE SHED. NO WAY.
LET'S GO, SLOW AND EASY.
I WISH THE MACHINE GUN WASN'T IN THE CAR.
ME TOO.
BLAM!
BLAM! BLAM!
DON'T RUN, BUT WALK A LITTLE FASTER. THE CHICKENS WON'T HOLD THEM LONG.
AAAWOOOOOO!

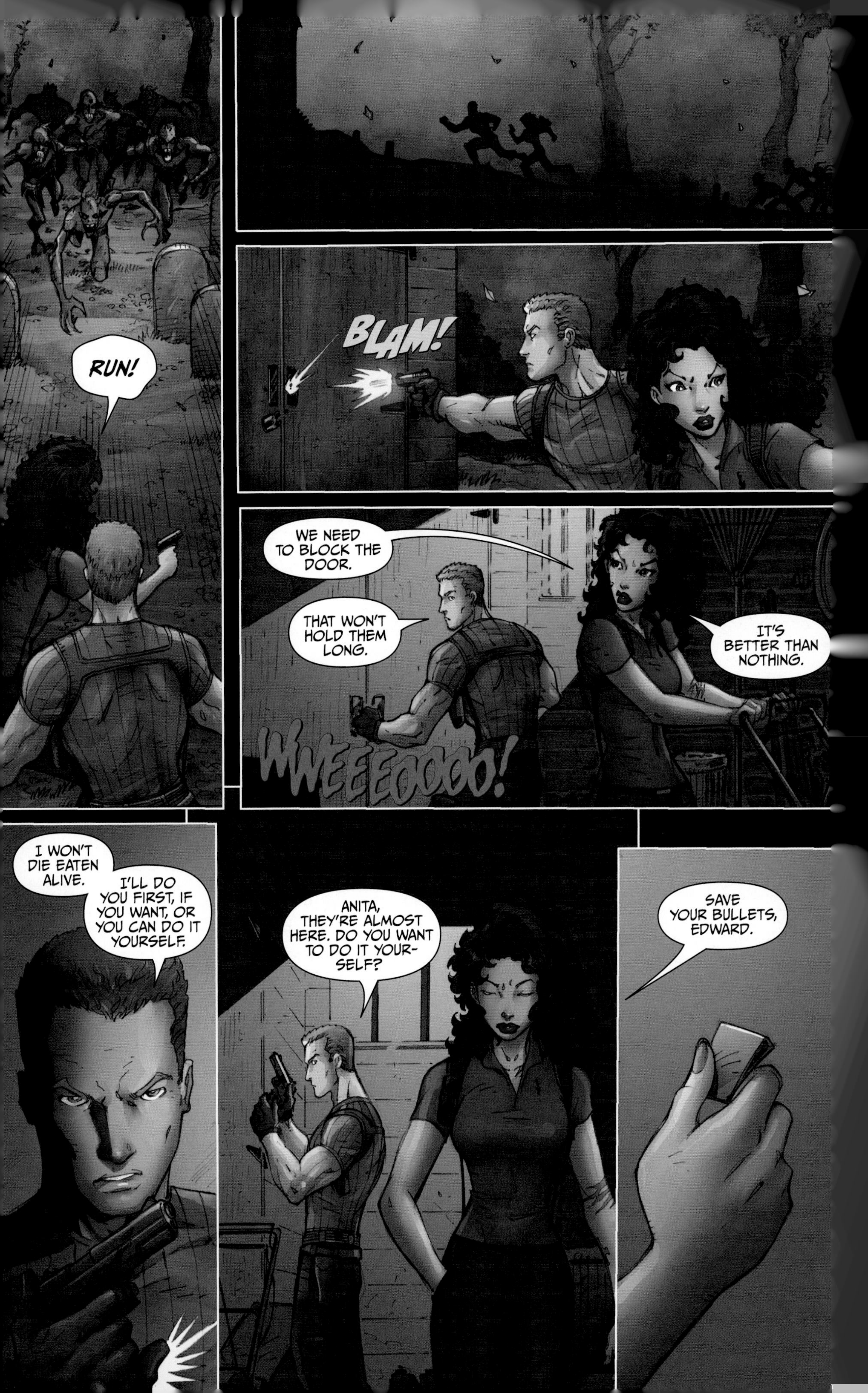
RUN!
BLAM!
WE NEED TO BLOCK THE DOOR.
THAT WON'T HOLD THEM LONG.
IT'S BETTER THAN NOTHING.
WWEEEOOOO!
I WON'T DIE EATEN ALIVE.
I'LL DO YOU FIRST, IF YOU WANT, OR YOU CAN DO IT YOURSELF.
ANITA, THEY'RE ALMOST HERE. DO YOU WANT TO DO IT YOUR-SELF?
SAVE YOUR BULLETS, EDWARD.

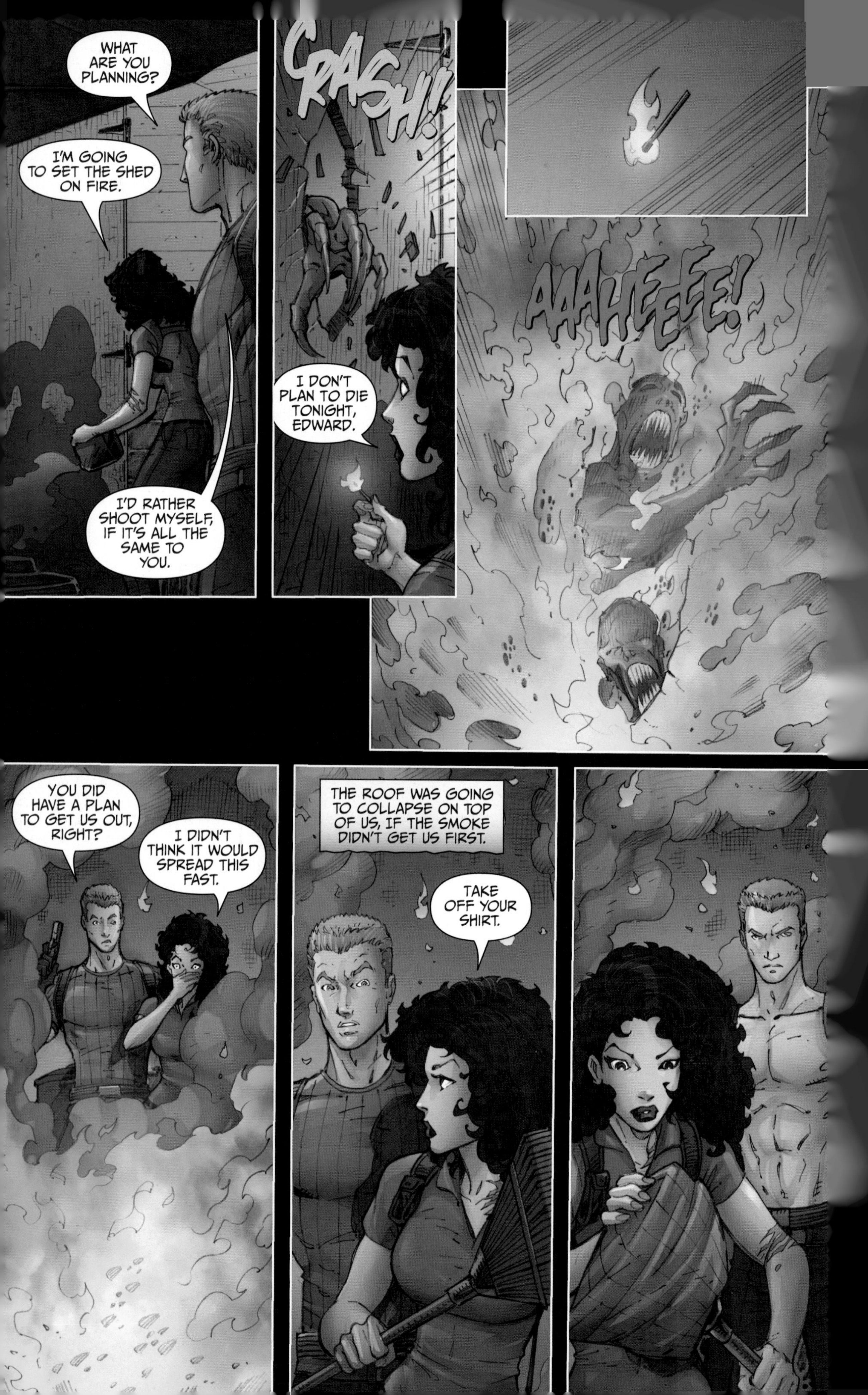
WHAT ARE YOU PLANNING?
I'M GOING TO SET THE SHED ON FIRE.
I'D RATHER SHOOT MYSELF, IF IT'S ALL THE SAME TO YOU.
CRASH!!
I DON'T PLAN TO DIE TONIGHT, EDWARD.
AAAHEEEE!
YOU DID HAVE A PLAN TO GET US OUT, RIGHT?
I DIDN'T THINK IT WOULD SPREAD THIS FAST.
THE ROOF WAS GOING TO COLLAPSE ON TOP OF US, IF THE SMOKE DIDN'T GET US FIRST.
TAKE OFF YOUR SHIRT.

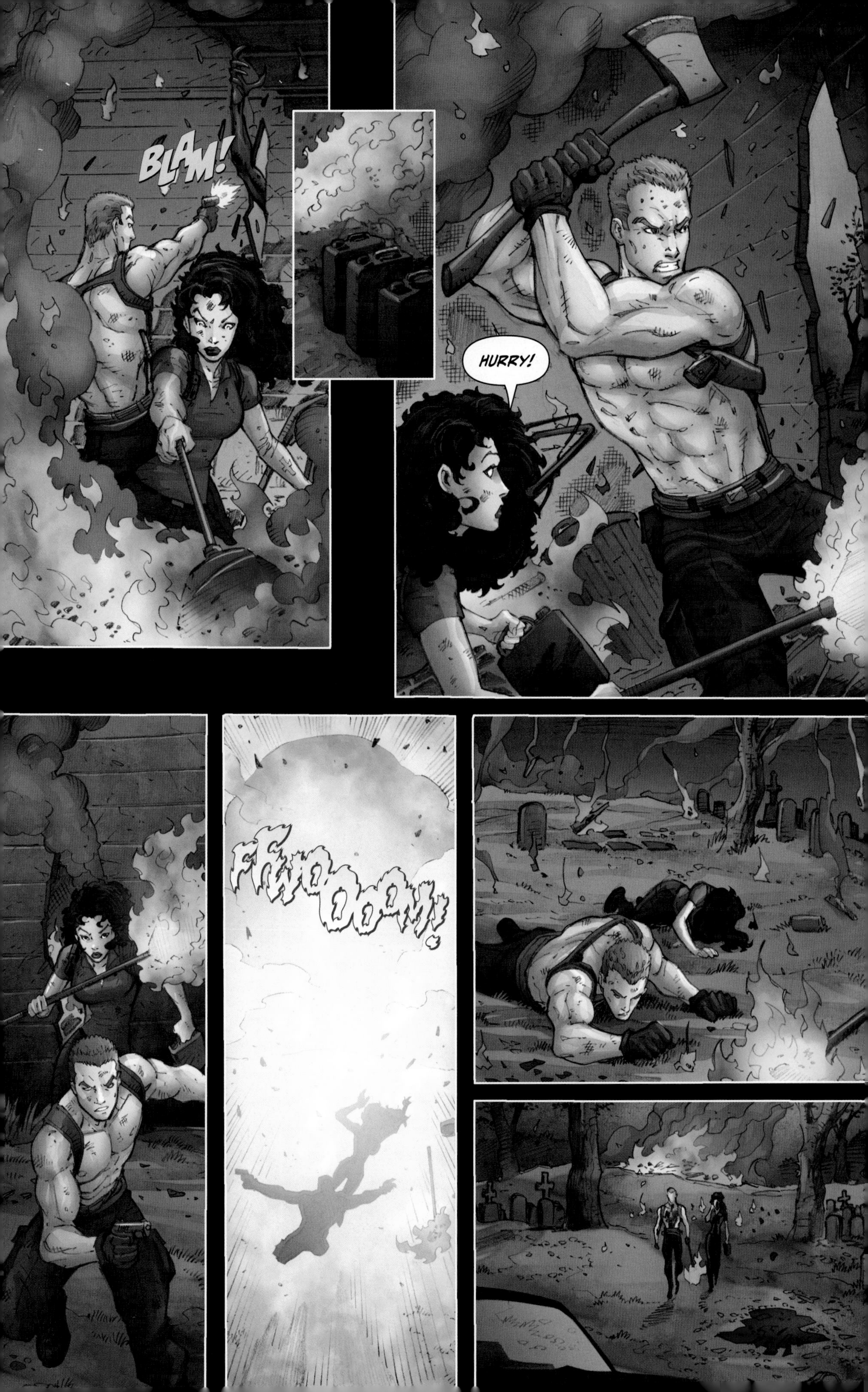
BLAM!
HURRY!
FWOOOM!

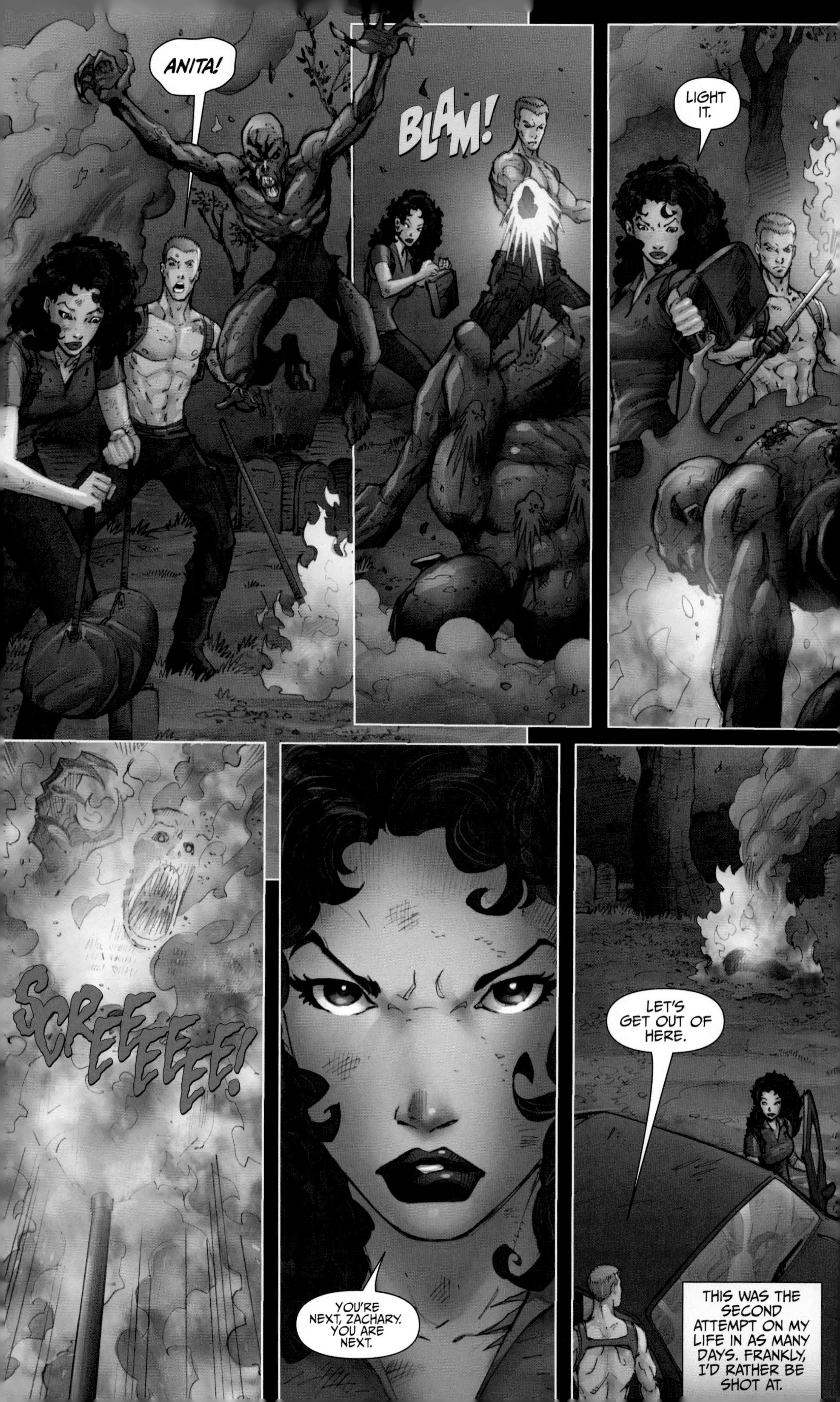
ANITA!
BLAM!
LIGHT IT.
SCREEEEEEE!
YOU'RE NEXT, ZACHARY. YOU ARE NEXT.
LET'S GET OUT OF HERE.
THIS WAS THE SECOND ATTEMPT ON MY LIFE IN AS MANY DAYS. FRANKLY, I'D RATHER BE SHOT AT.

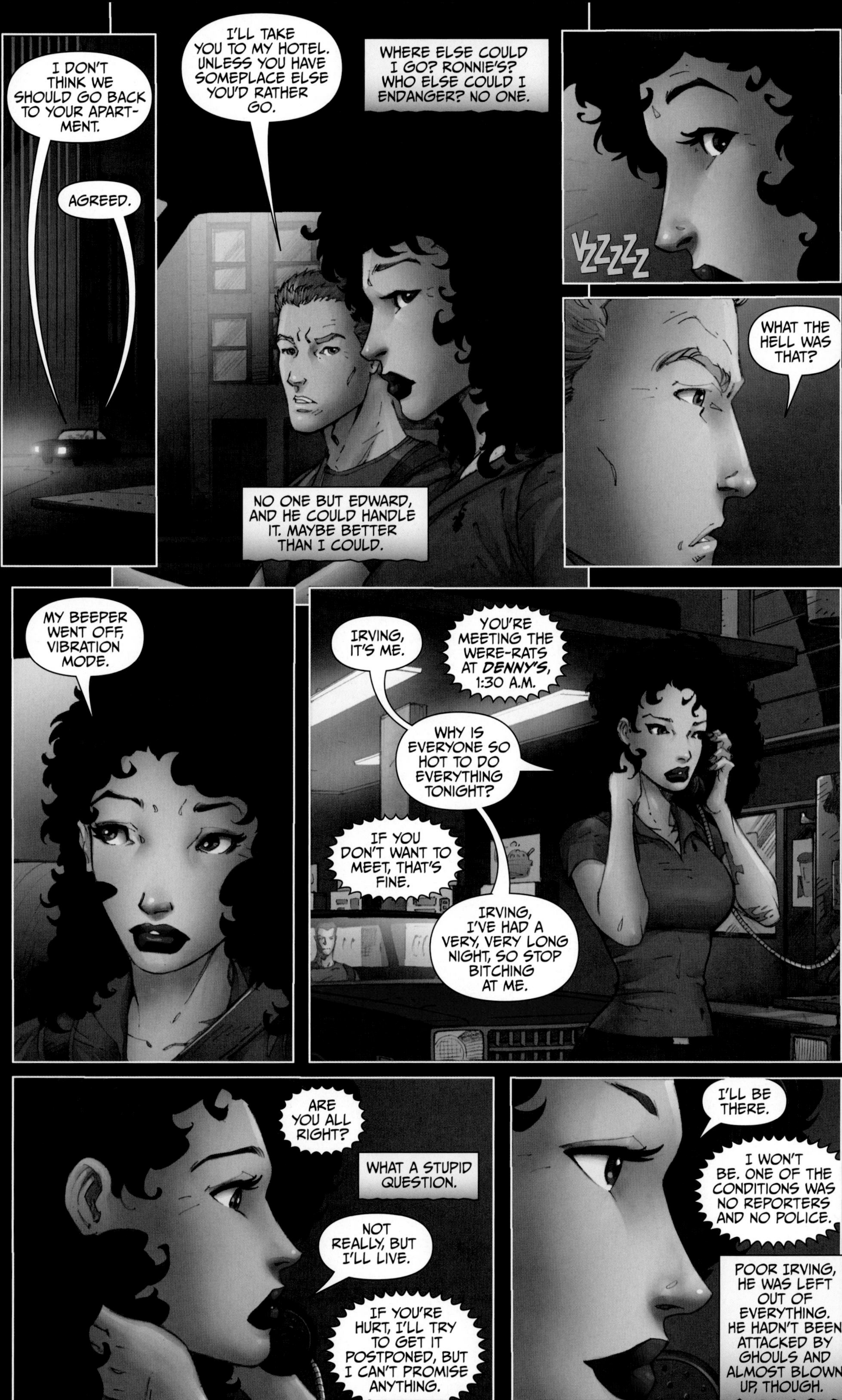
I DON'T THINK WE SHOULD GO BACK TO YOUR APARTMENT.
AGREED.
I'LL TAKE YOU TO MY HOTEL. UNLESS YOU HAVE SOMEPLACE ELSE YOU'D RATHER GO.
WHERE ELSE COULD I GO? RONNIE'S? WHO ELSE COULD I ENDANGER? NO ONE.
NO ONE BUT EDWARD, AND HE COULD HANDLE IT. MAYBE BETTER THAN I COULD.
VZZZZZ
WHAT THE HELL WAS THAT?
MY BEEPER WENT OFF, VIBRATION MODE.
IRVING, IT'S ME.
YOU'RE MEETING THE WERE-RATS AT DENNY'S, 1:30 A.M.
WHY IS EVERYONE SO HOT TO DO EVERYTHING TONIGHT?
IF YOU DON'T WANT TO MEET, THAT'S FINE.
IRVING, I'VE HAD A VERY, VERY LONG NIGHT, SO STOP BITCHING AT ME.
ARE YOU ALL RIGHT?
WHAT A STUPID QUESTION.
NOT REALLY, BUT I'LL LIVE.
IF YOU'RE HURT, I'LL TRY TO GET IT POSTPONED, BUT I CAN'T PROMISE ANYTHING.
I'LL BE THERE.
I WON'T BE. ONE OF THE CONDITIONS WAS NO REPORTERS AND NO POLICE.
POOR IRVING, HE WAS LEFT OUT OF EVERYTHING. HE HADN'T BEEN ATTACKED BY GHOULS AND ALMOST BLOWN UP, THOUGH.

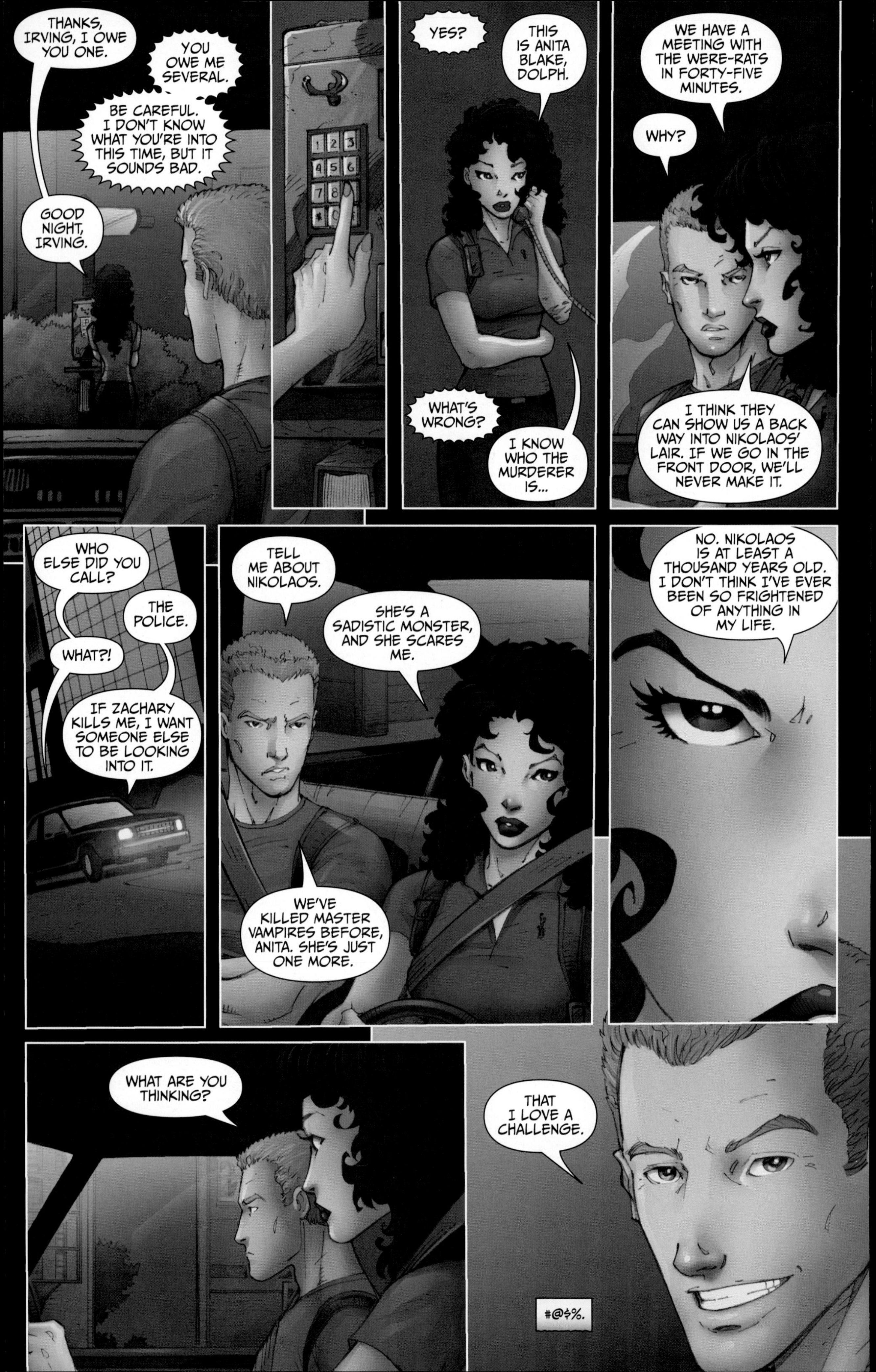
THANKS, IRVING, I OWE YOU ONE.
YOU OWE ME SEVERAL.
BE CAREFUL. I DON'T KNOW WHAT YOU'RE INTO THIS TIME, BUT IT SOUNDS BAD.
GOOD NIGHT, IRVING.
YES?
THIS IS ANITA BLAKE, DOLPH.
WHAT'S WRONG?
I KNOW WHO THE MURDERER IS...
WE HAVE A MEETING WITH THE WERE-RATS IN FORTY-FIVE MINUTES.
WHY?
I THINK THEY CAN SHOW US A BACK WAY INTO NIKOLAOS' LAIR. IF WE GO IN THE FRONT DOOR, WE'LL NEVER MAKE IT.
WHO ELSE DID YOU CALL?
THE POLICE.
WHAT?!
IF ZACHARY KILLS ME, I WANT SOMEONE ELSE TO BE LOOKING INTO IT.
TELL ME ABOUT NIKOLAOS.
SHE'S A SADISTIC MONSTER, AND SHE SCARES ME.
WE'VE KILLED MASTER VAMPIRES BEFORE, ANITA. SHE'S JUST ONE MORE.
NO. NIKOLAOS IS AT LEAST A THOUSAND YEARS OLD. I DON'T THINK I'VE EVER BEEN SO FRIGHTENED OF ANYTHING IN MY LIFE.
WHAT ARE YOU THINKING?
THAT I LOVE A CHALLENGE.
#@$%.

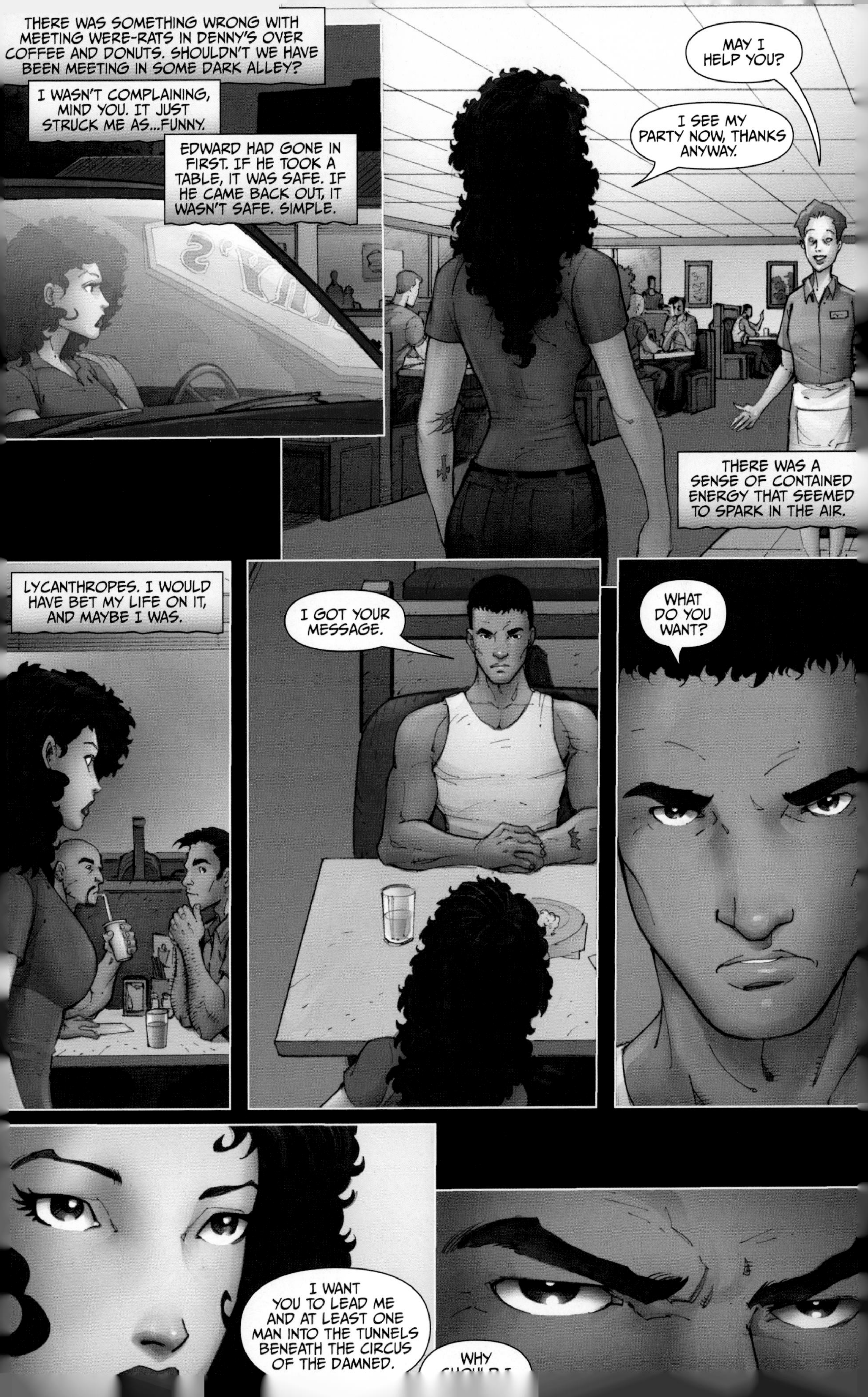

THERE WAS SOMETHING WRONG WITH MEETING WERE-RATS IN DENNY'S OVER COFFEE AND DONUTS. SHOULDN'T WE HAVE BEEN MEETING IN SOME DARK ALLEY?
I WASN'T COMPLAINING, MIND YOU. IT JUST STRUCK ME AS...FUNNY.
EDWARD HAD GONE IN FIRST. IF HE TOOK A TABLE, IT WAS SAFE. IF HE CAME BACK OUT, IT WASN'T SAFE. SIMPLE.
MAY I HELP YOU?
I SEE MY PARTY NOW, THANKS ANYWAY.
THERE WAS A SENSE OF CONTAINED ENERGY THAT SEEMED TO SPARK IN THE AIR.
LYCANTHROPES. I WOULD HAVE BET MY LIFE ON IT, AND MAYBE I WAS.
I GOT YOUR MESSAGE.
WHAT DO YOU WANT?
I WANT YOU TO LEAD ME AND AT LEAST ONE MAN INTO THE TUNNELS BENEATH THE CIRCUS OF THE DAMNED.
WHY

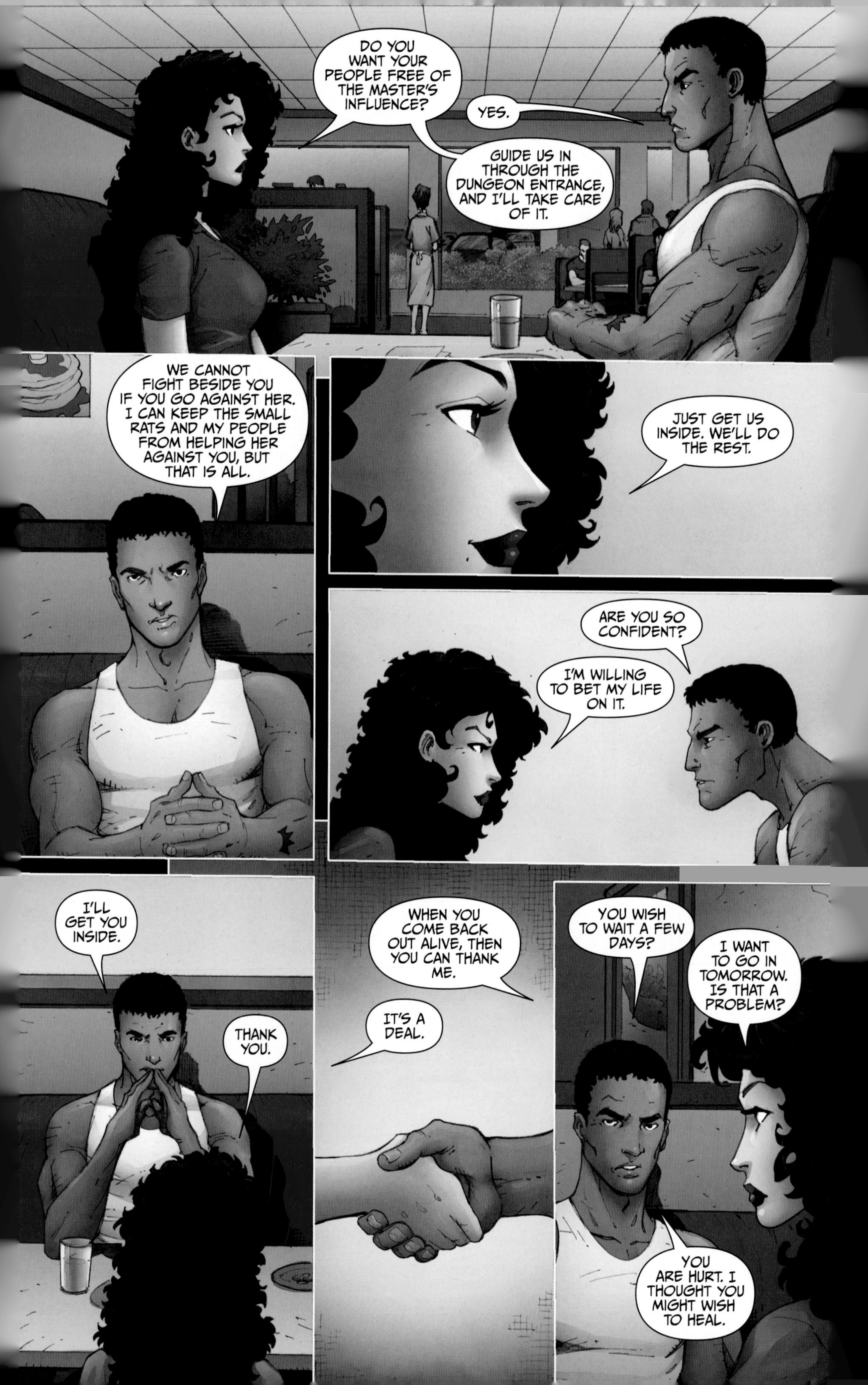
DO YOU WANT YOUR PEOPLE FREE OF THE MASTER'S INFLUENCE?
YES.
GUIDE US IN THROUGH THE DUNGEON ENTRANCE, AND I'LL TAKE CARE OF IT.
WE CANNOT FIGHT BESIDE YOU IF YOU GO AGAINST HER. I CAN KEEP THE SMALL RATS AND MY PEOPLE FROM HELPING HER AGAINST YOU, BUT THAT IS ALL.
JUST GET US INSIDE. WE'LL DO THE REST.
ARE YOU SO CONFIDENT?
I'M WILLING TO BET MY LIFE ON IT.
I'LL GET YOU INSIDE.
THANK YOU.
WHEN YOU COME BACK OUT ALIVE, THEN YOU CAN THANK ME.
IT'S A DEAL.
YOU WISH TO WAIT A FEW DAYS?
I WANT TO GO IN TOMORROW. IS THAT A PROBLEM?
YOU ARE HURT. I THOUGHT YOU MIGHT WISH TO HEAL.

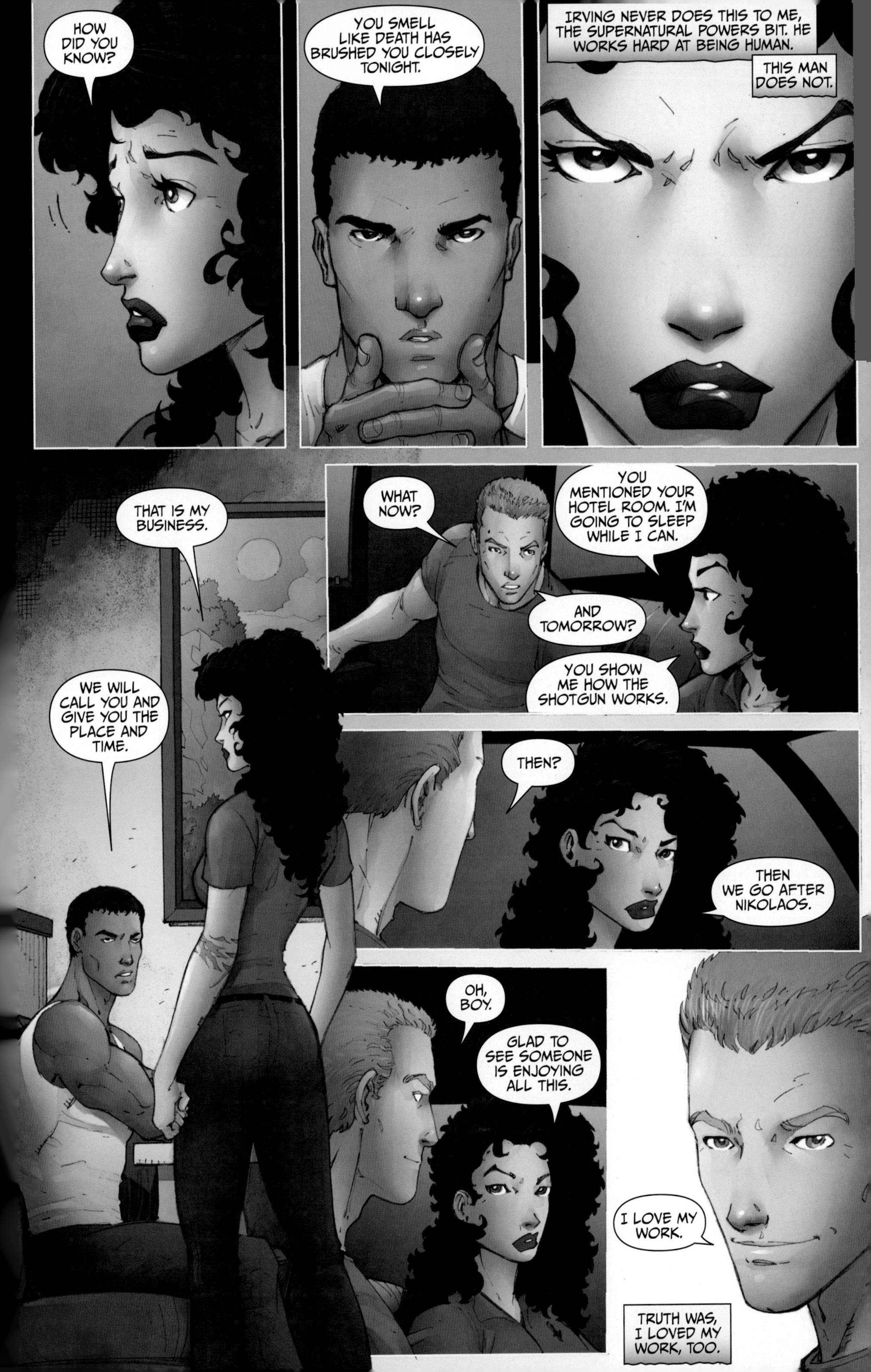
HOW DID YOU KNOW?
YOU SMELL LIKE DEATH HAS BRUSHED YOU CLOSELY TONIGHT.
IRVING NEVER DOES THIS TO ME, THE SUPERNATURAL POWERS BIT. HE WORKS HARD AT BEING HUMAN.
THIS MAN DOES NOT.
THAT IS MY BUSINESS.
WE WILL CALL YOU AND GIVE YOU THE PLACE AND TIME.
WHAT NOW?
YOU MENTIONED YOUR HOTEL ROOM. I'M GOING TO SLEEP WHILE I CAN.
AND TOMORROW?
YOU SHOW ME HOW THE SHOTGUN WORKS.
THEN?
THEN WE GO AFTER NIKOLAOS.
OH, BOY.
GLAD TO SEE SOMEONE IS ENJOYING ALL THIS.
I LOVE MY WORK.
TRUTH WAS, I LOVED MY WORK, TOO.

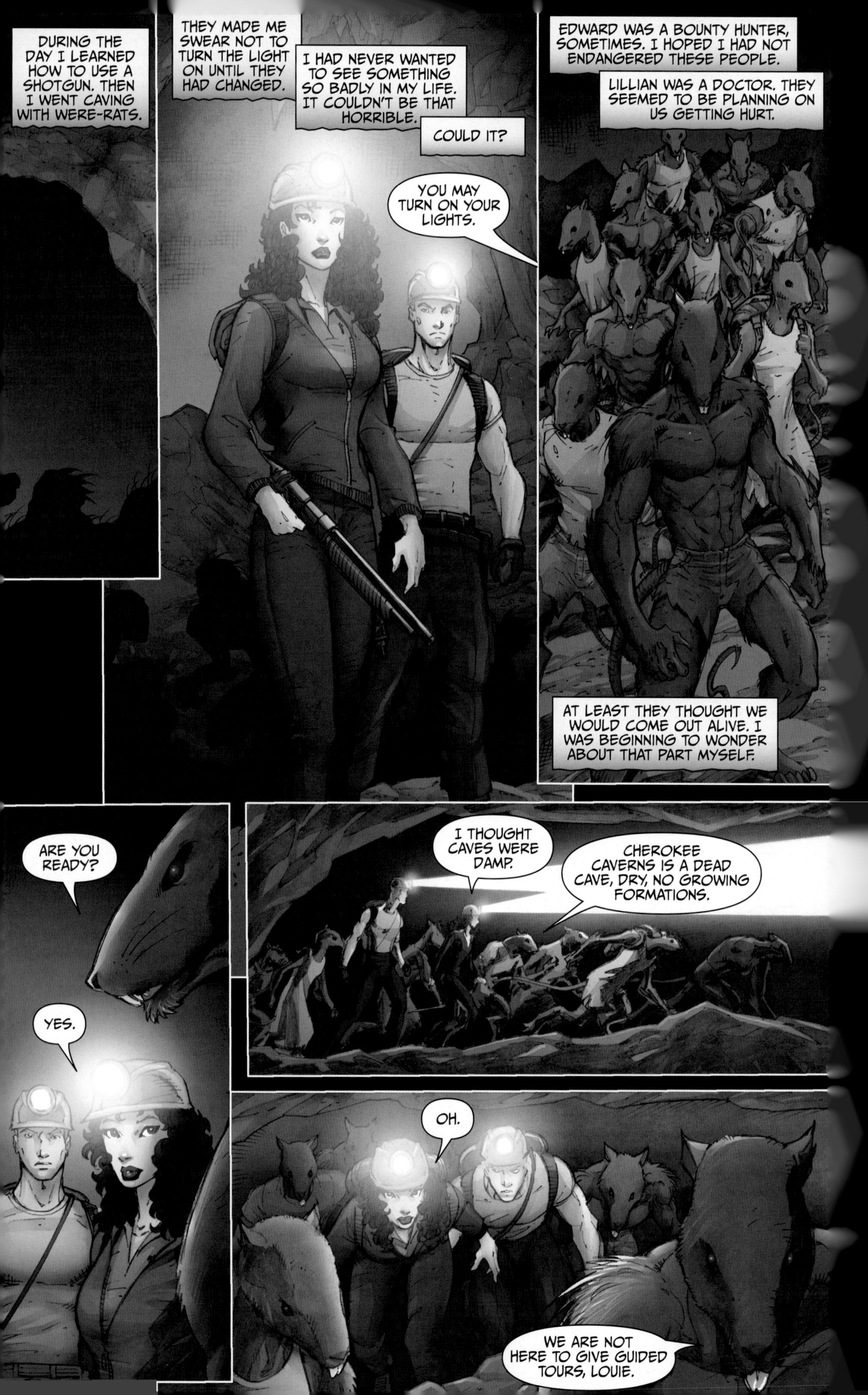
DURING THE DAY I LEARNED HOW TO USE A SHOTGUN. THEN I WENT CAVING WITH WERE-RATS.
THEY MADE ME SWEAR NOT TO TURN THE LIGHT ON UNTIL THEY HAD CHANGED.
I HAD NEVER WANTED TO SEE SOMETHING SO BADLY IN MY LIFE. IT COULDN'T BE THAT HORRIBLE.
COULD IT?
YOU MAY TURN ON YOUR LIGHTS.
EDWARD WAS A BOUNTY HUNTER, SOMETIMES. I HOPED I HAD NOT ENDANGERED THESE PEOPLE.
LILLIAN WAS A DOCTOR. THEY SEEMED TO BE PLANNING ON US GETTING HURT.
AT LEAST THEY THOUGHT WE WOULD COME OUT ALIVE. I WAS BEGINNING TO WONDER ABOUT THAT PART MYSELF.
ARE YOU READY?
YES.
I THOUGHT CAVES WERE DAMP.
CHEROKEE CAVERNS IS A DEAD CAVE, DRY, NO GROWING FORMATIONS.
OH.
WE ARE NOT HERE TO GIVE GUIDED TOURS, LOUIE.

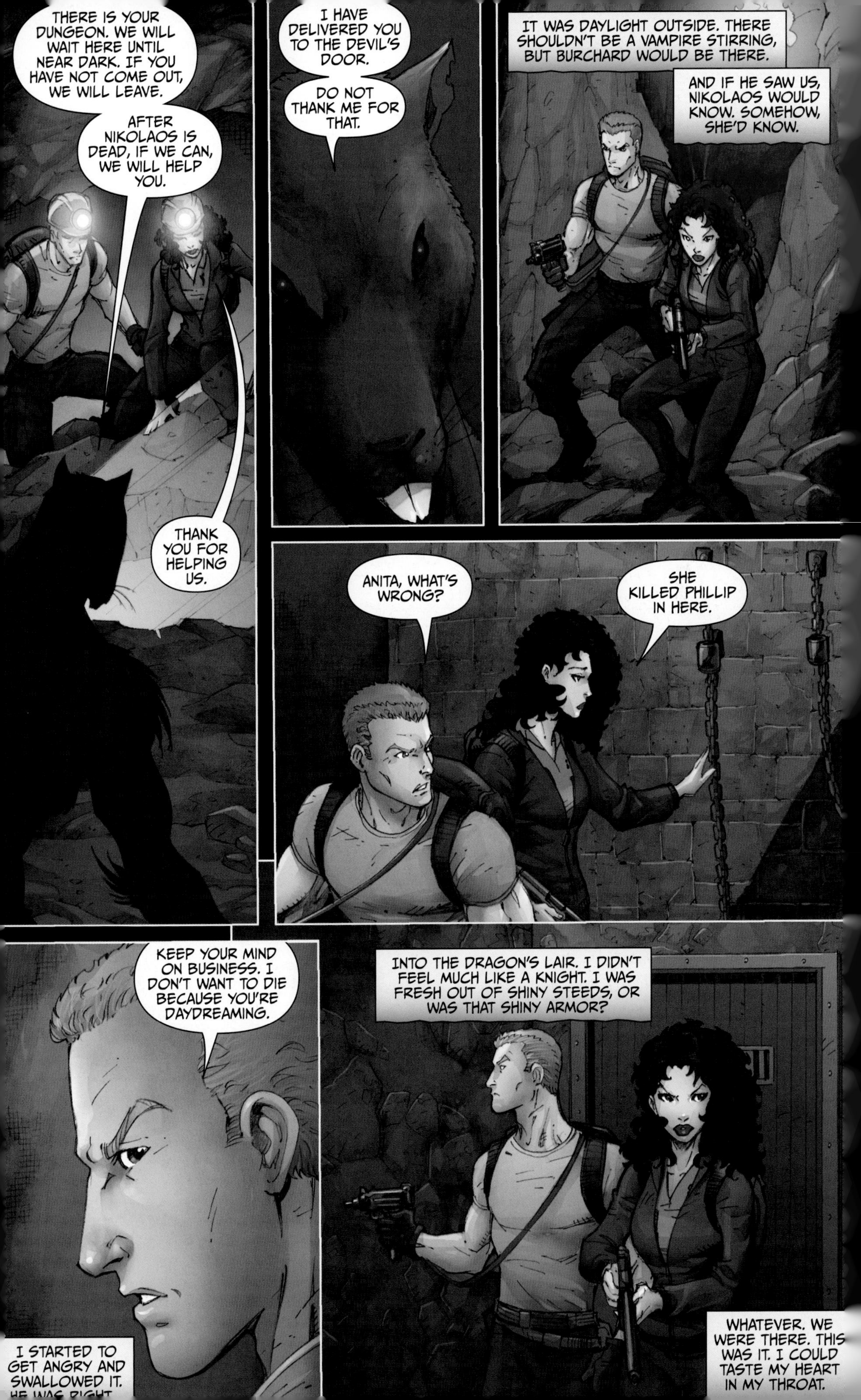
THERE IS YOUR DUNGEON. WE WILL WAIT HERE UNTIL NEAR DARK. IF YOU HAVE NOT COME OUT, WE WILL LEAVE.
AFTER NIKOLAOS IS DEAD, IF WE CAN, WE WILL HELP YOU.
THANK YOU FOR HELPING US.
I HAVE DELIVERED YOU TO THE DEVIL'S DOOR.
DO NOT THANK ME FOR THAT.
IT WAS DAYLIGHT OUTSIDE. THERE SHOULDN'T BE A VAMPIRE STIRRING, BUT BURCHARD WOULD BE THERE.
AND IF HE SAW US, NIKOLAOS WOULD KNOW. SOMEHOW, SHE'D KNOW.
ANITA, WHAT'S WRONG?
SHE KILLED PHILLIP IN HERE.
KEEP YOUR MIND ON BUSINESS. I DON'T WANT TO DIE BECAUSE YOU'RE DAYDREAMING.
I STARTED TO GET ANGRY AND SWALLOWED IT.
INTO THE DRAGON'S LAIR. I DIDN'T FEEL MUCH LIKE A KNIGHT. I WAS FRESH OUT OF SHINY STEEDS, OR WAS THAT SHINY ARMOR?
WHATEVER. WE WERE THERE. THIS WAS IT. I COULD TASTE MY HEART IN MY THROAT.

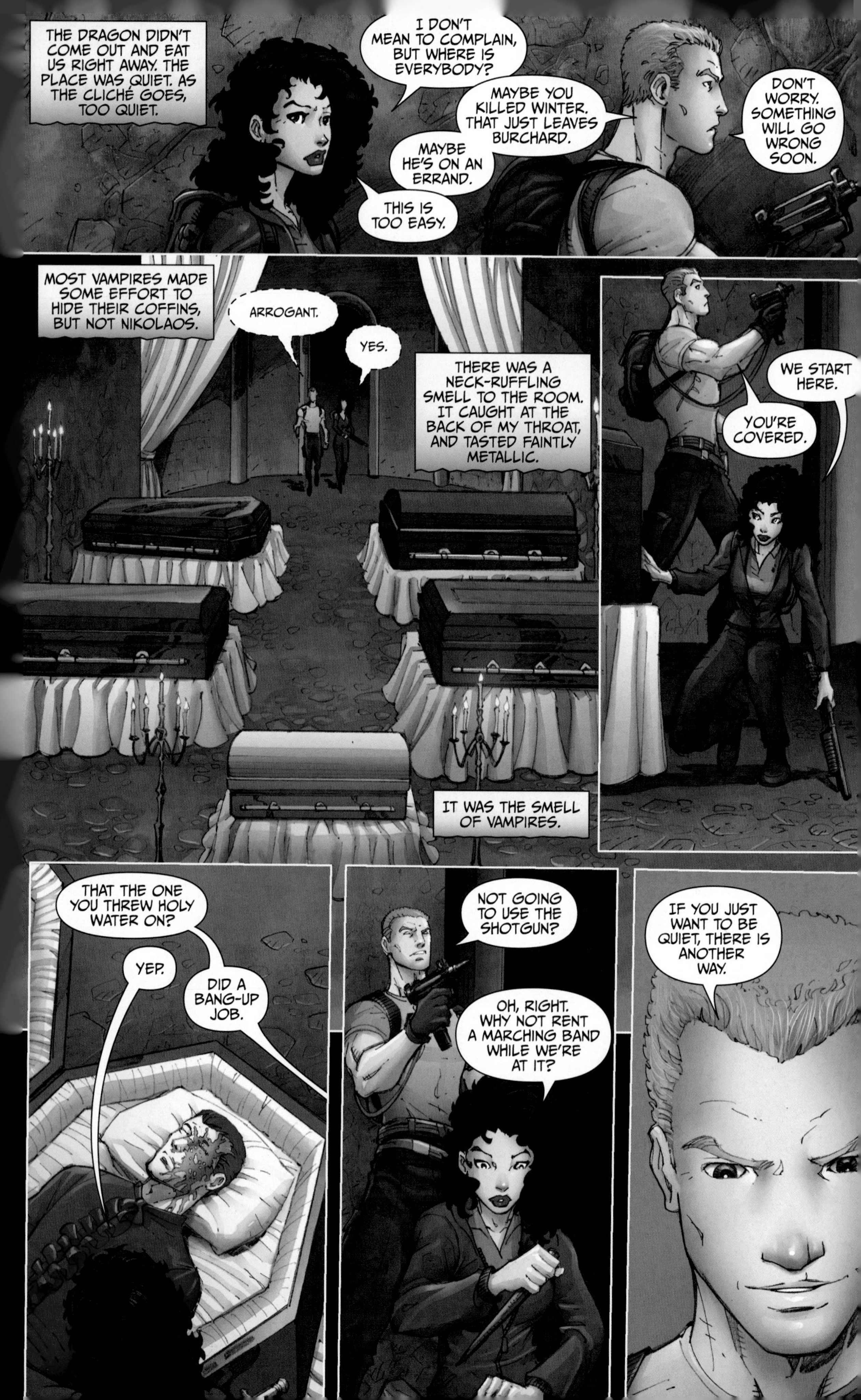
THE DRAGON DIDN'T COME OUT AND EAT US RIGHT AWAY. THE PLACE WAS QUIET. AS THE CLICHÉ GOES, TOO QUIET.
I DON'T MEAN TO COMPLAIN, BUT WHERE IS EVERYBODY?
MAYBE YOU KILLED WINTER. THAT JUST LEAVES BURCHARD.
MAYBE HE'S ON AN ERRAND.
THIS IS TOO EASY.
DON'T WORRY. SOMETHING WILL GO WRONG SOON.
MOST VAMPIRES MADE SOME EFFORT TO HIDE THEIR COFFINS, BUT NOT NIKOLAOS.
ARROGANT.
YES.
THERE WAS A NECK-RUFFLING SMELL TO THE ROOM. IT CAUGHT AT THE BACK OF MY THROAT, AND TASTED FAINTLY METALLIC.
IT WAS THE SMELL OF VAMPIRES.
WE START HERE.
YOU'RE COVERED.
THAT THE ONE YOU THREW HOLY WATER ON?
YEP.
DID A BANG-UP JOB.
NOT GOING TO USE THE SHOTGUN?
OH, RIGHT. WHY NOT RENT A MARCHING BAND WHILE WE'RE AT IT?
IF YOU JUST WANT TO BE QUIET, THERE IS ANOTHER WAY.

I'VE STAKED MOST OF THE VAMPIRES THAT I'VE KILLED. IT IS HARD, MESSY WORK, THOUGH I DON'T THROW UP ANYMORE.

I AM A PROFESSIONAL, AFTER ALL.

SILVER NITRATE.

DOES IT WORK?

IT WORKS.

HOW OLD IS THIS ONE?

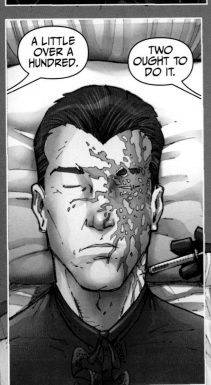

A LITTLE OVER A HUNDRED.

TWO OUGHT TO DO IT.

HE DOESN'T LOOK VERY DEAD.

THEY NEVER DO.

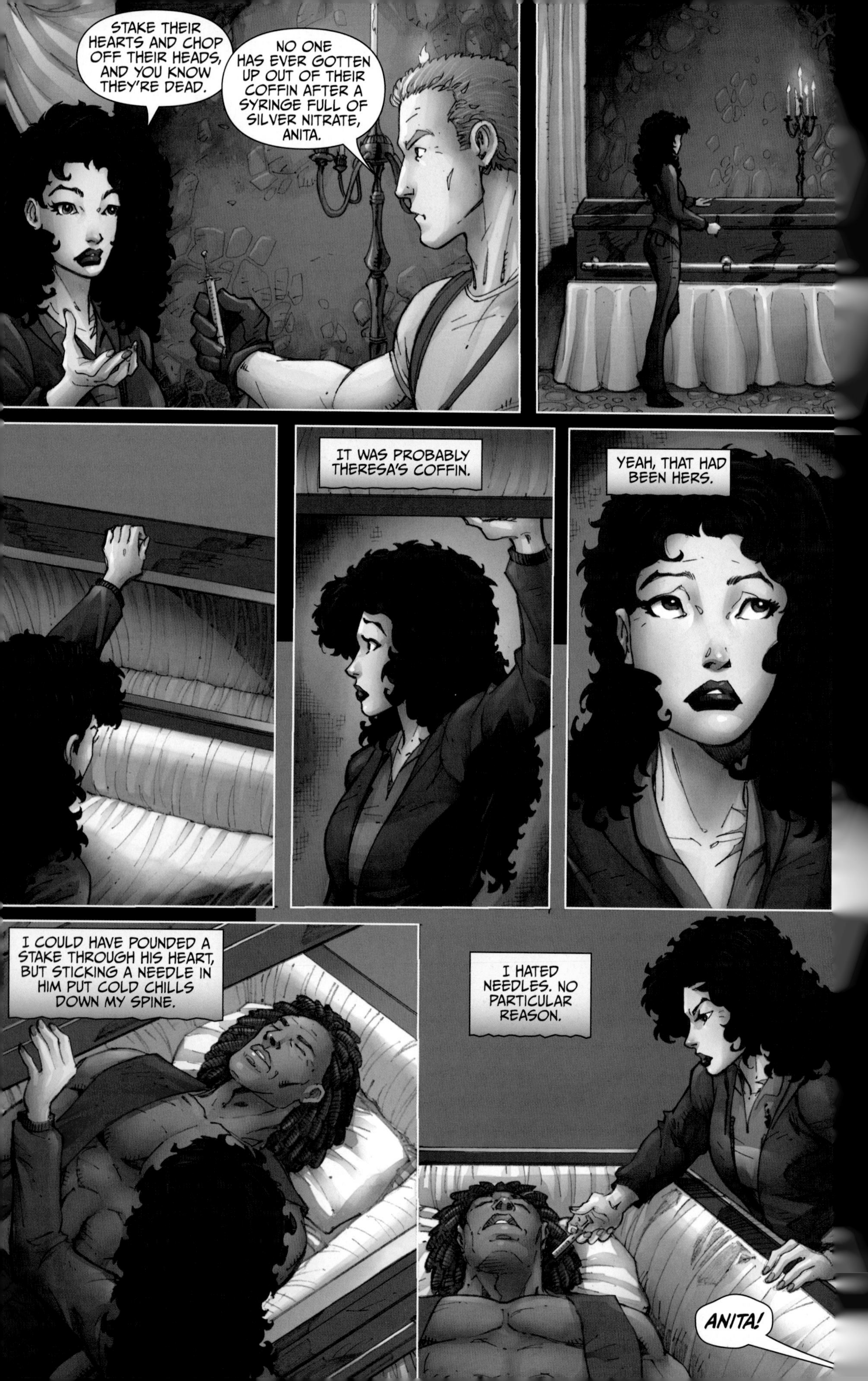
STAKE THEIR HEARTS AND CHOP OFF THEIR HEADS, AND YOU KNOW THEY'RE DEAD.
NO ONE HAS EVER GOTTEN UP OUT OF THEIR COFFIN AFTER A SYRINGE FULL OF SILVER NITRATE, ANITA.
IT WAS PROBABLY THERESA'S COFFIN.
YEAH, THAT HAD BEEN HERS.
I COULD HAVE POUNDED A STAKE THROUGH HIS HEART, BUT STICKING A NEEDLE IN HIM PUT COLD CHILLS DOWN MY SPINE.
I HATED NEEDLES. NO PARTICULAR REASON.
ANITA!

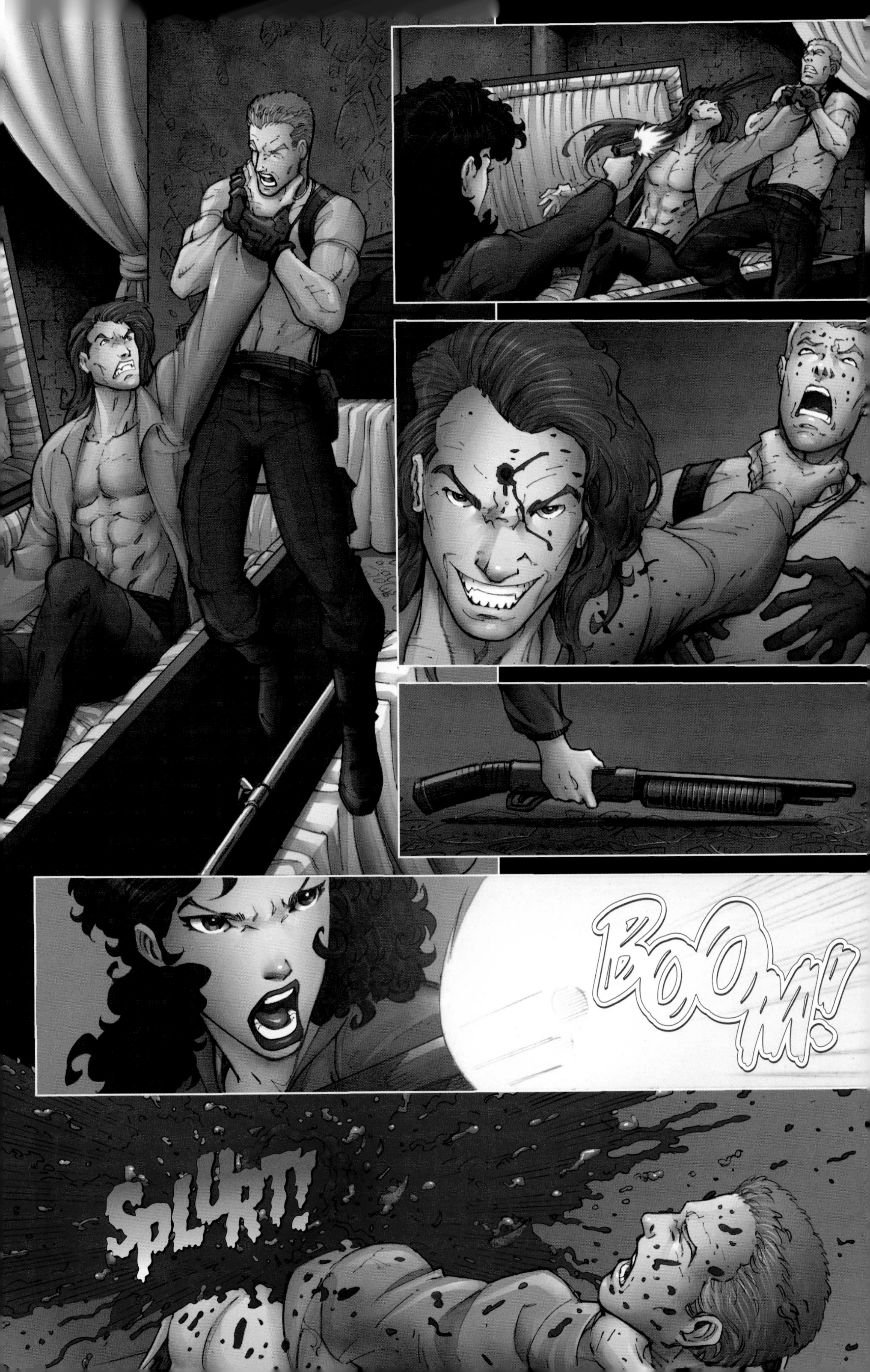
BOOM!
SPLURT!

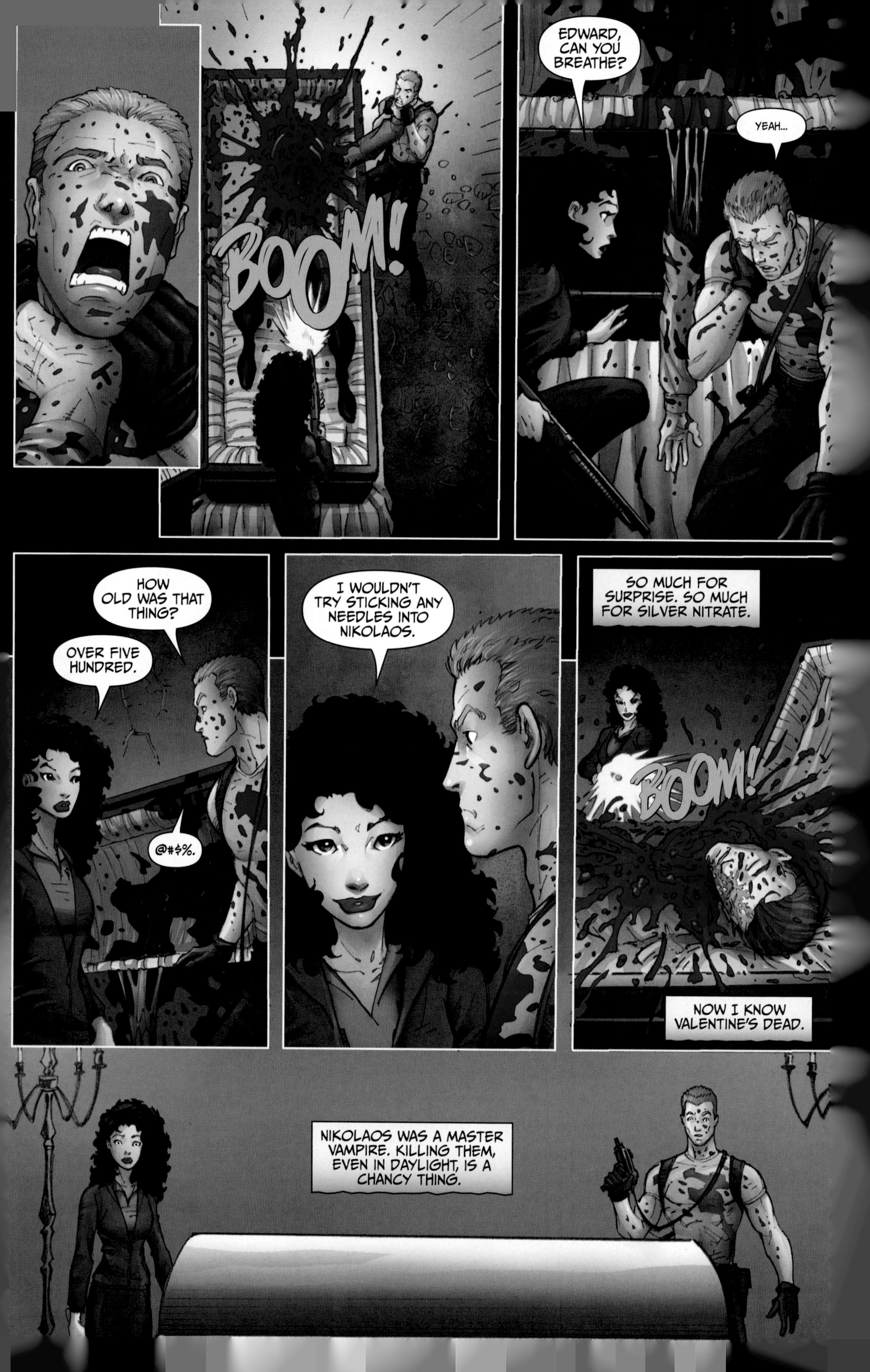
BOOM!
EDWARD, CAN YOU BREATHE?
YEAH...
HOW OLD WAS THAT THING?
OVER FIVE HUNDRED.
@#$%.
I WOULDN'T TRY STICKING ANY NEEDLES INTO NIKOLAOS.
SO MUCH FOR SURPRISE. SO MUCH FOR SILVER NITRATE.
BOOM!
NOW I KNOW VALENTINE'S DEAD.
NIKOLAOS WAS A MASTER VAMPIRE. KILLING THEM, EVEN IN DAYLIGHT, IS A CHANCY THING.

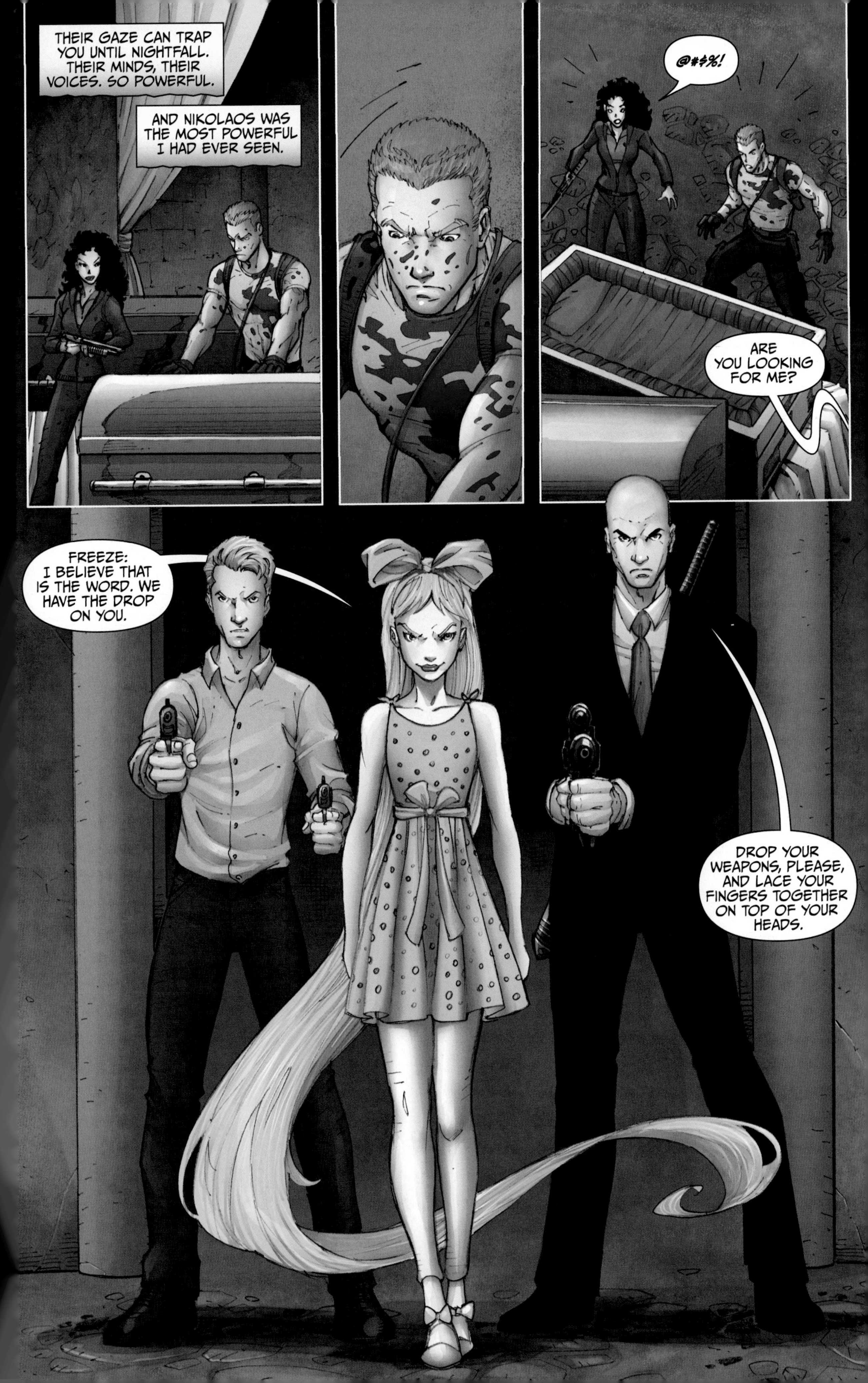
THEIR GAZE CAN TRAP YOU UNTIL NIGHTFALL. THEIR MINDS, THEIR VOICES. SO POWERFUL.
AND NIKOLAOS WAS THE MOST POWERFUL I HAD EVER SEEN.
@#$%!
ARE YOU LOOKING FOR ME?
FREEZE: I BELIEVE THAT IS THE WORD. WE HAVE THE DROP ON YOU.
DROP YOUR WEAPONS, PLEASE, AND LACE YOUR FINGERS TOGETHER ON TOP OF YOUR HEADS.

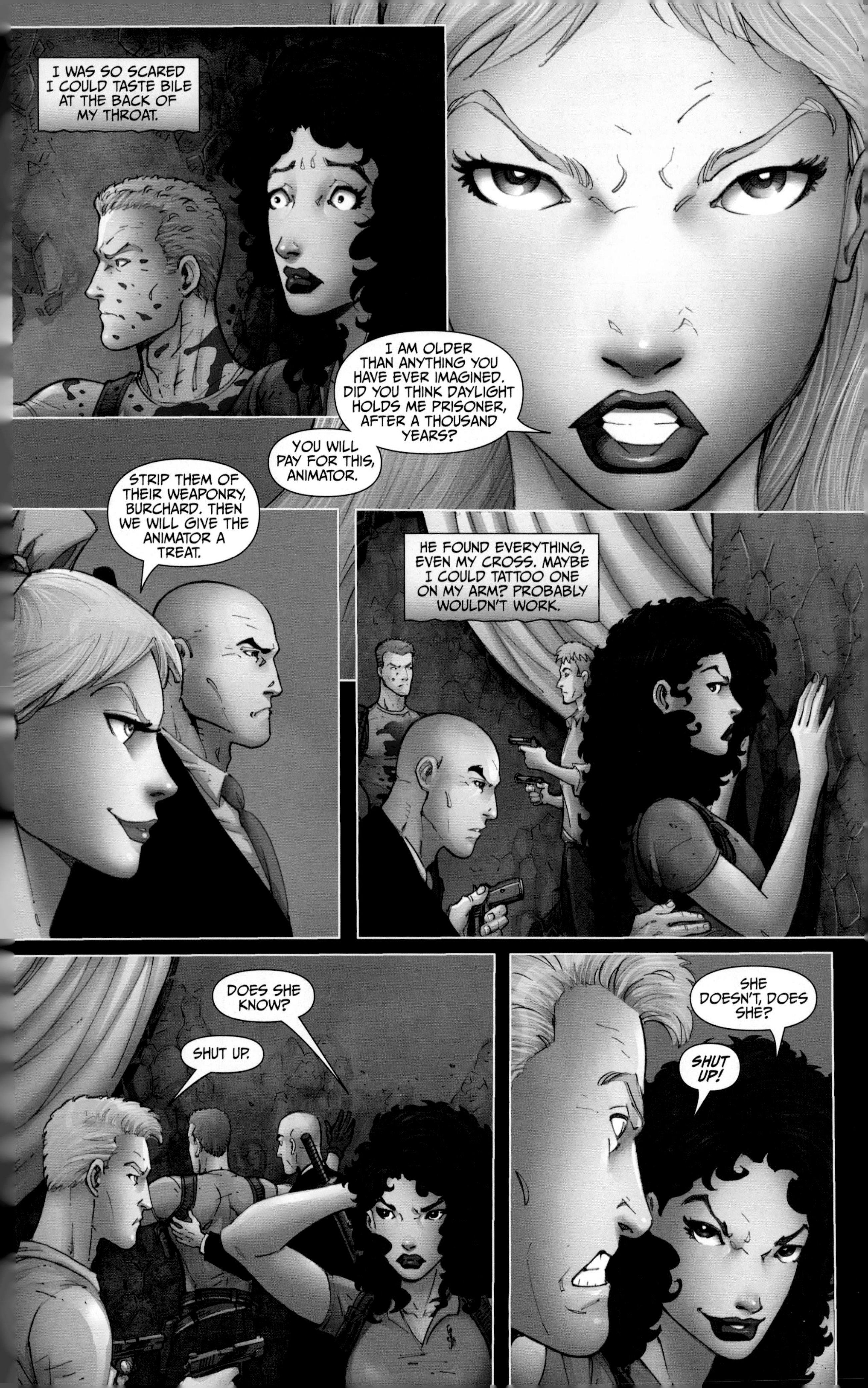

I WAS SO SCARED I COULD TASTE BILE AT THE BACK OF MY THROAT.
I AM OLDER THAN ANYTHING YOU HAVE EVER IMAGINED. DID YOU THINK DAYLIGHT HOLDS ME PRISONER, AFTER A THOUSAND YEARS?
YOU WILL PAY FOR THIS, ANIMATOR.
STRIP THEM OF THEIR WEAPONRY, BURCHARD. THEN WE WILL GIVE THE ANIMATOR A TREAT.
HE FOUND EVERYTHING, EVEN MY CROSS. MAYBE I COULD TATTOO ONE ON MY ARM? PROBABLY WOULDN'T WORK.
DOES SHE KNOW?
SHUT UP.
SHE DOESN'T, DOES SHE?
SHUT UP!

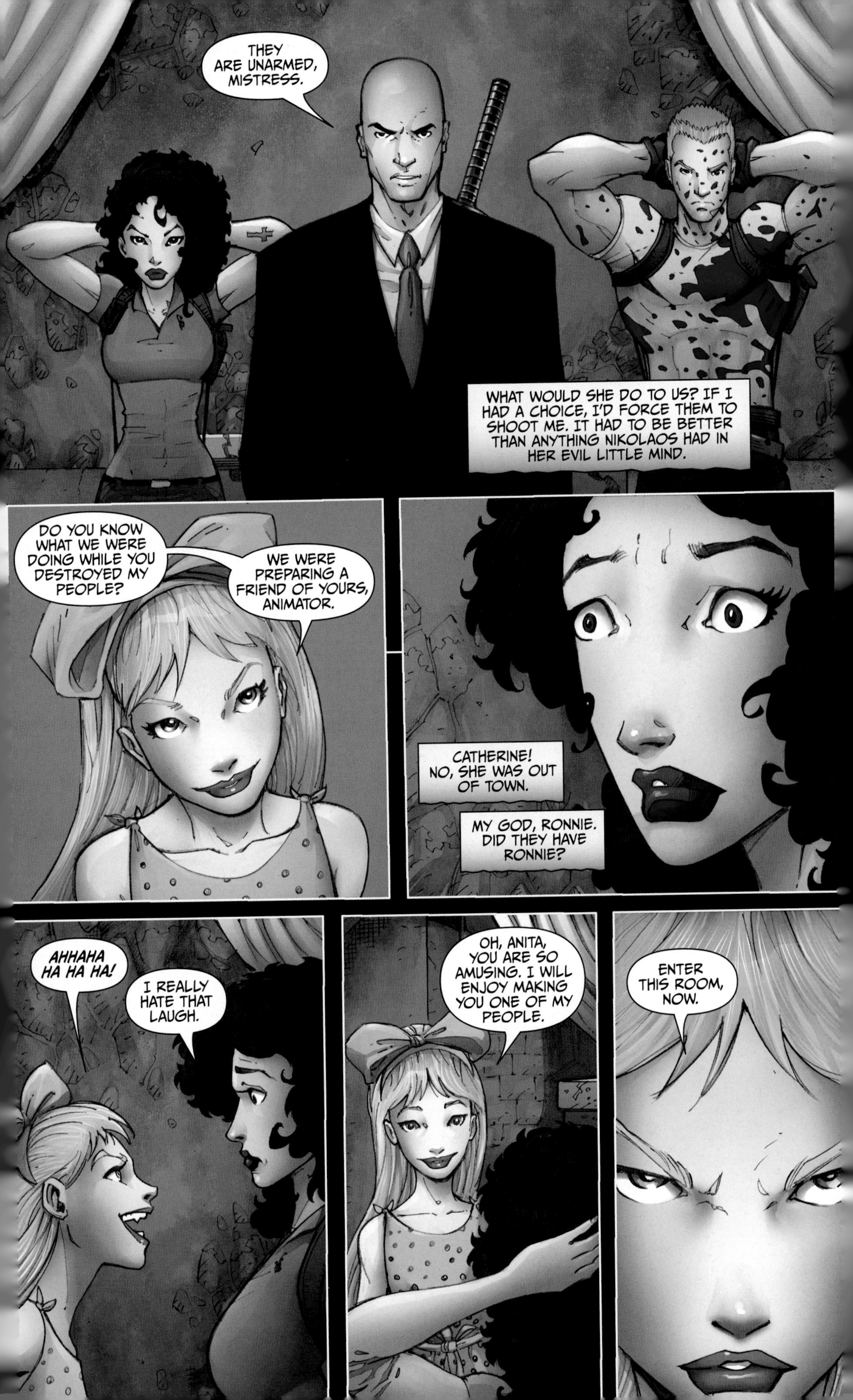
THEY ARE UNARMED, MISTRESS.
WHAT WOULD SHE DO TO US? IF I HAD A CHOICE, I'D FORCE THEM TO SHOOT ME. IT HAD TO BE BETTER THAN ANYTHING NIKOLAOS HAD IN HER EVIL LITTLE MIND.
DO YOU KNOW WHAT WE WERE DOING WHILE YOU DESTROYED MY PEOPLE?
WE WERE PREPARING A FRIEND OF YOURS, ANIMATOR.
CATHERINE! NO, SHE WAS OUT OF TOWN.
MY GOD, RONNIE. DID THEY HAVE RONNIE?
AHHAHA HA HA HA!
I REALLY HATE THAT LAUGH.
OH, ANITA, YOU ARE SO AMUSING. I WILL ENJOY MAKING YOU ONE OF MY PEOPLE.
ENTER THIS ROOM, NOW.

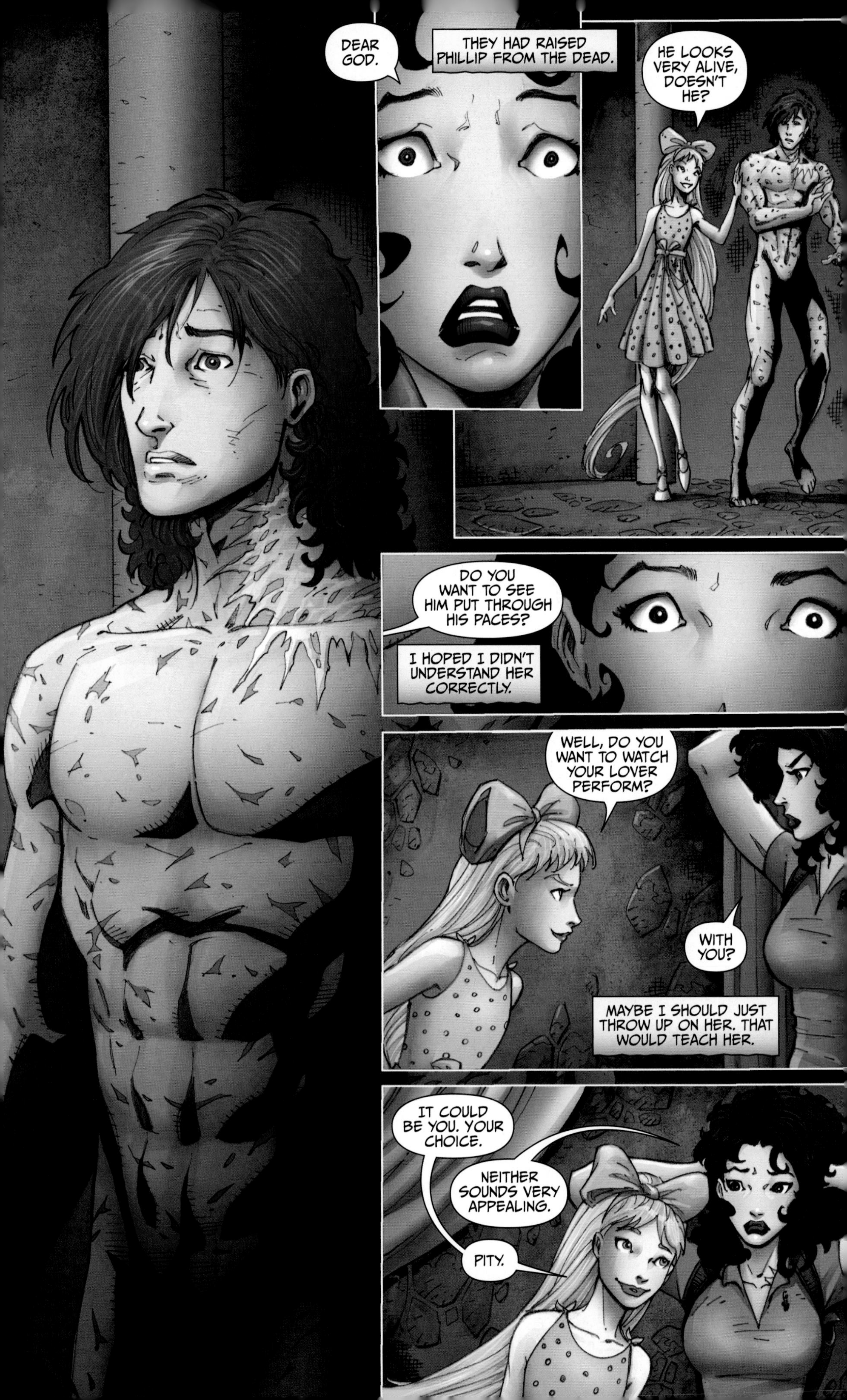
DEAR GOD.
THEY HAD RAISED PHILLIP FROM THE DEAD.
HE LOOKS VERY ALIVE, DOESN'T HE?
DO YOU WANT TO SEE HIM PUT THROUGH HIS PACES?
I HOPED I DIDN'T UNDERSTAND HER CORRECTLY.
WELL, DO YOU WANT TO WATCH YOUR LOVER PERFORM?
WITH YOU?
MAYBE I SHOULD JUST THROW UP ON HER. THAT WOULD TEACH HER.
IT COULD BE YOU. YOUR CHOICE.
NEITHER SOUNDS VERY APPEALING.
PITY.

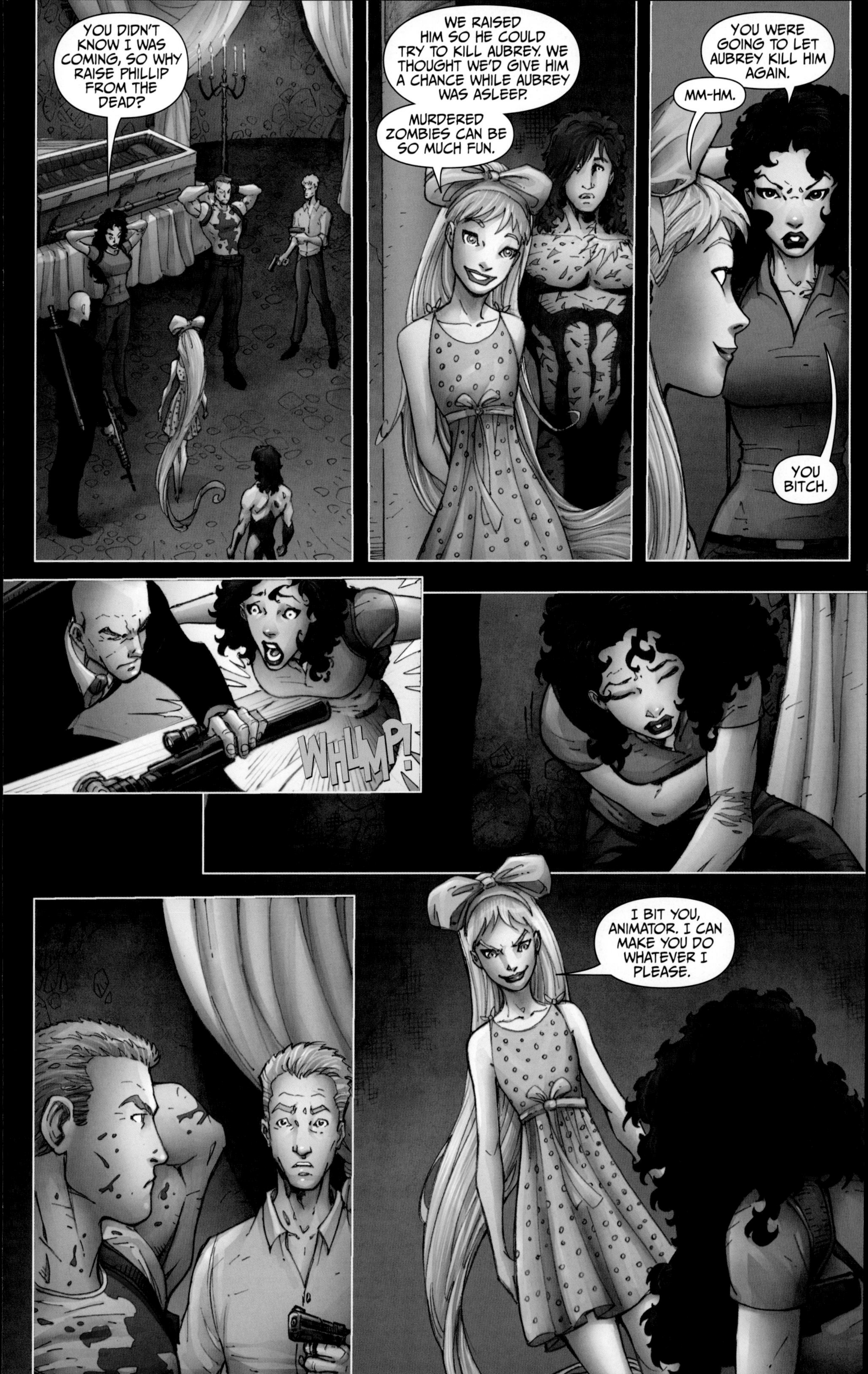
YOU DIDN'T KNOW I WAS COMING, SO WHY RAISE PHILLIP FROM THE DEAD?
WE RAISED HIM SO HE COULD TRY TO KILL AUBREY. WE THOUGHT WE'D GIVE HIM A CHANCE WHILE AUBREY WAS ASLEEP.
MURDERED ZOMBIES CAN BE SO MUCH FUN.
YOU WERE GOING TO LET AUBREY KILL HIM AGAIN.
MM-HM.
YOU BITCH.
WHUMP!
I BIT YOU, ANIMATOR. I CAN MAKE YOU DO WHATEVER I PLEASE.

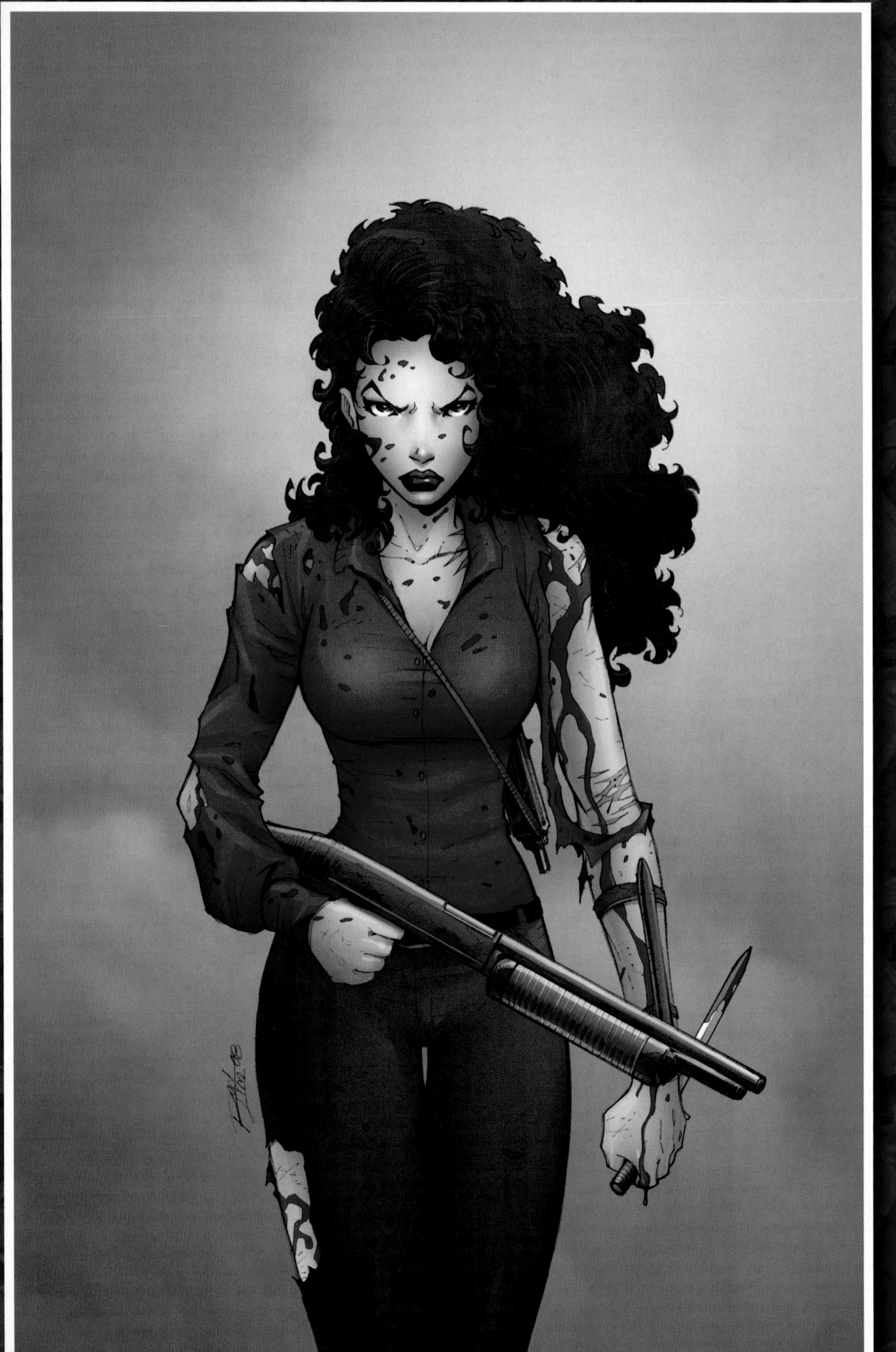

TWELVE

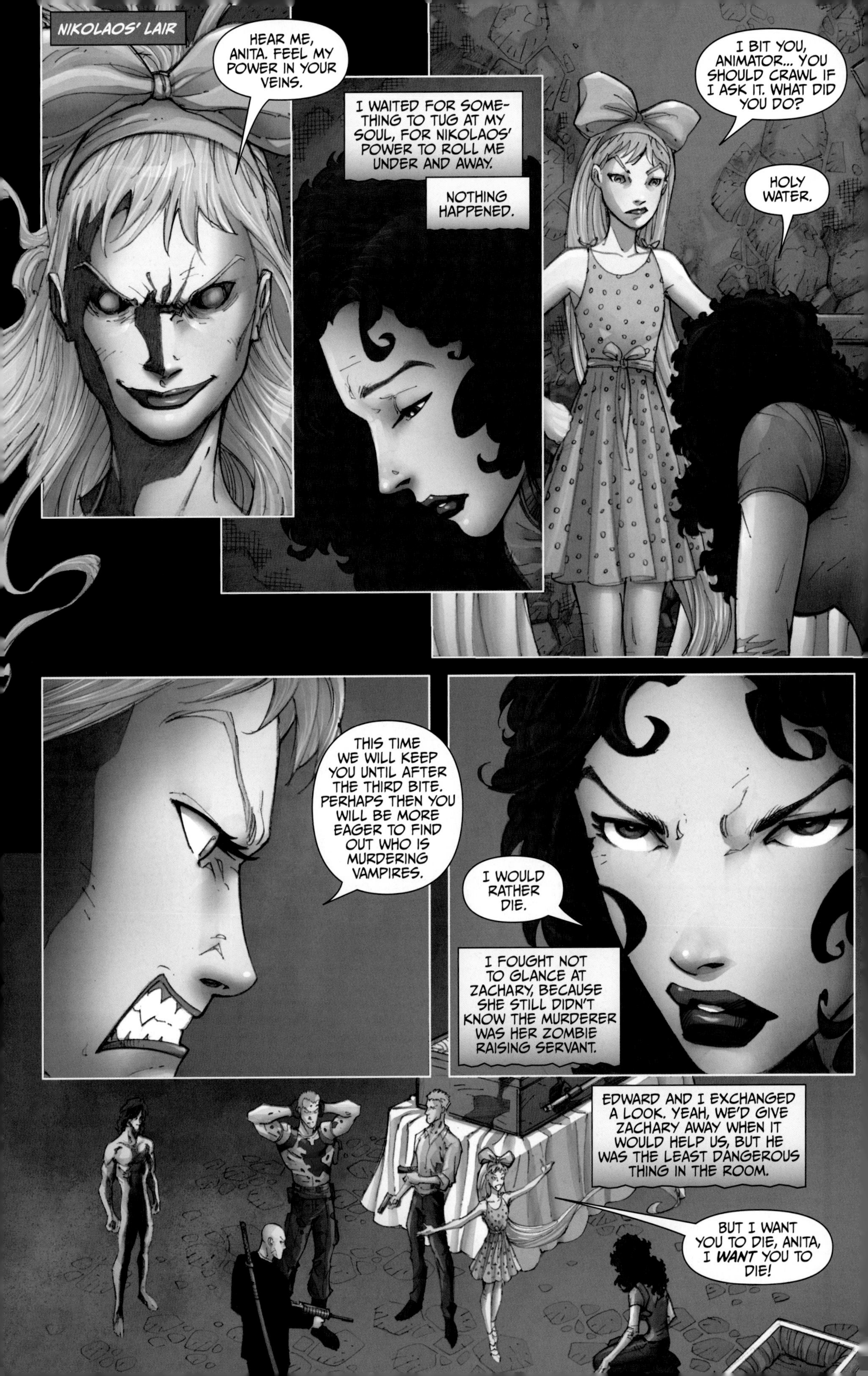
NIKOLAOS' LAIR
HEAR ME, ANITA. FEEL MY POWER IN YOUR VEINS.
I WAITED FOR SOMETHING TO TUG AT MY SOUL, FOR NIKOLAOS' POWER TO ROLL ME UNDER AND AWAY.
NOTHING HAPPENED.
I BIT YOU, ANIMATOR... YOU SHOULD CRAWL IF I ASK IT. WHAT DID YOU DO?
HOLY WATER.
THIS TIME WE WILL KEEP YOU UNTIL AFTER THE THIRD BITE. PERHAPS THEN YOU WILL BE MORE EAGER TO FIND OUT WHO IS MURDERING VAMPIRES.
I WOULD RATHER DIE.
I FOUGHT NOT TO GLANCE AT ZACHARY, BECAUSE SHE STILL DIDN'T KNOW THE MURDERER WAS HER ZOMBIE RAISING SERVANT.
EDWARD AND I EXCHANGED A LOOK. YEAH, WE'D GIVE ZACHARY AWAY WHEN IT WOULD HELP US, BUT HE WAS THE LEAST DANGEROUS THING IN THE ROOM.
BUT I WANT YOU TO DIE, ANITA, I *WANT* YOU TO DIE!

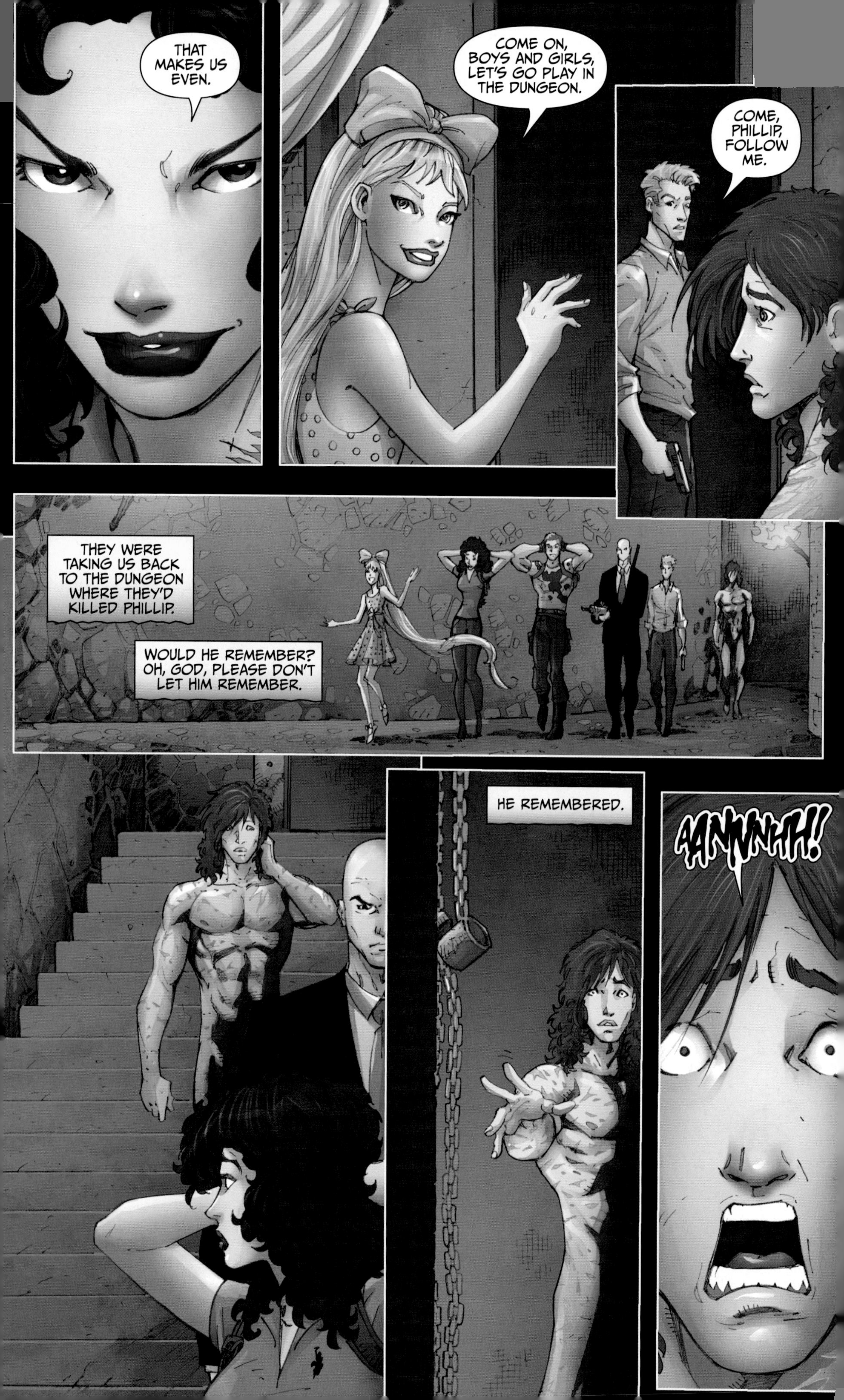
THAT MAKES US EVEN.
COME ON, BOYS AND GIRLS, LET'S GO PLAY IN THE DUNGEON.
COME, PHILLIP, FOLLOW ME.
THEY WERE TAKING US BACK TO THE DUNGEON WHERE THEY'D KILLED PHILLIP.
WOULD HE REMEMBER? OH, GOD, PLEASE DON'T LET HIM REMEMBER.
HE REMEMBERED.
AANNNHH!

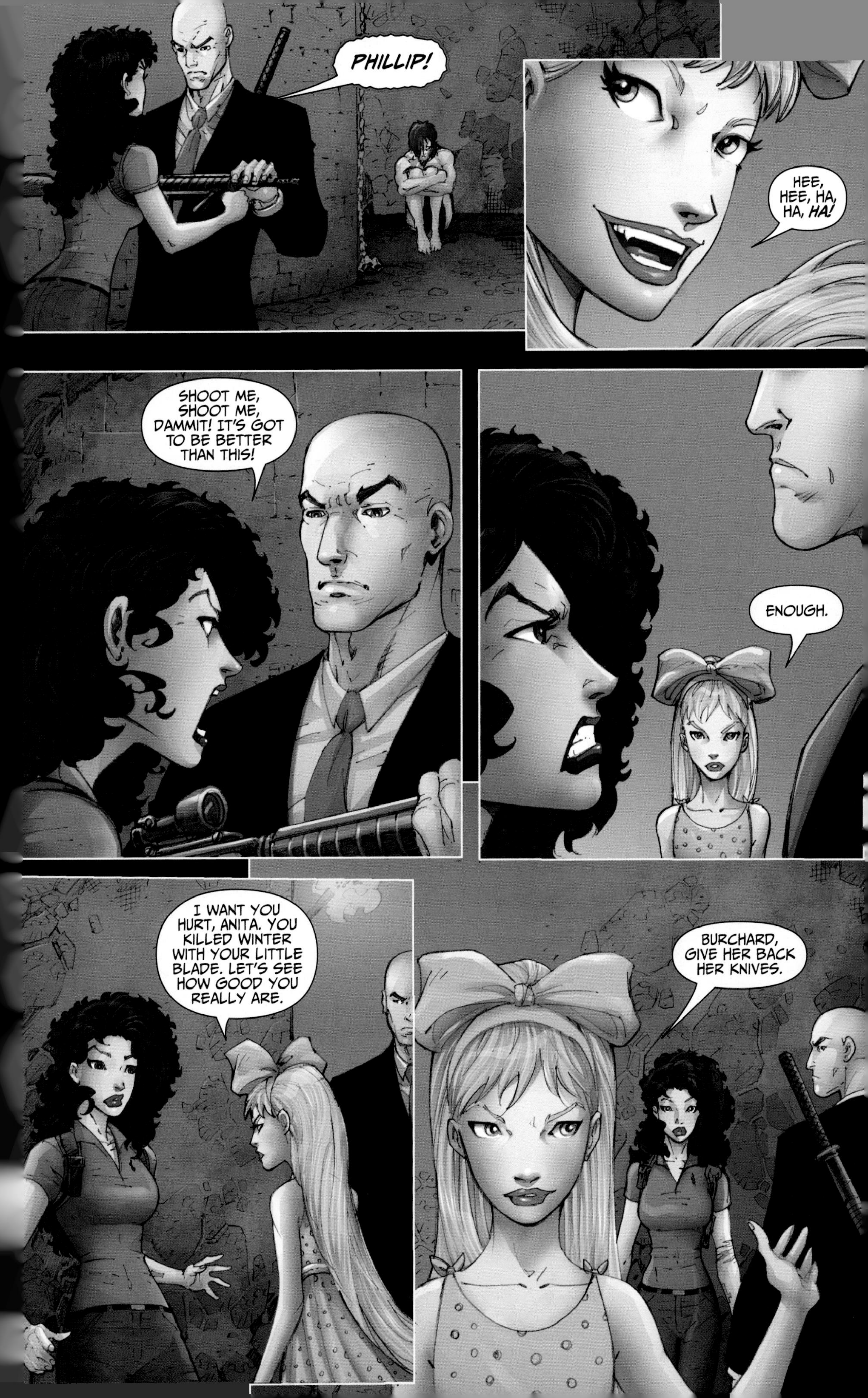
PHILLIP!
HEE, HEE, HA, HA, HA!
SHOOT ME, SHOOT ME, DAMMIT! IT'S GOT TO BE BETTER THAN THIS!
ENOUGH.
I WANT YOU HURT, ANITA. YOU KILLED WINTER WITH YOUR LITTLE BLADE. LET'S SEE HOW GOOD YOU REALLY ARE.
BURCHARD, GIVE HER BACK HER KNIVES.

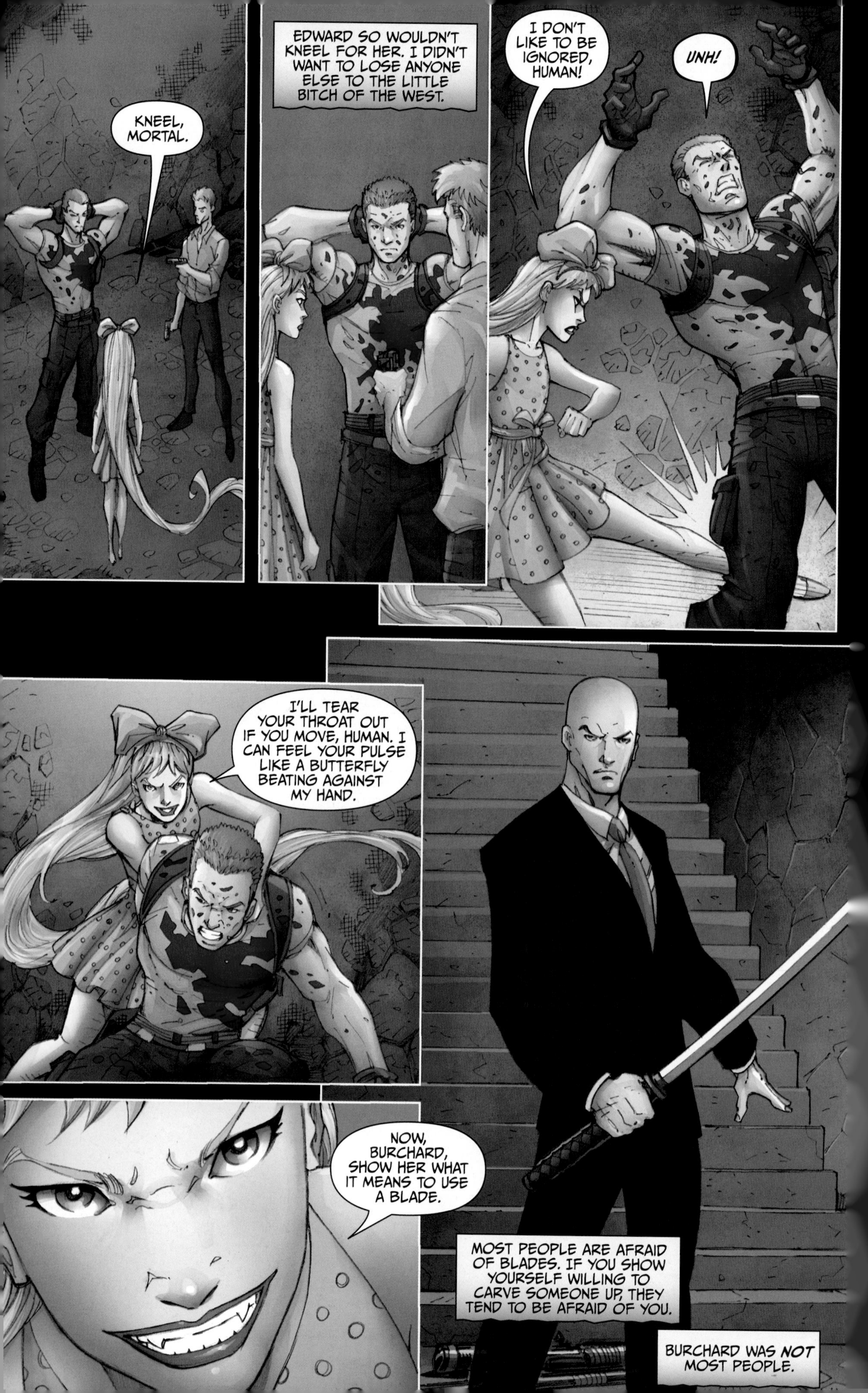
KNEEL, MORTAL.
EDWARD SO WOULDN'T KNEEL FOR HER. I DIDN'T WANT TO LOSE ANYONE ELSE TO THE LITTLE BITCH OF THE WEST.
I DON'T LIKE TO BE IGNORED, HUMAN!
UNH!
I'LL TEAR YOUR THROAT OUT IF YOU MOVE, HUMAN. I CAN FEEL YOUR PULSE LIKE A BUTTERFLY BEATING AGAINST MY HAND.
NOW, BURCHARD, SHOW HER WHAT IT MEANS TO USE A BLADE.
MOST PEOPLE ARE AFRAID OF BLADES. IF YOU SHOW YOURSELF WILLING TO CARVE SOMEONE UP, THEY TEND TO BE AFRAID OF YOU.
BURCHARD WAS NOT MOST PEOPLE.

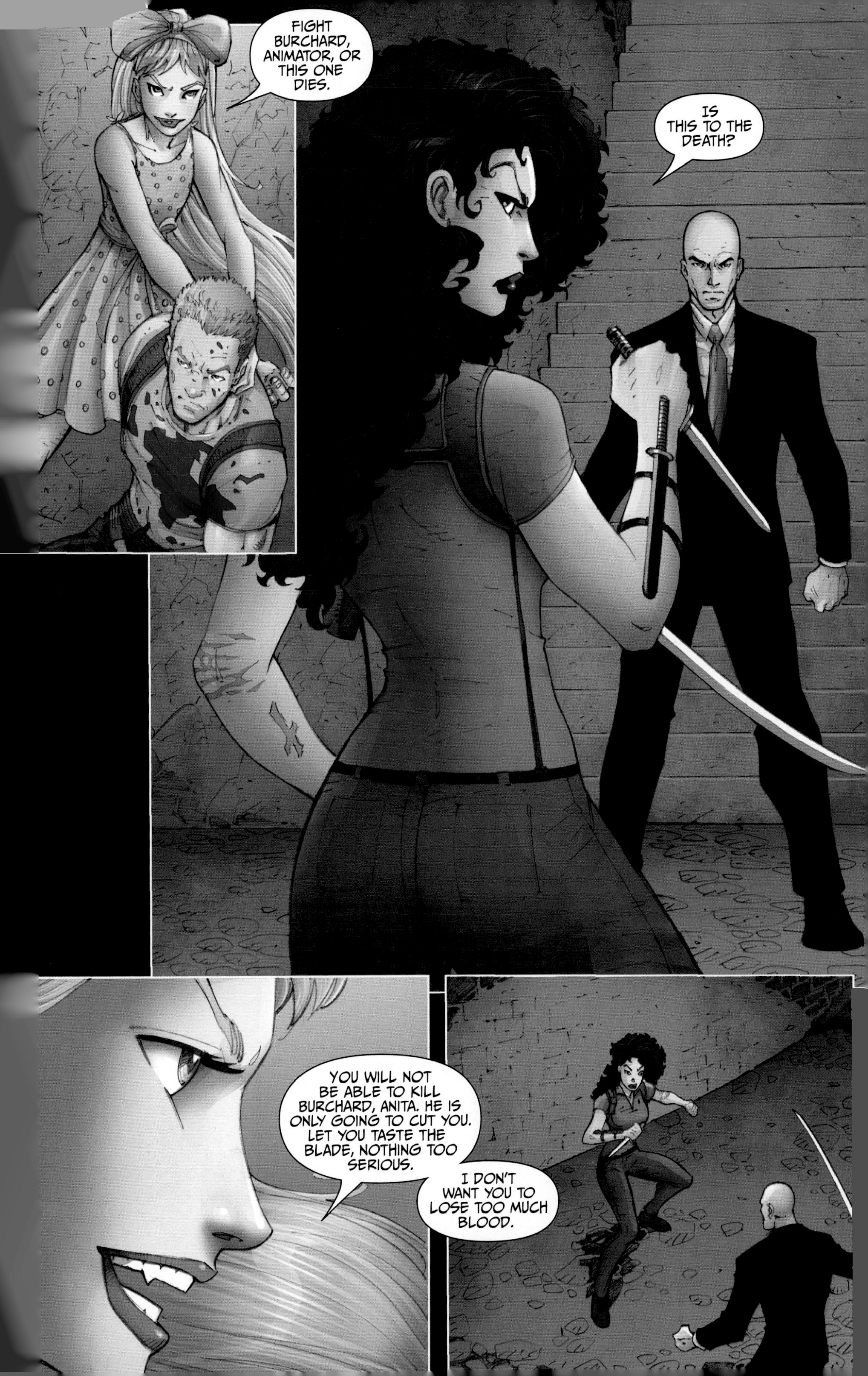

FIGHT BURCHARD, ANIMATOR, OR THIS ONE DIES.
IS THIS TO THE DEATH?
YOU WILL NOT BE ABLE TO KILL BURCHARD, ANITA. HE IS ONLY GOING TO CUT YOU. LET YOU TASTE THE BLADE, NOTHING TOO SERIOUS.
I DON'T WANT YOU TO LOSE TOO MUCH BLOOD.

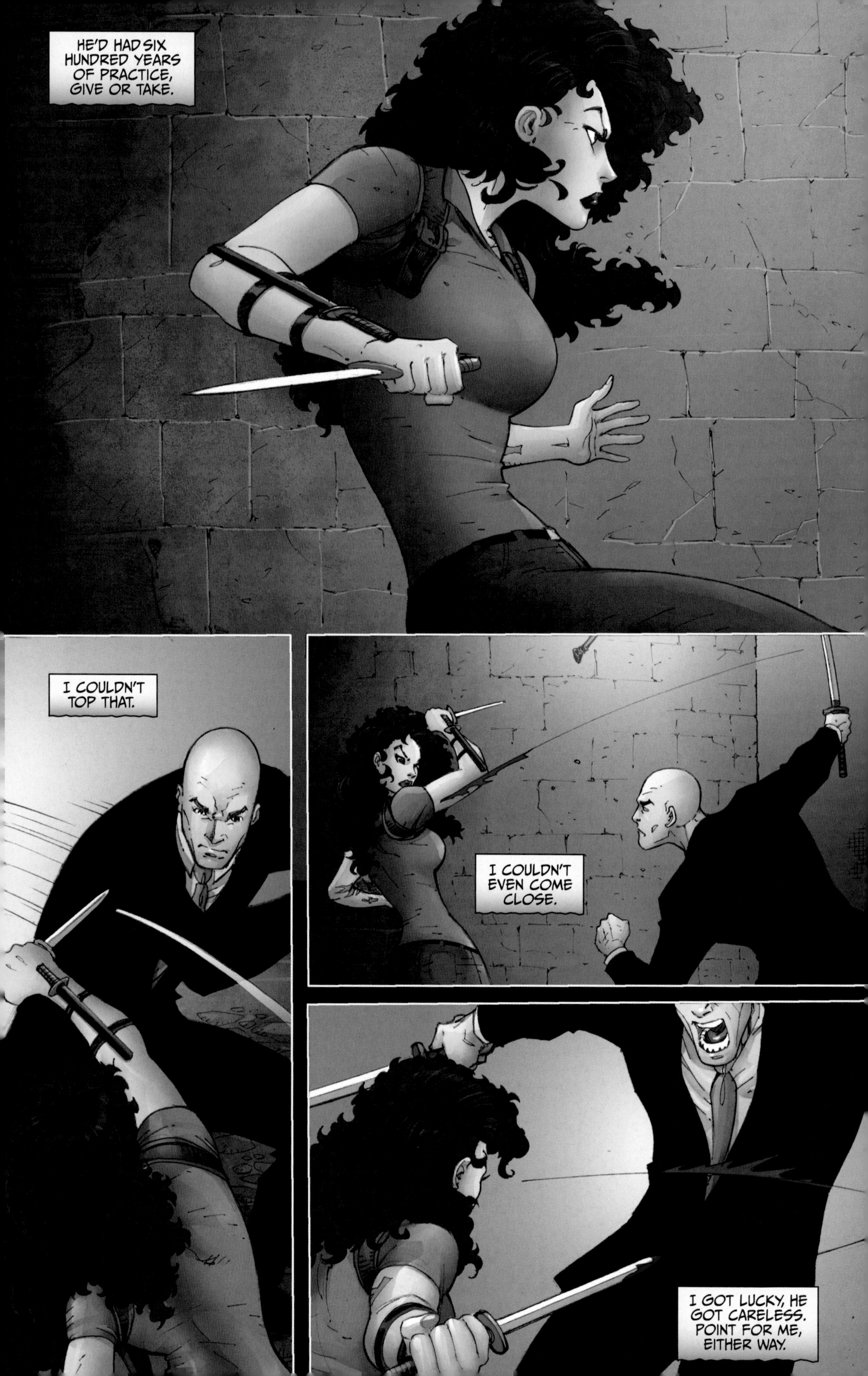
HE'D HAD SIX HUNDRED YEARS OF PRACTICE, GIVE OR TAKE.
I COULDN'T TOP THAT.
I COULDN'T EVEN COME CLOSE.
I GOT LUCKY, HE GOT CARELESS. POINT FOR ME, EITHER WAY.

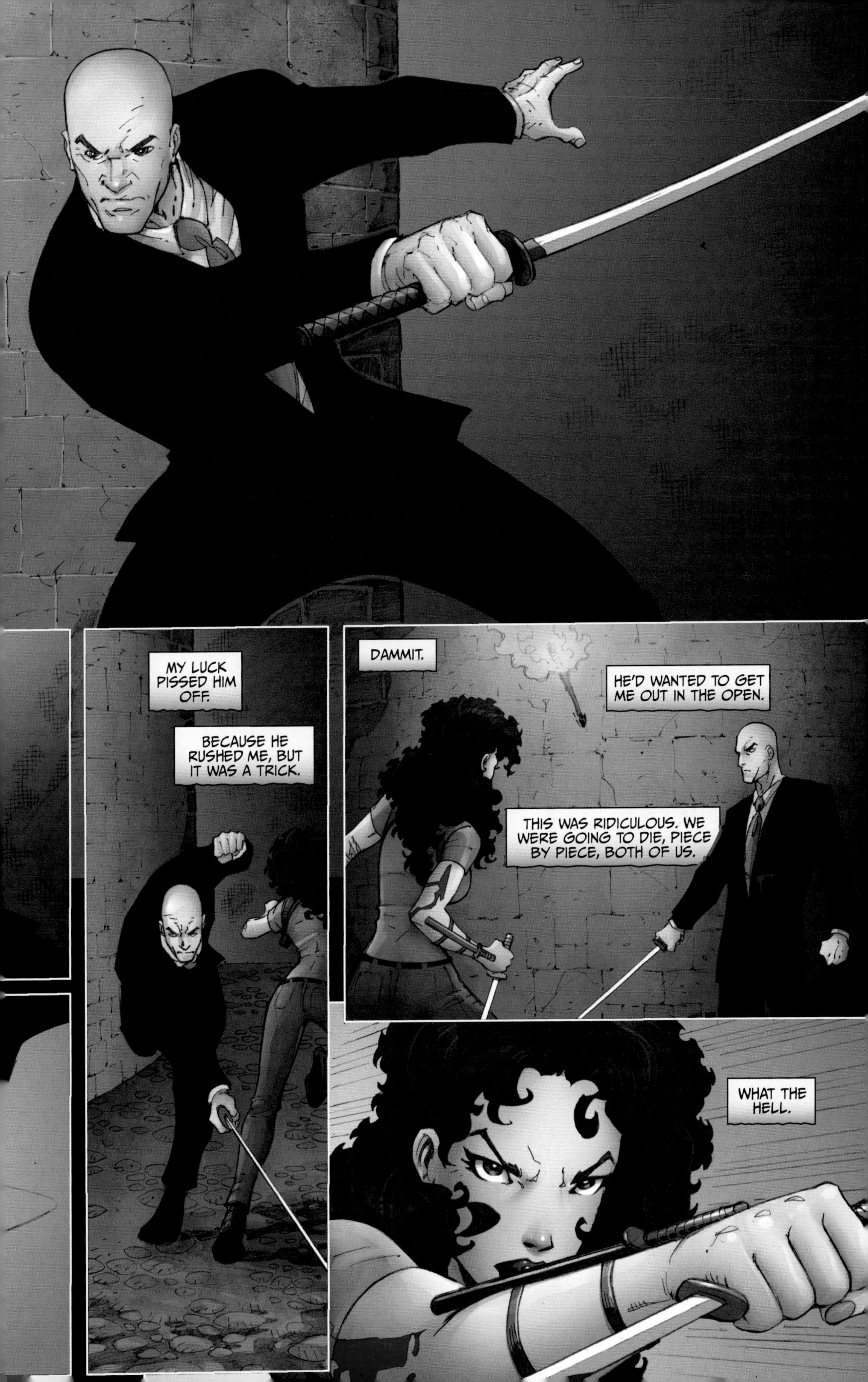

MY LUCK PISSED HIM OFF.
BECAUSE HE RUSHED ME, BUT IT WAS A TRICK.
DAMMIT.
HE'D WANTED TO GET ME OUT IN THE OPEN.
THIS WAS RIDICULOUS. WE WERE GOING TO DIE, PIECE BY PIECE, BOTH OF US.
WHAT THE HELL.

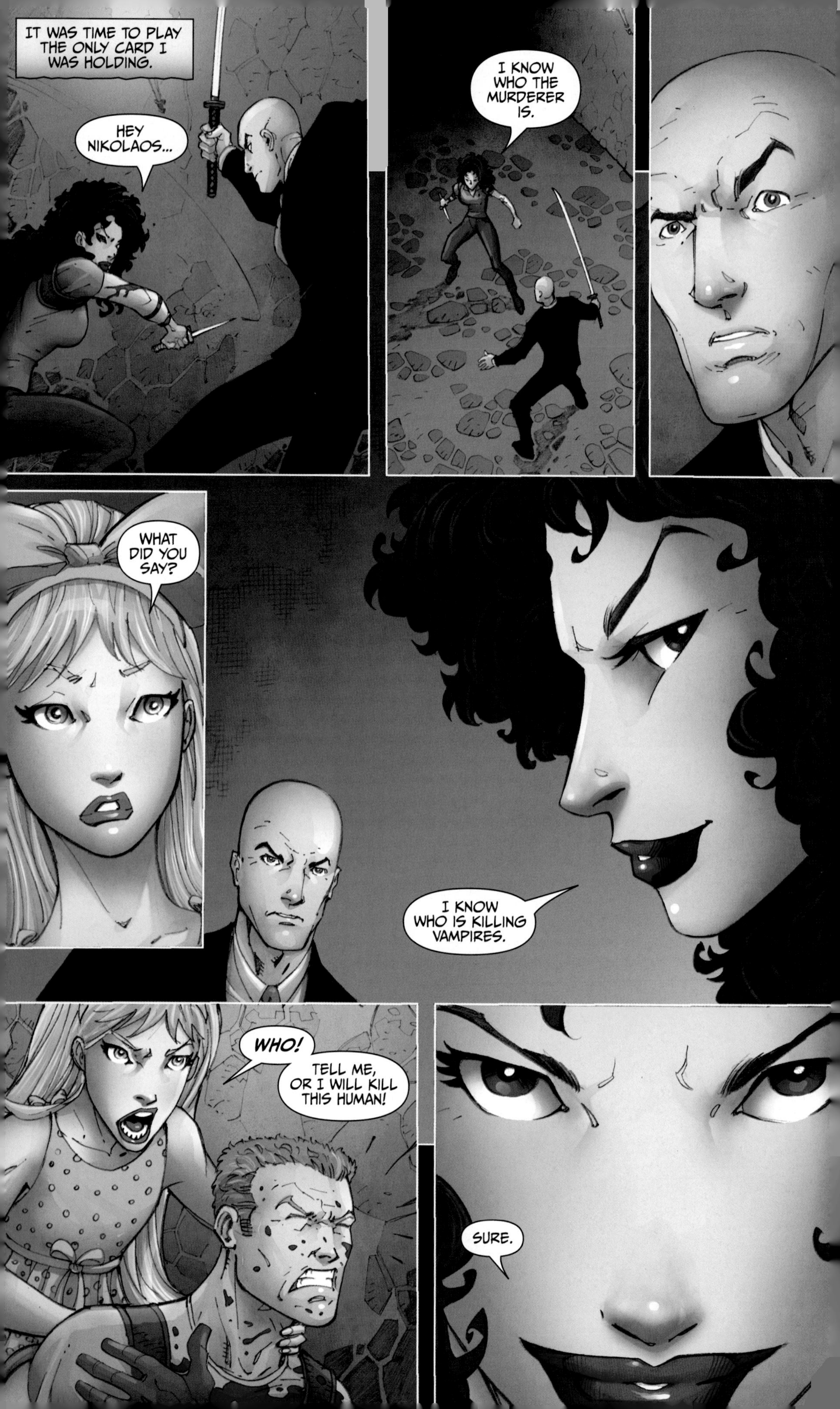
IT WAS TIME TO PLAY THE ONLY CARD I WAS HOLDING.
HEY NIKOLAOS...
I KNOW WHO THE MURDERER IS.
WHAT DID YOU SAY?
I KNOW WHO IS KILLING VAMPIRES.
WHO!
TELL ME, OR I WILL KILL THIS HUMAN!
SURE.

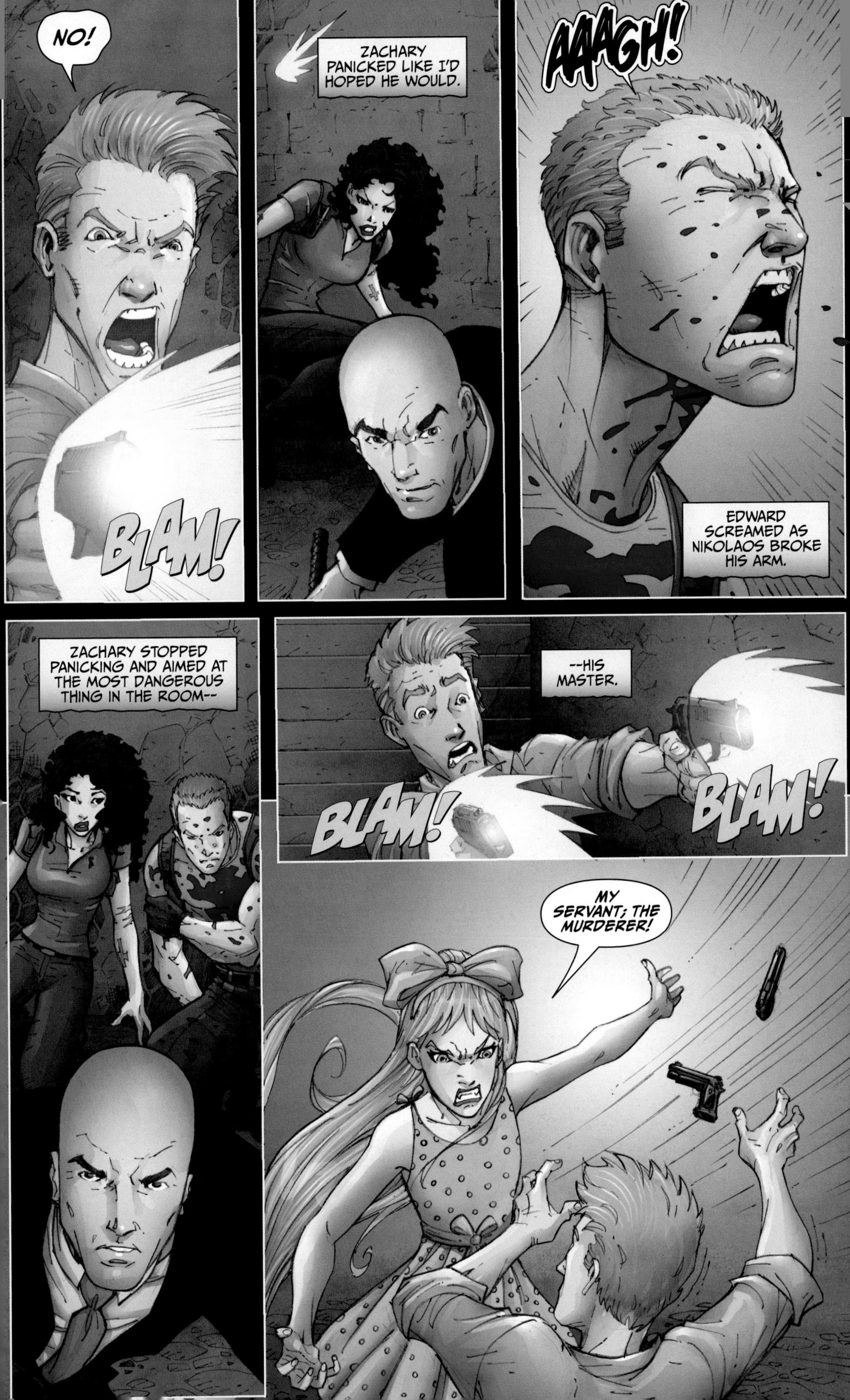
NO!
BLAM!
ZACHARY PANICKED LIKE I'D HOPED HE WOULD.
AAAGH!
EDWARD SCREAMED AS NIKOLAOS BROKE HIS ARM.
ZACHARY STOPPED PANICKING AND AIMED AT THE MOST DANGEROUS THING IN THE ROOM--
--HIS MASTER.
BLAM!
BLAM!
MY SERVANT; THE MURDERER!

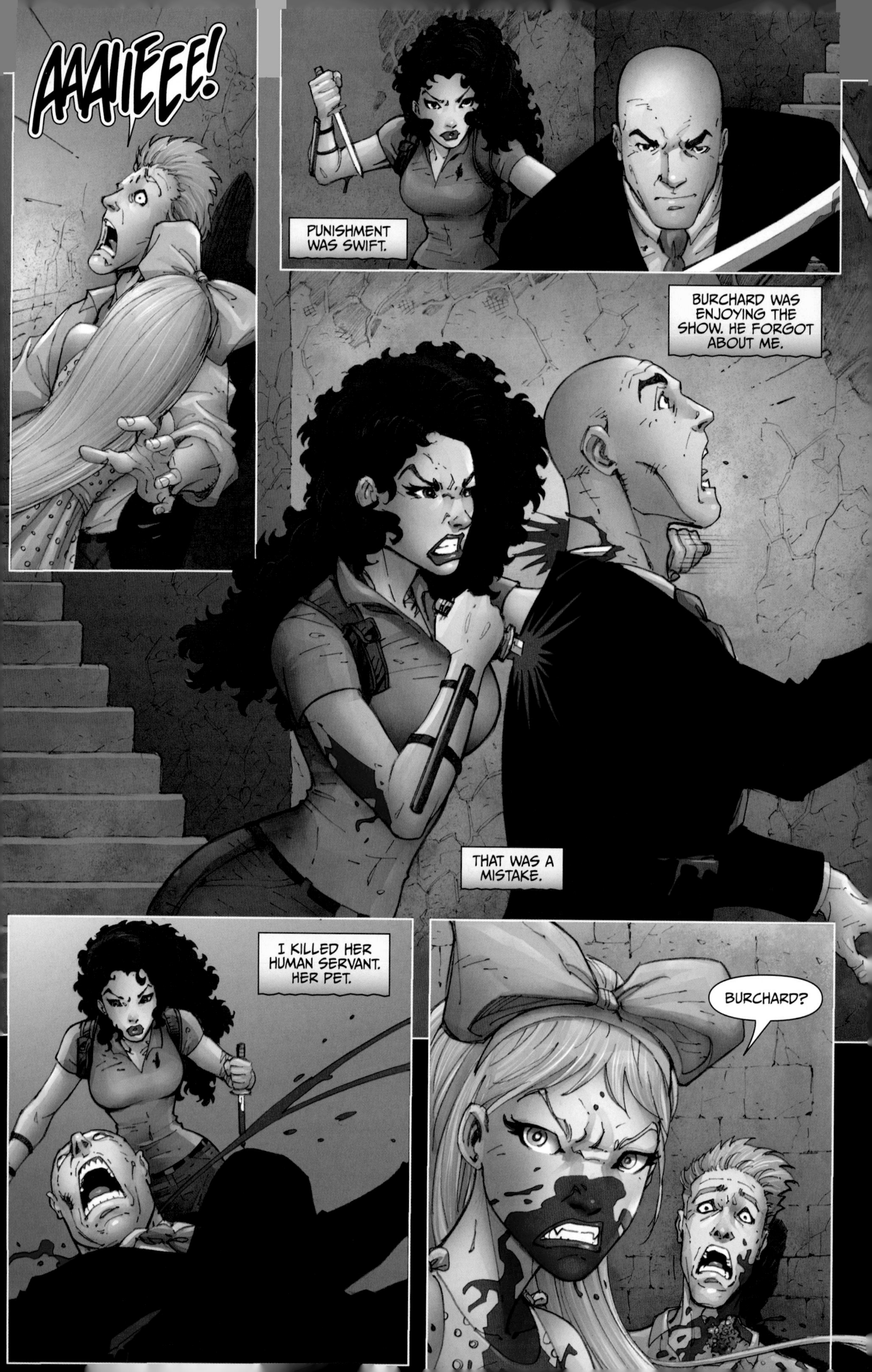
AAAIIEEE!
PUNISHMENT WAS SWIFT.
BURCHARD WAS ENJOYING THE SHOW. HE FORGOT ABOUT ME.
THAT WAS A MISTAKE.
I KILLED HER HUMAN SERVANT. HER PET.
BURCHARD?

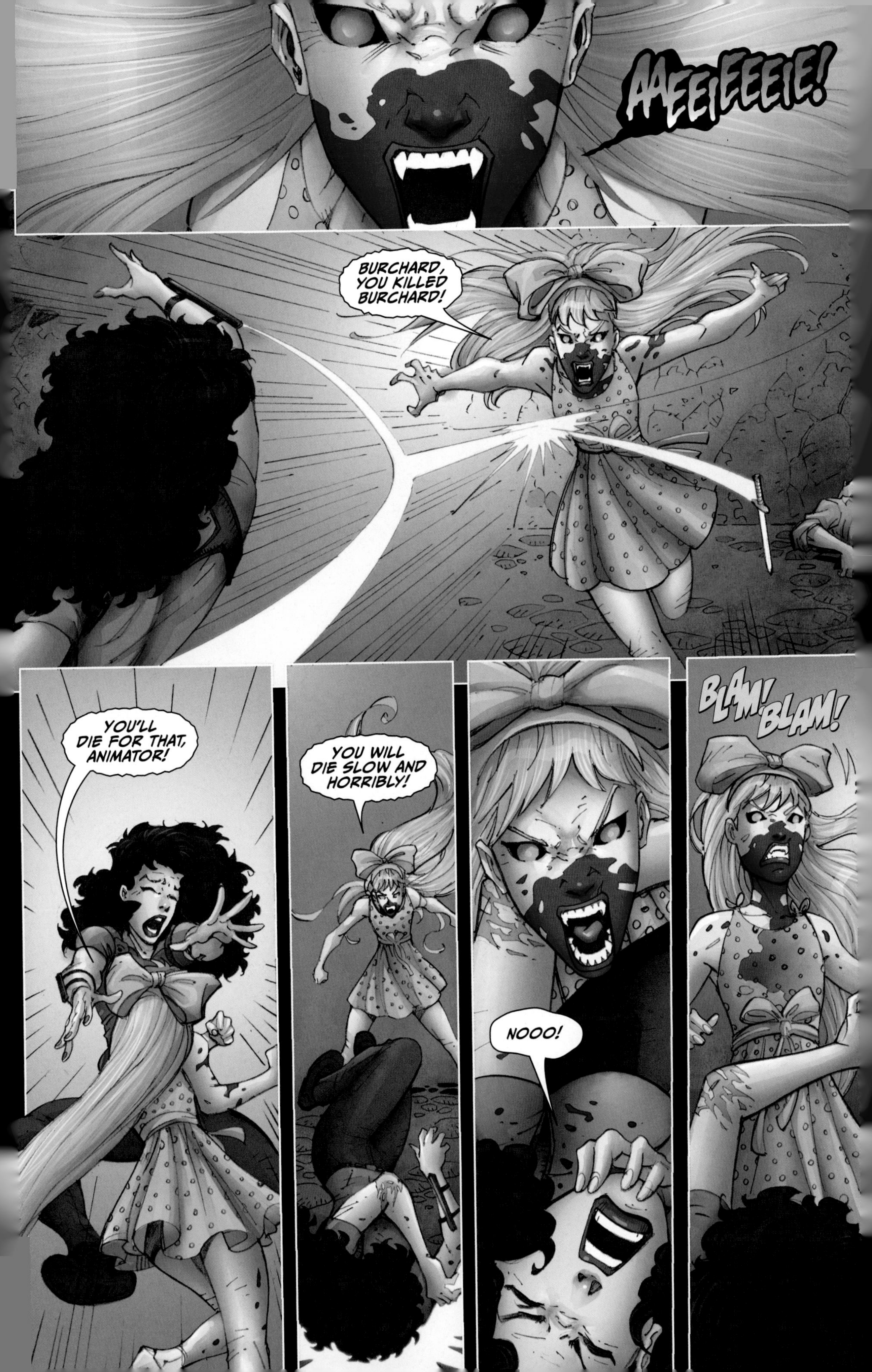
AAEEIEEEIE!
BURCHARD, YOU KILLED BURCHARD!
YOU'LL DIE FOR THAT, ANIMATOR!
YOU WILL DIE SLOW AND HORRIBLY!
NOOO!
BLAM! BLAM!

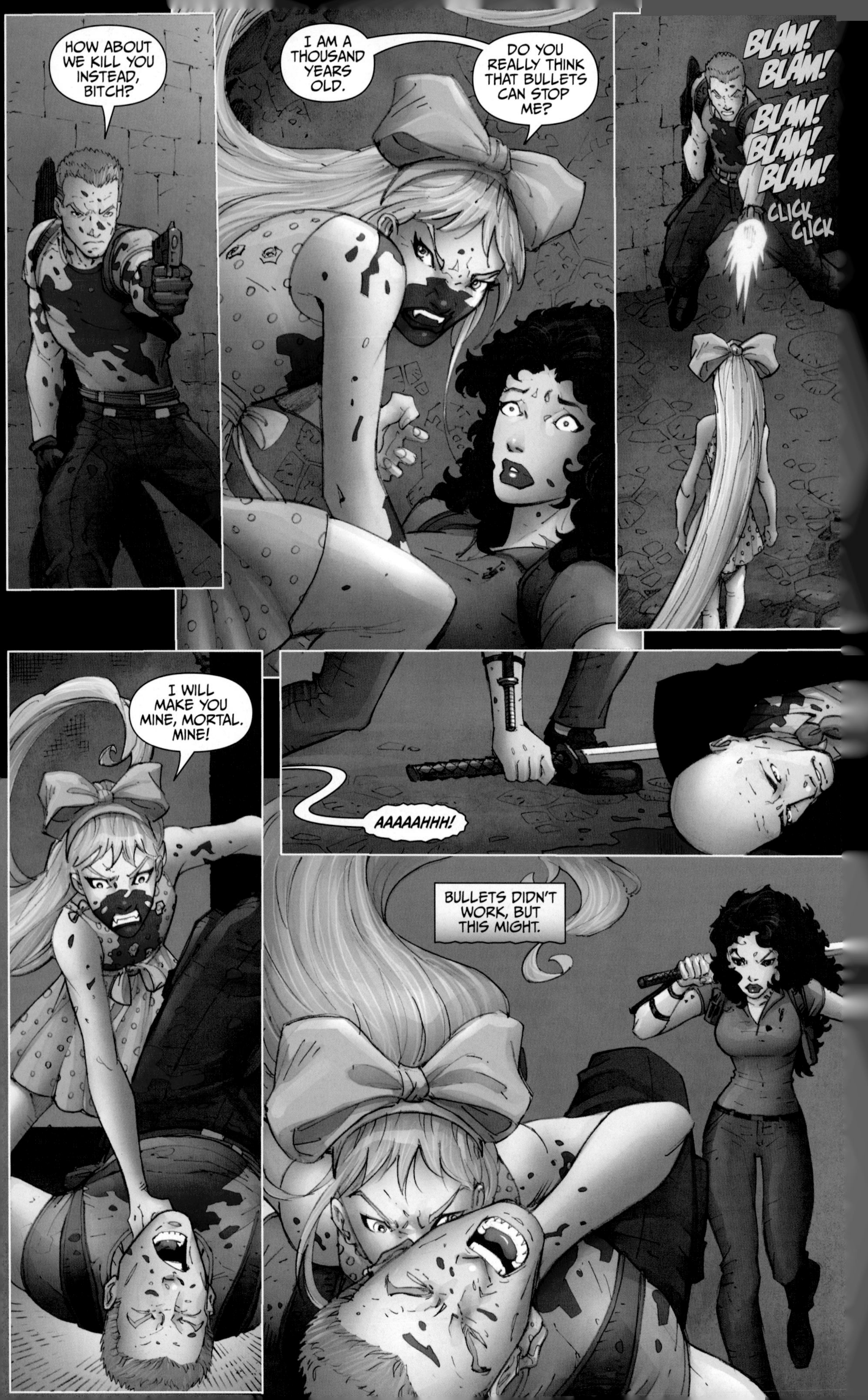
HOW ABOUT WE KILL YOU INSTEAD, BITCH?
I AM A THOUSAND YEARS OLD.
DO YOU REALLY THINK THAT BULLETS CAN STOP ME?
BLAM! BLAM!
BLAM! BLAM! BLAM!
CLICK CLICK
I WILL MAKE YOU MINE, MORTAL. MINE!
AAAAAHHH!
BULLETS DIDN'T WORK, BUT THIS MIGHT.

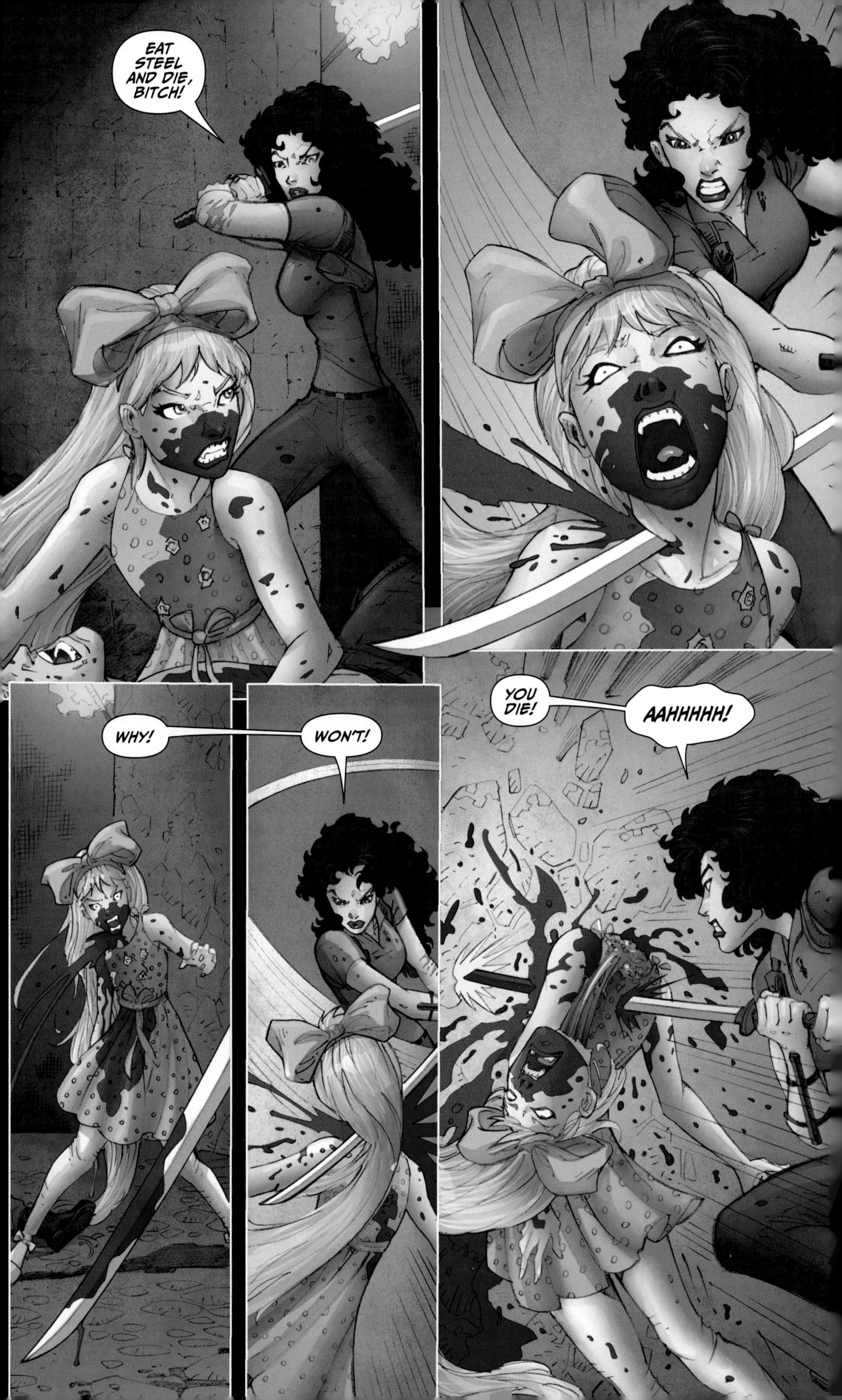
EAT STEEL AND DIE, BITCH!
WHY!
WON'T!
YOU DIE!
AAHHHHH!

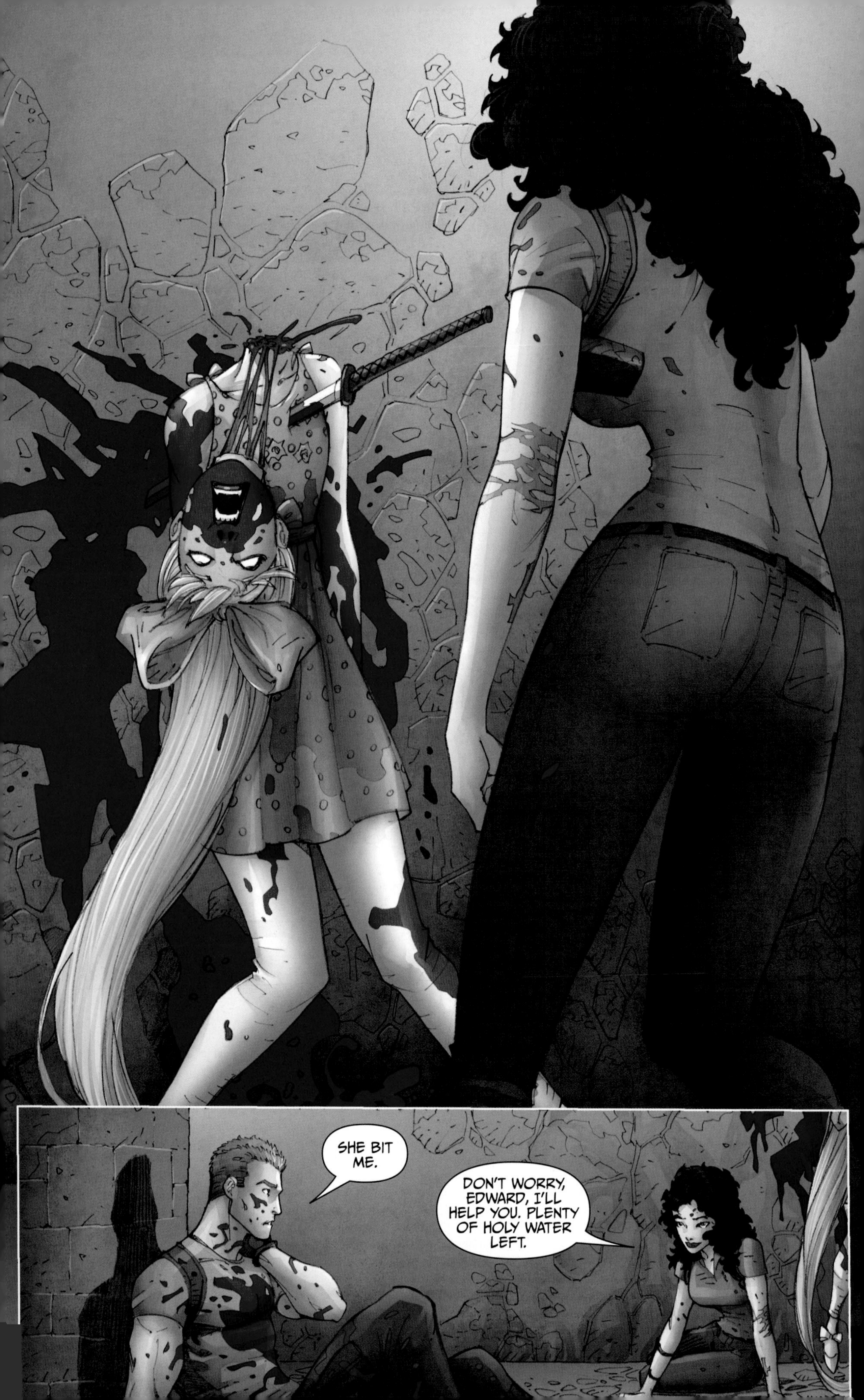
SHE BIT ME.
DON'T WORRY, EDWARD, I'LL HELP YOU. PLENTY OF HOLY WATER LEFT.

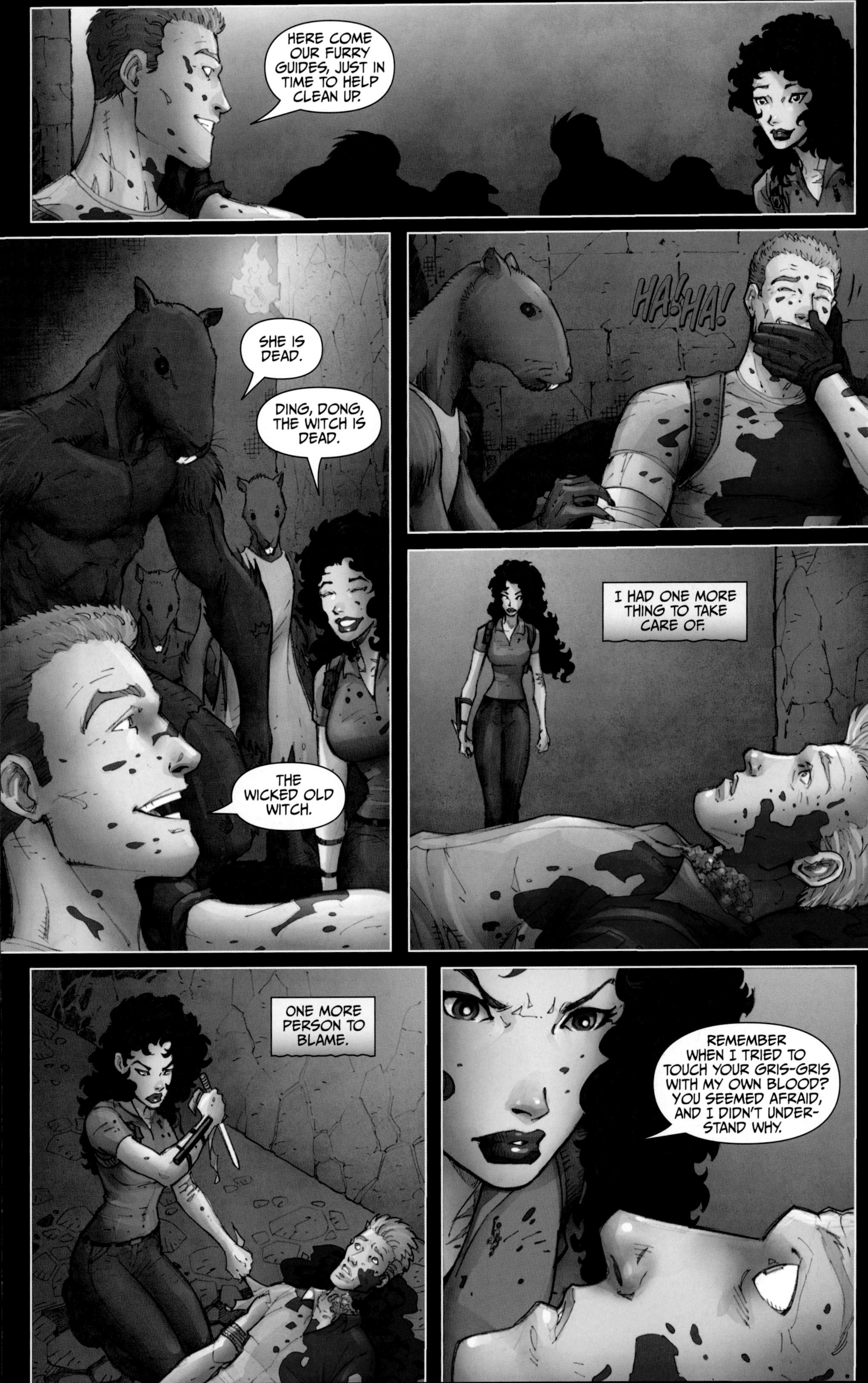
HERE COME OUR FURRY GUIDES, JUST IN TIME TO HELP CLEAN UP.
SHE IS DEAD.
DING, DONG, THE WITCH IS DEAD.
THE WICKED OLD WITCH.
HA! HA!
I HAD ONE MORE THING TO TAKE CARE OF.
ONE MORE PERSON TO BLAME.
REMEMBER WHEN I TRIED TO TOUCH YOUR GRIS-GRIS WITH MY OWN BLOOD? YOU SEEMED AFRAID, AND I DIDN'T UNDER-STAND WHY.

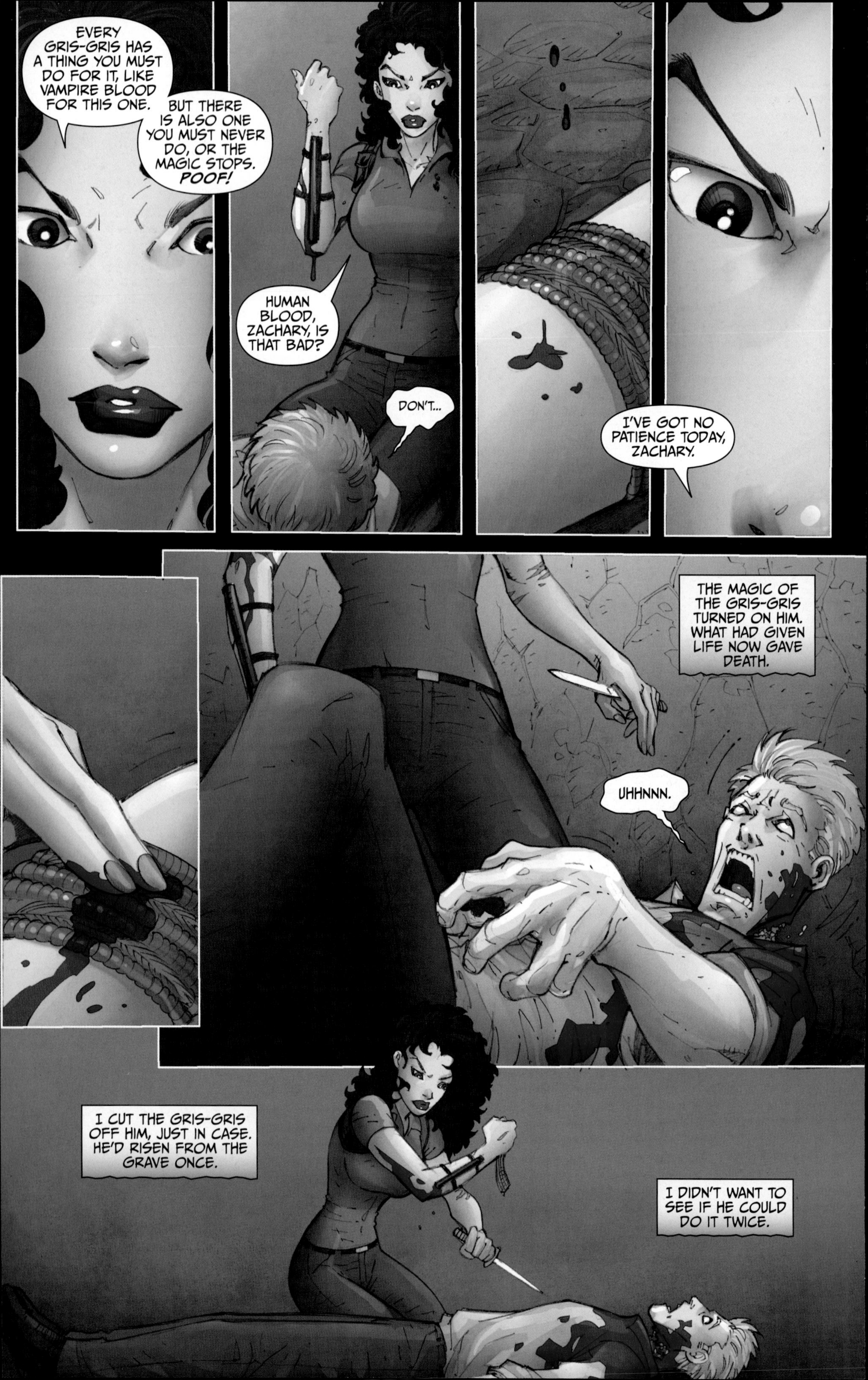

EVERY GRIS-GRIS HAS A THING YOU MUST DO FOR IT, LIKE VAMPIRE BLOOD FOR THIS ONE.
BUT THERE IS ALSO ONE YOU MUST NEVER DO, OR THE MAGIC STOPS. POOF!
HUMAN BLOOD, ZACHARY, IS THAT BAD?
DON'T...
I'VE GOT NO PATIENCE TODAY, ZACHARY.
THE MAGIC OF THE GRIS-GRIS TURNED ON HIM. WHAT HAD GIVEN LIFE NOW GAVE DEATH.
UHHNNN.
I CUT THE GRIS-GRIS OFF HIM, JUST IN CASE. HE'D RISEN FROM THE GRAVE ONCE.
I DIDN'T WANT TO SEE IF HE COULD DO IT TWICE.

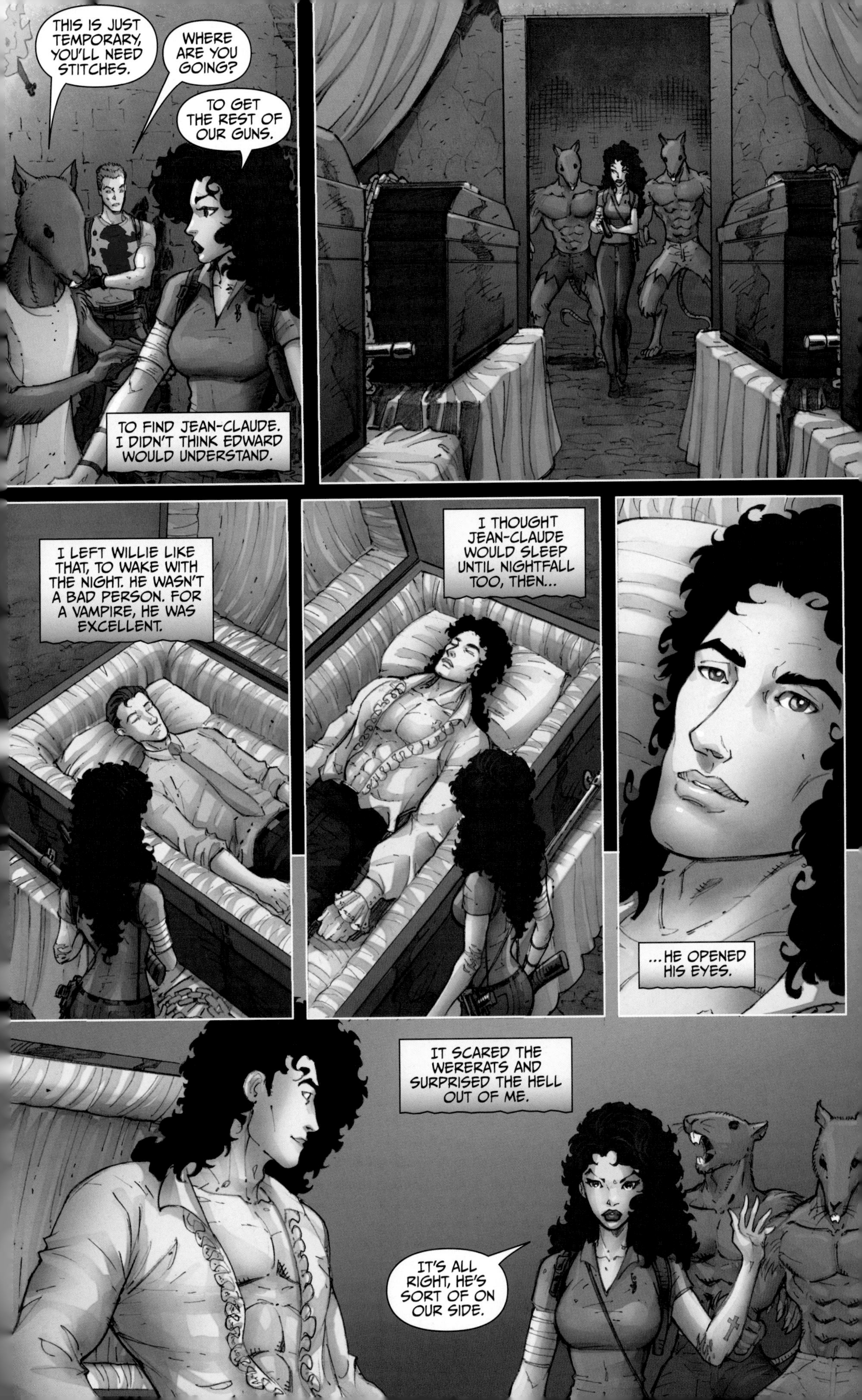
THIS IS JUST TEMPORARY, YOU'LL NEED STITCHES.
WHERE ARE YOU GOING?
TO GET THE REST OF OUR GUNS.
TO FIND JEAN-CLAUDE. I DIDN'T THINK EDWARD WOULD UNDERSTAND.
I LEFT WILLIE LIKE THAT, TO WAKE WITH THE NIGHT. HE WASN'T A BAD PERSON. FOR A VAMPIRE, HE WAS EXCELLENT.
I THOUGHT JEAN-CLAUDE WOULD SLEEP UNTIL NIGHTFALL TOO, THEN...
...HE OPENED HIS EYES.
IT SCARED THE WERERATS AND SURPRISED THE HELL OUT OF ME.
IT'S ALL RIGHT, HE'S SORT OF ON OUR SIDE.

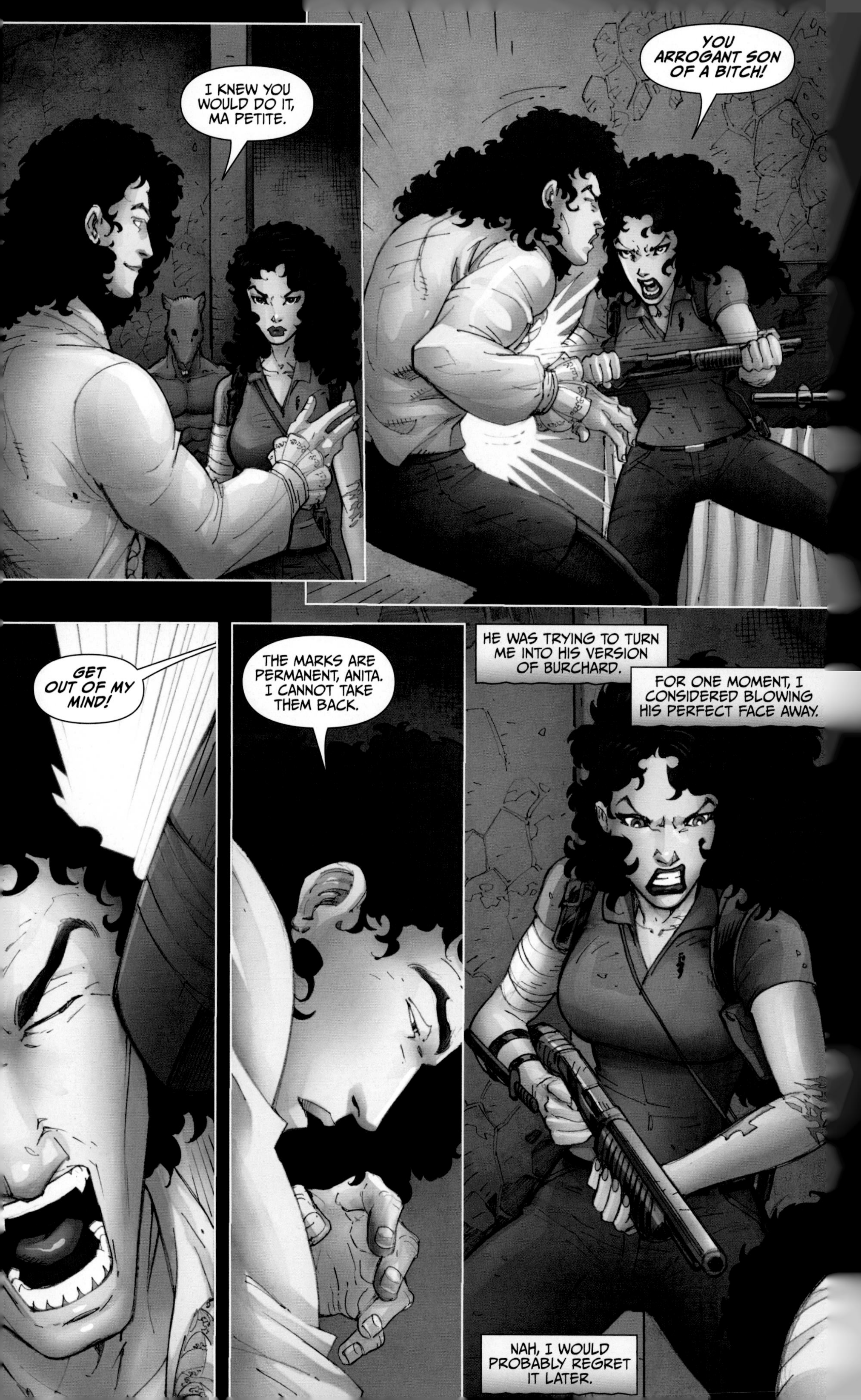
I KNEW YOU WOULD DO IT, MA PETITE.
YOU ARROGANT SON OF A BITCH!
GET OUT OF MY MIND!
THE MARKS ARE PERMANENT, ANITA. I CANNOT TAKE THEM BACK.
HE WAS TRYING TO TURN ME INTO HIS VERSION OF BURCHARD.
FOR ONE MOMENT, I CONSIDERED BLOWING HIS PERFECT FACE AWAY.
NAH, I WOULD PROBABLY REGRET IT LATER.

CAN YOU STAY OUT OF MY DREAMS, AT LEAST?

THAT I CAN DO.

I AM SORRY, MA PETITE.

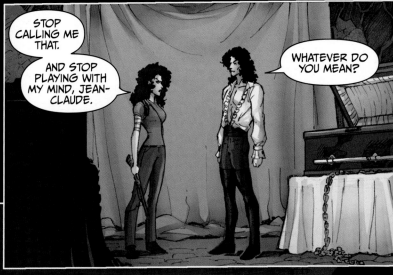

STOP CALLING ME THAT.

AND STOP PLAYING WITH MY MIND, JEAN-CLAUDE.

WHATEVER DO YOU MEAN?

I KNOW THE OTHERWORLDLY BEAUTY IS A TRICK. SO STOP IT.

I AM NOT DOING IT.

WHAT IS THAT SUPPOSED TO MEAN?

WHEN YOU HAVE THE ANSWER, ANITA, COME BACK TO ME, AND WE WILL TALK.

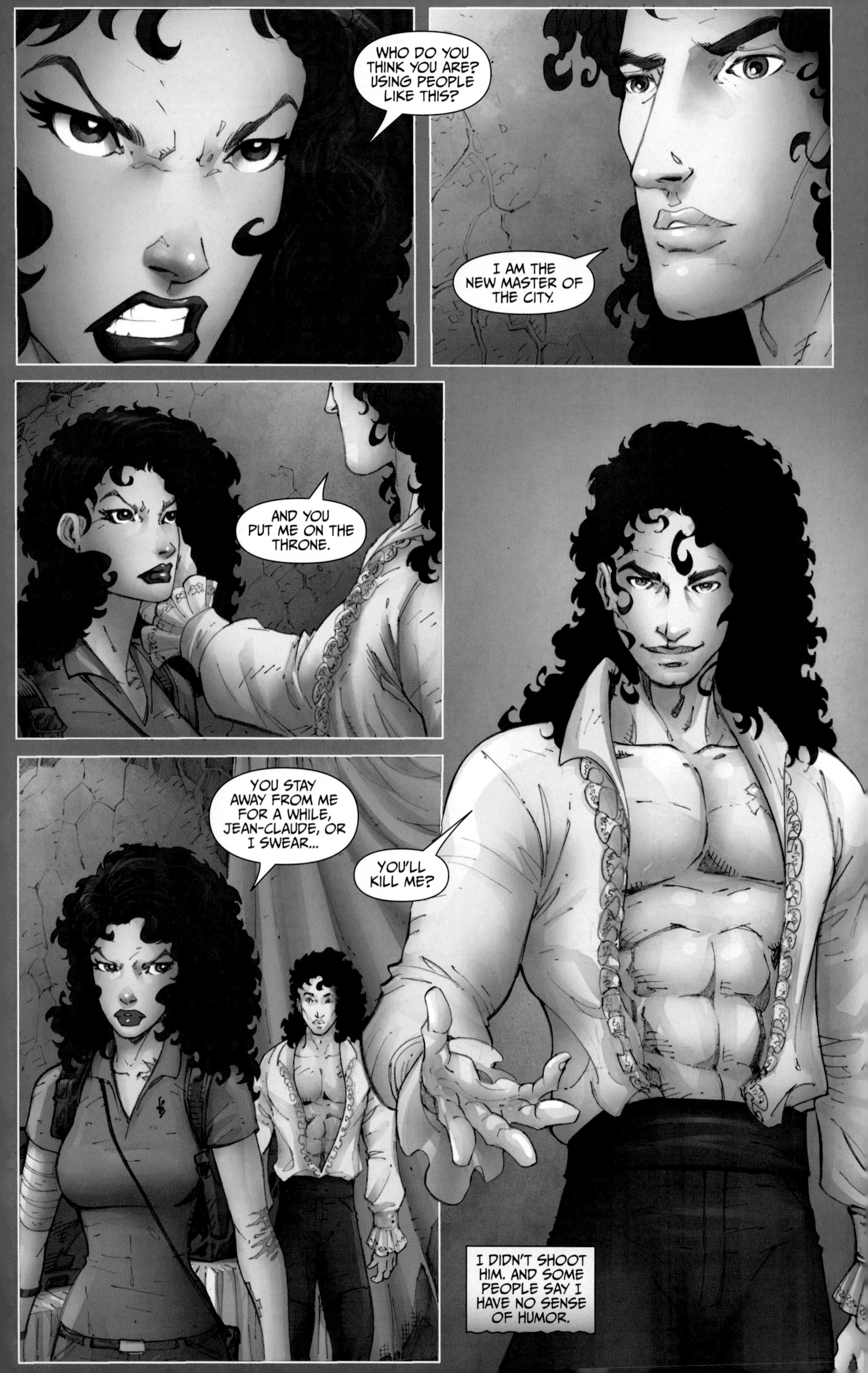
WHO DO YOU THINK YOU ARE? USING PEOPLE LIKE THIS?
I AM THE NEW MASTER OF THE CITY.
AND YOU PUT ME ON THE THRONE.
YOU STAY AWAY FROM ME FOR A WHILE, JEAN-CLAUDE, OR I SWEAR...
YOU'LL KILL ME?
I DIDN'T SHOOT HIM. AND SOME PEOPLE SAY I HAVE NO SENSE OF HUMOR.

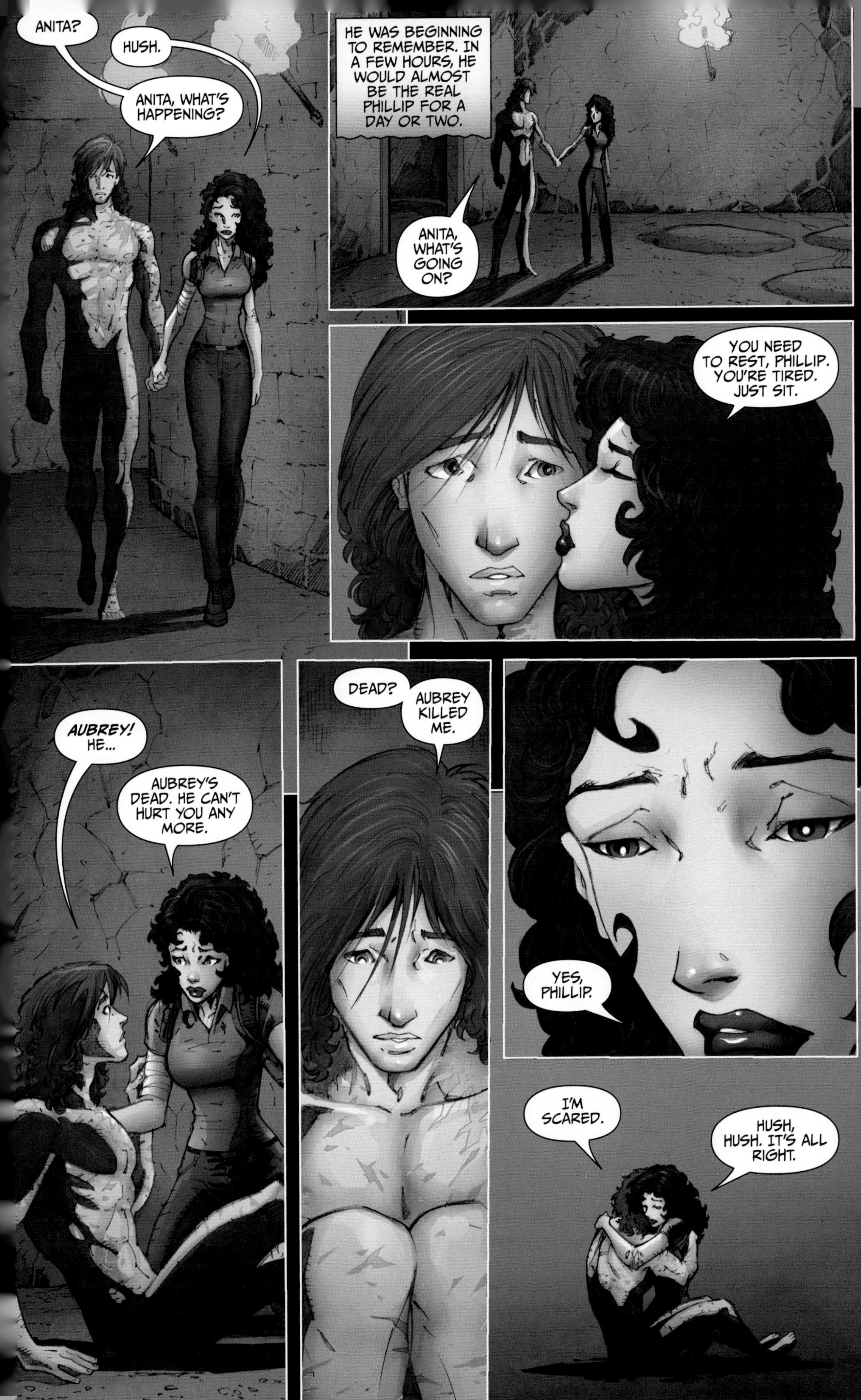
ANITA?
HUSH.
ANITA, WHAT'S HAPPENING?
HE WAS BEGINNING TO REMEMBER. IN A FEW HOURS, HE WOULD ALMOST BE THE REAL PHILLIP FOR A DAY OR TWO.
ANITA, WHAT'S GOING ON?
YOU NEED TO REST, PHILLIP. YOU'RE TIRED. JUST SIT.
AUBREY! HE...
AUBREY'S DEAD. HE CAN'T HURT YOU ANY MORE.
DEAD?
AUBREY KILLED ME.
YES, PHILLIP.
I'M SCARED.
HUSH, HUSH. IT'S ALL RIGHT.

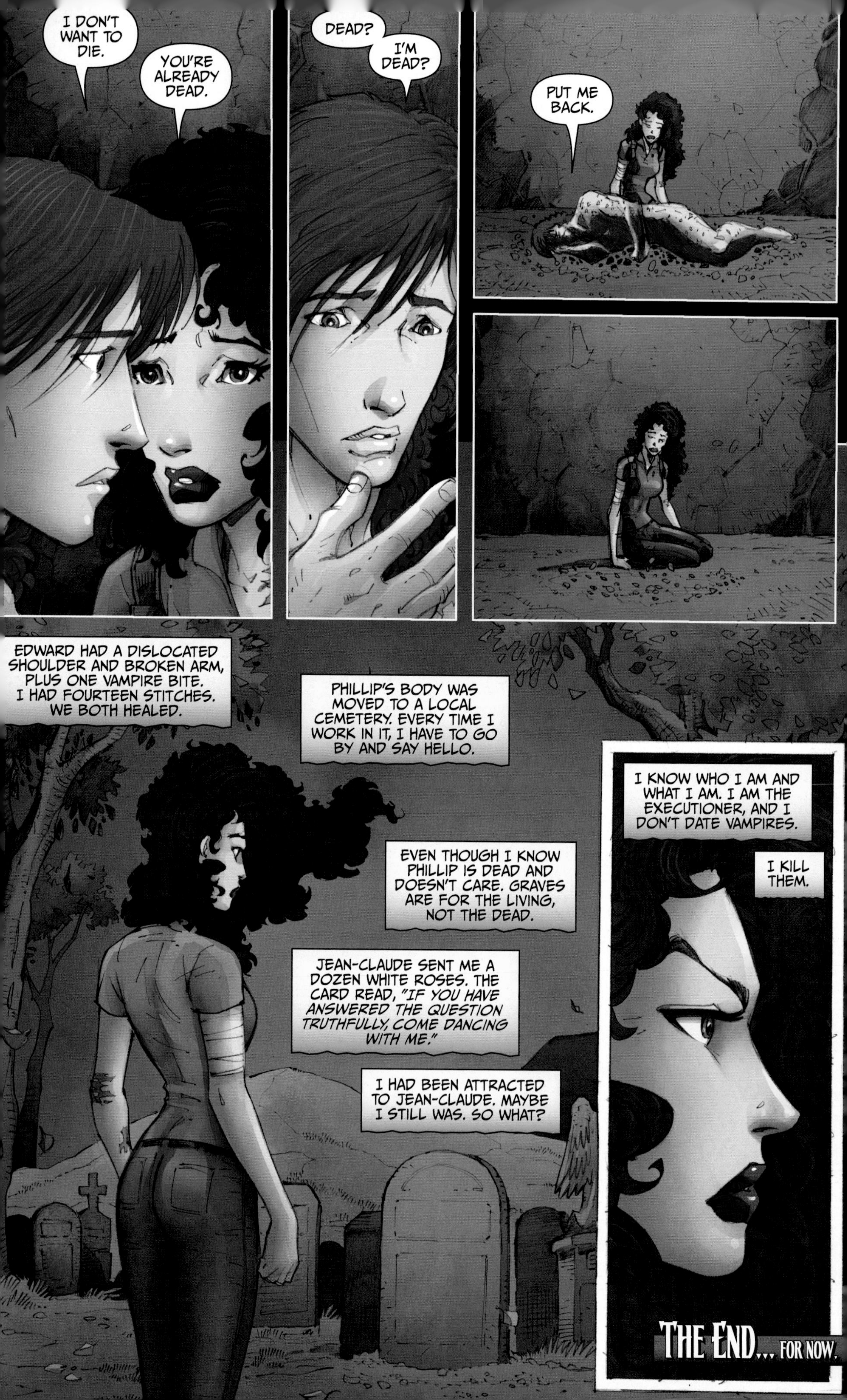
I DON'T WANT TO DIE.
YOU'RE ALREADY DEAD.
DEAD?
I'M DEAD?
PUT ME BACK.
EDWARD HAD A DISLOCATED SHOULDER AND BROKEN ARM, PLUS ONE VAMPIRE BITE. I HAD FOURTEEN STITCHES. WE BOTH HEALED.
PHILLIP'S BODY WAS MOVED TO A LOCAL CEMETERY. EVERY TIME I WORK IN IT, I HAVE TO GO BY AND SAY HELLO.
EVEN THOUGH I KNOW PHILLIP IS DEAD AND DOESN'T CARE. GRAVES ARE FOR THE LIVING, NOT THE DEAD.
JEAN-CLAUDE SENT ME A DOZEN WHITE ROSES. THE CARD READ, "IF YOU HAVE ANSWERED THE QUESTION TRUTHFULLY, COME DANCING WITH ME."
I HAD BEEN ATTRACTED TO JEAN-CLAUDE. MAYBE I STILL WAS. SO WHAT?
I KNOW WHO I AM AND WHAT I AM. I AM THE EXECUTIONER, AND I DON'T DATE VAMPIRES.
I KILL THEM.
THE END... FOR NOW.

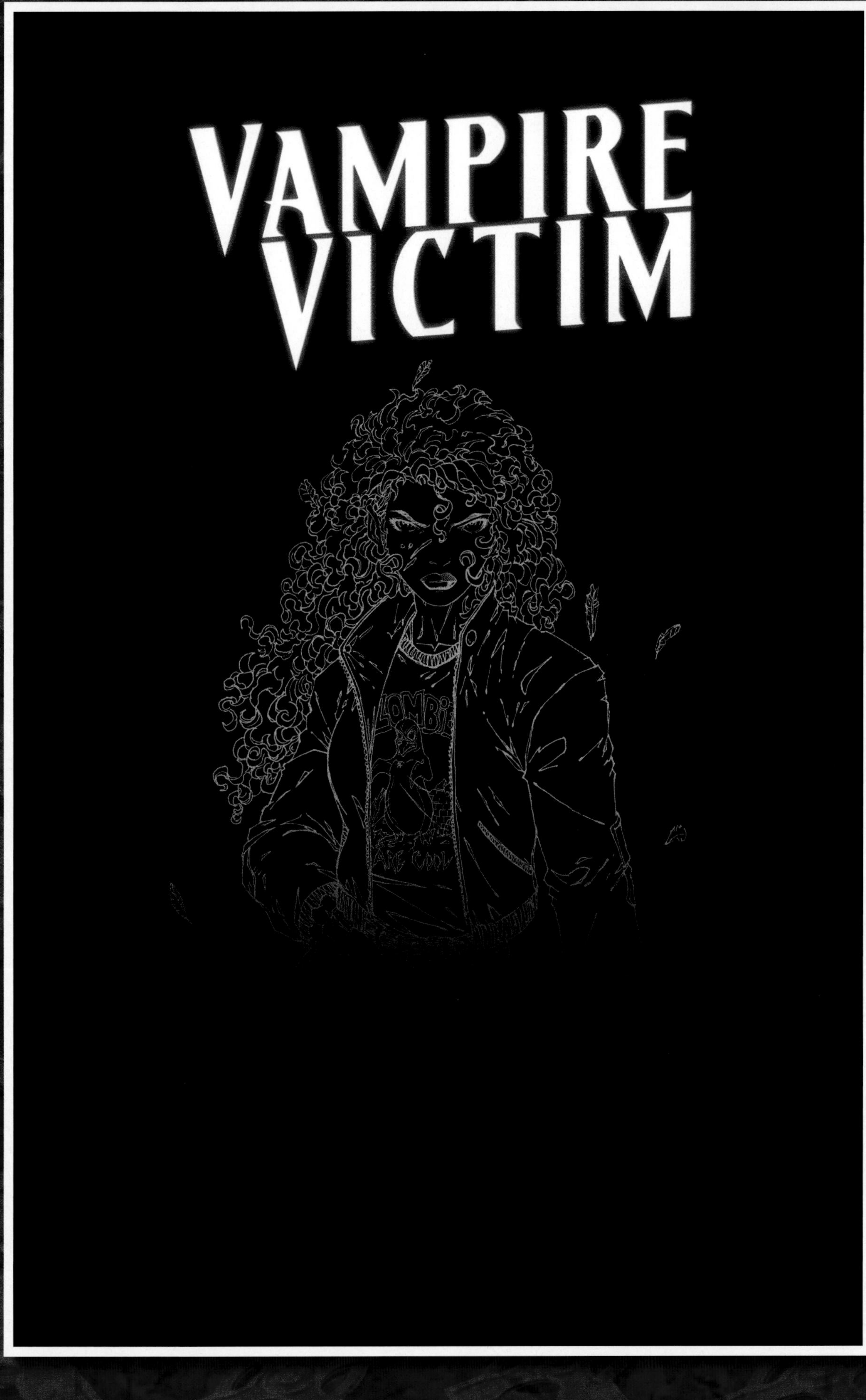
VAMPIRE
VICTIM
ARE COOL

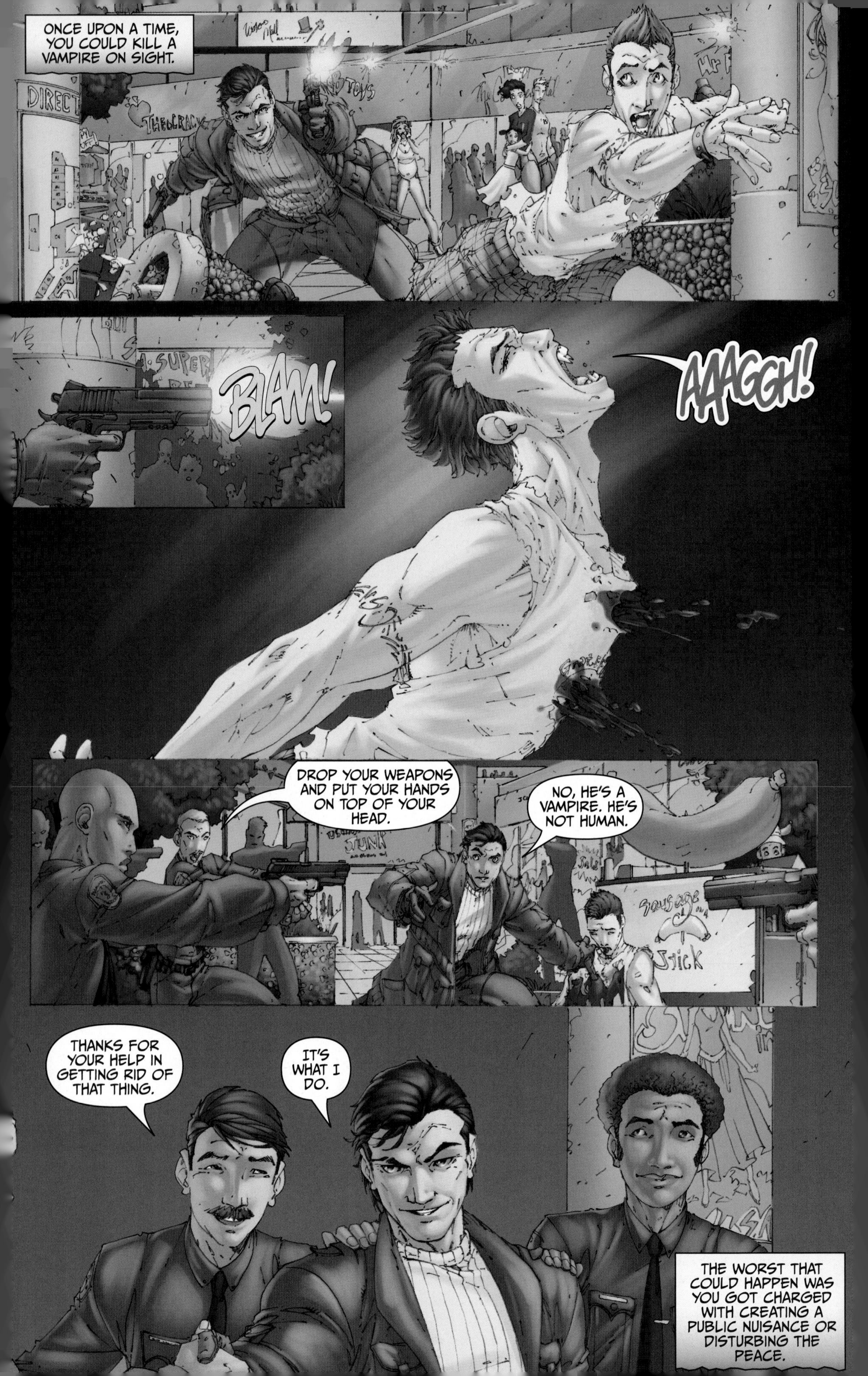
ONCE UPON A TIME, YOU COULD KILL A VAMPIRE ON SIGHT.
BLAM!
AAAGGH!
DROP YOUR WEAPONS AND PUT YOUR HANDS ON TOP OF YOUR HEAD.
NO, HE'S A VAMPIRE. HE'S NOT HUMAN.
THANKS FOR YOUR HELP IN GETTING RID OF THAT THING.
IT'S WHAT I DO.
THE WORST THAT COULD HAPPEN WAS YOU GOT CHARGED WITH CREATING A PUBLIC NUISANCE OR DISTURBING THE PEACE.

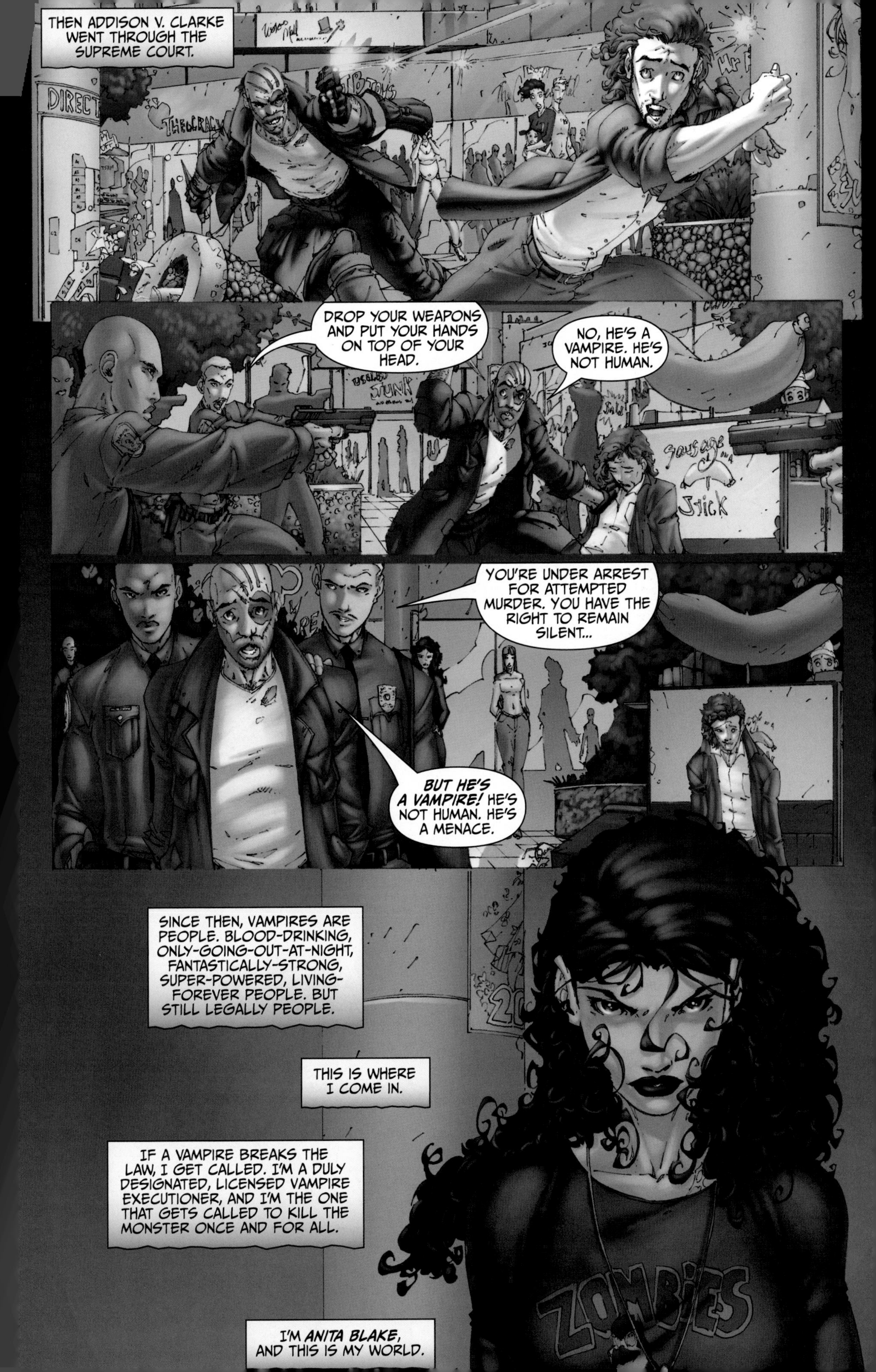

THEN ADDISON V. CLARKE WENT THROUGH THE SUPREME COURT.
DROP YOUR WEAPONS AND PUT YOUR HANDS ON TOP OF YOUR HEAD.
NO, HE'S A VAMPIRE. HE'S NOT HUMAN.
YOU'RE UNDER ARREST FOR ATTEMPTED MURDER. YOU HAVE THE RIGHT TO REMAIN SILENT...
BUT HE'S A VAMPIRE! HE'S NOT HUMAN. HE'S A MENACE.
SINCE THEN, VAMPIRES ARE PEOPLE. BLOOD-DRINKING, ONLY-GOING-OUT-AT-NIGHT, FANTASTICALLY-STRONG, SUPER-POWERED, LIVING-FOREVER PEOPLE. BUT STILL LEGALLY PEOPLE.
THIS IS WHERE I COME IN.
IF A VAMPIRE BREAKS THE LAW, I GET CALLED. I'M A DULY DESIGNATED, LICENSED VAMPIRE EXECUTIONER, AND I'M THE ONE THAT GETS CALLED TO KILL THE MONSTER ONCE AND FOR ALL.
I'M *ANITA BLAKE*, AND THIS IS MY WORLD.

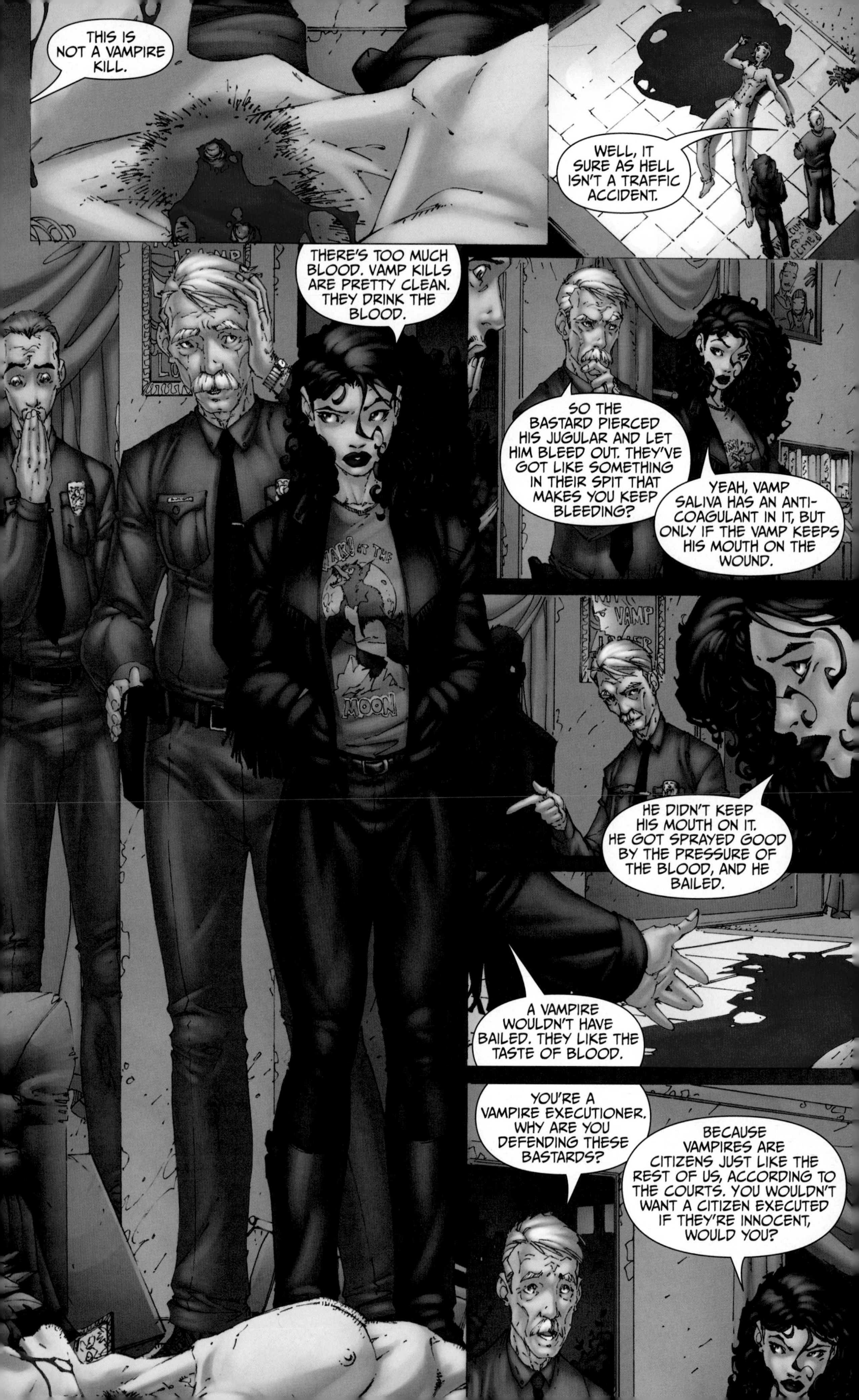
THIS IS NOT A VAMPIRE KILL.
WELL, IT SURE AS HELL ISN'T A TRAFFIC ACCIDENT.
THERE'S TOO MUCH BLOOD. VAMP KILLS ARE PRETTY CLEAN. THEY DRINK THE BLOOD.
SO THE BASTARD PIERCED HIS JUGULAR AND LET HIM BLEED OUT. THEY'VE GOT LIKE SOMETHING IN THEIR SPIT THAT MAKES YOU KEEP BLEEDING?
YEAH, VAMP SALIVA HAS AN ANTI-COAGULANT IN IT, BUT ONLY IF THE VAMP KEEPS HIS MOUTH ON THE WOUND.
HE DIDN'T KEEP HIS MOUTH ON IT. HE GOT SPRAYED GOOD BY THE PRESSURE OF THE BLOOD, AND HE BAILED.
A VAMPIRE WOULDN'T HAVE BAILED. THEY LIKE THE TASTE OF BLOOD.
YOU'RE A VAMPIRE EXECUTIONER. WHY ARE YOU DEFENDING THESE BASTARDS?
BECAUSE VAMPIRES ARE CITIZENS JUST LIKE THE REST OF US, ACCORDING TO THE COURTS. YOU WOULDN'T WANT A CITIZEN EXECUTED IF THEY'RE INNOCENT, WOULD YOU?

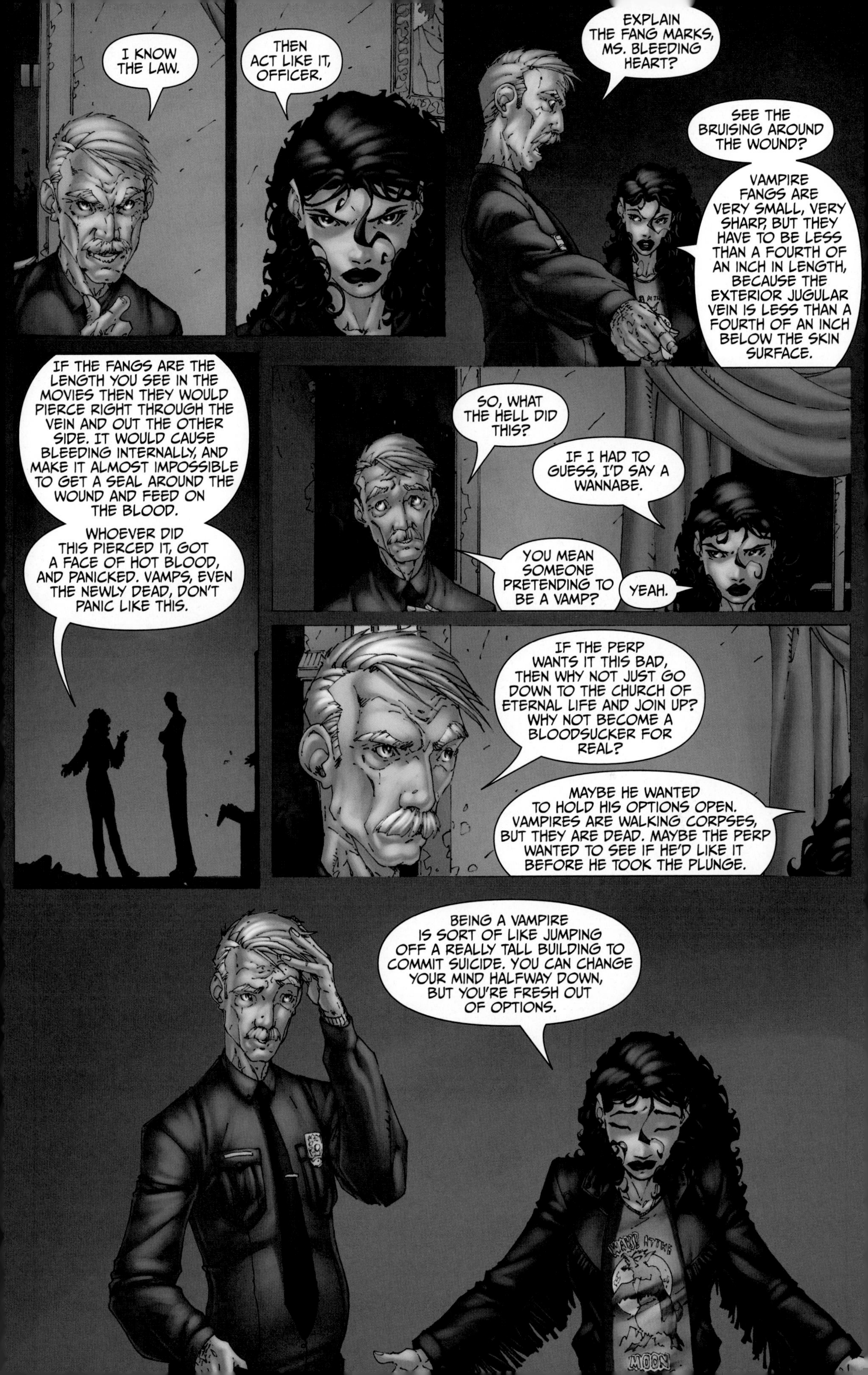
I KNOW THE LAW.
THEN ACT LIKE IT, OFFICER.
EXPLAIN THE FANG MARKS, MS. BLEEDING HEART?
SEE THE BRUISING AROUND THE WOUND?
VAMPIRE FANGS ARE VERY SMALL, VERY SHARP, BUT THEY HAVE TO BE LESS THAN A FOURTH OF AN INCH IN LENGTH, BECAUSE THE EXTERIOR JUGULAR VEIN IS LESS THAN A FOURTH OF AN INCH BELOW THE SKIN SURFACE.
IF THE FANGS ARE THE LENGTH YOU SEE IN THE MOVIES THEN THEY WOULD PIERCE RIGHT THROUGH THE VEIN AND OUT THE OTHER SIDE. IT WOULD CAUSE BLEEDING INTERNALLY, AND MAKE IT ALMOST IMPOSSIBLE TO GET A SEAL AROUND THE WOUND AND FEED ON THE BLOOD.
WHOEVER DID THIS PIERCED IT, GOT A FACE OF HOT BLOOD, AND PANICKED. VAMPS, EVEN THE NEWLY DEAD, DON'T PANIC LIKE THIS.
SO, WHAT THE HELL DID THIS?
IF I HAD TO GUESS, I'D SAY A WANNABE.
YOU MEAN SOMEONE PRETENDING TO BE A VAMP?
YEAH.
IF THE PERP WANTS IT THIS BAD, THEN WHY NOT JUST GO DOWN TO THE CHURCH OF ETERNAL LIFE AND JOIN UP? WHY NOT BECOME A BLOODSUCKER FOR REAL?
MAYBE HE WANTED TO HOLD HIS OPTIONS OPEN. VAMPIRES ARE WALKING CORPSES, BUT THEY ARE DEAD. MAYBE THE PERP WANTED TO SEE IF HE'D LIKE IT BEFORE HE TOOK THE PLUNGE.
BEING A VAMPIRE IS SORT OF LIKE JUMPING OFF A REALLY TALL BUILDING TO COMMIT SUICIDE. YOU CAN CHANGE YOUR MIND HALFWAY DOWN, BUT YOU'RE FRESH OUT OF OPTIONS.
MOON

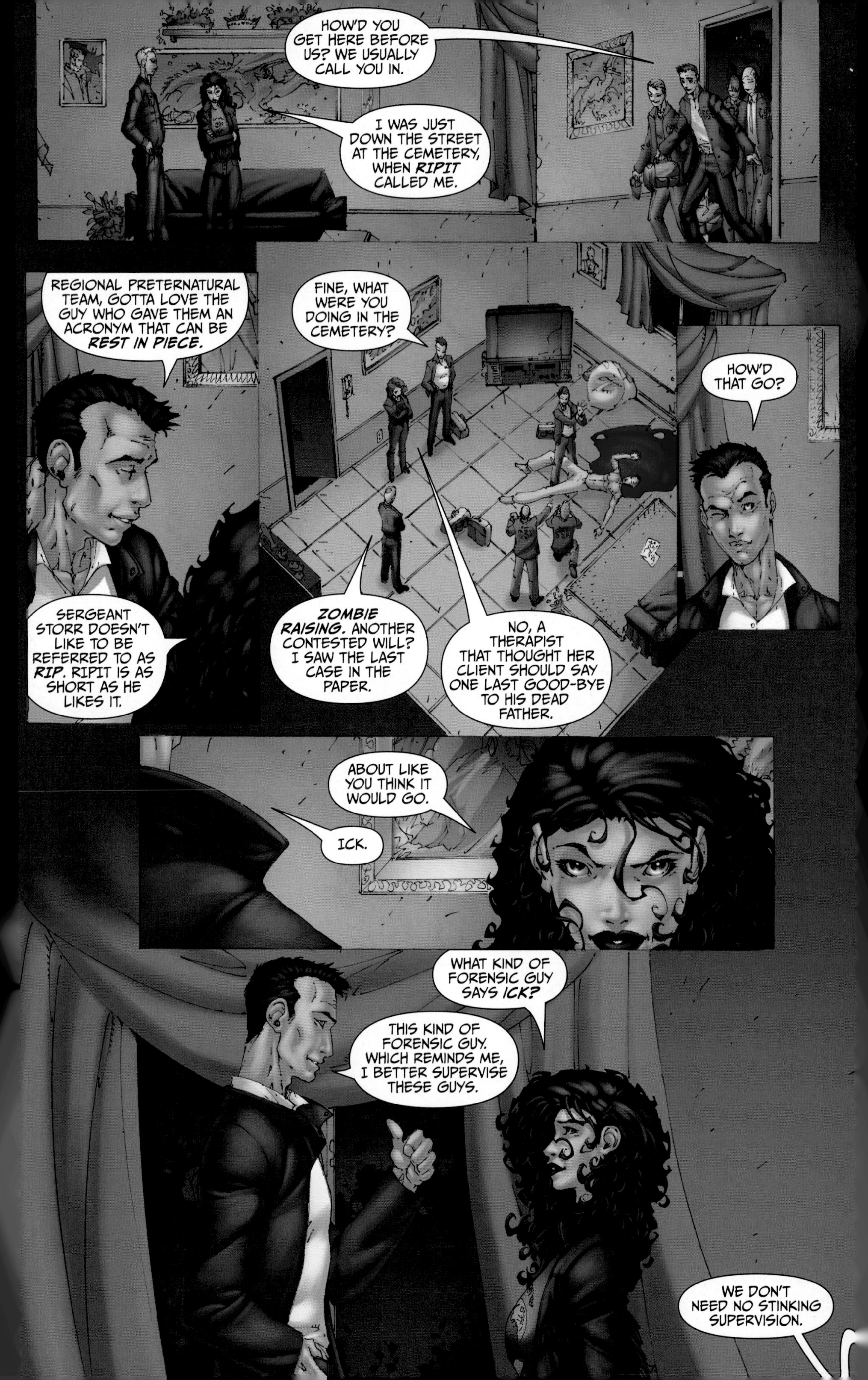
HOW'D YOU GET HERE BEFORE US? WE USUALLY CALL YOU IN.
I WAS JUST DOWN THE STREET AT THE CEMETERY, WHEN RIPIT CALLED ME.
REGIONAL PRETERNATURAL TEAM, GOTTA LOVE THE GUY WHO GAVE THEM AN ACRONYM THAT CAN BE REST IN PIECE.
SERGEANT STORR DOESN'T LIKE TO BE REFERRED TO AS RIP. RIPIT IS AS SHORT AS HE LIKES IT.
FINE, WHAT WERE YOU DOING IN THE CEMETERY?
ZOMBIE RAISING. ANOTHER CONTESTED WILL? I SAW THE LAST CASE IN THE PAPER.
NO, A THERAPIST THAT THOUGHT HER CLIENT SHOULD SAY ONE LAST GOOD-BYE TO HIS DEAD FATHER.
HOW'D THAT GO?
ABOUT LIKE YOU THINK IT WOULD GO.
ICK.
WHAT KIND OF FORENSIC GUY SAYS ICK?
THIS KIND OF FORENSIC GUY. WHICH REMINDS ME, I BETTER SUPERVISE THESE GUYS.
WE DON'T NEED NO STINKING SUPERVISION.

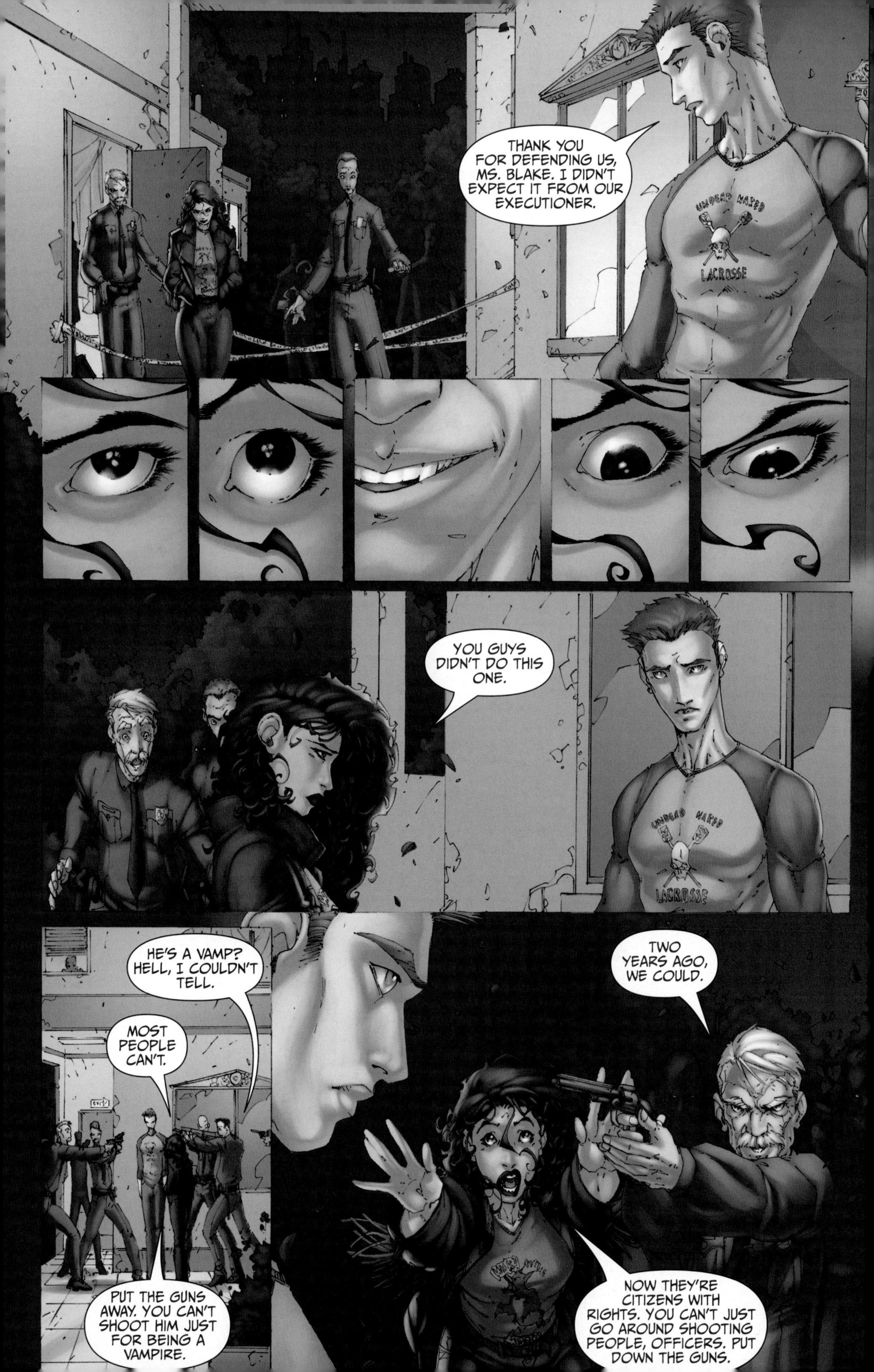
THANK YOU FOR DEFENDING US, MS. BLAKE. I DIDN'T EXPECT IT FROM OUR EXECUTIONER.
UNDEAD NAKED LACROSSE
YOU GUYS DIDN'T DO THIS ONE.
UNDEAD NAKED LACROSSE
HE'S A VAMP? HELL, I COULDN'T TELL.
MOST PEOPLE CAN'T.
PUT THE GUNS AWAY. YOU CAN'T SHOOT HIM JUST FOR BEING A VAMPIRE.
TWO YEARS AGO, WE COULD.
NOW THEY'RE CITIZENS WITH RIGHTS. YOU CAN'T JUST GO AROUND SHOOTING PEOPLE, OFFICERS. PUT DOWN THE GUNS.

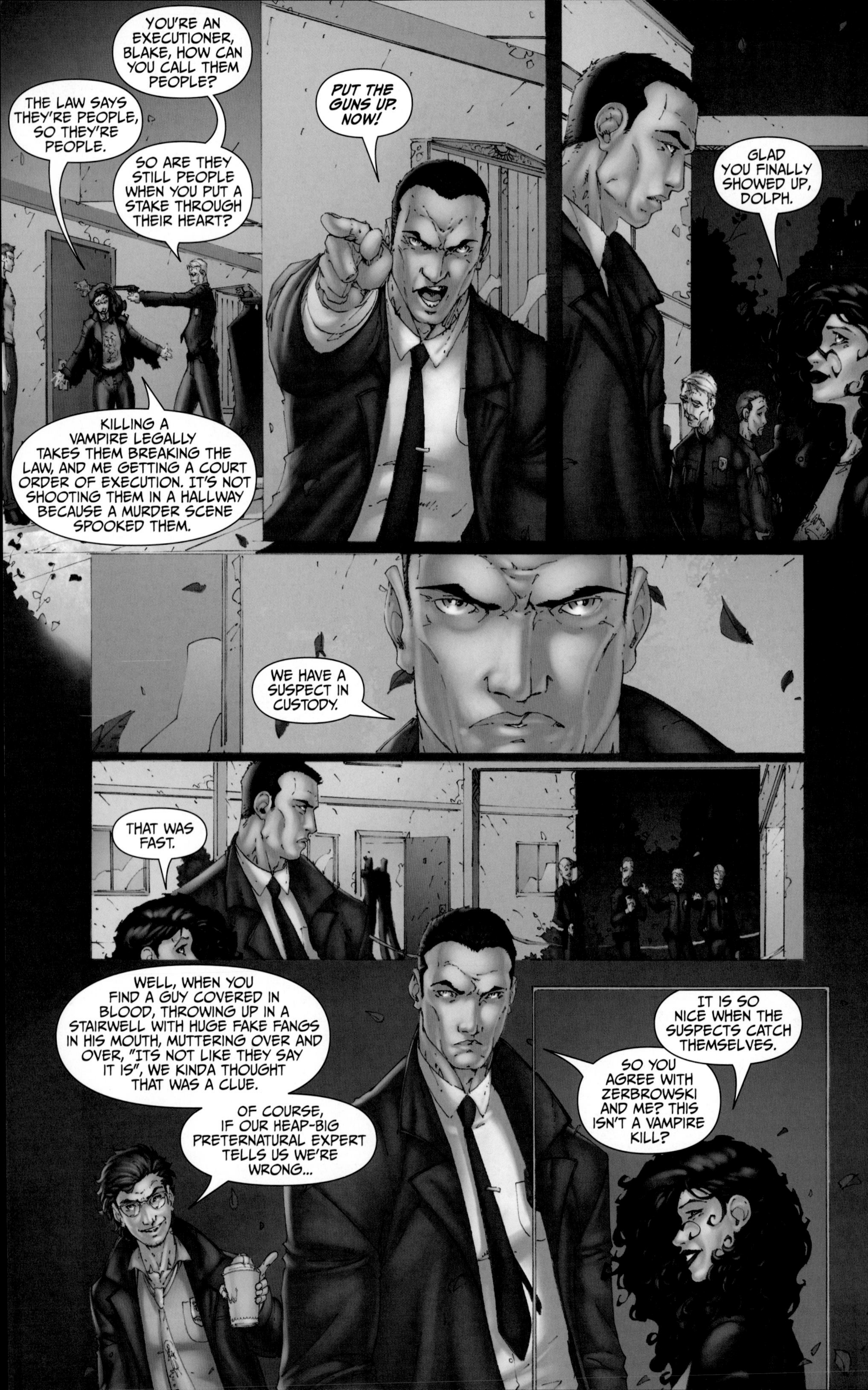
THE LAW SAYS THEY'RE PEOPLE, SO THEY'RE PEOPLE.
YOU'RE AN EXECUTIONER, BLAKE, HOW CAN YOU CALL THEM PEOPLE?
SO ARE THEY STILL PEOPLE WHEN YOU PUT A STAKE THROUGH THEIR HEART?
KILLING A VAMPIRE LEGALLY TAKES THEM BREAKING THE LAW, AND ME GETTING A COURT ORDER OF EXECUTION. IT'S NOT SHOOTING THEM IN A HALLWAY BECAUSE A MURDER SCENE SPOOKED THEM.
PUT THE GUNS UP. NOW!
GLAD YOU FINALLY SHOWED UP, DOLPH.
WE HAVE A SUSPECT IN CUSTODY.
THAT WAS FAST.
WELL, WHEN YOU FIND A GUY COVERED IN BLOOD, THROWING UP IN A STAIRWELL WITH HUGE FAKE FANGS IN HIS MOUTH, MUTTERING OVER AND OVER, "ITS NOT LIKE THEY SAY IT IS", WE KINDA THOUGHT THAT WAS A CLUE.
OF COURSE, IF OUR HEAP-BIG PRETERNATURAL EXPERT TELLS US WE'RE WRONG...
IT IS SO NICE WHEN THE SUSPECTS CATCH THEMSELVES.
SO YOU AGREE WITH ZERBROWSKI AND ME? THIS ISN'T A VAMPIRE KILL?

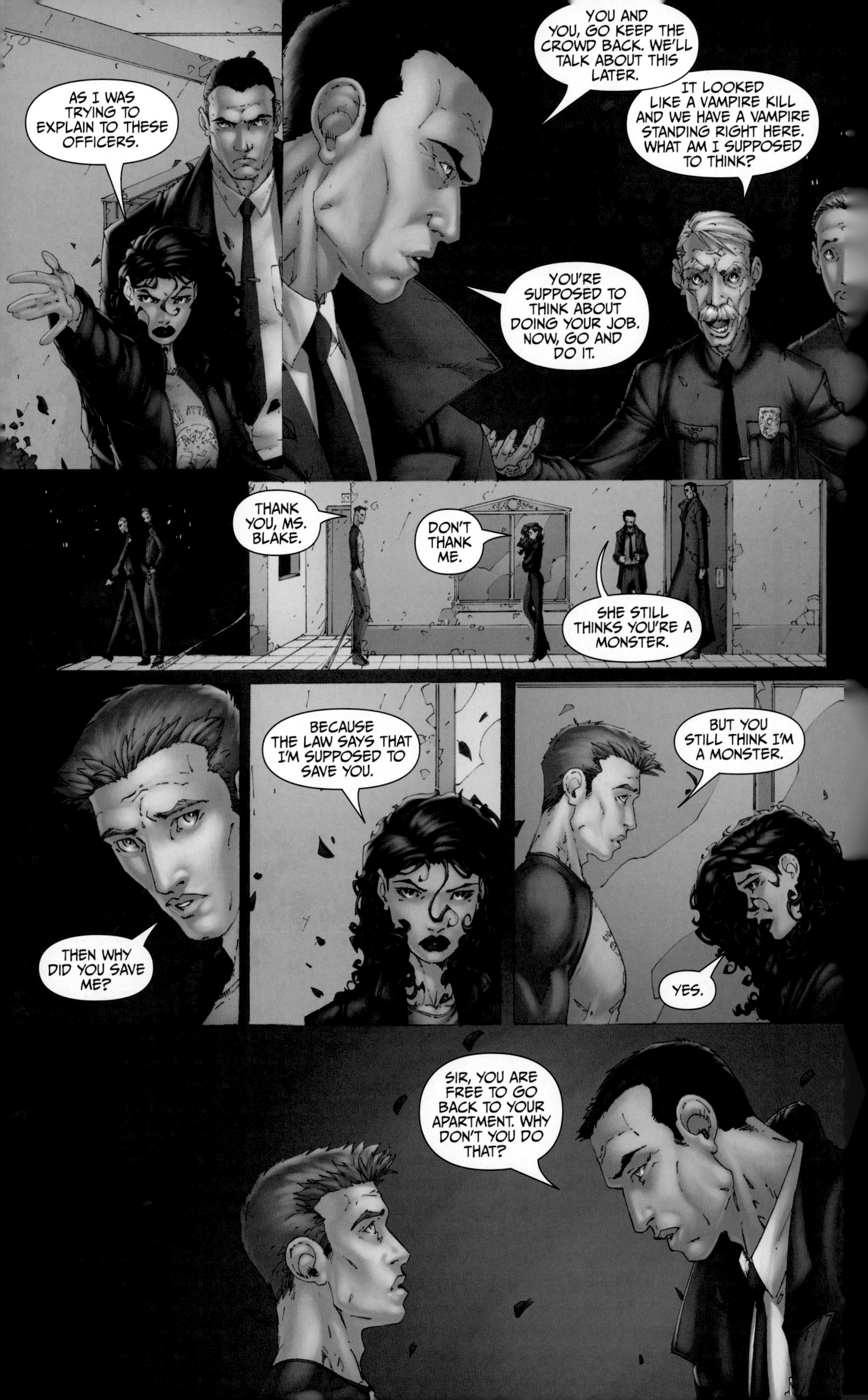
AS I WAS TRYING TO EXPLAIN TO THESE OFFICERS.
YOU AND YOU, GO KEEP THE CROWD BACK. WE'LL TALK ABOUT THIS LATER.
IT LOOKED LIKE A VAMPIRE KILL AND WE HAVE A VAMPIRE STANDING RIGHT HERE. WHAT AM I SUPPOSED TO THINK?
YOU'RE SUPPOSED TO THINK ABOUT DOING YOUR JOB. NOW, GO AND DO IT.
THANK YOU, MS. BLAKE.
DON'T THANK ME.
SHE STILL THINKS YOU'RE A MONSTER.
THEN WHY DID YOU SAVE ME?
BECAUSE THE LAW SAYS THAT I'M SUPPOSED TO SAVE YOU.
BUT YOU STILL THINK I'M A MONSTER.
YES.
SIR, YOU ARE FREE TO GO BACK TO YOUR APARTMENT. WHY DON'T YOU DO THAT?

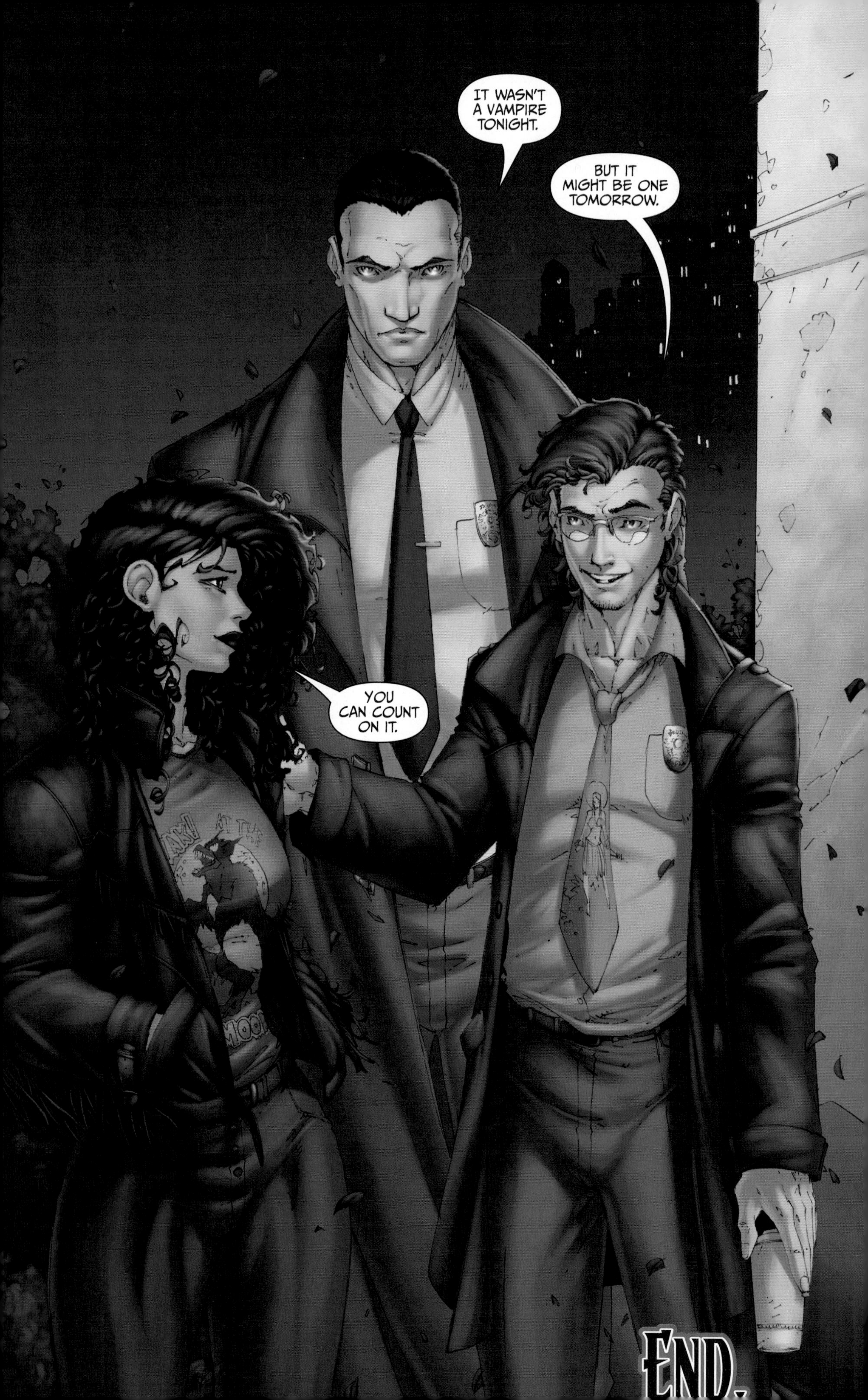
IT WASN'T A VAMPIRE TONIGHT.
BUT IT MIGHT BE ONE TOMORROW.
YOU CAN COUNT ON IT.
END.

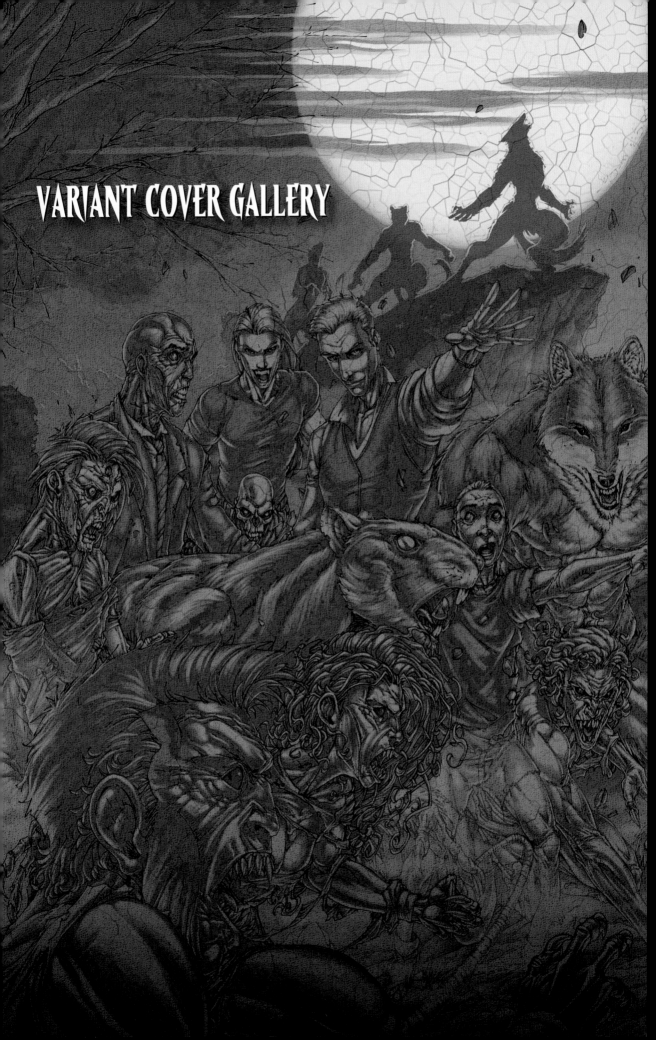

VARIANT COVER GALLERY

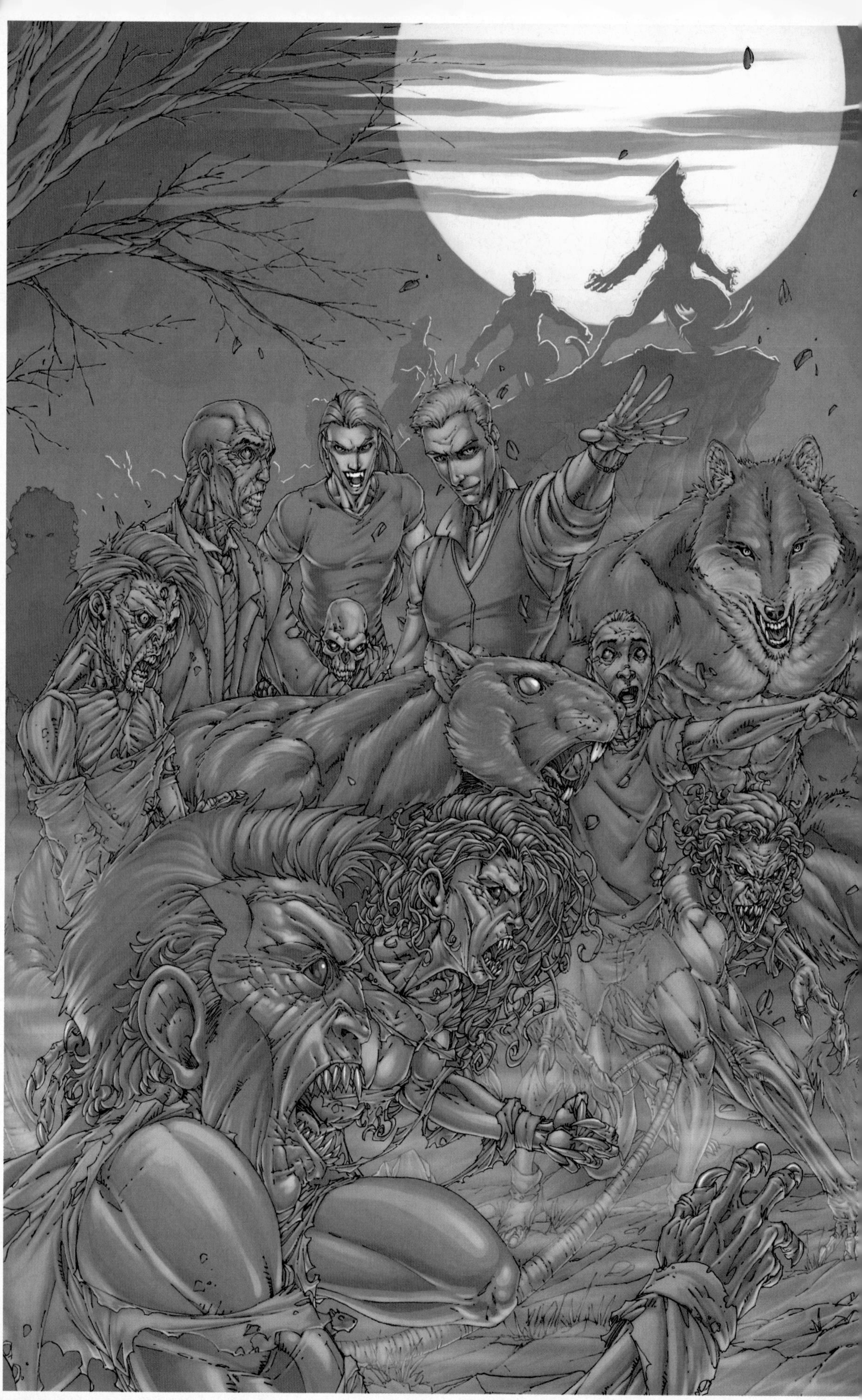

ISSUE ONE VARIANT BY BRETT BOOTH & JESS RUFFNER-BOOTH

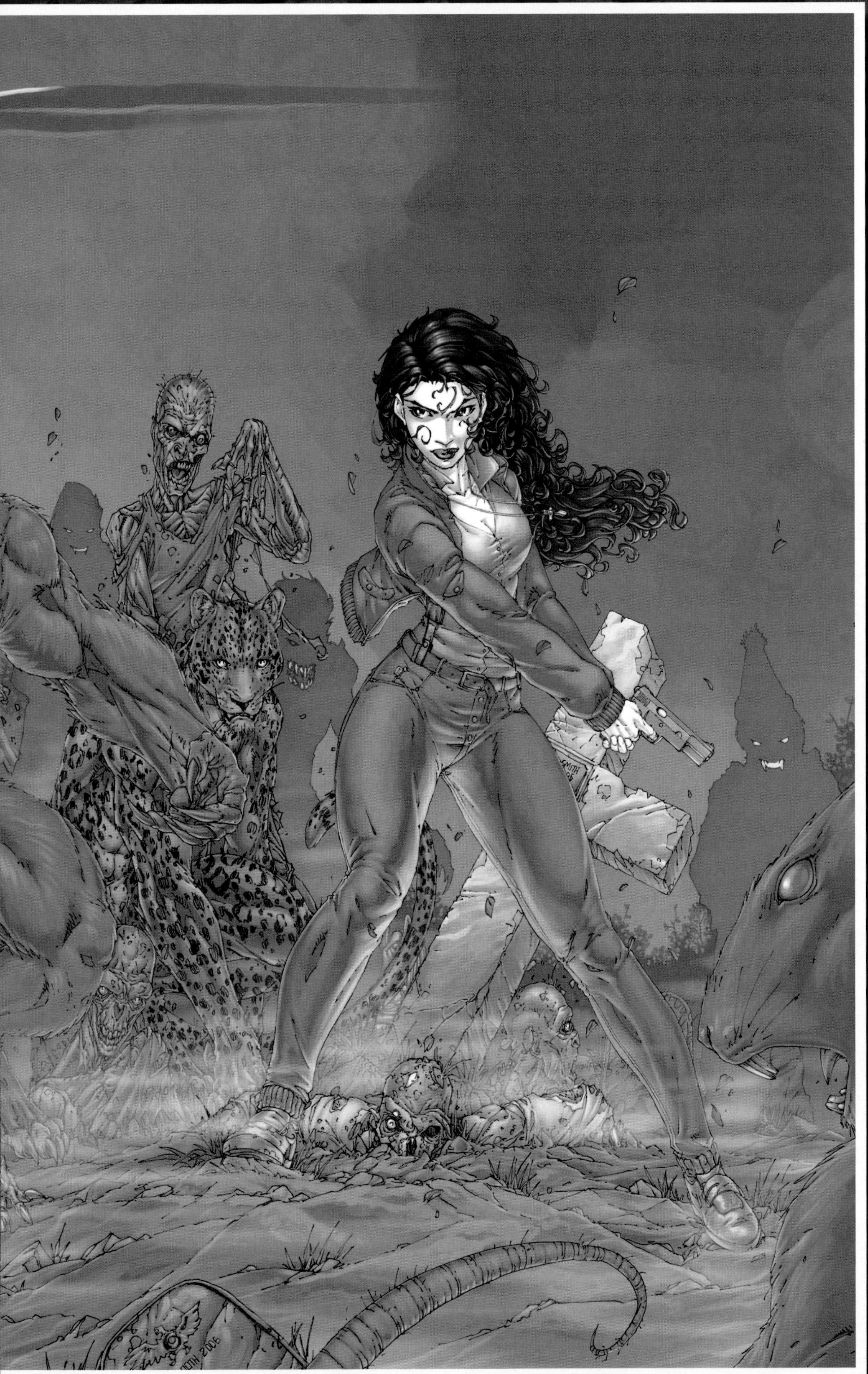

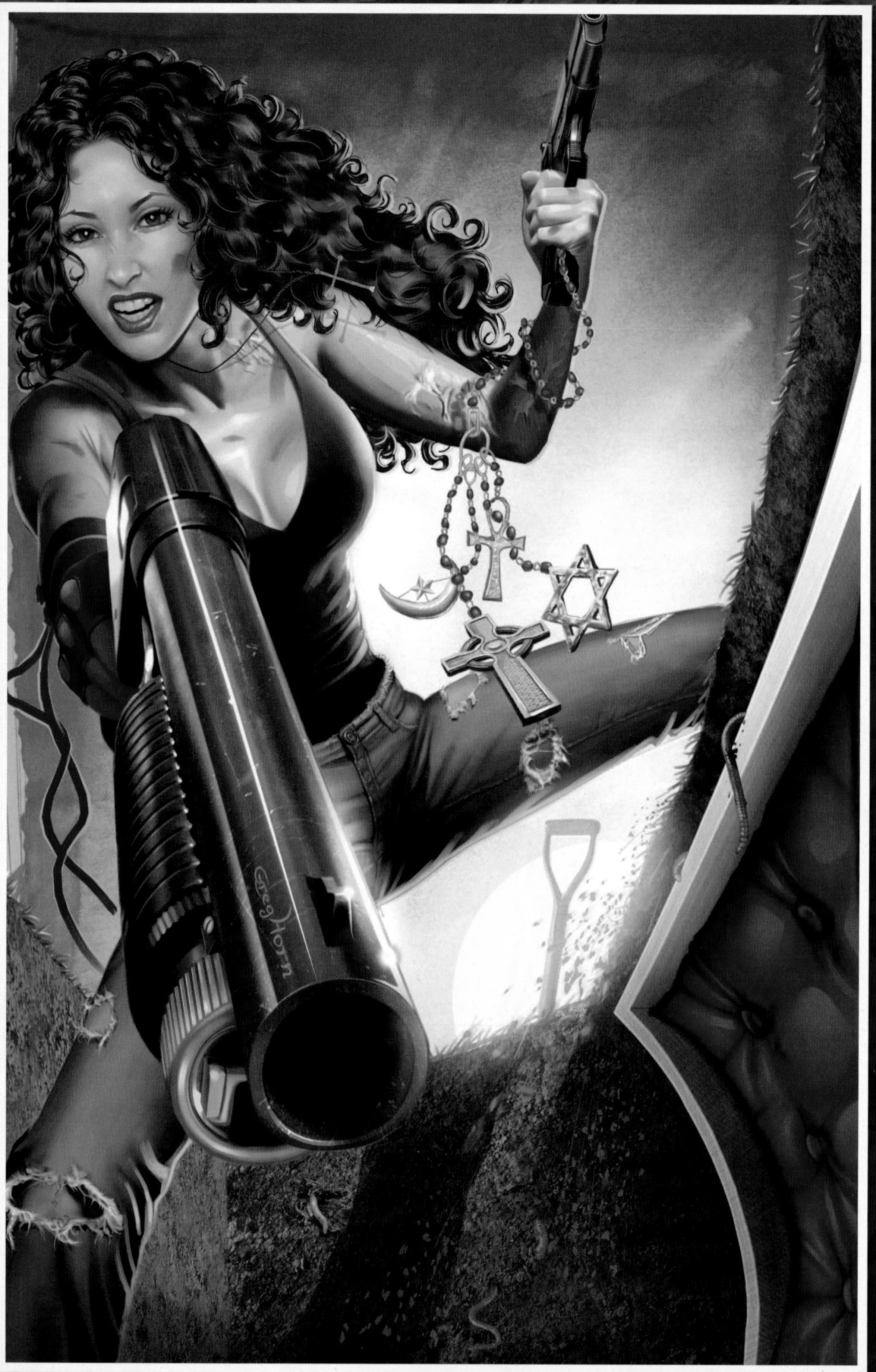
Greg Horn

ISSUE ONE VARIANT BY GREG HORN

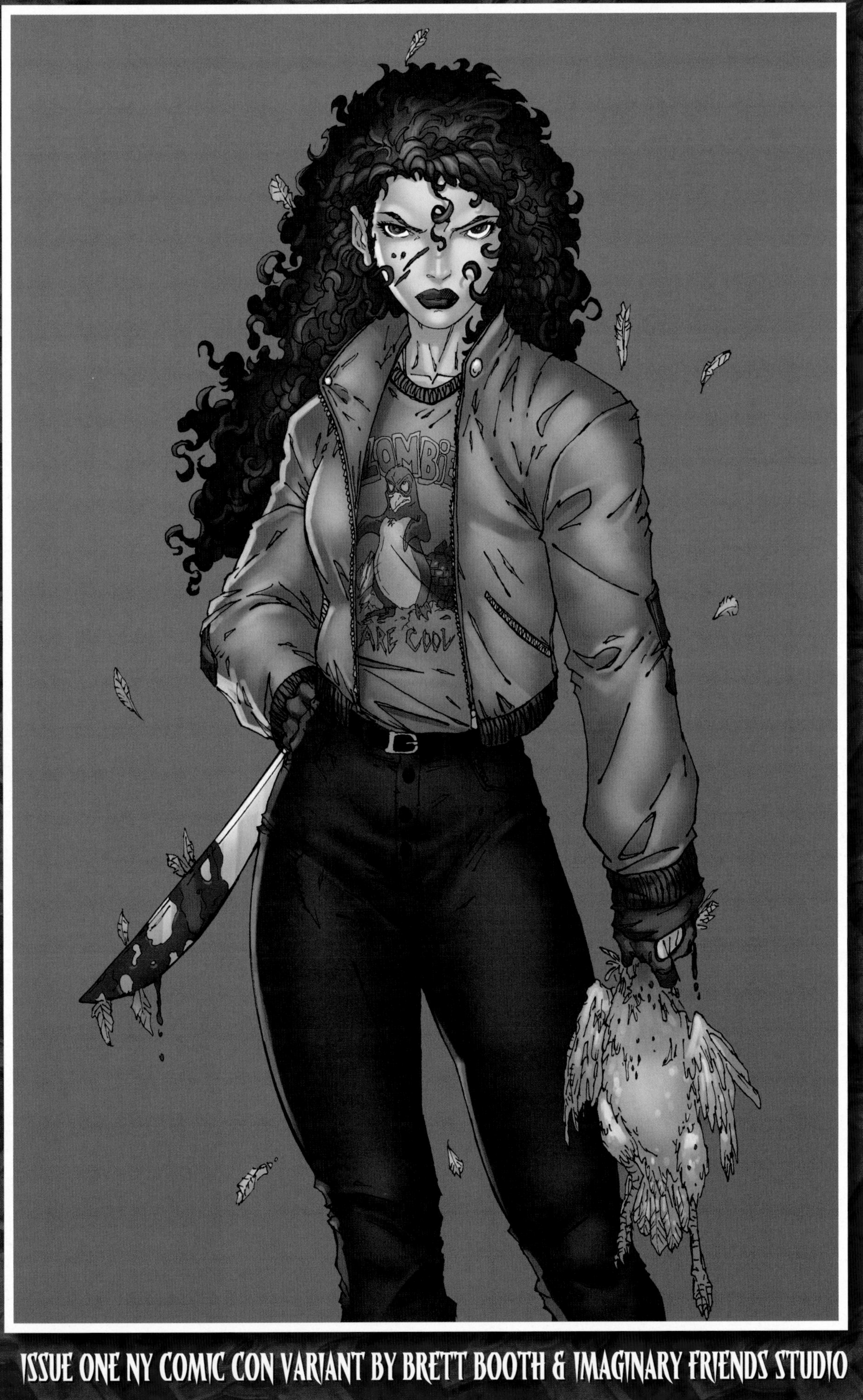
ARE COOL

ISSUE ONE NY COMIC CON VARIANT BY BRETT BOOTH & IMAGINARY FRIENDS STUDIO

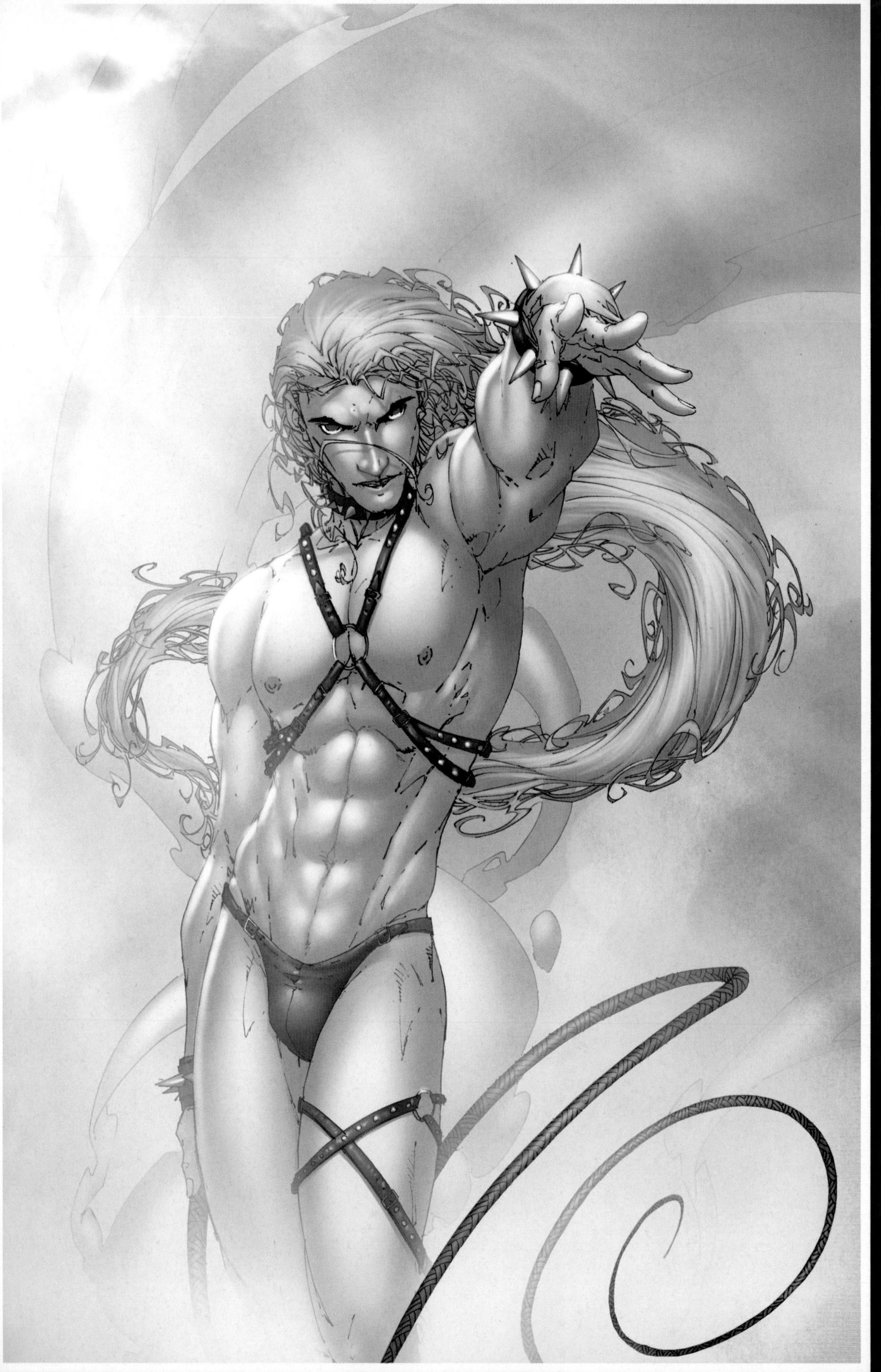

ISSUE ONE 3RD PRINTING VARIANT BY BRETT BOOTH & JESS RUFFNER-BOOTH

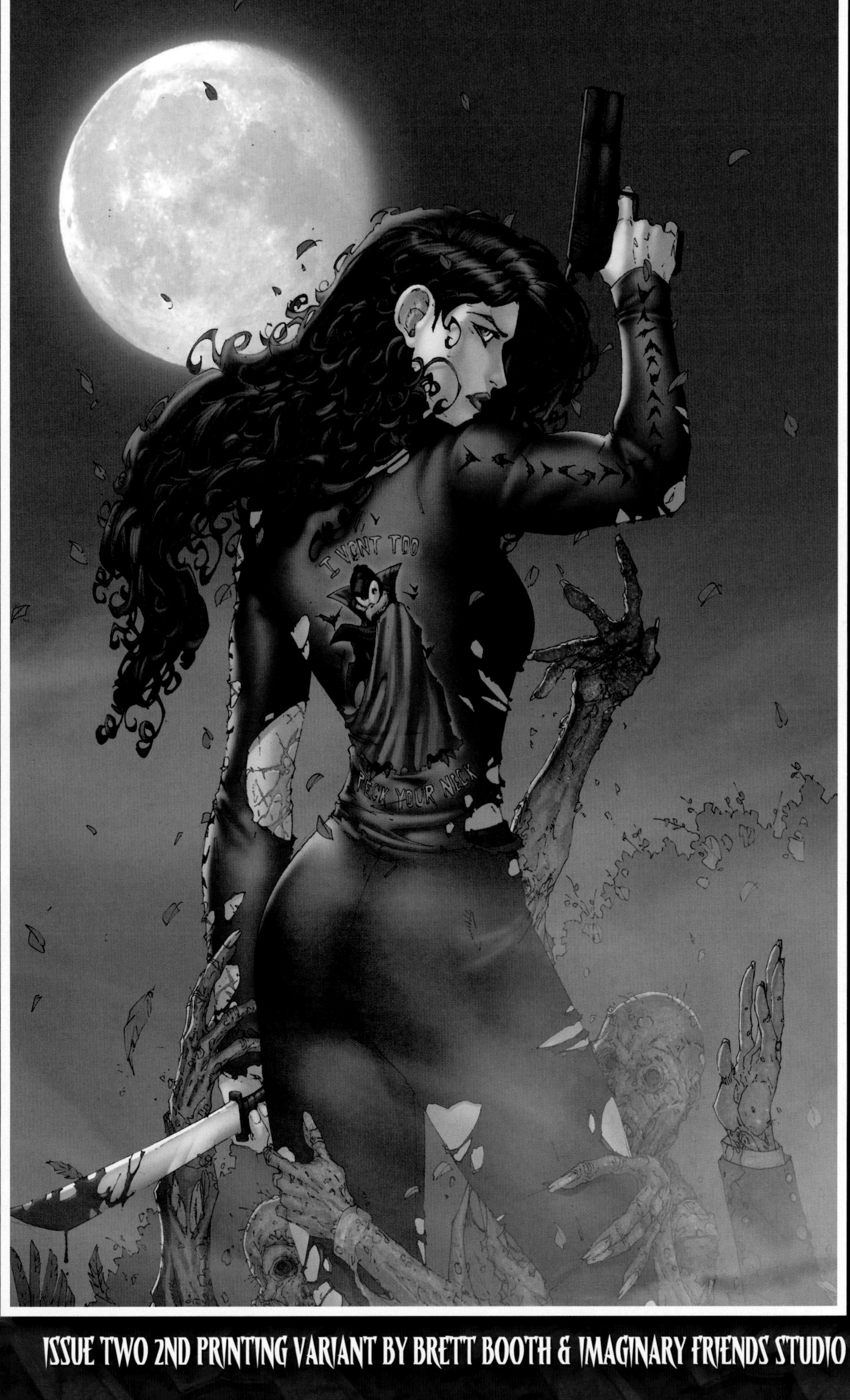
I VANT TOO
PECK YOUR NECK

ISSUE TWO 2ND PRINTING VARIANT BY BRETT BOOTH & IMAGINARY FRIENDS STUDIO

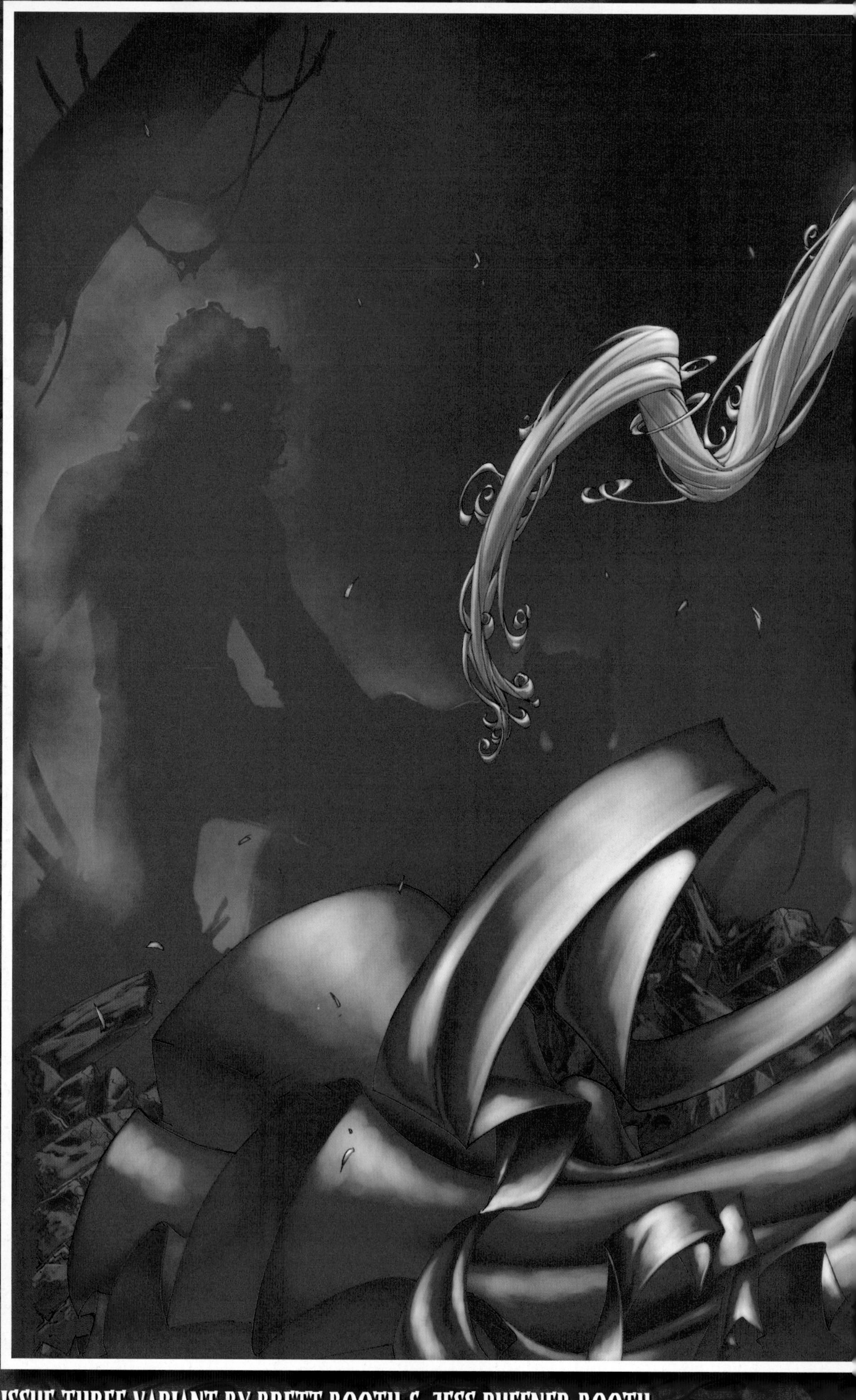

ISSUE THREE VARIANT BY BRETT BOOTH & JESS RUFFNER-BOOTH

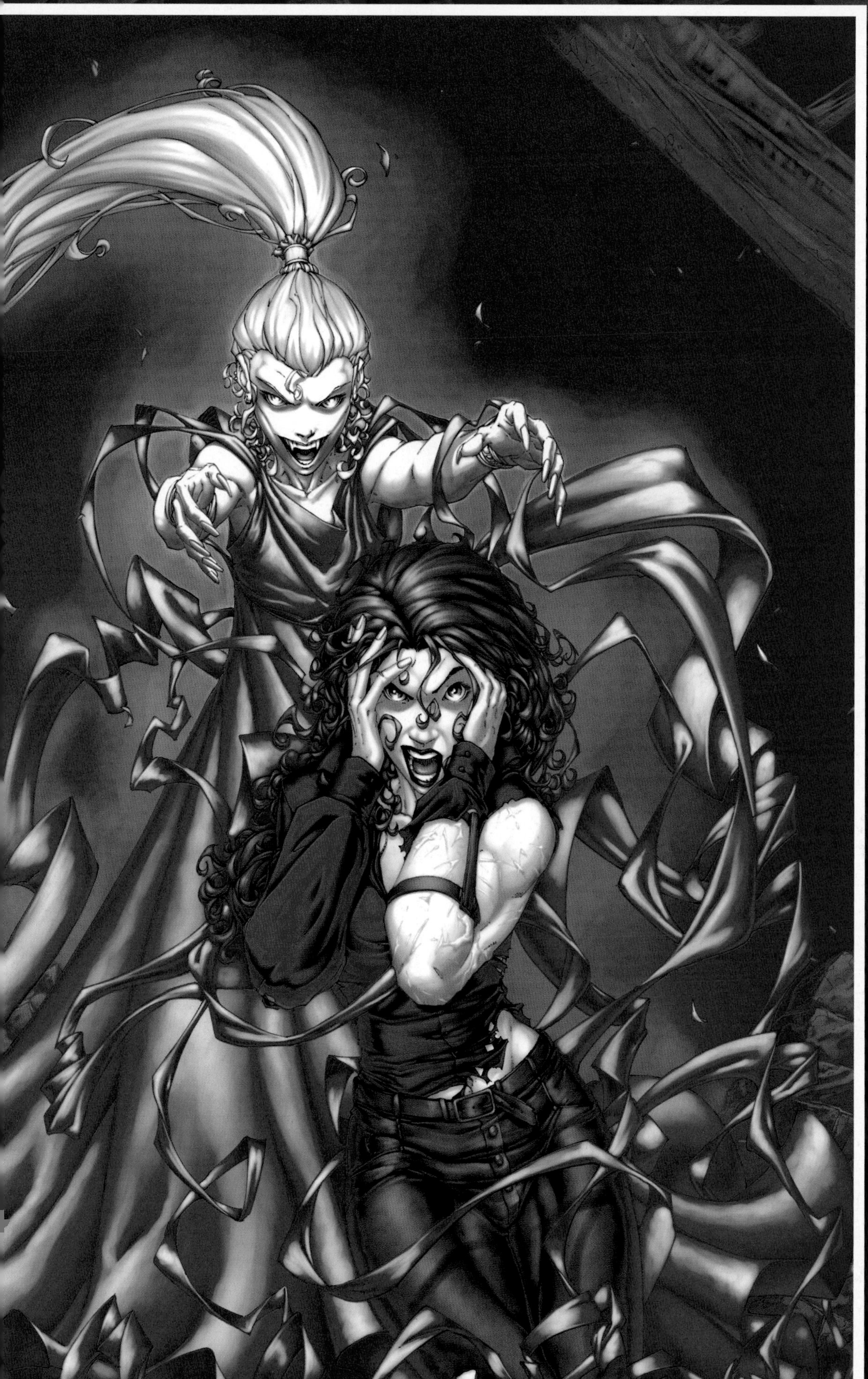

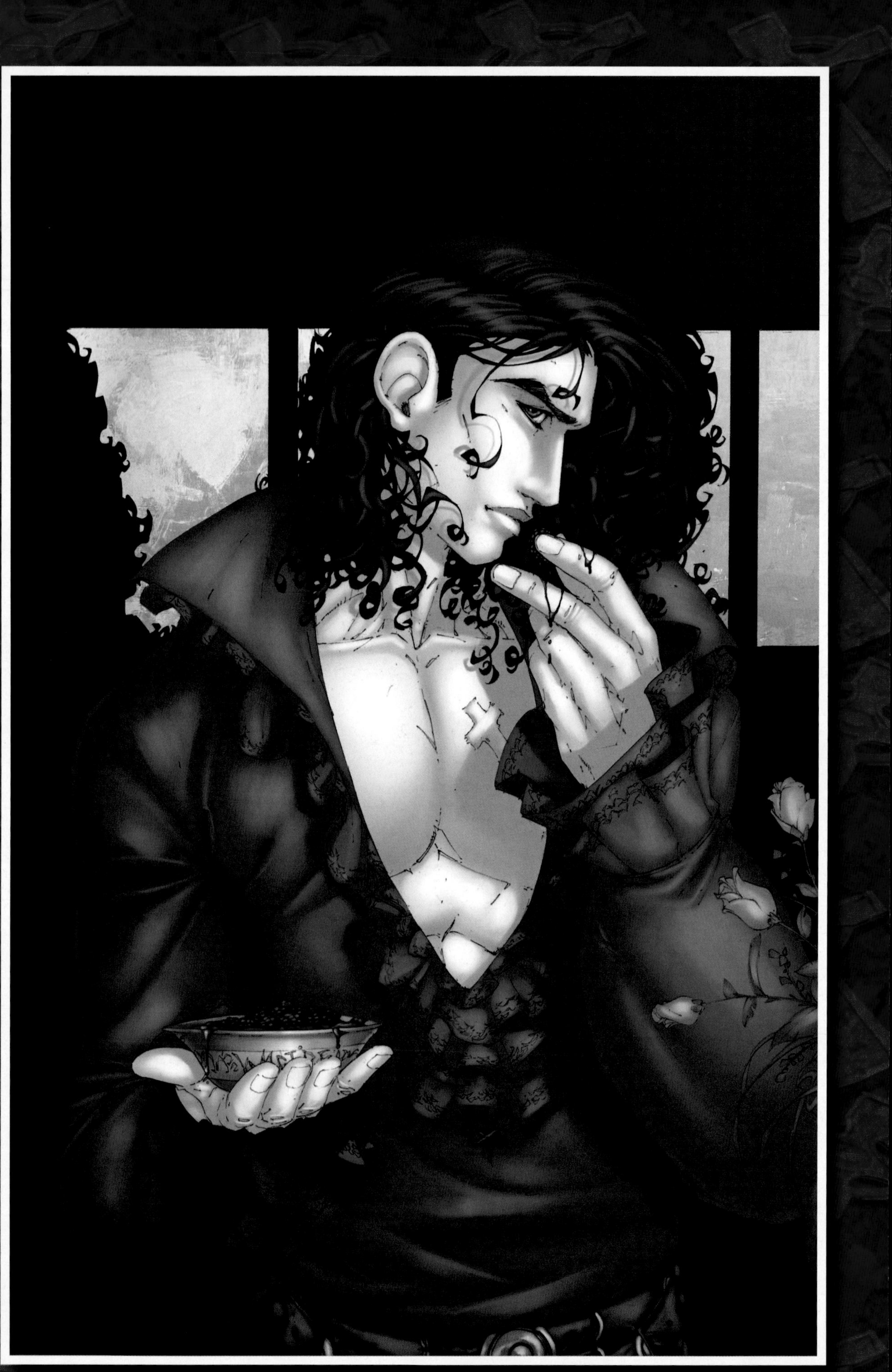

ISSUE EIGHT VARIANT BY BRETT BOOTH

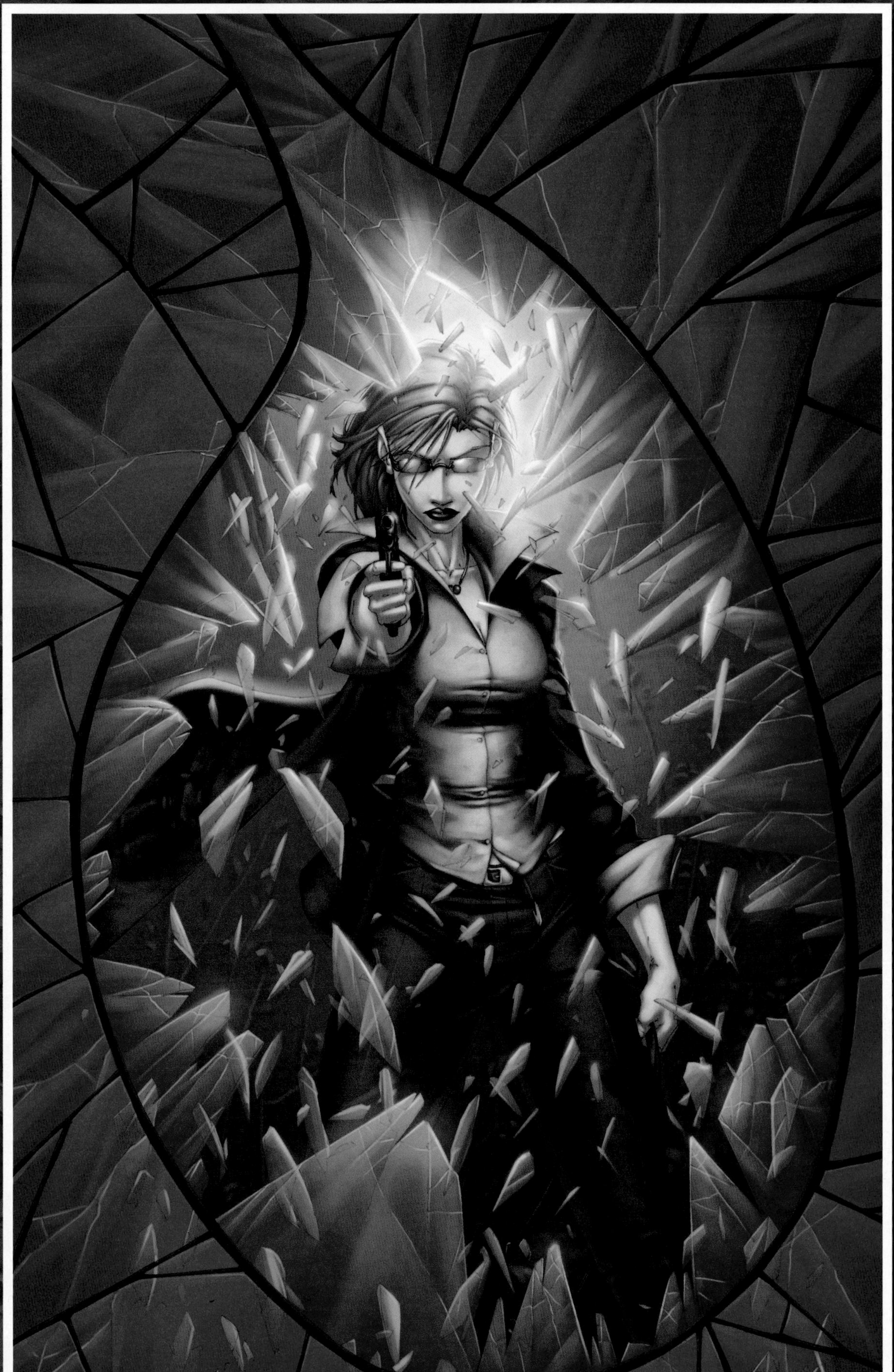

ISSUE NINE VARIANT BY BRETT BOOTH

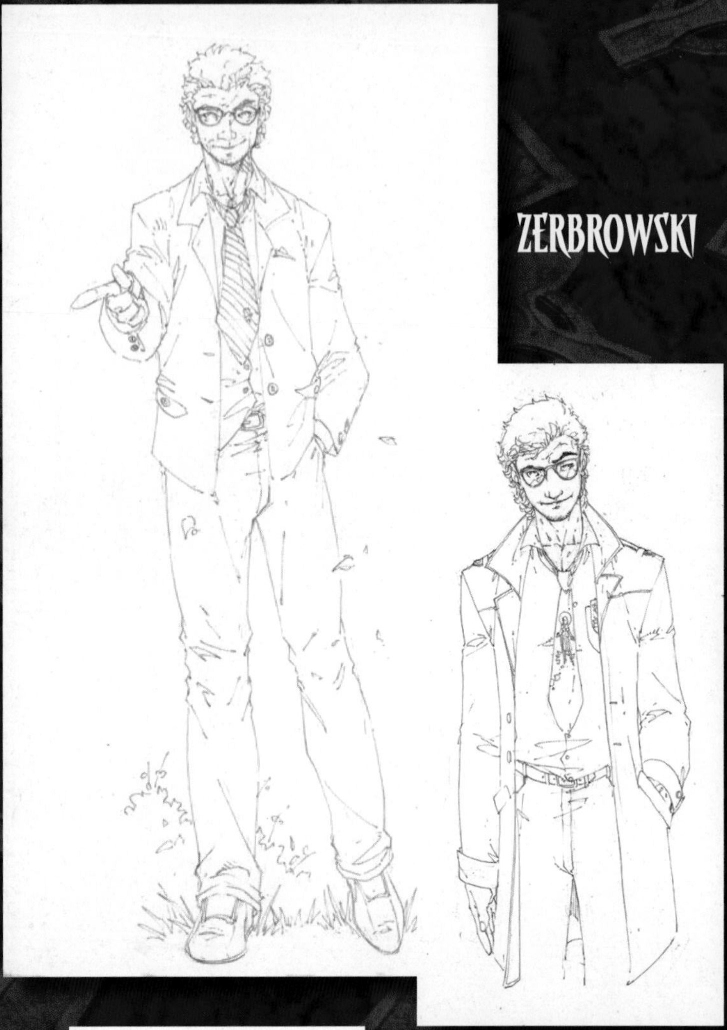

ZERBROWSKI

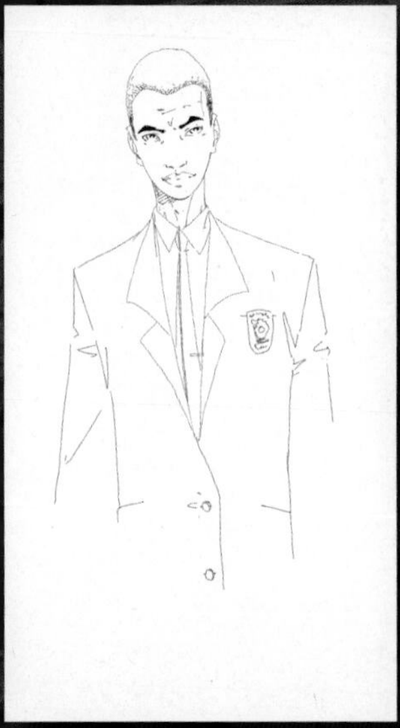

CLIVE

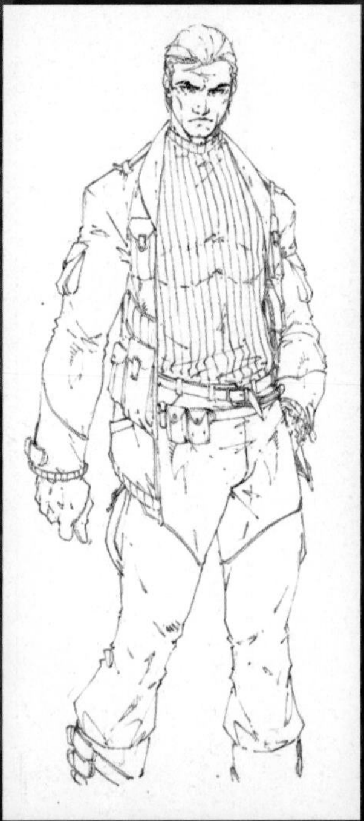

ORLANDO

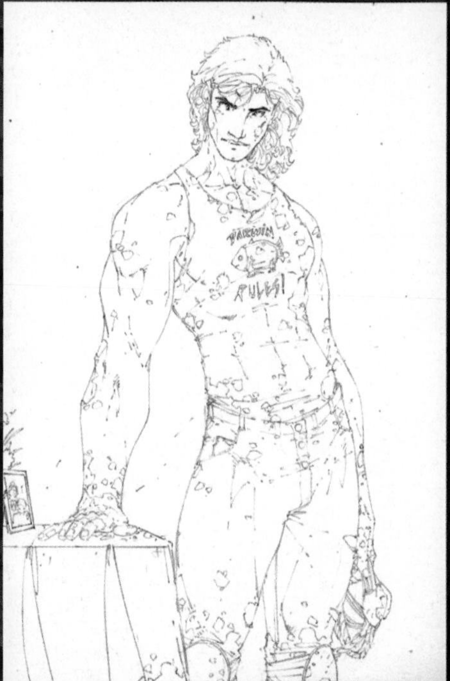

RICHARD

CHARACTER SKETCHES BY BRETT BOOTH

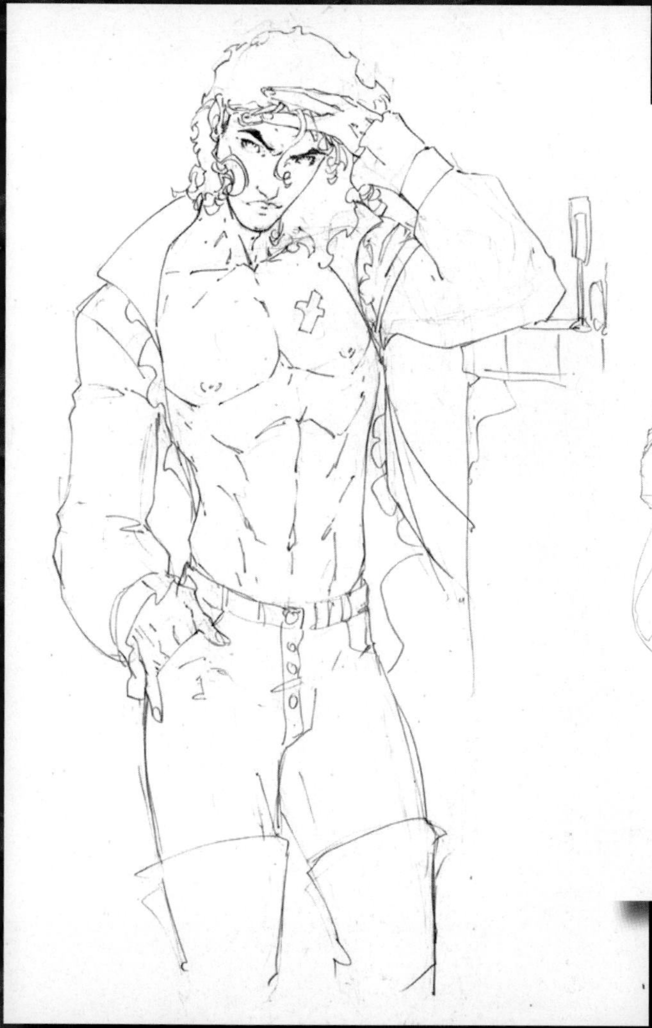

JEAN-CLAUDE

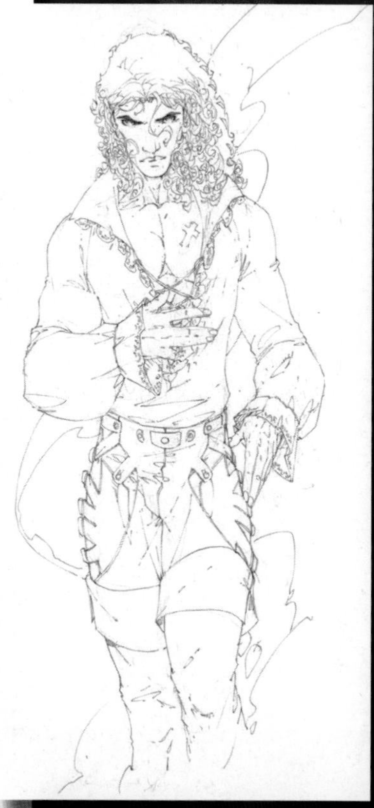

ANITA

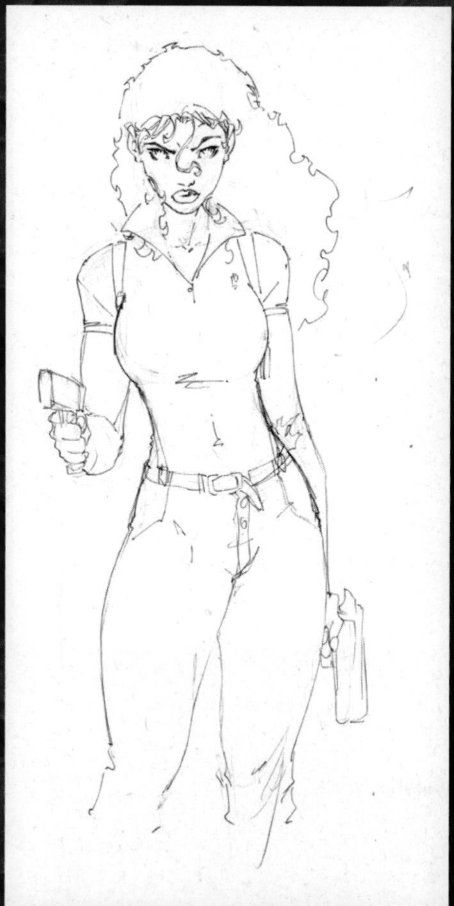

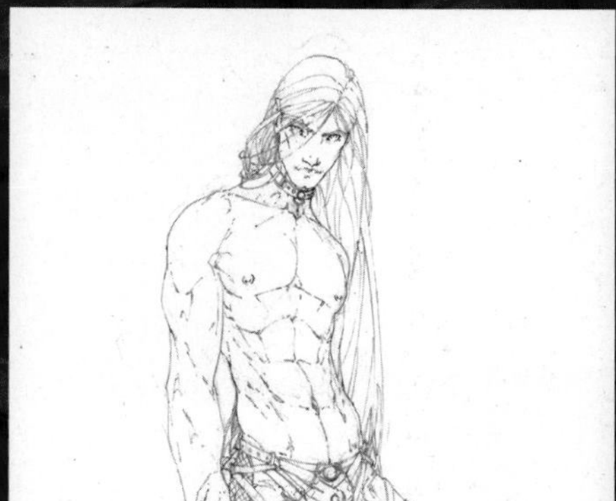

NATHANIEL

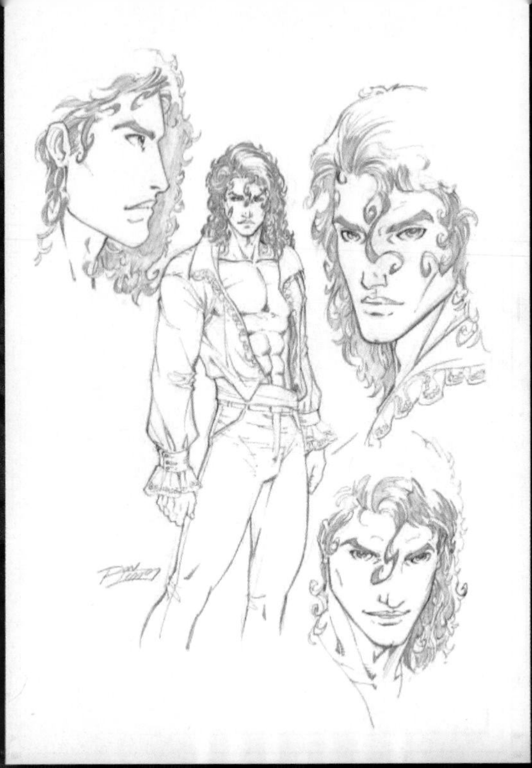

JEAN-CLAUDE

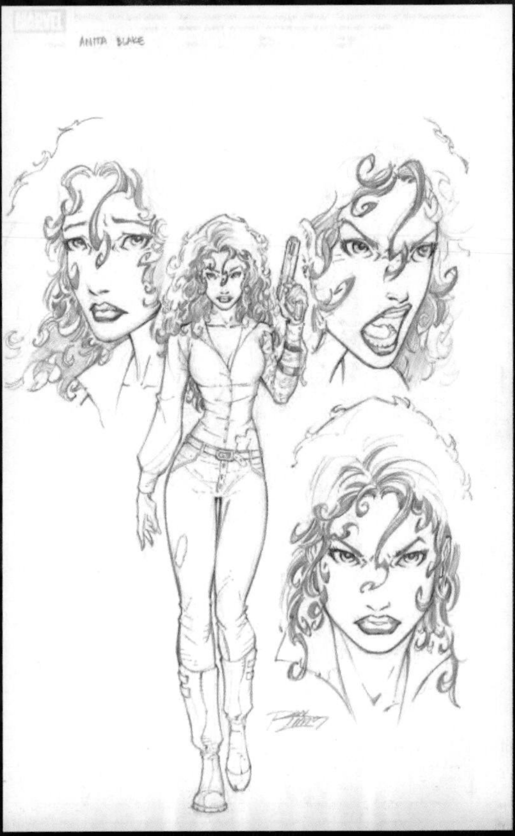
ANITA BLAKE

ANITA

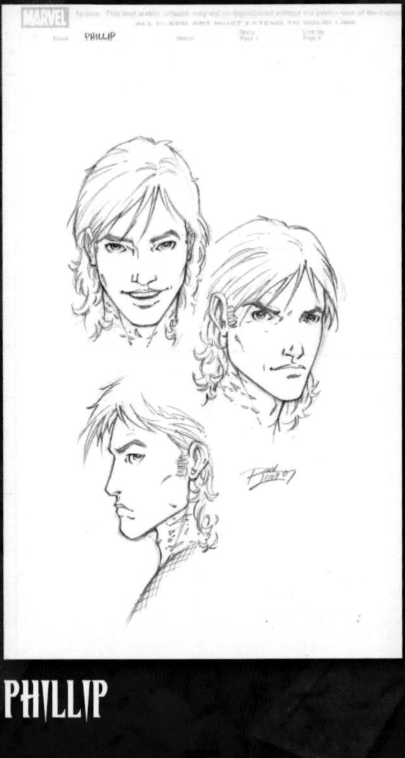
PHILLIP

PHILLIP

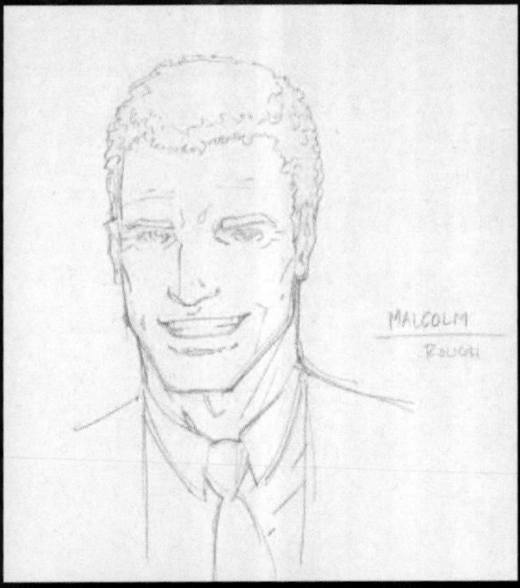
MALCOLM

MALCOLM

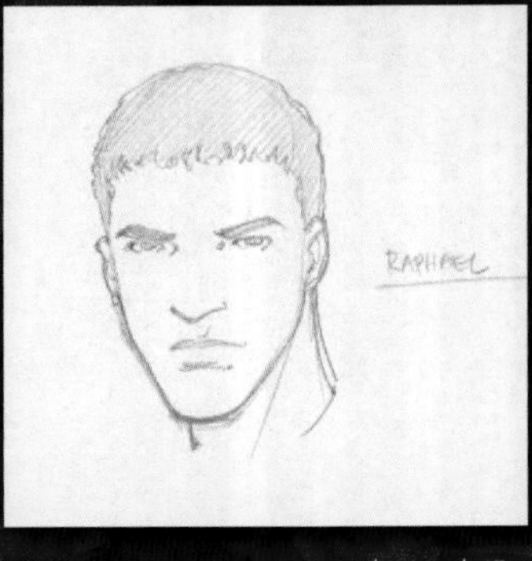
RAPHAEL

RAPHAEL

CHARACTER SKETCHES BY RON LIM

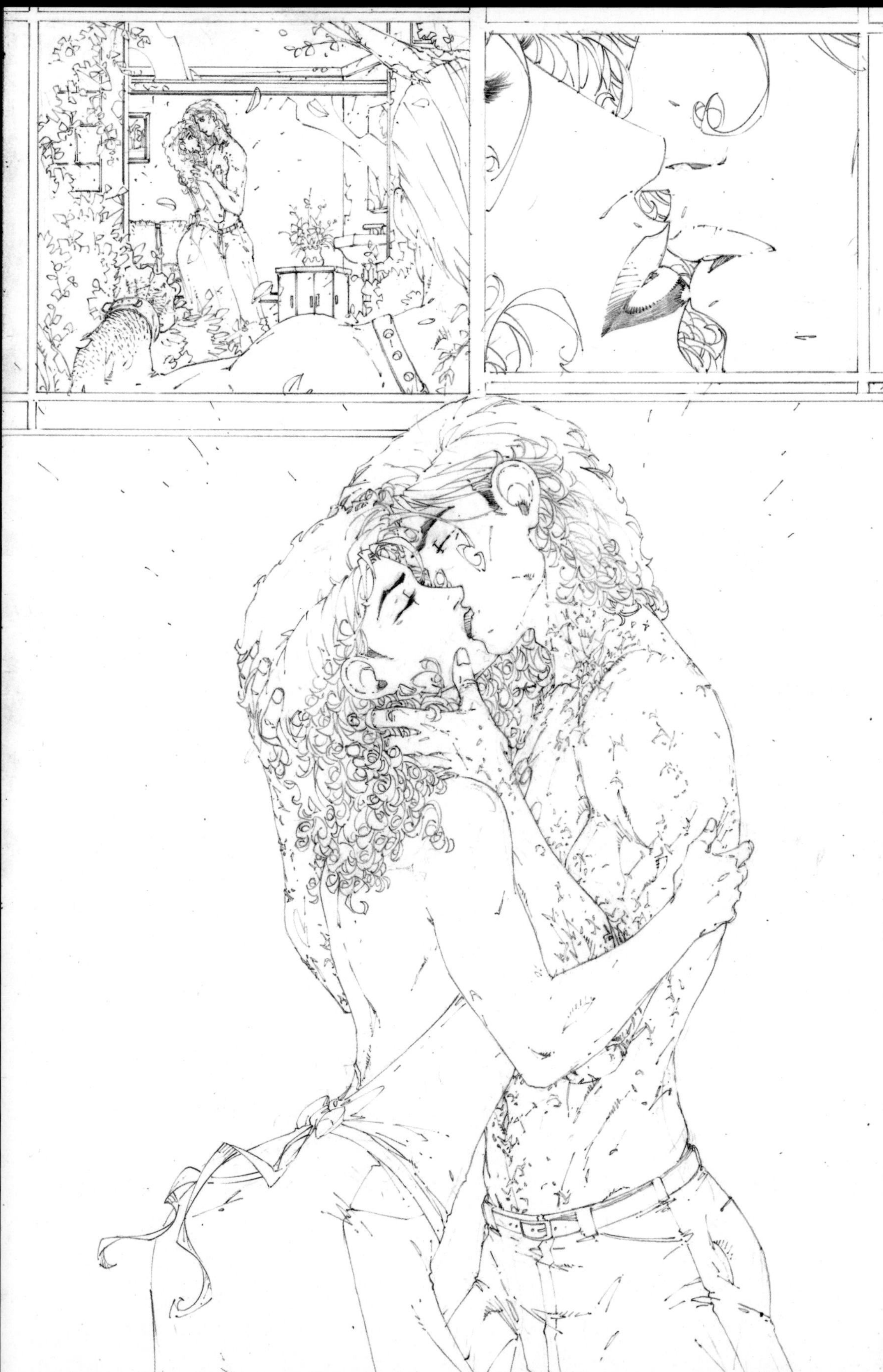

ISSUE #7 PENCILS BY BRETT BOOTH

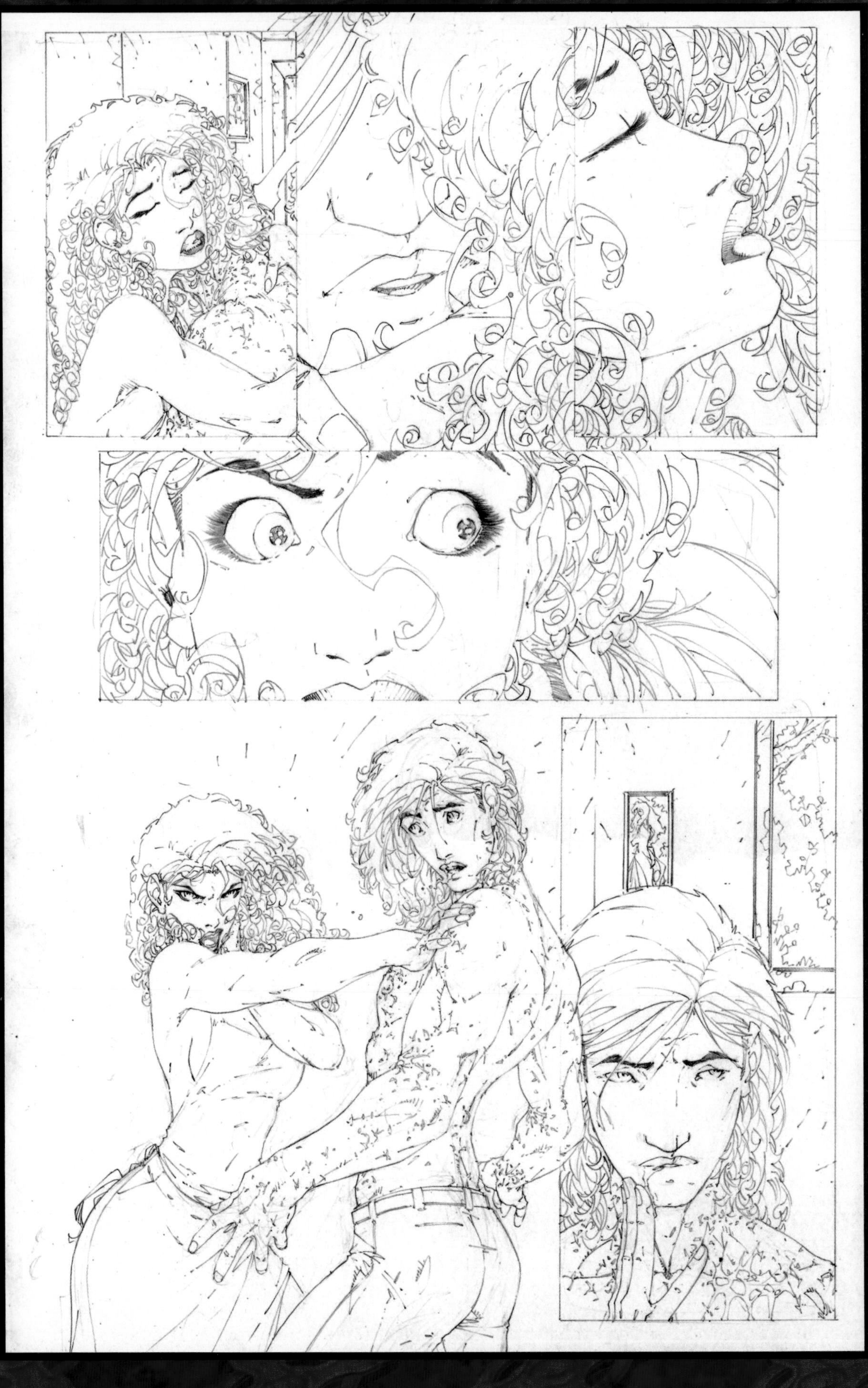

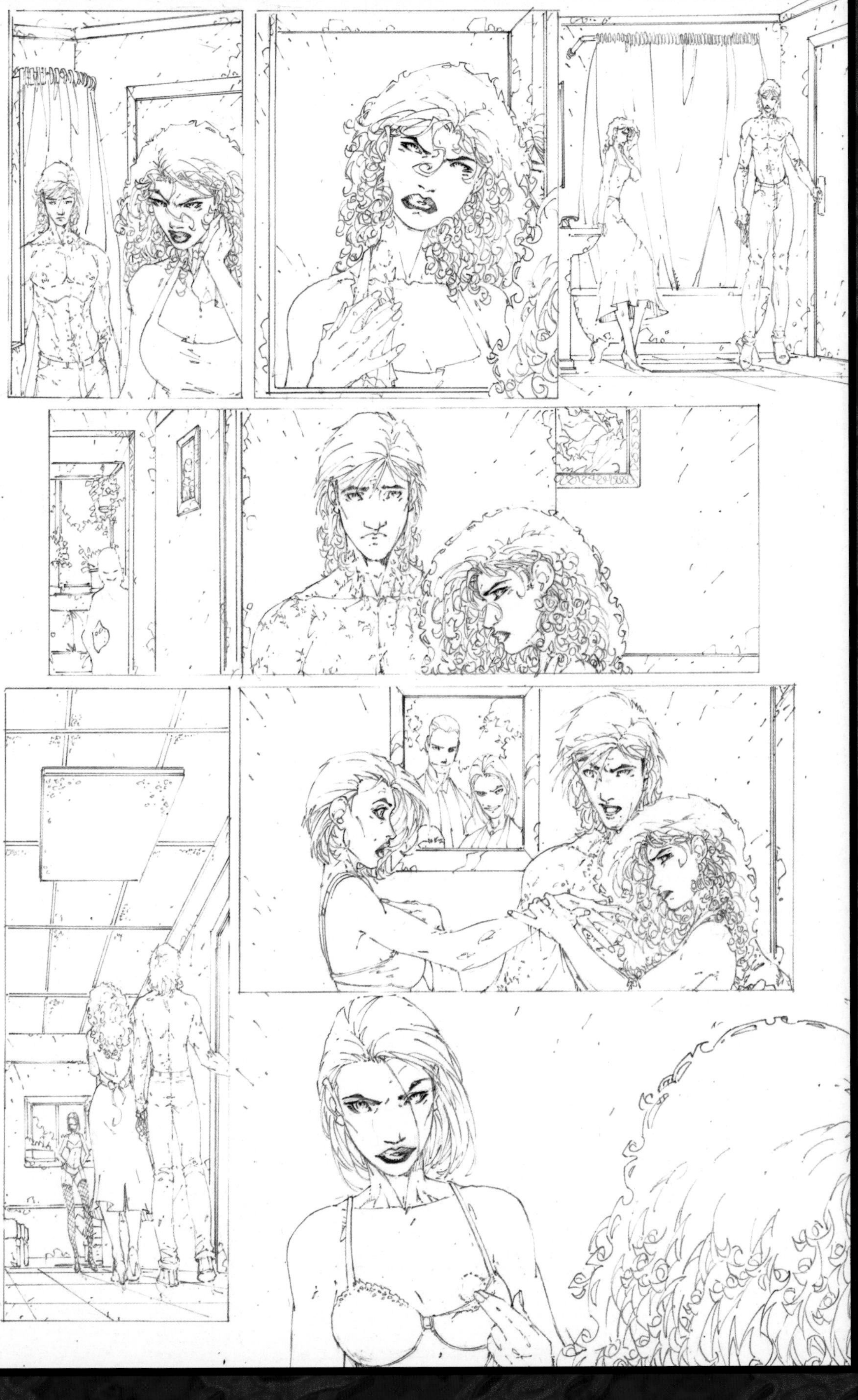

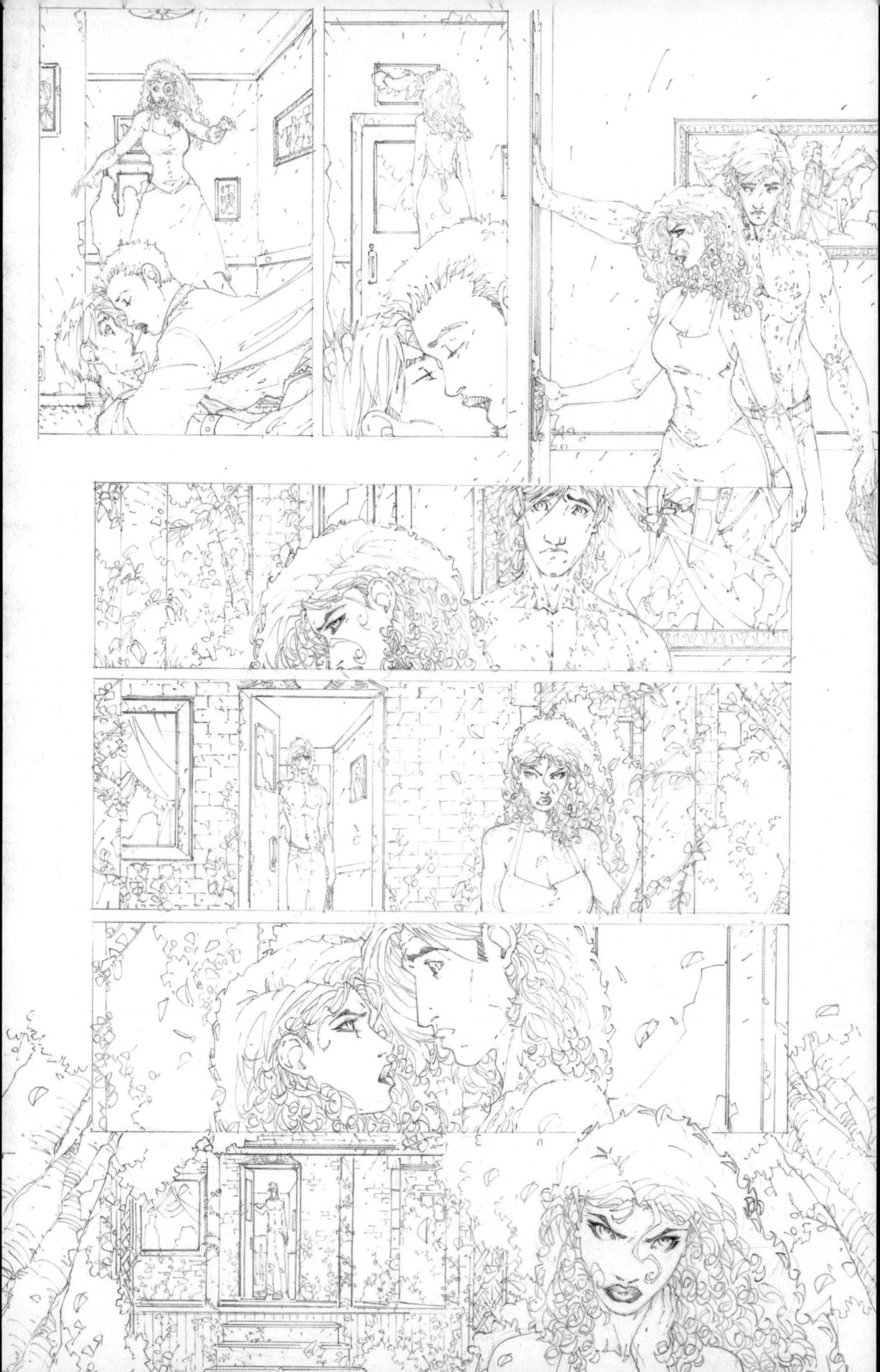

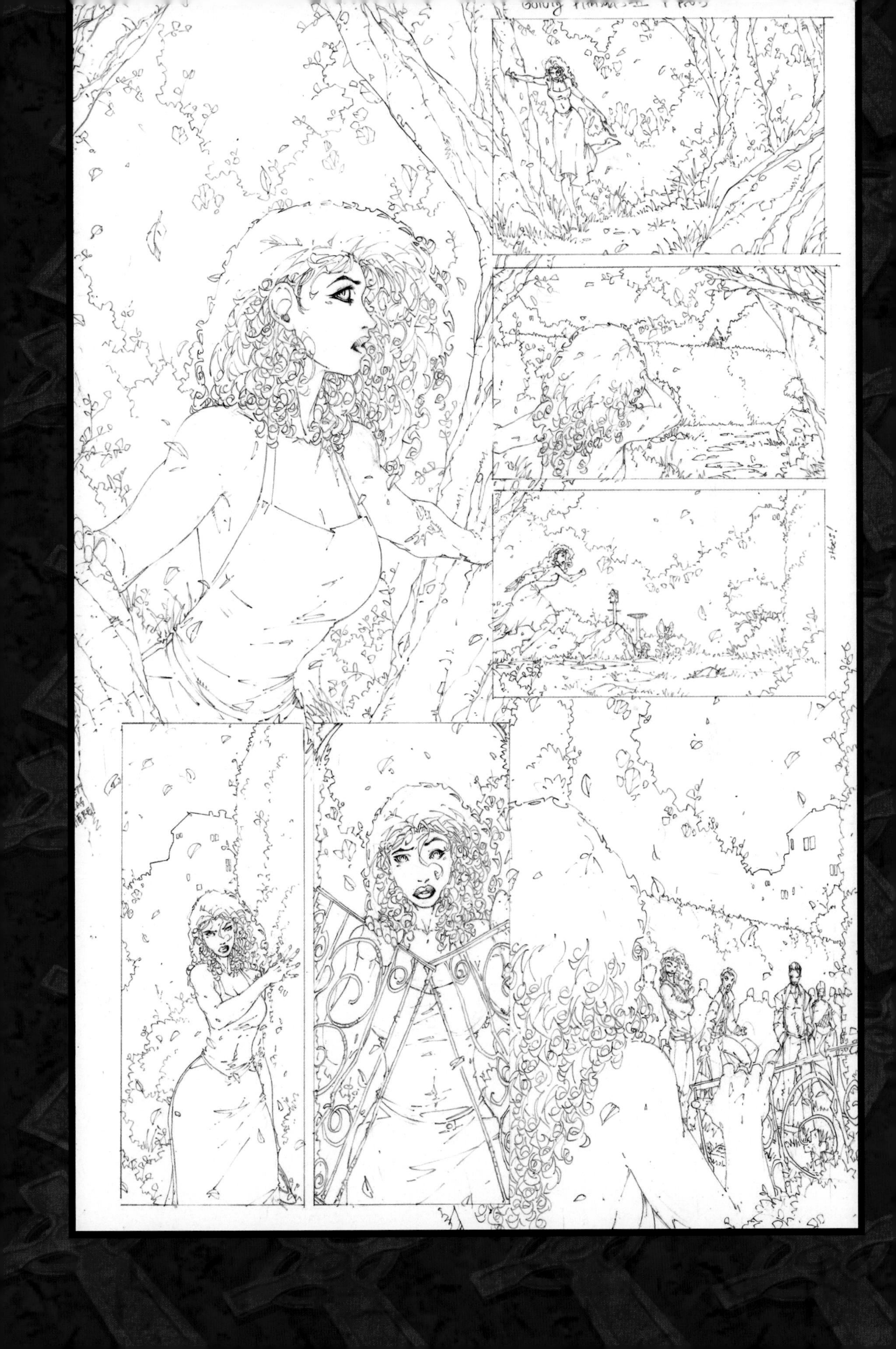
SHOES!

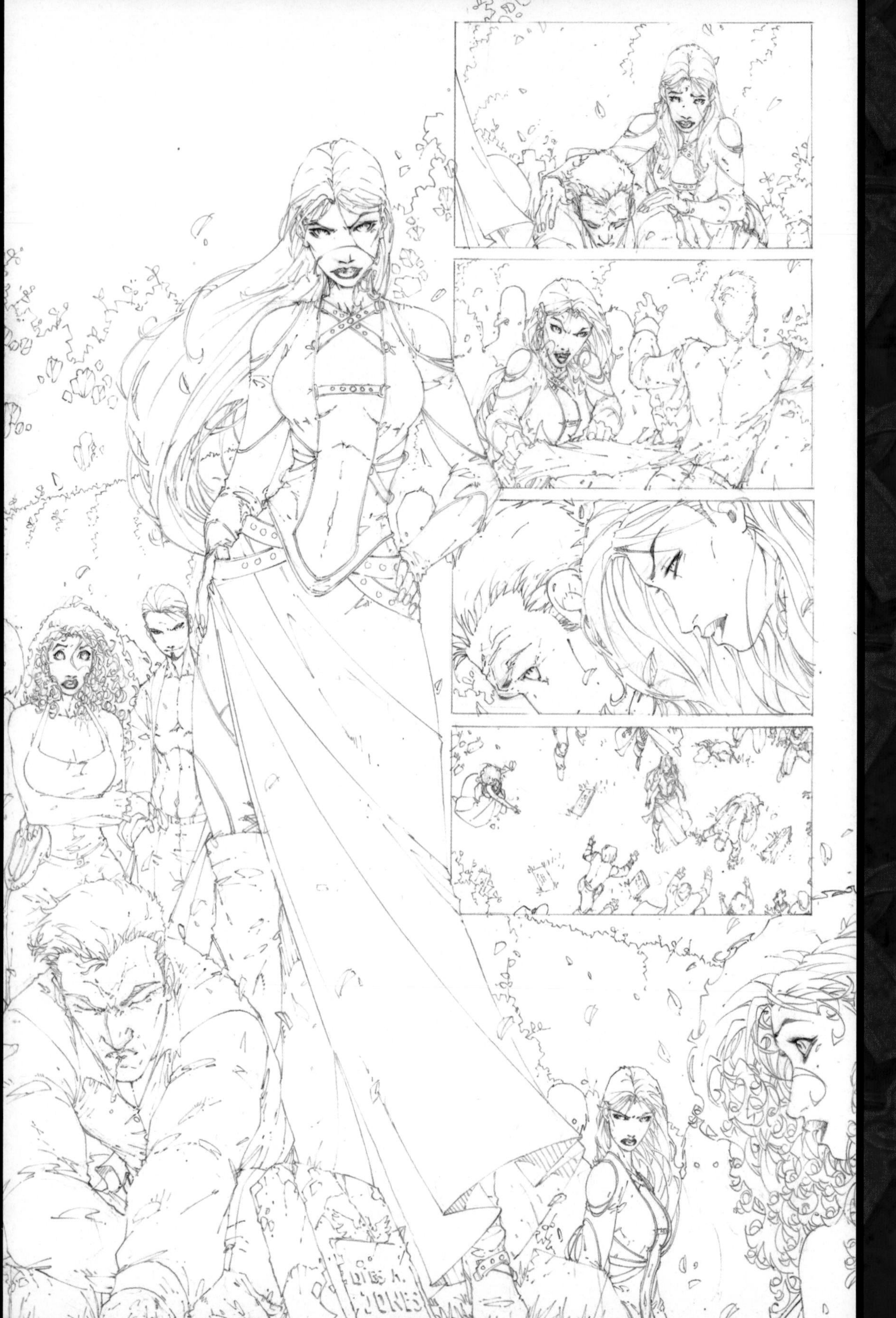
JONES

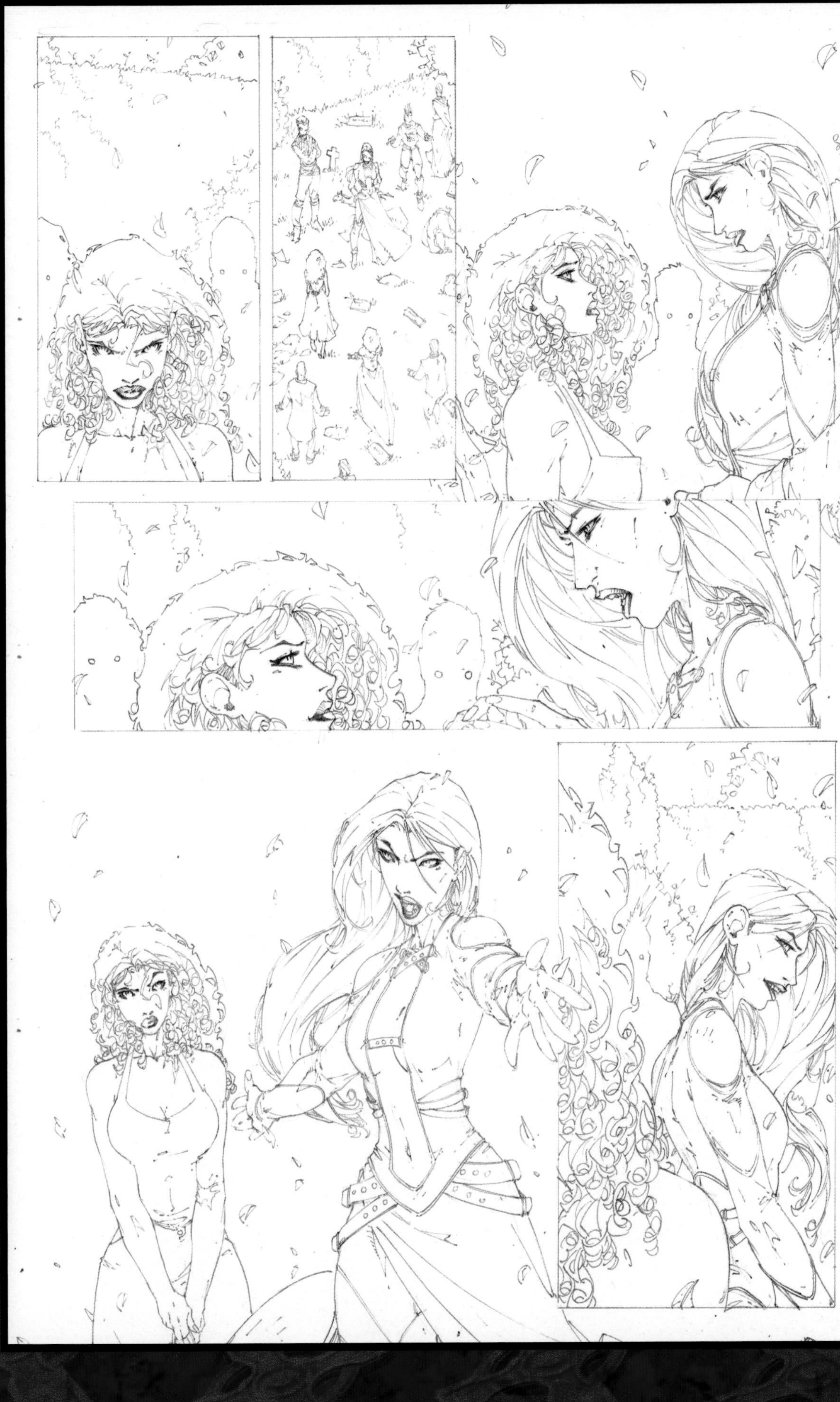

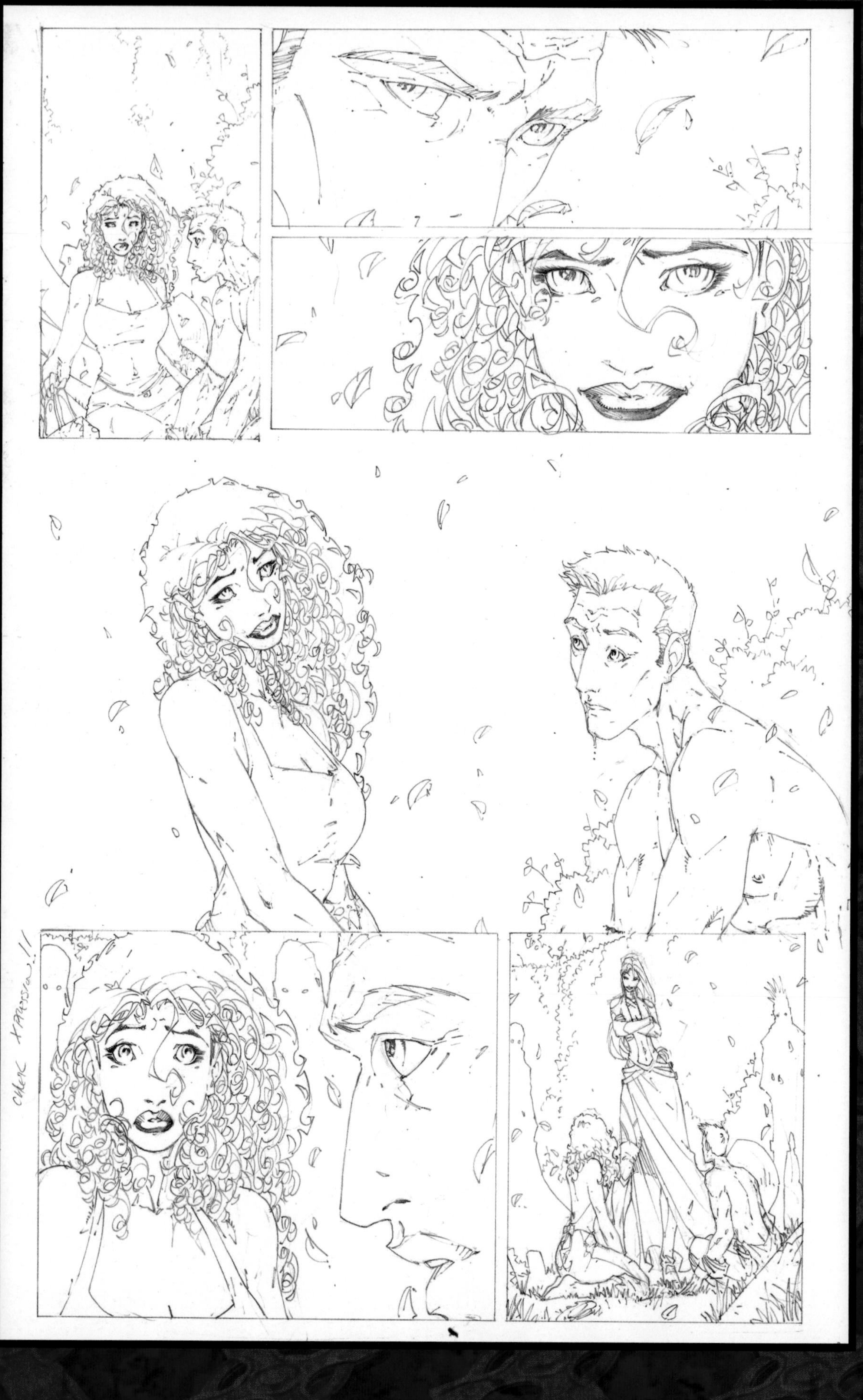

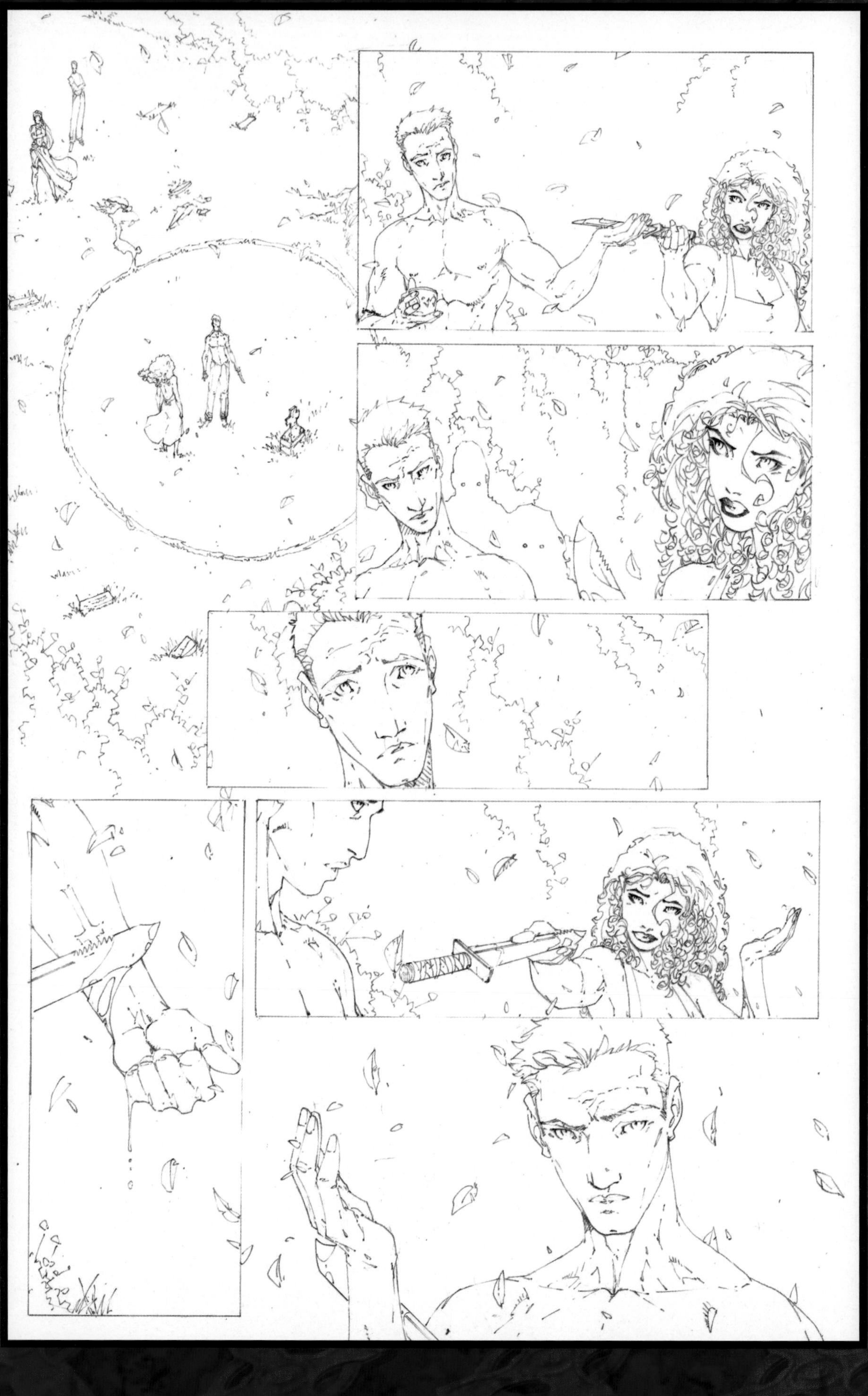

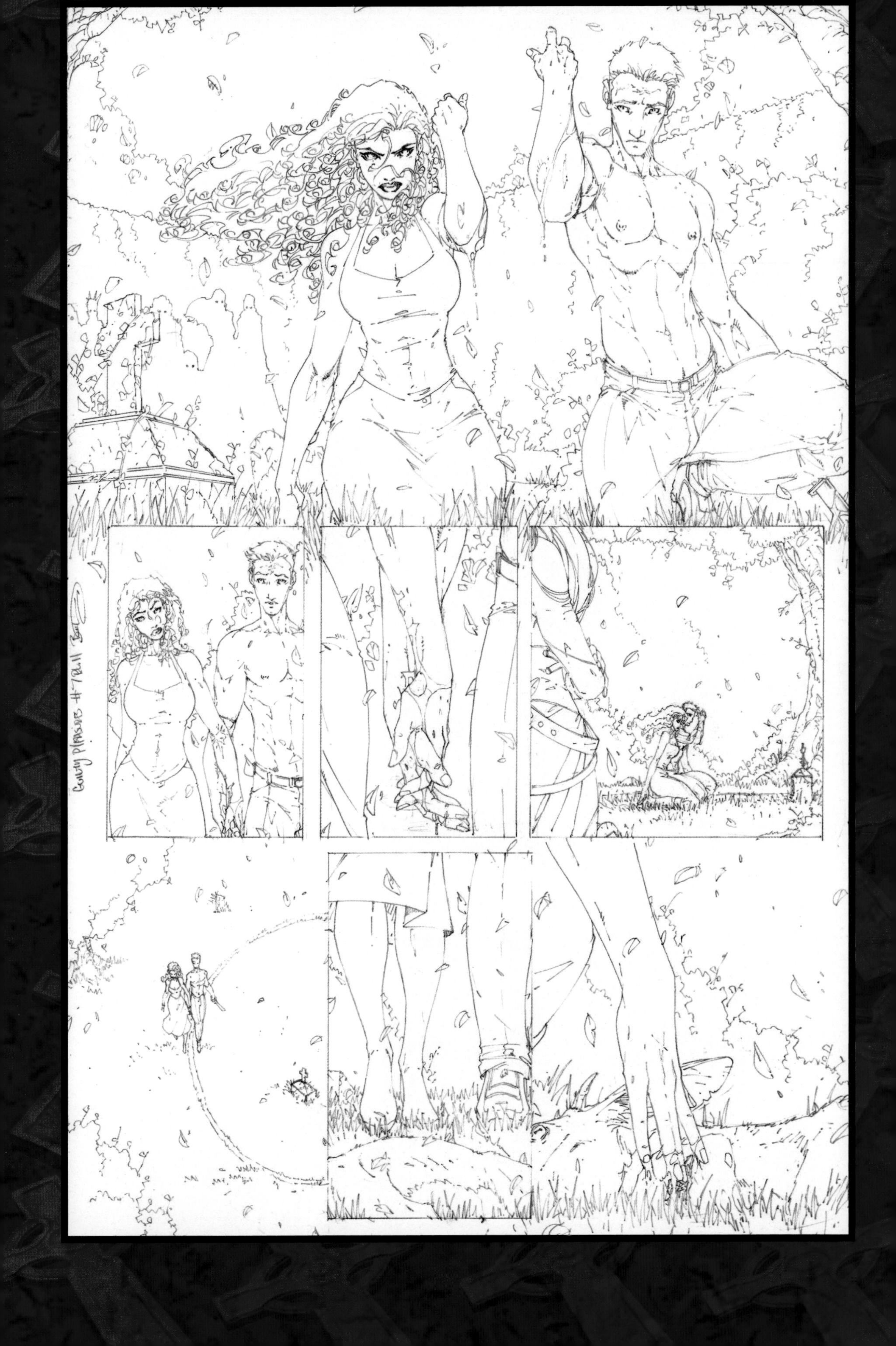
Guilty Pleasures #7 pg.11

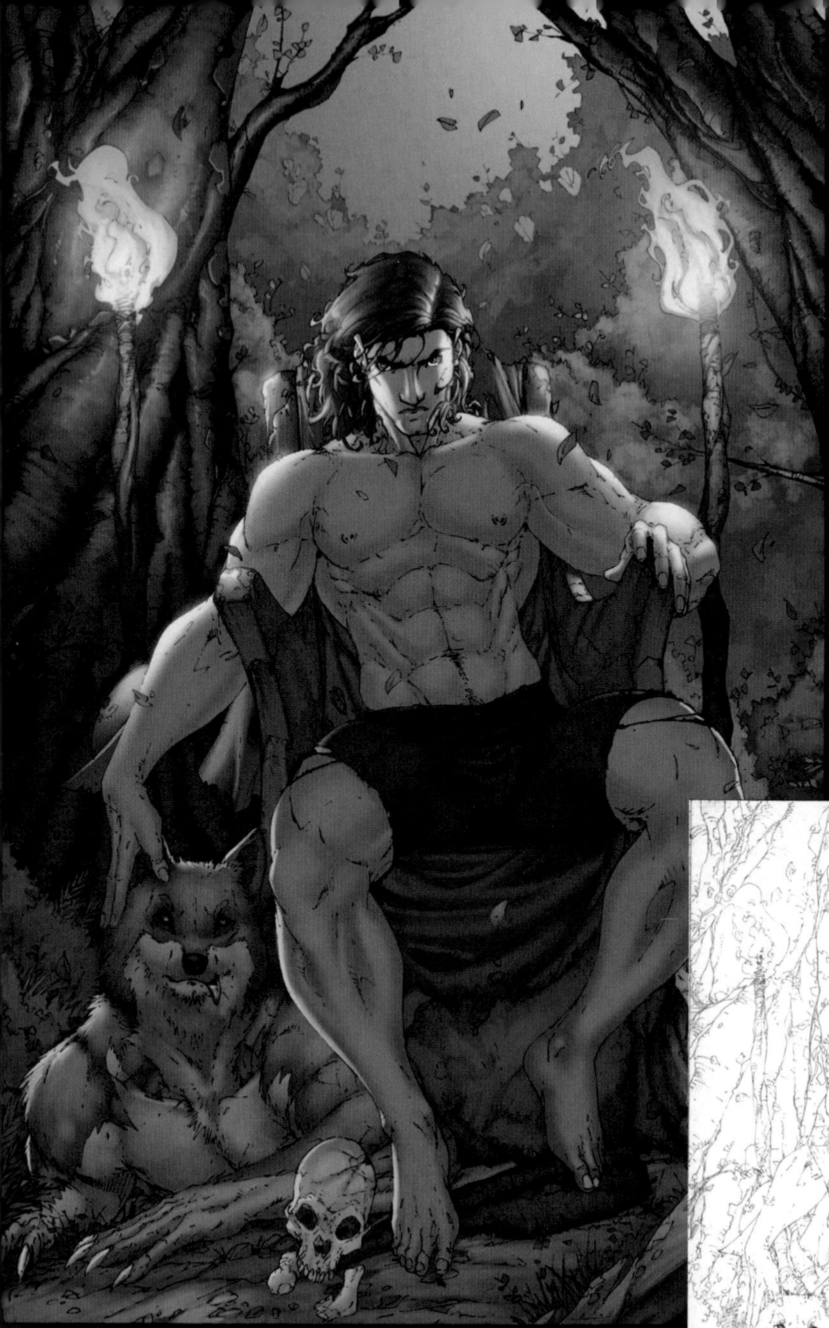

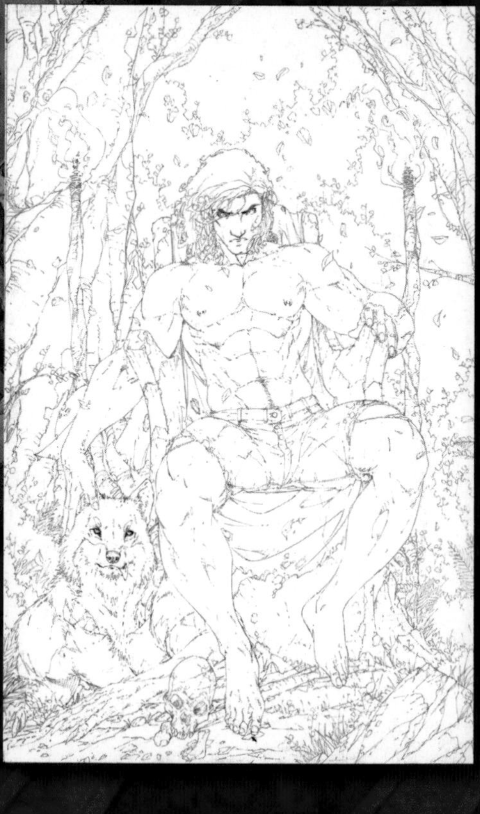

UNUSED PINUP BY BRETT BOOTH

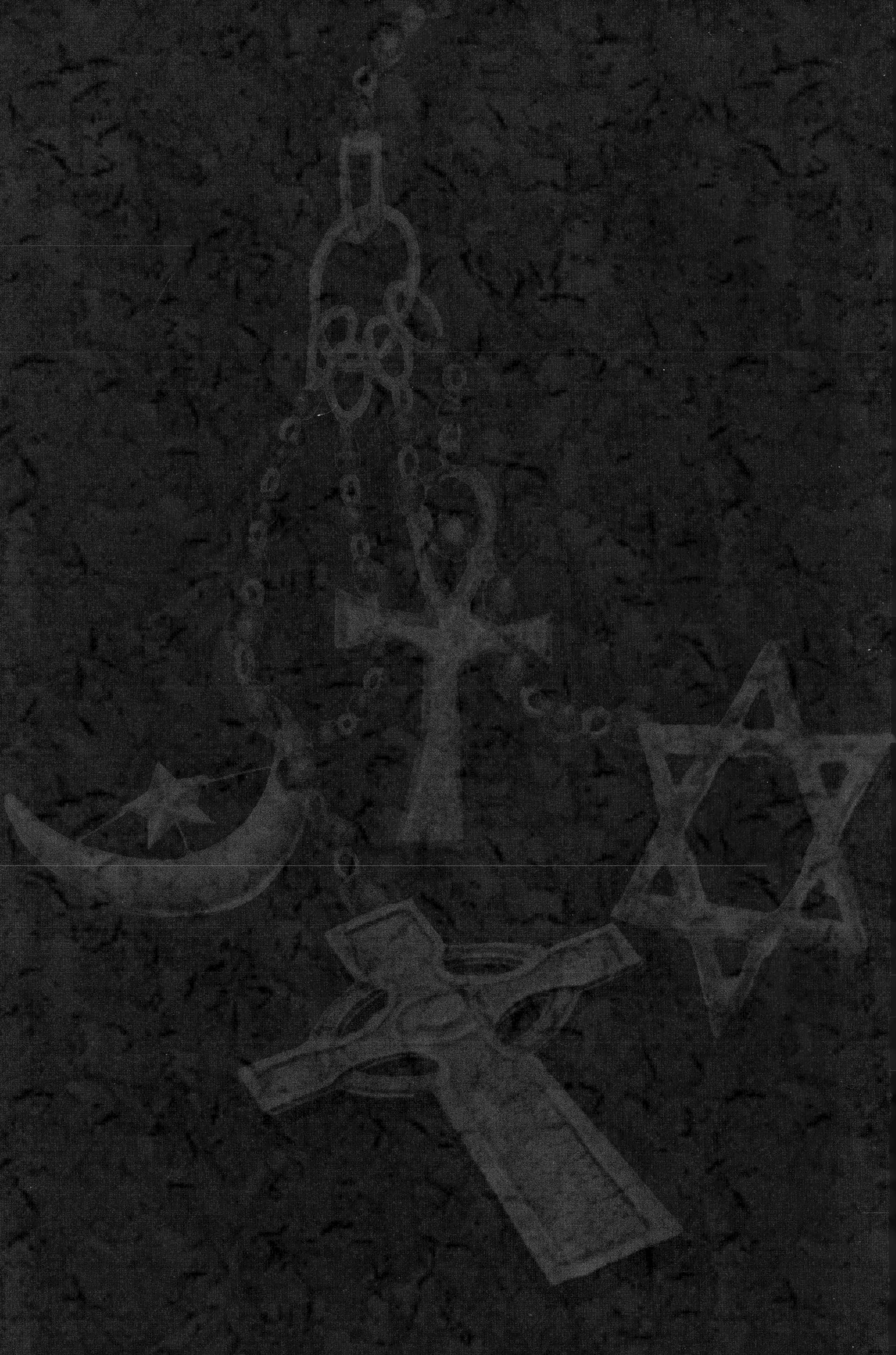

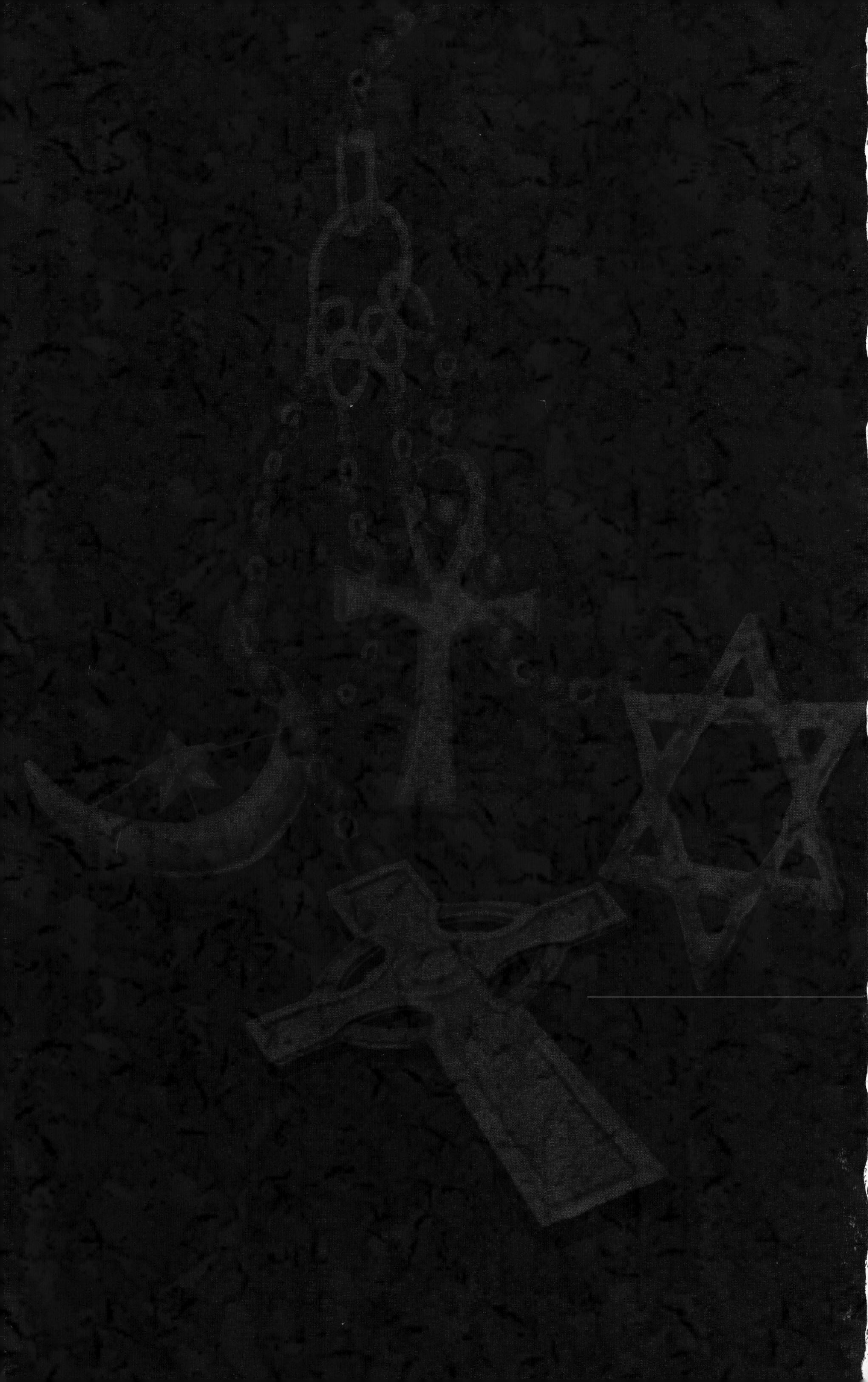